...thanks
...ur support,
...ay your path be
starlit...

The Greening

For the Animals!
Pxx

This edition is published by Wild Spirit Books, Wells, Somerset, UK
Typeset by Poppy Palin

Printed and bound by Anthony Rowe Ltd, 2 Whittel Drive, Highfield Industrial Estate, Eastbourne, East Sussex, BN23 6QT.

Cover Illustrations by Poppy Palin
Cover Design by Dave Kendall/Poppy Palin

ISBN 0-9543417-0-8

For further information on Poppy Palin please e-mail
poppypalin@gypsymoondesign.fsnet.co.uk
or see www.poppypalin.org

The Greening

Rise of the Faerytide

Written and Illustrated by

Poppy Palin

Wild Spirit Books
Somerset, UK

Poppy Palin B.Ed (Hons) writes on the themes of psychic awareness, green spirituality and wild enchantment. She is also a soul-poet and singer. As a trained artist she illustrates her own work and that of other green-spirited writers, most notably the respected hedge witch Rae Beth. Poppy's art has appeared in magazines across the UK and USA.

Poppy has formerly been a leather jacket artist, a care worker and a Head of Art in a London school. It was during the latter that she developed the much misunderstood illness M.E. Despite this long term (and very real) disability, which includes daily migraine and pain, she is also a sacred tattooist specialising in one-off sacred pieces for the purpose of personal transformation.

After living in several regions of England, Poppy Palin currently lives in Somerset, UK

Other books by Poppy Palin

Season of Sorcery (Capall Bann, 1998)
Wildwitch (Capall Bann, 1999)
Walking with Spirit (Capall Bann, 2000)
Soul Resurgence (Capall Bann, 2000)
Waking the Wild Spirit Tarot deck/book set (Llewellyn, 2002)
Craft of the Wild Witch- Green Spirituality and Natural Enchantment (Llewellyn 2004)
Spellcaster*(Llewellyn 2005)**

As Rosa Romani

Green Spirituality- Magic in the Midst of Life (Green Magic, 2004)

In preparation

Greening the Spirit-*Guidance for the Wild Soul**
Spiritwalking
The Hidden Goddess*
Sacred Skin Art- The Tattoo as a Tool for Transformation*

**Provisional title* ***Poppy wrote a chapter of this collective work*

PRAISE FOR THE WORK OF POPPY PALIN

'Poppy Palin is adept at parting the veils between the everyday world and the realms of wild spirit. Her approach is unpretentious, friendly and down-to-earth. It is also poetic. She is a clear medium for teachings of a wise wild beauty, much like a bird call in silver light after rain, luring us all deeper into the forest. Her work is a pilgrimage that can teach how to live magically, heart and soul.'
Rae Beth, author of the popular **Hedge Witch** series, two of which are illustrated by Poppy Palin.

'This tarot is one of the most original I have ever seen...thank you Poppy for something new and wonderful.'
Silver Wheel Magazine, UK

'This is a wonderful card set which will unfold a realm of visionary delight and profound realisation to all who use it.'
Elen Hawke, author

'A beautiful reverent approach to green spirituality...highly recommended'
Witchcraft Magazine, USA

'...colourful, imaginative, free-spirited and even iconoclastic'
Avalon Magazine, UK

'In a lovely and very poetic way the author gives us a multitude of new ideas, rituals, journeys, meditations - especially for those who think there's nothing new published in this area within the last years. The beautiful warm and caring way in which the author shows you how to make your very own unique experiences is...absolutely highly recommendable for all those interested to walk the green way off the beaten track. My heartfelt thanks to the author for this brilliant book'
Review for '***Craft of the Wild Witch***' on **Amazon.co.uk**

' Poppy Palin's designs are unique, and occasionally troubling - shocking your awareness like the wild nature spirits which seem to have inspired them.'
Alan Richardson, author.

ACKNOWLEDGMENTS

I would like to thank the completely generous, infinitely talented and much loved Dave Kendall, as ever, without whom this book wouldn't exist! To the fab Pete and Chris at Counter Culture, again without whom...And of course to my bemused but ever-loving parents, definitely without whom...bless you M and D. Likewise my wonderful guardian spirits and the Fey (*now I see you, now I don't!*).

Thanks to the magical Mark Austin, who gave me permission back in 1995/6 to use the evocative name Treeface. I hope that I have done him justice and I thank you, Mark, for our wonderful time together. I wish a long and happy life for you.

I would also like to thank Lisa Tenzin Dolma who is a massive inspiration, possessed as she is of super-human abilities. Thanks also to Jill Smith, another very inspiring friend, and to beautiful, shining Bobcat...*fifteen minutes with you, well, I wouldn't say no.* My gratitude for their loving friendship to Becky Haynes, Jenny Russell-Smith, Germaine Knight, Rae Beth and Sue Mac Donald-King And to friends that were: Barbara Mackay, Helen and Harry Knibb, Lou Driver, Alice Pink, Giovanni Camisa, Kate, Liz-ness Brown, Barry 'Sir Barrold' of Stead, Seb, Kes Hatton, David Mantripp, Ball Corey, Caroline Khalil, Pam Hider, Trish Anderton and Simon Barr...I wish you well, dear ones. You were all precious to me in different ways. Likewise Karl Randles and Auntie Rene, *still greatly missed.*

I would especially like to mention Claire Louise (Ciel) Ruffle-Brandt who deserved so much more than she got from me. I am so sorry C-L but I know words are not enough. I hope that you have found your own personal Greening. *You deserve all the love in the world.*

This book was brought to you courtesy of Joy Division and The Waterboys '*Dream Harder*' album. Also Albinoni's *Adagio*, Barber's *Adagio*, early-ish Cure and Siouxsie, Ed Alleyne Johnson, And Also The Trees, Nick Drake, Robin Williamson's rare and wonderful '*The Road The Gypsies Go*' album, '*The Sensual World' by* Kate Bush, Sinead O'Connor's '*Universal Mother*' and '*All that You Can't Leave Behind*' by U2. Oh, and Paul Weller...*always* Paul Weller! In memory of John Peel, who brought so much to the table yet made us hungry. And to John Thaw, for many happy Morse hours. Also to the memories of the wonderful Kirsty MacColl and Malcolm Owen, who were both underated. And to Dury, Harrison and Lennon, who were not.

AUTHORS NOTE

Firstly thank you for buying this book. It is a self-published venture and so for me it is more important that it reaches people than ever as I have put even more of my heart, soul, time and energy into it than usual. And, as those of you who know me will appreciate, each word that I write causes me physical pain so it really has been a hard and complicated labour, as well as a difficult birth, for me.

So, let me introduce you to what this book is. Not what it is about, persay, but *what it is.* It is my intention that it be a 'teaching novel', a work of magical fiction that includes some serious advice on how to work with energies, spirits and the Otherworlds. It also includes spirit-full ideas that I wanted to discuss - about the nature of the soul that dwells inside a human form, about 'soul mates' and 'soul links' and the complicated webs we weave, energetically. In this it is far from a 'straight' work of fiction. Yes, it has a beginning, middle and end (as all good tales should) and plausible characters (I hope) but it also contains much in the way of spiritual concepts and actual practical advice on psychic, or 'unseen', interactions. Because of its nature The Greening would never have found a mainstream publisher and even the smaller independent places didn't know what to do with it. It is a *cross-over*, perhaps ground-breaking, perhaps unworkable, that is for you to decide. But please, even if it doesn't work for you then please take something from it; be that Lian's journey though anger to personal power, or Treeface's struggle with deep-seated fear, or Alicia's selfless sharing of her gifts, or Lydia's courage and conviction. Or perhaps you may take the teachings parts and add them into your own practices, as do my characters. Or maybe you'll recognise my musings on the Fey and the idea of 'faery souls in human forms' will move you. Who knows.

However you take it (or leave it) let something of The Greening remain with you for good and all...and for the good of the All. Because regardless of how its written, or how it affects you, the underlying message is a shining thread we can all pick up and it is this: *to bring the magic back to life we have to acknowledge our individual and collective magical power.* It is that simple. Instead of changing nothing we can change *everything,* right now, with thought, kind words,green-spirited deeds, focussed intent, prayer and creativity. May our personal Greening be that of the All. *So may it be!*

To those who stand against the tide of consumerism with quiet temerity

To those with wrinkled skin, silvered hair and tired bones who are beautiful and wise in their advanced years but who are written off by society's 'cult of youth'

To the unseen spirits who guide us with infinite love and patience

To every peace campaigner or green activist that ever took issue against the cruel and foolish ways of men and to every person who ever died for someone else's cause. And, lest we forget, to every horse slain in battle and every other creature that has been killed by bombs, guns or deadly gases

To the forgotten carers of those who are soul-sick or disabled and to those who society has deemed worthless because of their infirm body

To those who grow and buy organic vegetarian/vegan produce, regardless of the personal cost

To the Mother Earth who supports us even as humanity disregards and disrespects her

To every gentle cow, innocent sheep or intelligent pig that faces the abattoir

And to those who dream and of the Greening and who work towards it tirelessly, without expecting praise...BLESS YOU ALL

ANY PROFITS FROM THIS BOOK WILL GO TO ETHICAL CHARITIES, THANK YOU!

Please support:
British Union for the Abolition of Vivisection (BUAV)
Hunt Saboteurs Association, Greenpeace, Animal Aid,
Save the Newchurch Guinea Pigs Campaign,
National Animal Welfare Trusts, Action for M.E.

Part One

The Yearning

May I speak for the Mother? I feel that I must try, even if I only end up speaking from my heart...

Chapter One

The Little Foxes

The woman swept the leaves.

Sweeping was good medicine she always thought; the rhythmic action was familiar and reassuring and it helped to soothe the unnameable anxiety that gnawed at her guts this day. She did not know it yet but there were leaves in the tangled skein of her hair too, russet against the frosted strands which looked more like a mass of moonlight now, no longer the shining raven's wing of years gone by. Everything was change; the years had somehow slipped furtively past and left Alicia Owens old, stealing her bright vigour and leaving her a silvered shadow of herself. Such was the curse, and the blessing, of life in a human form. In such a fast-flowing mortal world only the motion of sweeping remained constant. For decades the same gesture each autumn into winter; the gentle brushing of swirling leaves, saffron, gold and cinnamon, the measure of the seasons marked by a prayerful gesture with a favourite besom.

The colours in the swirling leaves reminded her of strange exotic places that she would never see, not in this life. She saw the leaves as spices, heaped on the market stalls of Marrakech. Oh, there was much she had not done, so little time to accomplish all there was to do in one incarnation! The rhythm of her besom could take her to places unseen though; the motion rocked her to that waking dreamworld where everything was possible. That otherworldly realm was the place in which Alicia had always been happiest. If only she could slip away there now.

But the nagging sensation in her solar plexus remained, unsettling her.

Alicia was a woman given to a slow pace and to mellow moments, to wistful dreams of souks and spices. She was an autumnal creature, as were all the ancient Shining Ones; it was their secret season of sorcery. She usually revelled in the drifting mist, the visible shifting of the veil between the worlds, yet on this day...

On this day she was drawn to look up and see the girl that stood alone at the bus stop across from her garden wall. For a moment her heart lurched painfully, frighteningly, and then settled. Her broom ceased its sweeping. Alicia's faded chambray eyes widened and she shook her head as if to clear her vision. How could the girl stand out as if in relief from her background without anyone else noticing? Everything, the road, the ordinary houses, the muddle of litter crumpled in the gutter, all of it became sepia toned and unfocused compared to this girl. This girl was separate, thought Alicia, this girl was *other*. She was compelling, terrible, like a road accident fatality who wandered the highway as a tormented wraith, unseen by passers by. Yet she was just a girl; a girl wearing a faded and torn black velvet frock coat, its worn collar studded with tears. Alicia saw her in minute detail, as if the girls own tears were somehow magnifying her, making her sharp and shining in her misery. Oh, she was so alone!

Some forty years ago, Alicia thought, pin-sharp and precise, I was just like her. And, under the sagging skin, she knew that in so many ways she still was.

Alicia had once shared the striking physical presence of this poor young woman as she had shared the pain that made her flare, bright and cold, in the careless lilac miasma of an autumn afternoon. This girl had tallow skin and angry hair which exploded around her waxen face, crowning it in fiery glory. Her eyes were strange, strangely familiar, emphasised by the streaks of black make-up she habitually wore; black which now, unbeknownst to her, had left tear-trails like tribal markings on her cheeks. She was not tall but held herself rigidly straight, perhaps through pride or maybe as if she were perpetually braced against any eventuality. She was not rumpled or forlorn, despite her weeping, she simply emanated *hurting.*

Alicia felt an overwhelming urge to call out to her whilst at the same time as experiencing an inner dread, worse than before. Her stomach knotted and her teeth clenched against the desire to reach out to the waif in the velvet coat. A girl with hair like wicked tongues of flame. As she gazed at that shock of vermillion-hued hair Alicia could smell burning, a sickening stench like cordite, and perhaps something worse, smouldering. What was real? This was the problem with autumn, it robbed rationality and replaced it with layer upon layer of memory. Past, present, future, swirling like dead leaves. She shook her head again, more vigorously. Images of normality, of autumn bonfires in back gardens, merged with a scene of stark horror, a market square, a blackened stake at its centre...

Alicia came to her senses in slow motion. The girl was still there as before, solid enough against the bare scratched metal of the bus stop. Alicia was torn, she longed to invite the girl in to share her sorrow and yet oh to hide and lock the door against her! The Faerytide was unbelievably strong in this fiery woman, too strong for this world, and it made the mortal Alicia reel. If her energy affected Alicia in such a way what would it do to other mortals, those without her *seeing* and *knowing*? Alicia in her faded floral smock and baggy cardigan, an elderly woman living alone with clothes hugged threadbare by a dozen other needy girls, felt her human-self fighting her spirit, forbidding her to touch this kindred. Her soul cried out even as her body rebelled...

(*Go to her now....no, stay away!*)

But she needs me, just as they all need me, but more...much more.

Oh yes, Alicia had certainly helped stray girls before; she had given them tea and healing, maybe a very basic tarot reading, nothing too scary, just words and images of more comforting futures maybe. Sometimes she had offered them no more than a hot bath, a warm bed and the benefit of her unobtrusive hospitality. Had it ever been safe to take in these drifters, these misfits? Right now it felt like the most perilous, and yet the most obvious, thing.

No matter how much her human-self struggled Alicia could not tear her gaze from this sight, nor extricate her heart which had been moved beyond words by the plight of another woman, of another Fey. This was indeed no usual or ordinary girl, no runaway, and no hapless, hopeless misfit. A strange woman who was almost incandescent in the afternoon mist, a woman who was weeping, one who looked as familiar as...

The crow flew at Alicia, cackling, and her torpor was broken. Instinctively she swiped at it with her broom but it still came close enough to brush her cheek with its iridescent oil-slick wings.

"I hear you, shining brother," Alicia acknowledged and lowered the broom in shame. The crow was her harbinger, the bringer of news, and it spoke most oftenly of death. It had an unpleasant job to do and it did it without balking; Alicia had no right to swat it away. The winged darkling was always true and was bringing her the clear knowledge that the girl, the blaze of woman-ness before her, was going to kill herself this day...

(*This night!*)

Alicia spat and made the sign, an involuntary action even though she had long since learned to honour death. Old superstitions from days of fear, long since passed, lingered in her depths, ready to surface at the slightest provocation.

The crow landed on the fence and bobbed its head, a beady eye fixed on the oblivious girl with her coat lapels studded with early stars, jewel bright tears of an unspoken grief. *Apart-ness* radiated from her; a young woman somehow physically removed from everyone and everything, from the whole world. This girl was as Alicia had been before the crow became her friend, before she had *re-membered.* She was a pariah, an enigma...in danger.

"Wait!"

Alicia opened her mouth and stepped over the fallen broom towards the crying girl. The word came out as a croak and the girl did not turn. How could she hear the pathetic voice of an elderly woman above the torrent of her own grief? And the bus was coming around the corner. The girl was focused on the bus but she had to be stopped. If she went away to her fate...

(*Holy Mother, help me now!*)

The girl had to be stopped but Alicia was frozen, gripped by a residual mortal fear of coming too close to one so powerful, so...*doomed.* Yet the Faerytide rose up and almost drowned her.

"Wait, please!"

It was said louder this time, beseeching, but the girl was moving and the noise of the bus's brakes were more obvious than the sound of an old woman's plea. The bus stopped and the girl stepped on. Alicia thought, even above the hiss of the doors opening for her and the hum of the engine, that she heard the girl sniff. One of the sad tear-stars on her collar broke free and made a celestial ice flow down the back of the tattered coat. Alicia saw...

(*or did she feel?*)

...the girl square her shoulders, defying the bus driver to notice her pain, challenging him to comment upon it. The driver was lost in the cab, shadowy in the October afternoon half-light.

('*It's always worse in October,*' Alicia's mind chattered, '*always worse for those with the* seeing *and the* knowing.')

The girl with the seductive spangles of misery on her velvety coat, the girl who had chosen to die rather than bear this burden of being alone, was getting away.

"No!"

Alicia broke free of her dream-like torpor once more and lurched stupidly towards her garden wall, on the other side of which a bus was closing its doors against her; a bus taking the girl to a fate more certain than any other. Alicia reached out, knowing she looked ridiculous, knowing nobody cared. The girl was going down the bus aisle now towards a seat, the bus was pulling away. The crow with eyes like asphalt after a car wreck, slick and shiny with a myriad of colours swirling on black, was cawing. Alicia wanted to scream at her ineffectual actions, the whole of her life condensing down into that pin-prick of feeling, that moment between choosing and letting go.

She turned away from the sight of the departing bus and ran for the house.

I am here because I do not wish to be there. Is that the only reason? Why am I getting on this bus, anyway? Wouldn't it have been better to go into one of those nice fields and dig myself a dark brown grave, like a little foxes earth, and curl up within it? How I would love to cease to think, to feel, cease being for a while! Are these my only choices now, to get on a bus to somewhere or dig myself a hole? Perhaps I want neither. Perhaps I should steal myself a van and drive myself to the edge of a cliff, right to the very edge, and drink strong coffee from a thermos flask while looking out to sea.

What would I see, perhaps, over that empty sea? Maybe lights reflecting in the distance, the lights of impossible cities, apricot on indigo as the night falls around me. I want to be cocooned in an eternal darkness, that's all. Everything comes back to darkness, oblivion, endings. Dark stars, cold crescent moons, anti-light and anti-love. I yearn for only oblivion and no more dreaming. Yet my treacherous feet, and that stupid human will of mine to keep going, make me board this bus that will take me into the city.

I am reaching for my money in this patchwork bag, a bag I once loved, made of scraps of velvet in rich colours, all stitched together. Whereas each jewel-bright scrap of fabric clings to its neighbour, sewn fast, I am coming undone and I welcome it. I wish my colourful bag was now big and softly black, a bag I could enfold myself in.

I imagine myself, the bare bones of my very existence gently grinding themselves into powder as they rub together, a powder which settles into the secret folds, the darkest recesses, of a soft deep black bag. Someone else could then tie up this sackful of meaningless memory and forgotten dreams and cast it into the sea, where it would fall through fathoms of cold indifference and come to rest with all the other bones of those who dared to live and die alone.

Then and only then I would be un-*seeing* and unseen, un-*knowing* and unknown...lost to the world. Maybe then I could rest in peace.

Yet now I am handing over money to the bus driver. I mouth a destination and he understands. Men only understand things that they can hear, instructions and lists, dry as dust to me. I reach into my bag once more as the bus pulls away, wishing I could find something so terrible in it that if I showed it to him, this stranger, he would truly understand where I have been and where I must go this night. Maybe I can still stop the bus and run. Run to my secret fox-hole, sleep before running some more. I want to be somewhere that is not here. Somewhere that is not anywhere. I am so tired of being me.

And I will not, I *must not*, turn to look at the old woman behind me in her pretty garden, even as she calls to me. For I do not want to be saved.

I do not know what people want to live for. I wish I could touch one of them and find out, somehow read the encrypted code of their motivations and transfer them to my own hard drive. I wish I could become like them. I want to know if maybe they feel like this sometimes too or is it only me that feels barren and blighted? They seem so stuffed with thoughts and plans and wants, just brimming with things. I can hear their thoughts all around me, buzzing like fat juicy flies, big dumb thoughts that I pick up from their overflowing minds. I can see all the people they have to see, I can know all the places they want to go, yet I cannot tell how they feel. And for me I ask, which people do I have to see and where shall I go? Because wherever there is, whoever there is, *I have to take me with me.*

Once I had a real heart and now I have one made of pitted, tarnished pewter which sits in the cavity of my chest like a bullet. Like a lie. I wish I could cough it up, shift it, and spit it out onto a pavement, into someone's face. Wish I could know what I cannot know even though I know too much. Who am I? Where am I? What am I for? The bus jolts me forward and I look out of the window onto a world that does not want me. I see my face reflected in the window and gaze into eyes the colour of moss on a granite slab, hair like flames that greedily lick my pale flickering face. I feel as if I am already only a memory. Wish it was over but it isn't, not yet.

Did I tell you I killed someone? And, strangely, that someone killed me? How do I begin?

"You shouldn't have done that!"

The girl looked down at her pixie boots and then up again, meeting Alicia's gaze which she tried hard to keep steady.

"How do you know, child? Who are either of us to say what should have been this day? All I know is that this is one version of events, and one I much prefer."

Alicia was working very hard to keep her voice even. It was an effort to be calm in the presence of this young-old woman, a strange girl who could have been millennia more ancient than herself. Close up she was even more mesmerising, more off-putting. Alicia gave a dry cough to ease her own tension. She reached over to the brown teapot which sat on the cluttered table between them and made to refill her cup; perhaps the fragrant chamomile brew would calm her. This was like the hardest exam, the most important test, and if Alicia failed then all this beauty would be lost to the world again...and it felt as if she was indeed failing. Her hand shook noticeably; how could she convince this girl of her wisdom, reach out to her innermost being, with a trembling hand?

"Who are you to weave fate, to know destiny, old woman? You think that you are some sort of...some sort of soothsayer, playing the venerable wisewoman? How dare you use your sorcery on me? How *dare* you!"

The girl was cruel but she spoke truly. Her slanted lichen coloured eyes met Alicia's and spoke only of agony and loss. But they were not the eyes of a fool, rather eyes that had seen too much and now longed to shut and stay shut forever. Alicia gave an involuntary shudder as she connected with the soul within and the torment it must have suffered to look through those desolate, almost-beautiful eyes.

The girl held the gaze and her tone softened somewhat but remained flat, potentially deadly.

"You stopped me from doing what I had to do and now I've got to live another night and tomorrow, when you're tired of playing benevolent mother, or martyr, or liberal middle class do-gooder, I will still have to live. Or choose not to, all over again. It just needs to STOP! *I* need to stop. I can't do this...this *living* thing...any more."

All the words the girl connected to herself and to her life were spat out with a disgust that made Alicia recoil. This incredible woman, this extraordinary being, was filled with self-loathing.

This was the voice of one who was not distorted with drugs, pathetic self-pity, psychosis or mindless rebellion. There was a chilling honesty, a callous objectivity, about her words which Alicia could not override with platitudes. Tears sprang to her eyes but she could not afford to become sentimental. Too much, a whole life, many lives, were at stake here...and it rested on Alicia to be the catalyst that tipped the balance in favour of this girl carrying on. For she had enormous gifts, this peculiar black clad Elf-woman. Yet there she was filled with anger, coiled tight as a spring with her pointed boots now curled up beneath her and her slender fingers clenched into a fist. A white, delicate fist that longed to drum a hole straight though the arm of the chair she perched upon.

Yes, this one was no sham, no false prophet of doom playing with glamourous mystery or dangerous subversion; this one had gifts so great they were crushing her. Alicia had seen the chalk-white, black eyed girls who lay claim to dark powers and cursed those who misunderstood their gauche social ineptitude. Alicia had made tea and stroked smooth the spiky hair of many a rebel-child who had no more real power than any other human in need of greater love and affection than they had found in the world so far. This one though, this one was authentic, may the Lady help her. She needed Alicia to show her how to use the gifts that became intolerable burdens if they were untrained, undisciplined, suppressed. For the gifts could be worked with, for the good of the All.

The *sight* could be a blessing as well as the curse this ragged haired girl had known for all her years on Earth.

What was there to latch on to, to appeal to in this woman who burned silently like a cold flame in Alicia's small, crowded kitchen? There was no accent to betray the girl's origins, she had not even given her name yet, and there were just no human markers to make conversations from. Alicia longed to touch her as a gesture of wordless comfort, hoping it would convey her genuine concern, but knew to do so would just make it worse for them both. If they touched, the girl would pick up Alicia's fear, Alicia would pick up more than she already knew about this...

(*witch, this was between witches!*)

...and then all would be lost. Best to remain impersonal for now, asking questions that did not delve too deeply, too fast. Alicia knew the girl was staying of her own free will so far, with only a little help from Alicia's own psychic bidding to hold her there in that safe haven of a house. One false move, one probing question too many, and the girl would bolt to her death, or to her destiny as she probably saw it. The girl was under the impression she was condemned anyway, as if she were somehow singled out for special, cruel treatment on Earth. And maybe she was singled out but cruelty was only her perception of the special response she elicited from those she encountered. She should have been a treasure, not a terror, to those around her with her phenomenal psychic ability and genuine gifts of healing and prophesy, yet she thought that she had nothing to lose by dying. Alicia saw that the world had everything to gain by this girl staying alive.

For the Greening. Yes, always for that.

Alicia hoped that she could tread very, very carefully and edge towards what she needed to know.

"I'll tell you, old woman, if you just ask me straight, it isn't any sort of secret. I've told all manner of nosy old bats, young ones too, if they asked me if they could help, wondering greedily if I needed to *share*."

This last word was sneered as the girl looked directly at Alicia, provoking her, reading her thoughts, anticipating her tentative questions.

"So stop thinking you're any different from them and get on with the compassionate looks and the seemingly casual employment of empathy. Stop your pussy-footing and let's just cut to the juicy bits shall we? I know it'll give them something to spice up their tea and scones at the women's institute when you tell them. '*Ooh I had a murderer in my house, you know, and I stopped her from murdering herself. Aren't I good and ever so slightly daring too?*' And they'll tut and nod and keep on nodding while the jam in their scones turns to so much gore in their mouths, a bit of ladies relish, a bit of something gristly to chew down and regurgitate at a thousand other dry old meetings."

"I don't go to meetings, I'm usually not welcome," Alicia said quietly, feeling as if the girl was slapping her in the face repeatedly, not wanting her to know it. But the girl was in her stride now, the vitriol and hurt kept coming out of her wide slash of a mouth, and she did not seem to hear the old woman.

"Bloody hypocrites the lot of you! You think you want to help but you want to gloat and wallow and say stuff about it being a shame and a waste. A '*deary, deary me*' and a donation to the collection box. You make me sick! So, lady, nice kind generous lady who hasn't got the faintest idea how I feel, shall I tell you about it now or shall I just go and get on with the inevitable? It's up to you; you're the one that had them stop the bus. You're the one that used whatever magic you have to make them believe that I'm your mad, sad granddaughter who has forgotten her vital medication; it was you that made me into more of a freak than I already am, had them all staring, wondering what I needed to be escorted off the bus for. As if I'm not enough of a weirdo already now I need some treatment too, eh? Do you know why I got off the bus and got into that taxi that you had sent for me with your witchy voodoo?"

Alicia shrugged, trying not to make the gesture seem too hopeless under the girl's attack.

"Well, I'll tell you...I didn't care where it was going to take me. I half hoped the driver was a maniac who would finish me off himself. Being dead in the city or dead in a country lay-by, hell, they were all the same to me! I didn't know why I was being called somebody's sick granddaughter, didn't really care, anything to escape from myself, from my own reality. I would have gone with an axe wielding madman if he would have offered to give me a release. So don't you feel special, lady. You think you saved me but you could have been anyone, anyone at all who intervened."

To protest would be useless, Alicia knew that. The girl needed to speak her piece to get some peace.

"What sort of magic trick did you pull on the bus company to get that to happen, anyway, and why couldn't you just have minded your own goddamn business? How did you get the taxi to turn up bang on time? More to the point, why did you bother? Who are you, some meddlesome old bag who wants to live vicariously through some hapless mad woman like me? Someone who thinks they're a witch, using your dubious power in a world that has long since stopped believing in you? Well I've seen it all before. The benevolent counsellors, the drippy-hippy '*why don't you let it all out creatively*' brigade, the fat mystics claiming they can cure me with a crystal pendulum. I've seen the whole gamut of professionals who are oh so incredibly generous as to accept my problems and *work* with them, as if I were some malleable thing that could be re-shaped it a more pleasing effigy of rightness, made into a less challenging changeling. Oh yeah, they all say they won't judge me and that may be true as long as they get something from me too, like cash, like a bloody good story to gossip about. You're just one of the many and I'll tell you what...*they all failed to make me normal*. And so, my dear, will you."

The girl leaned forward, unclenched one fist and pointed one very long, white finger at Alicia.

"Now, you're the one that's holding me here so shall I just tell you and have done with it? Spill the big dark secretive stuff and make you feel like you've lived dangerously by proxy? Then you can ask me to leave and I can do what it is I have to."

Alicia was reeling from this assault, the sheer fury of it, but managed to find something to respond with.

(*Holy Mother, this girl can use the* seeing *better than I can and she has decades less experience, what do I do? She is no fool, nobody's problem but her own. I do not wish to add to her pain, I do not want to help destroy that which is already so deeply damaged. Give me the words, guide me, I beg you!*)

"I won't ask you to leave, whatever it is you want to say to me. You are welcome in my home. Do not be angry because you cannot use your *seeing* on me to know what I am, child, for I am well protected in a way that you are not. If you stay I will teach you how to work with that *seeing* wisely and then you will know what we two are all about, for we are of one spirit, you and I, like it or no. But, beloved, if you choose to go then I wish you well. The choice is truly yours, brightling."

Alicia spoke softly but with conviction, grateful that the right words had flowed through her. She had now made this girl an offer, not a demand.

"Do you think you know what I am going to say next? Do you?

Have you truly the faintest idea of what it's like to *see* what can't be seen and *know* that which shouldn't be known? I mean, look at you, how can you know what it's like for me with your comfy chair and your warm hearth and..."

"I lost my daughter through it," Alicia cut in. These were the words she needed.

The girl stopped her litany and gazed steadily at the older woman once more.

"Go on?"

"My daughter left me."

"She died, you're saying? Well, why don't you just say it, '*my daughter, she bloody died on me, and now I'd like to pretend you're her?*'?"

Alicia was calm but the voice became glass, smooth but hard and shiny with pain.

"I mean, madam, that she left me because of who I am and what I be. Walked away in disgust, it was, in shame. She still lives, oh yes, but she prefers to be on the other side of the world than to be close to a mother who is a witch."

The old dialect was creeping in; its inflections and turns of phrase suddenly making Alicia seem more *other* than the girl had first seen. Although her attention was caught, the girl laughed, a harsh bark.

"Witch is it now? You're owning up to using your stupid craft?"

"Aye mistress, a witch, but not a frivolous one playing for effects in the world. Oh no, a shunned, spurned, feared woman, a born *seer*, born to be reviled, that kind of witch...*your* kind of witch, beloved! The one oft called sorceress, the one spat on more often than revered. The gentle-woman who people ask for things when they are needy but who they turn from when she tells them what it is they cannot, will not, know. And a Faery-woman too, one of the Shining Ones who has come back to this Earth, time and again, to try and bring the Greening. Just to try."

Alicia threw her hands up in her own exasperation.

"Accch, so, I'm the wyrd-woman who lives alone, doing her best by those who ask of her help, her hearth, her nice comfy chair, her spells, her healing arts...."

"I ask for nothing"

The girl made as if to rise, her voice quiet.

"Your soul spoke to me and asked me for something, the flibberty-gibbet that is your human self is too proud to ask anyone! Your soul knows what your mortal self is too a-feared to face and it calls out child...*it calls out!*"

"Too proud, is it? Too stupid? Or is it that I just don't want your help and that my soul is actually a stupid dumb messed up thing that should keep its own damn council!"

The chair scraped back as the girl rose, pulling on her coat and nearly toppling backwards in her haste.

"What the hell am I doing here anyway, this is crazy!"

"Crazier than death beloved? Crazier than ending your own life?"

The girl struggled frantically with her sleeves, trying to get her arms in to her coat as her jumper got pushed up to her elbows.

"That's not madness, its sanity! It's sane to get out of pain isn't it? Sane to end torment? And it's definitely sane to get out of your house, old woman, that's for sure. What a waste of time! What did you think this was going to achieve? Maybe you wanted to initiate me into the ways of the devil? Well, I think I'm pretty much *au fait* with those thanks very much."

Alicia stood up and met the girl as she steadied herself. Eye to eye they were more or less the same height. They locked their gazes, entering a battle of wits. Whose will was stronger, the one that sought life or the one that sought death? For a moment they enacted an age-old dance, youth and age, season upon season, one fighting for supremacy over another. Youth could not defy age's wisdom yet age was destined to become innocent youth again, in the endless cycle... and who was to say who was the Elder, in spirit?

What they discovered, eye to eye and toe to toe in the crowded little kitchen, was that they were equals. More than that, they knew one another.

(*A flash as the torch was lit, a flare of orange against the grey, the pitiful cry of the woman straining against the stake to which she was tied. Across the marketplace, with her one good eye closing against the rising smoke, she saw the face of her beloved friend, a friend whose dear face wavered and faded as there tears began to fall, tears that could never put out that blistering, searing agony of the all-consuming fire. Who was the woman at the stake and who was the friend? The edges were blurred by smoke and the boundaries were melting away, both felt each other's anguish and cried out...*)

"Marguerite! *Maman*!"

"Allette!"

The two women, Alicia and the red-haired girl, drew apart gasping.

"I know you!"

The girl sat down with an audible thud and put her head in her hands. There was silence save for the ticking of the kitchen clock and the gentle rubbing sound as the girl worked at her tears in shame and confusion. Finally she raised her head again and her face was a pale candle of pain in the twilight.

"Okay, I give up. Just please, please tell me what's happening to me. What am I?"

Alicia sat down too and tried to gather herself. She had won the girl back, but for how long? And what did it all mean? There was too much going on at once, even for an experienced wisewoman like Alicia, a woman of over seventy summers and countless incarnations. There were too many emotions, too many thoughts flying freely; thoughts that were being wrongly read and misinterpreted. Impressions and images danced behind her eyes from the contact with the girl. The link they had forged was like plugging herself into the middle of a particularly vivid dream, it would have been easy to drift into the scene she saw echoed in the shadows of herself, yet she need to think clearly...what best to say to keep the girl safe, to reassure her not to smother her...

"Tell me what has happened to you?" Alicia said at last.

"Why don't you tell me about your bloody daughter instead?"

"I need to know what has happened to you, beloved. And I need to know who you are."

"Why? I want *you* to tell *me* who I am! You are the wise one, not me! I mean, I don't bloody well know, do I? That's the problem!"

"Ah, child but you do know, you have only forgotten and when you *re-member* your *knowing* will be well beyond mine. But for now at least we are in two mortal forms and you are a guest in this house, therefore I need to observe common courtesies. And because I would like to know your story even if no one else ever has wanted to hear it. Even if you still choose to die I want to have heard it. And most of all because I knew you and I want to know you and even if we never meet again I will have gained by that knowing. Humour me if nothing else. Then do as you must, or as you will."

The girl raked her hands through her wild crop of red hair and looked up. The face had grown even paler, the chin thrust more determinedly forward than ever.

"My name is Lian and I killed someone."

She pronounced it like lion. There was a pride in the way she said it and a terrible anger, unquenched by accquiescent tears alone.

Alicia chose to ignore the bait. There was plenty of time to be told of death.

"Lian, you mean on account of your wonderful hair? Or your temperament, perhaps?"

Alicia ventured a small crooked smile.

"My mother named me before she died. I killed her too, apparently, or so my father seems to believe. I don't bloody know, do I? I was only a baby, hardly accountable. I don't consider her as being someone I killed because I was just a horrible freaky kid, I didn't know any better. It would have been an accident my killing her, see? Not like the other one, not like Robert. I *really* killed him. My mother? Well, that was...that *wasn't* the same...I was too young.

I often think that she must have loved me a bit before she left me..."

Lian paused and looked at Alicia beseechingly with her huge eyes, suddenly seeming like a child desperately needing comfort and reassurance, yet she didn't wait for Alicia to speak the words she so needed to hear..

"...yeah, she must have, mustn't she? All mothers have to love their children; she wouldn't have been able to help herself, it'd have been like a rotten itch she just had to scratch. But she didn't love me enough to stick around, that was for sure, and how could she? I don't blame her for going at all, I mean who'd want the responsibility of bringing up a sodding mutant?"

Lian sighed deeply.

"Anyway, she named me because I had a mane and a fierce roar....apparently. It's all hearsay isn't it? She was Irish, that much I do know, from Thurles, which I am told is pronounced *Tur-less.* She had red hair too but *normal* auburn hair, not like my incandescent mop. The old man, dear Daddy, never mentions her anymore even though she gave up everything and alienated her good Catholic family just to be with him and bear his child. Don't know what she could have seen in him! I'd say he was as much responsible for her death as me but he'd never, ever take that on, the bastard, not while he's got his ugly, weird kid to pass the buck to."

Lian grimaced at the thought and played with a sprig of that fantastic flame-hued hair.

('*Irish blood in her, Welsh in me, it's the Faerytide seeking its old wild haunts*,' thought Alicia.)

Lian was talking again, almost distractedly as if she were watching a film of her life at the same time.

"At school they kept calling me Lee-Ann when they took a roll-call, on account that the spelling looks that way. Or does it? L-i-a-n...well, really its just lion without the 'o', isn't it? Teachers are stupid, really stupid, sometimes. I never bothered to correct them but it's meant to sound like lion...Lie-Ann. Eventually no one called me anything ''cos they didn't need to. In the end no one spoke to me at all. The lion thing, it's scary, but it's not all of why they found me scary. I don't even have to *do* anything to be scary. They just looked...and then they didn't want to look again, not properly. They never looked right at me, only ever at a point just above my head, like they would find a label therc that'd tell them what I was. God, you know, thinking of it I'm amazed I ever got close enough to Robert to kill him at all..."

Alicia nodded. She daren't speak. Oh Lian, poor little Lian!

"After he died, after I *killed* him, there wasn't any time. Time got all souped up, soupy. We all sat around a table, that's all I really remember. We put one finger each on this dirty glass tumbler and...*just don't let them tell you that I didn't do it, okay*?"

Lian leaned forward and grabbed Alicia's wrist. The jolt was electric and there was a jumble of images...

(*the truck and the bike and the boy, all in a slow motion ballet with no choreography. The boy Robert becoming several boys at once, all dancing in different directions, becoming nothing but a corpse in a graceless descent onto tarmac. Dreams exploding, sparks and bright poppies petals falling onto a field of withered corn. The wind moaning, a mother moaning, someone screaming...*)

Lian was staring hard at Alicia and she released her grip. Her eyes snapping green fire spoke silent messages. '*I know you can see this but I want you to feel it, feel how alone I am with this pain. Please...come with me!*'

Alicia nodded her assent, swallowed.

Lian spoke again.

"We lived in the North, myself and Robert. He was my best friend, maybe my only one, and now he has gone. What sort of a person kills the only thing that loves them? I want someone to blame me for his death but nobody will. I want to wear the badge that says '*I did it, I was responsible!*'. He's too precious to put in the ground without someone taking the blame for such a crime but they wouldn't even give me credit for that. Denied me, they did. And I never had a badge, not even at Girl Guides. Those nice badges embroidered with artist's palettes and tennis racquets, I never even achieved one of those, and I was always cast out from the things I joined. But I should have gotten an award, some sort of medal, just for surviving our town and my school. I mean, you put a freak like me into such a cauldron of sarcasm and prejudice and something's got to give. They are vindictive, divisive gutter-snipes in my town, my *ex*-town, and they dropped me into a vat of their own bile. What did they think would happen, that I would come out smiling? Oh no, I emerged as a killer, pitted and scarred, brutalised and brutal.

But they didn't even call me murderer, privilege denied, they just sent me away. Said it was a shame, an accident, and no more. They called his death *misadventure* or some other nicety, making it sound like he'd just got lost or something. They negated my part in it by saying I was having mental problems. If only it were that simple! *I killed him!*"

"I believe you, but I can't believe you meant to?"

Lian's eyes were wild and for a moment Alicia wondered if Lian were really only a mad, strange girl on the run and no visionary, no *seer*. But Lian was just distraught beyond measure or reason. She had suffered too long and too hard, alone, and now she was simply offloading and really truly feeling it, maybe for the first time in her life. Alicia bore with it and Lian continued with a new and terrible strain to her voice.

"Can you believe, after our dismal northern town, that they send me off to live in this beautiful place? I would have laughed if I hadn't been crying so much, crying so hard I could barely see the sign at the train station. They, my Dad and my aunt, put me in a Georgian flat that cost a fortune, even though I'm not worth one. Well, they didn't put me there, they just paid for it. Couldn't even be bothered to see me off. I just made my own way to this strange place, the only mercy being that my tears blurred everything anyway. I couldn't tell if people still stared at me, not at first. I just sat in this unfamiliar empty room and thought that it was as good, or as bad, as anywhere else. The sash windows looked like pretty enough bars to me so I pretended I was in prison. A self-inflicted penance as no one else was prepared to sentence me. They called it *rehabilitation*, I called it *solitary confinement.*

I never see the view from those windows, even though I know it's there 'cos I the house is high up on a hill which I am told is beautiful. I am on one of the seven hills that surround the city, I should be grateful but I can't see..."

She raked her fingers through her hair, an established gesture of torment and despair.

"...I can't see out of any window anymore 'cos my reflection, this stupid face, gets in the way. My face which swims up the glass and clouds it before I get a chance to see out. My face looks ruined to me even though I'm only twenty eight...

('*She doesn't even look eighteen!*' thought Alicia)

...and mirrors always catch me out. I see this thing looking back at me. Sometimes I look twisted and ancient, there are bruises under my eyes like dark fruit and my mouth looks like a bullet through a rose petal, a dumb ragged 'o', permanently horrified by everything and everyone. But mostly I am horrified by myself. Even in this beautiful, genteel city I am still me, no escaping that one. Me still getting the dreams, still seeing the stuff that isn't supposed to be there. And then it gets worse!"

Lian laughed that horrible barking laugh again and Alicia thought of little foxes in their dark earth, baying for their mother and food, of vixens calling for a mate, of those persecuted red-furred creatures running for their lives from the hounds. She wanted Lian to continue but didn't want to just nod. She was already well aware of Lian's opinion of so-called magnanimous counsellors who just sat in silent observation.

"In what way was it worse?" she asked, putting all her genuine love and concern into her words.

"In all ways! All summer those strange green insects drifted into my room on warm breezes and I just sat there thinking, *knowing*, that I'm somehow on fire and dying and I want someone to come but he never does...one minute I am Lian, in a rented room in the *Now*, in twentieth century England, the next I'm someone else, somewhere else and Robert never existed and there's cold stone and dried herbs (*I can smell them*!) and *the man* with the nut-brown hair who comes to call on me... and I go from seeing the buildings of the city all around me like Robert's dirty bones, all stained and lonely in the purple dusk, and then I'm..."

('*You're having far- memories of France*,' thought Alicia, *'its Thirteen Twenty Five, the year before they take us both to Avignon, and we are sitting in the kitchen of the Lord. His name is Roger Antoine and I am Allette. I work in his kitchens and you are training me as your successor for you, mistress, are Marguerite, the Maman, and childless. You are valued by the Lord, as midwife and lace maker to his estate, and you live in the one roomed dwelling on the edge of the wood, as your mother did before you. There is much activity around us as we stand together at the scrubbed wooden table; the Lady Veronique is with child and we are happy...so happy!*)

"I think I am in France and there is so much to do. I can see my hands; they are small and quick, always working. Yet a part of me is always listening, I am waiting for him...*the man*..." Lian's brow furrowed and she paused, "what am I talking about?"

Alicia said gently, "tell me about Robert? Let's get back to him and why you think that you killed him?"

Lian clutched at her hair hard enough to hurt and nodded miserably.

"There was this photo of him, of Robert as a boy. His mother used to get it out of her handbag when she was really drunk and she'd tell me he was a lovely little boy, she'd slur it into my ear. The photo became slurred too, blurry from the sweaty mauling his stupid, fat mother gave it when she was all smashed and sentimental on gin. That one pock-marked photograph, it sticks in my mind more than the man Robert was. That kills me, you know, I feel so bad that I know the face of a toddler, grubby and unfocussed, more than a man I was supposed to love."

One tear fell onto the black jeans Lian wore and soaked in to the fabric while she visibly held herself in check. Alicia felt her own chest tighten and heave. Her throat burned.

"What's your name? I can't tell you any more till I know who you are." Lian plucked at the damp fabric and looked up at Alicia with swimming eyes.

(*Allette! You can call me Allette!*)

"Mary Alicia Owens. But we can dispense with the Mary. Echoes of my convent days and big Nuns with hard hands. I prefer the middle name."

"Alicia, that's good. A good name to have. Robert's mother was called...she doesn't deserve a name, does she? Let's call her bitch. Bitch that she was she would take his cigarettes and any booze he could find, she wasn't discriminating, and make him ride all the way up to the Lake District on his bike just to deliver some booty to her."

"What sort of bike did he ride?"

"Would you really care if I told you? I mean, Alicia, would you even know what it was?"

"I have a son too, you see, and he likes...I mean, he *liked*... bikes. When I knew him."

"It was a Norton. Commando. Black. A Six-Fifty. Now it's nothing."

"My Davey would have approved. He liked British motorcycles. Do carry on with your story, I apologise for my interruption."

Lian threw the old woman a quizzical look and continued slowly.

"His mother would get all maudlin, not so much for Robert's lost youth but for her own. She was a selfish baggage, the bitch. She wasn't bothered about anything except her drink and the exploitation of any man that would come along, even her own, her only, son. Her son, the child with the sun-bleached hair and freckly nose, captured forever in a square of dingy Kodak paper, his bright, laughing eyes and his tiny, eager hands, digging in the dirty northern sand. I always thought of him more as my little boy than hers. I won't ever drink alcohol, no matter how bad my pain is, because I want to be nothing like her. I wanted to be his good mother, not that clinically obese, terminally selfish, neglectful hag that was his bad Ma.

So, that night, the night I killed him, he was going up to see her. He got on his bike, all shiny and well-maintained it was, not like me. I was nothing but a sketch done on tatty grey paper that night, I was *foul*. I had Robert's baby inside me but I was deciding. Deciding! Oh the luxury I had to make a decision! I told him to give me time while I, the great me, decided whether our seedling, sapling baby should flourish or be terminated, up-rooted. I wanted time to see if I needed to prune and weed or water and nurture. A bee-sting baby that was Robert's...oh, it seems like another world and it probably was...I like to think that there is another world where that baby still exists and so does he. But in this world...*nothing, no baby, no Robert*...because then he was speeding on his bike because he knew...

(Alicia knew too)

....knew that the baby inside me would become nothing. That I would decide to still the idea of its beating heart. Even after Robert had said he would love to marry me, to start a family. Even then! Even when I knew how much he wanted to do it right for this child, right in a way neither of us had ever known. But no, I had to decide didn't I? I had to know best and I had to take it upon myself to decree that there could never be, would never be, a perfect world for our child. Or a child at all. The only human being that ever loved me in this life and I had to push him away and test him and spurn his love..."

"Your mother loved you," said Alicia.

"My mother died on me! And Robert was the only one who would have seen it through and weathered the taunts and the teasing he got for being with freaky Lian Smythe. But because of me and my pathetic display of controlling him, of *destroying* him, he was speeding on his beautiful bike, hoping to crash because he knew...he *knew* that I would chose to obliterate our lovely child and so he wanted to eradicate that inevitability. I killed him on a lonely road in an unknown county at midnight. He put his head down and rode into certainty above my uncertainty; he opened the throttle but it was me that was pushing him, making him do it, just so I could feel powerful when I had never had power. Just so I could cause hurt when I had always been hurt. I was deliberating with fate and dancing with my stupid self-absorption while he was going too fast for the road."

Lian drew breath as if she were about to dive under water.

"And do you know why I didn't want his baby? Because of the *visions.* The ridiculous, wretched visions based on nothing and no one real, the notion that somewhere there was another man, another life and I must search for him and go towards it. I should forsake Robert, ditch reality, and meander off on a quest for a man with green eyes like mine but less verdant somehow, with more granite than moss. I could always see *the man* and not Robert, my dearest friend and lover Robert, who I had never wanted, not truly. Always the bloody visions! Stupid damnable things, thwarting my only chance of happiness in this world. Making me kill him, making the baby die in favour of some nebulous, irresponsible, illusive piece of junk that my mind kept showing me."

('*It wasn't junk,*' Alicia thought, '*it was medieval France you were seeing and the man was Julien, Julien De St. Pierre. But we shall come to this later, later my precious.*')

"So, Robert braced himself and the thirty two ton lorry, fully loaded, using the back roads when it should never have been allowed to, finished it for him. He became free like he never wanted to be and the crow circled the gatepost and I screamed even though I was not there because I was never really anywhere. I could hear it all though I was not with him, I was never really with him, and I felt the glass and metal rain down upon me and the dead weight of a body hitting the ground. And I knew...I knew because I always *know*...that part of him landed somewhere else. That there was a softer thud as the head of a boy, a dear boy who had once been Robert John Tindall, hit the dry earth in a field. The engine was ticking and his intestines were dripping and Robert's poor head lay in the field, pulped and pitiful and still staring at me."

Lian lurched forward and Alicia reached out, not caring if she felt and saw the images, just needing to comfort this girl. Needing to hold her as no one, not even Robert, ever had. To hold Lian Smythe with tenderness and compassion yes, but also with complete and utter understanding of who she was and why she saw, heard and felt things as she did.

She was a witch, Alicia's kin.

She was one of the Fey.

"Cariad," Alicia's hands stroked back the damp red fringe from the waxy brow and Lian moaned softly against the shoulder of the old woman's nubbly cardigan.

"Hold me, lady! I keep drifting away from it but I need to remember. I need to face his face, that kissing part of him, the deaf ears that would never hear my rejection, the blind eyes he turned to my lack of faith in him. I need to witness..."

"I'll hold you steady, girl, that's all right now. You just follow the thread and let it flow. Talk to me, Lian and I will hold you."

The two women began to rock gently, one on each chair but meeting in an embrace that spanned centuries, holding and rocking until Lian moved her damp mouth from the rough wool of the cardigan and continued.

"So, they parceled him up, his remains and put him into a body-shaped box when he wasn't body-shaped anymore. My best friend, my darling, in bits and all the love in my world gone! We weren't meant to know that but I could *see*, the wood of a casket can't stop my vision. No amount of earth shovelled onto its lid can keep the truth from me! He was denied a beautiful corpse, denied it by me. He became nothing more than an urban myth, a warning to errant sons. '*Don't ride those death-trap motorbikes, boy, see what happens to foolish young men who do*'. He became the legendary 'Biker with no Head' on every lonely road in the North. He became a monster, a ghost, a figure of fun. No son would ever heed the warnings, no one else had Robert's pain, or his beauty, and they would all live, the sons of bitches. Robert was the dead son of a bitch and so he remained, still and cold."

Alicia, despite protecting herself, could hear Lian screaming inside her own her head. Tears poured down their faces unchecked as they grieved and, just for a moment, railed against the world as one.

Lian took control of herself and sat up poker-straight, once again bracing herself against the reality of the world. Despite her dignified pose her chest was heaving.

"Do you want to hear any more?"

"Child, I want to hear whatever you want to tell and more besides. Just you take it steady beloved, breathe..."

Lian nodded and, taking a huge hitching breath, she plunged back into the horror of her tale.

"So, I went there, to the scene of his death. I hitched a lift and searched and became a pilgrim. I saw nothing except a stain on the ground, a bloodstain, the same size and shape as an unborn baby in its early stages. I saw everything, blood and bone, tangled limbs, bright diamonds of glass in the maw of a big black bird. I wanted to keep Robert's skull, pristine and arcane, to remind me, and keep a candlelit vigil eternally. At least then he would have been with me, loving me, somehow. But I just stood there, hapless, seeing an empty field, a broken gatepost. *knowing* that I would never possess one of his sacred bones.

I was no mourner but a murderer who had not yet seen the scene of their own crime. Or had I? For a while I became a time-traveller, lost in space. I do know that I placed a pumpkin head at the cross-roads, not flowers, and it stared at those few passers by that used the road, reminding them of the hour of their own death. It said it them '*hurry home lest your loved ones miss you. Love them for time is short, give them the care they deserve now*'.

I hated that pumpkin head yet I carved it lovingly and it spoke to me, *sotto voce*, of inevitability and fate. Like meeting a silent doppelganger in a misty county garden it was a foretelling of mortality and it whispered to me of death's coldness and lack of guile. It mocked me, tormented me and gave me all I deserved. I wish I could have been all Robert deserved. But I wasn't, not ever.

I was better than his mother though, oh yes of that we can be sure. Or can we? It's my fault isn't it? Everything is!"

Alicia wordlessly shook her head and squeezed Lian's hands, pouring love through each fingertip into her quivering form, strung tight as a bow but vibrating as if unseen fingers continually plucked at it. Lian attempted a smile, perhaps her first in many many long months, and it faltered badly. She swallowed hard and continued.

"All is death! Every one of us will see that guileless smile of inevitability. But maybe...maybe not so soon as I saw it. It was my companion in the crib, after all.

I've been to the cross-roads and now there's no turning back. I saw Hecate on that lost day and I feel like we made some sort of deal, she and I. And I think she took away time, or some time, because I don't remember much after I saw the place where Robert had died. They found me and the pumpkin man, on a lonely road, collecting tiny slivers of glass. Shivering. I'd set fire to that treacherous gatepost and it stood charred and horribly black while I screamed at it. Then there was a fat silence and for a long time, or a matter of moments, I became a yawning shadow, wandering.

And then...then..."

Lian screwed up her face as if peering at something indistinct.

"Yes, then the clouds thinned and I saw something. It was after Robert's death and we gathered in a tenement flat to place one finger each onto a dirty glass tumbler. We were nobody much and there were so few of us, we couldn't get his biker friends to help us. Robert's noisy, beer-swilling, well-meaning friends, they wouldn't play although it would have been so much more powerful if they'd have been there too. But that was my fault, of course it was, because to them I had become the ultimate pariah, an *untouchable*. They had so much raw hate for me yet they never called me murderer, they just skirted around me, left me bereft, drowned out my wails with the roar of their big bike engines and drowned their own sorrow in drink. I would not follow them into pubs to become un-*seeing*, blinded by alcohol, temporarily numbed. I wanted to stay alert; I had to contact Robert so that I could make amends and so we had the Ouija board."

Alicia moved back a little in alarm, she could not help herself. The Ouija was somehow more affecting, more terrifying, than the death of that poor boy. Ouija, used by an undisciplined but brilliant *seer* in high distress? By the Lady, it could be disastrous beyond measure!

"Who were the people who helped you with this, Lian, you need to tell me exactly what you did, you need to be very clear now...try and remember!"

Lian pulled a face that was child-like in its openly perplexed state. She looked like a somnambulist waking up to find themselves in a totally foreign place.

"It smelled bad. Yes, that I remember. It was a horrible place. The funeral had been near where Robert had grown up, not in the town where we had both lived, and the North can be so depressing. No wonder Robert had grown up so..."

"Try to focus for me, girl, come on now!"

"Robert used drugs when he lived there. He moved to our town when he became clean and we met..."

Again the frown of concentration.

"We met at a college party, Robert and I. I don't even really know why I was there. No one really spoke to me except for the other misfits and even they had no idea what I was about; I was always too far out, even for other outcasts to relate to. Robert was there in a long black coat and battered boots; he had stopped the drugs but he drank spirits and he was quite drunk I think. He had a kind of...poetic melancholy. He didn't look like the typical biker, more like a would-be Byron with dirty nails. Bovine eyes, liquid brown. Freckles I could count. He put the same record on the jukebox four times...the one that goes '*this is the end, beautiful friend*' and I knew he didn't find me weird, that he wouldn't mind my visions and my intuitions and the way my eyes looked. Most people hated my eyes, feared what was behind them, but some men found them exotic, even exciting, until they discovered what *does* lay behind them. Those other boys...men...I could pick up every scrap of distaste and confusion they felt as they took their leave of me, not like Robert; all I ever picked up from him was love. I knew that he wouldn't call me witch and pelt me with excrement, that he would never lock me in dark cupboards after school or pull my hair out by the handful and laugh. No, he would never wilfully hurt me, me with my black jumper and my faded jeans, trying to look normal after a fashion, looking like a confused cockatoo with my stupid crest of hair. Nobody believed all this red hair was natural, you know, except him; he accepted everything about me. As if I'd try to look this conspicuous on purpose! But he, that angel called Robert, he just loved it...I mean, he loved me. It was like a miracle!"

Alicia gave a small sad smile. How unpretentious this girl was, how little she realised of her own potent pull, her power. That was why she had to speak of what they had done after Robert's death. Goodness, to have her power, the *seeing* and *knowing* of the Fey ones and to use the Ouija...

"Tell me about the Ouija, beloved? Please?"

"Don't you want to know about him?"

"Yes, but I need to know about what you did, this is very important!"

Alicia was aware that she had started to talk to Lian as if she were a child but Lian, having spoken of the event of Robert's death, had slipped into a childlike state. Dreamy, rambling, hopelessly lost in terms of time and place. Any reference point to that was seized upon and followed aimlessly. They could spend hours trying to find their way back to the events that followed if Alicia did not guide them now. Lian was close to unravelling.

"We asked Robert's biker friends to do the Ouija with us but they just cursed me. Bernie, the one-armed pillion passenger of Kev, Robert's best friend, he threw his flowers into there stagnant canal in disgust. They all looked like Tolkien figures in denim and leather, hopping mad, with old-young eyes accusing me without words. I had once admired them, I thought they exuded this calm sagacity that somehow always eluded me. I was fascinated by their wild beards and crinkly hair; Vikings and warriors, they were, in my mind, and goblins and dwarves too. But after Robert left me, they didn't smile at me anymore, they just used their engines to make me silent. I cried out, my face all contorted and disgusting, a mask of snot and tears, and they cursed me. I heard them in my head, like I hear everything.

Damned me to hell, they did, me with my kooky ideas and ludicrous fancies, my supposed visions. As if I wasn't already in hell! They blamed me with the uproar of their engines, made me patsy, and called me sorceress for turning Robert from an ordinary boy into a dead one. Truth was, Robert had never been as ordinary as they supposed. I found it sad that they had not seen that Robert too had his dreams and his needs, complex desires beyond pistons and gaskets.

All their anger focused on me and I absorbed it in penance. It was as it should be. I couldn't argue with it so I turned from it and found others that would play with me. There were two boys, ones from Robert's lost drug days in that dismal northern city, two poets, two patchouli-scented, smacked up fools. Both had sick cream-cheese complexions, stilton veins standing proud in skinny arms. They saw Robert as achieving what they had always wanted, an early death, an ending, and they welcomed me and my idea of the Ouija. They liked death, wanted to play with it, and they even liked me. I was strange and these two courted the outlandish and the lost for that is what they were, all at sea and wrecked on the rocks. They didn't really see me, their drugs saw to that, but it didn't matter, they would do. They were the dregs, the losers, the only hope I had of ever speaking to Robert again.

I knew they would be gone soon, too. They were close to him in subtle ways, balancing on the edge of the abyss. They had cheap copper bangles that clicked like mandibles during the church service, distracting me, making my head full of insects. They had hands that moved like the dried out, bleached limbs of dead crabs caught in a restless tide. And they looked at me and almost smiled, these wild-eyed marionettes with their sleeping sickness and their scuttling, desiccated souls. Drug-raddled addicts who looked like the physical embodiment of my pain and two who must, I reasoned, be close to the Otherworlds, looking death in the face as they did daily. Their connection to ghosts had to be extraordinary because they were forged from little but cheesecloth and ectoplasm anyway and with them I knew I could talk to Robert again."

Lian looked up, suddenly lucid, the soul-poetry of her rambling descriptions ceasing for a moment.

"Tell me, Alicia, do people or situations really sap our hope or do we let it trickle away ourselves?"

Alicia could not answer, for to respond would take them too far from the path they were on, and Lian would welcome the diversion from her terrible story. No, even if it risked Lian's wrath they must say on this track; there would, she hoped, be plenty of time for the discussion spiritual philosophy when this nightmare was all talked out. So Alicia cocked her head like a bird and spoke directly to Lian's spirit, asking it to fly them swiftly back to the place they needed to be.

"The Ouija, Lian?"

"The Ouija, yes. That bloody thing. It sucked me in, you know. I just needed something to do with my grief, grief, grief and I had no safe haven in drugs, no oblivion in drink. Sleep for me has always been tormented and tinged with the regret that it wasn't deeper, darker, *permanent* and so there was no escape from it there either. But I had to find a release, a way to apologise. I thought of killing myself too so as I could find Robert again and love him properly but was afraid I would become one of those empty shells I always see, grey and ephemeral, hanging around the humans who don't know they are there. I didn't want to become stuck in that fog where the lost ones go, just a ghost of my own self with my pain still intact, I needed to remain corporeal and finally use my dubious abilities to talk to things...to people...that no one else could see.Yes, I needed to contact a Robert who I could no longer see. How ironic, I spend a lifetime seeing spooks and finally when I want to see him...nothing!"

('*That's because suicides aren't like other spirits*,' thought Alicia, '*they can't be contacted, not for a long while. You know that yet you ignore the facts and now court such a death yourself. Oh child how much you have to learn of your Craft! How is it that you can now commit yourself to suicide when you know what will happen? How desperate are you my little Elf-woman*?')

"So," Lian continued, " I enlisted the help of those two imps, two remnants from a particularly hellish Bosch painting. Jamie and Aaron they were called, still are called as far as I know; such normal names for two such wasted specimens! They were barely male and fading fast, unthreatening as dandelion seeds in a breeze. I loved them because they were more messed up than me and my father would have hated them. But he didn't know where I was, my dear old Dad, I had disappeared into another city's soft greyish underbelly. After the hideous funeral, after the bikers had left, after that bitch, Robert's anti-mother, had snorted and wailed her last and sloped off to the pub, then I fell into step with these two revenants and we made our little plans. They knew people who dabbled in the occult, like all of society's rejects do, and so we plotted."

Lian was coherent but Alicia feared at any moment she may lose her thread and the vital information, the story of what happened with the Ouija, may get lost in a maelstrom of disjointed, distressing memory. It was vital that Alicia know what she was dealing with.

"Dear one, can you just tell me about the session you had with the boys and the Ouija; was it a proper séance? Did anyone there have any experience in what they were undertaking?"

"Oh I doubt it! If they had it would never have happened the way it did!"

Alicia shuddered. At least now Lian was letting her give endearments without balking, in fact she barely seemed to notice Alicia at all as she went on with the distressing tale.

"My knuckles were raw from chewing on them when we arrived at their squatted flat. I bet you've never imagined how sordid the life is that some people try not to live. You wouldn't believe the combined smell of the damp, dirty blankets and sour milk, the spilled beer and the patina of greasy dust on everything you touch. The vomit and the urine on the stairs, the stench of unwashed skin, the claustrophobic fug of anti-matter and stained mattresses. I wondered how Robert, precious child that he had been, could have lived there, but I knew deep down that the heroin had taken away any disgust for these surroundings, replacing it with self-disgust. How strong he had been, my lover, to kick the habit? And for what? I wept that he had been so miserable as to have taken drugs with these two in the first place. I cried for the fact that he had pulled himself out of this mire only to meet me and perish anyway.

I sobbed as we climbed the sorry stairs, edging our way past shrunken, quivering dogs and rubbish. I wept harder when I found there was nowhere to sit in a room designed only for those who lay down, comatose, and my tears fell onto a carpet of indeterminable colour. It was like a modern day opium den but worse, far worse. I saw faded, wilting David Bowie posters leering at me with those crazy mis-matched eyes of his across the gloom and I clung hopelessly to those two puzzled boys with distemper coloured hair who had known the only man who had ever loved me. I held them for comfort but was afraid they would snap, made of gossamer and glue, brittle and tarnished, two empty carapace boys, the toxic twins that were my only hope.

We needed a table but there was no table. We needed chairs, the letters of the alphabet written on neat squares of card, a glass. The boys said they would get these things. They liked to have something to do that was different from their usual routine of scoring drugs and using drugs and hoping to never return. They needed to make phone calls, connections, deals. They would arrange things for me. And I believed them because they had more compassion in the dried out husks of themselves than my father, or my counsellor, or any other supposedly upright, uptight citizen. They could still feel, still cry, even though they were broken and polluted beyond repair.

I was touched by their concern, their offers of drinks and drugs which I declined. They genuinely wanted me to feel better even if they never could succeed. They accepted me as those who claimed to care never had...excepting Robert of course, he meant every word he had ever said. Including '*I can't live without you*'."

A sob, stifled, hitched Lian's chest. She struggled on.

"I trusted them where I had no trust, before or since. Because, by association, I was trusting Robert, albeit belatedly. Once upon a time, before I had known his freckly face, he had loved these two boys as brothers. Brothers in punctured arms.

As the light faded a space was cleared. Piles of things left on the floor for countless weeks were shifted aside, placed deeper into the gloom at the corners. I could feel something gathering even before we stole the table from the adjoining flat. We had to prop it up straight on bricks but it was adequate. It needed to be shiny so I bought some polish from a twenty four hour convenience store, run by nervous looking Asians. I bought children's coloured paper, scissors and a ruler and jauntily coloured felt tip pens and began work on lovingly crafting the alphabet onto inch squares which I meticulously measured. A motley collection of five chairs were assembled, some with makeshift legs; one even had castors still attached like a reminder of those who had such luxuries in their homes, a sign of some other civilisation.

It was became possible, our Ouija, through our unified need, or our collective madness. Jamie went out, hunching his shoulders against the foulness of the outside world, and returned with candles which he stuck in saucers and then, running out of plates of any kind, directly onto the mantelpiece so that the wax dripped there and held them in place. They added to the eerie ambience, I guess. But, to me, this was no horror-movie effect for spooky atmospherics, it was reality. The candles draw the spirits, just like I seem to. Maybe we both shine, attracting the moth-like visitors, the half-seen, only my own light must be corrupted somehow for I only attract the damned it seems.

I felt the presences coming even before we started, my skin was creeping, hairs standing to attention on my frigid skin. Aaron said it was cold. Of course it was. They always made it cold, the dead. It was normal to me. I was used to it. A life time of unseen and uninvited guests, all with icy fingers, had been mine. I hoped that this time one of them was my dearest Robert, sucking all my energy to give himself form, nourishing his cadaverous self on my vital essence, making himself real again. I welcomed the cold for the first time ever."

('*Oh no,*' Alicia was thinking, *'this is dreadful! If I only I could step back in time and stop it but I cannot and powerlessness is a terrible thing.'*)

Lian went on, eyes fixed and staring, looking inward at some stark and terrible memory.

"The others arrived; a bizarre collection now in a room filled with flickering shadows and flame. We stood awkwardly in a tawdry hell of mismatched chairs, fluttering scraps of bright paper, drifting sandalwood from cheap incense sticks and the sweet smoke from the endless joints the boys lit. The three newcomers were misfits all...a fat woman dressed in a voluminous kaftan, an elderly scrawny man with tattoos and a sinister black clad, bald youth. Were these the folk to help me talk to my darling? They had to be, I supposed.

In a corner I caught a movement and realised there had always been another woman there, a whispering pile of rags. This was Jocelyn-who-Did-Not-Speak, Robert had mentioned her to me. Sister of Aaron, a girl who survived on black coffee and biscuits and the ragged skin from around her splintered, yellowed fingernails.

Jocelyn; seeing her filled my mind with tangents and logarithms. I realised that already I was getting the vision...the *sight*. It would be easy to contact Robert; it *should* have been easy! Jocelyn was a special lucky/unlucky charm I thought; she was a creature who lived but had long since transcended this Earth-life and dwelled on another plane and she would help my communion with the beloved dead. She was visible then invisible in the electric blue drift of dope smoke. My tears made her legion as she fragmented further. She was all the lonely people condensed into one and she could have slid down a crack in a skirting board and vanished and no one would ever have noticed, except the two lost boys and me...and who were we to remember anything? She smelled bad, musty and forsaken and her scent would linger on long after she was remains...

is remains..."

Lian sighed heavily again. She seemed so weary.

"She was like all of us misfits, remaindered from society, but somehow she was more than us, or less, it was difficult to tell. How was it possible that she been so outlawed into this anti-life by the status quo? Hadn't someone ever noticed her presence and reached out to help her? She was like a little mushroom in a dark clammy place, sprouting despite itself. Her fetid essence clogged my pores and made me feel unbearably tainted as if I were already sharing space with a corpse, breathing in fragments of its spongy flesh as it decomposed. I could have howled in my desolation but I did not, I had work to do, I needed all of my energy for that.

We assembled ourselves at the small circular table and the room grew heavy with the hiss of static and tinted with shades of alchemy. If you've never been a ...what shall I call it...?"

"A psychic? A *seer*?" offered Alicia, silently urging Lian towards the crux of the tale.

"Yes, a *seer* I suppose, although it makes it sound grander than it is in reality. Well, if you've never been one you won't know that feeling. It's like being suspended in some primeval ooze, some treacly thick, electrically sparking darkness..."

"I know that feeling well," confirmed Alicia, "I feel it each time I have been asked to clear up some psychic mess that humans have made."

"But no one else felt it, only me that night, even though these people were supposedly occultists...thrill seekers more like. Crowley's devotees, followers of Madame Blatvatsky, dribbling sycophants and acolytes of any weird, alien concept. But none of them felt it but me. I supposed that was enough, at least I could be the conduit. And Jamie and Aaron could too, I supposed. But then Aaron got scared and wouldn't play so the love Jamie had for Robert in the dregs of his worn-out soul would have to suffice to boost my own connection. Would it be enough? I willed it to be so!

We just needed to sit around that table and to *concentrate*.

I wondered how Jamie and Aaron had convinced these people to come and play? Three strangers had somehow listened to two spindly boys with cobweb hair and narcotic stares and just how they had made them listen I never found out. Maybe they were so mad they'd have done any strange thing for a thrill. And they must have been quite, quite mad to have done it. I mean, I was me...always half way to insanity anyway and apocalyptic with grief, and the two boys were drugged up delinquents who were out of their heads already. But these other three must have had a modicum of sense between them? But no, it seems not, because they sat down with us and entered into it. The most dangerous game you can play. Worse than drugs."

"Yes," Alicia was leaning forward clutching her chair. This was going to be bad. *Bad*! What had the poor girl done?

"We begin."

Chapter Two

Gone to Ground

Alicia looked across at the small woman curled in her familiar kitchen chair, the one usually covered by books and balls of wool, and paled at the prospect of hearing what she needed to hear from her. For anyone to have undertaken an Ouija board session with a bunch of unknowns was dangerous in itself. For Lian, an adept but completely untrained *seer* to have even attempted a haphazard, unprotected séance of any kind, was akin to having opened a door and invited any unscrupulous, devious entity to enter in to her life. It was rather like leaving her house keys with a total stranger, thus giving them free reign to use her home. Ultimately she may have been safe but it was a foolish risk to take without adequate precautions and protective measures in place.

It was easy and indeed tempting for a manipulative or plain dangerous spirit to take advantage of one so gullible. And they surely had, hadn't they? Lian had effectively advertised her presence between-the-worlds and not been particularly choosy about who she welcomed in. And she would have been fortunate indeed if she had attracted the attentions of a wandering human soul. More likely she had contacted a collection of astral rubbish which enjoyed and thrived on pretending to be all sorts of fascinating people or things. Some called this detritus thought-forms, amalgamations of human wishes and unpleasant imaginings. Others perceived them as demonic spirits in their own right, ranging from the mischievous to the outright perverse. However you perceived them the result was the same. Lian was being haunted by more than her own grief and longing.

The small red-haired *seer* licked her unusually shaped lips. All of her features seemed exaggerated and the more Alicia looked at her in the half-light the more she seemed to change into something otherworldly. Her skin was like tallow and glowed with a strange radiance in the evening gloom. Her eyes seemed even more slanted, curiously wide and tapered in a way no human eye should be. Lian was almost a physical impossibility but she seemed painfully familiar to Alicia. The older woman felt a further pang of protective compassion towards this poor lost child who surely had suffered for looking as she did in a society not known for its tolerance of the unorthodox. And why did Lian look this way? Well, t'was the Fey soul inside Lian which made her human self look as it did for the Fey aspect was so much more potent than the human self. Her inherent wild soul-energy would always make its presence known, both through the flesh and through the *feel* of her. Lian's body simply took on the attributes of her soul-self, of the essence she held inside her temporary human vessel, and so consequently the effect was bound to be startling, not mundane. The essence of a green-spirited Faery, a Shining One, could be observed in every nuance and gesture of the girl, may the Lady bless her!

Lian spoke, drawing Alicia's attention back in to the harrowing tale.

"The bald man, Gregory I think he was called, asked the questions. I thought he was rather po-faced and I had the urge to laugh. Jamie did laugh, quite a few times, a bit too maniacally, like he was already mad. We all tried to concentrate but it was so hard at first, hearing this dead-pan voice intone '*spirit of the glass, are you there?*' in this dreadful, dank little room."

"That's all he asked, not for Robert to come through specifically?"

Alicia was leaning forward, straining to hear Lian's muttered, rambling speech. There was such a fine line to be walked between prodding the girl too hard for details and consequently upsetting her totally or letting Lian's painful memories to meander radically off course, away from valuable information.

"Not at first, no," Lian was chewing at her thumb now, obviously getting more distressed as the event was replayed in her mind. " He just kept repeating '*spirit of the glass, are you there?*' until it moved. It stumbled jerkily across the table, like an incoherent drunk lurching for a lamppost. It came towards me, I was sitting by the letter 'I' and then it just wobbled. It was as if someone was pushing it and so this Gregory chap, he got even more pompous. Gave Jamie a really foul look and told him to stop pressing his finger down so hard. Jamie looked really indignant, even I could see we all had just our finger tips resting gently on the glass as we had discussed before we began. So it must have been real, even if it did look clumsy and forced."

"I don't doubt it, child," Alicia nodded.

"You'd have to have had a white fingertip to have been pressing as hard as Gregory suggested and none of us did. We had all obeyed orders, fingertips barely resting on the opaque tumbler. You know, we all wanted it to work, it wasn't some teenage party game. Gregory started up with his '*spirit of the glass*' spiel again but the glass moved before he even got the words out. This time it did one little shuffle then it whizzed across the rest of the way and hit the letter 'I' then back to the 'W'.

Jamie got excited and called Aaron over to make a note of what it was spelling out but Aaron was too scared, or too stoned, and so we had to try and read what the glass was spelling ourselves. But it was so fast! Faster than I had hoped. I just wanted to know if it was Robert but I guessed that it had to be, it being so keen to speak to us."

Alicia groaned inwardly.

"Didn't you ask who it was?"

"It said, or it spelled out, '*I will come back through glass*'. It worked! It was real! Not that it made much sense, I was hoping for it to be relevant to me straight away but it doesn't work like that, does it?"

"No," Alicia said, tersely, thinking how much she detested this mode of spirit-communication. It was so risky, especially so for their kind. Oh the sadness she felt for a fellow Fey one having to reduce herself to such a level...it just showed how far removed they had become from their own *knowing*. Society had all but bludgeoned it out of them and now it was up to those like Alicia, those who had *re-membered*, to help her kindred to find their true selves again too.

Lian continued.

"I was so pleased that it had spelled something decipherable at least, I mean if it worked that easily then I could talk to Robert! *Just like that!*" Lian snapped her slender fingers, "and Robert had been going to study stained glass at University, it was what he had wanted to do, and so maybe he was trying to say something in a kind of code, like something that only I would understand. I waited for the next part of the sentence, knowing it had to make more sense to me, but then it stopped so Gregory asked who was speaking to us. This solemn atonal voice of his made me even more impatient '*welcome spirit, speak with us, identify yourself!*' so I butted in and started asking if it was Robert Tindall and if he had a message for me but it had already started to reply to Gregory."

Lian scowled, her animation suddenly gone as she remembered her disappointment. " It said '*I am Henry the Eighth*'."

"Oh dear Lady!"Alicia was feeling sick. She had witnessed so many false spirits claiming to be everyone from Adolf Hitler to Jesus Christ. She had seen many unprotected and blasé mediums and countless foolish teenagers attacked and deluded by such intrusive astral entities. Never a peasant or a fool among the legion of historical figures these spirits claimed to be, always aiming for the most dramatic effect, the nasty tricksters! It was just as foolish to believe the claim of such an entity as to believe someone dressed up in period costume on stage actually was the historical character concerned. It was more than an act, it was a con to illicit something (fear usually, despair often), from the people at the Ouija board. Yet she had to hear Lian out.

"Everyone got quite excited except for me of course. I mean, I didn't want a former British monarch, thrilling as it may have been. I wanted to say sorry to my Robert, my love. I got cross when the woman asked him what he wanted."

"And what did the spirit say?"

"It told us to stay quiet and listen but I didn't want to. I wanted Robert! I didn't know how listening could help me."

"What did you do?" Alicia was silently praising that Lian had done something...anything...other than being quiet. A spirit that asked for silence was playing for time, trying to discover who was the easiest prey, who could be most readily influenced, possessed of its qualities. It was a cheap trick used by the flotsam and jetsam of the low spirit realms which undisciplined use of divinatory tools attracted. It would then proceed, no doubt, with some amazing revelation or snippet that only the person concerned would have known. It was mind-reading, a trick, a cheap sham. Ugh!

So predictable was this routine that Alicia could have laid what little money she had on what it would do once it had rapt attention and blind belief in its authenticity. The cosmic con-artist could, and would, then frighten anyone innocent enough to believe this tomfoolery with prophesies and threats. It was control and fear it wanted, as a rule. Such was the sustenance of a low astral being.

To attempt such a séance, Lian would have needed a psychic handbook the equivalent of the sort of manual one had to memorise for becoming a motorist. One should not enter the realms of spirit blithely unaware of the codes of conduct required, it was as much an act of idiocy as getting into a car without knowing the rules of the road. But how could she blame Lian? Alicia knew her intentions had been heartfelt but her pain was a beacon...and a liability. The girl had been wandering about open and receptive for years with no protection and so it was no wonder she was so unhappy and unsettled; she was constantly at the mercy of any energy, any spirit, that sought her bright flame out. What was Alicia to do about it?

Lian went on, not knowing why the older woman was frowning.

"I interrupted Gregory again and said I wanted to talk to Robert John Tindall, at once! No time wasting! The other three looked daggers at me in the gloom but I could sense Jamie was keen for me to take control rather than Gregory. After all, he wanted to talk to Robert too. I think they had just come along to use us to make up the numbers for their own agenda...whatever that may have been."

"That's very astute of you," Alicia ventured.

"I dunno about that. Anyway, so Jamie said '*Yeah, man! Let's talk to Robert, this is just going to divert us*'. And the glass moved off again, unbidden, spelling out a whole string of things.

It felt *angry*; it kind of jabbed at the letters and I started feeling properly frightened for the first time that night, my elation ebbing away. I became pathetically scared, just like I used to be when *the voices* would get really loud when I was in my bedroom as a child and it was as dark and my Dad didn't believe me so he shut the door on me. I was afraid I was a sitting target watching this glass just moving on its own. Feeling that anger from it, whatever *it* was, I *knew* that sooner or later it would make a bee-line for me. I started to feel the pain of realisation that Robert wasn't there at all. Or if he was he was very, very mad at me. As soon as these thoughts entered my consciousness it was as if the thing we had summoned with the Ouija sensed the change in me and began to taunt me. The more I stared at the jittering glass the more I felt all the despair of my life welling up, complete with fragments of imagery...me having my coat ripped off and stamped on in the school playground...me being cornered in the school lavatories and being called a freak while they tried to flush my head down the toilet...me being rejected by one boy, one man, after another..."

This was what Alicia had been dreading. Lian's fear, coupled with her psychic brilliance, would prove easy pickings for a malicious and dirty spirit.

"Gregory kept on with his ridiculous '*speak with us, is there anybody there?*' mantra and I felt like slapping him. Of course someone was there. Robert was out there somewhere, wasn't he, all he had to do was ask for him by name? The glass skittered in response to my thoughts and Jamie kicked me under the table; I think he was getting unnerved too. I knew he'd blame me somehow, people always do when the lights flicker or there are weird noises. And all the while he was kicking me the glass was skidding wildly about and bumping letters and reminding me, with seemingly meaningless strings of letters, of all the people who ever mocked me or bullied me."

"I'm sorry to hear..." Alicia was set to comfort her but Lian waved her hand impatiently.

"That table, I'd polished it within an inch of its sad little life and now I could almost see my face in it, contorted by grief. For a moment I lost my bearings completely, seeing only a circle of faces reversed, staring blankly upwards. Where was I? Incense, pious faces...was it a monastery? Then I heard Jamie's reedy little voice pipe up '*come on, Robert, man! We're you're friends, say something...we miss you, are you okay? Rob?*' and the glass did this pirouette that wasn't possible and I implored my dead boy to talk to me.

It felt as if it were going to thunder....thunder inside that room..."

Lian shook her head, her habitual gesture of trying to rid herself of these impressions, the psychic overload her life had been burdened by. She continued, her face becoming more blank and unreadable.

"Sweat began to stand out in little moonstone droplets on Jamie's milk-white forehead. There was storm brewing right there around us and everyone was fighting the urge to take their hands off the glass and wipe their own brow; it was stifling. The glass, the thing in the glass, told us that we weren't to stop, must not remove our fingers from it, that we had to maintain the connection or we would be in grave danger. I became aware of Jocelyn standing close behind me; I could smell her damage and her dankness, and little guttural grunts were escaping her. The glass did a perfect glide and hit the letter 'R' so hard it fell to the floor.

'*Robert!*' I remember me starting up my own mantra to rival Gregory's. I kept on '*Robert, I'm so sorry! Can you hear me Robert?*' but my mind was reeling back and forth, round and around, from corn dolly babies to the swish of a scythe, flesh of my flesh losing cohesion and...I could see myself from above."

Alicia's skin prickled with terror and once more she reached forward to hold Lian but the girl was locked into the memory. Instead she quickly sent her companion spirits to comfort Lian, to calm her, for the memory was getting on top of her again, threatening to swamp her lucidity.

"I was floating. I had lost my own body. I was looking down on the plump woman and the scrawny man who was sounding tired and desperate, beseeching the stupid glass '*speak to us more slowly, we beg you!*'. I could see the ludicrous spun sugar quiff of Jamie's bleached hair and see into my own mouth which hung open, gaping obscenely, a face completely devoid of any expression for I was above it...and I could see them all now looking at my body's shell with a mixture of alarm and concern. Didn't they know where I was? Couldn't they see me?

As I stared down I thought distractedly that Jamie might have been a good friend to Robert if they had played in the dirty northern sand and had plastic sailing boats instead of syringes. Poor Jamie, an insubstantial stick-boy with his sick, waxy complexion and his dish-water eyes, looking at my silly body as it drooled and slumped back in a stolen chair below me. I saw a table of frightened strangers and a glass that moved with random jerky movements, spilling letters onto a filthy carpet nobody remembered the colour of.

I was out of my body yet my body was moving, yawning, eyes rolling, grinning. There was a blizzard all around us now and a voice kept crackling in and out like a badly tuned radio. There was a stream of dancing, electrically charged air being sucked into my wide, wide mouth. I didn't like that, not at all. Even if I was outside of my husk-self I didn't want it invaded by that...that *whatever it was.*

'*Do it, do it NOW!*' a voice came out of the static and I sucked that up too like some phosphorescent spaghetti. I watched that body of mine inhale the effervescent stream of words until it became nothing but vapour, green tinged, being drawn into my nostrils. My poor body took it in and sighed, a little death. It shuddered and I was being drawn back into it, into that empty female shell. I could have fought it, stayed where I was, floating, weightless, could have gone off into the ether, to the stars, to meet Robert. But I was back and there was a horrible jolt, like when you fall downstairs in a dream. Then a pain.

'*Blood, blood*!' Aaron was babbling and Jocelyn screamed like nails on a blackboard while I licked the spittle from my chin and sat up. Our hands had left the glass, the circle was broken."

Alicia could no longer be strong for the girl. She began to weep.

Lian broke out of her internal reverie and reached over to touch Alicia's quivering shoulder, a gesture that was infinitely poignant, achingingly sad.

"It's okay. The baby left me of its own volition to be with its father and I was trapped back in this sordid flesh, the cheap little body of Lian Smythe. The candle flames wavered and grew unnaturally thin and long. Bright sparks ignited and red roses of raw agony bloomed before my eyes. There was a tingling in my hands, my body twitched in little spasms of searing pain. I was sitting in a thick pool of blood, sat on a chair that belonged to no one in the sad collection of matter that had been the fruit of my union with a quiet young man who had his whole life ahead of him. The plump woman's hair flew backwards in the unseen breeze and someone was saying a Hail Mary. I fainted.

I could still hear them though. '*We should never have broken the circle!*' someone wailed and I heard the glass break... '*he will come back through glass,*' I remembered...and there was a wind rushing in my temples that became a gale.The scattered letters blew around me like the confetti I would never have in my hair from my wedding to Robert John Tindall, a man who was no longer alive. Dead! Slow motion and shapes moving in the twilight of my quivering vision, chairs sliding back over a greasy carpet and Jamie sick with fright, his vomit brightly coloured like a child's.

A voice was coming from somewhere like a slowed down record of a song that never was, never could be, the air buzzing, my head filled with fat flies. Everything was shimmering and distorting with a blast of heat that could not be felt. The humming, whirring air and this terrible crashing discord of pain in me, in my womb, releasing, contracting, expelling. What a death to have, in that sordid room that had never been filled with love and laughter. Our baby was dead and I wished it would suck me down and away with it...

I hadn't really know that it was there until it wasn't.

I hadn't wanted it, that poor lost child, I had just wanted Robert back! It had been like a souvenir of him and that was all. And, you know, while I was unconscious, or dreaming, I actually saw Robert, finally. I almost...almost...had him back. He was walking out of the mist, surrounded by the blackest night, a beautiful, gently swirling velvet sky studded with stars. He looked calm. '*I'm so sorry!*' I said to him and he smiled. I realised he was only a boy, a small boy from a photograph taken when he was three or maybe four, his image grainy and the colours fading but he still smiled and gave me his hand. Freckles..."

Lian had tears running down her face again now, a face distorted with grief. She was a shining flame-haired girl with a broken heart but not a broken spirit, at least not yet. She was also a brave, intelligent and naturally gifted witch, a Fey *seer*. She must complete the story. Despite the tears, despite her own heart ache, Alicia had to hear the rest.

"In my vision Robert took me by the hand and he showed me something from his past. He showed me that once his mother, that appaling, desperate bitch, had left him alone for a whole weekend while she went off to Blackpool with her latest boyfriend; 'Uncle Pete' Robert had to call him, a man who wasn't too fond of children. So Robert had to remain locked in an oppressive little flat while Ma went off for her dirty, slovenly weekend with a strange bad man.

There were no windows open and it was July. Robert was too small to open the windows and was afraid to stand on a chair to reach the latches. If he had fallen and hurt himself his mother would be angry at the inconvenience, he had known that even as a tiny lad. So he just sweated and moaned in his confusion and loneliness. Even at his tender age he felt self-disgust when he had peed his own pants. The heat was stifling and soon Robert began to cry and feel naughty for being soiled and cowardly.

And the little boy Robert had been showed me how he had scrabbled around in a low kitchen cupboard and found himself a few old, dry cornflakes to eat. He couldn't reach their taps so he had taken water from the toilet to drink like a disobedient dog. Then he had curled himself up in a tight ball and hid in the only cool place he could find, between the toilet and the sink. And he had waited for forty eight long hours for his errant mother to come back.

I was crying even in this dream place, or in this death-place as I thought that surely I must be dead now to be with him again? And I held him to me and said I was sorry, so sorry and that it was all my fault! And...and he held me away from him and I could see him again, as a teenager, wracked by heroin withdrawal and thin as a rake and I closed my eyes against the scrawny youth he had been, with eyes like dirty saucers in a pallid, broken face...a face with so many beautiful freckles...

And when I looked again he was the Robert I had known, and yes damn it, had loved. And he told me, without any words, that I was not responsible and that, in his own way, he had chosen how to respond to the things that had happened to him. He told me gently, (*he was a gentle man!*) that I should know that things would never be that bad again, for him or for me, because we had seen *how not to be.* He explained to me, quietly, soothingly...*lovingly*...that we were both wrong, both reacting to our own pain, clinging to our own hurt, our own patterns of need and abuse. We could never have responded to each other in the state we were both in. Not properly. It drew us together, yes, but it flung us apart too.

And he squeezed my hand, *I really felt it*, and told me he had to go now because he had to get better, to become well again. Told me there was a place where he could be healed along with all the other souls who had died in despair, by their own hand. And he said that we would not see each other for a while but there was no need for me to worry because where he was there was love, more love than we could ever imagine from our perspective as human beings. And he said...he said..."

Alicia tried to wipe away her own tears but Lian touched the older woman's wet cheek and gave a small, twisted smile.

"He said that it was me that needed looking after and that I had the harder road for now. He said he'd send someone to take care of me. And then I realised that there were two boys walking away from me, hand in freckled hand, and a clock was ticking as from several floors below me. I heard a baby cry, just once, and I almost reached out to it. There was a damp, fetid cloth pressed to my forehead and a plump face peering down anxiously at me...not Robert's face...and I blinked and sat up to see that it was the fat woman. I asked her where my baby was and she said nothing and that nothing said everything.

I was wet and hurting and empty as hell. It was only then that I realised how truly bereft I was. I felt a twinge and doubled over, clutching at my uninhabited body. I couldn't bear it, not another moment of it.

I longed for oblivion to slide over me and for once it obliged.

I think I dreamed again, Robert at six with a red and blue beach-ball, bobbing on a clean green sea. Then it was raining and Robert was fourteen, smoking a joint by a curtainless window. I dreamed on and on, about little glass babies and of Jocelyn, translucent and many-limbed, blowing in through my window, awash in spells and charms and thin pinkish blood. A thousand reflections shone at me from fragments of lives, lives that glittered, flames that gutted, life-lines that broke and spilt apart, and I heard the prayers for all those lost souls slipping away even as I lay in my drenched slumbers, even as I twisted and moaned in my own sweat.

And at some point I was taken home again by my father who '*re-assessed my situation,*' based on the assumption that I had lost my mind. I mean, why else would I have been in that squalid flat, mis-carrying a baby I should never have been having, trying to contact the dead?

They...always *they*...knowing what was best for me. My Da and my aunt conspired, or worked out as they saw it, what I needed and until I was packed off to this city on an Intercity train with a suitcase they kept me too doped up to protest. Legal, prescribed drugs of course, they are respectable people after all, not like Jamie and

Aaron. Or so they think.

'BATH SPA' said the sign at the train station. I stepped onto the platform and spoke to that would-be welcoming sign. I had never felt so alone in my life and my head was numb from sedatives. I liked the sign; it informed me but remained impassive, not wishing to get involved. I liked it better than all the people that pushed past me. I placed my hand on the sign, it neither resisted nor protested, a bit like me, this sign. Or was it a bit like them, clean and somehow blandly appropriate? My head was so stuffed with wadding I had no idea.

I walked to my flat, ignoring the taxi rank. People and contact were not to be pursued in any shape or form. I had a map of directions to my new home, drawn on a piece of paper torn from one of my Dad's books. On the paper lingered a hint of him, his thoughts and a distilled essence of how he felt about me. I got a sense of his honest belief in my 'temporary breakdown' and in Robert's 'unfortunate death' and how both things were abhorrent to his orderly, regimented world view. I was part of things that should not be so. I touched the map and caressed the fringes of his disgust and disbelief. How could I have happened to him? Well, I thought, how did I even happen to myself?

How cruel a gift I have that enables me to see, feel, *experience* the disgust my own Dad has for me, his only, sad little mistake of a daughter?

I walked on. Why not be here? It was as good as anywhere else! After all, I wasn't paying for any of it, my '*relocation package*'. I was just an irresponsible mess. I held the map and read its subtle, horrible psychic messages.

I *see* and *know* too much. I sit in an empty flat in a beautiful city and I don't care and I care too much. The previous tenant's thoughts and dreams seep into my fuzzy mind. I hardly have the strength to move. I eat biscuits, bite my nails and drink coffee, just like Jocelyn. Tears fall, regardless.

Someone sprinkles sand and splinters into my open, staring, kohl-smudged eyes. I clutch a tiny sliver of glass with a hope that someday Robert will come back through it, as the Ouija board said. But I doubt it. I know that I am just a dream-weaver and that he is the dead.

And I also know that somewhere, getting closer but still so terribly far away, there is another man calling to me. I know that when I stop taking their stupid tablets I will get the full-force of my vision back and the man...

(*the man!*)

...will be with me. I am haunted by everything but especially him.

Who is he to make me kill my true lover in his favour? WHO IS HE, damn it, and why does he make me yearn?"

Lian looked at Alicia and the older woman had a vision of her own, that of a brighter time when a different Lian was singing in the surf at midnight and the *seeing* and the *knowing* were celebrated not sedated, negated. For a while she was lost in her own pain. She yearned too...they all did, the lost Children.

"And what ails me? Why am I so haunted? Is it that...that *thing*...from the Ouija making things one hundred, one thousand times worse for me? Just when I didn't think things could get any worse I'm made to feel even more hopeless, confused, despairing..."

She looked at Alicia, beseeching her with those enchanting eyes, to appreciate the gravity of the situation.

"Despair is the worst of it, for sure. And then there's the usual gamut of Poltergeist stuff, and *the voices*, all the bloody time, *the voices*...Can you make it stop? Can we make it stop together?"

"Yes, child, yes! We can do it, if you'll only stay a while and hear what I have to say first. I promise you...

(*'I can promise,'* thought Alicia, *'it's my job to do this sort of work in the world and I'm good at it, so I am!'*)

...I promise that we have the power to change things, for the better. We can make a new life for you, sweetling."

"And can you absolve me of my crimes against Robert, against the only man who ever, ever cared for me? Do you believe I killed him, lady, as I believe it?"

Lian's naked hurt and longing were terrible, yet beautiful, to behold. Such strength and depth of feeling there! Such passion! Surely if this were turned positively and outwards instead of negatively and inwards there would be such transformation in the world, a real Faerytide of emotion!

Alicia shook her head again in sadness.

"No my love, I do not believe that you killed him for in that you negate Robert's own free will to choose and afford yourself the power to control his spirit. Each of us is bound free by the laws of nature and of our own spirit; it is only us who can give away our free will to another and so disrespect our own sacred gift of choice. And, as for absolution, well only you can give yourself that; forgiveness of the self is a powerful thing that we all fail to give credence to, so busy are we seeking approval from outside of ourselves. It's time that we learned to take our own counsel, beloved, time for us to be strong in our own inner *knowing*. And I have hope, real hope, that we can achieve this together. When we have spoken of the meaning of our lives..."

"Our lives?"

"Yes, mine as well as yours and, when we have brought clarity where there is only darkness, then you will be able to absolve yourself fully, for good and all. I am going to help empower you cariad, to find inner knowledge and trust your own *knowing*, and with such wisdom comes peace, peace the like of which you've never had before...at least, not in this life."

"Peace," Lian savoured the word as if it were a foreign delicacy in her mouth, disbelieving of its sweet taste.

"Aye, peace, child. Lasting, true and deep. It can be yours I swear it! Just please, please stay with me a while. Give me time, I beg you mistress!"

"You beg?" Lian was child-like again, slanted eyes almost round with wonder. "*You* beg *me*? Surely I am not worthy to be begged after all I have wrought? I am well used to being the beggar in this life; as a powerful witch you may not beg me, your lesser!"

Alicia leaned forward and clasped the slender white hand to her bosom again. Lian could feel the old woman's heart beating through her faded smock. Summoning up all her passion, all of her will and all of her love, Alicia spoke.

"Yes, I beg you Lian. You are no underling, we are equals you and I; sisters of spirit under the skin."

She replaced the younger woman's hand back gently into her lap with such tenderness Lian was visibly moved by it. The emotions in that little cluttered room had swung from hostility to grace and back round again so many times in those last few hours as to leave them both reeling but still they continued, seeking safe purchase in the slippery scree of their temporary human-ness, both desperately wanting to discover a place free from searing soul-pain from which to relate.

Lian bowed her head in acknowledgement of the older woman's generosity of spirit, her volatile disposition, born of long torment, tempered for a time.

"Then I will stay."

After a silence which was filled only by the comforting ticking of her own kitchen clock Alicia leaned forward, conscious of the fact that Lian would probably not like to be touched now.

"I have a suggestion," she said, as gently as she could.

"Yes?" Lian looked up, her eyes dry but the face marked with ghostly silver trails where her grief had poured forth from her. Her black make-up had long since been washed away in the emotional deluge and now she sat exposed, with a face scrubbed naked by fists clenched from frustration and fear. She seemed made of alabaster, flawless yet unearthly, and there was a shimmer in those eyes that no human ever should have possessed. Even Alicia had to suppress a shiver when meeting those eyes...such potency, such potential!

"I suggest that I make us tea and sandwiches, maybe a heat up a little soup, I made a great pot yesterday and now I know why. I grow all the vegetables myself, of course, we need to be close to the land you and I."

"I grew some cress in an egg box once," Lian smiled despite herself, "but that's about it. I'm the product of cities, Alicia, not like you."

"You'll learn, sweetling. And then..."

For all her years Alicia still felt nervous at saying the next vital thing. Lian sat, staring straight into her eyes and she had to go on.

"And then I will share with you what I know of...those who are different. Those like yourself and...*the man*. Those who have been born...

(*Oh Lady, give me the words, I beg you!*)

...with the *seeing* and the *knowing*. Those who have a hard road indeed but one which can lead to places of great beauty. I will speak of people who walk in human form just as you and I do but those who are...the Shining Ones."

Lian's gaze was steady, penetrating. For the first time she noticed that Alicia was clearly visible to her even in the darkness that had long since fallen. Not only that but Alicia had eyes that reflected the light like silver sixpences and a lambent glow around her, a nimbus of dancing gold like a halo crowning her head. Lian had seen such crazy sparkling coronas around her own self; it had caught her out many times when she looked up into a bathroom mirror whilst cleaning her teeth, or when walking past a shop window. There was curious inevitability about the hearing of what this old, wise, infinitely kind woman had to say. And she was certain now that Alicia was not another detached do-gooder, her tears and her involvement with all that Lian had poured out...her loving embrace...had confirmed that Alicia was indeed different. Hadn't it?

Lian let out a long breath and dropped her gaze at last.

"I would like that very well, lady, and I would know what it is that you are."

Lian started at her own voice, the turn of phrase and inflections so familiar yet deeply strange

(*Marguerite! Allette!*)

"In fact, I believe that when I understand what you are I will come to know, for the first time, who I might be. Beyond this body, beyond this moment, beyond the pain of being here...I want to know why I am as I am."

Alicia smiled at last, the tension easing between them a little.

"I am as you are and it is well," she said softly, and got up to prepare their simple meal.

And as Alicia cut the thick wholemeal bread that she had baked only this morning, not expecting to share it but somehow knowing that she would by nightfall, she considered how she would rid this flame-haired Fey kindred of the spectres that haunted her. All in good time and gently, she thought. The main thing was to keep her here, safe, until she could explain what is was that they were because by doing this Lian's life may have some meaning at last.

And then she may not want to leave.

Chapter Three

Before

"We are not of this world yet we are of the Earth, for we grew here like the grass, or so it seems. Like grass, we grow naturally, turning our faces to the light only to be cut back or poisoned by some of those who walk in human form. Yet, like all green things, we experience a resurgence. The wheel of life turns and so we *become.* From bush and berry, beyond bright bubbles in a stream, behind sun-warmed stone in the subtle play of light and shadow, we return. Rising again, falling and laughing, in the joy and the pain of our eternal *returning.*

To try to stop the way of *returning* is to stem the natural flow of life. No wise one would ever attempt such a thing, even if it meant the end of all they held dear. *All of it !* They must, if they are truly wise, let go. Even in the face of destruction, even as they hear the last breath of their beloved, there must be a letting go. Never be afraid, my dear one, for the way of *returning* simply is. How do I know? Why, for I have returned. No, *we* have returned.

We do not need to be afraid any longer. We can speak out and be heard by those with the blood dancing in their veins and by those with a wild singing spirit. To them, to *you,* I tell our creation story. I know you look for your own lineage, a sense of ancestral place, and our story may shed some long-lost light on that which you yearn for. Share with me a dream of belonging, your soul's birth-rite of *being.* Take hold of the silver thread of these words and follow. For we are *re-membering* ourselves in the time before and beyond, before the darkness descended and our hiding commenced."

Alicia was rocking gently backwards and forwards in her chair, eyes closed, seemingly oblivious to Lian who hunched over towards her, straining to hear the old woman's sing-song words. She had switched from being a genial, if shrewd, old woman into some sort of bard, commanding yet lyrical and full of romantic whimsy. Should Lian laugh or sit rapt? Then those clear, calm faded chambray eyes opened and Alicia addressed her directly. It was more than a little disconcerting for one used to making others feel disconcerted.

"Let me ask you before I truly begin, do you think sometimes that you do not belong here, in this harsh reality? Do you feel that you are too sensitive, cariad, to live in this time, in this place? Do you call out in your soul to go home or even to know home?"

"Of course!"

"Then perhaps these words will resonate deep within you and wake up the wild spirit once more. I pray that it is so in the name of all that is wholly holy, in the names of the Creator Spirit, the Old Green Ones, and of our Mother Earth, that these words remind you of your origins, of your creation, of your destination..."

Lian made as if to answer but Alicia held up one wizened finger, adorned with a single plain silver band worn thin and narrow on one side. The old woman seemed then to be unfeasibly ancient and incredibly powerful, her face made in turns ghostly and luminescent as the night's shadows moved across it like clouds across the moon. Lian had no choice but to pay attention even though her instinct was to rebel and question Alicia's authority. '*She is a half-remembered destination, both weaver and the broken loom,*' Lian thought, without quite knowing why.

"Listen!"

It was not a command but it held more authority than any one word Lian had ever heard before. She listened and the old woman, she who was wise beyond knowing and generous beyond measure, spoke to her.

"Once upon a tide of time, before we lost the shining forms we wore so well and became dusty memory...before we lost sight of the starlight and became a frosty parody...before we hid the truth in the silent stones, in the deep pools, in the land herself and withdrew into her welcoming womb to that place between realms...

...yes, there was a before!

Before there was fear there was love. Love was natural and free and love was the Way. At the heart of all creation there was love and transformation. Out of this pure love, the Way birthed the web of existence and fashioned from these sacred shining strands the citizens of Itself. For the Way wished to make love with Itself, over and onwards and eternally, a great sensual spiritual unfolding, lapping and entwining with Itself in the bliss of reunion and the pain of separation. In the desire to experience its own great love reflecting back It *birthed.*

Fountains of love fuelled the process. A process of illumination, a great light that was only given meaning by its opposite, the velvet dark of dreaming depths. The dark was not greedy, it willingly gave up the gems of glittering, sparkling life that tumbled from the womb of Itself. It was a nurturing darkness, the polar opposite of the brightness but not its lesser partner, and they danced as equals for without the light there could be no shade by which to appreciate it; without the dark the light could not be discerned. So they danced on, eternally and blissfully cycling towards union, and from this ever-spiralling tunnel of love burst the stars, gleaming with new-ness. And the stars in turn birthed the citizens of themselves, the Shining Ones. The dreaming dark bore the Children of Light.

These Star Children were miraculous, beings of pure energy and raw power, fired by sacred intent, sustained on the pure harmonious tones of a cosmos in tune with itself. There was a universal shimmering and shuddering rippling throughout the All as it experienced for the first time the passionate throws of creating. As It created, these glowing Star Children danced the dream of being to the ululating rhythm of the beginning. They were the singers of the song that accompanied this birthing, these opalescent and marvellous creatures of gossamer and gold, the beloved ones of All-that-Was. In this bliss of white light, in the heat of the eternal moment, they danced the web of starlight and dreamed the Milky Way of the Mother."

Alicia rocked forwards and opened her eyes.

"Is everything clear to you so far, sweetling? You may stop me to ask questions at any time if you wish."

The jolt of hearing Alicia speak again as a mortal woman, not a bard, was unwelcome. Lian, for the first time in her mortal life, was spell-bound by another's magic instead of crushed by her own and she wanted more of it. Impatience crept back in and she tried to swallow it down.

"Yes, yes, please carry on!"

"So," Alicia shuffled and got comfortable again and commenced that steady hypnotic rocking in her chair, "for aeons they worked enchantments, self-seeding, glorious and giving, the precious, nebulous Children of Light. Of that tide of time, there is no abiding memory for all was one; all was created by a flight of communal fancy, a *melding*. These primeval beings shone in the darkness, expressing themselves freely and with infinite love. Their thoughts and feelings rose up on the heavenly fountain of *becoming* and made worlds. Their dreams of all possibility brought colour and sound and texture. They were the original artists and the architects, the first visionaries and poets, working with the essential essence of everything for the sheer unbridled pleasure of just being a part of it all. It was an age of beauty and freedom without boundary or limitation.

But that age, like all ages, had to pass.

Let us not lament that passing but instead remember its being."

Lian nodded her agreement and encouragement but Alicia did not see her as she had become lost in the magical pull of her narrative once more.

"It was right and it was good that these original seeds of change spread their fiery wings and headed out into the infinitely expanding oceans of space and place, the seas of swirling constellations and galaxies full of promise. Their original stars grew hot then cold, their light winking out and their time and tide moving into another phase. From the embers of their original homes, the Star Children moved to other levels and dimensions, forming new and fantastic dwelling places in an infinite, unfolding universe. Blessed by their loving Creator, their kisses rained down on astral winds and where they fell the Children followed, filled with the spirit of adventure.

And so it was that some of the Children came to Earth.

The sacred marriage between the heavens and Earth was made, the snaking serpentine flow of energy grounded by the Children as they walked with wonder on this new and verdant planet. Their cosmic energy seeped into the Mother's soil, touching her molten core, only to pour forth from places upon her, rising up at natural centres of energy on her lush and beautiful body. She had been resting after her own birthing process and now she was fully awake. She called the Children to her bosom and there were heart-vows made, in love, for her honour.

This was a living planet, one amongst the millions which seethed and boiled in their own processes of death and re-birth, a place of unlimited possibility and breath-taking beauty. A planet with her own awareness, uniquely washed by the seas which themselves followed the tide of the universal flow, guided by the enigmatic moon mother, the Lady of Mystery. It was a planet inspired by the haunting, fluctuating face of Luna but it was doubly blessed by the warm embrace of Brother Sun who kept his benevolent distance in Father Sky. Light and dark, hot and cold, matter and spirit all danced the dream with their sacred duality.

It was a good place to call home.

So it was that all of the inhabitants of the small blue-green planet named Earth were awoken by the presence of the Star Children, the Shining Ones, and they flourished. From river to mountain peak and from fiery pit to greenest hill the creatures woke up and danced the dream too. All beings knew their place in the dance, their unique sacred awareness of their part in creation, and they understood their interdependence on each other and the land. This *knowing* allowed them to move with a lightness of step on the Mother, for the good of the All. Yet more difficult than this awakening of the feathered, finned and land-footed was the meeting of dense mind and matter with free-flowing imagination...the meeting of the human-kind with the Children of Light.

The indigenous human-kind of planet Earth were worthy in that they were still fresh from the Creator's own touch and so they had reverence for their own manifest being. However, they were simple people whose love only extended as far as that which they could physically see, touch, hear, and smell. Their senses were honed and sharp, their wits worked well for them. Yet they were dense, grounded in matter and the reality of existence, they were not opened to their own spark of spirit.

They had no concept of the universal energies, of the cosmic ebb and flow that the Children were fashioned directly from. They were essentially of the Earth, used to working with her in often trying conditions. They were beings fashioned from the very body of the Earth, moulded like clay from her substance, grounded beings of flesh and bone and they had known nothing but their own manifestation from that fascinating corporeal landscape. Even though they had the potential within them to experience the same glow of life-force within them that the Children of the Stars had knowledge of, they remained focused on the task of staying alive in a purely physical way. The human-kind remained spiritually asleep while their bodies toiled and maintained and strove to endure. It was easier that way.

They were brown and red skinned, these humans, burned dark or left pale, as the climate dictated, as nature intended. They had simple eloquence and a grace and harmony with their surroundings. They were of the soil and waters, hardened by a nomadic existence, accustomed to looking no further than their next meal. Oh yes, and these first human-kind with their uncomplicated souls, they had respect. For without respect for the land, there was no next meal, and where the next meal came from was of ultimate importance. They did not deplete the land or her resources because that meant individual human depletion. They moved on from place to place and took only what they needed without awareness of anything save shelter and the seemingly constant rumble of hunger in their gut.

Bare, essential survival was their only motivation. And yet they had understanding of Earth's ways, of their fellow creatures, of the seasonal cycles. They even spoke of the moon and sun and stars around their fires at night, but only in terms of the observation of their movements, never in glorious inspiring tales based on the sacred energy involved. These people, they knew only what they could experience by direct bodily contact, they were motivated by the body alone. These humans were no myth-makers, no *seers*. Their lives had no real joy, they were dreamless sleep-walkers, survivors. They were the first beings to take part in the *forgetting* and so the balance of life, of spirit and matter, dark and light, was overlooked and then buried in the day to day nitty gritty of existence."

Alicia opened her eyes and fixed them unflinchingly on Lian's, searching for soul-connection, for recognition.

"Are you still with me, dear one?"

Lian felt a little more impatient now.

"Yes, yes, don't worry about me, I'm not so stupid and messed up that I can't grasp a simple story! Please go on!"

"As you like," Alicia replied, unruffled. "So, all the humans knew was how to exist. The need to exist meant they needed to resist...to resist death. To cease focusing single-mindedly on the goal of seeing another dawn would mean certain death. And death was, in the human sense of existing, an ending. When something died it was no longer there and so death was considered to be final and consequently to be avoided for as long as possible! The humans closed their minds and hearts to what they saw in the seasons and cycles of renewal and stripping bare in the land; they disregarded their inner *knowing*, the wisdom of the Creator that was inherent to all creatures, and instead they relied solely on their physical seeing. They saw themselves as something apart from the growing and dying back of other species. They did not believe in renewal for themselves; they simply put their heads down and concentrated only on the task in hand rather than seeing the bigger picture.

Had they observed things with more open-minded sensitivity they would have seen a continuation of life after death and life before birth as was seen in the natural cycle of *all* things. Just because the plant withered and its seed was hidden from the eye in the dark loam did not mean there had been a permanent death. By no means were there endings in nature! Even carcasses were broken down, eaten by scavenging creatures or absorbed back into the soil to feed another plant while the spirit of the beast concerned flew on as pure soul-energy. There was always transformation and continuation. But the human-kind had not the capacity to visualise transformation. They could not believe in anything that was not obvious, for they had not the imagination, nor the inclination, to pursue thought beyond the need to survive. Their creative faculty for perceiving that which was hidden lay dormant and inspiration did not flourish in the parched, infertile soil of their limited existences. They simply lacked the drive to make such connections, or leaps of faith and conciousness, at all. This was why their lives were empty of passion and romance, pleasure and real purpose.

In this limited human sense, existing is not fully being for to fully *be* one needs awareness of the whole of one's *be-ing.* An understanding is needed not only of the physical inter-connectedness of lives, to ensure survival, but of the spiritual essence which enhances it. To give meaning and purpose there needs to be knowledge of what it is that animates the life one strives to keep; to not only witness nature's *physical* transformation through cycles of dying and growing but also to feel it on an *energetic* level...witnessing the unseen, but still tangible, force that is behind the process. And what is this force? Why, it is creation! And what do we need to create something from nothing? Imagination! It is only with a direct experience of the endless energetic creative force of nature in all beings that one can truly appreciate life as a miraculous and joyful unfurling, not a purposeless trudge from beginning to end, a trudge which needs to be endured and prolonged to avoid the oblivion of physical death!

So, the way of the first human-kind was essentially good, yes, but it could certainly be bettered. Their resourcefulness and earthy practicality could be enhanced so that they were truly living, more completely walking in beauty. With the imagination to create, to *envision* that which is unseen, and with the sensitivity to *feel* the unseen, then life could be beautiful and not just a struggle. The humans simply needed encouragement and for their spirits to be re-awoken to the gifts of the Creator so that they may dance the dream of life into being. And so the universe, with creation at its wild heart, gave of Itself and sent the Star Children to Earth with the gift of the *dreaming.*

When the Children of the Stars first came among the human-kind there was confusion and blind awe. They, the solid and hirsute children of Earth, saw radiant beings, made seemingly of some less dense source of inner luminosity. They could see no expression on the strange faces which seemed to shape-shift and remain beyond description. They were not in the human range of categorisation and for a time there was complete bewilderment. But the Shining Ones did not reach the humans with their visual impact so much as with their emanation, something so pure and affecting that it made the people weep for the first time in human memory.

Surely such beings were their superiors? Or their masters? Or their enemies? Surely not their enemies, these gossamer beings who floated on the wind and gave....gave....

No, the first human tears were not tears of grief, for when a loved one died it was as nature intended and hunting and eating and sheltering went on just the same in their passing. Endings were inevitable and to be avoided if possible, but they were always final, were they not? Suddenly, the possibility that there was something beyond that terrible nothingness, beyond physical death, decay and endings, brought hope. No, those first precious human tears were tears of joy, awe and utter unbridled wonder.

There was a period of confusion as the two species met but there was no killing. The common, natural sense and rational way of the human-kind came back to the fore. How dangerous were these beings if the animals and birds did not shy from them, rather they came to them and played around them in a way they did not with people? How dominant could these beings be if they did not command or demand, but simply stretched out their long limbs to reach out with the utmost gentleness?

There was no way that a human would as attempt to kill such a being, for killing was for food and these light-creatures were not food. Nor did they appear to have a useful hide or pelt, like the creatures of Earth. There was no sign of where they came from but they walked in peace. Their nebulous hands extended in a friendship which was alien and yet deeply touching. For the first time the human-kind saw something beyond themselves and were touched by another being which could not be utilised for survival purposes. They experienced connection for the sake of connection, love apart from physical gratification. It was a pleasure.

Moreover, the Children of Light brought new benefits to the physical side of being on Earth. They came to understand the folk of fur, feather and fin who also dwelled harmoniously upon that wonderful flourishing planet and they came to work with the plant-beings, the green indigenous people of the land, who were patient teachers and generous healers. They then healed the Earth-children who did not thrive. They saved the mothers who laboured long and painfully. They showed the way to work with the plant life so that it yielded its secrets and explained which plants should be respected for their poisonous aspects. Likewise, the Children of Starlight knew which creature-kin dwelled where and how best to work with their individual spirits to ensure an honourable, clean death. How could anyone find it in their hearts to despise or ostentatiously revere any being so extraordinarily virtuous yet totally simple?

The human-kind had for a countless time moved across continents which shifted, experiencing climates that fluctuated, with no certainty in their lives other than death. They had travelled through through terrain which could be harsh or nurturing and dwelled among creatures both deadly and charming, with no thoughts beyond surviving. Oh yes, the human ancestors *endured.* But with the life enhancing gifts of the Shining Ones there was now celebration as well as thanks-giving for another day without death by starvation, disaster or disease.

So it was that the inhabitants of planet Earth came to know these new and beautiful star-people as the *Children of the Greening*, for they sang new life into that which was and would be and inspired every living being to be the best, most bountiful version of themselves. The Greening was life at its best, a *flourishing*. Theirs was an energy of *resurgence,* of *returns* and *renewal.* They had brought new elements to existence, these being inspired dreaming, the enchantment of *en-visioning* and the creative joy of a healthy imagination, amongst many other things.

These qualities were the Children's biggest blessings to a diligent, practical species such as human-kind. The gift of imagination, the belief that one could picture what *wasn't* and make it so, for the sake of the joy of creation, was amazing. This was the ultimate gift of the universal consciousness - that for no other reason but sheer pleasure or entertainment there could be fantasy and invention. A being could share in the ultimate experience of being a part of their Creator, at the heart of existence, by bringing something to bear from nothing, by *en-visioning* it. In this way, through imagination and dreaming, they could connect with the Source. It was extraordinary, and they were extraordinary, these shining, selfless intermediaries between the Creator and creation, the Children of the Greening.

To bring the art of imagination to life on Earth, the children taught that a being could picture the type of animal it would be good to eat, even though it had not physically been sighted. Using the old motivation of filling the belly well, the Children wisely showed ways of dreaming that could prove physically useful. From that premise, it was possible to teach that anything which could not yet be seen, touched, experienced could exist in side the minds-eye and felt in the soul. This was how the Creator Itself worked, dreaming that which never was, then giving it form and spirit so that the Creator may have a broader experience of Itself through its creation. The Children taught that, in essence, we are all the Creator and imagination was the tool to achieve this *re-membering*. Imagination aided practical problem solving and to humanity this was, after the initial wariness, warmly welcomed and encouraged. For the first time, human-kind had fun while remaining fed and watered and was opened to the infinite possibility of existence once more.

On a cave wall, in daubs made from the Earth's own pigments, there could be a prancing heard of beasts where before there was only bare rock. Adornment could be made for the human self from shells, seed-cones and stones, strung together in visually stimulating ways. There could be vessels fashioned from the body of the Earth which looked beautiful and enhanced the experience of drinking. There could be music plucked from the air by the creation of a simple gut-strung instrument, obtained with honour to the donor creature, or from a reed-pipe, played with respect to the donor reed. A story could be woven from fragments of fact about a man who never was, for the sake of hearing another's laughter. With all these new creative pursuits, and with a new-found fascination with aesthetically pleasing attributes, the human-kind learned about the quality of life. And about the possibilities it had to offer.

So, life was now lived to its fullest. Song and dance became a vital part of daily life. The stories of the stars were woven into the fabric of daily living, as the Children saw much beauty in their origins and wished to enhance life with the re-telling of the Mystery they had experienced, over countless seasons. They would accept no *forgetting* of connection, for the *forgetting* would bring confusion, isolation and fear of the unknown. It was understood that without the root, the route back to Source, there was no connection. It was the *knowing* of truth, the belief in connection, that linked all to All and so their tales were knitted into the every fabric of this fecund landscape and so brought harmony, balance and growth.

With these things came a full belly, a happier heart and a warm hearth. There was security balanced with pleasure, safety offset by the spirit of adventure, a desire to grow beyond *what was* into *what may be.*

Because of this telling and expressing of truths, every being was equal and had the knowledge of who they were. It was believed in the blood and bones of the two and four-leggeds, in the sap of the leafed ones and in the minds of the winged ones, it was felt, tasted and touched to the last root, grain of sand and shiny scale. Life was simple and beautiful. Life was born to the Way and the Way was present at the heart of all things so that in each individual coming together there would be an experience of the Divine. Separation and distance from each other was unthought-of of...*inconceivable!*..as who would dream to be disconnected from the Source, alone in a meaningless universe?

The time of grinding, gruelling existence was over.

At this time of creation, bonds were made which could never be broken, for the oath was made by the Children to protect their fellow citizens and to respect the land herself. In honour of the divine spark which each being *re-membered* and acknowledged at the heart of themselves there was ritual and celebration in keeping with the cycles of *being*. The Children of the Greening brought forth the stone-people who grew from the Earth at their touch, mirroring the cosmos from which the Children came; stone-people seeking the sky in concentric circles and rings. Between Earth and sky a new union commenced as the Star Children walked with spirit, the stone-people standing as reminders of that connection. The Children brought to life, through lilting melody and prose, the sheer pleasure, the profound beauty of *being*. While these things were marked, the land was blessed and the citizens of planet Earth were fruitful, purposeful and in love with it all."

Once again Alicia stopped to take stock of her audience of one.

"You'll stop me again if you need to?"

"Yes!"

Lian flicked her hair impatiently. She was leaning forward in the semi-darkness, straining to drink in every syllable of Alicia 's precious tale.

"Fair enough, cariad, I will continue. So, although each of the beings on Earth had the gift of spirit, the overseers of this sacred breath on the Earth-plane were the Wise Ones of the Bark, clad in mantles of green, gold and russet. These tree-citizens, the green standing nation, were the unique Earthly connection between the Mother and the heavens, feeling the free-flowing power from above and below, their bodies being mirrors on both levels, reaching up, reaching down, drawing on energy, breathing out life-breath. They were so strong and wise as they were especially able to refresh themselves by taking the Creator's raw power within themselves daily, for the benefit of all. The pulse of life was felt most fluently within them and the Children and the other Earth-dwellers held them in high esteem.

The Tree-People still covered much of the land; the burgeoning primal forest of which they were a part had once been even more vast and it had been said that in the elder days a being, if they were particularly dextrous, could cross the whole of the Isles from bough to bough without touching the ground. This strong and united tree-nation grew in love, nurtured by the Children who came to serve their needs. The Children knew that the Tree-People were most sacred and so, in this enchanted realm of long ago, did the humans."

Alicia paused to smile beneficently at Lian who gazed back at her, lips slightly parted, wild eyes wide, and an air of great expectancy about her. She was spell-bound yet even in her entranced state her naturally questing mind roved over the brightly woven words, picking them apart for further meaning. The mean spirit-entities around her shifted restlessly. Againh Alicia could sense their destructive presence more strongly now. How dare they do this to her, feeding off the life-elixir of this weary sensitive child! Yet this was not the time to speak of them, this was the time for their tale to be told.

Alicia took a sip of her cold tea. To get up and make more now would be an unwelcome diversion. She focussed in on Lian again, Lian as she could be...as she *would* be...whole and pure in her magic.

"Yes, I hear your thoughts, child! You are thinking that you know of Tree-People, of oak, ash and thorn. You know them though now there are woefully few and those who still stand are understandably reticent...but what of the Star Children, the Children of the Greening? I know that this is your soul's question...what were they like, truly?"

Lian nodded, willing the old woman to continue.

"Well, the Children brought great joy to the Earth level, and more so because they held themselves no greater or lesser than any other being. The Children came to the world flexing their pointed feet as if making to dance, only because it was hard not to dance when you heard the rhythm of *being*, never for the purpose of gaining praise. Born gently smiling on their distant stars, their remarkable slanted eyes were wide with wonder and they moved like ripples on a sunlit pool, like graceful silver fish swimming through the tides of life. Their long tapered hands reached up only to touch, never to grasp. The Children were magic incarnate; enchantment was born into the world in the form of their poetry, sung or spoken, or in motion and enchantment was the manifestation of imagination on the Earth.

Their desire, unique of all creations, was to entertain for the sake of bringing joy alone. Joy and the enhancement of life, that was their purpose. In so much as a bird sings to *be* in moments when unconcerned with territory and courtship, so did the Children sing, to celebrate *be-ing*. They were like liquid starlight fashioned into slender two-legged forms. Willowy and sexless, for they had no limit of gender, of structure. Fluid and perpetually in motion, yet filled with calm serenity. They were terribly beautiful. Frighteningly radiant.

Alien.

The Children were Earth Aliens, born of the first starlight but grounded through choice, and because of their enchantment life was as life is. Life was good.

Within the family of the Children there were many races, as there were within the human, bird or fish family. The longer they dwelled on the Earth-plane the more variations of themselves they dreamed into being. They did not need to mate or breed, although there were certainly instances of humans and the Children of the Greening lying together for the sheer unbridled pleasure of union and these acts resulted in strange and marvellous offspring. More oftenly though the Children simply *be-came f*rom the fabric of existence, mingling with the Earth, birthing themselves from a blend of starlight and soil. They asked the question '*what if?*' and created, so becoming a myriad of expressions of themselves, inspired by their surroundings, acting in perfect empathy with the Earth, creatively sculpting fluid forms from their environment. There was no pulsing desire to replicate themselves, for their essence was eternal and unique, there was simply a joy in finding new ways of expressing who they were, by blending with the fibre of the living Earth that gave them a home.

Thus the Children walked in many guises that we could recognise. There were the small ones with their pointed ears and long fingers and toes, frog like, climbing and leaping. There were the tall ones with their swift feet and dextrous hands and the green and the brown and the pale skinned, all dancing as One. They were the Faery and their kin, the Pixies, Sprites, Nymphs, Gnomes, Elves....all manifestations of the union of starlight with Earth 's elements. The grounded and the ariel, the watery and the tempestuous, they were mischievous and nebulous both.

The Children of the Greening were the Fey ones...the fair fate-weavers, the enchanters, the poets, mystics and dreamers of the soul.

Some still shone with distant starlight, others glowed. Some remained in indistinct and had nebulous, elongated forms which slipped between time and tide, distinct from human solidity. Others earthed themselves and wore the mantles of nature, taking pleasure in creating new and interesting manifestations of themselves. They had fun in their *becoming* and because they were as children they remained filled with caperings, laughter and song. Their lives were playful, artful; their soul-poetry resonated with the music of the spheres and there was peace because of it. Peace between the two-leggeds and the four, accord between the hunter and the hunted. Allegiance between Earth and sky, concord between land and sea.

There is no way to peace, it is said, for peace is the Way. And it was. Peace *was.*

Where the land met the sea in lush, seemingly endless forests, The Children of the Greening would lie down with the red fox and run with the young hare, mad with happiness. They could spend the passage of Lady Moon just staring into the clear waters of the streams, each moment lost in the movement of the tiny fishes, time slipping by as they became entranced by the flash of the silver scales on their backs. They would gaze into moon-pools, seeing themselves shimmering reflections of all that was and would be. As Brother Sun journeyed across their skies they could lose themselves in sensation and smell and in the beautiful rhythms of life. They called out their greetings to the day, '*Hail and well met, my friend, and blessings upon you!*' and they laughed and the All echoed their laughter.

There were no roofs and no walls, nothing to keep one apart from another. Even the humans had their portable dwellings, often open to sky and season, simple round huts, domed structures and framed tents, all touching lightly on the Earth. All beings connected with the Earth and did not elevate themselves from her rhythms. The canopy above them was the gently moving swirl of stars, the floor beneath them was the soft and yielding skin of the Earth. All inhabitants of the Earth were free to move across it as they pleased, leaving only tracks, walking gently on the skin of the Mother.

One being was safely able to lay down with another and sleep. While the Children slept on their mossy pillows they let their spirits fly free, their dreams themselves birthing new planets, new creations. For they knew that they were a part of the Way and that they had the power. And humanity dreamed its own dreams having been granted that gift by the Children. They smiled as they slept and anticipated a new dawn, not seeking the oblivion of sleep but the joy of it. The difference between all states of being and between all beings was a positive source of delight.

The dreams on Earth were peaceful for a boundless time, for it was a time of no time save the marking of the seasons within and without. The season of abundance, sometimes yellow-gold, other times green and glistening, other times white and sparkling had simply been for a seemingly endless age. Humans passed away, to be reborn into other lives, other selves. Their spirits returned, as did all creatures, into new bodies to gain new experiences. This was accepted, welcomed. But the Children were not mortal but eternal; ethereal. They simply evolved without shedding their nebulous forms. They did not remain static, they grew, adapting, changing. Just like the seasons.

Like seasons too, all things must pass...even those deemed immortal must pass...into something, somewhere, else...someday....

Un-peace was about to be birthed.

As the patterns of life formed and re-formed there was no warning of the universal shifting. There was no conception of un-peace to imagine how a shift may occur. How could this be if it were unimaginable? So it was that bears still hunted, the insects still darted and so did the Children play. But everything is change and flux in the cycles of life and some dances have to end for others to begin. Stars turn cold, their energy passing on into other expressions. Everything has a season. The citizens of the Way began to feel the unimaginable shift, like a cold, bitter wind that blew relentlessly for no purpose other than to chill. One day it simply was. The rhythmic, unfolding pattern was over-ridden by another foreign vibration. It was not born of love and its harmony was nothing more than a discord. The children had become used to aeons of bliss and were unprepared for this intrusion. This...

What?

A lack of peace.

It was a birthing of something which did not come to pass gladly and with joy. The All was shaking with the birth of a reluctant creation, one which trembled and spat, kicked and screamed. One which did not *see*. And as the Children were such a sensitive part of the All they felt it deeply, at their very core. It was not their way to feel sorrow, yet an unsettling ache began inside them. The Creator had to birth the opposite of what was to give choices, so that all beings may exercise their free will. In order to choose peace, one must first have something to contrast peace with. The All had to experience every possible expression of Itself. That was the way of creation. Yet it was a hard way indeed.

So it was that the tales of the Children, their tunes and their beautiful visions became a little distorted, discordant and misshapen. The image came of a terrible blight, a dark cloud upon their horizon which did not rain and pass on its way as was the way of the cloud-people. This cloud was filled with rage and noise and strange shapes fell from its broiling centre. Things of dull colours, hard and angular and heavy. Things that the Children could not recognise. Things with points and brutal edges, wrought of dark metal with no shine. The Way was of curves and spirals, the Dance of Life was round like the belly of a mother. These sharp planes were the harbingers of another era.

The Children asked the Wise Ones of the Bark, '*dear Tree-People, in our visions we see terrible things coming. Tell us, trusted friends and mentors, what is it that we see? What is this thing that rains hard rains upon us, that which fills us with foreboding, casting an angular shadow that we cannot understand? There is no flow to the beings that issue forth from these nightmares, they will not speak with us yet they continue to fall upon us, devouring our peace. How may we love them?'*

The trees bowed their mighty bodies and whispered low into the ears of the Children.

'It is difficult to love what you cannot understand, it is difficult to understand that which cannot love. What is it that you do best, Children?'

'We love, for all is born of love and all benefit from being reminded of it, gently.'

'What else do you do?'

'We dance, for all being is a part of the Dance of Life and we all benefit from being reminded of it, with kindness.'

'And?'

'We sing for the sake of celebrating this day. We grow, for all is change and flux and flow. We be. *We are as we are and we act according to that Way. Our lives are truth and truth is beauty. What else is there that we should do?'*

The trees spread their branches out around them and were filled with the sadness of caring parents whose little ones must learn a hard lesson in order to grow. Even though the Shining Ones were filled with starlight and the wisdom of an aeon of experience and *be-ing*, it was the trees who had the task of grounding the energy that flowed. It was the solid, infinitely compassionate givers of life-breath that had the responsibility of holding fast in the times ahead, even as they shook and bent to the wind of change, so they must remain rooted. They spoke gently but firmly.

'Now you will also learn to do something else, my precious ones, you must learn to do all these things inside yourselves. When the hard rain is falling and the love is hidden by mountains of useless things and the rivers are empty and the sky is turning to dust then you must learn to dance within.. *'*

'But we shine, venerable ones, we cannot hide the very light we are forged from! How may we keep the light within and not without? Surely there must be balance as there has always been?'

'But we love and we play!' a Small One spoke with the natural exuberance of the Children.

'How may we do these things inside and not in the world? How can something not have its own reflection in the world, if it is created within us?'

The trees held their breath, searching for an answer to reassure their beloved friends. In that silence, the Children clung to each other and to the Great Ones of the Bark and all the small animals of the forest floor came between them and trembled there while the humankind cowered in huddles. A fire kindled amongst them suddenly felt cold; seeing the Children who had brought enlightenment and joy so dejected, extinguished, was chilling beyond measure. The humans retreated into their family groups, wondering what ill-fate may befall them, they who had for generations been healthy and fulfiled. It was profoundly unsettling.

The trees exhaled and found words, hoping they were the most appropriate ones to bring comfort, or at least, an understanding.

'*And so you shall shine again, my beloved friends, for there are always* returns. *Yet now you must be strong, for a new season is nearly upon us all. And the Mother will need us to be strong for them, these poor misguided incomers, and strong for each other. To be strong we must learn to do all that we do inside our very spirits. We can keep our lights burning there and all who are of our spirit will see this flame in our eyes and recognise us as kin. And we will shine together until the new way is passed and the old way of things has its* returns, *when it will become transformed and fresher, deeper than before. Old becomes new becomes old again, so it is and so it must be. Time may seem to pass slowly, there may seem no end to the terrible season, but with faith we know...*'

'*There are always* returns...' the Children whispered to each other and the whisper spread out in concentric rings across the land, translating into the many languages of the creatures there. Then the whisper went within the spirit of all who moved upon the precious Earth at that time and there was an uncanny stillness upon the land.

The tree spoke, a voice heavy with sorrow but still firm, '*until then we will be silent until we are spoken to, for we must hold our secrets and be the Keepers of the Old Wisdom.*'

'*But tell us, Tree-People, shall we die if we cannot dance the dream alive?*'

'*We do not want this new time, we do not want this hard rain! We need to sing and to play and to love for it has always been this way and without the expression of love in the world how will the dance go on?*'

'*Oh tree, what does it all mean, why has this come to pass?*' the tiny, reedy voice of a sad faced Small One was heard and the others parted so that the form of a green and brown clad figure may come forward and hold the beloved Bark-Skin of a Wise One.

A tear, the first tear of pure grief ever shed, ran down his cheek and another Small One licked it away, tasting the precious salty pearl and the pain within.

'*Where has our wild power gone?*'

The trees sighed and their leaves rustled. '*It has not gone, it can never go, it has just been drawn within you for a time, like the precious sap we ourselves draw deep into our roots in winter, in order for you to become stronger when the time comes to* return. *If you continue to believe in the power, to have faith in it, it exists. You know that energy cannot die and your energy is enchantment, the magical and healing power of joy. Just know that you do not know yet why you must hide your light but trust that you must. Understand only this, that the power remains even when it is not seen. You are going to be acting out that which you yourselves taught the human-kind so long ago...that which cannot be seen with the eye can be imagined, felt, acknowledged none-the-less.*

Remember who you be, *even if that expression of* be-ing *is not seen in the world, and you will always have the power. The power was a gift to you and the gift remains, as does the love of the All which birthed us. Keep shining inside and their foul rain cannot dampen the spirit. Sometimes there must be dark for the light to come again, there must be sorrow for us to learn to rejoice at its passing. Does not Brother Sun surrender to Lady Moon each dusk, only to find a return again each dawn? Dark has always given birth to light and light has always been swallowed by the womb-tomb of darkness, and round again. Only by contrast and comparison may there be deeper meaning to what we perceive as joy, renewed pleasure in what is good as opposed to what is...not beneficial, not holy. And so, above all things remember this, and let it be a part of your understanding lest you lose hope. There is meaning in all things. There must be hate and hard things for us to learn* how not to be...'

The trees, their many voices uniting in one voice, paused and seemed to shrink into themselves, some of their magnificent size and colour lost. The Children clustered round them and the Tree-People felt their unconditional love. Someone had to keep the faith and the Tree-People knew they were the Keepers, they alone would be left standing when most of their beloved kindred had fallen to the new order. It was a heavy burden but they were the strongest and most powerful of all Earth-dwellers and even the Shining Ones bowed to their inconceivable depths of *knowing*. For the Earth Mother had chosen them to monitor the breath of life on the planet and so they had been entrusted to oversee life in that realm. How could they not be listened to now?

'*Truly Children, we do not know why fully for we are not at the Source of Life but only guardians of its truth, connected to the Way but not at its core...all we know is that we shall meet again if we have faith in that eternal, unshakeable connection. We will keep the faith as shall all our kind who are spared. When you are gone we shall remain for you until you* return. *Do not feel alone or abandoned, ever, for while we stand and there is life on Earth we will be there for you even if you cannot speak with us. Go in peace and flow in peace, for we are with you always. Know that our love travels from one to another, through the Earth herself and above your heads through the moving air. From the motion of the worm to the whisper of the wind in the leaves we will spread our message of hope.*

Those who are to come will not feel our presence as beings, as Wise Ones. They will have no clue as to our ability to communicate. Those with no ears to hear we need not fear for they will never know our secrets. For now, we will seem silent but you will know better my friends. They will think us dumb and so they will not question or torture us. They will try to obliterate us for their own selfish ends but we will not be seen as their enemy for they will regard us no more than they regard any creature or being who does not speak plainly in their language. They will have no fear of us and will not seek to destroy us as threatening adversaries...' The Tree-People paused, bracing themselves, sensing the pain that was to come, standing firm and resolute in spite of it. Their link was strong and they felt each *other's connection now. 'But they shall never conquer us for they will underestimate us. They will perceive us as voiceless and to the new ones who will come coherent speech is the only thing that shows life. We shall appear as silent sentinels and they will assume we are of no importance.*'

The Children and all about them gasped aloud and cringed at this disrespect to the great Tree-Folk and there was a moment of terrible and all-abiding distress. But before the Children could experience the first stirrings of their own anger the trees continued.

'Oh, but we are the life-givers, whose breath is the sacred exhalation and inhalation of the Mother, we are those who hold the key to wisdom and until they realise our worth they will be lost in pitiful ignorance. We will never forget and we will be there for the re-membering'

The trees spread their many and various mantles of gold and green around their wide eyed people.

'Oh, that this could be avoided, that we, the Wise Ones of the Bark, could protect you forever. But avoidance is alien to us. We are honest, as you the Children have inspired us to be and as the Tree-People have always encouraged themselves to be, we cannot not hide from anything as to do so is to turn from our own self. Our belief in the inter-connectedness of life means that we cannot escape from any aspect of life that we do not find easy. To do so is to shun a part of our own nature.'

It was a simple, pure and shining way that the Tree-People described. The trees knew that this old wisdom meant that they should go with the flow without obstructing. Denial lead to *dis-ease.* To block the energies of the dance of life was to hold back the Source. Without the Source they were as nothing.

The trees knew how to bend to the winds, not holding themselves rigid against them. They must help the little Children bend to the new, for like the strongest wind, the bitterest blast, it would pass. It was the Way.

Oh yes, there must be hate and hard things for us to learn how not to be and the light needs the darkness to become visible, ever and onwards. The trees could accept and so they would teach acceptance...and resilience.

The Tree-People said to their friends, '*do not weep, for they cannot kill what they cannot see. Even if the last tree is cut down there will still be the seeds in the dark earth, waiting, holding the old wisdom. The seed-people will tell of our time and our Way, they will tell the small creatures of the dark land. They will tell the worms and the worms will speak in the bellies of the birds who are free to fly away. The birds will sing of our wisdom from coast to coast but the new ones will not understand what they are singing. They will find their twittering dull and dismiss them.*

So it is that all we hold dear will be kept safe until the day that one of our kin awakes from a long slumber to hear the meaning in the chorus that marks the start of a new dawn. The song of truth will always be sung, even in our passing, the birds will be our messengers, the Earth herself will keep the faith. So there is no need to sorrow, Children of the Greening, Children of the Stars, and now of the Earth. Hold the faith of this truth, little ones, beautiful friends. Keep our secrets....'

From that moment, the forests and woodlands were completely silent for the first time since creation. The trees had ceased to talk aloud. The whispers of their leaves was but a pale reflection of their true voices, the creak of their limbs but a meaningless creaking of old bones.

And so it was that the Children who had never needed to do anything but simply *be* found themselves needing to fear. They were born of truth and honour and natural justice, of hope and free-will. They did not really know how to be afraid, or how to judge, or how to be bound to another's will. They did not know how not to hope. They were open-hearted, not defensive; receiving, not reactionary. But when the Makers of the hard rain came to the forest they had but a short time in which to understand these new rules.

Oh, the Makers. Who were they? Child, I had hoped to speak to you in a time when their era is passed but I fear it is not over yet. The Makers were your earthly fore-fathers, the Makers were *human.* They were not a race apart. Oh no, not they! They did not descend pure and shining as the Children once did, born of starlight, as a different kind of entity. The Makers were human-kind turned wrong by a spirit of disharmony that some say is pure evil but is only the spirit of *un-peace* which was born of the Way to show the universe *how not to be*. It was a spirit like a virus, infecting the simple souls of humanity as they slept, and all viruses are natural, are they not? And do they not teach the body how to adapt itself and become stronger?"

Lian did not answer, she simply scowled.

Alicia gave a barely audible sigh and continued.

"This virus-spirit infested and manifested on Earth and slowly slipped into the dreams of the weakest human kind, ensnaring them with tempting images, filling them with insidious greed and an overwhelming desire to behave in a way that was not beneficial to anyone or anything but themselves. It stole into the consciousness of a species and seized it. It twisted the gift of imagination, through dream-sleep, and corrupted. It showed a way not born of bare survival as in the old times, nor of joy and pleasure as in the good times, but a third way...

These poor humans were your human ancestors, they who fell prey to the offer of power and the choice to be either passive or dominant. These fools who had the free will to choose may be the gaolers of your true essence even now, or perhaps they are your closest kin. How I hope that you may know the end of their reign! Can you believe the Makers made, not for joy or new experience but for the sake of making, of simply amassing more of something? Can you understand how these people make just for the sake of ownership, as if it could make them more prestigious?"

Lian shook her head vehemently, child-like once more. The older woman's eyes flashed starlight in the gloom.

"Then it is well for you child, for such behaviour makes a prisoner of the soul, right enough. It is true that the Makers made, not for beauty, not for pleasure or giving joy but for power, for pressure, for prestige. What rhyme or reason is there in owning something earthly that we were not born with, cannot take with us when we die, and do not even need? As far as the Makers were concerned, to have the most things...possessions...was to have the most worth. To have most things made barriers and delineation's that never before existed.

They spoke of separation and ownership; 't*his is mine, that is not yours*' and '*I have and you have not,*' as if those born to the planet Earth had a hierarchy, or some right to preside over another! As if one being could stake a claim on the free and bountiful Earth Herself and divide her up for the sake of setting themselves apart or above. What folly, what tragedy! They began the separation of above and below, light and dark, as if one were better than the other! They placed human values on that which was equal and judged it according to human law, not universal law. They called their own values and opinions, measured in wealth and based on status, the Way. Where there had never been judgements, and hence no injustice, now there was.

As you were born to them, of them, into their era, I feel sadness for you. I feel love for you too, for that is what you need now to break the bonds the Makers have placed upon you. *Re-member* yourself, child! Recall the spirit within you, that which was not man-made and is not owned by any but your own eternal self. Acknowledge the gift of spirit, bestowed by the Creator, a gift never to be retracted, bought up in a market place or apportioned to another! It is *precious!*

Even now as I speak to you kindly, after boundless time when you have learned to mis-trust, I feel the stirrings of your dissent and your shying away from my words. How can I advise your *re-membering*, who am I that dares to offer you solutions? What knowledge have I of the Makers and the suffering they caused? How may I re-awaken in you what is only sleeping, never dead? By what authority?

I myself have no authority. I just hope.

Aye, hope. For I have the knowledge first-hand even though I am no chosen one. Sweetling, we *all* have the knowledge if we care to *re-member* it and I have *re-membered* so that I may pass this on! Yes, I was born of the first starlight and I have been burned, broken, beaten, boxed in by these human-kind, by these Makers and Takers. So, I speak from experience, as well as from knowledge, but not with bitterness, only ever with hope. I know something of the pain of times past, maybe the pain of your present, so please, bear with me, for I have been through the *re-membering* and I can help you in yours.

Have faith in me when I say that the Makers were *forget-full* of their true selves and their spiritual origins at the heart of creation; instead they actively sought disconnection and separation. How difficult it is to comprehend that a spirit born into a body, born free, born connected to the Source, actually wished to be so bound, tied, alone! They wished to build walls, doors, fences, defences. They wished to *man*-ufacture, to fracture, to cause disharmony and rape, reap, ruin. For the sake of money and power they welcomed the *forgetting* as to *re-member* was to recall connection and harmony, peace and equality. To wilfully take part in the *forgetting* was to believe that they could be all-powerful, to be gods apart from the Creator; yes, they convinced themselves that they could rule and govern and own, above Creation's plan of unity.

The Makers had *forgotten* and welcomed it. They *forgot* that they came into the world with nought but a spirit and body of flesh to walk in, equal to but no better than any other created being. *Forgot* that they would die, no matter what they made, did or said; no matter how big the pile of gold, bodies, things on their graves their human selves would still be die and decay. They had become as their dulled human forebears but did not live with their simple harmony. Harmony meant balance and these human-kind sought to tip the balance of power in their favour, not honestly plod on in an elementary mode of survival.

The Makers hated anything that would not submit, serve or satisfy their immediate needs, an attitude that was based in their *forgetfullness* that they had a soul which craved balance, in accordance with the harmony of the universal Way. They despised free-thinkers, creative spirits, the weak, the mild, the unusual. They despised the life-givers and nurturers for these attributes had no real worth that could be quantified; they had no reason and too much rhyme. In a world devoid of charm, women were useless except as commodities - prostitutes, slaves, heir-givers. Anything that was Fey, inspirational, compassionate, or creative for the sake of creation not profit, was laughable, contemptible or expendable. The Makers desired order, rank, file. They liked a bottom so that they may stay on top. They craved authority and dominion. They used the sacred gift of imagination not to bring pleasure but to dream up weapons of destruction, to envision new ways to kill, new methods to make mess.

They turned the precious gift that the Children had once bestowed on Earth-beings against the very Children themselves who the Makers perceived as the worst, most useless and somehow most irritating of all Earth-dwellers. For the Children did not know how to submit or to subdue themselves, to cease to be just as they always had been seemed an insult to the Creator. Moreover, the Makers were more deeply afraid of the Children than of any other living thing. They were terrified of their languorous or vigorous alien forms, of their enormous slanted eyes that seemed to look within them, making them feel uncomfortably naked. They hated their differences, the Children's seemingly insubstantial bodies, the way they could change shape at will....and, of course, their latent power which they craved as a drug.

The Children did not know why their natural way should be such an anathema to these folk or for it to cause so much anger. The more upset the Children became the more they changed shape in order to try and regain a sense of something pleasing, calming. The more they shimmered and became insubstantial, elemental, intangible, the more the Children intimidated the Makers. Even their bodies were slight and ethereal, even though they knew neither violent art nor any form of devious magic, they were rivals that the Makers could not ignore. Physically they posed no threat but on every other level the Makers sensed their awesome abilities and sought to exterminate these seemingly passive, yet deeply potent, life-forms.

They wanted to eradicate all they envied for it belittled them, a most disagreeable sensation, but mostly they wanted to do it because they *could.*

The Makers met their opposites in the Children and the Children saw all they did not wish to imagine in the Makers. The Makers chose to annihilate those that were *other* while the Children chose to learn how not to respond. In this there was both unbridled horror and great sorrow on planet Earth.

Aggression and discord were an abhorrence to the Children and the use of violence upon them and their fellow citizens left them reeling and sick. The Makers ran amok among the wild places, flattening and clearing, taunting and torturing, violating and taking. The Makers just wanted above all needing, they wanted it NOW and it had to be bigger, faster, better...never mind who or what it hurt. How may the Children and their closest Earth-kin have been prepared for such an invasion? In their confusion they broke apart from their relations and fled from this fierce onslaught.

They did not wish to learn the cruel arts of cunning that they had inflicted upon them and their places of dwelling. They did not wish to understand how to anticipate such barbarous actions, to play power games or to join hierarchies of control. The souls of the Children of the Greening, the Shining Ones, were truly innocent of atrocity and had no frame of reference for such monstrous behaviours.

But learn they had to. For they would be killed and killed again by these newcomers with their weapons and their words. These Makers and Takers were big and strong and smelled of grease and ale, sweat and tainted metal, ownership and slaughter. The things they acquired made them seem even bigger and rendered them even heavier and more restricted. They did not dance freely and their songs were only reflections of their affiliations to the things that they wanted to possess...women, servants, land, wealth, prestige. They used unyielding thought and wielded dull, brutal metal to cut and cull what was in their way. The Makers and the Takers seemed to want to own everything, including each other.

They had no respect for the life-force. They massacred the Tree-People, the Sacred Wise Guardians, to build their barricades against nature and each other. They dammed and drained and poisoned the waters. They filled the air with foul smoke and fouler words. They claimed themselves rulers of the Earth and they refused to consider the inter-connected sacredness of the All. Their domination of the weak was not born of hunger, like the lion's, but on selfish acquisition. Single-mindedness was against nature and a denial of the collective awareness of the One. The Children who tried to tell them of the Way were annihilated, enslaved or ignored. The human-kind bowed to the Maker's wishes or perished at the sword, or worse. To save themselves they had to integrate and ingratiate themselves to these brutal thugs.

It was heart-breaking.

Sometimes death seemed favourable to a life amongst those who appeared so grotesque to the Children. To suffer defilement in a realm made by the Makers greedy, grasping hands may be worse than going to meet death and, indeed, going to the cold ground like a fox hiding in its earth seemed infinitely more comforting. Death was new to the Children. They had previously waxed and waned, slept or grown, according to the season, an endless cycle of regeneration and rest. Now there seemed to be only a vast and heartless void to claim them as their pale spirit-blood ebbed away on some chilly stone floor. They died crude and stupid soul-deaths away from the gentle gaze of Sister Moon, away from the loving embrace of the Great Mother Earth. That, to the Children, was sacrilege.

For the Children, to shed their sacred bodies apart from the soft soil, away from the kiss and caress of the wind, was a profanation, a blatant disregard of the natural Way. The prospect of having their sacred soul-breath snuffed out in man-made, enclosed spaces was more agonising to them than any physical torment. They felt they had betrayed the Great Spirit of Creation by going against the Way. So it was that having their bright life-flames quenched, their hopes set coldly ablaze, was doubly destroying for the Children. In confusion they reeled; how could they return to the Source if they died apart from It?

It was not their bodies being abused that killed them beloved, oh no, although they were indeed pierced and bludgeoned in a vile host of ways. No, it was their souls which became sick and languished; their hearts which were broken. Their deaths were due to the soul no longer wishing to be housed in such a place and their death was a soul migration, a fleeing. The Children did not ordinarily die but they could be terminated, unnaturally. Their lives could indeed be ended by weapons, if they so decided it to be, but more usually their lives were ended by despair. Despair was such an alien concept to the Children that it hurt them as effectively as any tumour and so caused them to languish and fade. When hope, their natural state of experiencing the world, turned to *anti-hope* then they were killed from within their deepest being, exterminated by joylessness.

Their tormentors were amazed at the bravery and the calmness that the Children showed in the face of their desecration and abuse yet the Makers did not appreciate dignity or respond to pathos. They wanted a display, a show of anguish and submissive pleading. They had no understanding of the real pain that they caused to these pure spirits. They were Immortals, remember, but could choose to die if the spirit-pain became too great, and die they did, their gossamer bodies shed as husks on unhallowed human ground. So it was that the new masters spent time devising further methods that would get these silent beings to react. If they could not get them to talk and tell of their secret powers and magics then they must be destroyed and destroyed in a way which gave entertainment and value for money for a death without reaction, with no screams, was no sport at all. There must be some way to break their will, wipe that sad, faraway look out of their strange slanted eyes!

The Makers used their imaginations to devise new ways to hurt."

Lian bared her teeth.

"Yes, 'tis a horror and an anathema to our kind, I know," Alicia sighed deeply, her shoulders sagging a little more, "yet in their eyes such insubordination and lack of co-operation as the Children showed was unacceptable to the Makers and had to be punished. Yet even co-operation would have been unacceptable, in the end. Death lay at the conclusion of any encounter with the Makers and the Takers. They just wanted the secrets of the Children of the Greening, they had no respect for their Way...for *our* Way, beloved. They only wanted their ingenious arts, their abilities to *see* and predict, their shape-shifting, their key to longevity. And what would they use the sacred knowledge for? To *see* into their supposed rival's minds, to anticipate, to have the edge over the next person in order to control, rob, conquer and dominate. Never for love, never to bring healing, not for the sake of having marvellous dreams of impossible beauty.

So The Children, the Small Ones and their kin, the Tall Folk, were broken under terrible burdens. To be burned using the very bodies of theTree-Folk or to be drowned in the water of life was more than the souls of the Children could bear. It was a blasphemy and a terrible abomination, a crime against the Way. It was never just their own pain that caused them to lose faith and sorrow, it was always their involuntary complicity in a violation of the Way. Oh, the sadness they felt for Sister Water, the regret for Brother Flame, for making them complicit in murder! Yet what choice was there but to remain reticent and be soul-killed in such a manner? Any and all of these ends seemed merciful compared to a life of subservience to a species that cared nothing for the Way.

The Children learned to weep bitterly but never openly. They leaned to keep secrets. Retreating into the remaining wildwoods, the inhospitable moorlands, windswept hilltops and remote caves they learned to hide. They recalled the words of the Tree-Folk, in the time when they had still spoken, and they went *within.*

And some of them did physically hide. In the hillsides and caves, within the rocks and in the wild places, they ceased to walk the Earth but walked *in it.* They became a part of her, watching in pain and sorrow as their bright kin were slaughtered for sport. Watching through the leaves of an ancient forest, emerging and disappearing into a stone, becoming part of the rolling mist on the moor, the Children integrated themselves in another way. They slipped into the Otherworld, another layer of the Mother Earth, one with less density, less form, one step away from the realm of killing and fear, behind the sun, shining in shadow, half hidden.

But alive in spirit, child. Oh yes, always alive in spirit!

And, oh, the strength it took for the Children to abandon their kin in order to preserve their Way and the courage it took to wait.

And keep waiting.

Breathing steadily and slowing themselves right down as if in hiberation or speeding their energies up so fast as to be imperceptible to human sight, they waited. As they watched and witnessed they learned for the first time to distrust and to be cunning,. They even learned how to frighten these human Makers and to cause distress; their peaceful, loving way becoming twisted in their growing resentment. They began to frighten these blunt idiotic human travesties as they lurched stupidly drunk off their beaten tracks. They took to gleefully terrorising the Makers as they strayed alone into the territory of the wild which became a means of release for some of their own grief. They would not hurt these humans but they could scare them even more witless than they already were and so they became those who haunted the land; the Shining Ones in the Darkness, the Pixies, Elves, Faery Folk, Knockers, Hobgoblins, the Tuatha, the Sidhe...a thousand local variations on the theme of the Children in hiding. They became those who chose to step out from the Otherworld to cause dread and superstitious panic when they were all supposed to be long dead and part of the *forgetting*.

The Children were becoming folklore and legend, not a living, breathing part of manifest reality. That was hurtful.

Yet nothing is ever forgotten...a sigh, a caress on the wind, a tiny, slender hand...

The Green Ones who had not slipped between the worlds to bide their time and play with the souls of mortal men carried on living and dying. Though their souls were damaged, they were made of energy as organic and free-flowing as any natural force. Their souls, still full of buried treasure, of faith and hope and longing, came back. The bodies of these Children were finally obliterated but their essence was not. Even when it was assumed that the last Small One was driven into the ground and their bodies were no more, the souls of the Children were still surging, waiting to find expression and new life.

Their souls could find no bodies of the extinct Small Ones or the Tall Folk to breath life into and so they had to come back into the bodies of the new breed. In *human form*, child! In human form! They could have incarnate on other planets, into other realms, but their pledge to the Earth Mother bound them to this world. So it was that the souls of the Children found themselves inside the fleshy shells of mortal men and women, inside the new-born bodies of the Makers and the Takers.

The Children of the Greening who hid between the worlds called out to them, offering their assistance, sensing the kindred soul within the human shell, but the souls were too damaged, too afraid to hear their hidden kin calling to them. They felt now that they walked alone, all meaning gone.

The fear caused the *forgetting*. Yet still they came back, searching the Earth for something they half-recalled at twilight. A yearning filling their spirit, blood and bones. Something that could never be truly forgotten but was not even half-remembered...

...yet.

Yes, at first the soul's of the Children were shocked and traumatised. How could this be, to be born into these slow, lazy, greedy, stupid human bodies...bodies that could inflict such suffering on the world? What a cruel punishment! Why had the Way forsaken them so? It was almost more than their souls could bear! But bear it they did. Just when they thought they could tolerate no more and were pushed to breaking point, they were pushed further. They despaired at being trapped inside those prisons of flesh but they could not stop their spirits from returning. There were always *returns* in the Way. And they were still part of the Way, of course, born of the one Source.

And so time and again the incarnated, their energy could not die, only be transmuted into new forms, and the only forms available to their soul-type were those of humanity. The soul's of the Children had to cope in clumsy bodies in a new realm of hate; a brutal world where once there had been love and the song of the spirit. The Children's Earth-walk was undertaken in within the fleshy framework of the Makers human-kind and that was the real torture; neither bloodied blade nor fiery tongs could match it for inflicting pain.

They returned and were killed, over and over. All the terrible ways to end a life were used upon their fleshy shells. Their souls staggered at the Makers seemingly endless ability to find progressively worse methods to wound and rend the human form. For a race once so dull, their creativity in the area of torture and pain was extraordinary. The souls of the Children wept for now being a part of that wicked, wicked race of masters and servants, Makers and Takers.

Although they were housed in human flesh, the Children's spirits still shone through their eyes, reflected in their deed and their manner. For a boundless time they had been as they were and such a way of *being* was hard to break. Their life-force essence had been so gloriously strong that to subdue it was very difficult indeed. The men of greed could smell their soul-difference, even though they wore a human form, and they hunted those with that smell, to subjugate or murder them. The Children's spirits inside those despised bodies learned to cower away from such attention. They learned to hide their natures as best they could, to avoid the pain and the humiliation of yet another torturous death at their hands.

Yet they could never hide completely, forever. Sooner or later the real spirit sang out and shone through and then they were caught, no matter how hard they tried to hide in a simple human guise. The scent on their skin sang of their difference no matter how they robed their bodies. They were nearly always discovered, and then, inevitably, they met with death, horribly.

Destruction was an addictive recreation for the men of greed, the Makers and Takers, and once they had begun this frenzy it was so hard to stop. They always found a new way to justify themselves, now manufacturing a Lord who could give them the right to act as they pleased. They gave this Lord their own attributes in order that he may sanction their abuses. And they appointed other men to be the representatives of this Lord, a Lord that they had ever met. They could justify any act as one of piety when they called upon the name of this distant and absent Lord.

It was true that sometimes a special charismatic emissary of the All came to Earth in human form and it was indeed true that sometimes they were revered and worshipped when all that they hoped for, in fact, was to be listened to. But more often than not they were persecuted or exiled. The Makers always preferred to *man*-ufacture a God for themselves rather than accept the true face of the divine Creator made manifest in a recognisable form.Why, wasn't the Creator visible in each of them...in each dog, fish, woman, spider and daisy...if only they'd have had their eyes open to truth? But they had willfully blinded themselves and such glimpses of the true Way made them feel uncomfortable and inferior and so they rebelled against it with all their might. However, the Way must offer choices and even in the darkest times, great spirits were sent to give the Makers and the Takers another perspective, an opportunity to experience another way of being. But they preferred to limit their experiences to that which could be measured in gold. They liked their Lords to be judgmental, cruel and biased towards those with financial worth.

Just as they themselves were.

And so it was that the Lord of the Trees, the earthy green spirit-patron of the wild way who had once walked the land freely, was redundant to them as they did not require the services of a Lord of joy or verdant strength. This wild Lord of the Green Dance was turned into an enemy for their convenience, an enemy of their newly invented, rigid, unbending Lord of Sorrows. And so the Dance itself became a pale memory, forgotten at best, outlawed at worst. The majesty and might of the Old Forest Lord were reduced to a moonlit shadow, a mist-cloaked form leaping alone at twilight, fading.

The Old Lord's consort, the Lady Of Mystery, was taken and distorted into a flat parody, a sterile shell which the people could neither hug nor love. Their version of the Lady gave no nurture, she was but a facade of womanly virtue, unsullied and unbloodied as no woman ever could be; made of some *man*-ufactured and unnatural fibre. And then they dared to hold up this figure as an example to real women, those who were bound to fail in the comparison to this deity of emptiness! And so it was that the men used this failure as an excuse to beat and burn and degrade all women that fell short of this hollow, barren icon.

Lady Luna of the Tides, she that was of the moon's mystery, wept bitter tears alone. She wrung her hands and gave a mother's lament, knowing that her Children were lost to her for a time. She would keep her hand upon them but she could not hold them tight for she too was fading. Soon all would simply view her as a dead rock in space, a cold thing to study with no resonance of her own; a place to invade, exploit and own. And, no matter how abhorrent this was to them, the Children must learn the lessons of this cruel season, which would pass...*it would pass!*...as everything must. Like a good mother, Lady Luna knew when to let go, holding the dream of *returns* lightly in her moonbeams.

Yes, child, it was a time of rending and tearing and of undoing. The Earth writhed and then fell silent, her citizens looked upon only by the unseeing eyes of a Lord and Lady who had been made in the image of humans and so were as deaf and as blind as the fools they served.

It was an *unholy* time; a time that was the antithesis of that which is holistic and all-encompassing; a time of conquerors, conquistadors and entrepreneurs with a single-minded view. It was a profane time, an age of isolation and desolation, a time when storms of rage whipped up a frenzy of fear and loathing; storms which would destroy and lay waste to all which grew, all which had hope, all which was born of love.

The remaining Tree-People, left estranged from the rest of their beloved citizens, pondered the greater meaning of a time which took so much and gave so little to the All. The Wise Ones of the Bark had time and yet more time to think and muse as their voices were now silent and their wisdoms drawn down deep within themselves. Drawn into the roots, roots into soft earth, and soft earth into the spirit of the worm...

It was a time to protect and survive. The *knowing* of the wise ancients must be protected for after the storm when the tranquillity of the Way be felt again and appreciated anew in the clarifying memory of its absence and denial. The trees slept and thought and tried not to grieve too much, for they were the Keepers of the memories and of dreams. Without these there could be no hope. They kept their counsel and waited whilst millions of their brothers and sisters fell in the name of 'progress', the true deity of the Makers and the Takers. The hidden Children whispered to them through feelings and vibrations deep in the cold Mother ground. They held on to the truth of the worm and the bird and sought solace in the creepings of the tiny insects amongst their deeply rooted tendrils. The Tree-People and the hidden Shining Ones still had faith, despite their pain. Oh yes, they still remembered something, something that was everything. And so they waited.

The storm seemed to rage on and on and oh, it was a bitter time even for those humans born into it with no knowledge of the old ways. It was a bleak and unending midwinter, a harsh and lonely time of reactions, of attack and defence. The sun that shone was weak and feeble as Brother Sun was no longer praised and thanked and regarded as more than just a pretty orange glow there for the benefit of humanity. He too was sad and lonely, longing to hear songs and poems from his Children again. When would the true springtime come? The new regime had no room for patterns and cycles, only for marching forwards and straight lines. Straight roads to the edge of a dead square world where an eternal death waited.

Straight into nowhere and nothing.

Laws and regulations by rulers with iron fists both came and went. The unsupported and the lost tried to find a way to live, stumbling like the blind lead by the blind and fuelled with raw fear. The life-force was low and the Dance was not danced. But the storm was set in motion and must be weathered, there could be no stepping backwards, only a hope that stepping onwards would bring renewal and new understanding of how not to be, a new appreciation of how to be.

In isolated pockets across the Earth, tribal communities tried to live in balance and beauty but even they found themselves floundering, overridden by neighbouring groups full of the warring spirit of the Makers...an infectious spirit that even the strongest found hard to resist when faced with the lost of their loved ones and their precious land. Territory and ownership replaced sharing and comradeship. Some still hung on, clung steadfast to their old ways, yet the *sight,* that precious gift of the Creator-spirit was dimming, shrinking, unused. Fear predominated.

But energy cannot cease to be. It can be diminished but it can surge back, replenished. Manifest will and iron could not truly defeat or completely stop the ebb and flow of the life-force within all natural things. Even though the Children of the Greening, inside their new mortal bodies, were killed and killed again by stone, sword, rope and fire, their allies and friends turned against them as weapons, their energies inverted, still they came back and with each earthly incarnation they learned how to cope with the new way.

...and to be strong again. Stronger than before.

So it was that the spirits of the Children, housed in unfamiliar shells of bodies, learned strength born of hardship not joy," Alicia met Lian's eyes, " just as you have in this life child. Just as I have in mine."

Lian nodded a little half-heartedly. It was getting late and it was such a long tale! But despite the selfish goading of her spirit-parasites, who were of course encouraging her to get up and leave, she had to hear it out. Without any further promting Alicia continued.

"Some of the dear Children had gotten by in the new world order by burying their true spirits. When the glimmer of *re-membering*, fired by this new inner strength, finally reached those in hiding they found that they could not fully deny their heritage any longer. And once one spirit *re-membered* this truth then the message spread out from them, the realisation ran in unseen ripples and the silent Tree-People smiled and offered their own energy to it. The memories of trees filtered into the thoughts and dreams of the people who sought a *re-membering.* Soul-connection occurred across the miles even though each spirit still did not physically encounter other familiar ones, remaining lonely in their Earth-walk, never recognising the kindred Fey behind the eyes of a human-kind.

Yes, there was still alone-ness but the loneliness began to diminish as re-connection began.

This *re-membering,* this *knowing,* was the realisation that they could be killed in body but not in spirit for subtle other-life memories came back which could not be ignored and with the images came feelings which welled up. The Children recalled other lives, other selves, other places that once were...they beagn to recall their other incarnations. They glimpsed, as a thread running through these memories, beauty and hope as well as trauma and loss. They knew that they were different inside and they sought to meet those who were like them, within these clumsy human frames. The answer was not to hide the spirit under a layer of fear. Fear did not mask their true scent anyway. As that wise Tree-Person had once said, many centuries earlier, the Shining was in their eyes.

These Fey souls realised at last that their old ways were being betrayed by their fear and silence. And, after all, what was the worst that could be inflicted upon them for being who they truly were? Death? Well, they had been killed before! They would *return,* stronger than before, it seemed. Once there was a recollection of soul-survival then all else followed, once the strands of starlight were followed back then there could be a going forward. Death was nothing...*nothing!* The only thing to fight was fear itself. The true battle was about to begin, that which was not between good and evil but between *knowing* and wilfully unknowing, knowledge and ignorance.

If the fear of death was no longer then what reason was there for denying the Way? And, by reflection, themselves? The sword of truth shone, an invisible but deadly weapon in the hands of those wearing the disguise of human peasants. The light in the eyes of those who appeared downtrodden, sick and abused, began to get brighter. Kill my body, will you? Then you make me stronger...for I will come back made invincible through my faith in my own *returning*. Ha!"

Lian, who had begun to weep silently in frustration at the recognition of her own plight, clenching her jaw and gripping the arms of her chair, relaxed a bit again. This tale was too familiar, too personal to her, for her not to have become deeply involved in it, even as her rational brain protested at being involved in such blatant escapist fantasy.

Alicia, who must have been bone-tired, continued, her voice as strong and clear as ever.

"But the freedom of the Children's spirits was a germ to be

cleansed in the Makers human world. Yet their inherent hope was a disease to be dealt with and eradicated. But the Makers and the Takers could not wipe it out. Year upon year, ruler after ruler and regime after regime could not rid the Earth of the spirits of her Fey Children. They were reborn to *re-member* what once was. They connected across oceans and through boundaries of stone, their spirits soaring above the walls and the barriers, to meet with their kin. They could feel their unity again, their blessed strength and their lost love. They were isolated and had to be strong, in faith. In the branches of a tree, a single egg in a rough nest broke open and

'*Resurgence!*' sang the Robin.

'*Resurgence!*' piped the Wren.

The Children were bruised and damaged inside but still full of the memory of beauty and of peace. They could not fight with their anger, they could not kill for death was an illusion caused by fear and division, but they could shine light on the way to *be*. And others, tired of the reigns of blood and the grips of steel, began to come to these beacons in the dark world. For not all humanity is cruel and corrupt as we ourselves know today. They were only weak, fearful and blinded to truth, for truth lead to pain in this world and was best not looked for. Some human souls were trapped in fear, a fear which prevented them from saying '*no!*' Fear which depended on death. The system that the Makers had created on Earth used the deterent of a lingering, agonising final death to quell any thoughts of disobedience. Fear flourished as long as there was a dread of this ultimate crushing device.

Without this fear and dread they would be lost.

So it was that when the Makers heard tell that their inferiors, the enslaved humans, were seeking solace in spiritual *returns,* they invented stories of a cruel and vengeful Overlord who would cast them out even in death if they, the virtuous Makers, were not obeyed in life. Horrific stories of an eternal suffering, far worse than its Earthly counterpart, were spread to quash the hope of the poor masses. The tales of a dreadful punishment after death, an obliteration of the possibility of *returns*, made the fear surge back again. Some believed the stories of devils and demons with all their humble hearts for they had no *re-membering* of their own to cling to, only the hope given to them by the Children in their Earthly guises. And so it was that the Children worked in the poorest parts of the teeming cities, in the rural areas blighted by ruthless landowners and in all places were dis-ease and hopelessness reigned, in order to bring back hope even as it was being consistently, brutally removed again.

The potent imagery and crushing might of the Makers threat of a hellish afterlife were too persuasive compared to the Children's gentle vision. Was it not better to obey to have the chance of peace, at least, in death by obeying the Makers? What reason would a poor human have to believe that there were *returns* if the rulers told them that obedience and subservience were the only guarantees of an eternal, blissful death?

Was it worth the risk of demons to die fighting the system? Was it worth protesting and standing up for your rights only to find in death an everlasting torment and not a welcome repose? Was it worth clinging to the vague chance there may be another way when the alternative reality was a purgatory in the domain of some vicious and greedy demon, he who was apparently the raging adversary of the Lord of the Makers? How was it possible to risk your poor, beleagured spirit, against the overwhelming odds of the Makers, for the vague hope of a *soul resurgence*?

The Makers used their imaginations to conjure up after-lives of unspeakable horror instead of bringing to bear images and thoughts of beauty and harmony. They misused the gift of imagination and deliberately (mis)took fantasy for reality. They fashioned cruel and bleak visions and sold them as unshakeable truths. So much so that, to some, they became indelibly etched in their way of seeing things. The Makers view of existence and permanent death was poisonous, dangerous and designed to crush. It was against the Way which sought to liberate and enhance through unfolding beauty and joyous expressions of life. Here we must remember the reality of these Makers lost in the *forgetting*...their pitiful unhappiness and discontent. Perhaps we may even feel a little compassion for their own barren and bitter existences?"

"Perhaps not!" Lian glowered and her green eyes flashed.

"Well, perhaps in time child. At least we can accept that the Way was experiencing Itself as its own opposite through the words and deeds of human Makers and Takers. It was the time of an ultimate expression of *how not to be* and reveals to us the dangers of becoming out of balance and negative or controlling to extremes. It was a fine example of walking in harmony, with respect to both the dark and the light, and not allowing anything to swing us to either polar opposite at the exclusion of the other. A seed's germination needs darkness and to grow to flower it needs light...so it is and so shall it always be. By this we understand that although this age was wholly out of balance we do need both good and bad aspects for us to exercise free will and enable the Creator to express Itself fully, in a fully rounded sense, through us. Make no mistake child, this was a time which taught us much. And it still teaches us, even now when we think we are free of such bondage!"

"Hmm," said Lian, her wide lips forming a hard line across her pale face.

"Give things time, sweetling, give all things time," Alicia stopped as she swept a long, loose piece of shimmering hair back from her face. She wore her long but pulled back like a much younger woman but it only served to make her look timeless, almost regal.

"So, I will continue. The Children could understand the fear brought on by the visions of these bitter, vindictive Makers but they had better news for these sad, lost people. Their spirits could fly and fly again. *They would go on!* The limiting and hierarchical concepts of Heaven and Hell now meant nothing to the Children whose *rememberings* of the universe did not bear witness to the fiction of punishment for all eternity. Just as the cunning Makers used storytelling and myth-making to put fear into the masses, so did the Children weave their own strands of memory into believable and far more pleasing tales of the time that once was and would be again. They used nature to illustrate their points, and, carefully, gently, they showed their magic so that the people would believe in them and their simple country enchantments.

Their method was far slower and more beguiling than that of the Makers, fear was a far more instantaneous method of getting a point across. They had to be subtle and easy on the bruised humans who came to them seeking hope. It was a lesson in patience and the Children had to rely on their inner *knowing* a great deal, for there was little in the world to support how they felt and saw things. They had to have faith in the bigger picture and believe that, in time, the message would seep into the consciousness of the poor beleaguered humans, like fresh water into the ocean.

Even if they, as incarnate humans, never saw the changes that their wisdom could bring, the Children had to try and share what they knew to be true.

The Children, in their human forms, began to perform their innocent miracles again, in order to make the human-kind *see.* Yet mistrust and fear were harder adversaries to crack than steel and flame. To reach a wounded human spirit, tied in knots by fear, was not easy. The Children sought means of reaching these simple folk through work as midwives, herbalists, healers, visionaries, artists, even as gentle Priests of the new Lord, who had some favourable aspects despite his dour demeanor and abhorrent symbolism. They taught by example, not just by words, for their words, although beautiful and tempting, were not as awesome and affecting as those hurled out by the Makers as truths. The Children took on human roles in a human realm but that was the only way to help and reach out, even if it meant risking their own transient human lives as a result.

It was hard work, the people were scared and cynical. Terrorised. And many, many Children lost their temporary human shells as a result of stepping from the shadows and helping out. The Devil, that adversary of the God of the Makers, a curious character that was created by their supposedly just and generous Lord yet who was all-fear, held too much sway in mortal lives to be obliterated by one kind word alone. Humanity had become a cowering, cringing parody of itself and the Children had to persevere to neutralise fear...persevering through many life-times, if needs be.

Ah, the faith that was required, then!

The good thing was that people begun to ask questions at all, after an aeon of not-thinking. In questioning, there was not blind acceptance, as there had been, but a slow groping towards truth and liberation, no matter how challenging and frightening that may be, initially. The Children inspired questions by their very being, even if at first these questions were belligerent and filled with mistrust.

'*How may we know your truth to be better than the one they feed us, like dry black bread?*' they were asked by the peasants, the poor, the sick and the neglected.

'*How can we trust you more than them, for at least they give us the bread whilst you make only shining promises and paint pretty pictures in our minds!*'

'*How may we know that what you say is true, that we shall not burn in the Hell of the Masters? How is it that we should take a risk on our souls to believe you? Why should we lose the little we have to starve and then go to Hell anyway?'*

The Children thought on this and loved the harder. Not all humanity was obsessed with money and gain and those born without could see the unfairness, the imbalance and the corruption. The downtrodden poor did not want what the rich had; they only wanted the right to grow their own seed, make their own bread and have the rights, dignity and freedom that come with self-sufficiency, not bitter dependence. But fences and tithes, beatings and fear of starvation or worse stood between them and a modest, honest living from the good land.

'Aye! We are poor and we live off their scraps, we don't have the money or the strength to stitch our poor souls together. We don't want to die because we can't afford an after-life! Their Lord won't let us in because we have no shoes and so we will perish for nought and rot forever, or worse be prodded by fiery pitchforks for all eternity! What say you to this? Will your Lord, or whoever it is that you offer us as an alternative, not do the same and spurn us for our lowliness? The poor don't have a right to eternal life, we can't even pay the rent in this one!'

'What use is courage and honour when it is only money which opens the doors? We don't want their money or their ways, we just want food and shelter, in this life and the next!'

'You're just as poor as us, who are you to tell us about everlasting life?'

'Aye, there's a chance they're right and you are tricking us out of our pittance. Is it not better to have a meagre sum than place our trust in something else that we have no experience of?'

'Perhaps you want to steal our souls for yourselves? How can we know it is better to trust in you than them? Are you but demons, then, for you are surely not as we are!'

'How may we decide for ourselves what is fiction, what is fact? How may we know what is not there to be seen?'

The Children listened and felt the pain and the need of real folk trapped in lives restricted by poverty and the greed of others. They experienced the dilemma of a human who could not trust their own spirit to know what was right and good. But the Children were pleased to note that at last people were acknowledging their own spirit, even the women, the sick and the dispossessed who were told by the Maker's sanctioned church and state that they had no rights, no souls to save, no hope at all. With acknowledgement of the human soul it was easier to speak of the spirit that connected all things and which dwelled in all.

And yes, slow steps and perseverance!

The Children would answer with their genuine smiles and with the love of their true soul-nature shining in their human eyes. They would not argue or defend themselves as a human would. They had no pride, only a need to share peace. The angry words of the humans were wrapped in the soft embrace of the Children's spirits as their words poured forth.

'*Oh, good people, we may tell you tales of other lives we have had here and we can take you on soul-journeys to show you that we too were once in fear and alone and with nothing. You may listen to the words and make mind-pictures and maybe travel within with us as we spin the thread of life for you. We can tell you of the times* before *and of our lives since. We cannot convince you by telling but by showing you too. So, listen and feel and open your hearts without fear and we will share our truths with you so that you may be free! We bring you the gift of imagination for you to en-vision a better world for yourselves.*'

The Children may not have realised yet exactly what they were inside their human forms but they knew what they were not! And by all that was wholly holy they would never shirk from their soul's kind-light again, no matter who railed or ranted against them; no matter who raised a hand to hurt them. And so, proving their sincerity by deed as well as by word, the Children would take the fever from a child, straighten the deformed leg of an elder who had suffered from birth, cure plague, heal leprosy, and sing a soul to health before the eyes of the people. The plant-people, related to with respect, once again yielded up their divine properties to aid the process and this co-operation opened up the connected-ness of the beings on the land once more. Amidst the gasps and cries of initial fear and complete wonderment, the Children practiced what they had known all along, that to tune into the Way, as they truly were inside, they could work with the energy unseen. Not to destroy or to crush, as they themselves had been mercilessly crushed, but to bring joy again!

It was an example of giving not to receive, and a demonstration of another way...of *the* Way. Remember, the Children never returned for vengeance, only to bring happiness and wholeness and healing!

And, for a second time on Earth, the Children sent the gift of the *dreaming* to the humans who suffered in slavery and those who could find the strength to face the fear took heart. They did not follow the Children, as leaders, but they followed their lead and stood firm as individuals even if it meant human death for them. This was true bravery. And because of this walking-with-truth, real emotion flowed again and the energies changed. Oppression remained the norm but for some, not all, repression of true feelings was ending. Any act of such courage, such powerful emotion, effects a change. When a being is speaking from the heart, in beauty, it is so.

There were *awakenings; returns, re-memberings!*

And so it was that because the Children were being true to their natures that the gifts returned to their human bodies via their spirit. They received strength and healing, just as it had once been, from the core of the Great Mystery. They no longer experienced the terrible separation of the light-less times. Although life was still far from easy they had inner help. And they even met with others of their soul-kind, the once hidden Children who had remained walking in the Earth, in the wild places; the ones who had kept their original etheric forms. The division between the hidden Fey realms and the human dimension continued but now there were ways of stepping between the two, for those who sought communion.

And, oh cariad, what rejoicing there was in that reunion! Even if, for a time, it remained secret, away from prying eyes. For the spirits of the Children who dwelled in human form to meet with their kin, the Shining Ones in the landscape, was a magical thing! The laughter that was expressed in the possibility of a Maker-human seeing these caperings! Oh yes, the blunt fear the humans would have felt if they had seen the scene, a woodland clearing or cliff top filled with dancing forms, some recognisably in human shape, while others...others remained resolutely *other.*

And let me tell you, child, there was a pleasure in our hiding , a pleasure in the fact we may be seen and cause a human to be filled with unnerving feelings of the unknown. That, my friend, was as far into a sort of revenge has our kind ever ventured. A harmless sort of nose-thumbing, don't you agree?!"

Lian clapped her hands together, the first movement she had made for some time.

"Damn right!" she snorted.

Alicia nodded and smiled.

"And when there is a magical act of communion between those of a kindred soul-type there is also transformation. The Children who dwelled in human form looked a little more like the Shining Ones that they truly were, in spirit, and as generations went by the traits deepened as the link was forged between Faery, the starlit Fey, and those who walked as people. The pointed ears, the slender tapering fingers, the gifts of *knowing* and sacred imagination, the slanting, all-seeing eyes. The open, generous hearts and the need to share...

Just as I am sharing with you this day, cariad!

And so the old stories, full of joy and colour and celebration, were told freely and came to heal the dispossessed and the hungry who listened to them truly. The spirits of the Children, undaunted by temporary boundaries and threats, opened and they flowed and so their will was done.

So, with the constant presence of their bright words of truth and their healing and their gentle magics came a belief in them; a belief in a better way. The Children sought no followers but only to empower the lonely and the lost, those crippled by the pain of their hopeless species. Their touch and breath poured out their essence and the people who came to them were moved and blessed.

You have heard the legends no doubt, of those who took over the forests, firing their Elf-arrows for the sake of the poor and dispossessed, seeking to give to those who had not? Well, never disregard a tale, Lian, there is some truth in it if there is simple good in it. Oh yes!

How could the humans doubt those who gave so much and asked for nothing but a smile in return? The ancient teachings of the Children were passed on to these open, good-hearted humans to be told around firesides and sung quietly to slumbering infants. A spark was re-kindled and the honest smile of a condemned man who no longer feared death was filled with possibilities. This lack of fear was a growing possibility, yes, but also a gentle kind of weapon.

The Children of the Greening had scarred souls but they also had quick wits as part of their human-being and a subtle understanding as part of their spirit-nature. They began to accept that if they hid or gave up, conformed or submitted, they would be sick in soul and this was not part of the Way, a way which spoke clearly of truth and honour. To wilfully make ones soul sick was not something that they would do, it was obvious now that such behaviour was against the Way. So they refused to fit into incompatible ways of being. They refused to be blunted with toil and bent with burdens of worry. Their refusal was another subtle weapon and so the possibility began to become a probability. The smile spread, like a realisation.

Just imagine what we could do if we *re-membered*, re-connected... ah, yes!

The sky and the waters and the trees and all the kin of those places needed the Children as they awoke their soul-selves and their pledged their healing strength. Added to the will of the Children were the magical wills of those humans who were open-hearted and who had learned, sometimes by terrible suffering, *how not to be*. They had been healed of their fear of death and without the fear became fearless. They saw that nothing was permanent but that it may only change its form, not cease to be. By observing the hidden cycles of nature the humans saw the purpose and the rhythm of all things; all things which they no longer wished to be kept apart from.

'Teach us to fly! Teach us to *see*! Teach us to *be*!' The humans cried and spun around and around on the Earth, trying to follow the wild dance, falling down and laughing. Their exuberance was refreshing, their excitement was catching. For them, this Dance was all new, even though it had been there all the time.

'*Grandmother Earth will be your teacher!*' the spirits of the Children cried out gladly and their Fey souls inside their human bodies shone more brightly than ever.

'*Grandfather Sky will be our protector!*' the humans replied, filled with the gladness of true *knowing* and the Fey gift of enchantment.

'*Resurgence!*' sang the blackbird in the burgeoning apple tree, always in perfect harmony.

So, it was not a time to be defeated or to be hopeless, rather it was a time of a new union, albeit a limited one, between the Fey Children of the Greening and the human-kind. Fey souls and Fey blood were interchanged with human flesh and bone and the magic of this rang out through the land as it made to wake as if from a particularly deep and unpleasant dream... *'as within, so without'*, child! The possibility of the Greening, of a renewal, grew stronger and, almost imperceptibly at first, the Faerytide began to rise again, bringing with it a heightened awareness and a frisson of glorious Otherworldly glamour. It was a time to adapt, to move, to change and to *re-member* for the sake of all creation. That adapting included passing the old starlit ways on to the humans of good heart and the sharing of wild, uninhibited love with them.

It was not possible to hate all of the human-kind and, you know, it never really had been. Their clumsy first steps at *be-ing* were, in their own way, beautiful. Some had been born to be Makers but who used free will to give this option back, untouched. Some were born to be Takers but were touched by the thought of giving instead. And oh, the power in this, cariad! The power of Creator-given free-will, exercised *knowingly*, with love, should never be under-estimated! And it was thanks to the teachings of the Children, to the ways of the Fey ones, that it had its *returns*.

Yes, the Children now knew that they could dance a wild dream for everyone, in their minds, and no one could stop them! It would never be quite like *before*, there would be differences, and the Children must move with those who wished to change and flow into a new way. The Children of the Greening learned how to be patient with this process, for human-generations they had grown practiced at waiting. They grew skilled at quietly *en-visioning* the way they wanted things to be and then infusing those thoughts and images with the dances of the stars while seeing those very stars reflected in the shimmering of dew on a spider's web.

Once more, after countless lost generations and an aeon of heartache, the Children began to *weave.*

Within this cosmic weaving the verdant strand of the Greening ran brightly as a shimmering warp thread to the glimmer of the weft which was itself the inevitability of *returns;* the eternal thread of the endless sacred round. This ethereal weaving was glorious with the potential for healing the land and, because of this, with the healing of the spirits of the land-dwellers...it was, as ever, as relevant *within* as *without*. The Makers had caused a terrible desolation upon the face of the Earth but the Children now knew, and accepted at their deepest level, that their power was stronger, that their could be a healing, a *re-wilding,* a fabulous Greening. They had taken back their power, that Creator-power of imagining and of creating through *en-visioning*, and were to wield it wisely and well, weaving its magic in both unseen and manifest ways; for no longer were they the victims of the Makers, rather they were the medicine these destructive, disturbed souls needed to come back to balance. By the hand of the star-born Fey and by their thought, kind word and song, there would a resurgence of love and respect, and kinship with, nature occur again. There would be a One-ness again, in love, truth and beauty.

Yes, there *will* be!

For just as they vowed in the greenwood of their spirits so it will be in the world. Always and eternally onward, within and without!

Yet in the year of their Lord Twelve Hundred and Eighty the possibility of such beauty seemed far, far away. For Marguerite, a Fey soul born into a hostile human world with her wild shining spirit, it seemed like a memory or a faint hope to cling to. For she, a poor woman born with the soul of a Child of the Greening, was about to enter the struggle, reborn into the fray for the sake of a peaceful fight for truth, honour and natural justice...for the good of the All."

Alicia stirred herself from the deep reverie of her tale-telling and fixed her eyes upon the small healer woman before her. Letting her epic telling settle into the ether all around them Alicia exhaled, long and slow.

The girl before her returned her look. Lian had the widest eyes that Alicia had ever seen in this life, eyes that held the very essence of the Greening in their verdant depths.

Lian smiled, a small smile that held a sweet, sweet sadness.

"That's about me, isn't it?" she said. "I was born of the Faerytide, I have a Fey soul, just as you do?"

"You know it to be so, cariad."

"And somehow, although I do not yet understand it, I am also a small healer woman named Marguerite who lived in Fourteenth century France and was killed, along side her precious friend Allette, and *the man...*"

"Yes, beloved. it is so. And soon we will revisit those dark days to bring forth the light that they contained."

"All of us, all burned...?" Lian's voice dropped to a whisper.

Alicia nodded, her throat suddenly terribly dry.

"I *saw* it! I keep *seeing* it! This has haunted me for so long! Oh lady!"

Lian gave a sob and threw herself into the open arms of her oldest dearest soul-friend who held her as tightly as her old body was able to do.

"Why us? Why now?" Lian sobbed.

"For the Greening, child. The Faerytide has risen up in us most strongly, just as it has in many others like us that we have not yet met, not in this life. We are awakening to our true soul-selves that we may fulfil the vows made so long ago for the safety and sanctity Earth Mother. It is a Greening of our spirits, child, a personal resurgence that is, turn and turn about, for the good of the All. Do not be afraid, there is no longer a need for fear. Be at peace, sweetling."

This time the tears that flowed down Lian's sculpted cheeks, hewn as it seemed from finest marble, were of relief as well as of sorrow and the old woman, one who shone with an inner light filled with all the mysteries of the moon, cried along with her.

As the roseate light of an October dawn stole between Alicia's threadbare rose-printed curtains she gave a start and realised that she had fallen asleep where she sat. She then realised that the girl was still alive, Lady be praised! Another morning, one stained with only a sunrise, no blood spilled, and no life taken by the cruel hand of fate. As Alicia realised this stark truth so did Lian as she too woke from a fitful slumber on the wooden seat. During that long night, a night of knives that twisted in unison in their bellies as the horror and the beauty of life was laid bare, the two had become closer. More than that, they had become connected; indeed it had always been so.

So many shared pictures had formed in their minds, maybe memories, maybe just the daydreams of two that were disenfranchised in that society. Two lonely women who had between them created an elaborate fantasy, a beautiful reality other to that which embraced concrete and iron, slavery and subjugation. A world that was filled with magic, the dancing light of Faery beings.

A reality long-since gone but never quite forgotten.

Maybe it was memory, a reality, or maybe it was a harmless fantasy. Did it matter when it meant so much?

Alicia had given Lian her own explanations for the way things were in glowing terms in a flowing, sometimes arcane, tongue. Yet, with the returning light, the Lian who had felt safe enough to listen appreciatively and talk in a lilting and lyrical stream for hour upon hour was overshadowed by her more familiar counterpart, the harsh and aggressive girl used to having to protect herself from foolish fancies. Maybe it was tiredness or maybe something else...a *something* that enjoyed her being isolated, prickly and defensive...which made her snap back into old habits. Whatever the reason, as she awoke she found herself once more becoming the sharp-edged Lian with her quick tongue and shielded heart...the one who could survive in a world seemingly free of Faery-light.

The human side of Lian Smythe, ruled by fear, stepped to the fore again even as she scrubbed blearily at sleepy eyes and stretched out her cramped body as best she could. She had no memory of falling asleep but the tale that had been told of lost lives was still fresh in her mind and it now did little to comfort her, rather instead its memory goaded her unreasonably, like a fiery itching. Images and words crowded into her, stabbing and jabbering where only a few precious hours ago they had been like a wonderful herbal balm to an old wound. So it was that even as she yawned as teased the tangles from her wild hair she found herself attacking the old woman.

"You think that because I am still here and not there, wherever there may be, that you have saved me?"

Lian stabbed the arm of her chair with her long slender index finger and Alicia flinched visibly. The night's shared experience with all its attendant loving feelings immediately melted away. The closeness it had brought them had done little to sweeten Lian's bitterness towards a woman who thought that she had answers. The spirits that had dogged Lian since that revolting Ouija she had fallen pray to circled, cackling, sucking in life, dimming Lian's perspective horribly. How could Alicia get this poor damaged girl back from their clutches when she had now obviously fallen under their influence again? Even though she knew that she would, somehow, Alicia shuddered and got up to rake out and re-build the fire which had long since gutted to ash. She couldn't bear Lian's inevitable cruel onslaught, not yet.

But it came anyway. In the cold light of day the realisation hit Lian hard. How could this elderly, staid lady know what it was like to be her? How could anyone? Lian shook her head savagely. How on Earth could she have, only hours before, have been buying into this patently ridiculous subterfuge that she herself had a Faery-soul and was here to help bring about the Greening of the land? It was extraordinary how, when tiredness and despair overwhelmed you, you could be convinced of any crack-pot delusion!

Anything rather than face the truth, eh? The lonely, desolate truth...

Lian watched as Alicia moved around the room, tending and tidying things. She noted the lines in Alicia's face seemed more deeply etched, the skin a little greyer than it had when they had met less than twenty four hours ago. Even in the curtained half-light of an autumn dawn Lian could see how she had aged. This indomitable, intensely caring woman was really old now, brittle and fragile as the skeleton of a leaf. A brief blossom of pain swelled, burst and was gone in her own breast. What was the point of forming an attachment to this kindly grandmother figure? Whoever Lian loved she saw dying before her eyes, or worse, turning from her when they found out who she really was. And who she really was had nothing to do with gossamer wings and fireflies, but had everything to do with being cursed in a barren world.

And to be born cursed, for no apparent reason, was to walk alone.

How could she have ever thought Alicia could help her? Why, look what she had done to her in a day! Aged her beyond belief, made her cry, burdened her with tales of victimisation and personal tragedy! No, to try and form human relationships was selfish. How could she inflict her cursed nature on hapless people who tried to help?

No, she would not risk that link again with another human. It was not fair on either party. She would be cold, distant. An uninhabitable, hostile star amongst the millions of other lost and lonely stars in a place behind the sun.

Alicia looked up from her bundle of kindling as she knelt at the grate, tentatively meeting Lian's gaze. Something in Lian felt even more annoyed by this weakness. Her own gaze hardened, she couldn't help it. It was as if she were being worked like a puppet even as her real soft centre, her Fey-ness, protested.

"Yeah, so what?" Lian said sneeringly to the staring old woman.

"The universe wants you to live," Alicia stated as calmly as she could.

It was hard to be calm when she was once again face to face with this seething, possessed girl and not the lovely Fey-souled one she knew and loved of old. The shadows of fatigue under Lian's impossible eyes only emphasised their sylvan depths and the mean spirits around her drew close with an almost audible hiss as the air around her head became dull and bruised.

Lian snorted rudely. She was possessed again, that was sure and certain. Alicia sighed heavily, concentrating on the sticks in her hands...hands that shook visibly. Please let this wonderful, terrible girl not be too awful to her, not after all they had been through so recently...and, of course, not so recently.

(*Please!*)

"Yeah right, that's a good one Alicia, full marks for a classic New-Age one liner. A real gem of meaningless, facile, banal..."

Something in Alicia snapped back when she heard the mocking voice coming from this slight and petite girl-woman. She would NOT let these cheap and tawdry entities speak to her this way! Even if her hands still shook and she inwardly cringed she would not go belly-up for them. She would not! This was a fight like any other and Alicia, given time, knew just how to win...gently...

Gently...

But her own voice came out harder than she had intended.

"Oh spare me the derision, mistress! I am tired and you are tired. Why don't we share some tea and toast and I can make you up a bed? Proper nourishing sleep is what we need now, not a fight!"

But Lian was roaring again, the rage spilling back out onto the poor wisewoman seemingly without her being able to keep herself it check. A part of her was horrified to hear herself insult the woman who had showed her nothing but compassion and genuine care, hospitality beyond need or greed. Yet she ploughed ahead mercilessly. She had to sever the link before it grew too strong and destroyed them both!

"I've had bloody Elves, Pixies, the works from you Alicia and now for the best bit of all, the universe loves me! Me, the one it cursed specifically with the apparent gift of knowing how much everyone fears me! The one it cursed with the *knowing* who died where and in how much pain! Of seeing things and hearing things when there should be quiet...of having no privacy because there's always someone's ghost needing to say their piece...

(Oh for goodness sake stop it Lian! Don't say anymore! She's trying to help you, is all! Shut up, damn it, and don't let those nasty spirit-entities ruin things for you again!)

...oh yes, and of being haunted by myself, it seems, in other lives, even I can't leave myself alone! What a farce! And to cap it all you tell me the universe, a bunch of swirling dust and burning gas, loves me and wants me for a sunbeam. Ahhh! So I am the chosen one after all! *Give me a break!*"

"Stop it, beloved! I've told you what you are but you chose not to hear. I've offered you solutions but you reject them. Fair enough, that is your prerogative, but do me the courtesy of not disregarding my hospitality. I ask you not to throw everything back in my face, child."

"Oh Alicia, I know you mean well but I can't spend another minute hearing this clap-trap about Faeries, or Feys, or fluffy niceness about when we all unite and peace reigns upon the Earth. I'll stop insulting you if you stop mocking my intelligence. I may be psychic, or Fey as you put it, but I'm not thick!"

"I speak only of your kin, your true family, and your role in this life. If you find that far-fetched I ask you to compare it to what you already know as reality...ghosts, things others cannot see, the rejection you feel by mainstream society..."

"Don't forget the *deep* admiration my family...and yeah, I mean my biological family not some flimsy fruitcake fantasy family...and the admiration they *don't* give me for being so apparently special and shiny. In fact, the time of day they *don't* pass with me."

"Blood connections are not as relevant as your spirit lineage, cariad."

"Oh, *whatever!* But fundamentally at the bottom of all that convoluted story you are telling me that the world doesn't want me, and I don't want the world, but the universe, that vast uninhabited wasteland, that which is colder and emptier than even humanity...you're telling me that the universe loves me? Oh please! And it went out of its way to save little old me. Really? Oh good, that's all right then."

Lian's voice was dripping invective and the viciousness cut Alicia deeper than ever. Those vicious, stupid spirit-entities that haunted Lian! Alicia swore she would see them gone, the nasty, cruel flotsam that they were.

Was there any point in trying to reach Lian when the dirty entities had a hold of her again? Alicia had to try!

"Lian, you need to separate out the world, the Earth herself, and the mess human-kind has made of it. Society is not the Earth! Human ways, the ways of the Makers, are not nature's ways! You cannot say the world does not want you, but may instead realise that human-kind has become so fearful and forgetful that it doesn't recognise you! You pose a threat because humanity has become hostile, even towards its own kind. It destroys the natural way for the sake of a transient, illusionary security and for profit. So, yes, I say that the Earth does not reject you, even if people seem to, for you are of the Earth and your true nature is akin to hers. And yes, I say the universe, the Creator-consciousness that fuels all things with love and creativity, saved you. What does *uni-verse* mean, beloved, but 'one song'...the song of creation! It created you, sweet one, and yes, it loves you."

"Well, that's just dandy! So, nice knowing you lady but before I go how about you explain to me how you reached that completely insane conclusion?"

Lian stopped short of adding that it was no wonder Alicia's children had abandoned her for being a mad old dear. That was too much even for her present mood. No dirty spirit's interference could make her Fey soul stoop that low.

"I know it, child, for the Creator is the universe and we are all the Creator....each one of us! I *re-member*, see? And I know, if you need more tangible proof, because of one simple fact. That is, apart from my own intuition, tried and tested over the course of this one lifetime in a disciplined manner with respect for my spiritual ancestors."

Alicia had once again adopted her strangely compelling tone, the accent slipping inevitably into the old inflections.

"That one fact is my telephone. The one I ran to use to stop you going into the city to a truly pointless death. The one that I called the bus company on. The one they received my call on. It has been disconnected for five, maybe even ten, years."

Lian got up and went without asking to the old fashioned olive green telephone which sat on a window seat next to a pile of books. She picked up the heavy handset. There was no dialling tone. Pressing it down firmly into the cradle she lifted it again. Again no tone, the phone was dead. She checked the wire going into the socket and saw a junction box made obsolete some years previously. Maddeningly it all seemed to suggest that the woman was telling the truth. Ah, it was infuriating!

"Why? What? I don't get it!"

Alicia picked at yet another loose thread on her cotton dress. Goodness, she was cold! But the fire would have to wait.

"Ever since my children, Davey and Rhiannon, stopped calling me, in fact ever since they stopped seeing me, I had no need of such reminders. A silent telephone that should ring is worse than one which cannot. When I didn't even know where they where and when I had gotten sick of anticipating their calls that never came I had it cut off."

"*How* long ago?"

"Five years, approximately, but it could be much longer. I trust you do not wish an *exact* date?"

Alicia could also be scathing and Lian flinched.

"I couldn't bear a phone that could ring but didn't so I had one that couldn't and wouldn't. Method in my madness, mistress, eh? No more phone! I still had the grief and pain but no tormenting silent telephone. Yet I knew that if I called the bus company to save your life, it would work"

"How do I know you didn't use a phone box?" Lian's eyes narrowed.

"Calculate the time it takes to run there and remember I am old now, well past seventy, so I am, and once I'd come in, found money, phone numbers, keys and ran slowly to the telephone box...do you think I did that, Lian? Go outside if you will, flibberty gibbet, and see how far away the public telephone actually is! Use your skills girl, *see* the truth for once! I don't even possess a telephone directory! I used magic, Fey magic, *our* magic, yours and mine! I used the imagining, my will-and-wishing, our creative *en-visioning...*its real, beloved! It *works!*"

"Lady, you're quite quite mad but it's quite reassuring to know that there really is someone madder than me. I thank you for your time but if you'll excuse me I have an existence to get on with...thanks to you."

Lian slipped into her beautiful, tattered and now crumpled frock coat and stood over Alicia. There were no tears now.

"If you ever need me, if you ever, ever think of your own death again, well you phone me on my special number and I'll be here for you. Remember, even if you choose to forget the other things I have told to you, that my phone worked last night because you, my dear, are what I say you are. You are needed in this world, child, your very being is valuable."

"So, if I'm in serious danger or thinking of killing myself I call a number that doesn't exist, right? Hell, most people call the Samaritans before committing suicide, you suggest I call a number that isn't real and get a lecture on the sanctity of life from a barking mad old woman. Great, thanks for the tip."

Alicia just stared back, composed.

"So, what's the number then, oh witchy one?"

Lian was almost laughing now but there was no humour in her, none at all.

"I will tell you and you will remember. It is our Fey number and it is between witches, yes. In fact I have no need of telling you, you will know. You do know, even now! Do you understand me, wild spirit? Can you, above the chattering of your pain and all those stupid, clamouring spirit-vampires, hear the truth? Accch!"

Alicia waved a hand at Lian, brushing her aside with a gesture which now spoke of her own very human frustration and anger. Then she seemed to get a hold of herself and, with visible effort, calmed herself down. She must remember that Lian was but a wounded child, one that had lost her beloved best friend, Robert, and done something very foolish; one who had not, until this moment, had any real spiritual guidance at all. Alicia sought her inner starlight and found her centre. Lian watched, fascinated despite her human-self, as the older woman collected herself and straightened up.

Alicia spoke again, with new authority.

"So, try it, its all I ask. But only when you are at your lowest, if your darkest hour returns. I cannot bear the thought of waiting to hear a dead phone ring so I will assume it never will. I hope, I *pray*, your thoughts never turn to such things again. Consider this a favour to me for my time... trust me. Trust someone!"

The two women stared at each other and again that connection...

(*the flames, always the flames*)

...passed between them.

"Ok, I will. Happy now?"

"Oh no, beloved, not happy!"

Alicia met her gaze squarely and then turned away.

" I am not happy, child, because I know that on the night that you did your foolish Ouija board experiment that you picked up the equivalent of a nasty spiritual virus. I know such bugs as thought-forms, *nasties*, and your particular spirit-parasites have been playing up to your fears and anxieties ever since that night and getting very well fed from them too, thank you very much.

Now, such horrible psychic pests, little vampires living off your plentiful spiritual energy, have tried and almost successfully convinced you to kill yourself. They are having a great deal of fun at your expense. I would like, very much, to get rid of them for you. For this, I need to do a serious session of trance work with your full consent, within a disciplined structure, with full psychic protection. We can send these thought-forms off to the place in the universe where they can receive healing. They don't belong with you and until we sever their links with you, you will be unhappy. More unhappy, in fact, than I am now seeing you leave in such a condition. Scorn my words, for now, if you must...but heed them child. Remember them! And know that I love you and am desperately sorry for the loss of your lover and friend. Know that I see you as no murderer but an innocent who does not yet know the ways of her own wild spirit. Know that I hurt for you, child, and will help you. Heed me now, I beg you!"

"Oh, enough of your words! I want no more of your talk!"

Lian shook her head vigorously as if trying to dislodge Alicia's truths. Part of her, the eternal Fey part, longed to stay and get Alicia's help, feeling gratitude beyond measure to her. But the wilful, damaged human part, encouraged by the dirty spirit-virus, was making her run away from it...from all that she truly held dear.

"And I will be happier still when I can teach you how to walk with spirit so that you may practice the Craft of the Wise, taking the path of the natural Fey *seer*. Until then," Alicia shook her own head, "I will be terribly sad. I'm tired Lian. If you must go, go now."

"I'll be off then. And thanks for the tea and soup and all. Oh, and the chair."

"See yourself out."

Lian paused briefly at the door, wanting to say more, but thinking the better of it slipped outside and was gone from view.

"I'll see you before the spring, cariad," Alicia whispered, "and, foolish, beautiful child, I will make us both happy."

Alicia saw, with her own inner Fey vision, a small, red haired young woman with hunched shoulders walking away from her with fresh tears, this time the tears of parting badly from a friend, glistening on her waxen cheeks...a small Fey woman who, despite her fearful, damaged human-ness and her spirit hangers-on, was *shining.*

And one who, thanks to the intervention of her ancient green-spirited kin, was resolutely alive.

Chapter Four

Watching from Underneath

I met him at a party and I wish that I had not.

That damn woman, that ingratiating old hag, she had made it all worse for me. If she hadn't intervened that night there would have been no party, no Dominic, no rejection and no more pain; pain which hurt me more deeply than ever. Why, I wouldn't have been alive at all! Instead I was devastated again which was, to my mind, worse than being dead.

It happened so suddenly that it caught me unawares, me that had vowed to never, ever let anyone near me again! How could I have been so stupid as to even try and fit in with their social games, their relationships? Always *them!* Hadn't I vowed to stay alone? Yet, I saw him and I thought that he might be...

(*Julien De St. Pierre, always the man in the woods of France, with his grey-green eyes and nut brown hair. My love! He who was other than them, just like me*)

...but of course he wasn't and I just ended up feeling even more hideous, more outcast and undesirable than ever.

Once I had gotten back into my life in the city, my solitary life (that was if you didn't count the endless *voices* and the indeterminable visions) I had tried to put my head down and get on with the lonely grind of being. I believe that I could have called it an existence, of sorts. Despite all of Alicia's administrations the simple fact remained that Robert had gone and I had not, and so there was nothing to do but live 'til I died, although the urge to end it all by my own hand had passed...for now at least. I had deliberately blocked out all I had heard from Alicia that night, I mean, I didn't need to think I was genuinely mad as well as cursed, did I? It wouldn't do me any good at all to start believing I had a mission to save the world as a reincarnated Fey-spirit, now would it?

How many nutters are there in the world believing they are the chosen ones anyway? And, on top of all that had been dished out to me as a punishment in this life, did I really need to cap it all by claiming to be a Faery-witch...that particularly vilified, feared, shunned and persecuted species of outsider? No, Alicia, kind as she may have been, was wrong to try and help me by making me stake a claim to an apparent truth that would have made me even more marginalised and afraid than I already was.

Bless her, the old crone, but she was wrong. And I wouldn't let her confuse me again.

So, I got on with it, the stuff that people do in order to get their little pay cheque, be that from an employer or as a government handout. I kept in line and did what millions of others do. Only I did it all on the fringes of society, the place where the sick and the disenfranchised dwelled.

I went to my therapy sessions, arranged by my not-so-doting Daddy, for the sake of being co-operative. I dread to think what they would have done with me if I had been as belligerent as I felt. I resented being analysed, broken down and re-constructed, it felt like homogenisation, a way of making me into someone fit to be in their social structure. I felt as if I was being transformed into a palatable, non-threatening figure rather than the aberration I was. If Alicia was right...big if, I know...but if she was right then *I was as I was* and it made me dislike their well-meaning but intrusive and frankly rude assumption that I wanted to be put right like the rest of them. I was different, end of story.

For the same accquiescent reasons I sat in the mental health care Centre once a week, too, feeling like a freak amongst people who were genuinely ill. I wasn't ill, I was just...mad, perhaps? Maybe, but certainly cursed by some unknown quantity to walk the Earth as someone who could hear, see and feel things that no sane individual could. I didn't fit into the box of someone who had delusions as part of a chemical imbalance, I didn't even really slot into the category of one who had been abused or deprived, things that may have triggered a response in my psychological make-up. I really was, for no apparent reason, born that way. I couldn't blame my dear Papa, he was just a bigot, an idiotic little man who may have chosen to blame me for the death of his wife and I certainly couldn't blame her, my mother, for dying when I was so young now could I?

No, I wasn't one for casting about looking for a place to lay my howling pain. I was one who liked to think it must have been my fault, in some way, for whatever it was to have hex me so grievously. I had to believe in such things as curses, if I heard *the voices*, saw the disembodied ones, smelled their scent and touched their essence, well, how could I deny magic and the spirit realms existed? So, by direct association, I had to believe in ill-wishing. Curses came to bad people, those who had done something...whenever...that deserved hexing, surely? I had to walk with that, live by it. I must have sinned, somehow, somewhere.

I was no sweet little Faery, then. I never had been.

Nor was I some latently powerful witch. I was just terminally different and very, very alone.

There were some bits of my life that I didn't mind, really. I did my recommended yoga class (prescribed to calm me down, make me even more accquiescent, no doubt) but was careful to avoid the obligatory meditative aspects of it. I found that if I relaxed into a state of peaceful repose then *the voices* would take it as an opportunity to start speaking to me. I envied those bright, contented looking women who were in the beginner's class with me. They all radiated some indefinable sense of being at ease which made me feel wistful. Why wasn't there anyone who emitted the same feeling that I did? There was never anyone like me...

(*except for Alicia, of course*)

...and that was such a dreadfully lonely feeling. No wonder I had wanted to die, regardless of my losing Robert.

I did not envy these placid, healthy women but I watched them with interest, these chirpy creatures that discussed homeopathy or visits to Jaipur in gushing terms with the equally scrub-faced, earnest instructor. It kind of hurt me that they looked at me, smiling, but still focused on that point somewhere above my head even if they meant to be welcoming. I would sigh quietly and turn away and wonder what they really thought of the odd-ball with the flame-red hair that shuffled her foam mat into the furthest corner and never contributed to chit-chat before or after the session?

Not that I couldn't guess, no matter how well-meaning they were. I was like an enigma, a puzzle people loved to try to solve even if they couldn't. Most, like these women, were content to speculate idly on my nature but some, infuriated by their ability to work me out, tried to change me by fair means or foul. Humans just loved to box you up and explain you away! They thought they liked mysteries but only in stories when they knew there would be a conclusion. '*Oh, she's like* that,' they longed to say, triumphantly. Well, let them have fun analysing what I might be, I knew I would never be whatever it was that anyone seemed to think that I was.

My favourite bit of my life was my discovery of the countryside around the city. At first I stomped off across the fields as a form of rebellion, in a temper for my being stuck in a city that maybe lovely but which was, ultimately, hostile to my nature. There hadn't been rural areas, like the fields and woods I found here, where I had grown up. I felt, sometimes, that my Dad and aunt may have done me a favour after all, even inadvertently. For the first time in my life I discovered that I liked being alone in nature. And away from the human clutter of city life I got more gentle, lucid images in my minds-eye and heard more poetic, less intrusive, gentler voices.

I saw deer and kestrels, buzzards, badgers and hares and I sensed a kinship with all of these creatures even though they still felt the need to dart away and cry out a warning when they heard me approach. I felt solidarity with the animals that hid from the prying attentions of humans and wished that I could tell them that although I walked in human form and smelled like one of their enemies, that I was *other* than human. But how to explain something I did not understand myself, fully, if at all? The creatures of the land and sky had clearly become inured to only seeing human two-leggeds and so they responded by habit to a species that caused them harm, destroying their habitats and hunting them down for sport. Occasionally though, around nightfall when I wandered alone and unafraid through the trees, there would be a lingering communion with a vixen or owl. I found the more that I spent time in the woods, especially at dusk or dawn, the more readily the beings of fur and feather would linger in my stead, curious, scenting me, not so keen to take flight as before.

I could live for that, if nothing else.

I yearned for a time when they would come to me, unafraid, and see beyond my Earthly form, to the spirit which, like their own, was wild and free.

I treasured those moments. If only *they* (always *they!*) could have left me be I could have subsisted that way until I did eventually died. Call it avoidance, call it shirking my responsibilities in the world, but until you've had the constant *voices*, pictures, feelings, you don't know how much you crave to be left alone. Really alone.

Nature respected that need in me.

I would sit and feel a curious sense amongst the elder and ash, lime and hazel trees of being home. I felt more at ease, even at peace, watching the elder berries and rosehips wither and die. Finding the beautiful silvery skeletons of long-dead leaves and watching puffed-up, pallid fungi release their spores was more soothing to me than any comfort I could have in the company of chattering people. I just would have liked to have had another other to share it with me. But I had not, would not, find another in that life of mine, so I enjoyed what I had.

Never within my own four walls had I felt so at home, safe and secure, as I felt with my kin the tree-folk, the four-legged and the feathered ones. I even felt at home in my own skin when I lay amongst the leaf litter, smelling rich, damp loam in my nostrils in the deeply appreciative way that some other humans scent fresh-brewed coffee or baking bread.

And sometimes I was almost glad that I wasn't dead yet I wouldn't go so far as to say I was happy to be alive. I could not thank Alicia for saving me but nor could I forget that without her intervention, meddlesome old bat, I wouldn't have had that communion with nature to enjoy. I would be dead, cold and forgotten.

The only thing that I didn't seem to have was a deeper sense of communion with the spirit of the land. I longed, body and soul, to be embraced by it; to have it understand me and me it. I yearned for a nameless melding, something that was beyond my own words and thoughts but primal and all-encompassing. I wanted to dissolve myself into the Earth as into the arms of a soul-lover and to feel as the land did, just as I would wish to feel all my lover felt. I needed to have the land's green sap in my veins as I pushed and pulsed in the soil, writhing and burrowing, seeking entrance to its very essence. It was a passionate desire in me to have this union even though I barely know how to describe it; it was just a throbbing deep within in me that was beyond my ability to soothe it. I craved the land's company although each time I walked in the countryside and each time I lay on the Earth's skin I felt this aching need more keenly. I became addicted to this fascinating feeling, this wild lusting, for at least in this addiction there was a focussing on something other than empty days and lost opportunities.

And, it is true to confess, that in some part of me, I yearned to see the land-spirits themselves, the Fey ones, the Faery-kin. If Alicia spoke even a little truly then why did these beings not step out to greet me as their own? Why did I not see their shining forms of gossamer and gold, stepping out from the eternal green of the mythic forest? But they did not come...no, not ever.

So, I just walked about in the woods on my own, yearning madly, greeting the creatures there with love for they alone seemed able to receive the precious little I had to give without question or even acknowledgement. They just *were* and I thanked them for it.

That was how it was for me, day upon day, until I tripped over Carmen's bag outside MacDonalds in the city on my way back from the social Centre. I avoided the town and normal people's lives as much as I could but fate has a nasty way of making you fall flat on your face just when you think you've cheated it by finding a loophole. Especially if, like me, you are cursed.

I was miserable as usual. I had spent an unprofitable hour listening to other people's woes and drinking horrible tea in the dismal Centre. I fluctuated between a figure sunk in sullen introspection and a proxy counsellor to the other 'clients'. I knew they found it easier to talk to me than to the busy, efficient care workers and voluntary support assistants as I myself offered no words of advice, no positive, upbeat ideas. I just sat, met their gaze, and let them speak.

I tried not to hear *the voices* but, as was only to be expected I suppose, most of the people diagnosed as long-term mentally ill had a host of spirit hangers-on who wanted to talk to me too. Not only did I hear the cries for help from sad, dysfunctional, unbalanced people, I was bombarded with the wishes and wills of their menagerie of ethereal companions. I always left the Centre feeling exhausted but no one seemed to notice. It did me no good at all going there, quite the reverse in fact, yet it was part of my 'treatment', apparently, as agreed by my absentee father. Oh, how I wanted to be left alone!

It was in that tired and overloaded state, in the forced Yuletide gaiety of the main high street, I stumbled over Carmen. Or, at least, her shopping. People loved to shop in this city, especially around Christmas. I just didn't understand it at all, that family-orientated, materially wasteful, drink-sodden frenzy once a year. What was it based on, this obscene frenzy? More lies from the Makers of Alicia's telling? All I knew was that it left me feeling more alienated than ever especially as the only contact I could expect over that supposedly festive season would be a cheap card from my dear Papa and maybe a hello from a fellow tenant of my building as they rushed off to a party or dinner somewhere. They never bothered me, the other residents of the flats, and I stayed well away from them, not needing to pick up yet more psychic baggage in my own home...such as it was. As I sadly contemplated the isolation that Christmas meant to me suddenly I was sprawled at the feet of a young woman in a tangle of bags marked 'Next' and 'Gap'; someone who was evidently heavily involved in all the stuff that I wasn't. It was as if some great hand had literally pushed me into the path of mainstream society, a whole way of being I had studiously avoided up to that moment.

"Oh! Oh shit, here, let me help you! I am so sorry, I mean, *really* sorry!"

Carmen was mortified, possibly by the fact I may have been injured in my graceless tumble, partly because she was alarmed that one so strange looking as myself was languishing amidst her shopping. I rearranged myself into a sitting position that may have almost looked deliberate if it hadn't been on a cold, wet pavement.

"It's okay," I brushed ineffectually at my coat. It was pavement that felt greasy and was strewn with fast food wrappings and possibly worse. It felt, I realised, quite alien to me.

"I suppose I should stand up."

Carmen took my hand and I wish that she hadn't. I got a stream of faded but concise images and feelings from that connection with her - of her making love with a feminine-looking blonde haired man, of her worries about what to buy her grandmother for Christmas, of her graduation ceremony outfit and of her jealousy about her colleague who got the promotion...and then more distant images, all of which would have come flooding through if I hadn't let go of her delicate hand.

"I can help myself, thanks," I said gruffly.

In order to disassociate myself from human psychic impressions, the omnipresent baggage they carried home as well as their shopping, I had to be so rude! I was just protecting myself but I know how it must have seemed.

Carmen looked taken aback but let me disentangle myself from her packages and lurch to my feet.

"I really am sorry, that must have hurt," she went to touch me in a further show of apologetic sincerity but thought the better of it. Perhaps she had got a shock of her own from me...a blast of horrible *otherness* to disconcert her.

"No problem. I should have been paying more attention. You get used to people cluttering up the pavements in this city."

I sniffed, hoping that I could get on my way now, not wanting to prolong that human exchange a minute longer. The Centre had depleted me, I didn't need any more images or voices that day. I went to walk off in the direction I had been heading but Carmen, either curious to know what sort of person I was, or genuinely keen to make amends, wouldn't let me go that easily.

"You live here? Oh, how wonderful! Me and my boyfriend, Seth, we're just down to visit his friends and go to a party. We live in Kingston but it must be amazing living here? Wow, I mean, it's *so* beautiful! Look, I really am sorry, stupid of me to leave my things in such a terrible heap like that. Do you know where I could get a coffee?"

"MacDonalds," I stated the obvious, gesturing to the building at our rear.

"Oh no, I mean, *proper* coffee! Would you like to join me for a cup if you can tell me where there's a decent cafe? I'm sure there must be loads here, a place as exciting and vibrant as this?"

"I wouldn't know," I said gruffly.

Why wouldn't this woman leave me be?

I could see her looking at me with deepening curiosity. Damn it! '*Stick around*,' I thought, '*your interest in this strange person will turn to revulsion, soon enough*!'

"Oh, let's find somewhere together then!"

She chattered gaily on and I could see she was dying to take my arm, and ask me a barrage of questions. What sort of young woman lived in Bath and didn't go to cafes? She must be intrigued. Could I blame her? I sighed. She was so gushy and enthusiastic, I was so surly and withdrawn, what an odd coupling! A fated meeting, Alicia would expound, no doubt.

"I hear that the Abbey courtyard has decent places, dunno if they're still open. Do you want to try there?"

Carmen smiled broadly. She had an unmade-up face and incredibly white, even teeth. I helped her pick up her many and various bags and that was it. I was hooked into humanity again, albeit temporarily. We went for a coffee and she invited me to the party.

I could have said no, that I was busy. I could have just ignored her and forgotten all about her stupid invitation. Yet not wanting to seem even more churlish, perhaps, or nursing some distant, almost-forgotten hope of acceptance, later that night I walked across the city centre to the address she had given to me. How foolish was I? How ridiculous had I become to have even considered acceptance at such an event? It was only ever Robert that had offered me acceptance and where had that gotten him...or me? Still, I shelved all my sensible thoughts and followed up Carmen's invitation to this stranger's party. Perhaps, if that wise old bird Alicia was right, it was just my own spiritual hangers-on encouraging me to do something dumb so they could feed themselves up on my sorrow. Yes, perhaps. But then I credit myself with enough stupidity of my own apart from any extraneous dubious influences.

So, the party was in a fashionably middle-class area on the other side of the city from where I was ensconced. I felt immediately out of place picking my way between Citroens with '*Keep Music Live!*' stickers and Volkswagen convertibles. It got worse when I entered the small town house. Maybe in another incarnation, *sans* visions and without *the voices,* I could have been a nice ceramicist with two children at the local alternative school and a husband who went mountaineering. I could have taken holidays to Peru and had a CD collection of world music....

...yes, in another more favoured life maybe.

As it was I felt poor and shabby and completely alien to that world. It was normal, successful and positive and I was none of those things. My *otherness* made me feel as if I was dragging a foul corpse behind me into their pristine world, a sensation I remembered from my failed college days with all of the attempts I made there to fit in at parties. The only one I had ever enjoyed was the one where I had met Robert.

('*This is the end, beautiful friend...*')

Oh, that he had been there with me now instead of his wispy spectre and all of my own ghosts, howling for my continued failure in life.

As soon as went into that house I felt panic. I had once been an art student but had half-heartedly studied graphic design, not the fine art these folk seemed to be into. As I silently panicked I thought about making a living, surviving in the world, the way the people that thronged the walls seemed to be able to. I could feel, or *see*, that these were privileged arty folk who somehow had been given the right to just be able to create without income being a problem. They terrified me with their easy laughter and broad knowledge, their expensive wine and discreet reefers. I felt as if I had been out of the world so long that

I had no idea how to be in it again, especially a world that I had never been qualified to enter. These people had listened to Mahler as children, my Dad had Burt Bacharach. I was suddenly not only an *other* at a human party but also a working class girl at a resolutely middle class party.

In every way possible I felt like a rank outsider, a freak of nature.

I stood in mild terror looking at solid pine bookshelves crammed with Penguin first editions, outsize art books and popular psychology. A kind of terror was welling in me as I realised to that if I didn't shut myself off from everyone and have only the most perfunctory contact that I would be overwhelmed. Not only by my own insecurity and lack of understanding of their world but by their stuff; their memories, thoughts, desires, past lives....Oh god! What was I doing? What had I been thinking of to even attempt it?

They were well meaning, these strangers, offering to take my coat and find me a seat but I felt so out of place, out of time. Was it possible to slip away again? I had been offered a drink but my mouth wouldn't work, my lips stuck together stubbornly as if I feared that a foreign, indecipherable language would pour forth if I opened them. I shook my head and pushed their drinks away whilst remaining rooted to the spot, making a concerted effort to shut everything out and to steady myself before ever so slowly leaving again. What a terrible mistake!

Oh yes, I was good at those.

When I opened my eyes I was not alone.

"Do you know that Demi Sec means fruity pig?"

I was looking down, slightly, at a short, dark man with an engaging smile. He had a simian brow and was clutching a bottle of wine.

"What?" I tried backing away but he only laughed. He was very drunk.

"You can get breasts made from the same stuff they make teeth from...ortho...orthodontic materials. Yeah, that's it!"

He seemed very pleased with himself and gyrated a little to the music being played, waving the bottle aloft. It wasn't just my social ineptitude and psychic overloading, he was speaking gibberish, surely?.

"Do you know where Carmen is? I shouldn't really be here, you know but..."

"Monastery?" said the small man, with reference to absolutely nothing that I could understand.

I stared at him, ready to run from yet more madness, yet I saw in his eyes, bleary as they were, that he was a simple and good soul. I detected around him a host of ancestor-spirits, all of a similar bent...eccentrics and poets to the last. There was no harm in him, none at all. I steadied myself as he did another comic dance in front of me, grinning wildly but warmly. He was affable enough and his Dada-esque behaviour finally made me smile, too. Here was someone who made about as much sense as me and who looked almost as odd.

" Carmen? Do you know where she is? Nice woman, I don't think she has prosthetic breasts. I need to, I mean, I think I will have to, go..."

I looked down into his open face and he looked up and me gleefully with his slightly poached eyes wide.

He held out his hand to me and as I took his clammy paw in mine tentatively I discovered that this man worked in a bank but that he wasn't exactly cut out for it. Too many hangovers had made him turn up late and dishevelled, if at all, and his humour had confused more than one elderly customer looking for advice on investment. His name was Gianni; he was almost thirty and his Catholic parents wanted to know why he had no wife. His passion, besides alcohol, was writing plays and I saw him in a large, sparse room listening to music and sucking on a joint at three a.m, an almost empty bottle of Jose Cuervo at his side and balled up paper round his ankles. The spirits around him intimated to me, in rapid Italian that somehow I could understand, that his passion would kill him someday in the not too distant future. Their spiritual role was to try and steer his life onto a better course but so far they were not making great headway. I smiled at this unseen host ruefully and Gianni obviously thought the smile was for him. And why shouldn't he? Most normal folk cannot converse with the dead at parties, let alone see them.

"You should never talk with your mouth full!" he admonished me pointlessly as he shook my hand vigorously. "More champagne?"

"What? Er, no, tea, I'd like some tea!"

I had to shout at him lest he misunderstood. I couldn't drink alcohol, I daren't risk letting go of my control and being overwhelmed by *the voices*. And I had vowed never to act like Robert's sodden, pointless bad Mama...

"Hey, man, have a popsicle!"

This was said in a jubilant voice that had a hint of faux-American in it. I looked up now to see that it belonged to a much taller man who had joined us from the kitchen. It was then that my heart lurched painfully and I swallowed. He looked...he must be...oh, surely this was *the man*? The nut brown hair, the eyes like moss on granite...ahhh...was *the man* was here, at last? So this was the meaning of Carmen and this stupid party? *The man!*

Or was it him? How could I be sure after all this time, after all that dreaming and seeing him...

I looked to him for some kind of clue or cue but he was talking to Gianni in some sort of in-joke code.

"No way!"

"But it's cold"

"No way!"

"But it's good for you! have a popsicle, go on!"

"Doh!"

After this seemingly meaningless exchange both men fell about laughing and I backed away still further but found myself pressed up against a very expensive wall-hanging made of some itchy wool. The two men had lit post in-joke cigarettes and looked at me, in unison. Was I expected to applaud or laugh? How was I to know? I felt like a tourist from another galaxy. I opened my mouth, stupidly, and nothing of worth came out, instead I just said the first foolish thing that I was thinking and by that I seemed to have insulted them.

"Why are you wearing that silly hat indoors?"

There was a moments silence as they both tried to comprehend that this woman, with her peculiar sense of sartorial style and scarlet hair, had questioned the tall man's choice of baseball cap. Why on Earth had I said something like that? For the lack of anything else to say that they might understand, I suppose. I could hardly start gibbering about this newcomer being *the man* now could I?

"Hey, my hair needed washing!"

The tall man was looking at me in genuine bewilderment. He was obviously not used to women questioning his choice of clothing. I knew he would be more used to females fawning over him, so beautiful was he. Maybe I made a refreshing change. Whatever, it hadn't been a deliberate ploy. I just didn't know what to say or do in this situation. To prove his point he removed the offending cap and raked his hand through the spill of dirty mousey brown hair that fell to his shoulders. I inhaled and caught a waft of his musky maleness. I suddenly longed to bury my face in hair like that.

Gianni had begun to dance awkwardly about. The powerful surge of feeling I had emitted towards this tall man had made him nervous, I couldn't help how powerfully my will could be sensed by people. That was one of the myriad of reasons why I tried, as a rule, to keep away from them. Gianni quickly improvised a poem about fish but the rhyme was so tenuous that he had to stop. He and the other man stared at me, perplexed again. They had alcohol to alleviate this social nightmare and they both swigged from their respective bottles simultaneously. I became aware that I had not so much disconcerted them, as I was used to, as intrigued them. I wasn't their standard fare, that was for sure, and maybe the drunken haze of their perception made me seem exotic or even desirable for a moment. Oh no, not again!

"You didn't come here with the dickweed in the overcoat did you?"

The tall man looked at me, one eyebrow raised in a delectable curve.

"I came here as I go everywhere, alone."

To me it was stating a fact, to them it was enigmatic.

"Oh."

The tall man stroked the light stubble on his strong chin. It was his turn to be lost for words, it seemed.

" I don't know if I like students. He looks like a student," he managed eventually. Gianni kept hopping about, visibly irritated by the tall man's having an almost sensible, if extremely halting, conversation with me.

"I used to be a student," I said, flatly.

What on Earth did people say to each other, anyway? It seemed so dull!

Gianni piped up, as if some strange competition had begun.

"I got a two-one in philosophy when I was a student."

"Well I got a second and I still got a job, man. I just don't like men who try and look as if they are at college. It's so pretentious."

The tall man had ripped jeans and a baggy hooded top on. He didn't look like as if he had made any particular effort with his attire, one so good looking as him surely had no need to worry about such things. I had no interest in the doings of people, especially men, so why was I even thinking about that? I just couldn't tear my eyes from his face. He looked like *the man, the man* from my visions. Was he? Oh surely...? I stared thinking of fate and what Alicia had said. Maybe there was some truth in it. This tall man, he looked so like *the man* in my memories and dreams. Please let it be, I had prayed, silently, to no one in particular.

I so wanted the yearning to stop!

"I'd like to kick him, that bloke in the overcoat!"

Gianni growled like a dog and waved his bottle in an attempt at being threatening. He really was very drunk. I guess I had arrived rather late at the party in an attempt not to really be there at all and most people were the worse for wear. There was a rather precarious moment when I thought that the small Italian was going to fall backwards into an open doorway but he steadied himself and staggered forwards.

"If I get him I want a kiss from you!" he leered at me.

If he hadn't been so amiable, so foolishly inebriated and ultimately harmless, I would have done something instinctive like spit at him. But off he went, swaying, on a pointless quest to harangue a man in a long coat. I marvelled at the things that entertained people and failed to understand them. I was becoming more removed from their doings by the day.

Fate.

If only Alicia had not introduced me to thinking about fate! I considered that it had left me alone with the tall man for a reason. I thought wrong, in the end, but right then...he smiled

(and I remembered Julien de St. Pierre and the woods)

...and I made some connections that were all based in fantasy; connections based in my raw longing, not in the turgid two-dimensional world of human social interaction.

He smiled at me uncertainly.

"Do you like music?"

His question was so startlingly inane yet to me at the time it seemed like he must know me, for all I ever took from the human world was its music. Why, I had even joined the main city library to borrow tapes and play them to myself in that flat I called home, reluctantly. He must be more than the handsome, long-limbed, rakish man I saw before me. He must know me! Oh, how I was clutching at straws!

"Sure. Doesn't everyone like music to some degree though?" I replied, slowly.

I seemed I had lost any social skill I had once perhaps possessed. How had I ever talked to Robert? I tried to recall, with little success.

"I like things that sound like autumn." I said, realising this was how I thought but not how people actually spoke. I couldn't help my strange perspectives and my social inpetitude any more than he could help being handsome, could I? And then, before I could stop myself I added "in as much as I love anything in this world I love October."

Before I could try to re-phrase he attempted to understand me. He must have liked me for some reason. I wish he hadn't given me hope.

"Ah, Halloween! Right! So, you like gothic music? Dark stuff? Morbid tunes? Yeah...I should have guessed from the fact you wear black. And your mad hair...it's...cool. Really, cool. I mean, you look very *distinctive.*"

For a university graduate he spoke in a very dumb way. He looked impressed with himself for using such a long word. Was I supposed to be flattered? Distinctive could mean I stood out for all the wrong reason, not because I looked good. Or even beautiful.

I looked at him in frank bewilderment. My favourite piece of music was Albinoni's Adagio for organ and strings, I had found it on an old tape I had bought from a charity shop. What did he mean, gothic?

"I like rock stuff, myself, you know, guitar based. But, hey, gothic, it's...mood...suits you. Yeah, it does!"

He appraised me favourably and smiled awkwardly. I realised I hadn't mentioned gothic at all. He was confusing me now. Did we all just clutch at straws when trying to relate to each other, turning everyone we interacted with into what we wanted them to be? At that moment I chose to mistake his foolish clutching at anything for mind-reading. He must know more about me than I did, then? If he knew I liked a music I had never even heard...

"*All this darkness must mean something...*" he was singing to me now and I found there were easy tears in my eyes.

His voice was sweet.

"*There couldn't be so much darkness if it didn't mean something...*"

"That's beautiful!" I managed.

In my dreams he might whisper '*so are you*' but in life he did not.

"Yeah, don't you know it? It's a really excellent tune, one of those old goth bands from the 'Eighties!"

He mentioned some obscure arcane sounding band name and I shook my head

"I must lend it to you, er, sometime," he ventured.

"You must," I replied, awkwardly.

I thought he may take his leave of me now, but he did not. Instead I watched him swig from his beer and take the conversational lead. He began speaking to me of himself now, snippets of what he did, what he liked. He told me what his friend Gianni did as if to make himself feel superior but I already knew. His complete lack of self-consciousness was awesome to me, even if he was drunk he was still effortless. I didn't even know how to position my hands and feet comfortably, let alone hold a me-centred conversation. Just being there seemed a chore. All I wanted was to have some affirmation of who he was, really, not this idle banter. And, by direct reflection, I would know then who I was.

(*Oh please help me someone! Please!*)

Between his inept attempt to chat me up and my own terse sounding responses we were set to get nowhere fast. I desperately dredged my memory for any strand that would lead me back into understanding how people connected but then I remembered I was playing a dangerous game. How could I connect with a person and not feel their 'stuff'...all of it? It was impossible! But I still met his eyes, searching for a connection...

(*green on grey, moss on granite...dizzying*)

....and instead of a man in a baseball cap and jeans I saw a man in the woods of medieval France in a cloak and stout boots, walking beside me.

"You look like Julien," I blurted to *the man* I saw before me, his face overlaid with the face of my dear one, my true love.

"Who? Is he good looking?! Er...a singer in a band? My names Dom, Dominic, by the way. Er, yeah, pleased to meet you and all that!"

He went to shake my hand, staggering slightly in his drunkenness, and I resisted the temptation to connect. He took my lack of response as something cool and smiled at me all the more. This was all so bizarre! I saw the face of Julien wreathing like mist across the face of this man Dominic and he laughed, a dumb sounding 'hurr-hurr' as if to shake me from my reverie. As if he could! He must have thought I was being deliberately weird, like his smaller friend Gianni was.

I shook my head, tried to focus on this man who was not Julien...was he?

Oh god!

"Where do you live?" I asked with an immense effort, remembering suddenly that it was polite to enquire.

"I came over from Bristol. Me and Seth, Carmen's bloke, we went to University with Gee...that's Gianni...there. We like to get together near Christmas and Bath seems the best choice so he can just pop on the train at Paddington with Carmen. Our mate Chris moved here too, it's his and Zita's bash, y'know? Chris always holds a party for us every year so that we can, er, y'know, re-connect and all that. I go to see Seth now and then, we go out in the West End, have a few beers. I like Bristol though, there's a lot happening. I do research out at...do you know Bristol at all?"

I pulled myself back to the moment with a tremendous force of will. There was no *man*, damn it Lian get a grip of yourself! There was only Dominic, a very good looking ex-student who smelled of musky hair and cigarettes. He seemed to have no spirits with him and be quite straightforward...what a relief!

I concentrated and managed to home back in on the limping conversation.

"No," I said.

Was I supposed to elaborate? He was discussing a city only a few miles away and I hadn't a clue what to say about it. Obviously he took my reticence for some strange mode of aloof mystery as it didn't deter him.

"I work with plants, anyway. I'm from near Aylesbury originally but I like it in the west, it's more laid back and it's cheaper to live, y'know? I play guitar in a band, we play at the Bierkeller in town a lot. We do cover versions of rock stuff and some of our own songs now, too," his chest puffed up with pride, "you should come, bring a friend."

"I don't know anyone," I said.

"No friends?"

"No."

For the first time he saw me as I am and not how he wanted me to be. I felt cross at his perplexed look and decided to go on the defensive.

"I could pretend I have some if it makes you feel more comfortable?"

"No, er, really. It's a shame though, you must be new here, I guess?"

"You could say that."

At that moment I felt pretty new to Earth.

"Maybe you could hook up with Zita, Chris's woman, it's her part too, y'know? Me and the lads met her when she was studying Fashion and Textiles. Her brother Zander is a great laugh. He's over in Cork at the moment. Excellent. Have you been to Ireland?"

"No, but I like traditional Irish music," I said. "I have roots there, somewhere."

"Oh, wow, where's that then?"

"Somewhere near Thurles, apparently."

"Where?"

"Thurles. Oh, look I don't really know. Forget it."

My tone didn't brook any further discussion on the matter and he clearly didn't seem to know what to say to me anyway. Was I rude or enigmatic, he was wondering, or worse, was I just plain weird? And obviously he didn't know what I meant by Irish music either. He shuffled his feet in their expensive boots. Took a swig of beer.

"You mean you like Irish music sort of like U2?"

"What?"

He frowned and took another deep gulp from his bottle.

"Er...do you ski?"

"I kicked him! Ask anyone! It's true!"

Gianni came hurtling back at us and I wondered once again what I was doing there. Dominic slapped Gianni amiably on his broad back and they both laughed again at some private witticism. If this was Julien, this man in the raggedy jeans and sweat-top, he seemed so different now...

(*Too different, Lian, face it!*)

...and he didn't understand me at all and I didn't know what to say to him either. But why would life give me a man who looked so like him, as I remembered him, if it was not him? And who was Julien anyway?

Confused and as frustrated as ever I stared at the thick beige carpet at my feet. I stared and the buzz of chatter around me faded out and my eyes blurred...

(*Slipping away*!)

... and the carpet turned into a drift of dry fallen leaves.

I looked up and saw a man in a grey woollen cloak.

"You must hurry, there's no time to lose now, lady. You need to make as much distance as you can before sun down."

"But I want you to come with me! Why won't you come? How can I go knowing you'll be here at the mercy of this mob! They'll not take kindly to you knowing you've had dealings here with me. They've seen us together, there's no harm in it, but they'll make something of it in the mood that's possessed them. How am I to leave you when I don't know if you'll suffer the same fate as my cottage? Anything connected to me will be destroyed, if they feel so angered of me. And I need you...*I need you,* Julien. I can't do this on my own. I don't know how! I don't know how to survive like you do! I'm used to my dealings with the big house, I don't know how to..."

"Shhh, lady. Don't let fear cloud your vision now, you have the wisdom of the Green Ones with you, they'll walk by you, unseen, and the spirits of the land will guide and protect you 'til you reach your dear sister's house. I'll come to you there when I can, when it's safe. This will die down and then I'll come but I'll not lead them to you, nor will I make you more conspicuous. Let me divert their attention here and put them off your trail. That is the best I can do for you. Come here to me, now..."

He reaches over to me and hands me the cloak he has fetched for me from the village. It was his own sister's garment, she had been a small woman like myself. It is the colour of woodland shade and will hide me well. He places it around my shoulders when I am shaking with sobs and cannot do it for myself. My own winter cloak, like everything I owned save my basket and the clothes on my back, were all burned when they set afire to the cottage.

I look up at the kindest man I have ever met and he is calm as ever but when I look through my tears I see the lines have deepened around his eyes. He looks older than I have ever seen him but his face...such a beloved, precious face...is like a shining winter star, to me. So pure and so generous a man he is, to be seen here in this place with me when there is such danger. What a beautiful man...those eyes, that gentle smile...

He whispers in my ear, breath like the wings of angels on my skin.

"And are we not sure that we have not conquered such loss before?"

(*Aye, Julien, Aye, my sweet soul-love! Yes!*)

"...such loss before!"

I fell forwards into Dominic's arms.

"Oh Jesus! She's fainted or something! Oh shit! What am I supposed to do? I don't even know her!"

I can hear Dominic and the contact with his body brings me pictures of him. He sits at a table in a pub reading a comic, waiting for a girl to meet him. She is five years younger than him, prettier than I could ever hope to be, simpler and funnier. He loves her, he thinks. I see him at work with Petri dishes, I see him practising bar chords on a Gibson guitar and I see him as a boy with a cricket bat in his back garden. And before...into the past...I see his other lives. He has not incarnated much. Basic lives, a soldier in Flanders fields, losing a leg. A craftsman in Venice. A farm hand. A woman at her embroidery. No magic, no connection.

He is not Julien. He was never Julien.

Carmen is with me and Dominic walks away reaching for beer and cigarettes. I hear his last thought.

(*...lucky escape. Mad!...*)

Mad witch he calls me and condemns me, like so many others before him. I pray he is the last to ever wound me so.

Gianni stays a while and pats me ineffectually. Carmen gets me coffee. She thinks I am drunk or drugged, I know she does. How would she know that I never touch a drink or a drug? She wishes that she had never asked me to her friend's party, I can read her thoughts quite plainly. And who can blame her? How was she to know I was as I was...

(*mad, bad, dangerous to know*!)

...such a liability?

"I'll phone you a taxi...er, Lian."

"Thank you, that would be well."

And I sit with my head in my hands waiting as Carmen and Gianni exchange looks over my head, looks that say '*thank goodness we aren't like her, how sad!' and 'poor thing, shouldn't be out wandering the streets alone, there should be a place where she can be looked after, surely?'.*

They were nice, these two. Really nice. No harsh condemnations there. If I were really a witch I would have wished them both be happy.

As happy as I could never be.

So, how had I gotten myself over that? So many ways, so many options! I could have hitch-hiked across the channel to France, walked to Scotland, flown to Dublin, or Thurles, or even Mexico if I could have stolen the money. I could have dug that nice comforting earth that I yearned for, becoming a little fox in hiding, gone permanently to ground. I could have sought the razor blade or the bottle, signed myself into a hospital, walked into the sea at midnight. Why have limits? Escaping pain is something I cannot do by half measures. I could have sought meaningless adventure or numbing oblivion to obliterate the crushing agony of humiliation and the heavier blow of loneliness that followed it but I knew that such things were not for me; the spirits would get me whatever I did, I knew that by now if nothing else. So instead I remained in my room, alone, and no one bothered me. It was as if, to all intents and purposes, I did not exist. I hardly dared to go out to the woods even, lest I bump into someone, anyone, on my way. I lived off crackers and jam washed down with water when the milk ran out for coffee or tea. My Christmas passed in a fragmented haze, crumbs and nightmares falling around me.

I even took some of their medication to dull the visions.

Desperation guided my hand badly but it was a respite, of sorts. I didn't want those moths, those dirty spirit-moths that whispered of suicide, drawing too close and the only way I could think of staving them off, for a while at least, was to hide my flame under a blanket of pharmaceuticals.

I still dreamed though, even though the prescribed drugs were meant to shut down my senses, to control who I was, quashing my natural self. Oh yes, I still dreamed, of slate grey eyes patterned with lichen green and of a small woman hurrying through the slender, dripping trees. In my sleep I played with possibilities and realities and when I was awake I moved through a thick colourless cloud which nearly obscured my *seeing*. Inside my head I heard my own voice, for a change, a banshee cry for justice. A terrible pleading for understanding. Why me?

(*Why? Help me, Mother!*)

I would have loved to be able to hold someone right then so I held myself and whispered the reassurances I needed to hear. The ticking clock ate up the minutes and I surveyed the moving hands. I thought of someone else who sat in silence, save for the fat ticking of her own clock with a phone that lay dormant. A woman whose children would not be with her for the festive season, not now or ever again, just because of who she was...

(*of who she is...of who I can be*)

...that brave and integrous woman!

Slowly, inch by inch, I edged my way to my purse. It contained crumpled receipts and copper coins, perhaps even enough to make a phone call. Would I need to pay to call a phantom phone? I had no idea. I myself had no phone, there was no need. My father, the fool, wrote me stiff little notes (I tried not to touch them for fear I would sense his loathing) and my Aunt sent me recipes and progress reports on how well her son, my cousin, was doing in the civil service. I got the occasional piece of official literature from the mental health organisation I was meant to be helped by but no, I had no need of a phone that would never ring.

So, I walked in the biting cold to a phone box. It was December the twenty eighth. The roads were quiet and a hoar-frost made bushes and wrought iron gates glitter with lacy filigree. It was beautiful.

I barely had the strength to open the door of the old-fashioned red call-box. When I touched the freezing metal I felt the lingering memory of the last person to open that door; a young man, a student, someone that may have attracted Dominic's stupid scorn, trying to call his Mum. It was his first Christmas away from home and I sent him my kind thoughts, whoever he was. I hated to think of another person being alone.

And so my fingers, made clumsy and stiff with cold, dialled her number, our special number.

(*Oh, please! Please let me do this before those stupid vengeful spirits get a measure of me again and stop me. PLEASE!*)

She answered on the first ring.

My voice was little more than a croak from lack of use and I shook my head to clear it from the residue of their fogging medication.

She had known it would be me, of course.

"Cariad," she said, " are you ready to hear me now, is it?"

I thrilled to the sound of her inflections, suddenly craving the old speech, and the old ways, badly.

"Aye, lady," my rusty voice creaked and I tried to gain purchase in the world. "I am so sorry...so very..."

"Accch, child!"

I sensed her brushing aside my fear.

"There's something you must do now, sweetling, and to do it you must come here, soon as you can now."

No small talk for Alicia. She, or we, had no need of it. We spoke the same language, she and I.

"Oh Alicia, I tried, really I did! I tried so hard to fit in with their world but I'm no good at it. I just don't know how! And I am so sorry I hurt you!"

"Ah, child, don't fret yourself. You know there's another way now, see. You're not alone, beloved, and your path is waiting to be walked. Just come to me, now."

"Yes! But..."

"Will you come to me, Lian?"

" I don't think I can make it to the bus station," I could hardly manage anything above a cracked whisper.

"I'll send a cab for you, beloved, have no fear now."

Her lilting soothed me and I saw her hearth fire already burning bright to welcome me.

"I have to tell you about Julien, cariad. He is close now. Very close. It's nearly time. Hold on for me now, child, look out for the cab. And Lian?"

"Yes?"

"It's not your fault, girl. Not Robert, not Dominic, not your mother..."

(*I had not even spoken Dominic's name...had she sent him to test me, this witchy woman? No, I would not think badly of her. WOULD NOT! Be gone, foul spirits!*)

"And, cariad, we will get rid of the things that haunt you, never doubt it, not for one second. We can do it, together, you and I, as friends, as Fey witches. It will be alright now, I promise."

I was going to give her my address but she didn't need it, of course.

After saying our goodbyes I replaced the receiver and stood, legs like pokers, tears studding the collar of my old velvet frock coat. Outside of the phone box I could see a tiny, distant star light up the night as the sky turned from deepest violet to inky indigo. A ripe crescent moon rose and it was waxing; I thought it must have wept for me too, big, fat tallow tears, watching me being so lost under its enchanted gaze. I raised my poor aching arms as if to dance with her, this Lady of the Night, my muse and mentor. No one was there to see me except the moving moon and the twinkling sandman's stars and so I stepped, slowly at first, in a dance of surrender. I finally had to give in to myself and to the starlit world I held within. I danced a quiet dance with myself and the moon ceased to weep for me, my own tears drying in the chill night air. I felt welcomed into an embrace older than time and kissed by a mystery beyond imagining.

I knew that things were changing, right there as I twirled, clumsily at first, on the pavement. Witches knew things, didn't they?

For I was born of the Faerytide and I believe and I believe...

I waited for a cab that I knew would come for me, just as she said it would.

Our kind did not lie.

Part Two

The Quickening

Chapter One

Second Fiddle

Rory had known for years now that the best way for him to survive was to keep his head down, to lie low, to slip through life like an otter through water. Even with that face of his it was still possible. If he withdrew his spirit into the tiny walnut shell he imagined inside of himself people would pass him by, leaving him be. He just had to pull in his energy, the energy which gave him away much more than his strange face ever could, and to picture himself walking in a cloak of anonymity. He half wished that instead of the facial markings he had been given at birth a message which read '*I am not here*' could have been indelibly etched onto his brow; a magic message with the power to avert gazes. As it was, people rarely saw his brow at all, the floppy cap he habitually favoured saw to that.

So, how was it that despite his own best efforts to walk quietly, without fuss, his own sister had drawn him into the spotlight, into the most terrible places of all for someone like him, into the public eye? And not just because she was, lets say, a famous gardener, or a dress maker or something innocuous yet creative. Oh no, his sister was Lydia Fentley, the acclaimed and controversial feminist writer, someone who attracted not only attention but blatant curiosity, in-depth discussion and controversy. Someone who was now flirting with danger, as far as Rory was concerned anyway, for today was the day when she publicised her new book, a collection of ritual poetry designed to wake the witch within.

How lightly she used that damnable word, how casually! Who would want to label themselves with such a word, a word that could invoke outright fear at best and flagrant brutality at worst? It seemed like madness to Rory Reynolds. Yet with '*Silver Beneath the Stone*', Lydia's new book of inspirational invocations for enchantment and empowerment, his sister's career was taking off and she wanted her doting brother by her side. She wanted this for many reasons, and if she asked she knew that he would do it, no matter what it cost him personally. So here he was, standing in a train station with her, waiting for a train that would take them to London for her to disseminate, and for him to stand with quaking legs in the background, at a bookshop lecture.

For Rory, it was as bad as if she were about to stand him on a podium in Covent Garden with the instruction '*to be burned, prodded, tested out...at your leisure*' tied on a placard around his scrawny neck. And Lydia knew this, didn't she? She, above all others, knew what he had been through and how much revulsion, and, damn it, terror he felt about the whole idea of witchery and magic.

Rory considered walking into Lydia's spotlight, as she herself basked in its temporary warmth, was like handing himself over. There would never be enough shadows for Rory to hide in, no matter how he stood behind her hoping that the brighter the light that shone on her, the deeper the cover for him. There would never be the cool leafy shade that he yearned for if he followed her into a very human reality of magazine interviews and book launches. He felt as out of place in a bewildering, frightening world of mobile phones and designer labels as a Neolithic hunter would in the centre of New York.

He was been sucked into a world, a world Lydia needed to publicise and promote her work, which filled him with a kind of sick, giddy disorientation, a vertiginous swirling of the senses. The curious, almost terrifying feeling of being alone in a place which no one else seemed to notice was wrong made Rory feel desolate beyond measure and tired well beyond his years. The more Lydia ventured, albeit tentatively, into the role of upfront career woman the more Rory's face took on a gaunt and haunted look. The longer he stood at his sister's side the more he noticed himself ageing and somehow fading, becoming less vivid in a vista of bright plastic and shiny chrome. The more she dazzled the greater his insecurity became.

And now she was bringing in witchery to the already trying equation. Oh dear Lady!

But he had to be there for Lydia, no matter how he felt about this intrusion into his own private world, the personal space he had fought long and ever so gently for. Rory was a very loyal man, he prided himself on his being a steadfast and steady presence in a world that shot past him in all directions. Sticking by his sister, who had suffered far too long on her own, was one of his core values. He believed in simple things, and family was simply about sticking with someone no matter what. Lydia was, to all intents and purposes, his only real family anyway and he would have cut of his right hand for her. But how could he have known, when he made his vow to protect his younger, more impetuous, sister that she would somehow home in on the very thing that petrified him and introduce it into their life together? It was too late for regrets and recriminations, he had to treat it as he treated most things in the modern age, things to be dealt with, and responsibilities to be grimly, diligently fulfiled. As Lydia's protective brother had pledged to support her and honour her in all that she chose to do....he just hadn't bargained on her doing this.

If only Shay hadn't been such a bastard then Lydia wouldn't need Rory so much, if at all. And if only Jane hadn't been such a stultifying mistake then perhaps Rory would have felt his true allegiance to be with his wife, not his sister. The truth was that both Lydia's and Rory's marriages had been disastrous, to one degree or another, and the brother and sister leaned heavily on each other, much as they had in childhood.

Lydia, as a highly intelligent but wild and wilful teenager, had chosen to get involved with a tempestuous but precocious Irish literature student. Soon after the start of their affair, a union in which abandoned passion had very often verged on violent abuse, Lydia proceeded to fall pregnant, thus putting an end to her own promising studies at a prestigious London University. The result of this ill-fated, but highly charged, union had been Donal, a charming little red haired boy who now lived somewhere across the sea with his father's family...a family who were, thankfully, more stable in both financial and emotional terms than Seamus Donnelly. Shay had, predictably enough, ended up in prison after one to many violent episodes in the pubs of Camden Town and as a result, or perhaps in sheer relief, Lydia had suffered a total breakdown.

Rory's parents had been cold at best and disparaging at worst over his sister's pregnancy and subsequent illness, blaming Lydia in entirety for the mess she was in. They had always seen the charming side of Shay and were, as ever, quick to find their own errant and disappointing offspring at fault. They had seen no reason why they should make a temporary home for Donal within their own walls while their daughter recovered her strength and sanity. Thus it had been that Donal had been whisked off in to the overwhelming embrace of his Irish kin, never to be seen again.

Subsequent to her rehabilitation and resurrection, Shay's indominitable family had responded to Lydia's pleas for the return of her boy by effectively vanishing the child into America to stay with yet more of their relations. Lydia had been devastated by this further disappearance and the fight for a mother to have access to her child obviously became one of the primary motivations for her re-invention as a doyenne of feminist thought. Women had been abused, plundered and discarded by the masculine force of society for too long and the rallying cry of Lydia's early work was that it was time to reclaim that which was constantly being taken...even in today's supposedly egalitarian world. Her success lay, in part, with the fact that she was living her cause, day by day, and her passion fired her. Her soulful eyes burned with it, their strange dark sherry wine colour aflame as she gazed from her book jackets and, later, from television screens. It wasn't only her radical rhetoric that got her noticed, that was for sure.

Once she had established herself in this way Lydia was constantly pushing to earn more money and gain more prestige so that, eventually, she could afford for the best lawyers and detectives to find Donal. Her motivation to reclaim her estranged son, a boy who would now be nearly ten years old and who probably had no actual memory of his birth-mother at all, was bound to be a driving force in her. She had always been such a sensitive person, profoundly so, but through the traumas of her adult life she become honed and sharp, seeming to the outside world strong as steel and ready to cut any to the quick if they dared stand in her way. Yet her ethereal beauty made her compelling, not disturbing, and her cutting edge was always rendered decorative, not deadly, by her charming appearance.

Oh yes, to the public she seemed like a keen blade shielded by a velvet scabbard and that way her incisive commentary and razor sharp ripostes never really cut too deeply...and that was just how folk liked it. She had the admiration of many from the average working woman to well-heeled professors and publishers, that was for sure. Her drive to know, and to understand, was as fierce as her intelligence...but not as fierce for the need to be reunited with her son...and so she made a formidable opponent even for the most starchy of academics. Lydia had indeed come through Shay's unpredictable rages and Donal's disappearance with a show of great bravery and inner strength and so the writing she forged from her inner suffering was strong too, born of a fire fuelled with real pain. Yet underneath it all Rory knew her to be as fragile and brittle as the silvered skeleton of an oak leaf, found amongst the litter after a hard storm. She always plumped up the protective cushion of her persona when she was in the spotlight but when that persona was put away she was just a scared little girl again. Without the glossy veneer of Lydia Fentley then Lydia Reynolds was just as lost as she had always been. She was just a mass of tangled contradictions and paradoxes, just like any poor, confused mortal being was. That was why he couldn't abandon her, not now. Not even as she veered inexorably into an arena Rory had sworn never to enter again.

Rory was her shield and her confidante, perhaps the only person in Lydia's new and glamorous world who could see her as she truly was. To others she was a figurehead, a willowy warrior with a will of iron and a tongue of satin. To Rory she would always be a frightened Rapunzel, reaching out for him to save her with her blonde tresses hanging down around a pale heart of a face. To him Lydia was still the bewildered and bewilderingly beautiful girl of his childhood, a girl who was filled with a lyricism that spoke of tempests and twilight with equal tenderness, a girl who trembled as she spoke. Lydia...the only one who had cried as they had sent him off to that dreadful school, the only one that had cared.

And what of Rory's marriage, did his own wife Jane not care for him? Far from it. For whilst Lydia had acted on her ardour Rory had played as safe as ever, far too safe it seemed, as his limiting and fruitless marriage to Jane had been as joyless as it was sexless and barren. His need for safety had been translated into a stultifying and passionless boredom which succeeded in protecting him whilst rendering him stunted and immobile. For all Rory's need to lie low in life he still needed love and romance and although Lydia, dear Lydia, couldn't provide the romance she certainly gave him love. So it was that while his sister gave him care in abundance, and he rewarded it with loyalty beyond the call of duty, his wife gave him nothing except, quite recently, disloyalty.

Was it any wonder that Rory had gone to Lydia, throwing himself into the job of protecting her and encouraging her as no other man ever had? Was it any wonder after his own wife, the one who he had also taken because he feared no other woman would have him, had finally rejected him? At the age of thirty seven what else was he to do? Who would have him in their life now save his own sister?

Yet after all he had told her about his life, about his lives, he could not believe that Lydia would be so insensitive to his needs as to drag him into the arena of witchcraft. Rory had never even dreamed, even he who dreamed of so much, so often, that she would take the path he himself so dreaded. Lydia Fentley (she had adopted a new sir name to elevate herself from the hurts of her past) was a woman who valued her own furtherance, or 'affirmation of her own creativity' as she preferred to put it, more than being Lydia Reynolds. Lydia Reynolds was only the sister of a man with facial scarring who played the fiddle and lived, in the main, from hand to mouth, while her alter ego was a star in the fickle literary firmament. Time was of the essence in her chosen field and she was a driven woman, not only for the purpose of gaining back her lost son but to prove something else too. But beyond this seemingly ruthless drive Rory would always see that lost girl with the tears dripping down her little face, waving him off as they took him away to school. And, further beyond still, another girl, herself being taken away to another, far crueller, fate.

Rory was free to spend as much time with Lydia as she decreed for as her fame increased so did her need for support and confirmation of her worth. The man that Jane had married was, after all, just an outlaw of society with no proper job; a raggle-taggle man with scarring both seen and unseen, scarring that meant he could never work in the mainstream of life. He could never be considered a career man or a high flyer himself and romantic as it seemed in theory, being an outcast reliant on a wife's nursing income was hard. Honourable as it may be doing only what was ethical and creative it was tough living on bits and broken pieces, the bobbins that people donated, and keeping house for a woman who never showed himany real, lasting affection. Oh yes, he had free time for Lydia for he himself could never hope to be needed or wanted by the world as was she.

Could Rory ever attempt to change this outlawed life he lead? How could he? For Rory was also Treeface and being Treeface was hardest of all. It was not a mantle to be cast off when it became too restricting, in favour of a new and exciting guise. Rory had never been play-acting at being an outlaw, a vagrant with an ability to make the sweetest, most affecting music whilst appearing like a wild-eyed man from a fantastic fable. No, it was a way of life for Rory, with no alternatives. A way of life that had become too unbearable, too humiliating, for a woman who was in love with Pete the plumber. And who could blame Jane, thought Rory.

Did he blame her?

She would have never made him do this, Rory couldn't help but think as he balefully eyed the back of his sister's shiny blonde hair as they stepped onto the train to London. Lydia looked like a soft-focus advertisement for organic shampoo, her beautiful hair was tied loosely with a green velvet ribbon and even in the dirty drab setting of a train station she could look country fresh and sweet. People were bound to admire her, even before they knew who she was; Rory knew Lydia was like a princess which made him more protective yet. But his resentment for having to follow her into the arena of (god forbid!) witchcraft simmered on a low heat in his guts. It was the illusive *she*, not his sister and certainly not his wife, who was his only bit of sanity in a world that appeared to be losing cohesion altogether.

(*But where was* she *anyway, the woman who had bright red hair instead of Lydia's pale golden spill? Where was that slim young woman with those glorious verdant eyes that spoke of lost love and terrible longing? In his own head? Probably, that was where most of the important things in Rory's life seemed to be. But* re-membering her *was the only thing that sweetened his increasingly stressful life, picturing her face on his pillow, an extraordinary Elven woman...*)

Was it possible to be in love with one who seemed to dwell only within the imagination? Was it *right*?

It was Lydia and not that fabulous *she* who held his hand tightly as they boarded the Intercity express train from Bath Spa to London Paddington, for *she* was not in a world of platforms and stations but dwelled in an imaginary world of wildflowers in a perfect, permanent summer. He had to try and forget this *she*, his autumn-haired angel, but it was difficult to forget that which seemed so intrinsically a part of him as his heart or lungs. It was possible to forget that you were breathing but still you kept right on doing it. So it was with his thoughts of the *she;* he wasn't conscious that his mind had drifted but when his heart pounded fit to burst, as if he had been holding his breath too long underwater, then he knew *she* had been there again and he had to come back, come away from the imaginary back to what reality had dished out to him, cold and unappetising.

Rory knew that he had fallen into the habit of escaping reality by fantasising. There was no harm in it usually but this imaginary flame-haired woman was stealing his very real heart, *her* shyness beguiling him, *her* whispering becoming ever more intimate, her essence seeping into his. How could that be? Rory blushed to the roots of his nut brown hair at the thought that he was being inattentive to Lydia. Even if he was angry with his sister for making him so vulnerable he shouldn't be distracted in her presence, should he? And Jane...well, did he owe her a scrap of loyalty now? Not really. He just couldn't let *her* out of his thoughts just in case she never came back; to let *her* go was to let himself slip into the fog, into that grey land between the dead and the undead.

Where had the *she* come from, anyway? For the last year *she* had just been there, when he closed his eyes to go to sleep and then in his dreams and in his music...

Rory swayed to the train's motion as it increased its speed and left the city behind. He became of his sister's eyes upon him and, no doubt, half the other passenger's curious eyes too. Lydia's eyes sought out his as he pulled his cap down further over his face, hiding his blushes from her and hiding himself from the insistent gazes of their fellow travellers. People couldn't seem to help themselves, they just had to stare at him and even if there was no harm in them he still felt hurt by each of them. Why could he never be left alone? His damnable face made it nigh on impossible and only a full-face balaclava, worn like a criminal, would have given him the coverage he would need to remain anonymous. He met Lydia's gaze reluctantly and prayed that she was not feeling confrontational. Her nerves, for surely as he was nervous about giving today's speech in London, often made her react hastily, lashing out at anyone she deemed to have distressed her precious older sibling.

Many was the time that they had boarded a bus in his teenage years only for her, a mere sapling of a girl, to challenge the passengers who stared openly at her brother's fascinating facial scarring. She'd stood, hands on hips, glaring with her fathomless black-cherry eyes, looking for all the world like a silky haired, shining Faery, her favoured tiered velvet skirt trailing in the discarded packets and cigarette butts. '*His name is Rory, Rory Reynolds, and he is worth ten of you! You just remember his name because you'll hear it again some day when he's famous and you're not!'* she would spit, with no particular measure of profundity. Back then she had been more artless, less sure of her own guile, less wordy and more fiery, and he had been so proud of her. But that had been so many years ago and things had changed. Well, at least Lydia had; the birth-marked scars on his face were just the same.

Still, here his sister was, two decades on and still surprisingly nervous of being a woman alone on a train. For one who seemingly needed to proclaim from the rooftops the magical power of being female she could be a trembling and nervous thing outside of her familiar surroundings. That was why he could never abandon Lydia, no matter how she hurt him by taking this public road instead of his own meandering green laned by-way through life, because he knew that he was stronger than her, for she did not know what it was like to be truly, deeply alone. More than that, she dreaded it.

It was a nightmare for the man known sometimes as Treeface to be among commuters, business people and families on day trips as opposed to his usual carefully monitored existence which only brought him into contact with artists, poets and other musicians who dwelled, for one reason or another, on the fringes of society. By and large Rory's acquaintances, for he had no real friends, were non-judgmental folk who all had their own idiosyncrasies and foibles. Rory made sure that he only socialised with those who were equally outcast, by choice or necessity, and when he went shopping in the local store he was then a harmless curiosity. Then the awful meandering birth-mark on his face only served to add to his odd and quirky appeal, providing a bit of well-meaning gossip for folk with run-of-the-mill lives.

His small circle of like-minded acquaintances accepted his facial abnormality as part of his whole carousing troubadour's persona when he was standing before them with his beautiful fiddle, his foot tapping to keep time in his funny old boots. It did not threaten them or confuse them when his crazily catchy music and his larger than life character could cheer them up. He was a little piece of the past, of another, long-forgotten and gentler age, there to entertain them. In this context alone he was not seen as a freak. Then, and then alone, he was Treeface the wild bard, not Rory the poor disfigured man.

Rory needed to put all thoughts of failure out of his mind, it was probably just jitters from being stuck so out of his natural environment on a train bound for central London. He knew that sitting there next to his lovely sister he would become either the token monstrosity to be stared at or Lydia's novelty partner in people's minds. Either way he would not be viewed as himself. It was enough to make him very edgy and insecure.

Rory plucked at his over-long salt-and-pepper moustache, grown to cover up still more of his marked face, as the train rocked and lurched on its inevitable way and he felt the dread burning his belly like cheap whiskey. She was not only his literary sister now, his gorgeous blonde sibling who had a fascinating way with words and an ineffable charm that went beyond her good-looks, she was now also his *witchy* sister. How could this have happened? How had he allowed himself to be drawn into his sister's dangerous arena? And, moreover, why had Lydia chosen this road, the only road he hated to follow her down? And, indeed, why had he allowed her, even enabled her, to?

How had he mis-heard the warning bells in her enthusiasm for other witchy women's success, instead telling himself that she just needed strong women as role models? How had he ignored the most obvious signs...Lydia clumsily hiding her library books on herbal remedies and folksy crafts when he called to see her unexpectedly and, more galling, the scribbled notes on 'casting a full moon spell' he had noted on top of her bureau? Why had he sat with her, for hour upon hour, discussing what he knew of magic and folklore from his thwarted attempt at becoming a healer? He should have heeded the small voice insistent voice that whispered in his ear, the one that said '*you know what she's doing, she wants to play at being a witch! She wants to reclaim the power she's lost...and how!*'

The whole area of witchery had always made him feel dread in the core of himself. Even now when he sat alone late at night in the restrictive safety of his home, his thoughts would turn, at some point, to being persecuted; of having what little he had removed and being branded, somehow, as a *sorcier*. It was irrational, he knew, and it felt like an all-pervading madness in the cool darkness of his own living room. Yet when he sat quietly at night, feeling vaguely frightened despite the relative sanctity of his home, he would acknowledge that familiar, aching yearning and allow the thought, that singularly pressing thought, to fill him with a raging fever...where was *she*? *Where,* damn it! And who...who was *she*?

And after this all-consuming yearning for her would come the burning, (*always the burning!*) and Rory would weep through the dark hours until a watery dawn saw him wrung dry by his own pain again.

The knowledge that Jane was upstairs sleeping had never helped the pain inside him. Jane could never have understood the torment within him, the terrible fear, the overriding yearning. From the first moment he had set eyes on Jane Bryant he had known that she was not his kindred, not like his own kin Lydia. And certainly not like *her*, whoever *she* was. To spend a life without a kindred in your bed...well, it had hurt. Yet Jane had taken matters into her own hands now and it need hurt him no more.

But now there was a new hurt. It hurt that Lydia, who was his kindred and so who should know better, may be throwing up the chance of being a great writer, a feminist icon of real influence, for the sake of being some trendy parody of a very dangerous thing. Oh yes, he knew that Lydia, god curse his psychic sight, wanted now to be a 'media witch', taking something someone should never wish to be called and making it a powerful, glamorous label to wear in public. It sickened him to sit back and let her do this, and yes, it *pained* him.

Why couldn't she have just continued to write about the nature of love and relationships as she had started out doing when she had to drop out of college? She had been good at that, it had made her a bit of extra cash. Granted, it had been pretty low key but that was because it had been teasingly harmless and mildly stimulating, not controversial. Now it had grown, mutated, from the nature of the empowered feminine into the nature the divine feminine...and so onto the nature of magic and magic of nature. Okay, he could understand why she wanted to attract more attention for her work by some manner of means but why did she have to bring in the thing that scared him the most? And yes, he could see that there was a gap in the market and of course he understood that the right moment had come for her to introduce her enchanting poetic concepts, symbolic references to a woman's bewitching power, but wasn't there some other subject besides modern witchcraft that interested or inspired people that much? His mouth went dry just thinking about it.

He looked across at her, sitting nearest to the train's window while he sat exposed nearest the aisle, aware that all eyes in the crowded train carriage were flicking back and forth between him and his lovely sister. She was looking demurely down at her small, pale hands which turned her false wedding band, the one she wore to deter the inevitable flood of men who wanted her, round and round. She was too nervous, too deeply absorbed in her own thoughts about that day and her own success which depended on it, to notice the stares and whispers this time. Rory sighed and settled back in his seat hoping the hat would hide his face in shadow, knowing that it wouldn't. He hated to think what they may be saying. Their imagined comments made him feel more intensely the rift that was forming between himself and his baby sister. Things like *'what's she doing with him, he looks a right sort!'* came to mind, just as such words more often came to his ears. People seemed to think that he were somehow mentally disabled or emotionally crippled, deaf or dumb, just because he had a disfigured face. It was ludicrous!

It was *painful.*

Yes, he had heard it all before but now, well, he didn't want to hear it anymore.

Did he love Lydia enough to put himself through this? In a few hours he would sit behind her dutifully while she read her work to a besotted, rapidly growing fan-base. He would sit passively while his sister labelled herself as a witch, perhaps, or at the very least as an *aspiring* witch. She would be unaware of how the audience would switch their gaze from her serene and elfin face to his lined and gnarled one, thinking that he, in his silent ugliness, must be the real witch, not this charming slender girl-woman. Lydia would read her work aloud and the crowd would be mesmerised for her words were stirring and affecting, even he knew that. She was good, she deserved her success and acclaim, and she would hold them in thrall for sure. But no matter how good she was they would always want to stare at him as he sat in her shadow and waited for it to be over...or that was how it had always seemed. Maybe the day would come when they wouldn't notice him at all, so great would Lydia's power be to hold their attention.

Clanging discordant bells boomed out in his soul, a soul that shrivelled at the thought of the next few hours. The acolytes of his sister would condemn him as being the one to blame for her conversion to witchery and, for him, it would be like his death knell sounding. Again.

Perhaps he was mentally defunct or crippled inside after all?

And did he have to be there with her? Couldn't he just skulk in a bar and wait for her and then escort her home? Oh no, her claims to personal power did not stop her from experiencing terrible stage fright. Lydia couldn't read if she thought he wasn't there behind her, it was an established pattern or a silly habit that she had gotten into which had now assumed levels of superstitious fear. She couldn't do it if she thought he wasn't silently supporting her from the wings, as it were. She would tremble and weep if he suggested she should play this one alone and he would wait somewhere less conspicuous. God, how they had talked that one out...over and over! He *had* to be there, she insisted, almost hysterical, he was her lucky charm! So, he must remain stoical even though inside he was in a turmoil of personal terrors, be the silent sentinel that he was, and take their covert glances. Covert glances? Not everyone was as polite...more often it was their frank and open appraisal of a face which was more unique, more intriguing, than any poem or piece of prose they would ever hear.

'*It must be hard for that woman to walk around with the likes of him...*'

'*She's so beautiful and he...well, he's interesting I suppose...*'

Rory, the man known as sometimes as Treeface, was Lydia's Fool while she wanted to be the High Priestess. Rory often thought of people in relation to his cards; he had his own well-thumbed Tarot deck, with simple wood-cut images, ones that Michael McAllister had given him when he was seventeen. Rory didn't read the cards for others but he did use them for himself, especially of late, but he didn't want anyone to think that he was publicly dabbling in the occult so he kept his readings secret. They were harmless, useful things Tarot cards, but people so easily got the wrong idea. Even when he had been a spiritual healer at the McAllister's centre, ostensibly at a centre with a Christian bias, there had been enquiries from concerned parties as regards Michael's support of Tarot counselling as a 'legitimate therapy'. They'd asked Michael, these 'concerned parties', why he allowed 'the devils arts' to be practiced by *that man*? It was as if people sniffed Rory out as some sort of heretic for having a strange face and, admittedly, real healing powers. But there was nothing dangerous in healing, healing was good, wasn't it? They had backed off when Michael had put them in their place with some very choice, astute words, but it had left Rory wary. Very wary indeed.

There was nothing wrong with his card reading, he knew that. Except he should never have taught Lydia what he knew about the Tarot because she had, of course, used this in her work, another magical art to be blend into something alluring and mysterious for her. Why did everything have to have attention drawn to it like that? The Tarot was harmless, *he* was harmless! He felt the old desire to justify himself rising up like bile, that aggressive urge to shout and scream his own innocence in the face of those 'concerned' people, and he immediately took a deep breath to calm himself. He hadn't stopped using Tarot as a useful tool but he did keep it away from Lydia now, lest she drew public attention to his using it.

Just lately he had been brooding on the 'Tower' card that had come up every time he asked about their lives and he hoped that it didn't signify her bringing his whole world crashing down around him in such a way. Sitting there rocking gently in that train seat it was the 'Tower' card that he thought of.

Change was coming.

But how, that was the worrying thing?

And the '*Lovers*' card was there in his readings too, with the '*Ace of Cups*'. Over and over.

(*Was it her? Oh Please, Lady, let it be her coming for him!*)

"Why is that man's face all full of lines?"

Rory was jolted unpleasantly back to the present reality of the train and caught the child's eye as he whispered to his mother. The child, an undersized boy with faded sandy hair and an open, freckled face was sitting on the adjacent seat and suddenly looked horrified at the realisation that this strange man, who he had deemed to be sleeping, had heard him. If Rory had been all he wished he could be he would have leaned across and pleasantly explained himself in gentle, patient words to this boy. He would have reassured him by smiling and perhaps performed a simple trick for his amusement. Rory was capable of all these responses but something always stopped him. The memories of other small boys taunting him so that he thought of all children, by gut instinct, as cruel and mean, rose up snarling inside him, strangling any kind words. And worse, as Rory closed his eyes to shut out this boy and his innocent but devastating remark, the flames rose up as they so often did when he felt anger or despair or distress and he was instantly swept away again.

Memories, far memories, so quick to take him back the minute he let his guard down. Rory knew that for all the psychic protection he practiced, and for all his ability to work with spiritual energies, he was powerless to resist when he closed his eyes. His body, sitting on a train seat next to his demure sister, was still. He looked, to the small boy that had inadvertently insulted him, like a strange, Faery-tale figure who had chosen to take a nap. Yet, inside...

Anger.

Rory was no longer himself, no longer Treeface. He was another man altogether but he was still alive, in a darkened room with soldiers leering over him, bound to a chair which lurched and tilted horribly on the stone floor as he tried to escape their administrations. He hadn't even been allowed the luxury of raising his slender white hands to his ears to block out their words because the ropes held him firm, rubbing maddeningly at skin already raw, any movement meant agony as his bonds caught on the ragged flesh where his fingernails had once been. But he could just about still speak, his mouth was coated in blood and he kept gagging but the words poured out none the less, a litany of pain and desperation.

"...not a witch, *am not a witch...*"

It was the truth!

He knew that his clothes where ribbons and his wits were rags. He knew how much they hated him, his pitiable state only adding to their disgust, never arousing compassion. He had been taunted, tortured, torn open and interrogated. And yet none of it would make any difference, he knew that now. Protestations and pleadings had not saved his sister, they had all but told him that, barely disguising their gratification. They knocked him senseless for his stubbornness and his body went down, the rough wooden chair breaking into bits around him. Julien de St. Pierre lay in a small but rapidly spreading pool of blood and splinters and then one of the men kicked him.

Over and over.

"*Tomorrow*," he heard them say.

Through the pounding in his temples he understood their snide whispers and wished that he believed in curses. He wished too that he could welcome death as a merciful release but he could not. He was so afraid.

"*...am not a...witch!*" he had croaked, blowing bubbles of blood through his cracked lips.

One of the guards crouched down next to him. In a haze of red and grey he saw the brutal shape of a boot next to his face. Then his head was yanked back and a fist full of his own hazel brown hair, turning white those last few days, was yanked out by the roots.

It was so real. More real than boys with sandy hair and wide eyes, more real than Lydia's thigh pressing against his own. The rocking motion of the train sent him back ...back...

Always the *re-membering.*

Always the memories.

In another room, more than six hundred years after Julien de St.. Pierre had fallen to the stone floor, Rory Reynolds, who had fallen into a trance during a group healing meditation, threw himself violently to the ground, his mouth moving rapidly but no sounds escaping, his body held in a rigid and unnatural pose. Saliva dribbled from his lips and his eyes rolled back in his head as he slammed his own skull onto the ground. Was it a fit? The other group members had broken themselves out of their own trance-states to help the man the all liked but never quite understood. The staff and members of Openings Centre for Spiritual Healing had never seen anything like it. The man was not an epileptic yet he appeared to be in a state of deep shock, going through some inner trauma although in that room he had been quite, quite safe.

When Michael McAllister, the man who was teaching Rory to become a first class healer at his centre in Glastonbury, had managed to get Rory up off the floor he had held him, somewhat warily, in his big arms. Rory was stiff and unyielding. Occasionally a slight tremor had rippled through his inert form. Michael had no experience of dealing with such freak events even though he had been around a few years and seen all manner of peculiar behaviours. You couldn't run a healing centre in Avalon in the mid-Nineteen Seventies and not witness the most extreme aspects of human behaviour. This Rory was a strange boy, though, stranger than most to be sure. He was given to moods and rantings, yes, but then he was still a teenager and what with the facial scarring and all he walked a hard road indeed. It was not so much his outbursts but his silences that were the most disconcerting. Yet he was a superb natural healer and when he forgot himself and let himself go with the tide of energy that came through when he laid his hands on the sick and unhappy he was outstanding.

What could have caused him, during a simple and routine healing circle that they had all done a dozen times before, to act so erratically?

Michael was used to being the best in his field and, although he welcomed new talent to be trained, couldn't help but feel bothered by this character that belligerently called himself Treeface one day and Rory the next. A man who, although without discipline, was far more advanced as a conduit for spiritual healing powers than he himself ever could be. That simple truth had caused Michael a few sleepless nights, both professionally and personally, as he was a man whose family relied on the hefty income reaped from his healing centre and he himself had become accustomed to his own reputation as being the best the West had to offer. Rory was a fly in the ointment alright, a threat to Michael's own hard-won security, but Michael was a fair man as well as a shrewd one and he had given Rory the benefit of all his years knowledge, regardless of how he felt about his own reputation as 'the master'.

It had been unspoken but hopefully understood that when Michael died, being past his sixtieth year now and more than a little portly and florid, he would hand over to Rory.

But Michael had only planned to hand it over to Rory if he would be Rory, a brilliant healer with strange facial scars, and not Treeface, an unervingly intense young man who would alienate the very people who needed his healing. He could run the centre and bring comfort and aid to a wider and wider audience, especially when they saw how he himself had transcended his own personal 'disability'. The scarring could actually attract more attention to the methods of natural healing the centre employed, Rory could be an excellent advertisement for achieving personal equilibrium in the face of adversity, if only he'd accept that. He seemed to want no attention and hated to be singled out. Still, Michael had been sure if Rory could be persuaded it was for a greater good...?

Michael had looked down at the man in his arms as he gently tried to rouse him from his torpor. Was it possible to overcome this whole 'Treeface' personality and make Rory assume the responsibility as the adept healer he was? Such a gift should be used, in service, above an individuals own needs. Yet could Michael trust his life's work to this man now?

So unpredictable, he was, but so incredibly talented.

Michael had carried Rory upstairs to his room on the third floor of the big manor house they worked from, to the room Rory had chosen with the view of the Levels. He looked down tenderly at the rigid form with it's washed out, clammy skin. The birth-marked tree-lines on his face stood out even more strongly against the pale flesh. Time to call a doctor, which seemed ironic when he was in a centre for healing which people travelled across the world to visit. Michael had sighed heavily. His own sons had not caused him as much heartache as this one strange young man. Michael wondered, as he had gone back down stairs to telephone, if that was because he had not loved them half as much as he did Rory Reynolds?

It was only upstairs in Rory's room, when Michael and his wife Bethany had later taken off his boots, shirt and trousers to put him into bed that they noticed the marks. At first it had seemed that maybe poor Rory was scarred on more than his face as there appeared to be red welts and lesions running across his chest and terrible patches of inflamed skin on his thighs and calves. It made Bethie close to weeping to see how this kind, gentle man, admittedly a bit of a loner who could be difficult at times, had been afflicted in such an ugly way.

It wasn't until they realised that he was running a fever in the morning when they drew open the curtains that they saw the marks on his body where not as those on his face. These new marks were raw, open, and suppurating. When the doctor was called in again later still he commented with some perplexity that some of these freak marks looked like burns and should, for the time being at least, be treated as such, whilst others looked consistent with a severe beating He eyed Michael and Bethany McAllister with distrust. What on earth did they do in these places to cause such a physical reaction? All he could do, as a physician, was treat what he saw. As a Christian man, he didn't want to ask what they had been up to, no need to trouble himself with the meddling that these people did. Interfering with God's work and God's will was a job for professionals like himself, not frauds and tricksters like the McAllister's and their peculiar, disfigured young protégé there.

Bethany had wept as she had dressed the horrible wounds as best she could. Burns from an unseen source of heat, and lacerations and deep bruising, were on every bit of Rory Reynolds body, except for a strip of skin down his back.

As Rory had lay twisting and writhing in discomfort with sweat coursing in rivulets down his strangely marked face he could have told then why, perhaps. The part of him tied to the stake did not get burned straight away. Not like the rest of him. Agony he could not let go of. Searing pain and anger both. Julien de St.. Pierre had died horribly but his spirit, a battered but beautiful spirit, was residing warily within the body of a brilliant young healer called Rory Reynolds. Across the centuries they grieved and felt their pain and the body on the bed at 'Openings' healing centre, had relived...

The train carriage shifted and swayed.

Rory came back once again to the present moment, to the shabby velour covering on his train seat that his hand was gripping so tightly. To the cool hand placed gently on top of his own.

"Do you think that people are ready to become empowered and awoken, as magical beings?"

Lydia leant over to her brother and his eyes opened.

"I mean, using enchantment as a way of accessing women's inner strength and beauty? And sorcery as a symbol of how men may reclaim their own innate power without resorting to dominance and violence?"

For a moment Rory stared straight through her. He couldn't believe that she was asking him this. Him, of all people! But Lydia was used to him looking askance and she just sighed and twisted the wedding band again. She wished...although she knew that she shouldn't...that Simon could be there instead of Rory. But Rory needed her, didn't he? Poor Rory.

"What I mean is, do you think people need me to write about the Craft of the Wise? Will it enrich them...ennoble them, even?"

Rory grunted non-commitally and shifted in the uncomfortable seat.

"So, do you think that we can work with the whole modern iconography of white, or rather, *green* witchcraft to enable women...no, not just women...*people...*"

She trailed off. Damn it, she was really trying to engage him again without threatening him. She knew how this whole witchcraft thing scared him but that was irrational, wasn't it? Surely she could talk him out of it, make him see the sense of it? If anyone needed empowering and awakening it was her poor brother, after all.

Rory could hear the beseeching quality in Lydia's voice. She was pitifully nervous yet he pushed down the protective urge to reassure her. To all intents and purposes she was on her own now, and served her right for trying to involve him in dangerous games.

"I wouldn't know about all this stuff, I'm not a witch."

Rory was looking at her now and she felt the familiar chill run up her spine as she did when she knew Rory spoke from his heart. He could be a very disconcerting man indeed. There was a time when they could have talked about anything, anything at all. Now he was so touchy and tense around her and her work. Not like Simon, her agent, who positively encouraged her to express herself. It had all been Simon's idea, this witchcraft slant, and it was proving to be very beneficial in all sorts of unexpected ways. Simon knew things, just as Rory knew things, but in his own more grounded way. She loved and trusted both men, which was an achievement in itself after all she had been through with the Donnelly clan, but her agent and her stubborn, fearful brother would never see eye to eye. After all, Simon wanted her to fly, both personally and professionally, whilst Rory...

She wished that Rory could embrace the term witch instead of running from it. He could reclaim his own power, just as she was, through making an artistic statement, an affirmation of magical creativity. It could be a way to earn respect, not something to be afraid of, it was quite an inspiring idea. Why, it could even make people wary of your power and that could be enough to get just what you wanted from them...not that she wanted to think like that, really. What she really wanted was for Rory to support her, as he always had. Why couldn't she have that? It was painful to see his blank stare, to feel him withdrawing from her. There must be a spell-casting to do with keeping a loved one?

Yes, Lydia knew that there were ways of binding a man, of hexing him really as it was going against his free will, but she wouldn't make Rory do anything he didn't want to do, not in that way at least. He was too powerful a natural psychic himself to let her get away with dabbling with the energies like that. He would know! And it wasn't ethical, of course, and...well, it wasn't really in her interest to make him stay at her side, not in the long term. Simon had made that more than clear to her.

"No, I don't suppose you can talk about being a witch...I'm sorry for asking," she said, wilting a little under his coldly absent gaze.

Lydia knew that it would be far better for her if she went back to her own thoughts. She had a lot to think about. One of the things that was bothering her was that she felt a tiny bit jealous that Rory had actually had a life as witch, in twelfth century France, when she herself just wanted to be one in this life. She had been through the past-life regression with him, of course, and hear it all from his own lips. Even though he had denied that he had been a witch in France, well, that was what he had been, wasn't it? She couldn't understand how he had such a glamourous and exciting incarnation, the stuff of legend, and yet sought to disown it. She could never get any clarity in her own past lives, not yet anyway, although Rory had always sworn that she had been there with him. What if she had? Well, if she truly had then surely he couldn't blame her for wanting to get back the power she had once had there, power that circumstance had cruelly taken from her in that dark age? No, he surely couldn't keep blaming her for being drawn back to the Craft! '*Once a witch, always a witch!*' that's what they said. And '*witches are born, not made*'. If that latter was true then surely she had been born to it? And if it were so then there was nothing that her brother could say or do to deter her from her true path. Discovering modern witchery had been like a homecoming for Lydia, and possibly a lucrative homecoming too, and she wasn't going to give up, not now. Too much was at stake.

The other thing that was nagging at Lydia was nothing to do with witchcraft, well, not directly. No, it was how to tell Rory about Simon and what he wanted her to do.

Chapter Two

Treeface

When I look back upon my life I know that I will not be able to use the milestones that other men measure their days by. I will not mark my memories with material successes, nor with achievements that are quantified with coins for I have never courted their power or prestige, nor would I have been able to. My successes will be synonymous with my mistakes and my joys, what few there are, realised through my learning. For me, as the man I am now and for the man I will be, in years to come, the reason for being is only learning. I came here to grow by acquiring wisdom and understanding, I was born only to share this learning and to tread lightly upon the Earth. Aye, for me there is only learning how to be. Or *how not to be.* For me, well, the pain is part of the process...a large part.

For the lad I was though it was different. He was not aware of the process of *becoming*, he was only aware of the pain, of his pain and the pain of all that was and is. He was used to distracting himself from this pain with his sling shot, shooting at tin cans when he learned that other things hurt as much as he did, and by walking for hours alone, captivated by the smell of burning on autumn afternoons, a smell which made him strangely sad. For you, then, I shall recount his suffering, this scared and scarred boy, and the lessons I learned on account of my understanding that pain. And yes, it is my personal pain of which I will speak, for I cannot speak for another even though I know that we all suffer, we all feel the pain of one amongst us. Like tiny insects wrapped in the silk of a spider spinning in September shadows, we feel the vibrations of each other poor, trapped individual as keenly as the she-spider detects the slightest tremor on her web.

Yes, I would like to share that with you, now. Please do not think me self indulgent, I am a story-teller by my very nature and if I could I would sing you my tale, with my fiddle as the leader of the dance of words, of worlds, I would. But I am sitting here in a room full of people while my sister speaks from her own heart, or at the very least, from her own mind, to them. For now, let my words be enough. For I need to speak too. Who will listen?

As I sit here behind Lydia, seeing the rapt faces of her followers blur and her own voice fade away into an unintelligible murmur, I realise that my ways have never been those of humans, by and large, but instead I am of the wild, my ways shared by the jay and the badger alike. Look, you! See the marks I was born with? Elf-shotten, I am, my kind half-forgotten at best, mocked and worse besides in the most part. How could I have come into this realm again, being so branded, and not realise that I am part of the land but not of the world? I may be Rory, Lydia's brother, Jane's unwanted husband, but I am also *Treeface* and he has a story to tell. It is my story but also it may be yours, in part, for perhaps you were one of those who tormented me, making me stronger? Maybe you were one who tortured me, making me gentler? Or...and I pray it is so...that you are one of my kind and that you too have an affliction, a gift that makes your physical reality echo your spiritual self?

For me, I bear scars. No, I *wear* them. My face is different for it is as though a tree has cast a shadow over it, permanently, a delicate tracery of line and dappled shade. I have the mark of the wildwood on me, just as I feel the deep, resonant reverberations of the roots of the oak, ash and thorn pulling through the loam of my soul. I pluck the strings of my heart, the roots of my spirit, and speak silver-tongued to you, a bard of the bark. Birth-marked, my birth-rite to be visible in the world as a man of the trees...a Green Man. Yet I am without leaves, no verdant canopy to peer through or hide behind, I have a face which is blatantly covered in branches, twigs, hollows, knot-swirls, thorns; I am a lightening tree, a blasted oak in a forest of one. I was born with these lines painted indelibly into my mortal flesh, echoing of all that was natural and wild, wise and eternally free within me and if the world of mortals were kinder I would not need to hide this.

Yet hide I do.

Many harmed me because of these soul-lines as a child. It was hard in middle-England in the early Nineteen 'Sixties, just before the hippy revolution reached the suburbs, before the new Pagans 'came out', before there was much real interest in ecology...before there was sophisticated laser surgery to remove such aberrations as facial scars. I was just a small boy in over long shorts and a cap, swinging his satchel, a small boy with nut brown hair and greenish eyes and a pale face with mahogany lines weaving their twisty, twiney way across it. A boy with a face like a tangle of riddles, confusing the many with my puzzling affliction, people longing to solve me with their prying eyes and interfering fingers. My mentors and peers longed to label me, to unravel the mystery spelt out in me, and eventually they did. Crudely. Cruelly.

At school I was only Reynolds or perhaps *boy*. Everyone there was only a sir-name or boy, yet I had another name, one which was special but made to sound sordid. I had a name that was an insult when it could have been a label worn gladly, one that should have raised my scars up more proudly from my white vulnerable flesh while instead it saw those birth-lines crawling across my cheeks, seeking a place to root more deeply in the black loam of my despair. Oh yes, my broken boughs yielded no fruit yet I was still ripe for their ridicule.

"Scrub it off, you dirty bugger! Scrub it harder you *freak*! TREEEEFACE!"

In the playground, pelted with mud concealing sharp bits of stone, I was Treeface. In the school lavatories, with my head forced down the toilet pan or into another basin of freezing water, I was Treeface. Under their swinging fists and barrages of abuse, I was he. From every school photograph, Nineteen Sixty to Nineteen Seventy, there smiles a smallish, skinny lad with a face mapped out with a wild root system, his body marked in a more vulgar fashion with bruises and pinch marks. And later with lacerations across his back, welts on his arse. The priests were the hardest of all to appease. They still believed in devils, after all.

I would have done almost anything to get out of my Catholic school, that corrupt melting pot, that breeding ground for all that was the worst in human behaviour. Humans can be so cruel but they teach you so much about *how not to be*. That is, if you can endure and survive, until the worst is over. Then, and only then, on reflection, you learn compassion for their half-crazed and foolish actions, their lack of subtly, their hate of something *other* in their midst. Even if I had been without the marks they would have known me for an *other*. The marks were an excuse, I was already the reason. I can tell you this now with compassion overriding my anger, with a sense of sadness for their hollow lives, the empty dread that makes people behave so badly. Yet, oh yes, I still have fear of what can be inflicted out of blind rage and pointless spite, both born of a terrible panic, a mindless hitting out at anything which is not safe and supportive to their view of how things should be.

That woeful, wilful ignorance I experienced among the young, and not so young, brutes of my school days firstly fashioned a bitter resolve in a vengeful lad and then, later, I realised that if I let that need to avenge my own hurt pass then I would be more whole, not less. I had sometimes feared that what may remain when I stripped myself bare of the grief and anguish would be nothing at all yet when I did find freedom from my past I discovered a stronger self with many inner resources and a kind of soul-poetry made more resounding by the pity I now felt for they who could not feel. Most people are so dreadfully lonely because they have forgotten who they are and ...

Oh stop me, I am surely preaching, making myself sound nobler than the average human being, separating people out into *us* and *them*? By no means is this my intention. Ah, to be singing this to you, a gentle melody, a lilting refrain, it would reach your heart and you may not judge my explanations too harshly. What I mean to say is this; just as the wild rose and the fox are both alive, but different to each other, no better or worse, so it is with my kind and the human kind. Only now we have to wear the same bodies so we all look like human beings instead of what we *be*, inside, as our natural Fey forms are so very hard to find these days.

You know, we're not very good at wearing human forms. Somehow the soul transforms us and always makes the body we wear look *other.* No matter what we do the humans can smell us, like a wolf in sheep's clothing, only we are more like lambs to their slaughter than the ravening wolves that they can be. I know it is as it is and there's no use lamenting it but it's a shame though, a crying shame, that the forms that we once wore in this world have become so rare. They were more fluid, those bodies we once had, our spiritual essence made manifest was formed of sweet music, sunbeams and smiles, not clumsy and capable of harm as these two-legged, miserable human shells are prone to being. Our Fey selves were gossamer light, bright and fresh as a posy of primroses, eternally changing like the light on the sea. It is hard not to weep as I recall, albeit vaguely, the shape I once wore. Now, I am wearing the countenance of a man for the bodies of men proliferate far more than that of the Fey and so we incarnate, the disenfranchised Fey ones, into the fleshy shells of humans.

To be seen as human...well it sometimes, no, *often*, makes me so ashamed.

Treeface was not a bad name to have, still isn't, and indeed I use it now myself, in private, with some degree of pleasure. My name sings by itself, it is a lyrical title that entices with the promise of a slightly mischievous, definitely mysterious, yet warm and welcoming elemental character. For a bard, a player of instruments who would sing for his supper if only the world allowed it, it is a fine name indeed. Oh yes, it was only the way they said it that harmed me. And that was as it was meant to be.

Had it not been for my 'affliction' I do not know how my academic career would have been. As it was it was far from impeccable. Long before the word 'dyslexia' was used with authority and without stigma I muddled letters and numbers willy-nilly. How could I concentrate when another beating or taunting lay outside the classroom's four walls? My words danced dizzyingly on the page as I gazed out of windows and looked into the strange alien eyes of dazed flies trapped in those stuffy classrooms with me. I was awkward and I was shy, I could not spell, I stuttered and tripped over myself, I lived in fear and I looked like hell. What could anyone do for me but at best turn a blind eye? They could have let me explore the things I did love, like working with wood, but instead they assumed that I would display my usual ineptitude at that too and so they sent me on pointless errands when I could have been lovingly caressing the bodies of trees into new and beautiful forms in the woodwork rooms.

In music lessons I was given the most basic and plodding of instruments, usually percussive, when my strength was not rhythm but melody. I would have learned the recorder as it was cheap enough to buy for myself but that would have compounded my position as the resident sissy and made me even more open to the teasing which was, in fact, more like outright verbal assault. I would have played guitar, or fiddle, as I do now, but no one thought...no one thought at all about Reynolds. My school was indifferent and would not provide me with a proper instrument whilst my parents did not see fit to encourage their son by asking which instrument, if any, he should like to take up. So my soul sang quietly to itself without accompaniment while they all kept assuming that a physical defect reflected a damaged intellect.

All of my parent's care, what little there was of it, went into my younger, more aesthetically pleasing sister. Lydia, the tiny lass with the white-blonde hair and the big burgundy eyes that were so startling in contrast to the spun silk of those flaxen tresses and her pale, pale skin. Ah, Lydia! Lydia who was clever and dainty and who got it what little there was *gratis*, including a beautiful guitar that she had no interest in, while I, after years of saving, bought my own fiddle at the age of twenty and taught myself. Ah, the beauty of an instrument crafted from living wood, seasoned and strung and just waiting for someone to awaken its magic! How I appreciated it! And how it healed me during those long days, and nights, alone, covering in weeping sores that no one but me could explain.

Lydia loved me and I her, and it was truly a love without question or condition, but by no fault of her own she wasn't there for me when I was alone with an adolescent's iron grip on my neck, or with a priest's sneering face inches from my own. She was far too young to know and anyway she wasn't at my school. No, she was allowed to stay close to home, not like me, her 'troublesome' brother. My parents assumed that with her angelic countenance would come an equivalent academic brilliance and in this alone they were right. With my face it was assumed that I would get by at my own level, the face I wore symbolising somehow some inner abhorration as, apparently, Lydia's signalled some extraordinary inner beauty and talent. How many lessons I have learned from their mistake of equating external charm for inner worth? Although Lydia was indeed beautiful inside and out this externalising was no way of judging a soul for how many handsome lads have I had beating me, how many deemed as angelic as choirboys snarling their contempt and spitting in my face? As if external appearances count for anything, in the long run! As if we can judge the worth of a soul by the mantle it has chosen to robe itself in, this time around...what folly!

You know, Lydia, for all her sweetness, wouldn't have taken the harming I took from these cruel thugs who masqueraded as schoolboys. Lydia would have punched and swore and charmed her way out of any situation. Lydia, sister of '*that boy with the birthmark*', sibling to '*that poor lonely little sod'*, would have given them as good as she got. This is how she was until she met Shay Donnelly with his car-crash personality and Greek God looks. Lydia was lovely but she was also feisty and I know that she would have saved me if she could have. So would my friend Matthew, a big burly boy from the next village whose winning pearly smile and golden hair pleased my parents more than I, of course, although I think his wealthy family pleased them too, to be fair. But Matt, despite his 'suitablity' as my friend, was sent to another, more expensive, private school and I only saw him in the holidays, more's the pity. Yet I knew, I *knew,* that if he would have been there with me he would never have let it happen! For Matt was *tough.* He, as I, had a father who was a bully and a bigot and he, unlike I, knew how to defend himself against such monstrous male behaviours from an early age. That's what drew me to him in the first place and, out of school, away from the parents and the prejudices, he and I just did what boys do, without fear. It was so precious to me, the swinging and the shouting and the shooting tin cans; there was real magic in our time together although I always wondered what Matt got out of it. I have no idea what he saw in me although I must have had something, some gentler quality, that he needed for he stayed true to me, never mentioning my scars, never teasing or using his sturdiness to his advantage against me. I never saw him as much as I would have liked but just the thought that Matty existed was enough, sometimes. He was my rock in a weary land, for sure, just as my sister was an oasis in my desert.

But at school there was no Matt and no Lydia.

No one could, or would, defend me.

There was no one there! Or, at least, no one like me.

The school system devoured those who were deemed crippled or backward in those days, maybe in all days, and I was seen as both. Those where the days of words like 'mongol', 'remedial' and 'spastic' and my parents behaved as if the lad they had first created between them was such a being. I wore no callipers, no overly large hearing aid, no dreadful National Health spectacles with lenses like milk bottle bottoms, yet I was branded, placed within this ugly, fearful bracketing of children, with all the other 'poor sods', and I was written off, effectively.

Didn't they know that those who chose to walk the Earth with a physical ailment or disfigurement have come to teach this unconditional acceptance of all differences and to help us see beyond appearances? It isn't a punishment to walk the Earth thus, by no means! It is a gift to those who incarnate alongside such strong souls, so that they may learn to love beyond the exterior of all beings. We are here in such forms to express how it is that our souls are eternal and important while the packaging is as 'throw away' as anything else we use in this society. Oh to have communicated this to my own parents! But now, it is too late, they chose not to bother with my inner self, deeming it deformed somehow, equating it with my face and so now they do not truly know me, nor I them. What a waste!

It was this sort of prejudice and fear that got our Fey selves exterminated in the first place. It is always a choice we make, how to respond, how not to react. Free will....

But I said I would not preach, did I not?

You may ask, didn't anyone at all ever even consider why I was bullied within an inch of my slender young life? Did they never equate my own facial deformity with why I couldn't think straight, let alone write a decent sentence? Obviously not is my retort, for it happened and continued to happen, unabated, for the duration.

Now do I sound bitter? I hope that I am not for I know that there were good times, times like no other, that resulted from these torments. I can see myself now, sat in the open arms of a protective oak, supported by its knotty veined bark as I whittled and hummed to myself. I would make wooden animals from windfallen branches and make songs for them as I worked, my hands suddenly dextrous and quick when in the open air, away from prying eyes, hidden for view by my friend, Talius the silent oak. My tongue was no longer tied when no human ears could overhear my refrain. I was blessed in the fact that we lived reasonably close to the woods and that no one save Lydia noticed if I vanished for hours.

There, in my natural element, with the trees, I was no longer a scrawny lad whose feet tangled together when he tried to walk; instead I was a bold and daring boy who hopped lightly through the ferns, bounding through the bracken to reach my favourite glade. Cupping the golden light in my hands and trying to clasp it to my chest, to keep it in me always, shadow-boxing like the hares that joined me, my eyes full of the glad fools-fire the humans so despised. I sang with the birds and worked little pieces of green wood I found windfallen around me and I would never have had such a deep relationship with my favourite oak of all if it hadn't been for them, the bullies. No, I wouldn't have known about the real mystery and magic of my beloved glade at all if they hadn't dunked me and scrubbed me that last time.

It had been a Wednesday afternoon, double physical education on a drizzly October day. I dreaded Wednesdays but there had seemed no escape. I was too obedient to drop out of school without a reason and too mild to ask if I may be excused. I was, as ever, left on the sidelines while the teams were picked and, once again, I suffered the humiliation of the master concerned putting me forcibly into a team that didn't want me. Amidst a chorus of muttered expletives and groans I would stand, head bowed, having a team's coloured ribbon dropped with disgust around my skinny neck and I would wonder why they didn't just let me slip away to the woodwork room to get on with a carving instead of making us all miserable like this. If no one wanted me present why force me to be there? It seemed like an unnecessary torture.

That afternoon, as on so many others, the cruel ritual of team choosing was completed and I was doomed to a miserable hour and a half of rugby in a chilly drizzle. As the game began I immediately slipped into the reverie that carried me through such lamentable situations. I gazed upwards at the birds, flying free across a slate grey sky, and prayed for my soul to join them as they swooped off to welcoming trees. I saw a heron that day and I longed for his grace, feeling the thrill of his omen moving through my wiry frame. The heron was always my messenger, he showed me how to stand still and wait, always observing, his solemn, long-legged beauty like fragment of my own potential, his shimmering reflection in a silver pool while I mirrored his action on the pitch. I usually stood alone in some obscure position hoping that the ball would never come my way. Like the heron I was fast but under their contemptuous gaze I was always clumsy. In my dreams I dipped and soared and my body stood still, willing itself to become gauzy and insubstantial, feather light and free.

As I stared upwards I could feel them rushing at me. Too late I responded and then they were upon me, a scrum of boys and a ball in a flurry of flailing arms and sturdy, dirty legs. Watching in horrified fascination, as if in slow motion, I saw the ball come to rest between my long, lean legs.

The pack descended on me as I stood, gawking like an idiot at the ball which had remained just behind my right foot. One lad, nearly a head taller than me, knocked me flying and I lay, winded, staring at the sky, almost uncomprehending. I was so seldom fully present 'in the world' that their physical contact always shocked me greatly; part of me always seemed to be absenting itself to fly unfettered from that body of mine and their physical contact jarred me horribly. Another boy, amidst distant shouts and roars, bent his head into my field of vision, his face contorted by anger framed by that swirling grey sky.

"You fool, you stupid bastard. I'll have you for that. I mean it. That's your lot, Reynolds."

His face disappeared and I sat up, struggling for breath. How I wish he'd have just kicked me there and then, something honest and open. Instead, it was the usual psychological warfare, the waiting game, how they loved a covert operation which kept my belly full of acid as I remained on tenterhooks until their wrath finally descended upon me. When would he and his friends strike back at me? And how? The one thing that was for certain, I would be alone in whatever happened.

Nature had made me like a willow, not an oak, in appearance; I was lithe, easily bent but rarely broken. Trees do not fight, they endure, yet if the trees wished to they could rise up, branches whipping, great roots ripping and tearing; like Tolkien's Ents they could turn the tables and wreak havoc upon the wreckers themselves if they so chose. Instead they endure, silently, solidly, just as I endured for we are kin, the trees and I. When a tree is chopped down it withdraws its spirit deep into its very roots, hiding its green essence in the soil below, and when I was attacked I became the tiniest, most inconspicuous thing hidden in the earth within myself. I was hardly there at all, buried deep, but my body remained to goad them and to bear their rage.

There were times at school that were inevitably worse than others and, worse than the rugby game itself, I always felt vulnerable and exposed in the showers after any physical education session. I was always silent, seeking to be inconspicuous, and usually I was quick to dress afterwards as to escape without too much notice. I withdrew the seed of my true self deep within and allowed only my trunk and branches be visible, hoping that my body would seem hollow, rotten and unworthy of attack. The only thing I had in my favour when I was exposed after games was that even the most aggressive and confident boys felt a little wary of me lest they themselves catch whatever 'disease' I had that made me so different and I used this fact as much as I could, making myself strange and distant. Sometimes it worked, sometimes not; I could never tell how things would go and so I lived in permanent dread.

After games or physical education there were never any masters to save me, or to calm any situation centred around me, for somehow they all disappeared as soon as the first boy would start his merciless bullying. I guessed that the masters thought that I deserved a good dressing down for all my weird ways and especially for my disturbing countenance. That day in the cloakroom, after that ill-fated rugby game, I remember how completely alone I felt. Each minute as I rubbed my hair with the rough old towel seemed to last an aeon and it seemed to take an age to tie the laces of my horrible regulation brogues. Although I seemed withdrawn and meditative, almost vacant, I heard the shrill bell that signalled the end of the school day in every part of my being; it signalled all hell being let loose, a time of lawlessness outside the bounds of what few school rules I had on my side. I was intensely aware of every sound and movement, each drip of water into the cracked washbasins, the scent of polished wood in the corridors and the steady thump and slap of feet on it as one by one the other normal boys poured from the building. The lads began to leave the changing room one by one and I honestly thought, just for a precious moment, that they would all go and forget about me. The silence which followed their departure was filled only by the clicks and rustles my own movements made as I fastened up my bag and my blazer buttons.

Then there was another noise behind me, the whispering of conspiratorial voices, the gentle swish of the door being closed, the awful clunk as the wood and metal fitted together, locking me in with the assailants. How many of them? I will never know. The first two gripped me so hard around my neck I feared I would black out, bilious spots exploded briefly in my fading vision and then they punched my back. The inadequate armour of the blazer with its badge and motto '*excellence for all*' was rent by many hands. I knew better than to struggle.

All I can tell you is that they left my eyes alone, more or less. Round and round the scouring pad went, procured from the school janitor's cupboard, opened at the end of school for his rounds. The stench of cheap bleach and my own blood as they scrubbed. I realised, with bitter irony, that this was the closest they, or maybe anyone, had ever been to me. Only Lydia had ever clung and held me like that.

I wish I could tell you that I protested but I did not. I could tell you that they insulted me or humiliated me verbally but they, as I, were silent. They were intent on the work in hand. And they were very good at it, remarkably thorough.

I knew that I could not go home afterwards. Mother had been in her room, on and off, for weeks, confused and weepy after finding out about Father and Miss Dillon...something I didn't really understand at the time. '*After all I've done!*' she had kept muttering, lying prone on her bed and not hearing when I had asked her if I could make her tea of an evening. The visual impact of seeing how much her disfigured son, the one she was never too sure of anyway, was hated may have tipped her over some indefinable edge and at my tender age, when mother-love is all pervasive no matter how they hurt you, I wasn't willing to take that risk. I was barely in my teens and was reluctant to show my parents how much a man-child supposedly made in their own image could be loathed and rejected. Their own flesh and blood had been beaten and scoured to a pulp and my face unrecognisable, perhaps even to a mother...especially one who barely seemed to see me anyway.

I knew that after the boy's merciless, sustained assault I must look horrendous and I felt that to be my own problem, pure and simple. I could never bear to cause anyone else hurt so I couldn't go home and reveal the truth to them, now could I? And Lydia, little Lydia, would have been frightened of me and I could never, ever have born that.

I myself was beyond pain. Yes, perhaps.

As I walked, poker legged, away from the school building in the gathering twilight I was glad that mirrors in young men's lavatories were considered an unnecessary indulgence. I looked down at my surprisingly clean hands as I walked although they soon blurred as my reddened yes narrowed even further as the swelling increased around them. I felt like the scrag end of myself, a survivor of some long war which had robbed me of something precious. How I would have loved to have been hugged by a mother then, despite my tender body and raw face, oh to have been welcomed like a hero who had somehow made it through a long and bloody, if pointless and futile, battle. But that would not be possible.

My back became straight as the trunk of a silver birch and with legs like stilts, just like heron's legs, I kept on walking. I knew exactly where I was going and that was away from humanity. I would find the hollow tree I particularly loved and then find, therein, safety. And there I would sleep for a thousand years until a new age had come and I would awake refreshed as the handsome Prince of the Greenwood.

So, I walked for miles to a place I could call home with the gathering darkness heavy around me like a wet, woollen cloak. No one saw me go, no one watched me as I passed. For a blessed time I was invisible, not incandescent, in my personal pain.

Somehow I found my tree and climbed in, like a Roo into its marsupial mother's welcoming pouch. I crouched within and prayed for sleep to obliterate my hurtings.

However, I did not sleep much at all and I certainly didn't wake up to find myself a Prince, rather over and over I woke in fresh agonies as the reality of my situation, and the trauma of it, racked my body and soul. The tree I loved seemed hospitable on a warm summer's afternoon, but as the late autumn evening turned to dead of night it was damp and cramped. I was shaking with cold, hunger and shock and still I continued to force my way in, further and further, into the deep cleft in the oak. I attempted to coil around myself foetally but the restricted space only allowed me to be wedged awkwardly in order to avoid contact with the skin on my face and the bruises on my back and neck.

There was nothing to fear within that silent tree's worn body. It held me yet it did not speak to me, or if it did then I could not hear it for the sounds of my own anguish. To block out all else I kept repeating in my own mind '*badgers and foxes, little foxes and owls*' over and over. On and on I chanted to myself, adding the names of all creatures of the wood, the tree names and the wonderful names of flowers that grew in dappled shade, finding theses things reassuring and unthreatening. Whereas most humans would have been terrified hearing the scuttling and scuffling of the wildwood as night fell, I sought great comfort in it. I sought aloneness save kinship with the creatures that also feared humanity and who grew apart from it. I whispered and croaked their names over and over, a wild mantra of personal power, a sweet and sad, yet defiantly wild, lullaby for a husk of a lost boy.

The only thing I felt fear of, hidden in my dark damp place, was the return of the faceless boys, their hands moving in that loathsome repetitive motion, scrubbing...

(*scrubbing*!)

...the memory of which caused me to tremble uncontrollably every few seconds.

'*Badgers and little foxes....hootle owl and weasley stoat*'...my own lullaby went on even as my voice failed me and night fell thick and fast like a muffling blanket.

Soon the damp was so far into my bones as to numb my body and only my mind and spirit remained. That was how I preferred it. I felt comforted without my body and so my body was able to sleep while I floated somewhere starlit, drinking in the un-peopled peace like nectar.

When I awoke I was cramped to the point of agony and I would have screeched with it but my face felt so tight as to rip like paper if I opened my mouth. I clenched my teeth, which was in itself a great effort. Slowly and excruciatingly painfully I turned myself so that I was facing outwards instead of towards the internal bark of my hole in the tree. It was almost light, a whole night had somehow slipped past me and as I blinked I saw that there was a small figure crouched outside the tree, peering at me intently. At first the person, if it was a person, was made up of only patches of misty lilac and pale gold, smooth brown and shimmering silver, a creature of chill mist and speckled stone. My eyes wouldn't open fully and the stinging in them had not abated; I expected to see only a wash of colour, a blur of an image, and so I thought this strangely hazy figure was a result of my injuries. The creature giggled although it seemed to have no mouth, nor even a clearly distinguishable face, yet it was a clear sound that rippled the air around it so that its form shifted slightly. I realised that like some sort of strange frog the little figure was clinging to the outside of the oak's bark and was perhaps no more than a foot in height.

"You should introduce yourself!" she said, if indeed it was a she. I thought I saw a flash of red on flaxen hair, a cap bobbing as she spoke. Suki Red Cap, I learned later. Although she, like all of her kind...

(*our* kind!)

...could appear in any way they chose her particular calling card was her little hat, always bright as a Yew berry amongst the green and grey of her ever-changing form.

"I'm sorry!"

I could not speak but realised my thoughts had reached her anyway because I was aware of her grinning with an intensity that lit her up like a lantern and made her small almost-face split in two. Grinning from ear to ear, I thought she was, and she nodded.

I had to smile too and I felt my skin rip open and I wanted to howl.

"Sylvan-One, Tree Fella, I go, I get Meggy!" the figure stated, her not-quite-head tilted coquettishly.

One finger, an impossibly long and eerily cold finger of her misty form, reached in and traced the new line in the riven flesh of my face. Instead of shivering I felt warmer. The figure withdrew the finger that left a shimmering, ghostly trail in the air. There was a sound of a snapping twig somewhere behind her and a pheasant flew up in a flurry of noise. At this sound, the figure's form elongated and tendrils, like smoke, emitted from the pointed head, ears, hair and hands. Then she became almost solid again, but this time looked more concerned.

"Poor boy," she said inside my head. "Shhh now. Getting Meggy....send Kefli to you too."

"What is kefli?"

My thoughts had spoken for me.

"Ha! Swindling and Swagling and Marsh Boggart!! He be all three and a vimmish Roguer besides! Skillern, Widderwadder, he's Kefli, he is your *friend*! One of us, pretty-puss!"

There was giggle and she was gone.

I felt a little cross that she should laugh at me in my state, mocking my plight. My indignation mixed with my pain and confusion creating a heady brew that was quite unpalatable yet still I drank it down. Then I think I must have blacked out. There was a welcome nothingness and then I saw myself as if from above, scuffling through the wildwood, pursued by a long, gangling figure whose head was crowned by a spill of silvery hair that shot upwards, all caught up with burrs and weeds. Flashes of red, cloth of gold, the touch of dry, stick-like fingers on my skin. Did I cry out? Words and images tumbled through my mind, performing somersaults with my senses, filigrees of shining spider silk brushing my face, seed pods cracking, the languid movements of a tall grey figure, wrapped in a cloak of heron's feathers.

'*Vervain, tansy, meadow-sweet and sorrel...mend me, bend me, beg, steal borrow!*' I heard myself sing-song as strange chants flowed like honeyed milk over my swollen tongue. I was just experiencing a delirium of sorts my rational self suggested, from somewhere deep within. It was only to be expected under the circumstances, I was in shock, after all! But during those...minutes...hours...I could feel their presence. It was no hallucination surely? No delirium! For in my hour of greatest need *they* came and even as I groaned in my own pitiful physical torment I was awakening to their reality.

To my reality. To *ours.*

When I half opened my eyes again I asked the strangely swirling air in front of my face what time it was. I formed the question in my mind and knew it would be answered if any were nearby. Even though I was almost overcome with the otherworldly atmosphere, with the Fey energy that had all but engulfed me, something of the well trained human in me started to protest about my current inertia. I wondered suddenly if I should be concerned with some other reality, the one that I had so recently left. Struggling to recall the nuts and bolts of human living it occurred to me to consider if the Police had been alerted to my disappearance and if so did I want them to be? Should I be getting back? I placed one hand hesitantly outside the hollow tree but could feel nothing but cool, damp air. Nobody there? Bark though. Bark nose, eyes...bark *person*? My hand became my eyes and I reached out stiffly, exploring a countenance more rippled and twisted than mine could ever be. It was a face made of living wood whereas mine was only stained with a veneer.

"OOH! Oy! Getoff!"

I pulled my hand back, somewhat embarrassed of my shameless groping.

"I'm terribly..." my voice cracked and splintered and my throat hitched with a sob, "sorry and...sore".

It was ridiculous that even hidden in a tree's dark, damp folds I could offend someone.

"T'isn't for you to go touching'!" the voice was harsh but had a lilt to it. More of a bark than a bite...bark *person?*

"Well now, Kefli, step aside there!"

Another presence, this time a man...or a nearly-man at least. I heard the bark person jump back, his movements sounding like brittle sticks and dry leaves, and he grumbled to himself as that more human presence came close to the entrance of my sanctuary. It was very odd that I could see nothing but blurry images yet I *felt* them...I could sense their differences and their similarities, their sugar-frosted spirits as cleanly sweet as freshly mown grass and as intriguing as that which lay beneath rotting logs. They had an *organic* presence that gave me a deeply comforting feeling. Vulnerable and hurt as I was I did not feel threatened or cornered by these individuals whoever they were, their essential essence was like a fragrant balm to me. Even if they were figments of a whirling delirium I welcomed them as they felt like my guardian spirits come to bring reassurance and good cheer.

"Did I hear the young fella enquire about the time, and all? How would I be knowing that? And why should it matter to a young 'un all hidden in a tree's knees?"

This voice was definitely not in my head this time, even if the strange little amorphous red-capped being and the man-of-bark had been. I was having trouble distinguishing what was my own fantasy and what was real, as ever, but this was heightened through my pain and fatigue. Had I spoken out loud? Had someone else? I tried to shift myself out of the hole but I couldn't make my limbs respond. A very real, very male face peered in at me; I could sense him as well as see his blurred features.

"Hello there!"

The man seemed to see me there in the shadows but I wasn't too sure what I could see in return as I couldn't seem to do anything usual that I had been able to do twenty four hours earlier. All my human faculties like speech and eyesight, previously taken for granted, seemed to be dwindling.

A hand reached in and touched my exposed belly, my school shirt, or what was left of it, had few buttons left. "What's this now? Are you alright?"

"Mmmuhhh..."

My voice was now a rasping thing full of sawdust.

The other hand, brown, gnarled and impossibly gentle for such large, capable looking man's hand, found me and, almost tenderly, began to feel for purchase on my poor bent body.

"We need to get you out of there boy, see? Can't be having you stuck in there like a hibernating squirrel! Got to take a look at those injuries of your'n."

His face, one I perceived as being dirty and delightfully wizened, broke into a smile, while his infinitely kind amber eyes shone brightly enough to be seen in the darkness by my own squinting blood-shot ones. To my mind, rather than to my eyes, he looked like a foxy man, wily and spry.

"I'm sorry," I rasped.

I wanted to spit but I couldn't find a way of doing so without it landing on my own person. Besides, it was impolite.

"What's that lad? No, don't be daft, there, *I'm* sorry. Sorry we live in a world that allows such things to happen to young 'uns like yerself, here. I'm Jack Tatterkin and t'was rude of me to start man-handling you without as much as an introduction. You can call me Tatty, they all do, you know."

"Treeface," I said without thinking, in a chipped voice that seemed alien to my ears.

My whole mouth seemed to be clogged up with wood-shavings and greasy ashes.

"Well then, Treeface," the man spoke as if such a name was the most usual thing in the world for a teenage lad stuck in a hollowed out oak, covered in his own blood, "we'll be having you out of here, then. Can I lift you? Will you help me?"

"Don't know if I can...move...aggh!"

My voice caught like shards in my throat as I gingerly tested each unresponsive limb.

"Will you trust me to reach in and pull you? Might be a little uncomfortable at first but we need to get you out of old Talius now, see, need to see what can be done for you. Can I help you now, son?"

I nodded my assent and closed my eyes as best I could. There was a moment of sharp pain as my body protested at its being moved and the world lurched and rolled around me in a nauseating fashion. Like a drunk or a novice sailor I felt my head spinning dangerously fast as my stomach threatened to spill its meagre contents all over my scuffed shoes. Then I was out, placed like a baby at the foot of the oak, still curled in my protective ball.

"Talius guarded you well, friend. Well met we are this day, the three of us!"

Jack Tatterkin spoke with great kindness as he crouched down beside me and lifted a lock of my damp hair away from my face. It was stuck to the caked blood there and it made a sickening crackling sound as it was dislodged. The man winced at my state, I could feel his horror at my plight. I knew by my inner *seeing*, if not by the sight of my eyes, that he was a sinewy, tanned individual dressed in a funny tail coat and a worn and mis-matched assortment of clothes. Even though he was all but invisible to my human eyes my soul warmed to him hugely.

"'Tis worse than I thought and yet it durn't surprise me at all!"

The gangly ragamuffin who called himself Tatty sighed heavily.

"What's wrong with folks, young Treeface, that they has to do the likes of this to a Fey one? What sort of day and age is this for human's to have forgotten themselves so completely?"

"When is it?" I asked him, my eyes blinking against what little light filtered in through my swollen, abraised eyelids.

I realised how much I must have cried to myself, in my sleep. My head pounded, green and pink bilious spots dancing before me.

"'Tis time enough for you, and all, and 'tis always somewhen, don't you think?" came a voice from behind the man. I tried to struggle upright at the sound of this female voice. Something of my adolescent pride would not allow a girl to see me this way! I tried, and failed, to regain a sense of my human self, the Rory Reynolds self that was so despised. But why should I want to go back to him, to his plight, to his cursed life?

"What do you mean?" I asked the girl, and realised I was speaking in my own head again. "I mean...that doesn't...mean...much to me," I rasped, this time out loud.

I managed to sit up a little, propped against the tree that I guessed must be old Talius. The owner of the musical female voice stepped forward and I *felt* her...felt her energy which flew like a swallow in September, proud and strong and free.

"Now then, Meg, he durn't need all that nonsensical stuff just now, do 'e?" Jack stood up.

"Ah sure he does, let me...oh!"

The girl saw me fully for the first time and said "oh!" again before toppling backwards to fall onto her plump behind. From what I could make out from feeling her energies and *seeing* her in my mind's eye she was a pale, fleshy, freckly sort of girl, with red hair in natural ringlets that bobbed as she moved. She was just the kind of person that would have been laughed at and picked on in my school had she of had the misfortune to attend it and I immediately loved her for that. I visualised her staring at me and I suddenly wanted to laugh for some reason; imagining her funny round face all surprised and wide-eyed tickled me greatly. She was a mad girl, I thought.

"That's as maybe, but at least I ain't in such a mess as you!"

She replied out loud as if she had heard my thoughts and it was my turn to try and form my bruised lips into an amazed 'o' shape.

Silently berating herself for her retort, for I could hear her speaking in my own head, she came towards me, reaching out to touch my ruined face. I tried to straighten myself up more fully at her approach; to be seen slumped in such a state in front of strangers, especially a female, was somehow improper. Oh, how well, or how very badly, my parents had influenced me with their parochial sense of what was proper! There I was, their strange son, sprawled and bloodied in a pile of fallen leaves and fretting about good manners while they were probably still having breakfast and cursing me for being a slug-a-bed! I had no doubt that they had not noticed my absence of the previous evening; Mother in her rumpled bed tossing and turning alone, Dad home late and expecting there to be order in his house.

To hell with their sense of propriety! It certainly wasn't right and proper for me to be so ill-used!

"Look, what time is it?"

This time I rasped out loud to these two raggle-taggles, my new croaky husk-voice sounding so strange to my ears. My rational side desperately wanted some frame of reference in the unorthodox situation whilst my soul was rejoicing. These were people, real people, but not as the people I had already encountered in my short, painful life already. No, these were humans but not humans...they were Fey wild cards and unlucky/lucky paradoxes, just like me! I had a link with them, a spirit connection that went beyond my reduced eyesight and allowed me to be with them in a way that allowed me to really *see*. In my mind's eye Meggy's blue eyes glittered mischievously and I noticed she had things caught in her thatch of coppery curls, teasels and small white feathers, whilst my human sight saw nought but a blurry wash of colour that was bereft of all detail. Did human's only ever see like this anyway, I wondered to myself, was the human gift of vision squandered and always reduced to a rough watercolour wash of the true reality?

With my inner eyes I could see much more clearly. The two people that were in front of me stood out in stark relief, beautiful and vital. I decided, there and then, that bright red hair was the very best sort to have and that I would always see things as clearly as I did that springy, recalcitrant mop on the head of a pale, mad girl.

"I'm not mad! And stop your mutterings about time! How should I know what the divveling human hour is? I don't need a watch. What fool does if they've got the sun above them and the shadows below them?"

Meggy spoke out loud again and I sensed her hand, small, white and warm, was hovering around my face. I knew, just by her proximity to me, that she wore a necklace made of snail shells and wooden beads; all polished to perfection it was, each containing the reflection of the trees, rocks and water that gave her so much joy. Ah yes, daft as a brush she was indeed, no matter what she told me to the contrary, for I could feel her giddy madness and it was as natural and right as the wild leaping of the hare. Hers was no human rage or befuddlement, instead Meggy had the glad madness of spring and was as perfectly right as a May morning. She made a flapping gesture at me, being careful not to brush my injured face, and laughed, those cornflower eyes crinkling, echoing an unseasonably clear sky. In my head I saw the clouds move across her vision as I knew they moved across my own, here was a *seer* like me who was, perhaps for the first time in this life, allowing me to really see too. Tatty too was of my kind, I could read the concern in his energies like Braille, but it was Meggy that held me spellbound despite the pain and the humiliation I felt.

Ah yes, the mad girl knew what I thought of her and her delight to be found so lovely coursed through me like clear spring water, bathing and refreshing my soul. Through my narrowed gaze I could take little in but through my heart and soul I drank her down. She was a draft, an elixir for my battered spirit, and, by all the old wild gods, she was as soul-pretty as a picture of something very pretty indeed.

Yet I was still dimly aware that somewhere, somewhen, school would have begun, or was about to. Who knew what the hour was? No one, it appeared. They were both staring at me I knew, drinking me in as I had them.

"They shouldn't have done this to you! That Toby Stevens and Philip Gloucester, they shouldn't! I can make them sorry, and all!"

Meggy held her hand lightly, lovingly, against my torn face and even her gentle contact made me wince a little. I thought that she may have been crying as she spoke. We had a soul-link, she and I, but how did she know...

"Curse that Philip Gloucester, so I do! Curse that Stevens boy!"

"Now then, Meggy my lover, there's no need for all that now, what we need is another lad to help me get Treeface here back to Aelfthamne and then we can clean him up a bit see, give him a brew or two, let him tell it his way, when he sees fit to. Run and get me Robbie, love, will you? I'll stay here and mind the lad, see if I can rub some life back into his limbs."

Meggy struggled back to her feet which she planted stubbornly apart. "They'll not hear the last of this, so! I'll have to..."

"Meggy, lass, will you do what's right by the wee fella here and go?"

I closed my eyes. The sickness washed in waves through me and my head spun. I could hear her footsteps moving off and I felt the loss of her warm caring keenly yet Jack was there and his kind-light was strong enough. The firm touch his work-strong hands gently but firmly kneaded my calf muscles and I felt his soul seeking mine to sing it a healing song. My soul responded to his and relaxed even as my human side balked; here was a stranger who was muttering over me as he kneaded and his hands were so strong! Should I be afraid of him? But I had no energy to be afraid and to stave off the wave upon wave of nausea that threatened to engulf me.

I steadied myself and took a few hitching deep breaths, trying to swallow down the nausea with a draft of fresh air. Had those boy's bleachy adiministrations poisoned me too? I willed myself to be calm as Tatty worked on my soul. Some part of me, the deepest part, knew that to be afraid of Jack Tatterkin was to be afraid of my own self for I knew this outcast, this wandering man of many colours, was truly of my kind. I allowed this deep inner knowing to rise up and swamp my worries and they gradually began to ease as my body winced and writhed, coming reluctantly back to life. Pins and needles prickled my extremities as my mind raced over all I was experiencing. Ah, the constant fight between soul-certainty and human fear! It is an ongoing friction, the battle between spirit and matter, *knowing* and *forgetting*, peace and paranoia. If only the soul could win for once and all then maybe we would no longer need to come here to this beautiful Earth to witness the terror one human, lost in his own *forgetting*, can inflict on another being.

Yes, maybe.

As I lay there with pins and needles distracting me and Tatty working his healing magics over me I thought I felt the strange bark-man returning, peering at me with curiosity, although my eyes had closed again.

'*He's like me!*' I imagined him, this Kefli creature, exclaiming to himself. '*Chirpy as a sparrow, bright as the Jackdaw's collection of silver and gold, all branchy and twined with wildwood spells, so he is and so I am! Naughty, too! Boldly sprouting acorns and dropping his prickly seeds! And hated bad, he is, just like Kefli and that makes Kefli angry!*'

And I imagined this bark person hopping mad and crackling like kindling on our behalf.

I imagined? No, I don't think so.

The next I knew I was being carried in a blanket that smelled of wood-smoke and damp earth.

"Where do you live? Where are you taking me?" I raspily asked whoever was with me. I heard their feet crunching on earth that had not quite lost its frosty coating. I realised then how cold I must have been. It was one of those crystal clear and sharp days of great beauty, found only as the ashes of October settle into November.

"My head hurts."

"Aye and I'm not surprised," said a rougher, deeper voice with a more familiar accent.

"Lie still boyo, we're nearly there."

"Where?"

"*Over here...*"

"Aelfthamne, beloved, always to Aelfthamne."

We appeared to be climbing a slope. I could hear the men's breath and remembered the plume of foggy breath that had emitted from Toby Stevens as he had challenged me the day before on the rugby field. His breath, wood-smoke...

"How did she know about Toby? Meggy...that girl...how did she know?"

My words came in short barking gasps. In hearing this alien voice breach my cracked lips I thought of the two wood blocks I had been given it to 'play' as percussion in music lessons; their well worn splintery surfaces chaffing each other as they made that unlovely, ineloquent sound in my hands, the sound of indifference and endless, lonely discomfort. It was like the noise my soul surely made when it too chaffed against the confines of my human skin.

I knew better than to sit up on their make-shift stretcher. I lay still and waited for someone to reply to me but no one did. Their breathing became more laboured as they crested a small hill and then I could hear other noises. Muted music, a dog barking, and the sound of a baby giggling with pleasure. I was being lowered gently to the ground to one side of what I perceived to be a sort of camp. My head was raised and a warm draught of something sweetened with honey was poured into my mouth. I almost gagged but sensed it was good, despite its pungent aroma, and swallowed it, gingerly at first but then with more enthusiasm. I would find out what it was. Drugs? I doubted it. Whatever it was it took me, for a while at least, away from the hurting.

And later when the sky had become dim I was able to sit up again, unaided, and I was clean, or at least, not caked in my own blood. I had a man's heavy itchy brown sweater over my torn school blazer and was wrapped into same blanket I had been transported in. When I raised my hand to my face it felt less tight but faintly greasy as if some salve had been applied. The dull throb of discomfort was still with me but was less than I expected it to be. I had no idea of my actual injuries but gathered they were quite severe. I felt as if I had been burned raw yet left tight as a badly tuned drum, as if the top layer of me had been stripped away and a new skin had been applied that was not a true fit. I was glad of the cream, or whatever it was, that coated my damaged skin.

Nobody noticed at first that I had my eyes partially open and was more alert.

It was Tatty who turned, as if by some instinct, from his stirring of the pot that hung over the fire and it was he who first came to hunker down beside me. I noticed that despite the chill he wore an open necked shirt, heavily patched and worn thin, and his chest was bony and brown. He had a slightly grubby neckerchief on, reminding me of the pictures of Romanies I had long since admired in my children's compendiums of Faery-tale stories, and like the Gypsies he wore one gold hooped earring. His hair was ratty and thin, partly grey, and to all intents and purposes he looked like a very shady sort of character indeed. I realised, to my dismay and distaste, that I was judging him by my parent's standards again, and I quickly reverted to how I felt about this wonderful saviour-man who said nothing.

Had he been from the world I was used to he would be plying me with questions, admonishing me for doing foolish things in trees, staring appraisingly at a pinched young face now not only lined but ruined. Yet he said nothing, just waited for me to speak, if I felt the need. As he stayed, crouched and calm, he removed a pouch of tobacco from his top pocket and deftly rolled a cigarette with one hand.

"If you ever take to smoking boy," he said, gesturing with the fragrant cigarette, "Make sure you use coltsfoot in the mixture, and chew elecampane root and all...'tis a good thing for the throat, soothing for the tubes, 'specially if you are going to be use your voice a lot....which I suspect you will be, one day."

He blew a perfect blue smoke ring and I thought of Meggy's eyes, bright with dancing firelight in the gathering gloom.

It was then that I realised, with a frisson of excitement, that I was in an adventure, of sorts. That these people were mine in the sense that I had long since dreamed with no little measure of guilt, that I was really born to travelling folk and not two suburban people who cared little for the things I held very dear. Moreover, this man seemed to not treat either my pulped face or its scarring as any reflection of how nice I was. Was it still scarred, I had suddenly wondered, or had those boys managed, somehow, to erase those life-lines of mine with their brutal bleachy scrubbing?

I felt a little panic. Were they gone now? Hadn't I prayed night and day for them to be gone? Yet in that smoky twilit moment I knew that I wanted my lines to remain with me for good and all. The thought was so dramatic and shocking to me that I almost gasped aloud. I wanted my birth markings to stay!

"Are they g...g...?"

I reached up in frustration to indicate my scars, the right side of my face and across to my left brow.

Tatty re-lit his thin cigarette.

"Oh yes..." he smiled.

Gone! Oh...

"...they're still there alright, for good and all too! They didn't take those from you boy, no, they couldn't see? They're *soul-lines*, boy, not things that can be removed by human hands. You can be proud of 'em, young 'un, blessed by Spirit you are! You're wearing the Greenwood as a mark of who you be, you're Treeface and 'tis an honour to be so! And 'tis a responsibility alright, I'll grant you that alright, but if you weren't up to the job you'd have not been given the marks, see?"

I *saw*. I really did.

"T'aint a burden, boy, 'tis a boon you've got sprouting on your face there. A blessin' that shows how strong that soul of your'n is and how you belong to the Earth. If I were you...well, safe to say I'd be respectin' the land and doing her work. I'd be speakin' out for all that's good and green and holy. I'd *be* Treeface."

"Holy?"

I whispered. I connected the word with sermons and hymns,

prayers that went on and on in draughty halls full of words that alienated me. I connected holiness with punishment; to me it was a chilly sort of word. I shivered involuntarily.

The man looked wistful.

"We try and live right, see? That's venerating the land, 'cos she's sacred. It's the Mother, boy, the only thing worth fighting for besides the right to be who you be, 'cos both are holy, see? Both are God given."

"Or Goddess given, depending on how you look at it!"

A tall, square jawed woman with long blonde braids stood to Tatty's right. He stood up in her presence.

"Aye, both God and Goddess given, beyond those two and each of them combined, The Creator, the All-That-Is. Whatever we call it, however we express it, it's all divine and holy. What's holy is harmonious, by its very nature, 'tis only the going against nature which is unholy...the trying to dominate and eradicate and carve up and own..."

"Human things!"

The tall woman said quietly but with conviction.

"'Tis only the humans who have forgotten how to be. You don't see no bluebells a-bickerin' and beatin' each other to a pulp over what football team is best, there ain't no cows in the fields debating over building another motorway across protected land for the sake of fast profit. Cows can't eat cash, nor can we, the bluebells and the cows know that, see? They *are* the land, see? They're a one-ness with it! We know that too, only most human-kinds, they're forgetful creatures when it suits 'em to be. They's got to thinkin' somehow they be separate and better and all the things that make them behave as if they own it so 'tis their right to destroy it!"

Tatty took a drag on his cigarette, crumpled it up small and then flicked it to the ground, spitting on it. I had never seen anyone so casual, so *natural*, before. And all this I saw with my spirit-eyes as well as my limited human ones. This way of being, these wild words, well it was all a revelation to me, the likes of which I hadn't had, not before and certainly never since.

"Creation is holy, wild nature is divine and you be part of it all, Treeface, *your* wild nature is divine! There ain't no need for divisions and hate, for separation from what we all are! Can you walk with it, boy? Can you live up to your name and your nature? Can you wear your scars with pride and know they are beautiful? Can you carry the burden of your blessing to the humans who need to remember?"

Tatty's spirit glowed as he spoke with such passion, a bright flame flickering briefly in the growing darkness. I had been away from 'normal' humanity almost twenty four hours now and I didn't care! I revelled in these people's presence, luxuriated in their energies as one would in a hot, deep bath. We all shared a companionable silence as I let their words sink into me, like the most beneficial balm I could have been anointed with. The woman laid a pale hand on Tatty's ragged coat as I lay and breathed in the fragrant wood smoke and their gentle, powerful vibrations. She, this almost regal traveller woman, seemed even taller than before and a feeling of great peace and serenity emanated from her still frame. I knew that she had turned to me even though my eyes were unable to perceive her adequately.

"He walks in peace, this boy, even though they make war on him. But now he needs to lift his head and not shirk. Now he needs to feel his roots strengthening him, gaining fresh purchase on the shallow earth of the human realm. He has to dig himself in and see it through, not give in and uproot his glorious soul. The marks will never leave his body until his spirit has fled, they are indelible lines from the *wild green beyond* and are like the clues on a treasure map. Follow them, Treeface, find the treasure at the heart of life! There is work for you in the world, boy, the Mother needs you and has called you back so strongly and with such love that she has laid her hand upon you and given you her blessing. You are her lover, the Green Man, bringer of the Greening to a harsh human age that appears not to care.

All things are given, all things just ARE, being neither positive nor negative in essence but potentially both. So it is with fire and water, both may kill or bring pleasure, and so it is with your scars."

I nodded slowly, knowing that the boy she spoke of with such love was me, *really me*. I felt in awe of this woman, even though I could only feel her presence next to me. She was firm and fair, this green lady, and she addressed me not with the customary pity of females who saw me, friends of Mother's who felt they should offer me some advice or sympathy. No, this one spoke with no sentimentality, only clarity. I could close my own swollen eyes with their gritty lids and know that her eyes were grey and her gaze steady, her flaxen hair threaded with both white-gold and silver threads.

"You must chose how the tree-lines will be used," this handsome woman continued, her voice lulling me, her words absorbing me. "Only you can make that choice although you have our support, either way. Only you can make the decision to walk with spirit, taking responsibility for the marks on your face that make you stand out. You can use them to attract attention and gain an audience or you can use them to make yourself a victim and hide from the work your soul has come here to do. Only you can see your affliction as a gift to be used. Can you love your life-lines, Treeface, can you love them and will you love them? They are not going to leave you, boy, not now, not ever!"

"I'm glad," I said. And I was, I truly was...at the time.

"You'll heal now, thanks to Ana."

I half opened my eyes as Tatty cocked his head to indicate the beautiful, serene woman beside him. I knew he was proud of her. And who wouldn't be? She was everything good that I could ever imagine, she was strength and hope and purity and she was endless compassion and selfless dedication. Like famine or fertility, plague or abundance she just *was*. Eternally, powerfully, she just *was*.

As are we all if we have the courage to let go of our simple mortal fear.

"Thank you Ana," I said, in my mind, and in my heart I felt her smile.

Behind these two wonderful figures I saw firelight and the flash of fingers moving in the rapidly gathering darkness, a woman knitting. I picked up the ululating sound of gentle voices raised in song, rising with the smoke, the notes of a mandolin pure and true flying like sparks into the twilight. I wanted to say thank you out loud but suddenly everything was becoming very blurred, the earth tilting away from me alarmingly, only to re-settle again, hard and cold as ever.

"What? How...?" I asked, feeling very inarticulate but still woolly headed from my ordeal.

I indicated my face again. The woman, Ana, crouched down by me and took my hand. I had never known anyone with such an ability to hold my attention, to keep me from drifting, a steadying influence like no other. I wished that she were my mother.

"Chemical burning, abrasions, blisters. It is not good, my

beloved, not good at all yet we shall heal it, you and I. No, I won't tell you what I used in my ointment but perhaps there's calendula and comfrey in it, lavender too. Lots of beeswax, too...the bees know how to labour for the good of the All. Loving thoughts are more important than ingredients to me and I put a lot of love into my work. The energies are what works the wonders, the energies are everything. *Our* energies are everything!"

"That's what Ana does, see. We've all got our jobs, here." Tatty was surely puffing out his scrawny chest with pride.

"Not jobs like my Dad would understand..."

I didn't want to insult Jack Tatterkin but my parents way of thinking seemed to infiltrate my thoughts at all times. I liked this wild man intensely, I certainly didn't want to offend him. I tried to pull a face of disapproval towards my Dad's ideology but found it impossible to get my facial muscles to respond.

Tatty only laughed. The sound reminded me of something that needed oiling in my Dad's workshop. Him again! Go away, Dad! Get out of my head like I am out of yours! GO!

"No, we've not jobs that most people can understand at all, young 'un. We here's a dyin' breed. We'll not fight our demise but we'll try and pass our energies on to the likes of you and then, y'see, our way gets passed on in your thoughts and deeds, ''cos you see we ain't the dirty, lazy scum we're painted as."

"Not scum!" I croaked, indignant.

Who could think such things of such generous, witty, poetic people? The same people who sought to torturously obliterate a young lad's facial abnormality I supposed.

Tatty sighed now.

"You'd not believe it, boy, even within our own family here there's talk of leaving to settle, a rejection of our own ideals held so dear for so long. We're the last of the wood-folk in these parts, just tryin' to live out a dream, tryin' to honour tradition. I'll never go into a house, away from the land, it but some of the younger ones..."

He shrugged in the gathering darkness, little more than a silhouette, yet I felt his pain acutely.

"Ironical, like, that some of the young 'uns not born into the travellin' life want to come and play at it when our own want the things they haven't got...stuff that the settled folk own. 'Tis a crazy thing, so!"

"I'd like to be as you are," I said in that awful crackling voice, surprising myself, "I'd like to...not play at it...but really BE it, to get away from...things. I'd LOVE to. Really."

"And that's why you'll have to go back, y'see, sonner," said Tatty, sadly, " 'cos running away from things, from your own path, ain't no good reason to be with us."

Ana had stood up.

"Best we be leaving the young man to sleep now."

"He's got so many questions though, lady, and where's he going to get his answers to when we're gone, eh?"

"In the morning, maybe," soothed Ana. "And if not then, well, the answers are within the lad. He knows that, we all know what it is that we need to know, 'tis the small, still voice inside that speaks true and all. What he needs to do is come out and sit by a tree, if the tree will have him so, and he'll *re-member* and *know*..."

The way she said it was like a charm, as if when she spoke she implanted a kernel of wisdom within my dark soul that would sprout and grow when the season came for it to do so.

I believed that what Tatty and Meggy said was right and real, but I really believed in Ana.

"I need to know!"

My poor voice sounded so rusty! But they couldn't go and leave me alone without a bit of help, could they? I needed to have some signposts for the hard road that lay ahead of me.

I sensed Tatty and Ana taking in my thoughts and feelings. Please, I sent them my plea with all my heart and soul. PLEASE!

"Meggy there'd be a good 'un to give him clues as to what it is he should be doin', that's if he wants to know, 'cos sometimes it takes someone who ain't so close to the whole thing to give an insight. Meg's a *seer*, lad, no doubt you've noticed."

Tatty spoke directly to me and I tried to let him know I understood but movement was increasingly hard to co-ordinate again. I sent him my grateful thoughts instead and I know that he acknowledged them.

"She can guide you with some vision and then, sure enough, you can find out the rest for yourself."

Tatty knew how lonely I was, I knew, and he just wanted me to get as much help as I could before they and I parted ways. I felt warm inside at his generosity. I knew Ana was hugely benevolent too, but her way was less personal and passionate, more objective and calmly compassionate, like a good mother.

"I'll say good evening, Treeface" she whispered and, touching Tatty lightly on the arm, left us to ourselves again.

Tatty gave another deep sigh. I could just about see him but he felt very close, very near to me.

"I doubt if this is your way, our travellin' way, elsewise you'd have been born with us, not somewhere else. We's all got our things to learn, our person-paths to find, and you've got things to do that you'll never do in this life if you run away for good and all now. You'll not believe me, I know, I know..."

He felt my despair as it rose up like a wave again. Would these wonderful wood-folk abandon me back to a life of loneliness and hurting too? I blinked back tears behind my swollen half-closed eyes.

"I can't help but think there's other things you'll have to do in this life of you'rn Treeface. If I'm wrong then your welcome to claim hearth-rite here with us one of these fine days, when you've been through school and all. 'Til then, well, trust that there's a reason for you bein' where you are and....well, Ana seems to think you've got work to do elsewhere and I trust that. It'd do you well to trust it too."

"You's not fillin' his head with all that are you?"

Meggy kicked at Tatty's behind gently. She was wrapped in a plaid shawl and her springy hair stood up around her face, a tangle of russet ringlets. I could see her in the darkness, a luminous creature, and her soul-light brought hope afresh to my own sagging spirit. Where Tatty and Ana had faded just a little along with the daylight, and with my failing sight, she stood out in sharp relief like a radiant being made from, and clothed in, the sun. Ah, Meggy!

"Let him do as he pleases, stay or go as he wants. I'd not want to go back to a horrible school, to *that*!" She gestured at my face. "Why should he want to go back to parents who don't know what's really valuable in their lives, to loneliness and cruelty? No, let him stay wi' us if that's what he wants. Isn't that right, lover?"

Meg must have only been a year or so my senior but to me she seemed wise beyond measure. I think that I fell in love with her, or with the idea of her, there and then.

It was Tatty's turn to hunker back down next to me. Meg was not as flexible as he was and looked almost comical trying to maintain her balance in a crouched position. Jack drew on another of his thin cigarettes and I smelled the sweetness of aromatic tobacco on the air.

"Hard roads bring strength, strength and compassion, the decidin' of how not to be, they make great teachers, and the best teachin's come regardless of schools and rules and such. This young 'un has chosen, yes girl, he *chose,* to be born there with those parents, to go through that to make himself strong and kind and wise in his own way. That's between him and his soul and if he opts out of that contract he made with his soul now then he'll not get back on the right path for him. Ana knows he has a role in the world...his own unique, special work to do on the Earth-walk. Ours is here, we *knows* that. His is...wherever he has to be to do the best job of it. Bein' alive's a job of work, 'tis the bit between the lives when we get our truest pleasure, but there ain't no good reason that we can't enjoy the work we have here. That's how we know's if we're doin' the right thing by our spirit, and all, if we love what we do and do what we love in the world.

We all know's about what dwells inside our humanly bodies, mine and his and yours, and it t'aint human, that's for sure and certain, so. 'Tis green and alien to them, all starry and bright as it is, and it *survives*! It is strong, STRONG! And he has it, the little tree-faced fella, and we both have it, Meggy. So, like the pointed ears that you have under that great squall of your of hair, like my own long taperin' fingers and like Ana's slanted eyes, like Rain's fine, pale gossamer hair and Irina's strange webbed toes...Treeface here's got the sign on him of what's within. He's kin to us, a Faery-soul. He's the strength of the Fey within him, he'll manage, same as we do when they taunt and move us on, makin' us beg..."

"But I'll not see him go back there to that Steven's boy and the beatings and..."

"Meggy darlin', sweet and precious girlie, 'tis for him to decide, not you, not us! All we must do is give him the time to decide his path, in peace. Now, you can give him a word of prophesy to give him hope or go stir the cunny-rabbit in yon pot for me and ask Ana if she can spare us some more of her salve for his face. And a fresh draught of that brew wouldn't go amiss either, he needs to keep his strength up for decisions to be made."

"I'll stay and speak my piece."

Meggy, that gorgeously plump and gloriously gamine young woman, had agreed to give me some signs for the way ahead and my soul rejoiced at hearing those six words. I saw her clearly in my soul-vision. Our link was so tenacious, so precious!

Meggy sat down heavily, her plaid blanket beneath her and around her, and screwed up her bright cornflower blue eyes tightly as she spoke words of fore-telling. I became aware that I was holding my breath.

"I'll say this to you, Rory Reynolds, *you are Treeface*."

I shivered, this time with a deep thrill at her certainty.

"You need to bear witness for the Earth and all your kin, tell stories, be the Fool. Follow the way of the wildest words, be lyrical, find our soul-poetry and tell it, tell it to those who most need to know. No preaching to the converted for you, instead intrepid footsteps, dancing feet, speaking our truth to the four winds. Let words be your peaceful weapon and your canniest tool, talk to the trees then speak to the people. Fashion words like daisy chains to connect them again, reintroduce them to the land! No harm will come to you this time if you hold true to your bright sword, sharpened by wit and whimsy, and take up the challenge. You can do it, brother, tree-lover!

I see you in another market square...no death for you this time, only joy and laughter. There's clapping for you and your fiddle. Sylvanius, the fiddle-friend, he tells you what to play and Kefli...he's your mentor...he gives you the stories to sing-song. You're the minstrel and the wild card, full of fool's-fire and brimming with the goodest of good hearts, twice married...once in love. The work is your life, you'll run many times but never lose your voice. The words are your way and the music is their means of getting birthed. And one day, lover, you'll be on the road, just like us, but not yet! So keep the faith and so may it be, Treeface, kind man, spirit of the trees in the form of a lovely leaping fool. Be it so!

BE IT!

So!"

I had already closed my eyes again and begun to drift, despite Meggy's intoxicating presence. Dreams and thoughts and ideas all swirled in the mist of myself. Wood-smoke...the sweetest smell along with the damp earth, wet leaves...

I opened my eyes as far as they would go.

"But how did you know their names, Meggy how did you know?"

My voice had been so quiet that they did not hear me for they were, once again, a circle of thirteen people around a campfire, silhouettes moving against the embers of a scarlet and vermillion sunset, surrounded by the silent oak, ash and thorn. Birdsong was dwindling into the last few calls before nightfall but a robin still trilled as one tear escaped and left a trail in the greasy salve on my burning skin. Meggy had gone back to her kin, joining the circle, and I was alone. The tears did not even speak of a fraction of the terrible pain in my heart, of my yearning, deep and wide, for my own kind. And I saw, beyond the long purple shadows, the forms of my kin, slender and willowy, bending and tending and loving with infinite patience and skill. And inside me a little human boy wept and I knew that he had been lost forever and I mourned his passing. I knew that only Treeface remained to face the loneliness of his own path in a changing world. If he could cope. Oh, if he could...

Later, just as beautiful as birdsong, I heard a flute and a violin, the notes intertwining then soaring upwards in a rippling, shimmering spiral. To me it was the most exquisite thing I had ever heard and it eased the loneliness, uniting me with the players and with the stars that wheeled above me. And, as I slept, the sweet music entered my dreaming, filling it not with bitterness and anxiety but with warmth and joy. As my poor body twitched in its slumbers I dreamed that there was a man of bark lying close to me, his wooden knees brushing my own, one skinny twigling hand covering mine, his great glowing eyes open and on me, filled with care. '*Never be alone again, no, not everly, neverly no!*' I heard him whisper, like the comforting shhh-shhh of leaves in a breeze, with the tenderness of a caress between a mother and her baby. And this man of wood told me all the old tales of the primal forests of long ago and I dreamed of trees. Just trees.

I knew, even in my sleep, that my soul had been awoken to its purpose and even in my awesome soul-pain I must go back to their world. Just as I knew why the tawny owl called to the night I knew why this must be for me, also. And when I finally awoke fully, whenever that may have been, to shafts of palest sunlight illuminating a clearing devoid of human life, I knew also that I would not see them again, at least not in this life. All that remained was a circle of flattened earth and the smell of wood-smoke. And a bright shard of loss that pierced my brimming heart, gladdening it even in its suffering.

Had I dreamed my saviours, conjured up my dearest, most motley assortment of friends? Did I imagine them to ease my grief and terrible loneliness? Were they just fragments of a fantasy created by a pain-crazed lad in a state of deep trauma? Whatever, my face had been cleaned and tended to. Did ghosts and fantasies and dying embers heal? If I had spent my last thirty six hours alone and they had been nought but drifting ashes of dreams in the twilight then it was ghosts that had washed me, visions who had wrapped me in the itchy woollen jumper I wore and delirious ravings that had made my face slick with salve.

And the stories stored at the heart of me...no, I could not believe them to be only the ravings of a sick boy.

They were setting fire to a cornfield as I made my way back, limping mile upon mile down fragrant smoky lanes with a face that burned like the stubble fields. But I was not alone. A small man made of dark, twisted bark, skewed and tumbling, full of wit and pitted with his own network of deep grooves and knots, was at my side, ever out of view of those who did not yet know. And what did I know, then? Not everything but one thing for sure...

To be spiritual is to be kind.

Compassion and care are *holy*.

And I knew this too, that to be more than my facial scars I had to look beyond myself. I had a purpose, all I had to ask was '*how do I be of service to you*?' just like a tall woman called Ana had, or a wild man called Jack Tatterkin, or a fiery minx called Meggy. Imaginary or no, these beings were teachers and I would honour them. Yes, I would! I had been shown a way of being that was both natural and free and I had gifts to be given equally freely to others. I wanted to be like them, even if they had no place in the 'real' world, no existence outside of my own head. They were loving and giving, not bitter and lonely. Ok, so I was different to other lads my age, but I was never as isolated and abandoned as I had previously thought because somewhere, beyond space and time maybe, I had true kin. The boys could scrub and scour and insult me but they couldn't remove my truest nature, a nature which connected me by a hidden, tangled root system to marvellous people, all quietly living a life that was good and real...and true.

(*Somewhere, somewhen!*)

All I had to do was look beyond what held me back and offer myself, as they had, unselfishly, as a channel for whatever energy worked through that body of mine. That wild individual energy blending with universal energy, forging gifts to be shared. Even when they were hurting me, as I knew they still would, I could still be me on the inside, that singularly magical creation, a unique and special spirit. That was my ultimate joy and the only way to defeat their cruel, shallow, human way of being. They could not eradicate me and my way, they could never erase what I held dear. It was deep in my eyes, too deep to ever dig out, and it was written all over my face.

There was a place within me that would be forever filled with firelight as opposed to cruel flames, hope instead of fear, and a face which would bear the mark of the trees just as surely as within my soul I had a heart that beat in time to the rhythm of the seasons, the thrum of the Earth. I had been given the tools of transformation, had been touched by the hand of a true god-made-flesh, and so I was made new, made true again. True to my soul so that even when those favoured handsome boys evaded punishment at school and so were emboldened to carry on with their tormenting I held fast. True to it even when my parents would send me, their disturbed, errant boy, away from dear Lydia to a far worse school, a place where hard-handed, deeply twisted Christian Brothers held all the powers of the God they preached and a double helping of the Devil's own cold cruelty. Yes, true to it no matter how much callous indifference or hateful vengeance was meted out to me like the unappetising fare served up at supper in my supposedly well-funded, expensive boarding school. However I was beaten or ignored, by my family and by my enemies alike, I would hang on to simple, transformative truth.

Wouldn't I?

WOULDN'T I?

No, I would not.

For all my *knowing* on that fateful day I was still a coward, am still a coward. For all my brave, bold words their subsequent threats and the pain they continued to cause me still made me hide. No matter what I know to be truth, I still have the fear!

I am a-feared! So help me, I cannot forget the burning. I AM AFRAID!

(*And I'm so terribly sorry if I let you down, Jack Tatterkin, beautiful Ana, lovely bubbly Meggy, I believed all you said to me, trusted all you did for me, yet my fears override my instincts so often. And to you Kefli, my brother, my elemental twin, I apologise for being more afraid than you of falling into human traps time and time again. But most of all to the Earth Mother, whose mark I bear, I hold up my hands and beg forgiveness for I am afraid of the hurting just as much as I long for the Greening. For all my* knowing *I still run from what I know to be my work in progress, this life of mine.*)

Oh yes, a terrible coward all the same, but working on it. I am, like all things, but a work in progress.

"...and the poetry is found in our struggle. Thank you!"

The small woman with the soulful eyes of dark burgundy and the fabulous fall of white-blonde hair concluded her talk. Almost coquettish, she gazed at her feet shod in shabby suede, and waited for her applause.

When it came, that startling sound of clapping, I realised that I was looking at my sister and that my sister had turned to look at me now, hoping for a similar reaction to that which her ecstatic audience bestowed upon her. I saw her poised and posed in tones of sepia against the harsh monochrome setting of the room. She smiled but I knew that she had practiced that smile in front of her chipped, liver-spotted bathroom mirror. This child-woman, this enticing blend of clued-up, straight talking feminist and vulnerable, sensitive poet was my own dear sister and yet she was not mine at all. She now belonged to the row upon row of bookish gentlemen in crumpled linen suits and the earnest women with sensible shoes. She had crossed the line to be with them and I sat behind her, watching her slip away from me, part of me relieved, part of me filled with sorrow, broken and defeated. I had let her down, too.

She amazes me, my sister, the woman I have shared so much with. She is like a stranger now, poised and dignified, and so very lovely even in her wash-faded attire. She looks so confident, so ready to walk into this new life filled with accolades which she so richly deserves. The audience loves her better than I ever could and it longs to heap praise on her the likes of which my humble encouragements could never convey. To her public she appears as she truly is, a star, only I know that Lydia washes her hands over and over after such workshops, for although she feigns intimacy when she talks, she hates their closeness. She fears that somehow the ordinariness of the public will seep through her pores and contaminate her, rendering her lack lustre and bereft of star-dust. She told me that once, lying on the sofa, a threadbare and uncomfortable affair, in her rented flat.

My sister has her neuroses, that's for sure, I wouldn't be there with her if she was truly as composed as they see her, would I? She certainly wouldn't need me if she was as together as the crowd think she is. But how could she be so, what with our parents being the way they were? And how could she be supremely confident after what happened with Shay and little Donal? Worse still how could Lydia hope to be free of all her fears when she had such a freak as me for a brother and had witnessed, albeit second-hand, how folk had treated me, over and over? How could she possibly have come through that one hundred percent unscathed?

Oh for those times when Lydia had been drunk on Elderflower wine and she had sung to the strains of my dear fiddle, Sylvanius!Oh for those simple uncomplicated times of sharing with each other, in perfect love and trust! Now our relationship was being invaded by other women in drooping charity shop clothes, their canvas bags filled with Lydia's slim volumes as they surged eagerly forward for her book signing. Even as they swarm towards her, these strangers, Lydia Fentley turns gladly away from me and from our secure times together. I wonder what my sister has seen on my face as I observe this. Bewilderment? Or worse, that impenetrable blankness she complained of so frequently of late? After all, I had not been fully present for her talk, not really. For even though my body sat there in the same space as her and I appeared to be Rory the protective presence, her talisman, my true self had been absent. I had been visiting the past, walking softly in my memory's dangerously painful places, even as my body sat there as a sentinel for her.

But for how much longer would she really need me, her lighthouse of a brother, whose only role these days was to make sure her jaunty vessel did not hit the rocks? I felt like a husk-man as I sat, redundant, behind my sister the star, removed from people's real joys and sorrows, lost for words but filled to overflowing with feelings from my past. What was I now? A mere Rottweiler of a man, kept leashed to snarl if necessary? Maybe so but certainly I was a just a dusty ornament sitting on her shelf, a keepsake from a simpler time. For Lydia I had become a figure made from some rare, resinous and impenetrable wood, an effigy of a man with a face patterned with twisted branches, a man who was losing his best friend and letting it all slip away from him.

There are bobbles of fluff on Lydia's cardigan at the back. I see them as she bends over to sign another book, her head cocked to one side. She is like a magpie or a jackdaw, collecting and collating other people's bright shiny comments about her work. She stores them up so that later, back at the cottage she now has, she can regurgitate what it is people want and so, by giving them exactly what they need, she will become famous. And, in that fame, be reunited with her boy.

Or is that even on the agenda now?

I watch only her back but I know exactly what her fans will be getting. For the men she is a Jane Morris or Lizzie Siddall, moon-eyed and sighing meaningfully, a magical woman. Most of them will invite her for a post-talk drink in the nearest bar. She will decline but not cite me as the reason. '*Wouldn't that be nice...*' she might say, and trail off, letting them think as they will of why she cannot, will never, join them. And for the women? For them she is the Goddess, urging them onwards, daring them to be like her. For everyone there she is an inspiration; an influence that will help them to leave their restrictive relationships and end their violent marriages, that will encourage them to write and maybe even to fight.

It is her time to shine and I will not hamper her.

Everything has its season and ours has, perhaps, turned cold.

And yes, of course, there is another woman.

She is coming at me through the crowds, this flame-haired vision, knocking a plastic chair aside in her hurry to reach me. Through the milling throng of men in corduroy and prickly hand-knitted sweaters she comes towards me, blazing. A woman on fire and my heart melts and I have no heart but am burning from the inside. We are incandescent for a moment and *she* is still coming for me and I stand up. *She* is the only person in this room looking at me now and for once I do not care that she stares at my face. The clouds in my mind have parted and I almost hear a name. *Her* name!

Our eyes meet, yielding moss on sparkling granite, and we are both suspended, behind the sun, arms flailing. We speak.

"I know you!"

Chapter Three

Of Stars and Scars

When I met him I didn't recognise him as Julien for he didn't look like him physically at all. But then I saw his eyes and that undeniable, indefinable something that shone out from behind their sad and soul-full gaze. Whatever it was that the man emanated, I walked towards him with more purpose than I had ever mustered in my lonely little life. He may not have looked like a romantic ideal as Dominic had, nor did he closely resemble the image of a Fourteenth Century holy man that I held very dear to me, but the feeling of recognition was too strong to deny and I was certain of that one thing.

"I know you!"

It was like a bell being struck down the years, a sound which sent ripples across the fabric of time, yet no one else in that room heard it. No one! Only *him* and I...only ever *him* and I!

Our eyes met, lush moss on glittering granite.

My natural reticence and shyness were forgotten in that instant. I had to reach out and touch what previously had been as insubstantial but tangible as a mist over a reedy river. This man made all my fancies and nebulous feelings real! There was no letting that one chance to substantiate my own memories pass me by for there was only one way to liberate myself from the clinging fog of my fantasies...if that was what they were. I had to connect with him to end the separation, to become more than just someone else's fiction. I had to connect...

(*lest I leave it and once more we shall only meet in death*)

...for if this man was nobody and I was wrong then that was that, Alicia was just a foolish liar and all my visions were the pathetic delusions of a madwoman after all. No more wishful thinking about Fey legacies and lineages. No more yearning, just life; life full of cold hard edges and a bitter little trudge to its restricting conclusion; life as a road of broken stones walked in a solitary fashion. If he were not Julien De St. Pierre born again, come once more into flesh to love me for good and all, then Julien was never more than an imaginary lover, a pathetic and tawdry attempt by me to assuage my crushing isolation. If he were just another man then there was no spiralling, spinning dream-weaving in the world, nor had there ever been, all that there was to hang onto were the concrete facts of existence. Birth, a long and lonely linear track to death. Then nothing, anti-hope.

But I *know* you!

(*Julien! Marguerite...Maman!*)

I met *his* eyes as I spoke the magic words and whirling eddies carried me along, leaves of ruby and amber blowing around me, everything subtly changing as I made it real. I made it so! Me, the nutter, the butt of the joke, me with all my idiosyncrasies and foibles suddenly becoming ME, she who could have faith in herself, her power coming from within rather than from some external source. Everything shifting into other ways of being just because I had stood up amidst the crowd and done the brave thing, off my own back, bringing the magic back to life by the simplest, most personally costly, gesture.

And all because *he* had answered me with my own words.

"I know you!"

The words eclipsed any others I had ever heard. No poetry could ever match the beautiful eternal mystery found in words more profound, perhaps, than those uttered more often, given more credence. Oh yes, to *know* was greater than to love, for in that knowing there was something more than a simple human exchange of emotion but aeons of feeling beyond the body's limitations, a universe of connection, bound in strands of starlight, shimmering with hope. *I know you!* The longing each individual feels for an inexplicable something is not merely the desire to be loved, it is an end to the separation which truly causes the heartache. The knowing is unconditional, unbound by ties of responsibility, heedless of the shape or colour or gender of a body.

I know you and in that *knowing* is an awareness of the divine spark, an experience of that energy being reflected back through another being with a full appreciation of its eternal beauty and our own connection to it. The most wonderful blessing of experiencing divinity made manifest is meeting a kindred in spirit who wears a body you do not yet recognise at all...but oh, how you want to hold that body, regardless of what it looks like, just to try and bury yourself in that holiest of all things, a soul which you resonate with! In itself, it is a small personal act, and yet it reflects the single most affecting moment of creation, the split-apart when the One first experienced Itself coming together with itself, in union. And the bliss, and the rending, of the separation before and after the union, forever...

So it was that day for two spirits housed in human form, for two insignificant not-quite-people walking the Earth who had wanted so much to *know*.

Yes, I know you!

And that knowing is the same between infant son and mother, between sister and beloved brother, between valued mentor and devoted student and between romantic partners, of course. It is the *knowing* of soul-mates, of those who connect at a level far beyond the skin into the realms of the essential essence. Our eternal soul-essence is ever unfolding, ever growing, always seeking to be the most effective expression of itself through learning and so it is that our soul-mates, our spirit-kin, are those with whom we experience most fluently the lessons that searing passion or profound pain teach us. These relationships can be trying, can be ecstatic, and without them, for good or ill, we are mediocre and dull. By them we expand who we be, at the deepest level, beyond flesh and blood. By them we open up fully to the experience of life.

And, for a time, we truly live with our hearts open, and it is glorious. Yet every thing has its season. In all beginnings are endings writ large...

Oh yes, I knew this even as I sat on the bus, travelling to his house, one Saturday in January, just as I had known it as a small child, standing looking at a summer sky in a field of wild grasses. It was a bitter sweet and exquisite feeling inside my deepest self, a pain which tells of the passing of all things, childhood safety, youthful exuberance, the passion of lovers...oh yes, even as I went to him at the start of our affair, I knew that we knew each other but we did not know how long we had together, not this time, not ever. How long would our union, this delicate, dazzling thing, last? How would the dance unfold? We loved, and would always love, while I knew that it would not always be as it was on that day. With that knowledge secure inside me somewhere, smouldering like a fire that would one day rise up and consume me when I least expected it, I tried to do what Alicia had advised me and I sat and savoured the moment. On that bus, at that time, travelling towards my love I was the moment...at least for a short while. I sat and treasured and relished that which was human and that which was timeless and free, the delicious anticipation of a connection, the development of a dream.

Ah yes, I wallowed in that deeply glorious beginning but the knowledge that even it would pass, this love which spanned universes, haunted me even as I struggled to stay in that shimmering *Now*, in that poignant, perfect beginning.

On the bus, driving slowly through our city's crowed streets, meandering towards him in his country home while the shoppers, eager for a bargain in the sales, crowded out the early tourists, I *remembered.* While Japanese couples tried to raise their video cameras without being jostled, I *saw.*

My soul saw his wife, the one who didn't care, who is not soul-kin to us. It marks her as irrelevant and moves on. It saw his sister, the dangerous one, so humble yet so charming, drawing people to her, people who have no sparkly, bright things like her in their lives. Ms. Lydia Fentley with her dainty hands emphasising a point as she reads her evocative prose. On that fateful day of our meeting I had hardly heard her invocations and elucidation's on themes that should have been relevant to me. I had looked at her hands, hands that looked as if they would be good with a needle and thread, and I felt a burning, acid jealousy in my gut, imagining her spending years with him when I had wandered alone in the world, bereft and hopeless.

I was filled with an unreasonable and incandescent rage at her presence in our world because I had seen him! I had seen him and the sight was intoxicating like moonlight on poteen, as delicate as the dusting of pollen on a butterflies torn wings, as strong as my hunger for the green shade of a gnarled oak in high summer. All these things he had given to me, like a honeyed benediction, as I laid my eyes upon him. As I thought of him now the waves of adoration that rolled over me, threatening to hold me under in deep waters, leaving me gasping and shaken, washing away my momentary irrational jealous hatred of Lydia. It was as if one simple glance could free me from all unhappiness as no words ever could. I had seen him and all ties placed upon me by my status, my looks, my class, my strange nature, fell into the dark well of yesterday and hit the bottom with a barely audible splash.

I had shivered as I struggled to hear the clever intonations of Lydia, his sister not his lover, and I knew they were as incisive as scissors on paper, sharper that scissors honed by stone, yet they were made as ashes by my inner fire and smothered in the dark molasses of my desire. I had no fear for I knew that my souls-longing could overwhelm the most heavenly, most intelligent, most eloquent of women...

...and I loved him then, just like that.

I saw him and in seeing my eyes took in an old man, almost. With a salt and paper moustache that need a trim he stood awkwardly, a lean gypsy Jesus with his neckerchief pulled just so and his hair brushing a worn old coat collar. I had a worn collar on my velvet coat too; we were two ragamuffins destined to be together come hell or high water, two renegade urchins all at sea. His floppy hat could not disguise his eyes which glittered and glinted like sunlight on deep water and the fine tracery of lines on his face was like filigree, as intricate and meaningful as the lines seen on a palm by a Romany Teller. I knew then why the people of my own age, people that I could never really relate to, took drugs as I could have chased the high of him seeing me, and of me seeing him, for the first time in this life, forever. Yes, I would have been a slave to that feeling, a sensation of being alive like no other while my veins hummed and my blood sang and my heart...

...oh god! I was melting and reforming each and every second as I walked towards him, just melting and reforming. But the feeling went beyond the physical for it was my soul which urged me on as I pushed chairs and, for all I know, people, out of my way. Couldn't they see I was drowning, had been drowning all my life, and my life raft was there, finally, in front of me? I would not sink before I reached him! Alicia had prepared me well for this moment and I was no longer at the mercy of *the voices*. I could pass through a crowd without picking up each and every spirit-voice, full volume. And besides, their voices were only a distant murmur compared to the timeless soul-song that sang between us in the air.

I fell forwards and righted myself. I tripped and pushed my way through orange plastic chairs, shoving aside discarded coats, moving in a strange slow motion towards a man who still sat, smiling slightly to himself. I shook the soul-sleep from my cold bones and awoke my heart which had lain slumbering in my chest and Lian Smythe, body and soul, lurched towards Rory Reynolds.

The man with the tree-face.

"I know you!"

There had been a savage beating in my chest, a resonant hum in my ears and we seemed to speak in a strange code, babbling in ancient tongues of summer evenings lost. To an outsider, our speech may have seemed nothing but glossolalia, meaningless syllables and sounds repeated over and over in an attempt to make sense of each other whilst deeper, unseen things were at work between us. We stood in a crowded room with only a veil of silk between us, a shower of silver sand in our eyes. We talked, Lydia's brother and I, and there was a blaze of a Romany fire nearby, created in some other dimension by our longing, tangible in its warmth, its wild heat. He began to eat me as we stood there, revealing the arcane arrangement of the pips within the sweet clean flesh of my inner self, the fruit first seen by him, first tasted.

He told me Lydia was his sister and the sigh of relief I gave was audible and so he smiled, a lopsided grin of pure joy. We laughed then, he and I, and he gave me a slip of paper which I clutched to my breast as if it were the only sacred, precious thing in the world.

Later I looked at the paper, for when he was with me my eyes would not leave his face. It was lilac and it had his name printed on it, an address. How had he known to have that paper ready for me?

(*Witches, cariad, this is between witches!*)

I tried to see us, Rory Reynolds and Lian, from an outsider's viewpoint. How was it we two had come to have that disjointed, ecstatic conversation? We were just two mis-matched strangers to all intents and purposes, two halves of a whole with our own fuzzy logic, meeting in the real world whilst we had always loved in some other place. We must have looked so awkward, staring and shuffling around each other when all the time we longed to plunge into each other at the deepest possible point. Or maybe, just maybe, we gleamed, partly cloaked in the Otherworldly mist that shrouded our union, becoming to the casual observer nothing more than rippling, shimmering air, something that may have been a heat haze or a trick of the light. We tried to work out where we may have met but we knew we never had, in this life.

He had said to me "where were you in Thirteen Twenty Six?" and I realised how bizarre that would sound to any other person. Even I, who had retained a little of my previous cynicism, regardless of Alicia's patient training, found it almost laughable. Yet Rory was serious and I opened my mouth to tell the truth, as I saw it, felt it, but

I never had chance to answer him. He already knew for his eyes filled with easy tears.

I did not answer him because then she had been there beside us. We had spent so long in our funny dreamy state that Lydia had finished signing books and shaking hands and soaking up praise. I looked down at her smooth and shining halo of hair, she was a good few inches smaller than me yet I knew her to be a strong woman, stronger than me by far in a worldly sense. How could a sister look so unlike a brother? Yet she too seemed familiar to me. Different, yet familiar. And she too looked at me with curiosity as if trying to place me. I was still fresh and green from my own cocoon where I had lived so long in torment and isolation and didn't know what to do next and so she took my hand in her equally small and pale one and shook it politely. Did the images come then? Did the spirit-voices speak as she touched me? Oh yes, for sure, but they were not as overwhelming as they had been before Alicia had taken me under her wing. I did not wish to intrude too far into Lydia's mind, the terrible jealousy would well up in me at the slightest glimpse of an enduring love between those two, so I pulled away and shut myself down to her. It must have looked quite rude.

"Have we met before?"

Lydia had enquired politely, confused. Had she felt something from me too? Yet I couldn't know her, could I? There had only been three stakes that day in Avignon and none of them were hers.

"No, you don't know me. I'm Lian."

She expected me to say more like who was I and what did I do but I had no explanations for myself. None at all.

"Well done...for the show, I mean. Well, not the show, the talk....thing...you just did. It was very good. Enlightening."

Lydia smiled, oblivious of my blithering. She was taking Rory's arm, keen to share her success with her brother. I saw her taking him from me into a world of pristine punctuation and restrictive margins. I could hardly string a coherent sentence together and she was taking him back, leaving me alone again, and I couldn't even cry out. He was smiling at me and then at her. I could have wept but I didn't. I could smell wood-smoke and whiskey. I had to hang on but I was slipping away, so I gripped the nearest orange vinyl chair and tried to smile back as they made to move away from me. Suddenly I was just Freaky Smythe again, the last lone straggler after the workshop, just a sad and lonely woman staring balefully after them. Elegant, nimble, diminutive Lydia was taking my man, my soul-love, and all I could do was gape. I felt silly in my crushed velvet dress, how I hated dresses! But Alicia had told me to wear red so that he would recognise me and I had found the dress in a charity shop at short notice, heeding her advice. Our spirits had codes, you see, he would wear blue and I red, yet I felt all tangled up in that flashy dress, momentarily threatened beyond all reason by Lydia Fentley and her uncluttered, natural look.

I was horribly conscious of my ruby red lipstick as my grin became a rictus of pain at his departure. Lydia's unadorned face had made me feel so grubby somehow, tacky and second rate. My lipstick, bought for the occasion, was called 'Excalibur'. How foolish! Clammy, clinging material wrapped around my legs and what had once seemed soft and flowing now felt like another weapon to trip me up and wrap me in my own clumsy ineptitude. Whereas moments before I had been all satin and bubbles, gliding, I was suddenly laden with over ripe fruit, bursting stickily. I felt so shabby next to Lydia and I thought that no matter what Rory would say to me, in some supposed future together, I would always feel as if she cast a shadow that engulfed me, making me dimmer, less effective and certainly uglier.

I thought of her clever words, of her golden image, aware of a piece of lilac paper in my sweaty hand. I slipped it into my patchwork bag.

"I'll see you soon eh, Lian? Go well!"

He turned and called back to me as I stood, bereft. He had such a deep voice, musical. A *manly* voice.

I saw their backs finally disappearing, his shabby dark blue coat, the floppy cap pulled down low, her pinkish cardigan with the incongruous bobbles of fluff. She held herself straight but was dragging him towards her by the arm and his head was bent in her direction, probably just excited to share the day's events with him...to talk it through, brother and sister.

They had gone.

My pirate had left his treasure behind. I sat down heavily in one of those horrible chairs and stared blankly. There was a piece of paper in my bag and that was all. That was *all*! People came in and began stacking the chairs and I knew that I had a train to catch because for some reason I was in London and I had to get back; back to my involuntarily adopted city, back to an empty flat high up on a hill, and not back with a doting brother for I was nobody's sister. How was I to know, in my own grief and disappointment, that the piece of paper had Bath written on it too, for it was also part of the address of Rory Reynolds? Would it have mattered to me then if I had known? After all, if he was with Lydia, or with anyone, and not with me then he may as well have been in Africa than southern England!

Pain had ripped through me. I picked up a flyer, a forgotten memento of the audience with Lydia Fentley and slipped that into my bag too. After all, she was a link to him. If I could get past the anguish, the raw, elemental rage that I felt when I saw her photograph on the leaflet then I could reach him through her. Somehow...

But it hadn't been necessary.

The bus was going down Walcott Street now as I recollected. I saw the alternative record shops, the second hand stores that had rails of funky, silly Nineteen Seventies fashions outside yet I couldn't stay in the present moment, no matter how precious it was. I smiled because I should have been there with those young people, people like Dominic and Gianni, having a beer in the 'Hat and Feather' pub and scouring the CD racks for a bargain. Yet instead I was travelling to see a man many years my senior, or so it seemed, and his wife...his *wife!* Who was she, anyway? And I was going because I had gotten a letter from him. Rory Reynolds had written to me, had sought me out! Even if it was via the Centre in the city where I still went, more as a helper now than a 'client', I convinced myself.

Apparently I had told him that I worked there (only a half-truth, surely?) when we had been trying to gauge if we had met before in the 'real world'. He hadn't mentioned a city where he lived so I presumed it to have been London as we were in London that day. He told me that he played the fiddle professionally and told stories too...

(*Oh Treeface, was that the only half-truth?*)

...and it had seemed wild and extraordinary to me that a writer and musician should make a living doing what they loved. How I had envied him and his literary sister! I presumed them both to be wealthy and had consequently imagined them living in bohemian Camden, Crouch End or possibly Hampstead, country-quaint but city sussed. I hadn't dreamed of them living in the same city as me because I hadn't looked at the piece of paper with that precious contact address on it since the meeting. That paper had become like a talisman to me, a sacrosanct thing to be kept pure and whole in its magic, and I hadn't dared to so much as glance at it lest my profane eyes had somehow made the writing fade or change. I hadn't known how I was to contact him if I couldn't face unfolding that precious piece of paper and I had never, not in my wildest fantasy, expected him to seek me out! I couldn't have done, it would have been too painful if he hadn't, you see. How could I have known they both lived in that fair city that somehow I had arrived in myself? Fate! I could have hugged Dad, for the first time, for ditching me there. But even as I silently thanked my dear Papa I cursed my own insecurity for if I had been brave enough to reveal the words on that precious fold of paper sooner I could have saved myself a lot of heartache and many sleepless nights.

Once I had been back in my flat after the meeting at Lydia's talk the whole affair had all seemed pointless and patently ridiculous, a simple event that I had no doubt blown up out of all proportion. I had endured a horribly lonely journey back to my city, never for a moment considering they would be on my train too, heading west towards beautiful Bath! What would I have done if I had known? Gone to find them in their carriage, asked to join them? Yet he had known I lived there and he hadn't invited me to share the journey home! That was why I felt even more lost and confused. Me and some stranger, past-life lovers? Reunited by chance on the say-so of some mad old lady who advised me...me the sad and ludicrous nut-case?

But I had been through that kind of thinking before, hadn't I, and it had gotten me nowhere but into a deep depression. I intended to talk it through with Alicia sensibly but with an openness of spirit, in case there was something in it, some truth, perhaps? But before I could go and see her the note arrived at the Centre, addressed only to '*Lian with the red hair, c/o the Co-ordinator*'.

Some psychic I was! In fact, when I had really needed help, be it reassurance about Robert or confirmation that I wasn't losing my mind over a man with a tree's empty boughs birth-marked on his face, then none was forthcoming! I had no intuition, let alone idea, that such a thing would happen...that it would be he who sought me out there. My own apprehension and fear stopped my intuition dead and also...well, it wasn't really good to get psychic guidance for yourself, was it? Alicia had told me so, had said that our own personal needs and worries obscured the truth when the matter in hand was too close to us, had explained that getting psychic guidance for one's own self was not beneficial because it left us open to illusions and delusions. Far easier, she believed, to work in service for others, giving them the guidance which was not so overlaid with our own human beliefs and fears...one step removed from us, as it were, was more objective.

Anyway, psychic skills were for service to the All, Alicia maintained, not for an individual to dwell on, concerned only with their own immediate future and well-being.

It had been Alicia's, not my, psychic guidance that had told me to go to an obscure venue in London's West End one Saturday in January, to listen to a women talk about 'waking the witch within'. It was she that had instructed me that I would meet him there, that mysterious he that had haunted me for so long, and to wear red so that *he* would know me beyond all shadow of a doubt. Yes she had told me to look out for....

(*Oh Alicia, how could I ever have thought you mad!*)

The man, Julien...Rory...

(*Treeface!*)

...wearing blue.

And now I was going to his house! The man who had disturbed my dreams, haunted my somnambulist's life, had invited me to his very real home! I looked out of the bus window and smiled. I smiled at all the young people with their bright jumpers and big boots, their breath coming out in a dragon's plume of white in the chill of a bright crisp day as they went about the business of living and loving and laughing. I would have felt so excluded from their purposeful lives just before Christmas when my own life had seemed so pointless. Now I held no such resentment as the bus moved on, I let their bold little figures blur and fade. I was leaving them behind forever, I felt. I was going somewhere myself for the first time. Somewhere real to me.

I didn't want to be too early for our day together, not too pedantic or too lackadaisical by being late. What would he want of me, this man I knew through death and desire, but whose favourite food did not know, nor his taste in music? The bus was up to the traffic lights and I could see the fields in a frosty landscape. I cherished the feel of everything at that moment, knowing now that I had someone to I cherished the feel of everything at that moment, knowing now that I had someone to go to and thoughts of my own and was no longer the confused, terrified girl I had been mere months before, boarding a bus to nowhere.

Thank you Alicia, thank you a million times over, you sweet witchy woman, for not letting me die!

I hugged myself, feeling toasty warm on the inside, loving the wonderful crispness of a new day unfurling, the sharp tang of adventure on the tip my tongue.

And what if this meeting came to naught?

That would mean the negation of all my dreams, my visions, of Alicia being a sound psychic guide. Everything I was would become a sham and a waste of time. It didn't bear thinking about, the stultifying prospect of life without the truth of this magic was unbearable...

...and I would not countenance it! To remove myself from such thoughts I took off my woollen gloves. My hands smelled of white chocolate, a cheap and comforting passion of mine, and I let it distract me from the unthinkable.

And when I stepped off the bus it made me wish, in what wouldn't be the first or last time, that I was Lydia Fentley and that I could find words to describe what I saw with fresh insight. I wanted to be able to fold up that moment as she could compress and wrap up her thoughts into enticing packages, stating '*this is how it is*' in words that would inspire others. All I had was a tune to hum to myself which spoke of the beauty, the weak sun and the wet grass; of a moment in time. My step had a bounce hitherto un-noticed and I repeated part of Alicia's guidance to myself '*be open to all possibilities yet remain, cariad, in the* the Now *as best you can. Do not try, flow with it, girl, go with it! It is soul-destiny and it belongs to the Faerytide, it is not of mortal ken.*'

Such beauty in her words! I clung to them even as two worlds began to collide, our union becoming a glorious inevitability. I could feel my part in the dance and how many eventualities shifted as I stepped closer.

His house was at the end of a terrace, up a steep incline, a red-bricked affair with a small, and surprisingly dead, garden filled with wood and clutter. If I had that garden I would have it like Alicia's, filled with herbs and native wildflowers, and small trees which bore glorious fruit and delicate blossom. There was at least a hedge for me to hide behind while I gathered myself, trying not to feel too awkward or inferior, trying to calm all the psychic impressions I would receive from Rory...

(*Treeface!*)

...by doing the simple visualisation that Alicia had taught me (*thank the heavens for that woman!*) which would leave me open enough to be sensitive but not so open as to be a conduit for every sensation, impression and spirit in the vicinity.

I closed my eyes and breathed deeply of the freezing air. I felt my feet planted squarely in their soft pointed boots on the pavement outside of his house. I felt my connection to the land and to that moment. I breathed in , letting my stomach, my diaphragm, expand. I held the breath for a count of three. I exhaled and felt my stomach contract as the breath was released. As I continued to do this I maintained the awareness of my roots in the earth, not slipping into a trance as was so easy for me but steadying myself in the world whilst creating a sacred space in which to travel through the day. I saw a going light around my body, pale clear blue edged with gold, and as I breathed I saw this expand around me. It was a blue bubble resembling the protective cloak of the Earth Mother's atmosphere and not a solid wall; a shining etheric light which would, by my own intent, keep out any unwanted or extraneous feelings or intrusive energies. It would protect me but still allow the natural flow of energies between me and my environment to occur.

It was all a matter of will, Alicia had told me. Yes my wise and generous mentor had told me that the energies were there to work with and were as real as the hedge I stood next to. At any time during the day I could strengthen my protective cloaking, even when using the lavatory or sitting still on a bus I could take a breath and see its light shining brightly. It would remain with me until ceased to 'feed' it by my visualising. It would fade gradually if not 'maintained' rather as a rainbow does. I need not constantly be aware of it for it to be there but if I wished it to remain for any great length of time I must keep topping it up. It was easy, really.

It was easy yet it had eluded me all those years, years of torment and intrusion, with *the voices* and all...

I could still hear *the voices*, of course, but as I chose to and in a safe space which kept me from any lasting attachment to them. I need not worry about such things when just visiting Rory, although I knew, what with the tension of meeting his wife...

(*His wife! God how that made me scream inside even though I knew, I really knew, that their marriage was over long before I came on the scene*)

...and my connection to him, that it would not be an easy day, in terms of our energies. Yet it would be a necessary day if I were ever to see him again, in any shape or form. For the old Lian, the one before Alicia's kind administrations, it would have been an overwhelming nightmare with thoughts and images coming in from all angles. For any person who was not a sensitive it would have been a potentially difficult situation. For me, as clued up psychically as I was that day, it was as it was.

Lian Smythe was going with the cosmic flow for the first time ever and, I have to say, it was good.

I walked up his garden path, up *their* path, with a host of adjectives welling up inside me to describe how I felt at that moment. None where particularly original...

(*Elated; apprehensive!*)

...and then there he was at the door, a lop- sided grin hiding under his freshly trimmed moustache, wearing a blue lambs-wool pull-over that was slightly too tight and faded, patched trousers. I saw a man that few others of my age could have called handsome with his twiney root-lined face. He was no granite-jawed hero but then I was no elongated blonde wearing strappy sandals, tripping daintily to meet him. I was looking at his boots rather than his eyes until he said my name and I thrilled at the sound. So sweet that moment as our eyes met, soul to soul, yet so potentially devastating!

There was a pause, like the moment before the bullet left the gun of Kennedy's assassin, a space between the worlds I which possibilities shifted forever. Then the imperceptible movement, a feeling of rightness as things changed for good and all and new patterns emerged. He reached out and took my hand.

"Treeface," I said.

It was like a statement of intent.

"Good to see you, so bloody good it is. Please come on in!"

He squeezed my hand and I felt, despite my impromptu psychic protection, his power and his passion. No protection could ever stop me from feeling as he did.

Did we have to speak as mortals do now, had the loving babbling of our spirits been negated in favour of a more formal conversing?

My eyes adjusted from the bright clear light outside the small house to the scene within, shades of grey and brown, a tortoiseshell cat on a rocking chair, a wood-burning stove in a tiled fireplace. Minor pleasantries were exchanged as I stood there in that subterranean world; old walls cried out for me to touch them and receive their secrets even as a well scrubbed pine table called to me. I knew that I could have laid my Fey hands upon that table's deeply grooved and pitted surface and read like a book. Yet I heard his voice above all others in that shady room. Tea or coffee? Pleasant journey? He flitted about me, plumping up cushions, rubbing at a mark on the back of a chair. I tried not to be overwhelmed by his presence which was singing its song to me from every inch of that cluttered room, so different from my own sparse little flat, so far removed from my Dad's house, a modern, barren affair. Where was his bloody wife? Where?!

It was hard for me to imagine that Lydia was not his wife, such had been the bond between them. How could I bear it if his wife had the same grace and good looks as his sister? Then there would be double the reason for me to feel fear and jealousy, two lovely women to worry about! It was bad enough that he was married at all, let alone that his wife should overshadow me too. Oh why couldn't he be free, like me? Even the spectre of Robert, poor dear Robert, had faded from my shoulders of late. This tree-faced man had replaced everything in me, everything, yet he was married...

I could smell his body as he moved around the kitchen, making me sugary tea. I saw her shoes, *Jane's* shoes, by the door, one heel was worn down and lop-sided. Why couldn't she afford better?

"Jane has gone to town today, she'll be back later for tea," he explained, reading my own mind as I had vowed I would not read his.

If she wasn't here why were we pretending? Had I imagined our connection? Was I too keen? Too stupid? Maybe he just wanted a fling, this older man with his knowing smile and me the flame-haired floozy? I twisted a strand of my scarlet hair and tried to stay calm. What should I say?

There was suddenly too much babble inside my head, I tried to breathe more slowly. I got up and stroked the cat which seemed not to notice. Breathe, damn it!

"Jane doesn't like Wil'o," Treeface said, as he came back to my side holding two chipped mugs. They were blue and white striped, Cornish-ware, so incredibly like the sort of crockery I'd imagined he would have. Or were they her cups?

Oh calm down Lian! Calm yourself!

"How can you not like a cat?" I asked.

He set the steaming mugs down beside the air and I felt his hand, lean and hard, against the side of my face.

"How can people be so cruel?" he responded, his voice so deep and low.

And I saw the square in Avignon and the pale sunlight falling in shafts on the ground, dust-motes dancing in the weak golden glow and I felt his hand mould to the contours my face as the rest of the world crumbled away into fragments of charred black wood. I wanted to cradle his holy face in my hands, his perfect face that was sanctified by sap and soft rain, but instead there was only a bitter wind and the darkness of the world between worlds, where we wandered alone, searching, holding cobwebs of years and ashes of kisses.

"Treeface, hold me!"

I never believed I could ask such a thing!

Or want it, *need* it, so much.

My hands went up to my own face and I nearly over balanced. That brought us back into the moment, to *the Now*. We were just two figures crouched on a hearth-rug next to a sleeping cat in a red-bricked house on the outskirts of Bath. Two figures, perhaps male and female, or perhaps something far simpler than that, perched on the precipice of a possibility. I saw a married man and his soon-to-be lover, I saw Treeface and Lian, I saw Julien and Marguerite and I saw a fiddler and a dancer turned to stone on the Sabbath day. I saw hope fade and I saw hope spring eternal. The cat was purring and I was breathing steadily. Who were we, though? And what were we doing?

"*For I was born on the Faerytide and I believe and I believe...*"

I think that he was singing, this half-man, perhaps to himself or to the All-that-Is. I looked at him, filled with meanings and greenings and with infinite love, and I *saw.*

Later, as we walked through the fallen leaves which had lost most of their glorious colour but were now so much mulch, returning to the soil to feed it, he told me tales, his voice weaving like fragrant smoke into the frigid air. I was whole for a glorious moment, just listening to him made me feel complete and sated. And when we reached the yew trees he stopped and drew me to him and I trembled and he held my gaze.

"Remember this," he said, "and remember it for all time for this is the moment when I tell you that I love you, beyond reason, in this life and all others and let the yew trees bear witness to it."

It sounded like a charm, an incantation, and my old, tormented self balked at his flowery-ness even as my eternal soul dissolved in bliss, moulding itself ever closer to his.

Under the yew trees, the dripping trees, the dryad and the druid stood. He was my flame, my holy man, and we were on fire of our own volition, never to be extinguished.

"They can never take this from you," he traced my cheek with his fingers his voice was sonorous, soporific, and I closed my eyes but he shook me gently and I saw him again.

To see him again, as if for the first time, was a benediction and a gift beyond measure and I revelled in it. Then the grace of seeing my love with my own eyes was abruptly taken from me without warning I saw him as the world would see him.

I felt a little shame.

He was a man with eyes like moss on granite with creases and pouches of skin beneath them denoting weariness, with thinning nut brown hair worn too long, too ragged, with shabby clothes and a greying moustache, with a mahogany coloured scar weaving across his cheek and reaching up to his brow in a tangled mass of twigs and shoots. There were deep grooves running from there corners of his mouth to his nose, showing strain and worry. His clothes were worn and he smelled of musty rooms...

(*Oh Treeface! Julien!*)

...and I knew that by his own considerable psychic power that he was making me take on the burden of how people would react to us, to him and I, seeing if I could cope with the real him as the world perceived him. His own insecurity made him force this vision over my own far sweeter one and I balked at it as I had balked at my own paranoid fearful responses, but he held me there and made me experience it. It was a test I did not want to take but I had to endure.

He whispered to me

"And this is the man you take on, often treated like a leper, spurned and outcast. Now what say you, lady? Do you want him now? Will you take him, body and soul?"

I felt the pain of his life, of our lives, and the fevered longing in me flickered and faltered as I shrank from the responsibility of bonding myself to someone else's problems. I made myself face the truth he offered me but in facing it knew it not for my own truth but for *theirs,* the non-Fey, and with a vast exertion of energy I rejected it and embraced him fully, finally, for I knew his soul and it was beautiful! It sang in a perfect refrain with my own of sorrow beyond bearing and of joy too great to be held inside the hearts in our imperfect, quivering bodies. I heard his voice and it was rich and even, his language and intonation vaguely archaic. Had I heard such words elsewhere they would not have rung true. As it was he wrung them from my very essence and there were impossible cathedral bells in my soul and the sound of larks ascending gladly, eternally.

"I did not tell you last time but I tell you now, lady; this is ours, this sacred bond that defies death, and I love you all there is, always."

I did not know how to speak as he did so I spoke as I could, fashioning my own feelings into something more simple but with no less heartfelt truth.

"I want to paint leaves on your branches, put birds amongst the leaves," I told him, tracing his sweet soul-lines with infinite care.

And then his eyes closed and I saw the tear, winding its way down a face that was wind-beaten, ravaged and lean but branded, a face that made him *other.* I traced the lines and entwined myself in them, imagining leaves of burned umber, baby hazel leaves of impossible softness. Empty branches that could be filled in any number of ways, my own hand as the Creator's hand, painting in colours and textures, bringing the tree to life. It seem unfair that this man's tree had no foliage, no Greening of its own.

"I don't know what to..."

I wished again that I had Lydia's way with words. The fear of sounding crass or clumsy made me fumble for anything that would match his poetic declarations. '*Go with it, child!*' I heard Alicia urge.

But I shouldn't have worried, I had touched him with my heartfelt simplicity.

"Thank you," he bowed his head and I made to lift his chin, I needed to see his fathomless eyes. He flinched a little but let me lift his face gently.

"I have not cried with such sweet sadness in more than quarter of a century," said Treeface, his eyes locked into mine, and I held him, not caring that they world would think us mad, not caring, just for a moment, how Jane (*his wife!*) would feel. And it grew darker and colder and still we clung as the yew trees, silent but present in every atom of their beings, bore witness.

Does it matter to you what he told me? Do you want to know what we ate and drank in the local pub that evening? I expect it matters what Jane thought when she came home though, finding, as she did, her husband absent. How did Jane feel after so many years of joyless marriage, letting herself in to an empty house with the fire gone out and a cat that had not been fed winding itself about her legs? Did it irritate her greatly or make her desperately sad and sorry? And how did *we* feel? Can you imagine the scene, two people in love with each other, each enveloped in that unique glow that comes from the thrill and anticipation of romance, each smelling a little of fragrant pipe smoke, meeting the third party in the eternal triangle....his wife? Did it hurt us and well as hurting her? Oh yes, and I shall tell you a little but not all of what transpired between us three. I leave to you to conjure up the rest, the scent of the night on our clothes and the taint of tears on the cold, wan cheeks of a scarlet Elven woman now made flesh.

Suppose that there is something called a soul within you and that soul has another part to it which belongs to another being who is incarnate in this life. Suppose that this being is your perfect match in this universe, your soul-mate, and just imagine now that you are holding them to you. This precious being possesses within them the soul-essence that makes your own eternal spirit sing, in completion. Imagine the person that would fill that role, satisfy that need in you, and *wish* for them! Wish hard! You smell their skin and it smells like home, you brush your lips across the back of their neck and whisper your needs to them with only your eyes and they respond, looking deep into your spirit. Just hold that thought and the hope that the world would support this union wholeheartedly (regardless of circumstance, of ethnicity, of age or religion...or marriage) if it existed. Picture a world where soul-mates meet and there is rejoicing because of it.

Now see a woman with short, hennaed hair and cold grey-blue eyes pick up a green glass vase to throw it in order to shatter this image, one that she finds displeasing beyond all others. She is his *wife,* damn it! What ill-fate had him marry her before me? We are soul-mates and all should celebrate our union, not stand it its way, protesting of stupid human things!

We did not cling together, Treeface and I, as she examined us and found us guilty. We were not linked by choking bindweed but by energies which entwined in our very essence, gently, with the ultimate tenacity. All was new and all was possible, even in the face of this angry woman. That moment of our lives, his and mine, was frozen and incorruptible, beyond reproaches and vicious threats of vile retribution. We were together, pure and whole, and even as we stood apart in that small, dark living room we were wreathed in the mist of the ancient woodland, kissed by sunsets and caressed by falling leaves of saffron, umber and pure gold. We were in love and the whispering of dry grasses on distant plains and the snap of brittle, frost-bitten branches in hedgerows were our language and our link. No amount of shouting or smashing of glass could touch us for there was only ever one choice for us; in the Otherworlds, the Summerlands...

(*Oh Alefthamne!*)

...our wrists were bound by ivy.

I thought, on that beautiful winter's night, with the shadows throwing Jane's face into an unthreatening abstract of gently shifting shapes, that I held a flaming sword of truth that would cut them apart cleanly.

I was wrong about that.

I felt a tiny flicker of irritation as Treeface left my side to re-stoke and light the wood-burning stove, seeing, as he was bound to do, that Jane was shivering. She was no oil painting, as my father used to say of women who were not overtly glamourous in his eyes. She was no Lydia, that is all I can say for sure, no Lydia with her skin like smooth sugared almonds and her eyes like mocha sprinkled with nut-meg. What a contrast there was between Lydia's pale, pale hair and her deep, dark eyes...she would be even more beautiful in her terrible anger than in her calm repose I supposed. Was Lydia Faery too, a Fey spirit in a lovely human shell? Yes, I knew this to be true. Yet Jane was just a woman, certainly no Fey, with no real distinguishing features. Maybe I thought this because the light that I perceived Treeface in was so bright as to make anyone else seem dull? Yet maybe I saw her this way because I could not bear to have another beautiful rival for his affections. All I know is that I do Jane a disservice for seeing her as bland and unimpressive but at the time I was capable of little else.

She pointed at me and said she wanted me out as she sat down on a wooden chair by the hearth. I fingered the damp hair at the nape of my neck and I knew that all the luminous life-forms that had surfaced in the empty ocean of my life would be swallowed up by her hungry gaze. I had to leave; the mistress of the house was ordering me to go home. Home? Home was Treeface, the skin of his neck against my lips. Everything had changed, everything was change. I could feel the familiar sensation of trance slipping me into non-ordinary reality.

I tried desperately to focus on something normal. There were a pack of cards on the table next to her and she picked one up without looking at it.

"'*Seven of Swords*,'" she said icily, "thief in the night!"

So he had taught Jane to read the cards too had he? The jealousy burned deep in my gut. I thought their relationship had been dead? I thought that she had another man she had loved for years and had finally gone to, as lover. I thought...

I thought that this marriage was already over, that it would fall down as a house of cards would when I appeared and someone would clear it all neatly away for us.

"'*The Tower*'," Treeface said with his back to us both, "inevitable destruction of a house built on sand!"

"She'll not get my house!" Jane pointed at me again with the card.

I felt the bolt of anger from her and I was slipping. I tried to ground myself but it was too late. Trance-vision was upon me, brought on, no doubt, by my desire to escape the stress of the situation, the unbearable pain of their confrontation in the wake of my own wildly flowering passion.

"'*Queen of Wands*'! '*King of Cups*'! He who was the Knight is the real usurper! The black haired man has already tipped the boat over. Who will sink and who will swim? Coins there are, five and six, in the water, confusion! And voices...a voice, trying to be kind...'*Will we do it in the spring? And how shall we tell Rory...I mean, what will he do without me?*'' Another voice now...harder, cold, '*the sad bastard will just have to manage, Janey. I mean, Jesus, you can't mother him forever! I need you now!*'

I could hear my own voice ringing out in the silent stone room but I myself was far away, far removed from the tragedy that was unfolding. My prophetic words sliced up the night and shards of truth fell to the cold paved floor between them.

"What is this *crap*?"

Jane threw the card at my feet disgustedly. I was dimly aware of her lunging at me as if to throw me out of her house but Treeface caught her arm.

"You'll hit me now, eh? Well, go ahead! It's about time you did something to show you're a man instead of a fool!"

She growled at him, trying to shake him off.

I was lost to them, seeing a small boat on a calm sea, me alone in a velvet place. The words that came were not my own. Voices speaking. Who? *What?* I tried to follow their lead but they were leading me on a fine dance. Always callling me, always leading me astray!

"Where have you been today, Jane?"

Treeface cut across my spirit-wanderings, asking in a tone made all the more deadly by its gentleness. He continued to hold his wife firmly, with the same soft but persistent touch. Later she said he had bruised her. Later I was not there to see if it were true.

"What? Oh no, oh *no* Rory, you can't switch the blame to me! Just because your silly little girl there spouts her strange prophesies. Soft in the head, is she? Well, you deserve each other!"

Jane suddenly burst into loud sobs.

"Were you with Pete?"

"Oh what if I was? I mean, does it really matter now? You've never loved me! At least I didn't bring him here like you and your....*witch*!"

"I tell you this, Janey, I will never be called a witch again, nor will I let Lian be called it. Your black haired Peter, 'the Knight', he will support you and doubtless he'll have you support him when he takes yet another day off from plumbing to visit the Bookmakers!"

Jane gasped.

"How *dare* you! Pete loves me and he loves who I am. He's not the equivalent of some mad little tart like this one here! And whatever she is, that's not being a true witch. She's just a...a nobody!"

Jane spluttered, her angry tears long since dried. Even in my place of stars that moved in an unfamiliar sky, swelling and swirling, I could feel her pain and her fear, her howling desolation at her perceived abandonment. Even if she loved another she did not want to lose what we had taken from her. How dare Rory, an ugly strange little man find someone he loved more than her? How *dare* he! Even if she didn't want him he should not, *would* not, reject *her*! After all she had done for him! Looking after him when any other woman wouldn't have given him house room. Protecting him from gossip, shielding him! It wasn't her fault she couldn't love him properly. It *wasn't*! How could he? HOW COULD HE THROW IT ALL BACK IN HER FACE?

It was she, Janey, that was meant to be the one leaving him not the other way round! She had loved him the best she could have under the circumstances. She *had*! And this was all the thanks she got...she who had even managed not to make a fuss when he had been unable to give her the baby she had so wanted. Perhaps it was just as well, it may well have been a stunted deformed little mite anyway, puling and squirming like its father did. Not robust like Pete's children; he had six by his ex-wives, all fine and strong and normal. Yes Peter would give her what she craved. He *would*!

I heard all this as if from a cold and distant star. I could understand Jane's selfish frustration, in a way, but I could not speak to empathise with her for I was lost to them, trapped in the trance, half-hearing the words, half-feeling their loss and their anger. I knew she was trying to break free of his restraining grip to reach me and hurt me. But why? I was no threat, not really, for he was already lost to her and her to him; they had never really found each other at all. Then it was me who lost myself in the darkness, seeing seeds of stars that could be new life. I shrugged off the curses and looked for blessings in the welcoming void of creation. I drank in the possibilities and I saw a star among the many that twinkled just for me... a future child, I wondered?

"LET GO OF ME!"

"She's what I want!"

"LET GO OF ME! I'll throw Little Miss Nobody out of my house be she witch, bitch or as mad as you are!!"

"Aye, she may be all of those things, or none, *but she's what I want*!"

I heard Treeface speak these words, emphatically yet softly, and felt my own burning arrow of grief pierce my heart. Could he not have defended me better, denied my 'nobody' status? I could not defend myself, I was too far gone into trance.

"LET GO OF ME! She'll not get a penny of mine no matter what you say. I know how charming you can be, how conveniently you can play the victim with your poor scarred face. Well let me tell you, *Treeface*, I won't be paying for your hopeless liaison with this little whore when you could have had half of what I owned when I went with Pete. I would have given it to you. I *loved* you..."

I hated to hear their intimacy! Even at a distance it sliced through the trancing and hurt me, plucking cruelly at the fresh, bright feathers of my fledgling love. Ah, their long-term bond...even in that place of quiet reflections in which I floated, unacknowledged, I could feel that it had strength. And, although I resisted now, I could feel all the things it had meant to them. They were wrapped in their own misery, the unspoken grievances of a whole pointless marriage weighing heavily in the air between them, recriminations hovering on tongues waiting to be spat out like so much hemlock. Too busy with their own grievances, they were, to notice I was no longer really there. My body sat down, slumped in front of the fire, but my wandering spirit was elsewhere. Not since the terrible night of Carmen's party had I been so absent from my body. Stars snapped blue and gold and I distracted myself from my own pain with their fiery dancing.

"And what of love? Do you love Pete?"

Treeface asked her, bringing me back a little to that ever unfolding *Now.*

"Do you love *her*?"

The retort was sneering. Was I really of so little consequence here?

"I do. And I would expect that you must love your Peter Latimer if you are going to be with him. So why are we fighting? Why can't we let each other go, with love?"

I could see his face, harrowed and narrow, a careworn tree-face hewn from living wood.

"I'll kill you if you say another word!"

Jane was struggling, managing to lash out with her foot and kick over another wooden chair. Treeface flinched, he hated violence, and in that momentary lapse of attention she got free of him and stood up, gasping. I could not see but I knew that his shoulders hunched against what he thought would come next. He steeled himself for her blow. Instead she picked up a cold mug of tea from the table and threw it at the wall. She swept the Tarot deck off the table and I was showered in cards. I felt the heat of thwarted passion in her and I too shrank from her. She had loved him in her own limited way and I couldn't bear it. I couldn't bear Lydia and I couldn't bear Jane! '*Get away from him!*' my soul screamed.

"'*Ace of Hearts*'! '*Queen of Cups*'!"

The words poured forth from me again, unbidden, as I began to see, against my own hearts-will, pictures of the life Rory and Jane had shared.

"She loved you that day you spent in Cambridge together, looking for velvet clothes. Chiming church bells, cobbled alleyways and a suitcase with someone else's name in it. She held your hand and you walked...."

"God! Did you tell her that? *Did you*?"

Jane sounded shrill, almost out of control.

"I did not." I dimly heard the reply, the deep voice of my lover tinged with awe and wonder.

There was a silence save the ticking of a watch and the settling of logs in the grate.

My words had the sharp clarity of my unhindered psychic vision and I spoke with direct relevance to her. My insights into their life together were mesmerising, temporarily stopping her litany of rage. The room became still. I could now hear the crackling of logs in the wood-burner as they caught. The room was getting warmer and I was returning. My words began to falter but I still spoke truly, incisively, to his wife.

(*Oh damn my vision, curse my* sight, *for making me see and feel the ghosts of their love*!)

"In...July...your mother died....you fed her soup from a spoon and rocked her gently....and you found no solace in your husband, although he tried so hard to support you. Then that October you started seeing Pete around the hospital, when you were on late shift. He was updating the boiler system...Peter...a fit man, muscular and hard...and he gave you comfort didn't he? You watched him as he worked, deftly, decisively, so unlike your Fey, ineffectual husband, and...and it wasn't anyone's fault, just fate...*just fate, is all.* And then Lydia, lovely Lydia, began to write about women's magic and you read her first draft for her didn't you? It was a manuscript of '*Novena*' and it encouraged you to move on, to go with your love for a new man, to believe in your woman-power. And while you read those charming words Rory felt so afraid that somehow the end of a peaceful era was coming...and his fear, his terrible fear...drove you back to Pete. Pete who was solid, not Fey like Rory. Pete who you could feel strong beside, not confused and lonely not like with poor Rory. And Rory, he loved Lydia too much to tell her how frightened he was of the world she wanted to be a part of, a new world full of attention and spotlights, and he loved you Janey, and he didn't want you to slip away...not yet...

Poor Rory.

Poor Janey. 'Tis fate, is all."

I was sitting up straight now and they swam back into my vision, both looking at me with tears brimming in wide eyes. I was almost aware of what I had said. I knew that they were words full of compassion for their plight. I also feared that what I had said would bring them together. I swallowed my own pain and tired to stand, thinking that they would want rid of me now, for the sake of their own reunion. Damn my supposed gift!

"Marguerite! Maman! *Fair one*!"

Now it was Treeface himself that seemed lost in trance. He shook himself.

"The *sight* is strong as ever in you! Lian, little Lian, forgive me!"

"Why should she forgive you when it is me you've hurt, idiot?" Jane was belligerent again.

"I hurt her too once. I know that I have wronged you both."

"Oh, so you've known her a long time then? *Ha*! Well don't you dare accuse me of adultery then! And don't go playing the victim or the damnable martyr now, Rory; I don't think I can stomach it if I have to feel pity for you!"

Jane had broken the mood. They would not be reconciled.

(*Would they?*)

I sighed, exhausted, and stood between them.

"I must leave now."

"If you go, I go with you!"

Treeface looked at me as if noticing me again truly for the first time.

"But what will I do?" Jane began to cry again. "What if Pete doesn't want me after all? I'll be alone! ALONE! And I have kept you safe for so long, just as you wanted me to. How could you do this to me?"

Abruptly she swept a row of small wooden sculptures from shelf behind her. I knew that they were his loving work.

Treeface turned even paler, his root-scars standing out in sharp relief. Jane seemed to enjoy the unpredictability her actions gave to the drama, the total opposite of her husband who hated it. Treeface loved security, stability and seclusion and this woman, who even now was stamping her foot as her reddened eyes bored gimlets into me, she loved tempests. How had they both lived together for so long? I stood foolishly in a heap of bright Tarot cards, raising my hands in supplication. Who was the real victim here? Me? Suddenly I longed to be away from it all, in my own space, with a mug of hot chocolate and a late-night play on the radio. It was draining me beyond measure being there with them both. Jane seemed to slip through a range of characters in quick session, the mad, vengeful, wronged woman...the poor pathetic hurt wife...it was deeply confusing for me and, I imagine, ten times worse for Treeface. I remembered how many emotions and behaviours I myself had go through in Alicia's own kitchen not so many months previously and I felt myself blush. I looked away. Would I be just as bad for him, in the long run?

"I really will go now."

"Do you honestly love her?"

Jane asked her husband (her *ex*-husband, surely?) in a tiny voice. His face had aged in those long, tense minutes and he looked wearier than ever in the flickering half-light. I wished he had looked at her and wielded the sword of truth but he merely nodded, an almost imperceptible gesture.

"You know I do."

"Yes, I know you do, you're not a frivolous man, not the kind to do something lightly. And you...Polly? Or is it Molly?"

"Her name is Lian."

"She looks like a Molly. She's got those mad eyes, dangerous eyes like a deep treacherous sea. Irish eyes. The sort of eyes you've always wanted, I'm sure! You never really wanted me, I suppose. So, do you love him, Lian, you peculiar little thing, will you be his colleen and dance a reel to his fiddle?"

She said my name like a foreign word she was trying out for pronunciation. I was now a factor in the equation, not just a strange shadowy third presence in their room.

"I'm not Irish, not really."

I felt guilty, sullied and tired, all the pleasure of my personal celebration was being rubbed away by the abrasives of their disintegration. All I wanted was to leave, preferably with Treeface. I had a momentary fantasy, that he would whisk me out of there and we could shake off Jane's mad sadness and celebrate our union and she could call up her Pete and love him properly too. I stared at their hearth rug, thinking it was nice, their little house, knowing that I would never see it again.

I also knew, deep down, that no matter how much more intelligent or conventionally lovely she was than me, she could not keep Treeface for she did not have a soul-link to him, as I did. Treeface and I, we had come into the world to join up again, in the flesh, and deal with our unfinished business. Despite appearances or worldly achievements, spirit-connections still mattered most.

Jane threw me a side-long sneering look as if she knew that too but wouldn't let me get away with it that easily. Her physical advantages over me were legion and she could use all she had in her weaponry to maim me, to lessen my appeal to him.

"Ah, you still look like a wee bog-trotting Celtic inbred whore with your funny cock-eyed face!"

Jane's attempt at a thick Irish accent was as insulting as it could have been.

"Don't start abusing her, it isn't her fault, not any of this! It was me that sent her a letter begging to see her, it was ME!"

Treeface was like a weeping willow, and the sight of him would have broken my heart there and then but my foolish heart was too full to be broken.

I made as if to confirm what her husband had said.

"You BASTARD!" Jane roared, not willing to hear me out.

It was more satisfying to curse than to bleed openly in front of me, a stranger. She bent and picked a face-up card from the pile at my feet.

"'*The Lovers*'! Well, how very appropriate! I understand things now, Rory, I know how you've used me to take care of you. Well, I have the power to make or break you now. I've spoken to Lydia about this..."

She paused to observe the horror that she knew would now be on her husband's face.

"...oh yes, *darling* husband, I've spoken to your spooky sister MANY times of late, that surprises you doesn't? DOESN'T IT my stupid bloody husband? *Ha*! We've spoken about *witching* to get what we want, or to get rid of what we don't want, and I know that I can use a symbol, a *fetish*, to work my magic! That's witchcraft, eh, Rory? That's what you're most afraid of, what makes you cry the nights away in fear of some stupid, stupid memory that isn't even real! Well, this is my witchery, this is how I use it and HOW I SEE IT becomes HOW IT IS! So, this is what I think of your desire for permanence with her! I TEAR YOU APART!"

And she tore 'The Lovers' card clean in two.

"You shouldn't! You didn't! You *won't!*"

Treeface stood aghast as I looked on, uncertain of the relevance of Jane's flamboyant gesture but feeling more and more uneasy. I needed to go! An awkward uneasy sensation was filling me, a sense of being out of place, an instinct to get out before I made it worse and all that we had brought to bear between us would be rendered null and void by words and gestures.

"And this is what I say to your union!" Jane yelled at him and flew past him, opening the door of the wood-burning stove and throwing the half of the torn card inside it. The other half she crumpled in her hand and the tears began again.

"You shouldn't have! You know what that means! You know what you just did!"

Treeface looked devastated as if Jane had burned something infinitely treasured.

"What? What does it mean?"

I spoke but my voice was lost in their arguing, his outrage and her bitter weeping.

I had to get out before they corrupted our love totally, before they split apart my delicate sugar spun dream, so carefully fashioned that very afternoon, pulled my love apart like so much thistledown and so many cobwebs. I moved unnoticed towards the big old wooden door.

"She's leaving you, Rory, aren't you going to go with her?"

"I'll call her a cab."

"Christ, he'd make me catch a bus! Rory never could afford luxuries like cabs for his wife! Oh no, Rory's wifey has to pay for him! Maybe I'm well shot of you! HA!"

"Lian is going home in a taxi," Rory stated calmly.

"I can walk, thanks."

I just wanted to get out. To hear no more personal recriminations and sordid accusations. To keep our love sacred, unsullied, cleanly away from this mess.

"Let me phone a taxi for you, please!"

Treeface was looking at me and I saw every line, every crease in his face. Oh my dearest one, my soul-love, why couldn't you have said that my home was with you?

"I'll wait outside for it then," I said. I felt as wooden as one of his little sculptures that now lay in a jumble on the rug.

I looked at Jane. I knew, just as I knew that I would take another breath, that she would be fine, given time. This was the best thing for her if she could just let go of her pride.

"You'll be pregnant by next May," I said, plucking prophesy from the heavy atmosphere, from the possibilities and probable futures densely swirling around all of our heads. I knew it was true. She shivered, I could see the movement even under the winter coat she was still wearing, a sure sign her soul felt it to be true too.

" You'll be a May Queen because you are, and always will be, a very lovely woman. Beside you I feel ridiculous and gauche and I know that it's only your hurting that makes you hateful now. I hope Peter makes you very happy, and the baby, because I think you deserve that, just as we may deserve it, one day.

You have a career where I have none, you have a home which I would never dream of taking from you and you chance of worldly success where I don't. I wish you well."

I did, truly, but I had to step away before she responded. I couldn't bear another tearful reproach, another barbed comment.

"Good night," I said, quietly and then I was outside.

Outside where it was freezing. A clear and razor sharp night, everything, including my feelings, flung into sharp definition, hard diamond white on indigo silk. I stood for a moment outside that door and then walked up their path towards the wooden gate and the steeply sloping road beyond. I did not know if he would follow me out. I did not think, I only responded to the throbbing in my own chest, the gnawing in my stomach. I knew that he was not the sort of man to enter into infidelity casually, or divorce proceedings for that matter. I knew what he had promised me and I trusted in it; he had offered me the chance of a life together if I was willing to risk being with a poor, scarred and almost middle-aged, man in a world that was not particularly amenable to such traits. It didn't sound much but I knew he had offered me all he had. He was open enough to tell me that life with him would be hard, that he came with no property, with no prospects. I had seen the pain and longing in his ravaged face as we had shared memories and experiences had said I would be with him, whatever happened....

but all that had been before Jane had come home.

He had asked me to trust him but I had not bargained on Janey being so volatile, so upset, even. How naive I was! I stood and my breath caught in my throat as I realised he may send me away in my solitary taxi and that may be the last of it. No notes, no contact at all. I tried to remember the remarkable rockets and Catherine wheels that had pierced the night when he had held me earlier, the shower of bright sparks that had flown as our skin had touched, briefly. I longed to be skin to skin and breath to breath with him while instead my foggy breath was swallowed by the empty night and my hands turned to stone and my heart to ice as I stood as I had always stood.

Alone.

And I waited but he came out only briefly, to whisper in my ear that he loved me and that my cab would be with me soon and that he would write. Oh yes, he would write because he promised and we would meet and he would, he promised, be leaving Jane and her charming house. Just not that night because that night belonged to Jane who needed Rory as much as I needed Treeface. She needed him just this one night, like the crutch he had always used her as during their marriage. She would need him to reassure her on practical matters, to prop up her damaged pride and bolster her self-image before he moved away from her for good. He wanted to make her understand the hugeness of this affair, the relevance, to make her feel the special nature of this union, the inevitability of it, so she didn't think he was throwing away their marriage for something shallow and short-lived. And yes, he wanted to know about her intentions with Pete; Peter Latimer, a knight in tarnished armour but with lovely curling black hair who would, we both knew...

(*because we could* see)

...give her one fine boy baby, then twins.

Oh yes, they had to talk as husband and wife for the last time, there were so many issues to discuss and put to rest....an entire marriage to sweep up, to sort out and clear away. It was like a bereavement, really, did I see?

I understood, I said. I saw. I truly thought I did.

(*Oh, good intentions, eh? Isn't the road to somewhere very unpleasant paved with those*?)

And I never saw Jane's husband, Rory Reynolds, again.

Chapter Four

From the Flames

"Once, there was a woman whose gifts were so great that the pain of bearing so much knowing seemed destined to break her. The name of this wisewoman was Lian, for at birth she had resembled a lion with her fiery, unruly hair, her disconcerting stare and loud roar of protest for being back in a hostile world. Even as a tiny infant there had been a wildness about the girl, as a child she had been set apart not only for her uncanny knack of speaking hidden, unwelcome truths to adults but for her very unnaturalness...although ironically her untamed way of being was far more as nature intended than that of those who sought to ostracise her.

Poor Lian, this ethereal, mystical child, lost her own mother when she was but an infant. This loss made the girl feel somehow guilty for she felt the discomfort of those around when she mentioned her Mama. Lian would stare disconcertingly at her Dad and her Aunt Maureen with her steady gaze and they would shiver involuntarily and look away, avoiding that greenish gaze, avoiding her innocent questions. How could she not feel that she had done something wrong when she alone amongst the children at her school had no mother? And, indeed, how could she feel that she was not to blame for being abandoned thus when she knew that her own father felt that way? For Lian picked up his thoughts and feelings, those of his own personal loss mingled with his resentment about this alien child for whom he felt no small amount of fear. It was true to say, even though Cliff Smythe was not a superstitious man, that he considered his only daughter to be a changeling. And maybe in this alone he was right.

What a terrible burden for a psychic child who can detect their only parent's hostility and remorse at having sired her, their own sense that she was somehow inherently *wrong.*

She knew that she was not wrong, for she was as bright as she was wise, but that somehow she realised that people did not welcome her intuitive intrusions, helpful as they could have been. She also knew that she would do well to hide her true nature as best she could for it seemed to provoke anger or rejection. So it was that the flame-haired oracle, she of the most resounding prophetic visions, went to ground. Lian Smythe became silent and shy. She became isolated and sad."

"Go on?"

"Lian's wild spirit was trapped in an earthly body without the knowledge of how to channel through her soul's gifts of *seeing* and *knowing* effectively. She had been given no instruction, nor any support, from any living soul. It seemed to her to be a cruel trick for her to be so dis-empowered when so much latent energy flowed unbidden through her small human frame. Scorned and ostracised by her peers, kept and arms length by her scant family, she had little self-worth left intact and felt fiercely angry at being so treated by the world. She thought of seeking her own demise to escape the cruel burden of gifts which weighed heavily on her small shoulders. She felt as if she could not go through the wearisome process of bearing all of this psychic information alone and so death seemed the only answer to her."

"You make it sound so stark!"

"Well, it was a hard time for her....

(*for you, Lian, my beloved*)

...and all she could think about, day or night, was how to be finally rid of *the voices* that told her that which she did not wish to know, the visions which showed he that which others did not see, that which they did not wish to see! Her revealing of these truths was an aberration to those who sought to travel through life incognito, heads down and scuttling, without any transformational information or insights to disrupt the orderly pattern of their existence. Oh, how it isolated her to be the bringer of revelations that nobody really wanted! The pain and confusion of others was hers to sense and experience, more often than their joy or kindness which came less frequently.

Lian was a sponge for the emotions and emanations of others, a sensitive spirit housed in the body of a small, striking woman..."

"Not beautiful, then?"

Lian teased, although she was half-serious. Her insecurity was a problem between them still.

"A strikingly beautiful woman who could not cope any longer with the suffering she had as her lot. On top of this she carried the burden of guilt from the untimely death of a lovely boy, Robert John, whose death was not her fault..."

Lian looked at him gratefully but her eyes filled with tears as they probably always would when Robert's name was mentioned. His face swam before her and yes it was blurring a little now but she could still see those freckles.

"...no, not her fault, only fate. And on top of that the trauma of losing their tiny baby..."

And the baby, of course, who posthumously, and only in her own mind, she had called Robin Rainbird.

So it was that one evening, when she had decided to put an end to the pain in her very soul, she was stopped from committing a grievous act by an elderly lady. This woman magically managed to get her to come into her home, a small cottage on the edge of a beautiful city, which was no mean feat considering how wary of people Lian had become and how close to suicide she felt. As if she were encouraging an injured fox to come and eat from her hand Alicia approached this wild girl, gently coaxing her closer with titbits of soul-information. Alicia did not rely just on her kindliness though for she claimed her own measure of psychic powers and assured Lian she was not alone and should not give up the fight. Moreover, this kindly woman said that she would teach Lian to be a great *seer*.

So long and fruitlessly had Lian searched for help and support, only to be rebuked, rebuffed and outcast, it made her suspicious of this woman who genuinely wished to be of service. Lian had sought the help of several self-proclaimed mystics before and they had lied to her although Lian was too canny to be conned by standard trickery and spiritual showmanship. She had become bitterly sick of those who would take her money, maybe grope her in the name of healing her, and then send her off into the world, as lonely and confused as ever...only angrier still. Lian had long since given up hope of meeting a genuine psychic in a world full of charlatans and was used to shaking her fist at a nameless, unyielding deity who had cursed her to wander so deeply alone.

Despite her misgivings, Lian let the old woman make her tea and eventually, after much feisty procrastination..."

"Downright rudeness! I was an utter bitch to Alicia!"

"...told her about her biggest problem, the hauntings that she had experienced since trying to connect a dead lover, Robert, using a badly organised Ouija board..."

"Completely dumb and irresponsible use of occult tools, more like!"

"...and the lady, being a generous and very wise spirit, listened and vowed to help the girl rid herself of the malignant presences that plagued her. Lian got cross and demanded that the woman remove all *the voices* and visions if she was capable but the lady saw those as gifts, not curses, and would only remove that which was harmful to Lian's own self, not banish her innate psychic gifts.

Well, Lian grew more and more agitated and insulted the woman..."

"Don't remind me!"

"...and then became even more agitated when the woman said she was a reincarnated Faery!"

"Do you have to put it quite like that?"

"That's how you told me the story!"

"Oh...and then Lian ran away from Alicia, thinking that she knew better, and got herself into another mess!"

Lian punched Treeface playfully in the arm. They were lying together on the floor of their flat, a place they could barely afford to keep in their hand-to-mouth existence. The place was empty of furniture and may well remain that way for some considerable time, neither of them had enough money to buy as much as a chair. Next to them on a blanket, a brightly coloured, Indian-style affair that Lian had salvaged from her father, lay a small picnic, bread and a variety of cheeses.

"It wasn't as simple as her calling me a reincarnated Faery! Alicia said that inside the human form there were different kinds of spirits...elemental ones that came originally from out there..." Lian gestured towards the ceiling.

"What, from Mrs Upstairs' flat?"

Their elderly upstairs neighbour remained nameless to them but had made her presence known in disapproving glances and sighs at their comings and goings.

Lian grabbed Treeface and they rolled over together, laughing. His elbow went in some soft French Brie, a special treat for themselves and Lian began to cry with laughter as she picked it from the sleeve of his blue-grey jumper.

"You look so lovely when you laugh!"

"Oh, and I don't when I look serious?"

Lian, in spite of her good humour, could never quite forget her own hang-ups about her appearance and self-worth. In fact, in the weeks that followed her meeting with Treeface, her own doubts about her odd looks compared to the pale, delicate Lydia, and even the earthy, curvaceous Janey, had mushroomed. Her continual fretting about how she appeared compared to most average people was bad enough but Lydia's casual, elegant charm had made her even more edgy about her ability to hang onto Treeface. It was unbearable sometimes to think that her man thought his own sister more beautiful than his soul-love. Her rampant insecurity seemed such a huge liability and her falling prey to it again and again made her feel as if she had failed him in some way; he was her perfect man and she couldn't afford to risk losing all that they had, that heart-link and soul-bond, for the sake of giving free rein to her fears. Every time he made a seemingly ambiguous remark she allowed her panic to rise up and almost swamp her in its murky waters, through which clear sight was impossible. *She must stop it!*

But, oh Lady, it was so hard! Would he leave her? How would she cope? How could she live with the fact that he had married Jane first? Even though he had been true to his word so far and braved the foul arguments with Jane and the tense meetings at Solicitors offices in town Lian still couldn't quite grasp that he loved her. Oh, the irrational thoughts she had every time he made one seemingly erroneous remark, probably something entirely harmless that she chose to read wrongly. It was hard enough being deeply sensitive, or 'as psychic as a fish' as he put it, without her unruly bright red hair and slanted eyes...

(*not to mention the ears, the ears that seemed to be growing ever more prominent and pointed*)

...which all made her feel more freakish still. She was so used to being laughed at and ostracised that it would take so long for her to trust him and his love. Could he wait that long? Had he the patience or the tolerance to dismantle her fears?

"Don't you know how I feel about you, little *seer*?" Treeface took her hand as she picked at the soiled sleeve.

"Yes...*no!* You've got to remember, I had twenty odd years of being the peculiar, impecunious outcast. You at least had the validation of being told you were a great healer by the McAllister's and had Lydia's approval for your natural way of being even if you didn't always want it! A few weeks of love, even from you, won't change the fact that I've only just been accepted fully by anyone in the last few months! Even Robert, bless him, was only really playing at being with me because he had his own deep-seated pain and I was a bizarre kind of mother-replacement for him. I wasn't really *me* to him, I think he just disregarded the more outlandish aspects of me in order to satisfy his own need. I don't think even he ever saw *me* ,not truly, so I can't say he gave me any true love for who and what I am and that's okay, I don't resent that. It's just that...well, I can just about handle the fact that I've endured no support at all so far but on top of that I've had *negative* feedback all my life too! It would have been easier to have just been ignored but I have been both outlawed, rejected *and* ridiculed."

Lian could see Treeface dying to reassure her but she carried on, wanting so desperately for him to understand her. He was so much better at talking, at expressing himself clearly, than she and it was easy for her to let him override what she was going to say. There seemed to be so many skills for her to learn in order to have a relationship! Most women had been in several by her age, maybe had even been married for years and here was she struggling with the basics!

('*Still, not every woman is a natural psychic with a Fey soul*' she reasoned quietly with herself. Not every woman had had *the voices* to contend with, let alone the visions!)

She took a breath, keen to maintain his attention while she had it. He was so apt to get lost in his own thoughts and sometimes she didn't know if he was really listening to her at all. Was it her own insecurity or inexperience that made her feel so uninteresting compared to Lydia, compared to anyone he had ever known? She would have to try harder to speak her truth plainly but the whole idea of being herself was new to Lian.

She continued, gathering what little confidence she had.

"So, I know it's a burden but you are the first man to truly give me any attention whilst fully knowing who I *be.* I know it's hard for you listening to my constant demands for reassurance but stick with the compliments and I may start to believe them by the time we are sixty!"

Treeface fiddled with his moustache, a sure sign that he was thinking his own deep thoughts again.

"And me...do you really think I am full of confidence with a face full of branches? Most people find that surplus to requirements in a man!"

The raw pain in each of them was easily touched.

"I love you even with your cheesy elbows!"

Lian kissed him lightly, aware of how he was sensitive around his face, especially after Jane had thrown hot coffee at him before he had finally packed up his meagre belongings and left her in an empty house, seething. Even Jane making such an outrageous gesture made Lian uneasy. Instead of thinking that it would turn Treeface further from his (*soon to be ex*) wife, Lian worried that it revealed an underlying passion to their relationship that Treeface would want to keep. She must stop herself thinking that way, she would spoil everything!

Alicia's advice shone at her in the darkness of her own fears...

('*Be in* the Now *beloved*!')

...and in *the Now* there was no danger. He loved her and she him. Rory Reynolds, Jane's husband, a man trying to be both normal and invisible was no longer an issue. Treeface was her man, was Lian's man, for good and all.

"Now, will you finish my Faery-story?"

Lian forced herself to smile brightly at her lover.

"I can't finish it until you tell me what happened with Alicia when you went back there after Yule?"

Treeface, like Alicia, used archaic sounding words for seasonal holidays. It still made Lian feel a bit strange.

"I can tell you now, if you'll make me a cup of your special tea?"

"With lots of love in it?" he asked, reaching to stroke her pale cheek, smiling his heartbreaking lop-sided smile.

"That's the stuff!"

Treeface unfolded himself gracefully and got to his feet, looking more than ever like a wading bird.

"Your wish, little *seer*, is my command, as ever," he said, bowing.

As Treeface moved out to the sparse, neat little kitchen Lian padded out after him in her black stocking feet. Treeface was very precious about them removing their boots before they came into the hallway, he couldn't afford for them to lose their deposit by ruining carpets, especially as they did so much walking in muddy woods together. He had altogether more experience of landlords and regulations and she let him take care of the official side of things. His authoritative air added to her feeling that at last in her life someone was in control and could tell her what was what. If Treeface thought that they should be extra careful with their money, with the landlord's rules, with anything at all, really, then she was happy to let him say so and for them to act accordingly.

Their studio flat was lovely; it was airy and bright, although very small, and she hugged herself at the prospect of her new life in it. From the single living/sleeping room there was view of the city of Bath, the city that now took on a whole new perspective than the one she had on it living as a single woman previously. Now it was a vibrant place full of street theatre and artists and beautiful buildings constructed in a lovely mellow stone. The lights of the Abbey shone out and the now familiar roads and alleyways all glowed with their orange street lamps. It was another flat on a hill but this time it contained two people bound together by the power of love and the burgeoning energies of kindred spirits. It had been no hardship to leave the one-bedroomed place that her father had so kindly...

(*cruelly?*)

...rented for her in order to move her few ragged possessions in with her soul-mate in a far tinier place. They could have kept Lian's old flat going but it had such strong associations with the past, and therefore with much unhappiness, that it seemed wise for them to begin afresh...even if that meant doing without her father's patronage. And the bonus was that although it was tiny the flat was *wonderful.* It was as if, finally, fate had smiled on her. She must not ruin things with jealous, petty thoughts. She must try to be secure in his love!

The clatter of Treeface moving their motley assortment of second hand cups and plates, bought for a few pence in charity shops, and the sound of the boiling water swishing around the big stripy teapot were the sounds of her new life, not howling despair and ravening spirit voices clamouring for attention. She could control *the voices* now, couldn't she? Of course she could! But even with that certainty Lian could never quite shake the sadness that haunted her, both her own sadness and that of others, thousands of others, all lost and yearning. Even with Julien De St. Pierre, as her had been last known to her, back by her side and now at last in her bed (or, temporarily on their floor, wrapped in blankets) she couldn't say she was truly happy.

Still, it would pass, surely? Everything had its season, after all.

'*It's just my getting accustomed to happiness*' she often counselled herself when the familiar ache inside returned unexpectedly. It was hard to adjust to anything new, at first, wasn't it? Trying to mentally shake off sadness that felt as much a part of her now as her blood and bones was a harder task than she could ever have imagined. And trying to lose society's labels, real or imagined, and, worse than this, her own ingrained stigma, would be a job in itself. There would be a lot of pressure on their new relationship, for sure, internal pressures as they both adjusted to a new kind of safety and acceptance and a lot of external expectations too, from family, from the world at large. Nothing ever changed in that respect, no matter what the situation or the era, when one was incarnate there were responsibilities and regulations. Unless, of course, one tried to live in isolation, as Lian had done, so far. The only responsibility that she had encountered in her strange little life up until meeting Alicia had been to keep herself out of other people's way as much as she possibly could...an arrangement that seemed to have suited everyone.

Treeface came through carrying her tea and sat down on the blanket in front of the door to their tiny balcony. It was a glass door and it afforded them with a stunning view of their beautiful adopted city. Lian followed close behind him as she had taken to doing, afraid to let him out of her sight in case he somehow vapourised and returned to some magical realm from which he seemed to have materialised for her. Treeface picked up his beer bottle and took a deep swig, he favoured real ales with lovely illustrations on the labels and names like '*Fiddler's Dram*'. They were his little indulgences in a strict financially monitored life-style. He looked contented, she thought, and a stab of envy went through her. She wished he could join him in a beer, instead of sipping her tea from an oversized mug, but she still couldn't tolerate its affects on her sensitive psychic state, no matter how much protection and grounding she did. He was much more earthy than she, much more able to cope with alcohol. It was a shame, it might have lightened her up a bit; made her laugh more and look beautiful for him.

'*Drugs and psychism do not mix! Fey ones can't abuse sub-stances like other folk can, it leads to madness and worse*!' Alicia had told her, sternly. It hadn't been so much a dire warning though, more a bald statement of fact. Lian recalled the rare occasion when she had given in, in the past, to a toke of a joint, a line of speed or a swig of cider in order to ease her own social nerves and to stop the litany of the endless, awful voices. What appaling consequences these numbing actions had heralded! While the other teenagers merely laughed and closed their eyes in apparent ecstasy, Lian had seen Roman legionaries materialise out of the walls, carpets take on the shape of demonic-looking figures and had fallen into black wells of sickness and depression for days afterward. So, she lived with yet another stigma of her gifts, the social alienation of being sober and abstentious when others could rely on ale and chemicals to alleviate their shyness and ineptitude.

Was her talent a hard road indeed, or a blessing? The jury remained out on that one despite Alicia's reassurances that it was the latter, of course.

Even looking at Treeface drinking gave Lian worries, she realised. She hoped that he didn't find her dull because of her tee-total life. She had so many fears of what may put him off her! She even worried that her worry would make her uptight and dull! She regularly chided herself over it but still it persisted, the habit of a lifetime...of lifetimes?

"So, my little wild Irish rose, are you going to tell me what Alicia told you that day? After all, I have to thank her for bringing us together. I'd love to meet her, as soon as we can."

Treeface was sporting some copper beech leaves, drawn onto his facial scars with brown and bronze eyeliner that morning by Lian. She noticed that some of them had smudged. How she loved him! Tears burned the back of her eyes and she put her cup down so that she could reach over and squeeze his leg. He was, as ever, clad in his faded grey-ish jeans, his legs out in front of him, long and lean as a heron's.

"If I tell you the rest of the Alicia story you'll have to listen to the...to the France bit too. It was all part of it, part of us too! Firstly, Alicia had to get rid of the stuff, the *spirit-detritus*, that was with me after I did that stupid Ouija board and then she wanted to show me why I had the visions and so much pain inside me."

"So? I can deal with hearing about Avignon!" Treeface sounded unusually belligerent. "Come on now, Lian, I know the story! Christ, I was *there* wasn't I? Come on, I'd like to hear it from your side of things. It's something I've waited to share with you for a lifetime...for hundreds of dead years..."

"Yes, but...well, I know what happened to you at Michael's healing centre when you regressed into that life yourself without any warning. I don't want to upset you or affect you, it's dangerous for us to do things like that, to dabble in...you know, *stuff.* I'm not the only sensitive person in this room, beloved. We have to be more careful than..."

"*Normal* people?"

Was there a hint of a sneer in his voice?

"Yes, if you like, other people, normal folk. So we have to watch how we go and I don't want to spark something off with tales of burning and..."

"Fair comment," Treeface said, abruptly cutting her off, " but I can take care of myself now and I want to know! I want to know everything about you, lover. I've told you all my tales, now its time for yours! I want us to share the *knowing* of it and I'm even willing to believe that hearing it may help me heal, as Alicia says, even though I am ninety nine percent sure I am healed, me being the wounded healer archetype and all that. I do know what I am doing so let's just start then shall we?"

Treeface lay back a little more on the blanket, his face set and determined, and the stubby candle they had stuck in a saucer to add ambience to the 'picnic' threw his flickering, giant shadow onto the bare wall. Lian wanted to remember every detail of each day in their new home but instead she forced her vision away from the somewhat grim countenance of her lover, letting her mind's eye see further back than the present.

Breathing deeply she reluctantly faded out the scene around her and easily found herself back in Alicia's kitchen where she had greeted the woman more warmly than the first time they had met.

She saw Alicia in as much detail as she had seen Treeface in front of her moments before; the older woman's hair a mass of different shades of grey, some almost lilac, framing her face like pale drifting mist. Alicia had entwined bits of shell and pine cone, acorn and silver ribbon into a braid at the back of her neck and Lian had seen her then not as a mad, interfering old busy body but as a special person with great knowledge, a Faery-tale Grandmother with a basket full of apples, each containing seeds of old wisdom. Yes, Lian *remembered* and then painted the mind-pictures for Treeface to share. Slowly she began the re-telling, speaking softly at first. Then, as the tale absorbed her back in, she quite un-self-conciously lapsed into the old inflections, her cadence a soul-song from the *wild green beyond.* And for Treeface, who considered himself a good storyteller if little else, there was something spellbinding about her, strangely compelling, and he found himself captivated by his own tale once more. Only this time it was not just his tale it was *theirs*, this impossible Elven woman and his, and that alone was enough to move him.

So, Lian sat on their blanket and she *saw*. She saw how Alicia had welcomed her into her home for a second time and how the embrace they had shared was long. That embrace had been filled with the first genuine love Lian had ever experienced from another woman, from another person, perhaps. She had hot tears on her cheeks as she pulled away.

"Now then, we'll have no need of tears between us two anymore, hmmm? I'll make us some sweet mugwort tea and you can talk the socks off me and hug me as much as you like but I'll have no more crying!"

Lian noticed with a crooked smile that Alicia had a shiny tear winding its way out of her own bleached blue eyes and knew that Alicia would only busy herself with the tea making to avoid her own pent up sadness. Lian would respect that. They had, she knew, work to do between them that would have no room for overly sentimental gestures or clinging.

It had been such a pleasure to see the lady again, Lian had realised, a genuine joy. How relieved she was that she had rung Alicia from that icy phone box and how relieved to find that there was indeed genuine magic about their link as the phone, the phone she knew to be disconnected, had indeed rung for her.

It was simply amazing that wonderful Fey magic could be, no, *was,* real in the world!

It was real!

She saw Alicia for a moment, not as the shrunken but sturdy woman she witnessed going about the uncomplicated task but as another lady, with black hair and starling eyes the shade of bluebells in late spring whose hands had never been still, either. Allette, a long lost friend, had been returned to her in another form, their friendship simply renewed, their bond never severed. Lian knew this as a shining truth just as she knew the red and white chequered fabric acting as a table-cloth was real.

Alicia moved and Lian noticed a nimbus of shimmering light around her as she went about the simple, almost ritualistic tasks of tea making, a task probably acted out a thousand times or more in a dozen different lives. It amazed Lian that suddenly one just knew things to be right, if one could remain open to a possibility rather than angrily railing against these strange feelings and thoughts, or brutally shutting them out. The realisation that Alicia had made tea for Lian in different bodies, in different rooms, throughout the cycles of incarnations seemed now to be a plain fact not a startling and half-mad insight to be blocked at all costs. It just *was*. The tea making, the houses, even the bodies involved were all props and stage-sets to the greater work...that of learning. Over tea they discussed and opened the channels for new thoughts, ideas and concepts to be shared.

So, how many times had they shared this little act? And did it matter?

The acceptance of other lives, of other selves, but most of all of an eternal spirit-self, just *was*.

It would have been very easy indeed to have sobbed that day. Not only for loss, and for *returns*, but in gratitude, for once, for a gift of *sight* that allowed her to *see* and recall such things. Without the *seeing* and the *knowing* all this inner yearning would just be as it had always been to countless thousands of incarnate humans, a wordless, nameless melancholy of the soul that made life seem almost unbearable. Many of the questions Lian had ever felt beating inside her like the frustrated wings of a butterfly caught behind glass came clear to her, the answers illustrated so perfectly and poignantly in the observation of a woman making tea.

How very natural and normal this profound realisation seemed to her, how widely it opened her as if she had been granted the unexpected privilege of seeing colours not usually afforded to human eyes; it was as if a veil had been lifted, as if the spectrum of life was greater than she had ever dared imagine. An unexpected gift, an insight, something that had clearly been with her all along but had been re-presented to her, somehow. Once it was given it was difficult to understand how it had not always been so. It was like growing an extra limb and not noticing it happen yet wondering how it was you could have ever managed without it...

'*Like magic*!' Lian thought.

"People need magic, you see," Alicia said, hearing her thought and responding to it.

"Yes!"

Oh, there was suddenly so much to see, to know, to understand! Lian smiled and accepted the organic wildflower honey the older woman spooned into her cup. Even the honey seemed to connect her into a world in which enchantment just *was*.

"Well you look happier for a bit of magic, my love, I'll say that!"

Lian took a sip of the scalding brew, bitter-sweet and familiar. She felt welcomed and warmed by it.

'*A flowering star*,' she thought, '*is what I am. A fiery blossom shining brighter still, older yet and wiser far...*'

Such thoughts!

"They are good thoughts child, welcome them, savour them, make them your allies!"

"Tell me what is happening to me, lady?"

Alicia licked her lips.

"The Elf-Arrow has been fired in the twilight of your ancient self and now your life will never be the same. He is looking for you, kindred, just as I believe you were looking for me. All connected, see? Things are set in motion by just one thought or wish. The longing of three individuals for renewal is strong magic, especially when the souls are of the same essence, resonating throughout the realms in unison. The wheel turns and so we *become*; the time of yearning has passed and the Quickening has started."

Lian had looked bewildered.

"Magic! Ah the grace of the enchantment we have been given! We're Children of the Greening, beloved, you didn't believe me last time and I don't know if it'll sink in this but I feel you'll at least give me more of a chance now for I have proved to you that magic exists, have I not? You are part of the *returning* of the rapture of life...Child of the *resurgence*, thrice blessed, never cursed. It was only temporary, the pain and grief, it was your own fear that blinded you to the *returning*."

"You're making no sense to me!"

Lian laughed nervously. The last thing that she had wanted to do was insult this wonderful old woman again. She was enjoying the poetic sounding statements but they still sounded like so much fantasy fiction to her, albeit lyrical and gripping fiction.

"Look now, child, don't you pull away from me again, not now!"

Alicia had sighed, leaning forward and clasping her hands around her steaming mug.

"I'll take it slowly, cariad, have no fear. I told you the story of *before*, yes? When we, that is, our kind, our spirit-selves, first came to this small blue-green planet and the Greening, the fabulous magical awakening, began? Yes? Well, now is the time of *resurgence*, see? We're coming back together, overcoming the fear and all...the fear of pain which kept us silent and dumb, the fear of eternal damnation which kept us meek and obedient, the fear of nothing but personal insecurity which kept us isolated!

Because of our own inner resurrection so will nature herself be revered and revived, for we are intertwined, the Earth Mother and the Children. It is so for we pledged it thus!"

These last words were spoken like an invocation and Lian felt its powerful intent echoing in her head, its raw energy coursing up and down her spine. She nodded in affirmation for Alicia to continue. The old woman shut her faded chambray eyes and smiled to herself before meeting Lian's own wide green-on-grey gaze again.

"We forgot for a while that it is all transient, we forgot that we chose new shapes, new bodies, have new chances and circumstances and always, mind, always the ability to recall it for ourselves. *Re-*

incarnation, they call it, and how right they are, though often it is written of as if we march from one end of our lives to another in some orderly historical progress, with some selfish motivation of ascension at the end of it! As if we are in some sort of race to pay off all debts in some strange bartering of good and bad deeds, as if the world revolved solely around our spirits progress in splendid isolation! Ah, the popular view of these matters...but never mind, it is a start to understand that we come back at all, I suppose!

Do you understand, do you feel how vital that one truth is, beloved? *We shall live again!* Yes, destroy our temporary body but we shall return! Has the moon ceased to be as it moves from dark to new, not visible to those who rake the sky for her presence? By no means! Just because a human cannot witness something directly doesn't mean it isn't there! Our spirits are invisible to humanity between lives yet they still exist and they still return! They do not need human belief to do this and nor does the moon need it in her eternal dancing from dark to bright, unseen to fully seen.

Yes, so called ordinary folk are beginning to accept certain elements of this truth for themselves at this time yet there is so much that we do not yet share with the populace, with mainstream society. We are not only they who have *re-membered* but we are not of their soul-race, we are just wearing their bodies, as our kind are not available to us at this dense energetic level! No, do not look so worried child, just listen and it will become clear! For you know this from your own first hand experience, you already have an understanding that we feel isolated from people, from real humans, because of this singular *knowing*. It is so easy to fall prey to loneliness and despair in this situation, the *knowing* can, for a time at least, make that harder still as we must face up to certain things which others do not have to...hard things like responsibility and ethical behaviours.

When we become aware of the spirit-essence within, be that human or star-born, be it beast or mineral or green growing one, we know we are all joined but that each expression is unique and so we have a singular as well as a collective task in our lives. When we *re-member* we know we have soul purpose as well as soul-type...a job to do, incarnate. Do you see? When you *re-member* you wake up and once awoken you cannot ever fully go back to ignorance, to the sleep of the sad human dreamer, even if it was easier that way!

So, here we both be, child, awoken!

Now what, I hear you ask? Well, it does get easier as well as harder, more beautiful as well as more painful. All is paradox, mysterious and magical and very simple too! Like riding a bike you'll just pick it up without noticing!"

"I never had a bike, Dad didn't want me on the road alone, no one would go out with me and he was too....busy."

Lian could hear the old voice, resentful and full of hurt. She stopped herself abruptly.

"I know what you mean, Alicia," she said, making herself stop her familiar victim's litany, "I felt an understanding of connectedness earlier when I had a realisation about the simple act of tea making running through all of our lives, valid to all of our incarnate selves...then it slipped away again as I became only aware of me, and my pain, right now. So, I do accept that one day this sort of thinking will be second nature to me but for now I will accept that I don't really get it fully. But I will accept, yes."

Alicia smiled broadly at her younger friend

"Yes! You will have full appreciation of what I say to you, one day. For now, know that we have much to discuss so please listen and do not be afraid. For we have each other and we must also accept that we have companion spirits, too, so that we are never alone and always supported. You see, even in our realisations of our inter-connectedness with all other life-forms we forget the spirits who surround us daily, the discarnates who guide and aid us. We always walk with spirit!

So, there are the guiding spirits who are discarnate but there are also the many who do not walk in human form with us but who long to share their experiences of life with us. I speak now, child, of our kindred who walk in four-legged form and in feathered, scaled or finned bodies. For the most part they are wise, they *know*, they have no need of the *re-membering* for they have never lost touch with their innate connection to the Source. They too are our companions and guides. We will return to these dear ones many times in the course of our working together child, many times.

"But Alicia," Lian had to bite back her urge to call her 'mistress', the need to talk in some archaic sounding tongue being so strong with this woman, "what of pain? You speak to me of good guiding spirits as if all we need to do is somehow feel the force within us, and them, and all will be well. Yet it isn't so, for I know we can hurt in these human forms and that the hurting overshadows all else. I can accept, in theory, that we are spiritual essence having a human experience and that all is transient but pain..." Lian shuddered involuntarily, " ...how very real it is at the time! And how hard it is to remain open and full of love when your soul, if that is what it is within us, screams in agony still. It is still harder to put trust in external spirits when your own internal, eternal essence is crying out!"

Lian shut her eyes against some vague memory, not yet quite clear but no less tangible for it

Alicia stared hard at Lian but Lian felt as if she were being looked *into*. It was not an unpleasant feeling, nor did she find it intrusive, but she suddenly realised why so many people had found her own intense stare so disconcerting. For *seers saw*, both within and without! Yes, she could understand a little of people's reluctance to be with her now. People did not want, necessarily, to be enlightened or to have their secrets known...particularly if those secrets were being hidden from themselves. Yet Lian had nothing to hide from Alicia and the old woman knew it.

At last Alicia spoke, her voice gentler than ever.

"Indelibly etched on your soul, it seems, are human pain and human fear and because of this there is a terrible resistance in you. This resistance makes your soul hurt and warp and twist. It creates blocks to your progress in this life because you are holding back from it. Part of your problem with psychic intrusions, unwanted visions, chaotic *sight*, stems from your blocking your own natural flow of energy, causing it to back up and explode around you rather than coming through gently like a stream. Fear, cariad, has been your motivating factor instead of love...fear of everything human that could hurt you!

Your soul, that fiery star spirit, it is elemental, *organic;* it can twist and warp but we can make it smooth and luminous again for it cannot be broken. Stars cannot be smashed, they burn and fade, ebb and flow, in accordance with the tides of life. Your energy flows, it grows or it gets temporarily distorted, but it is mutable, not rigid. It cannot snap like brittle toffee no matter how rigidly you hold it in check; it stretches and is pulled about but it can be made new again. Sometimes we lose a little, here and there; like wax from a candle we drip parts of our soul and they get stuck in other places. But they can be retrieved.

Listen, child, your soul cannot be broken, nor can it hurt forever!

Is that not marvellous? Is that not magic? In order to undo the knots ours human lives tie our eternal souls in, in order to smooth out our energies so that they may move freely, in harmony again, we must heal the past hurts."

"How so?"

Lian drained her cup. What a strange drink and a stranger conversation, yet neither felt unpleasant, only deeply familiar.

"How can I be healed of my fear of pain and enjoy being alive in this vulnerable body?"

"We need to remember what we are afraid of, to see it as a transient human thing, of no real lasting substance. If we accept that we, as souls, cannot be crushed, even after being abused in the body, then we know it is, in the greater scheme of things, a small thing only. All things must pass! I know it seems like the world to a human but in terms of a soul-life, all eternity, it is but a...*blip.* Yes, that's it, a blip of hurting. A blip which can warp us, none the less, if we let it. Oh yes, there are always choices!

We can feel the anger and release it; we can experience the regret but we need to let it go and then we can heal from the inside. All the soul's ills reflect on the external human shell, the body, sooner or later. You, my child, have so much work to do in the world that I needed to catch you before your soul's ills hurt your body permanently. Soul-hurts can cause so many diseases...what is disease but *dis-ease* within ourselves, what is illness but being out of balance? In extremis we can see soul-hurt manifest itself as madness or malign tumours. All things suppressed in spirit will out in the manifest realms. Energy can be corked, like liquid, but the pressure builds and..."

"And we get the desire to kill ourselves?"

"Perhaps, if that inner frenzy turns bad and rank, into depression and self-hate, encouraged by other unscrupulous forces. Or perhaps it bursts free like a bubbling geyser, enabling to kill another, our soul's turmoil wrecking havoc, again encouraged by corrupt external entities or energies. All acts of destruction, be they to the self or to the planet or to another being, stem from repressed spirit-energies and more, to the point, energies out of balance. For harmony, Lian, is the natural way, a creative and unconditional desire to *be* is the motivation of the All-That-Is of which we are a part. Any imbalance in spirit can cause an external reaction. Fear-driven reactions cause illness and accidents where as what we want is a measured response, made in peace, love and beauty."

"What of evil in this view? What of these malign external forces?"

Lian looked intently at Alicia who couldn't resist a smile.

"Accch, cariad, we cannot deal with such matters in a sentence but I pledged to answer all questions as they arose so here is a thought on evil, for now. Just a thought to be going on with, mind! Evil is, clearly, energy out of balance. No one thing or being is inherently evil, it is only an act, or an intent, which can be out of balance, against harmonious being. The Creator, the Source, can experience itself, manifestly, as destructive or creative, as opposite ends of its own self which, ultimately, meet back in perfect balance in the centre, at the fulcrum. Now, lady, we can accept that we have choices just as the Creator gave us the choice to use all energy, thought and deed for positive or negative ends. You recall in the story of '*before*', the Makers were the Great Mystery's way of showing us *how not to be* ? Well, they were also an expression of extreme negative reactions performed against the Star Children's backdrop of profound positive responses. And why? For the purpose of revealing the spectrum of choices we have when we respond to anything life offers us as a learning experience. They were as night and day to eachother, and as we had all become familiar with the cycling of night and day, dark and light, this taught us to look for polarity in a new way, negative and positive, that we may learn *response*-ability. Of course there are a whole range of ways of being between negative and positive; like dawn and dusk things can sometimes be neither wholly dark or light. But these two core principles are the paint which is blended to make many shades between and so we must witness them.

As for external forces, negative entities, rogue energies, well these too are born of free will and often of humanity's destructive, abusive, fearful, harmful thoughts. There are some spirits, it is true, who are the Creator's energy expressed in a disruptive fashion yet most of the entities we humans encounter are nought but angry, jealous, ignorant thought-forms that have gotten too big for their etheric boots. We will come back to this soon, beloved but do you see, at least a little, for now? None of us live in isolation, sweetling, neither from other spirit energies nor from our own spirits! There are a myriad of interactions we can discuss and learn to deal, or to work, with but will that do for now as we have other matters to attend to?"

"I suppose!" Lian laughed and Alicia rejoiced inside to see this woman, once so uptight, reactionary and horribly prickly, relaxing and enjoying the discussion. Lian went on, "I guess it's a big area to cover in one go...and one question segues into another and we could be here forever, or at least for this lifetime, just discussing these aspects of being and getting nothing else done at all!"

"That's right, beloved, and remember, what you most need to know now...and quite urgently too, before the moment is passed...is how to gain more wholeness and equilibrium through meeting with your soul's-love. Before you can do that you need to understand your connection and gain healing though that experience.

Part of your destiny in this incarnation is to meet with the man you once knew as Julien de St. Pierre and to heal his warped spirit, his wounded soul. He needs to be reconciled with who he is, inside. He has rejected his essential soul-nature because of negative connotations that have become attached to him being who he truly is, in the world. So he hides it and worse, actively rejects it. His wife, who he shall leave, have no fear to the contrary, has not helped him in this matter, enforcing his isolation through her own shame and insecurity. She once felt sorry for him as you would a stray cat or limping puppy and guarded him thus, keeping him safe and trying to put him right, but the novelty of such a relationship soon wore off. Afraid of him she is, cariad, afraid to meet his eyes and afraid of the ridicule he may bring on her. Accch, she is no wife to him save in name! Yet his sister, who shares our Fey soul-nature, has tried to bring him closer to his natural way of being but still he shies away because she uses the emotive word *witch.*

It will be part of your life's purpose, beloved, to heal his terrors as much as he can help heal yours, by reflection...so closely mirrored are your two spirits. You will be part of his *becoming*, a process that has been faltering because of the use of witch-words which make his spirit cringe back in fear...even though they are what he most needs to hear."

"How can she say that? She has no idea! NO IDEA!"

Treeface butted in to Lian's story. Lian felt her spirit jar as she was jolted back from her gentle recollections by her lover.

"You are beginning to sound like me, all rebellious protestations!"

She tried to soothe him but he looked quite perturbed. She tried not to panic at his sudden withdrawal from her. '*Two little psychic peas in a Pixie's pod'* he had called them yet she could almost feel him slipping away from her, to a cave somewhere deep inside of himself, to safety. What could she do?

"I know that feeling well, beloved, that trying to slink away from what is so hideously painful, reacting with anger to any mention of it being healed. Why, I didn't want to be healed...I wanted to be ANGRY!"

"I am healed!" Treeface muttered, crossly.

Lian spoke quickly.

(*Oh, please let me not lose him again!*)

"Bear with me and I'll explain to me how she convinced me of the worth of such a healing."

Lian tried not to sound to cajoling. He had to come to this of his own free will, no use dragging him kicking and screaming...that was precisely what he didn't need! She stroked the back of one of his hands gently and felt him relax a little.

"Look , if it wasn't for Alicia's truths then I'd still be locked up all alone in a flat, hearing *the voices* and seeing ghosts. I would be miserable and suicidal, maybe even dead by now, and you'd be living with a woman you knew was going to leave you for her plumber boyfriend any day! I would never have come to London to see Lydia's talk if she hadn't have told me to go and so we wouldn't even be here if it wasn't for Alicia! Can't you trust her just a little for that alone?"

Treeface shrugged and frowned.

"Okay, carry on," he said somewhat grudgingly, his face creasing into new lines, deeper pouches forming under his eyes. The reluctance was palpable, as was the fear, but Lian could not focus on those if she was to heal him, as she had agreed to do, as well as healing her own self through their shared process. Instead of fretting over his tense and withdrawn figure she concentrated on making the pictures of herself and Alicia form in her mind again and then she was back in that moment, with the old woman, her present worries about losing Treeface fading back a little.

Alicia!

"Lian, you can help him, and help others like you in the world, because you will have encountered it for yourself, you will have first hand experience of both your spirit's own damage and its healing ...for we *will* heal you, cariad! All it takes is for your spirit to get back on the level. There's an analogy for you, girl, a spirit-level, one of those little devices that the builders use, see? Imagine one of those showing you when you are all lined up and equal at both ends, your positive and negative sides both in alignment, both present but harmoniously held."

"I can understand things when you give me an analogy, that's good," affirmed Lian, "but some of it's more complex and harder for me to grasp. I need mind-pictures to learn and assimilate concepts, I think. Let me get this straight with you, you are saying that my desire to cease to be was the result of me as Lian being out of harmony with the me inside? And that I can put the me back together again by looking at what first distorted it?"

"Yes! That's it, girl; 'the me inside' is a good way to describe the soul. But 'the me inside' isn't broken, only mis-shapen, it needs to be made whole but not in a sense of mending broken crockery. The soul is elastic, 'twill be more like more like re-shaping clay. There will be no loss of identity, only a more profound understanding of the self, we are talking about the eternal me, not Lian, not Marguerite..."

"I want to know who she is, this Marguerite?"

The name tasted foreign but deeply satisfying on her tongue, like the first forkful of an exotic dish.

"And so you shall, cariad, so that you may face her fears and so know Lian's fears and heal your pain as best as we are able so that you, the you inside, can live out Lian's life as the very best expression of all she can be."

"I see, I think, but how? How do you know all this?"

"I *re-membered* because I was open, child, open because of my own past pain and dis-harmony having driven me to seek help. In my younger days I was lucky enough to come across a few talented people who were willing to include me in their Circle, so I had some good solid instruction to start me off safely, too. I know, in that respect I was far luckier than you, but it didn't last. People die, they move, they argue or get bored of things. My little group broke up too soon. Yet my best learning came on my own, out of experience, learning through hardship and through my communing with the spirits, moment by moment..."

"But at least you had some grounding! At least you met others!"

Lian interrupted, keen to make the point that Alicia had it easier, somehow, that Lian's road had been singularly hard and torturous.

"And you met me, beloved, when the time was right!" Alicia spoke a little sternly. "It was never easy for me either, child, not even with my little group, for those were different days, people in general were more afraid of the occult, less open to magics. I don't patronise you ever when I speak to you for I have my own memories of isolation and I do understand how hard it was for you. Even though I cannot claim to have had exactly the same experiences I can still feel your pain! How can I have been through precisely what you have in your life? I am me! But I can empathise, anyway, for we are one in spirit. I need not be a dolphin to know they will suffer terribly if caught in the tuna fisherman's net! I feel for all sentient beings but especially for you, sister, as you are my soul-kin, a Fey one. So do not assume for one minute that I am coming from some privileged position above you. Let us leave behind Lian's victim-consciousness!"

Lian smiled a little and shrugged.

"I'll try!"

" You will do better than try, in time! There is a time, a season, for all things and all things, even your beloved victim mentality, must pass! One day you will no longer need it, believe me!"

"I believe you!"

Lian relaxed again. How could she have remained so irate with this woman on her last meeting?

"And believe me also that learning can be best achieved when in a place of greatest suffering, or upon our subsequent reflection on it. Wisdom, or Sophia as the Gnostics once named her, is the illumination in the eternal darkness, the darkness which gives the brightest light, see? It is the dazzling darkness of which the mystics speak and it is en-*lightenment*! From the darkness and the silence we are born and reborn, star-children of bright wisdom, come to illuminate and ruminate before returning once more to the fertile void of the cosmic womb. There needs to be darkness for us to perceive the light and for pain for us to distinguish gladness. The trick is to witness them both as equally valuable and not mutually exclusive; the balance we seek to walk in is the application of this witnessing."

Lian shook her head, making tongues of flame my up around her pale face.

"Again, my dear Alicia, you are going too far, too fast, for me!"

Alicia smiled in acknowledgement.

"I beg your pardon, child, there is just so much, so very much, to share with you! But I will simplify, if I can. So, then..." Alicia breathed deeply as if to steady her own racing mind and eager soul, "...know this beloved, that joy is only the string that binds the pearls of wisdom, forged deep in the ocean of suffering and longing, to make a shining strand; it is joy that allows us to have something that can be worn with pride, a thing of simple beauty, yet it is pain that creates the precious gems therein. Indeed, it was my own desperation and suffering that drove me to asking really pertinent questions about existence and it was my own sensitivity that made me feel the need to understand, and to *connect,* so keenly. But child, it was also my own ability, which is as keen as your own, that made me able to hear clear responses from my own spirit and those of others as well as from those who crossed my path, inadvertently or purposefully.

I didn't always like what I heard back, mind, but I was looking for answers, unafraid to ask the questions I had inside of me, questions such as all Fey-spirited ones have within them. As I listened to that small voice within me, as well as to the communications of my spirit-guides, who I trusted more than most physical people, I experienced what needed to be cleansed and I healed myself. And if one heals then we heal all, and if all heal then so shall you, precious Fey one!

That is why you came you me, Lian, as you are part of me, linked by our soul-heritage, entwined by starlight and bound by verdant promises...and we are the All." Alicia looked very pleased with herself, not smug but satisfied she had made a point well. "I'm not at the centre of the circle, see, I'm but a shining dewdroplet on the web of life, just as you are, so don't go thinking I'm special and you can't do what I can. No matter how deep the pain or how severe the soul's trauma is we can heal it! I have no more power than you to do; I am just at a different point on the web than you, one with more perspective, or, at least, a different one. We two are linked by our shared soul-type; like called to like across the fibres of time and space and being and you came to me at the moment when you had almost given up, when you were, in fact, at your most open as you had stopped *resisting.*

Ironic, isn't it, you were actually the most open you had ever been when you were going with that flow, wrong as it was, towards your death! You were most open because you were no longer holding yourself back and had given in to a tide, one that you felt to be inevitable. Your expression of misery had become it's own extreme and in that abandonment to what you saw as fate, a desire for an obliterating darkness and for endless, mindless rest, you broke through into the light! Not all suicidal people are so blessed, my child, but you being you, a Shining One and a kindred of wild witches like myself, you gave off a vibration much stronger than your usual restrained and stifled one.

So, at the moment of your desperate decision to give up I felt your vibration and you felt mine. Some part of you felt the pull on the threads that weave us all into creation, the astral call I sent out to guide you to me in order that I may make you safe and well again, and here you are! I did not know how you would arrive, nor did I even know who you were, but I felt you and in your giving in to despair and letting down your guard you felt me, on some hidden level, too! Healing will be yours! Magic, see?"

"Look, I really still find this a bit much. How can I possibly see my own desire to die as my most openly intuitive moment? It's weird! And how can I accept I will be healed, fully and for good and all, just because you saved me? Surely it was just a lucky coincidence that we ended up in each others company ag..." Lian nearly said again. Had she known this woman before or was it all fancy? "Whatever!" She went on quickly. "I just don't know about being healed so easily, Alicia. I mean, in this life it was only cruel words, being ostracised and the constant threat of violence that hurt me, yet in other lives....and I know that such things exist because I feel *in here*!" Lian thumped her own breast bone " I have been injured, tortured, *murdered* in other bodies and I don't know how to pass that off as temporary trivial human stuff! I don't know if I can brush it aside as something that can be healed and forgotten! And anyway, how do I know what I am meant to forgive and forget if I don't *re-member* it properly yet?"

"There's no need to ever forget who you were and are, sweet one, but you can know and heal the wound and have only a scar not a gaping slash in the fabric of your being. And as for memory, I feel you need to go back and look at the life that most hurts your soul, the life in France. We can do this, I can take you there, in a controlled manner, through a regression session. Safety is paramount, cariad, and that's the invaluable part of my experience, see, that I know how valuable it is. You messing about with energies, with *entities,* in an unprotected way just as you did with the Ouija...well, it isn't going to happen again! We will do this with care and with respect and, well, can you have faith in me, beloved? I don't care why, for whatever reason you like, but can you just trust me and be still and experience and *feel* it even if you cannot yet accept it?"

Lian's eyebrows had raised and she looked alarmed.

"I don't want to feel some things again, Alicia, with all due respect. I mean, I don't actually want to go back to France and feel all that physical pain..." Lian swallowed hard, "....again."

"Acccch, no, don't be daft, we won't *physically* go there, we will *psychically* travel. That you, the body once called Marguerite, is dead, child! At least, it is in this reality..."

"Don't get complicated!"

"No, sorry, beloved. So, the body of Marguerite is no more, and the *human* identity dies with the shell, but the soul goes on. When Lian is the ground *you'll* still be around, eh, my love? The 'me inside', remember; that which is eternal and above such temporary identities as Lian and Marguerite? Bodies pass away but the real 'you' is eternal. We call that 'you' the self. We will access that part of your self that holds the far-memory of that life but you will not become her again any more than you can actually *bodily* become the Lian you were as a child, or even the Lian you were ten minutes ago! Marguerite was a role performed 'in costume', a fleshy mantle if you will, a character just as Lian is..."

Lian's face crinkled in an even more bemused way.

"...yes, I know, love, 'tis hard to understand so you'll have to imagine. Try to forget what you've been taught and have mind-pictures of what I tell you; *feel* it! Marguerite is long dead but your soul, that which now dwells within a lovely human-shaped body which goes by the name of Lian Smythe feels Marguerite's pain still. After all, if time is a circle then its all happening I the moment anyway and all we have to do is take a look through the veil of the illusion of time..."

"Woah!"

Lian was laughing at Alicia's audacity.

"That's quite enough of that sort of talk! You've got to keep it basic for me Alicia, at least for now! This is still new to Lian! Maybe its not new to that funny old soul-self bit of me inside but poor old Lian's just woken up and you'll have to be gentle with her fuzzy brain!"

"You're quite right, cariad! Try and just imagine for now though, if you can. Accept the possibility even if you cannot fully grasp it yet.

Such openness to possibilities is the way of assimilating much wisdom."

Alicia patted her hand and offered her an incredible and inedible looking rock cake from a plate of three such things.

"You make a grand soup Mother, for sure, but your cakes!"

Lian chewed, with obvious effort.

Alicia smiled, not least because Lian had called her Mother. It had been so long since anyone had.

"True enough, my love, they aren't so special are they? But we need to eat because we're burning vital energy with all this thinking! Now, I'll stop my teaching talk for a while and all I will say is this, that before we do *anything* we need to get you cleaned up, psychically, and once I do it for you you'll know how to do it for yourself because I surely won't always be there to bail you out. A sensitive such as your self, of rare talent, should know how to do her own psychic maintenance."

Alicia had tutted after she had tried her own cake.

"Tough as my old boots and not half as nutritious, I'll be bound!"

She unceremoniously spat the lump of cake unto her wash-worn handkerchief.

Lian snorted with laughter. How could she not trust this wild, wonderful lady whose own children had missed out on so much by rejecting her out of hand? This woman, above all else, was willing to give up her time (when she had little enough of that left at her age), her hospitality (even if that meant tough cakes) and her wisdom (even if she were prone to ramble on in a perplexing sort of way). How could Lian judge her as anything but kind?

'*To be spiritual is to be kind*' Lian heard someone saying, somewhere. It was one of '*the voices*', for sure. No need to be afraid of it, not anymore. It spoke wisely, it felt *right.*

Thinking of Alicia's errant offspring, Lian scanned the room surreptitiously for a Christmas card that may be from a son or daughter. She regretted not sending the woman one herself.

"No, they didn't send me one, beloved, and I tried not to expect it after all these years," Alicia anticipated her question, reading her thoughts again. "I didn't think that they would, now, but the heart has foolish hopes. Never mind that, it's trivial, after all. Let you and I get on to more important things..."

Alicia's eyes showed her pain and Lian felt anger for the wayward

Rhiannon and for Davey's lack of courtesy or concern to his mother. Had she grandchildren too that she never saw? Poor, good, kind Alicia to be treated so!

"As I say, we will clear you up in a psychic sense which means sending back any rogue entities that have become attached to your powerful spiritual aura to their rightful place in the universe."

Lian paid attention again, she knew that Alicia needed not to dwell on her lost children.

"Where is their place in the universe, whatever *they* are?"

"That's not for us to wonder about or rationalise. We've just got to send 'em packing, girl! But we do it with love even though they're right royal pains to us. We don't psychically bomb them, see, instead we put them gently where they should be for everything has a place and even a purpose. This is all we do, we send them 'home'; it isn't for us to go into it any more than that!"

"Why?"

"'Tis good you are asking questions, child but that's one I can't answer in too much detail. It's not good to dwell on the 'things', the nasty entities or the lost human spirits, you send off. It isn't up to us to analyse them and reform them. No, it is ours to simply send them to wherever they are meant to be. Engaging with them and dwelling upon them draws them back to the Earth-plane, makes a fresh link with them. In the case of *nasties,* as I call the tiresome things that float around the human astral levels, they are the energetic rubbish that gets left about by psychic meddling or the residue from too many thoughts that go array. *Nasties* just get all puffed up and proud if we keep on pontificating on them. Us discussing them is like giving them food, it makes them bigger and it links us back to them. And *hey presto!*...psychic problems all over again! As for other spirits who we send on for healing, trapped spirits..."

"Ghosts?"

"Sometimes, yes. For those spirits who get sent on to 'the light' as it were, well, if we keep mooning about over them when they should be allowed to go free then it holds them back. 'Tis why the Romany Gypsies burned the wagons and personal effects of a family member after the death, even if the possessions were very beautiful and all; it was a severing of connections done out of compassion and generosity to the free-flying spirit. Soul-links are all very well but to hang onto the spirit when its in that tender stage, just after a physical death or even after its been freed to move on, is a hindrance and stops the progress intended to occur.

When we die we should not hang about on the Earth-level too long, nor should we, as living people, try to keep our departed love ones with us 'in the manifest'. Even that which can't be seen can be felt, its all links, sweetheart, all connected, see?"

"I think I do but it seems a bit mercenary."

"We can't be sentimental, cariad but we can love compassionately without cloying slushiness and a desperate need to cling on to what is free to go. Anyway, the *nasties* place isn't with you, that's all we need to know and so we can compel it to leave. They, like all energy, like all matter, have a place where they should be in the *Now*. And there we should send them, with kindness and never hate or bitterness. So, that is what we will do. It was the most urgent thing I felt when I saw you first, beloved; I had to know what you'd down with the Ouija to know the extent of the *nasties* you had been carrying...not to mention all the other energetic detritus attracted to your bright spirit-light across the years."

Lian shook herself, impulsively looking over her shoulder as if she could see whatever tacky little entity clung to her there.

"It's not a nice thought, Mother!"

"No indeed, cariad, so we shall be tackling this issue first. And then, after we clean you up in spirit, we'll have a look at France..."

"A look?"

"Don't look so alarmed, child! Other-life regression is not necessarily deep hypnosis, you will always remain in control of the proceedings and the whole thing will be taped on this..."

Alicia shifted some papers which slid to the floor. An old, flat and highly dusty cassette recorder with out-moded controls was revealed.

"Davey left it when he went. Not exactly state-of-the-art but it'll tape the session to prove to you it's just YOU speaking and *re-membering*, and not some jiggery pokery manipulated or manufactured by an irascible old baggage like myself."

"You're not!"

Lian couldn't believe she had ever thought such cruel things of Alicia.

"Finish your cake up if you can bear it before I remind you of what you called me last time we met!"

Lian blushed as Alicia met her gaze levelly, the eyes full of warmth and humour.

"When you're ready we'll go through to my other room. I use it as my quiet room, my place for connecting with All-That-Is. Some may call it a 'home temple' but that's far too fancy a term, I've never much been one for altars and formal temples, any space is sacred if you make it so in the moment! I just use that room as its quietest and going there instantly puts me in the mind to connect with the Unseen. So, there we'll set up a sacred space for us and we'll do the work. It is work, mind, you'll have to pay attention! It's essential you do so that we can heal you, beloved, but also I'm teaching you so that when I am gone...no, don't protest...when I am gone you'll know and do the work yourself, and for others as well as yourself. The only pity is we that didn't meet sooner. All those years you've had of no discipline or understanding...."

"Yes, why did I have to go through that? No matter which way we look at it, it seems so unfair!"

"I don't know for sure, cariad, but I believe it made you stronger than you'll be more compassionate when dealing with others...

(*to be spiritual is to be kind*)

...as you'd never want to treat anyone as you've been treated. It's helped you see beyond the face value of folk to what lies beneath. That's crucial for being a good witch. No, don't look at me like that! Witch is just one word for it, there's wonder-worker, wisewoman, shaman, *seer*, visionary, mystic, cunning man, spiritwalker....you don't need a label, child, but these are terms to be proud of and they describe you well. We are wildwitches, you and I, being as nature intended; we're Fey-souled fate-weavers and natural *seers*! Part of your healing process, aye, and *his* too, will be to stop seeing your birth-rite as a curse...and that goes for the names that describe your way of being and all! Human words they are, yes, but not they are not dirty or shameful. Remember, everything is both positive and negative, in essence, even a word...''tis only how we, or others, choose to use it. Witch, then, can be an insult or a term of high praise. It is we who will decide that from now on!

You can make your own words up for what you are or you can silently know inside what you are, it matters not, as long as you do not hide from the truth just for the fear of one word! Words are powerful and can enchant as well as repel but it isn't just about words, it is about not blocking natural energies. If you reclaim that word that describes who you be in the world then you can stand in the light rather than skulking with shame and that lets the power flow freely. It means that you can shine!

Believe me, child, for they will know you for what you are even if you do not use any title to go by. Believe me because my own children had to abandon me out of their own shame for I could no longer forsake the beautiful name that was mine to keep throughout the centuries, the one that described natural wisdom, innate psychic gifts. Aye, it was worth everything to me, beyond even holding on to my own dear son and daughter by pretending to be that which I was not. To hide who you are is an affront to the All-That-Is that created us! No, I shall never deny my soul's-nature again just because one name or the other may have been used to degrade me, once or twice, out of some silly fear or prejudice! I may have been killed, branded with such a name, in some other time or place but I have returned, have I not?"

Alicia smiled, the mischievious smile of a little girl, not a woman of advanced years, and Lian, unable to help herself, returned it.

"Anyway, my Fey witch-mistress, I think that's why you had to suffer by not meeting me sooner. The pain and isolation strengthened you just as my own road of loss and hardships made me more able, more considerate. But I am still sorry it was so, we could have had you an adept by now! Still, no matter, child, we have the day that's been given to us to make a start. Let's get on shall we?"

It always seemed to be twilight in Alicia's house, a time of otherworldly enchantment. The two women had moved in to a small sitting room which had been converted to a curious state of part shrine/part surgery, such a place that Lian had never seen before. A couch was covered with a clean cream cotton cloth, making it look professional, yet a wooden chest bedecked with ivy next to it made it seem mysterious. Everywhere Lian looked there were small, intriguing items such as painted icons in sumptous jewel-bright colours. These included a black madonna and a fascinating image of a woman with large soulful eyes and green hair, the like of which Lian had only ever seen in her dreams. There was also a magnificent, intricately carved staff, a simple ceramic chalice, a collection of stones, shells, ribbons and silver charms hanging from a equal armed cross of woven twigs. In one corner stood a bare bough of what Lian recognised to be hawthorn which had its own formidable presence and above the empty hearth hung a strange black mirror. The room was fascinating and a little scary to a wide-eyed Lian, apprehensive of what was to come, accustomed as she was to confusion and psychic burdens, not safety or clarity.

"There was a bit of you that was reluctant to let go of all that psychic baggage?"

Treeface suddenly asked Lian, cutting through her focussed vision of the scene once more.

It was the second time he had interrupted her story's telling and she felt a little irritated; she wasn't a natural tale-weaver like him, how could she regain her flow? She was deeply involved in the images she saw before her, the feel of the cloth on the couch on which she sat, she gentle tinkle of bells as Alicia closed the heavy velvet curtains next to her fantastic twig -sculpture, and his interruption had disturbed the steady silver stream of her *seeing*. Never mind, it wasn't his fault, he was only interested and how long had she wished for someone who would be?

"I may have been reluctant on some level, yes," Lian murmured, thinking back, projecting herself into that room, into the moment experienced only a handful of weeks earlier but seemingly in another time altogether. An almost unthinkable time, a time before Treeface. How could she possibly be angry with a man that she loved so much?

"I was used to carrying all that psychic rubbish didn't know how I'd feel without it," she said to him, softly, and then let him fade from her vision once more.

Lian drifted away from her lover and focused on Alicia's ceramic chalice in her minds-eye, its glaze a wash of delicate blues and greys.

"What if I become, you know, *different*, after you take the spirits away?"

Lian had asked Alicia shyly as the older woman lit incense and candles.

"Accch, you mean 'what if I become ordinary and boring without my spiritual hangers-on'?"

Alicia had blown out the match and smiled reassuringly
"Believe me, lady, you'll be far more yourself that you've ever been without these parasites, especially whatever it was you attracted up in the North doing that Ouija!"

Alicia had spat out the last word with some distaste as if it were unclean.

"Now, you'll be tidy and clear with bright vision and more energy.

Your own dear companion spirits will be able to commune with you more clearly and effectively once it's done and that's what we will pray for, in sacred space, once we get started. Is that alright, dear one?"

Lian had nodded mutely. Praying? And what did getting started mean? Couldn't they just go back to the safety of the kitchen and keep talking at Alicia's cluttered old table? Horrifying pictures surfaced from Lian's memory, images gleaned furtively from library books, sensational tomes on witchery that were all that had been available to her at a time when she had been so desperate for understanding of her 'condition'. The thought made her cringe. What else would Alicia suggest, chanting and dancing like some hideously embarrassing amateur production of 'Macbeth'? Gabbling in weird voices? Nudity? Worse yet, a sacrifice? Why did Alicia keep using witch-words to describe what she did? Lian felt naive and ill-equipped to deal with the world Alicia had brought her into. Lian's cynicism and mortal fear fought with her newly acquired faith in the old woman.

As usual, Alicia had anticipated her worries.

"It'll all be nice and easy, in fact you may say what I do is quite tame by public mis-conceptions of witchery and the psychic arts. What we will do is very basic, in magical terms, no fancy rites, no flashing lights, probably not a patch on what you are used to with your colourful spirit manifestations, Lian! We will protect ourselves, set up an safe astral space to do the work, pray for assistance and guidance in it and then both call up and send our energetic intrusions packing. Poltergeists, cheap little thought-forms, menaces to your well-being which you do not need, will be gone to where they should be!

So, shall we begin child?"

Lian nodded the affirmative.

"Sit down then, beloved, yes, there on the couch...and be at peace. Close your eyes, hands on knees, legs uncrossed, feet firmly on the floor. For this exercise it is important to align with our beloved mentors, the Wise Ones of the Bark, our Earthly guardians the Tree-People, so please ensure that your spine is straight like the trunk of an ash in our native woodland. This spinal trunk allows the energy to travel up towards your spiritual branches whilst grounding you deep in the Earth's nurturing darkness. When I ask you to breathe in deeply, imagine your life-force, your *spirit-sap*, travelling up, connecting you to Father Sky, to the eternal spiritual aspect of yourself, and as you breath out imagine your energy travelling down, the spine becoming a tap root, anchoring you firmly in rich dark soil, re-affirming your temporal link to the Mother who so generously sustains us for the duration of the Earth-walk."

Alicia's manner had taken on something of a friendly but firm headmistress. Lian wondered, stifling a hiccup of nervous laughter, if Alicia had a teaching career lurking in her past. Had she ever had a normal career? Or even a husband? Well...she must have had one for who had paid for the cottage she lived in? Who had sired her children? Lian's mind had instantly filed with panicky babble...anything but think of the work in hand! Yet her still small voice spoke to her firmly saying '*think...when have you had such frantic thoughts before*?' Oh yes, at the Ouija board, when the spirit had wanted them to be quiet...yes! Her mind had thrown up a resistance to it and now she had felt it again then. What was the connection?

Lian knew, in a moment of sharp realisation, that the 'spirit-nuisances' she had attached to her didn't want to leave and were trying to get her to sabotage Alicia's meditation, just as the self same *nasties* had tried to stop her internal chatter in order to creep in! But she *would* concentrate! Whatever happened, she wanted them gone!

How long had it been since she had been 'alone' without them? Damn them all, she wanted to be free!

"Now breathe into your belly. No, like this, in through the nose and the belly puffs out...hold the breath and out through the mouth so the belly deflates. Your belly, your diaphragm, is breathing in life, puffing up like a balloon with it and then deflating and each time you do it you become more relaxed, more relaxed. Breathe in...and out. How easy it is for us to forget that which is most natural to us, how to breathe properly! And in...and out. Good! Remember, you are as one of our Wisdom Keepers, you are like a tree...and breathe in slowly as the energy rises and out as the energy grounds itself.

Now we visualise our protection. We need protection as to travel Between-the-Worlds without a psychic version of the Highway Code is like stepping onto a main road with no idea how traffic works. There are things out in the ether, on astral levels, that can harm you, just like the *nasties* you have already picked up. Protection is a safe-guard, it backs up your safe psychic workings when you begin, it stops you from being ploughed down by a rogue spirit-jugonaut. Yes, I know you like my analogies!

Now, here's where you get to use your imagination creatively as the manner in which you do this in is up to you in future, child, and it can be any variation on the theme that I am about to give you. You must surrounded yourself with bright blue light edged with shining gold for these are colours well suited to creating a radiant, healing aura around you that none can penetrate; the Mother earth has such a protective aura herself, does she not? Remember, it is your will and sacred intent that matter as much as a strong visual image. So, see the bright blue glow and spread the light of your brilliant protective shield above and below you, left and right, all around you, so you are covered. This can be an egg of light, a sphere like a bubble, a cloud or cloak, as long as you are inside it and completely surrounded by it. It can be a garment that covers head and feet and all in between. It must be *organic,* just as the Earth's atmosphere is, and it should be able to flex and move with you, shining as clearly as your wild spirit does.

Breathe...*yes, that's it!*...now see your protective veil breathe with you, it moves and expands and contacts you do, with your breath. *see* it now, see it glowing. Yes, that's good! You have the ability to imagine with strength and clarity."

"How does she know?" thought Lian

"Clear your mind! And breathe and see your beautiful protective light around you. None may penetrate its glorious bright shield, affirm this to yourself and it will be so. Now imagine a silver star, a wonderfully wrought silver star, crafted by the soul-smiths of the Underworld, the likes of which pinned the cloaks of the Shining Ones in the days both *before* and *beyond*....yes, you see it! This star is your protective talisman, you place it upon your brow, between the eyes but slightly above. See the star pour forth its light into the universe. Let none penetrate its rays, or cloud its shining protection of your mind's-eye area, which is needed so that your sight may be clear and true as we journey. Excellent!"

Lian was finding it easier than she had anticipated. Alicia's calm, authority and simple instructions immediately conjured up the appropriate response deep within her. Little did she know then how long and hard Alicia had worked to get those that she worked with to respond so well. Alicia was completely tuned into, and at one with, her clients needs. Lian was being guided by a Mistress of her wild soul-craft.

"Now, we are about to walk between the worlds but first we ground ourselves in this manifest one, re-affirming our link to the Earth Mother as we walk into the Unseen, opening ourselves to the universal energies. Like the trees we root ourselves firmly in the good supporting, nourishing earth, our tap root travelling down our spine, the network of supporting roots branching off from it, travelling far below us, making us stable and connected. Yes!

Now, imagine that you are standing in a circle of cold blue fire. Do not fear for this fire can never burn you, it only protects with its steady glow. It marks your sacred space in the universe, creating a border past none can travel unless invited, it is the third strand of our protective ritual. Imagine also that in on the ground in front of you is another circle, this time empty but created of a similar blue flame. See the tiny flames with their golden tips licking at the air. This is important, it is the space in the universe that you are creating for whatever it is that 'haunts' you to appear in. Anything which is attached to you, spiritually, which has no right to be with you, which has hitched an astral ride with you to feed upon you, must appear in this second flaming circle when we request it to be so. But first we ask for back-up and state our intent.

'*We ask now that Lian's true spiritual guides, her mentors in the otherworldly realms who watch over and assist her, those who love her, be present. May we feel their benign and beneficial essence even if we cannot see them at this time. We wish for assistance to remove those presences which have become attracted to Lian's bright self, that they may be sent to the place which can best bring them healing at this time. We seek to banish but not to harm, to restore harmony and balance by removing that which has no right to be present here. We ask this for the good of the All, may there be healing for Lian and so for every being by direct reflection. So may it be*!'

And now we wait for a moment for the guides to join us in our work."

Lian pictured herself standing in the circle of harmless, heatless turquoise blue fire which flickered with gold. As she waited she felt something shift behind her, a subtle change in the energies which meant that she was no longer alone in her task. Her companion guides, two of them, she thought, flanked her, remaining indistinct. She quashed the urge to turn and look over her shoulder at them. But how marvellous that they had come, just like that!

(*Was it really that easy? How many times had she asked for help when times had been hard, begged for it, even, and felt nothing?*)

"The reason you have not felt their presence before is that your constant fear and panic destroyed your true and natural ability to discern more subtle spirit emanations. The companion spirit guides do not clomp around in hobnail boots announcing their arrival; it is only the mischievous and downright dangerous astral energies or entities which will make loud noises and crude gestures like knocking things over or creating a foul smell in a room. The true guiding spirits will always come if we ask for them to assist us, even if our despair or anger prevents them from becoming clear to us, as they have vowed to help us in this incarnate life, this being their role or, if you will, their job. They will not resort to shock tactics unless it is strictly neccessary and can be experienced or perceived most clearly as presences in our lives when we ourselves are at peace. Our airwaves need to be 'neutral' and open for transmission, not clogged with the hissing and disruptive static of panic or anger. It is hard for them to penetrate our erratic energies when we are distressed and so it is beneficial for us to learn to be calm, measured and responsive. The natural psychic, the Fey *seer*, learns to create sacred, still space, for the good of the All.

And here we are in peace and stillness, that which is sacred, allowing for an exchange of pure energy. Be calm and feel the guide's energies now. One day soon you will meet the spirits that guide you 'in person', realising their unique forms in a more manifest sense so that you may discern their shape. Remember that 'in spirit' all shapes are assumed for our human need and will only reflect a human principle for our sake for when we are discarnate all is energy and we need no props. For now be content to experience their loving spiritual nearness as a shift in the energies around you and know that any form you may see is purely for identification in a human sense."

Lian breathed deeply as she let Alicia's words sink in and, to her surprise, felt calm, an almost alien but highly pleasant sensation. It was akin to slipping into warm and luxuriously scented waters after being in the wilderness for month, even years, without a bath. She felt tears spring to her eyes as she was enveloped in a soothingly tranquil yet infinitely loving feeling, an unconditional sense of being cared for that was non-intrusive yet all pervading. Her physical body felt ripples as it experienced the electric touch of spirit-nearness. '*They're here*!' she whispered, in her mind.

"Yes, we welcome you, treasured friends!" Alicia addressed the beings who remained just outside of Lian's field of vision, somewhere behind her yet at her side, a comforting distance away. "We appreciate your assistance at this time and thank you for being. We ask now that the harmful and invasive presences that have been causing Lian problems show themselves to us so that they may torment her and drain her no more! We accept that you may not interven unless we bid you do so, such is our own spiritual autonomy, but now we ask you, with all due respect, help us!" Alicia's voice became even more crisp and authoritative. "Appear in the circle of flame, you spirits, you entities, you energies, in the name of All-That-Is, the Creator!"

Lian found herself, in the dark space in her minds-eye, pointing at the flaming circle, her finger emitting a stream of bright light. '*Show yourselves!*' she echoed to herself, to embarrassed as yet to speak aloud.

To her surprise there was a movement in the circle and a tangle of shapes appeared.

"We did it!" this time she spoke out loud.

"Concentrate on shining the light of truth upon these who have appeared for us!" Alicia instructed. "We ask you, invasive energies, to show yourselves truly! Are you the spirit-entities which have cause Lian trouble? We ask for these energies to be present, we command it just as she has been have commanded, against her will! Now show yourselves as you truly are! Be revealed, be revealed, BE REVEALED!"

Lian wanted to shrink back but instinctively felt the hand of an unseen companion guide on hers, invisible but reassuringly firm, pointing the finger of light at the strange bundle of forms that writhed uncomfortably in the spotlight. She saw a long beak, three black legs of a brackish hue and an assortment of eyes, a veritable jumble of features in an ever changing arrangement. And it was this mess that had had the audacity to name itself Henry the Eighth! How dare this monstrous mish-mash of seething negativity seek to trick her or try to take her too her doom? What writhed before them in the circle of fire was quite horrible, very disconcerting, but no worse than her now nightmares had been for years. Now she knew why, perhaps? Ah yes, she wanted them gone, for good and all!

"Do not concentrate on discerning the forms you see, for they too are just assumed for human identification, but this time for negative purposes rather than good. These entities are energy gone awry and display themselves thus to scare you and confuse you. Pay no heed to their mindless showing off!

We ask now that these spirit-entities, these rogue energies, be sent to the place in the universe where they may best find healing and we ask that all ties with Lian may be severed, for the good of the All. We cut the ties and we ask that they may be sent off..."

Lian felt something heavy and clammy fall away from her chest. She *saw* it in her mind's-eye as a greasy coil of black rope which fell into the flaming circle she stood within. It vanished in smoke.

" ...and may it not return..."

Another almost audible plop as something fell away from he wetly, releasing her throat as if previously it had been constricted.

"...and may it be healed and transformed as is appropriate. SO MAY IT BE!"

There was a moment in which nothing happened except the multi-faceted strange form twisted and turned uncomfortably.

"It is done!"

The circle was suddenly empty.

"It's gone!" Lian said, amazed.

"Now, before we close the circle of flame and return to the world, we ask that Lian be filled with love and light, her energy portals being sealed and healed from the assault of the spirits who clung to her for so long. May she be given protection as she walks from this place into what is manifest. May spirit and matter be aligned here and may Lian be balanced again, to walk in beauty and work for the Greening in the world."

Lian felt her earthly body jolt on the couch, her head seeming to tilt back as a sensation of pure joy flooded through her, tears coming once more to her eyes as she felt buoyed up on pure light and elevated beyond all that had previously held her captive. It was blissful, an ecstatic communion. Or a *re-union.*

After a seemingly boundless time Alicia said, "we thank the companion spirits for the wise and prudent gestures they have made this day and express our heartfelt gratitude for their being. May we work together again very soon. Blessings upon us all, this day, be we incarnate or discarnate! Go in peace, friends! And Lian, may you now find yourself breathing deeply...slowly...and feel yourself firmly within our own manifest body, becoming aware of your feet, wiggling your toes, moving your fingers...

...and opening your eyes, slowly."

Lian felt herself returning from the deep trance-like state, leaving the bright cleansing light she had finally been bathed in. If that was real psychic work then Alicia could count her in! In all of her twenty eight, soon to be twenty nine, years she had never known the like of it, her own limited and fearful spiritual encounters seemed so silly now, so needlessly difficult. She saw Alicia, now just a little old woman before her, not the owner of a powerful voice which inspired confidence and trust but a simple country-woman with a broad smile and gnarled fingers steepled to her chin. Yes, she saw her mentor and soul-friend and she was glad, for the first time in this incarnation life, to be herself. What a revelation! Lian was actually glad to be Lian Smythe! It was almost miraculous but felt, paradoxically, very normal and natural suddenly.

(Lian, deep into her tale, thought that somewhere she heard Treeface say *'hallelujah!'*. Was he being sarcastic? Surely not?)

"Magic?" she asked Alicia, her slanted green eyes twinkling.

"Absolutely!" said Alicia, her face showing her joy and relief. "And now we'll break for tea and then..."

"We'll visit medieval France, yes, I know! It's all action here isn't it?" Lian smiled at her teacher, her dearest friend. "I love you Alicia but you're a hard task-mistress!"

And on saying that Lian knew that once again Alicia had turned away from her, ostensibly to go and prepare more mugwort tea but primarily because she was weeping tears of real happiness, welling up from a deep, hidden place within her of both infinite wisdom and profound personal pain. Lian had spoken of love!

"Now the hard bit..."

Lian visibly took a hold of herself and brought herself back to the moment in the flat, making herself face Treeface. The time had flown by and they were in deep darkness, save for the guttering candle.

"Shall I put the light on?"

She peered up at the bare bulb hanging from the ceiling. They hadn't gotten round for finding a cheap shade yet. Could they even afford to put the light on?

"No, my one-ness, let's stay in darkness...its suits the purple prose. This telling wouldn't be the same in bright spring sunshine and it definitely isn't suited to harsh human electricity!"

Lian nodded, stretching her slender limbs, cat-like. She was always happy to let him decide things.

"But I think I'll get that other beer if I am going to go back to

Avignon with you," Treeface said, smiling not entirely convincingly. On his wolfish face, in the flickering shadows, that sardonic half-smile looked more like a leer.

Lian did not notice.

For all his wiry flexibility he struggled to his feet. He had been so entranced by Lian's animated talk that he had forgotten to move and he had pins and needles....and she thought that she was no story-teller! An unexpected pang of jealousy went through him as he acknowledged another of her latent skills. What was he good at, really, when he compared his few abilities to her many gifts? He couldn't believe she had so little confidence in herself, often wondering if she were putting it on for more attention. He couldn't bear the fact that he may feel as threatened by her, as she gained in courage and capability, as he had felt by Lydia when she had learned to shine in the world. *He wouldn't let it happen!* He was stronger than that and Lian was his soul-mate after all, wasn't she? He would do anything for her...

...yet his guts churned at the thought of the next part of the tale. More beer, then.

Lian sat and waited for him to come back from their empty kitchen. It wasn't easy for her to go back through this, even now. But easier than for him, perhaps, as she was half way to a sort of healing whereas Treeface seemed to want to hang on to his past, using it as some sort of reason for his rejection of people, or some sort of righteous shield to keep the world at bay. Without his own anger where would he be? He would have to change, just as she had when her ghosts and hangers-on had finally gone. But she had *wanted* to change...

"Can you get me a glass of water?" she called to him.

In future, she would make sure that it was he that was telling her the stories, it seemed a bit odd to her that she had spent the major part of her earthly existence barely speaking to another human being and yet there she was pouring out all this information to a man she had known for a matter of weeks. Besides, it felt to Lian as if she were perhaps usurping Treeface's position a little, he was, after all, the bard whilst she was...well, she was *something,* a something that remained to be discovered. Hopefully. Perhaps she was a *seer* of sorts, if such an ambiguous, antiquated thing as a *seer* was needed in the modern world.

Treeface returned, prancing inelegantly, a battered tin tray held aloft with their drinks perched precariously on it.

"Waiter service!" he proclaimed loftily, trying to be make her laugh. Was he already a little drunk? For all his fooling she could tell that he was as nervous as she, underneath. She knew that his marriage to Jane had compounded his desire to hide his true feelings, his insecurities, just as he had done for years with his parents. Never with Lydia though, bloody lovely Lydia...

('*Stop it Lian! Stop torturing yourself!*' she berated herself silently, '*He does love you more than her. He does! He'll prove that when we meet her, I know he will!*')

Treeface flopped down next to her after placing the tray between them on the rug. She couldn't read his expression but opening up a little to his vibration made Lian shrink away a little. There was a curious mixture of anger and barely contained dread overlaid with a dull, depressed sort of resignation. So complex he was, the man that she loved, so multi-faceted and mysterious. And she herself, could she really judge him for wasn't she a more than a little enigmatic too? Was it not the case that she was still reluctant to share all of her foibles and feelings lest they put Treeface off her? Looking at him so made her empathise immediately with his conflicting emotions.

(*Oh my poor lost love!*)

Feeling lost she resorted to her usual means of contact, reaching over she touched his leg, hoping it would convey some of her intense adoration and immense understanding of what he went through on daily basis.

Lian had never been physically attracted to a man before, not even Robert, finding as she did the whole of human relating rather strange and alien. The feelings of a powerful attraction to another physical body had never been hers before...until now. Yes, she desired Treeface. She particularly liked his legs. He was a thin yet deceptively strong man who rarely exerted the amount of physical force he was capable of. Years spent out of doors trying to walk off his perpetual fear had made him leaner and harder than his already naturally wiry build dictated. His own poverty-stricken and frugal existence since had done little to put meat on his long bones and he still walked everywhere, come rain or shine, and ate only light meat-free meals. The beer he drank was a treat as it had been on special offer at the supermarket and it was, after all, for an exceptional moment such as the celebration of their new home.

Had she ever had such a home before? Had he?

(*Memories slid over her, soft shaded and silvery, a wash of green and grey shadows moving between green boughs; the sound of a brook a constant musical accompaniment to sunny days, dappled and delicious...Ah, the Summerlands of home, distant and yet a breath away, enticing her and making her weep for the sweetness of something lost that would only be found again in her own passing...Aelfthamne!*)

"Do you want to carry on now, sweetheart?"

Treeface was looking at her and briefly she saw the sketch of another man's face over his own dear one. This face was smooth and unlined, a spirit face, sculpted as if of tide-washed, moon-kissed stone and framed with pale hair like a nebula, milky and swirling. It was beautiful and it was terrible for it carried all of his soul's unique creative bounty, all of its capacity to love, and yet all of its wounds that made it howl and twist and squirm overlaid it. His soul was a fragile husk, it's once dazzling precious essence was tarnished by the brackish depths he had plummeted to in life, in *lives.* But behind all those ravaged human faces was the perfect face of her twin, a Fey face, alien, enchanting.

"I will grant a boon or bring devastation," Lian said, half in trance, mesmerised by the remarkable perfect Elven face of the spirit-being she knew and loved. Oh he was in pain, her soul-love! She could help to heal him by telling him their story, giving him her side of the French tale of love and grief, couldn't she? Alicia had said she could! Alicia knew. Didn't she? She had to trust someone...

(*Help me Mother!*)

...or would she just succeed in harming him further by involving him in a memory of death and destruction? If he refused to let go of that appaling recollection, the legacy of its cruel and brutal aspects, he may blame her for compounding his internal injuries. The choice was, as ever, his own to make.

He could focus on their enduring love and find solace and renewal in the eternal nature of their souls, seeking healing for his own essential essence, or he could dwell on the hideous crimes that humans committed, on the harsh reality of being incarnate, choosing to continue to carry that bitterness and hurt with him through "til death. Lian had a hard choice of her own to make and the responsibility weighed heavily on her slender frame.

"I have my own pain, beloved," she whispered, coming back to the present, seeing again his scarred face, the concerned, tender expression in his oh-so familiar eyes. "Do not...do not judge me too harshly if I do more harm than good by telling you this tale again for I am only trying to...to help. To heal. We heal...our kind...we..."

For one horrible moment Lian psychically picked up Treeface's immediate response and it was a loud cry of pure anger from deep within his soul...

('HELP ME, WILL YOU? WHAT KNOW YOU OF MY PAIN, WOMAN? HOW MAY YOU HELP, DO-GOODER?')

...and she recognised it as the same sort of astral sound her own spirit had gotten used to making Between-the-Worlds, a note of raw and passionate outrage at injustice, a rebellious yell of protest. Then she felt him consciously subdue that urge to react against her. As if she were hearing his own synapses snap and his mind click and whirr she experienced him trying to be more rational and calm. He steadied himself and took a draught of beer.

"No blame, Lian, never any blame to you. I want to hear our story from your side, to fill in the gaps. I want to know what happened to you after I left you there..."

He gazed at her beseechingly, naked pain making is face look more harrowed than ever.

"Under the dripping trees?" Lian smiled sadly and it was enough on its own to break his heart.

"Yes!"

"For what reason though, beloved? I don't know how to tell you my tale when I don't really understand why you want to hear it. I know that you won't tell me your side for fear that it will bring back the burns of your past *re-membering* so why do you wish to hear mine, truly? All I know is that knowing my own story brought me a healing to fully accept who I have been and why I feel, or *felt,* so damaged inside. The 'me inside' responded to my *re-membering* and I grew as a result of taking on board that we live again, over and over, and that no amount of hurting my body can destroy my essence. I also learned, well, compassion I suppose, for those who sought to injure and destroy me. Their aim to wipe me so completely away by means of fire, to humiliate me, to make me suffer before they erased me, eradicating my existence, or so they assumed, was absolute and yet I found forgiveness and yes, compassion, in re-living it.

I now know that we *return* and in our *returning* to the Earth-walk it is never the agony of retribution that we seek but the ecstasy of our unions with others. We seek love and our lovers, not our tormentors, we seek solace, not revenge. We seek to heal, only ever to heal, through magics from the *wild green beyond*. And if a soul chooses to return then..."

"You can spare me the spiritual sermon, I do already understand the ways of re-birth and death, you know!"

Lian tried not to show her hurt at his snapping at her again.

"I know but, well, it's all new to me and I guess I am just testing out what I know by means of explaining it back to you, 'cos you are undoubtedly wiser and more experienced than me and..."

"Flattery will get you nowhere, girl!"

Lian balked at his barked words and felt hurt. Where had the pained looking man gone that she had been speaking to only a few minutes before? Who was this snarling stranger that wore her beloved's body? What could she do to get her Treeface back and get him to love her again? She knew she was trying to appease him but not only that, for there was truth in what she said, truth that he needed to hear. There was never a minute that went by without her being aware that he was older and wiser than her. And stronger yet more well, *fragile*, if that were possible; vulnerable, yes. Yet his constant interrupting of her sentences and rebuttals were a little goading. She took a breath.

"I just wanted to say that we choose to come back to try and get it right. We don't blame anyone else if we can't but we do take on personal responsibility and, if the soul is willing, we agree to re-incarnate in order to re-address particular human situations which we messed up last time around. Or whenever..." Lian trailed off, unsure of herself.

"Yeah, I was taught all that too. Michael made sure I was all clued up on esoteric law, remember." Treeface spoke almost laconically.

This was a new side to him, this dismissive and condescending aspect. Still, maybe he was just little drunk? How would Lian know how to measure what amount of ale would make a man inebriated? Robert had seldom touched any substance in her presence, after all. He had been so good, Robert had. And she had given him up, given everything up, just to pursue this man, this dream, and now here she was. She had to try, for his sake, yes for Robert's sake, or it had all been a waste of time...

...a waste of life! Of two lives...

She swallowed hard.

"So, I don't need to explain it all to you. I just wanted to explain it to myself, I guess, testing out loud. Am I making sense?"

Lian could have kicked herself for her deferential and self-effacing responses, it wasn't like her at all to cow-tow to another who over-ruled her, but then she had never loved another like this so maybe it was different? Never mind. They would, she hoped, find a level when the subject matter wasn't quite so volatile and loaded with personal hurt.

"Will you just get on and tell me the story now?"

Treeface was smiling at her, almost teasingly, as if she had just been waffling on in a silly way. Or it may have just been the dark room and the spluttering candle casting shadows on his face which made it appear to leer a little.

"Okay."

Lian settled herself into an upright position, legs loosely crossed and palms resting on her knees. She took another deep breath and then projected herself back into Alicia's house. Oh to be able to tell a tale without having to physically go back to the memory in such an experiential way!

Alicia was looking at her in her mind's-eye and speaking. What was she saying? She let the old woman's voice fade back in

"...and you need to ground yourself now, see? To 'earth' the body before we go onto the next session. We'll take a half hour break."

Lian realised that Alicia was offering her the last one of her dreadful rock-buns. She took it, suddenly feeling ravenous even though she was a light eater and the cake was hardly tempting fare.

"Does psychic work always make you hungry?"

Lian spoke with a mouth full of crumbs as she followed Alicia out from the 'quiet room' into the kitchen. Her body did indeed feel lighter than she had ever experienced it before and more buoyant than she would have thought possible of a bag of flesh and bone. She was elated, in fact. Surely if anything could, Alicia's stodgy cake could make her more Earth-bound again? But did she want to be?

"Well, it can make you a bit peckish because it's work, see? Real serious psychic work is a considerable undertaking which depletes us physically as surely as if we were doing hard manual work; yes, it takes etheric energy to do the job in hand, *soul* energy. We have to sustain the body because it houses the spirit and we can nourish the etheric by taking in healing psychically, as we did for you in that session." Alicia filled the kettle and swilled out the teapot, the greenish leaves falling into the sink.

"'Tis a terrible messy business, making a herbal brew!" she sighed, scooping up the soggy congealed leaves and putting them into a little lidded bucket on her draining board. "For the compost, see?" she explained, seeing Lian's curiosity. The child didn't have the first clue about country wildcraft but she would learn! Alicia had smiled and continued. "Anyway...what was I saying? Oh yes, as you get more adept at working on the astral levels you'll use less of your etheric energy and take in more healing as a matter of good practice. But mind you always ground yourself after a session, child, ''tis essential, that. Even if you feel no real hunger, nibble a biscuit, drink a little water, write some notes. Which reminds me..."

Alicia spooned some dried herbs into the clean pot and turned to open a drawer to her right. Lian could see it was heaped with papers but that one the top lay a slim but sturdy volume. Her friend came over to her and presented Lian with a beautiful bound book, its cover was reddish brown and of a strangely soft material, embellished by slightly raised, and very elaborate, silver lettering.

"What does it, I can't read it?"

"Ah, but you will child! It's the old speech, long lost to even our souls now although we can learn to read it again, with practice. It says '*Ele mai ka te se kele mak'ei*' which means..."

Alicia paused and her faded eyes, dancing with joyful life, met Lian's eager gaze which snapped with green spirit-fire.

"Yes?"

"Which means, child, '*the words of my soul dance freely here'*."

Lian shivered but it was not an unpleasant feeling.

"That's beautiful!"

"That's right, star-ling, and'tis your book of bright shadows! Secret, see? I give you this book to build bridges Between-the-Worlds with, to make your notes and keep a journal of all soul-dramas and psychic workings and experiences as they happen. It is a valuable tool and maybe one of the few you'll need. It isn't an expensive thing!" Alicia tried to assure her, feeling Lian's unease at what she perceived to be a lavish gift.

"It's just a special thing, a tool, nothing more. We don't need much in the way of stuff to be *seers*, girl, t'aint a job for those who want to be surrounded by paraphernalia,''cos you've got to be able to do it anywhere, anytime! Just paper and a pen, willingness and compassion, a few candles and a little incense maybe, or fragrant, pure essential oils to bring about a state of peace and well being conducive to the work. Oh, and we need herbs, yes! Always the herbs, our green spirit helpers!"

Alicia took the kettle from the hob and poured the scalding water into her fat brown teapot, sniffing the aroma indulgently.
"Mugwort, for the *sight*. Yarrow and Vervain. Eyebright too. Oh, there's so many! I love them all, my little green allies!"

Lian laughed, clutching the lovely book to her breast.

"I don't know what to say!"

"About herbs?"

"About my book, you're not reading my mind, for once!"

"Accch! I'm not perfect, child! And the book, I won't hear another word, you know how few chances I get to give gifts to those I love..." Alicia busied herself with cups. "I want it used, mind, that'll be my thanks! And I also want you to learn about herbs. But not yet, don't worry! For now, just get used to drinking them!"

"They are somewhat of an acquired taste. You let me off lightly with a sweet chamomile infusion and ordinary English Breakfast tea when I came here first!"

Alicia gestured for Lian to follow her back through to the small sitting room.

"Organic and fairly traded English Breakfast tea I'll have you know! Well, such stuff as that is for confused, haunted and sad little healer girls, not wild Fey witches," she said.

"Don't Faery folk usually drink normal tea then?" Lian joked.

"The Faery-folk...our kin...would spit if you gave them that muck! They would never touch cow's milk and besides, they like flowery, light, sweet airy things! '*A glamour, a glimmer, a dismal dim-dimmer, we won't drink that muck 'cos we like things that shimmer!*'"

Alicia set the tray down between them and Lian took up her perch on the covered couch once more. She liked that room a great deal and longed to look at all of Alicia's treasures.

"Where did you get that rhyme? Did you *re-member* it from *before*?" she asked.

"Good grief, bless you cariad, no! I made it up! I used to be an English teacher, not a poet, in the far distant past before you were born!"

Alicia threw her hands up and laughed as if it were the most hilarious and outlandish thing in the world.

"Really?"

Lian was suddenly desperate to hear more about this fantastic woman, about her life. After all, how much time did Alicia have left to tell her secrets? She could have been eighty years old for all Lian could guess!

Too late she realised her mistake. Alicia may have once been a teacher but she was now a formidable psychic.

" Accch! I'm not planning on dying yet and you'll have to work harder than that to get all my secrets!"

Lian blushed but Alicia beamed at her.

"Now drink your tea and you'll grow up to be a big, strong old witch like me!"

"I'm not a witch, you know..."

Lian had muttered as she opened her new, deliciously empty magical journal, its soft creamy pages making her long for new psychic adventures to fill it with. She ran her hands over the blank sheets, feeling a vague fuzziness to them, like soft skin. What a fantastic gift this was, it made her feel as if she was the Creator with a blank canvas, a universe of choices as yet un-made, just dreaming of the possibilities to fill it with! To pick up a pen would be like taking up a tool to fill a universe, creating out of nothingness with a touch of a pen on parchment. It was magical! All creative folk were shaman, hadn't someone once said that? When she wrote in this book she would be creating her life afresh, making the dream of a new life real by committing it to the page. Oh yes, it seemed like a good as way as any to justify her existence, chronicling her progress into deeper understanding, recording her journey into the way of the *seer*, unfolding the mystery of herself in words and images.

Alicia busied herself in lighting more candles and setting up her tape recorder as Lian jotted a few notes own on the first page. She was hesitant at first but soon such fear of inadequacy deserted her and her mark making grew bolder.

"...the thing that had haunted me had many eyes..." Lian wrote and felt Alicia start from the task of emptying the incense burner.

"Accch! No, child! Don't dwell on descriptions of things you are trying to set free! I warned you of making links! And I told you, did I not, that these forms are not real in any manifest sense, they're only illusions for us to know the energies of the spirit involved, for good or ill. What you do in your book there is to record the process and the desired outcome, not get all entwined into the physicality of the whole affair. You are bridge-building with the Otherworlds, not hanging onto astral debris!"

Lian looked hurt and scribbled a line through her efforts. Now she had made a mess on her first page!

"You can't be afraid to make mistakes in psychic work and not in life, either! Take this book as a good analogy for the first day of the rest of your incarnation, girl. Each time you write in it and turn a page, 'tis a fresh start and it makes no odds to me, or your soul, if you've twenty pages filled with scratchily written, crossed through substance as opposed to twenty half empty pages written neatly but containing nought of true worth. Maybe I should have bought you a scrappy old note pad as to not have intimidated you so!"

"No! I mean, I love this book and I'll try not to be so precious!"

Alicia smiled at her, her eyes crinkling at the corners.

"Take each thing as a lesson in life, Lian, and you won't go far wrong. Be less precious and self-critical on the page and your life will reflect that! Be expressive and as accurate as you can without being sensational or restrained for the sake of anyone else's approval and you'll do fine in the world, also! Seek only your soul's authorisation and be authentic in all you do. Write from the heart and be inspired! But for now, can you stop and we shall proceed. Plenty of time for us to make notes later...and we will have the tape to help us recall this next session."

"The regression?" Lian placed the book down on the floor and took up her sweetened tea.

"That's right, a guided journey into the far-memories of your soul. Are you ready, then, to experience that which hurts your inner being the most? 'Tis not a light undertaking and nor should any delving into 'other lives' be attempted with the attitude of a spiritual tourist!" Alicia looked as if she had swallowed something unpleasant as she spoke these words. "No, the exploration of other lives, not past lives mind, for we are talking about levels of our incarnate being that are all happening, in terms of the cycles of life and Earth, at this very moment, but on other planes, in other realities..."

"I really can't grasp this, yet, lady!"

"You don't need to and do please forgive me if I push you too fast, too soon, it is just that I realises your potential for understanding is great and so I perhaps go at my teaching a-pace when I should be easier on you as a beginner....or, at least, a relative newcomer to *re-membering*! I'll not confuse you with further esoteric understanding at this stage, not when we have such difficult work ahead, but do you trust me, child? Do you?"

(Lian heard a voice within her say '*she'll know if you lie!*')

"I do trust you, now, even though I didn't at first. Probably because I have nothing to lose and possibly because I feel you to be honest and true!"

Lian grinned openly, disarmingly, and her mentor smiled back.

There was moment which could have been filled with hugs and affirmations of love but instead the two women stared into each others eyes and drank deeply of what they found there...eternal kinship that was stronger than temporary declarations of friendship. Most of a soul-friends relationship was affirmed in a non-verbal but profoundly affecting way it seemed.

"Ah, well, if you trust me, trust this...that we only look at the lives that our eternal self has had incarnate in order to address and then put to rest any material difficulty we have in this tangible life as a result of it. In other words, if we have memories and visions, as you indeed do, then we need to explore the life that is being *re-membered* spontaneously of its own accord for a soul-purpose, a human incarnate reason. We can tackle the origins of phobias and fears, relationships and personal issues, in this way. Before we do this though we should eliminate the possibility that the causes of these things may be a result of events that have transpired in our current life. If I say 'current' you'll know that I mean the one we experience as current even if 'the present' is only one way of experiencing reality."

Lian looked blank.

"Ah no, cariad, you don't have to understand me fully yet, just accept and trust!"

"I'll have faith!" Lian said, "what have I to lose?"

"You have everything to gain by placing your faith in the wisdom of the spirit, child, so it is well that you have chosen to do so!"

Alicia settled back in her plain wooden backed chair and Lian knew they were about to get down to business.

"So, beloved, can you accept that we only look at our far memories when we see the causes of our problems do not lie in the events of the current life, but rather *beyond* the reality of this life? And can you understand, and so accept, that we enter this exploration without frivolity but through necessity to get to the root of your current problems? And do you swear to enter into this with a positive and focused intent?" Alicia waited for Lian to nod. "Good, for we want no spiritual sight-seeing or tourism here, only proper spirit-work from which to learn! Now, lie down please! Comfortably mind, as you'll be that way for some time, and with limbs straight!"

That headmistressy tone again!

"Now, close your eyes, deep breaths, inflate the stomach and let it out through your mouth...two...three. Good. We are going to go through the protection again and then I will guide you back into the life in France which you already half-remember. A life which you have been guided through spontaneous vision to explore. A life in which you knew Julien...

('*And a lady named Allette,*' Lian added to herself, knowing Alicia would probably pick up the thought)

...and a life in which you had peace and fulfilment as well as pain and suffering. If you are ready?"

Lian nodded.

Alicia took her through the deep breathing and protection visualisation that they had recently completed for her spirit-cleansing trance work. Already the blue and gold flames of protection and the cloak of light seemed familiar and comfortable to Lian. Little thrills of anticipation ran through her as she tried to keep her mind still and calm and her body relaxed. She especially liked the visualisation or her 'tree roots' which anchored her in the world while her spirit was working with other realms and energies.

"We are now ready to make the journey into the deepest parts of your spiritual self to access the memory of Marguerite. This is our purpose and we ask blessings upon this work, in the name of understanding and personal growth. Let there be healing because of what we find, let there be deep soul healing...*and breathe!*...and now imagine that you are walking in a field on a summer's afternoon."

Lian was amazed that from the blackness of her protective space she was instantly in the place that Alicia had suggested to her. Her psychic vision behind her closed eyes flooded with sunlight and she immediately heard the birds calling overhead and felt a light, warm breeze on her cheek.

"Good! Remember, I am with you, you will hear my voice at all times and remember also that in our world there is a tape recorder running to make a record of all that transpires here and so nothing can happen without your knowledge or against your will. So, pause now and ask that your companion guides be with you also...yes, that's right...and as you hear my voice, and feel my support and theirs, you will see that you are following a badgers track, an indentation in the waving grass that is leading you an indentation in the waving grass that is leading you somewhere...

(*Yes!*)

...and you are aware of the feeling of the earth under your feet and the breeze on your skin and the smell of the meadow and the sounds of the wild creatures who are also enjoying this beautiful day, this wonderful countryside and you follow the track until it becomes a path into the woods. See how the light changes as you walk there, note the scent of the trees and the cool shade they provide for you at this time. You walk. You walk and the path leads you on, winding through beds of fern and moss, small woodland flowers of yellow and blue. A wood pigeon calls to its mate...

('*It does!*' Lian thought in wonder, observing everything in this amazing place, the contrast in the subtle hues of a silver birch and bright blossoming hawthorn at the fringes while the lush green of the petal strewn grass spoke of burgeoning life, bursting forth in her and in her surroundings. It was a true marvel!)

...and see, a doe brings her fawn to show you as you move on your way through the trees. See the patterns of light and shade dapple her rich red hide. Greet her and thank her for her presence on your path! And then look ahead of you to the large oak that seems to block your way. Approach it but do not touch it. Observe the intricate patterns in its skin, note the tiny creatures which live between each interlocking piece, feel the strength and the vitality of this Wise One of the Bark.

Now, notice with amazement that it is hollow! Yes, there is a gap at its base that you can, if you bend down, see right though. There! You must ask if it is appropriate for you to pass through this sacred being to the other side of understanding beyond it. Ask!"

Alicia was skilled at leaving Lian enough time to assimilate all she was being shown and asked to experience. It was as if she could see all that transpired in Lian's mind's-eye and was truly walking alongside her in the *beyond*. Alicia let her approach and speak to the tree in her spirit-journey, while constantly remaining attuned to Lian's energies, monitoring her subtle responses.

Lian found herself fumbling for words in her state of trance-vision. She did not know how to address an oak tree! She reached out for guidance, knowing her protective spirits were nearby, not wishing to ask Alicia out loud. What a self-conscious fool she felt! Alicia would know she needed help but had not offered any. Was it a test? Lian's physical self on the couch took a deep breath while her spirit-body asked in its still, small voice '*how do I speak to a tree?*'

And the response came not from an external source but from the tree itself.

"Oh come now, has it really been so long that we have not spoken to each other, your kind and mine? Welcome, fair-child, you who are all starry eyed and dreaming, welcome wild-spirited one! Do you wish to pass through my portal this day?"

Lian's Otherworld self shrank back in surprise and then smiled. How foolish! All she had to do was to speak as if to a valued friend. She *re-membered*!

"Please, beloved oak, I wish to move through your great hollow body to the realm beyond in order to find a part of myself which suffers and hurts me still, in its grief. I seek wisdom and understanding and you are, as ever, Keeper of Wisdoms!"

There was a pause, silence save for the bird-song and a creaking of boughs. Had she got it wrong? No, she would not react in human way, she would wait as was befitting to her kind.

"Pass and go well!" said the tree.

Lian waited. It all seemed so simple! She saw a shimmery presence to her right and knew that Alicia's spirit was nearby and she heard the older woman's spirit-voice

('*Pass! It is well!*').

Lian crouched down and made her way through the hollow oak. She found herself on the other side of the tree, the path leading from where she stood away into yet more woodland.

"Now," Alicia's reassuring human voice cut in, firm and friendly, "you may proceed. Follow the path until you reach the brook and cross it by the three stepping stones. As you use each one, focus on your intent a little more. Three stones become three wishes so as you step lightly upon each one make the purpose of your journey be a wish for success! And then in front of you filling your vision from side to side, you will see a bank. Do not climb this bank until I tell you."

Lian's astral body walked the path and came to a delightful babbling brook. She was aware of several spirit-presences hovering around the water, darting away from her and flitting rapidly back again, but now was not the time for conversing with nature spirits or water elementals, she knew. There was work to be done!

She stepped onto the first broad, flat, pinkish-grey stone which shone just under the surface of the clear water.

"I wish for a clear vision of Marguerite..."

Step two...

"I wish for a greater understanding of Marguerite!"

Three!

"I WISH FOR A HEALING FOR MYSELF AS MARGUERITE!"

And Lian, in spirit, was across the water and facing a grassy bank which obscured her view.

"You may climb this bank now but when you reach the top be sure of this, you will see a dwelling on the other side and this dwelling is unique to you, your special place which holds the secrets of your soul. It is safe and secure, it stands for you alone and will fit your requirements. There is no right or wrong thing to see, whatever you see just *is*; try not to judge it for it is appropriate for you at this time. When you see the dwelling clearly, approach it with certainty. When you feel able to, take the key which lies outside on a step and open the door.

Once inside you will see staircases, one running up, the other running down. Choose but one direction and choose it quickly, for your instinct must override the rationality of thought that will creep in if you start to assess. Remember, there is no good or bad way of approaching this, only your way. Ascend or descend, whichever feels right, and stop at the level which seems to be fitting for you at this time. There you will see a corridor filled with closed doors. Walk in the direction that feels right for you until you get to the door that feels appropriate...wait there. I shall guide you from that point onwards."

Lian was eager, in spirit. All her human reservations fell away as her spirit-self easily ran up the steep bank. At the top she saw spread below her a grassy and almost featureless plain. On it, nearest to her, stood a house. She ran down the bank and across the flat field towards it.

A Tudor house, all rickety and with many layers sticking out over each other, a black timbered affair, lathe and plaster built with criss-cross leaded mullion windows. Lian breathed deeply. The key? It was on the stone step, huge and solid, its top shaped like a golden clover. With her long white spirit hands she opened the door and went inside.

It was dimmer and cooler but not unpleasant within the walls of the house, dust-motes danced in shafts of sunlight which spilled in through the windows making diamond shaped patterns on the floor. The hall was tiled in black and white, reminding her of those crazy pictures of skewed perspective she had been mesmerised by as a child, surreal and impossible images. She heard Alicia's gentle voice...

"Do not give in to fear of this place even if it throws up images that seem unsettling or disturbing for it is yours and at your command. Remember, have no fear, for you are safe here! Now, with a questing and bold nature, take the staircase, both are quite safe, that appeals to you at this time."

(*Going down!*)

Suddenly the stairs were not in keeping with a Tudor dwelling at all but the winding broad stone stairs of a castle. Wide, deep stairs descending. Lian instinctively knew to count each one as she went down, round and around.

'*Thirteen...fourteen...deeper and deeper...*' she sang to her self as she proceeded, quite spontaneously and easily, to send herself down further into her own self's *knowing*. Deeper into a healing trance.

('*My*', Alicia, wondered in approval on observing her friend, '*she truly is a natural! Oh Fair One!*')

Soon Lian's spirit-self stood in front of a wooden door. It looked old and a sense of foreboding filled her with as much ease as she had found herself deepening her own trance-state.

'*Breathe! And remember, this is my own reality, I am safe!*' she spoke to herself and waited with as much patience and calm as she could manage. The door was clearly defined before her although it was dimmer still in this strange cool corridor that seemed to twist in a way unfeasible for a Tudor Manor. No matter that everything did not match up, it still worked, didn't it? Lian figured that the house, her visionary creation, was bound to be as full of contradictions and hidden aspects as she herself was. She concentrated her attention on what she could see. The door was an arch shape, dark stained wood studded with heavy squarish nails. It repelled and attracted her in equal measures. It was *her* door!

"Now you will open your door and step over the threshold. The door never disappears, it remains for you, ever open for your safe return. Whenever you choose to return to ordinary reality you may see the door and come back through it safely and with ease. *You* are in control. Now, when you step through the door and cross the threshold I want you to look down at your feet. Not at the view around or before you but at your feet. Ready, one...two...three...

('*Now!*')

....open the door onto a scene from the life of Marguerite."

('*Look down at your feet...at your feet!!*')

('Nothing!')

('*Wait!*')

('Black, swirling darkness, empty space!')

('*Look at your feet!*')

Mud! Urgh! All over the hem of her only decent skirt! It was all she needed on top of everything else!

"What can you see when you look at your feet?" Alicia's question reached Lian even as she stood looking crossly at this new set of circumstances that had finally become very clear to her as she stepped through the door.

Lian knew that she must speak aloud, realising that some part of her was still on the couch in Alicia's sitting room, the reassuring voice of the old woman alerting her to it, reminding her of it. She had to speak to be recorded on the tape, didn't she?

(*But all this stinking mud!*)

"A whole day, I've wasted, bringing my lace to this mob and what do I get for it! Dirt thrown in my eye and my only dress caked in their filthy muck. My cloak was a rag before I began and now I've torn it half to shreds getting through the accursed bramble thicket! All for this, people and animals, and mud, mud, mud! How can they live like this in such close quarters?"

"Where are you, lady?" Alicia had guessed that once she had used the standard visual trigger of 'looking at the feet' that Lian would probably kick-start herself into the deep-memory. Most would just describe their footwear, but not her! Lian was very gifted indeed. She had already saved Alicia the task of bringing her vision through clearer by dwelling on the details of footwear and they were now into the story, spontaneously.

"I am at their market! 'Tis the first time I've been to such an affair and believe me t'will be my last, and all! This mess, 'tis quite, quite foul!"

In her trance-vision, which was all encompassing to her now, Lian shook at the heavy, dark-dyed, rough hewn skirt she wore.

"What finds you at the market, mistress?"

Lian seem to accept Alicia's voice as if it were a natural part of the experience. Others Alicia had 'regressed' to what they saw as past lives had had scanty far-memory and had struggled with the basics, finding the voice of their guide Alicia intrusive or too much of a crutch. Lian, however, just spoke as if it were completely real and normal for her to be in character and speaking to her friend in such a way, even though Alicia wasn't 'there' in the sense that Lian was.

"I was trying to sell my blessed lace but they laughed at me! Laughed as if I'd made some jest! Humph! My lace is the finest they've ever seen, I don't doubt, but they still turn their backs and blank me, after they've had their fun jeering, that is! And then...just because I didn't go away but kept asking '*who'll buy my lace, today?*' they start to pelting me with muck. Stinking people, dirty place! That I have come to this now! Accch!

I cannot think straight for all their unholy din! And all their animals, pigs and goats, thronging about, a chicken flying up at me squawking, and they're throwing shit at me! It really is too much for me to countenance, madam!"

Alicia thought quickly of how best to guide Lian out of this scene and into another one but Lian had already done this for herself, muttering out loud as she did so .

"I'll have to leave with my basket still full of lace and lace that's filthy now, too! No bread for me today, nor butter either. No milk! Nothing to eat! And so far to walk back through the woods! Oh! Leave me be, have you not caused me enough distress? Be off with you!" Lian, lying on Alicia's couch, made a flapping gesture with her hand as if to fend something off. "I'm going, I tell you! Oh!"

The despair in the voice was unmistakable but the dialogue too natural to dismiss. A good job the tape as rolling to record the session; it was, even for a seasoned psychic worker like Alicia, truly special. All the more so because she knew she had been in that life too and soon enough would recognise that which Lian described to her with her superb psychic vision.

"A day wasted and nought to eat! Me, alone again, with no one left to turn to. All fled, they are, all of them!"

"Who...?"

Lian, lying on the couch waved her hand impatiently. She was obviously completely involved in her visionary experience. Alicia could see the brow creased into furrows of consternation.

"The Lady, see, and the Lord, himself....my benefactors and protectors, one dead and one disappeared! She died on me, while I was tending her, and now he's gone, taken the household away with him, so he has! Gone in the space of a day, maybe two, for t'was difficult for me to tell the passing of the time when I was so head-sore and injured by his raging. Now 'e's gone and taken all of them...and I would have liked to say goodbye at least, especially to....oh, no matter! Nothing matters now! I just want to go home!"

The voice faded a little, trailing into a string of unhappy sounds, mournful whimperings.

"Tell me more about the Lord and his Mistress, lady?"

"Ah, everyone knows! What is this, a trick? That'd be a dirty thing to do to me in the state I am in! You know they all blamed me! Everyone knows! That's why he took them all away, abandoned the Manor, left me at the mercy of...oh!"

"Where are you now?"

"Why I'm making my way home, of course! Foolish questions when you can see plainly I am in a bad way! Have to try to get home before 'tis too dark to see for I thought to bring no lantern. It's no place for a woman alone. Julien has told me such tales of these places at night, such tales you'd not believe what the world is coming to! No respect for an old maid like myself, no pity either! I cannot bear this yet...Ah! Damnation! Brambles and thorns, tearing me limb from limb, things waiting to trip me!" A wail issued from her, a miserable keening "They left me! Why? Am I so bad? So terrible? I did my best for the Lady, in Mary's holy name as Mother of All, so I did! Who would doubt me, a Good-Mother as I am, pledged to remedy ills as I am, striving to bring healing and only that! *Only ever that!* I didn't mean to...oh!"

Lian thrashed a little on the couch and Alicia knew that she must bring Lian forward to her homecoming as the journey was too distressing a process for her.

"You are home, now, beloved. The journey is completed and you have reached your home and you are safe now. Safe to..."

"NO!" Lian's recumbent figure jerked upright and fell back again. She was clearly perspiring now, licking her lips. "It cannot be...say I am dreaming! Please, I beg you, take this sight from my eyes! It CANNOT BE!"

"My lady? Marguerite, Good-Mother, fair Mistress, pray tell me, what is amiss at your homestead?" Alicia found herself lapsing into the old manner of speaking and pulled herself back from her involvement. Detachment, a caring but professional distancing, was required in such circumstances but, oh dear Lady, how hard to maintain in the face of such personal angst! Had this been such a good idea, to embroil herself in her beloved friend's *re-membering* in such a way? She must take care of her own reactions and stay calm, focused, responding with patience and clarity!

"Burned!" The wailing from Lian was dreadful and Alicia half felt inclined to end the thing there and then. It was to be too traumatic, perhaps, for one who felt and recalled things with such lucidity. Yet, for healing there must be a descent into the pit of pain, into the darkest regions of experience and being. They must, despite Alicia's misgivings at witnessing Lian/Marguerite in such a traumatised state, carry on through this.

"Julien! Julien! Where is *the man* when I need him? Never here...never! It is a cruel world, you mark me well, a cruel and cold world for a woman alone! These are dark times, lady, you'd be best to find a man to be your protector." Lian spoke as if Alicia were next to her in the scene she was seeing played out behind her eyelids. "Don't wait for love as I have! What did my true love do for me? WHERE IS HE NOW WHEN I AM LEFT TO WATCH MY

WHOLE WORLD BURNING? All I have now is a charred remnant instead of my little house. That," Lian, on the couch, pointed a finger, indicating something in her psychic vision, "that smoking heap there, that was my life! Aye, and my own Mama's life before me and her'n before her and so...and so....Look!" Lian flung out an arm and in Alicia's own minds-eye there flashed a picture of a small hut-like dwelling still smouldering in the he deep twilight, burned a deeper black than the encroaching shadows of the night.

"Who did this?" Lian was sobbing uncontrollably. "My herbs! My beloved green ones, all gone to ashes! Oh, my precious balms and potions! Mama's too! Oh, and Celandine and Armandine, my cats! My babies! *Ele mor ka te, es ka ra de!* I am undone!"

Alicia stood and moved to Lian. Very gently, as not to alert Lian to her physical presence she ran her hand in a light sweeping motion across Lian's energy field, close to her body but not touching it. Working quickly she flooded the small body with healing light. This was going to be a long night in so many senses. Alicia must main an impartial distance away and after she had soothed Lian's aura she sat down and gathered herself. The sobbing eased to a soft weeping and then ceased.

When Lian's voice continued it was harder, more resigned. Chillingly distant.

"My home is burned! They have burned me out. They hate me because I lost the Lady Veronique and Roger's child. Roger, Comte De St. Antoine, my Lord, he was a good man and his father was a better one yet but he has been gone many years now and the son has been a good Master in his way. And I, the Maman, midwifer to his kin, have served him as faithfully as Mama did his father before him. I have no harsh words for Lord Roger, he guarded me and sheltered me, let me stay on the Manor and make the lace his ladies loved so well, let me go about healing them too when the need arose, as Mother had done before me. But how he beat me when I lost them, his beloved wife and child! What a side I saw to him then!

So young, she was, sweet Veronique, so much blood she lost! Ah, she was too tiny herself, that was why Roger loved her so; delicate, aye, and all but split apart by the wee babe. Tragic, so it was, but not my fault, I swear! I did all that was humanly possible, calling on all the saints and angels, upon my own dead Mama's skill and wisdom. I even called upon the Old Green Ones, the spirits of wildwood and bright starlight, but silently so that none could tell. Well, none at least but Allette for she alone has sought my wisdoms in the stead of my own child....the child that has never been born through me. Like my own is Allette and we laboured along with the Lady as one flesh, so we did! Yet nothing could save the poor Lady once she ruptured like that. The babe was not ready to leave her, all upside down and back to front it was and we could not give her safe passage from her moter's womb into the world. No! It *was as it was*, I tell you! T'was fate and all, and the blessed saints and angels had decreed it so. And even the Ancestors could not make it otherwise even though I prayed heartily for their intercession. Ah yes, pray we did, until our soul's were raw!

And we used the poultices and the brews and the amulets...all of these, with the appropriate incantations, invocations for love and light and for increased healing in our hands...but the babe did not wish to enter this world rightly and the shoulders would not come free and so there was a tearing and...oh...the Lady, she was so young, so pale and frail to start with. That was why Lord Roger loved her, so it was, for she was like a little flower. Veronique, as white as a lily and gilded with his gifts of precious stones and ...so much love could not save her! Blood on my hands...on mine alone!"

Alicia knew this scene. She had been present, as one of Veronique's ladies, her women. Yes she had been Allette, called to help Marguerite, the Maman as she was known to them. Alicia, as the hand-maiden Allette, had been young and inexperienced in the ways of child-birthing and the sight of the blood had made her sick and faint but the Good-Mother Marguerite was labouring for the Lady and she had to help, fetching the water and the cloths, the steaming infusions of raspberry leaf, lady's mantle, white dead nettle and yarrow. She and Maman Marguerite had indeed worked as one flesh through the day and into the long, cold night.

Yes, Allette herself had looked down transfixed at her Mistress's life ebbed away from her. Even as Alicia heard Lian, as Marguerite, tell her tale, an image came to her unbidden of that doomed fevered noble woman lying a-bed with the cool dry hands of the ever-calm, always gentle Maman kneading and rubbing and stroking and cajoling. The memory was of silence save the mutterings of muslin, the hissing of steam and the Maman whispering her magics into the air as she applied the cloths. Allette had heard the small bones at the back of Veronique's neck pop and crack in protest, shocking in the silence, as Marguerite lifted the weak noble woman's head. the Lady had writhed and bucked in the tossed bed, all nobility gone, as animal as any labouring cow in the stalls. '*Maman is here,*' Allette had reassured herself, '*she will make it right!*' And Allette had kept up this mantra even as Marguerite's clever hands had reached in to ease the blueish baby out and the blood had flowed the more.

The silent scene was rent and torn from Allette, the screams of a dying woman being ripped asunder filled her ears and the picture turned from shades of milk-white to red, red, red.

Allette had focused on the huge wooden bed-head, anything but the terrible vision before her. The voices of the other attendants filtered through her own fear.

"'Tis an overly-large child for the little Mistress!"

"The Lord is a good man, and strong too, his seed produces fine stock, see!"

"Aye, virile, so he is! I'd wager there's a thousand women who'd long to be in the place of our good Lady here this day; 'Tis the woman's place to suffer to bring forth the child of such a man! T'will be fine...fine..."

The simple serving women spoke nervously, trying to keep a sense of optimism and gaiety in the face of what seemed to be an inevitable tragedy.

Allette had forced herself to look at Maman and it made her feel a little less queasy and panicked. Marguerite's face had betrayed none of her own fears.

"His progeny cannot fail to thrive!"

Could it be so? Could the child die and the mother along with it?

"So much blood!" Lian was wringing her hands on there couch in Alicia's room. Alicia took hold of herself, pulling back again from her own life as Allette and her own deeply personal involvement with the memory. Perhaps it had been folly to regress a woman she had shared this life with? No, for who else was there to do the job?

Just as Marguerite had once been strong where she, as Allette, had been the weaker young servant girl, so it was that Alicia was now the one who could help the little healer woman, she who relived the horror of being a midwife who lost her benefactors wife and child.

"So long that night seemed to me! So long and hard we all

laboured! And when the Lady Veronique could fight no more I poured my light of love into her and willed her strong so that she may keep on with us to expel the babe fully from her torn body. I thought then that we may save at least the child...ahhh..." Lian's voice faded into a sigh. "But we did not, it was not to be. We did not and past midnight on that second day we had to let her slip away." A single sob issued from Lian. So much pain to be held in her spirit for so long! "...and then...past four he came in, Roger, always so kind to me before...'*My Lord*,' say I, weeping openly and still having her blood about me even though we had cleaned her and laid her properly as was seemly, '*I tried my best, so I did!*' Believe me, we had done everything to ensure that in death her spirit was safe and at peace...*everything!*...but the blood about me, on my hands and even my face where I had lifted my fingers to wipe at tears which threatened to blind me that night...

(*Ahh! The memory! The pain!*)

...and so it was that he struck me even before he flung himself upon her. In repose as she was and almost cold in her eternal slumber, may God rest her and the holy Mother and all the Old Ones protect her soul! And for some time he lay across her until he took a hold of himself and stood up, trembling and crying out to the heavens. It was then that he lunged at me spitting 'YOU! *YOU!*' and he set about me with his belt and his fists and all of my friends who had helped me, the serving girls, Veronique's own ladies and hand-maidens, they scattered back as he let go his terrible agony upon me. My small body found itself curled into the tightest ball as he struck me..."

Lian's body tensed then slumped and she let out a long sigh.

"And later they dumped me outside the big house, the groom and his boy, in a terrible blind state. Half dead myself, I was, and for a seemingly endless time I remained in the dirt where they had left me. I could hear the spirits calling to me, calling me back to them, even then, but one strong clear voice came to me in my terrible black stupor and urged me to crawl homewards. The spirits of the Wild Ones, my Ancestors, comforted me as I dragged myself blindly homewards, on my belly, like a snake in the dust. I just wanted to reach my house to get out of the cold, and that terrible penetrating damp, to hide my shame.

When at last I regained my senses and was able to move more

freely I crawled on all fours until I could stand and I entered my house, a home with no fire in its hearth, and I lay in a swoon for a boundless time.

And when I came around again I knew that I must attend the Manor, even after what Roger had said and done, for I wanted to make reparations, somehow, I knew not how but had to do something! I walked, oh yes, even after what had been done to me, I walked up to the big house and then I saw the most terrible thing yet..."

Lian's eyes moved rapidly behind her lids. She was looking at the empty Manor before her and not a horse, nor a dog nor any beast was left in it or its grounds. No noises save the wind whipping up straw in the courtyard and the banging of a door in the stable block. Deserted! The Lord had gone while she had been unconscious and taken his household with him to who knows where. Left abandoned she was, given over to her fate. The fate of any woman alone in those times was hard enough without the protection of benefactor. But the fate of a midwife who had lost the Lord's wife and child, only to have him leave her all alone...it did not bode well, not at all!

"Roger, he'd always given me what little I needed to sustain me while I lived on his land like Mama before me; yes, he had been kind, in his way. I had my tiny house, and my privacy, my security and the freedom to gather my herbs and make my brews and create the lace that delighted the ladies that came calling to his household. And later his good lady, Veronique, that poor unfortunate who was barely more than a babe herself, took great pleasure in my work, especially as she was with child and had much time to idle away, chatting and admiring fine things. So with her dead, with his lovely bride gone and his hope of an heir dashed so horribly, he had left, stricken, to set up home in one of his other houses. Where? Well, even if I had not fallen so dramatically out of favour he wouldn't have discussed such matters with his midwife, now would he? I had not been party to such information, for my place, although valued in its way, was little more than that of the dogs that hunted for him. In fact who knows if the dogs had not been valued more highly for their pedigree? I was a poor-wife, a baggage, a chattel, and resolutely of serving class despite my skill. I had limited use but was an indulgence for the ladies. The age when my Grand-Mama's had been given more status and credence was long past; I was but a reminder of a more earthy, less reasoned age, and the Lord was ever a man of the times.

Oh, I can understand why he went, his grief would not allow him to remain in the house where she had died so tragically and he had other estates, of course he did! But he had just gone without a word, leaving me broken and battered at the mercy of a pack of wild dogs, the 'good people' of this harsh age! Had he not an ounce of pity for me? I know I was the least of his worries yet I do not know if he meant me to suffer. I do not know if he thought of me at all. I was like a rabbit, vulnerable to predators, left in my burrow to my fate. I would be sniffed out. I knew that. I knew it because Julien had seen it happen elsewhere and had told me so."

"Julien?" Alicia asked, gently.

"Julien...he who I would have had as my lover but he was given to wandering off.. 'tis in his blood, see? A hunter, a healer, a wild man, he is, a cunning man and many things to many people! Aye, a Green Man, straight and flexible as a wand of willow, crafty as a fox, strong as an ox and slippery as an eel! He has the skills I do not possess to make his way in the world, travelling and trapping and offering his wares to the villages beyond my own small world. Oh yes, he's seen more than I ever shall, more faces than I could imagine, why he has even been into the towns! An adventurer, he is. But he prefers the cool shade of the wood above the chatter and clamour of the human strongholds, he told me so, and that gave me hope in his returning to me.

Ah yes, he told me many things but it was never enough for me. I craved him but he was not to be caught and captured and I understood that for it was better to see him little and often than never again! Each time I chanced upon him I knew the time would come for me to let him go. He was like the creatures I nurtured by my hearth to make them well; I set them free to go their own way in their natural environs once my work was done, once the sharing was over, and so I would do the same with him once our talking was done, once our soul-communing had ended. Yes, I watched him saunter off, a-whistling, once his time with me had passed. I held him ever with an open palm, like the fledgling linnet I hand-reared until she was ready to fly. That was my love, a fleeting thing, but precious as water and just as refreshing to me.

Julien, he collected stories and recipes, he mended and he tended, as was required. He sold the fur of creatures he killed with great love, cleanly, quickly. T'was almost as if they came to him for the taking! He respected all that gave their lives to provide for his own, no heartless killer nor greedy slaughterer, he! He knew the way of the wildwood, see, whereas Mama had only ever taught me about the herbs and plants that flower, not the creatures that shared it with us. My Mama, Mari, had lived off the good will of the Lord, the Baron in those days, in return for her healing arts and midwifery; she did not have a need to learn hunting skills and so I was never taught them. We ate mostly bread and what table scraps we were given, along with the flowering, fruiting gifts of the greenwood. So I was ever a scrawny baggage, never good enough for my beautiful strong Julien, my Green Man. What woman would have turned down the chance to lie with him, my Elf-Arrow, my fair one?

Mama Mari, she was known as the Blessing Woman and she taught me all she knew within her limits. She left me her home and her ways, simple things, good things, but not exciting enough, perhaps, for Julien. What I had was enough, see, my needs were met and that was enough for me. But Julien...he was different, he was beautiful and he brought me the life I did not have, adventure and colour and laughter."

A dreamy look passed over Lian's face, replacing her pained expression for a moment.

"Julien was special but he was never mine, not really, he came and went with the seasons and long days passed before I would find him outside my door or crouching in the woods whittling sticks. He gave me lucky holy stones, given power by sacred waters to the north, and he told me tales of firelight in other parishes, of days gone by in other worlds. He had a face like the purest winter star and was often silent but we were comfortable with that for he painted pictures with his slender fingers, working wood in a way which was eloquent beyond any talking. He sold his crafts too, lovely little carvings, fine staffs and sticks turned like a snake or topped the head of a bird. A man of many talents yet humble and honest as the day was long and that's the middle and both ends of it. He was as he was.

When he did speak, though, he had the whole world to share with me and... and I needed him! I NEEDED HIM! Yet I knew not where he was when they, the ones that wanted sport with me, burned me out of house and home. There was no man to comfort me or to shield me and so alone I had to suffer for loss of the Lord who was most beloved to the people. A homestead without its Lord in its bounds was a weak place, open to vagabonds and thieves, dissenters and despots and so out of spite, out of rage and for the sheer power of it they destroyed my poor house. And in that house..."

Lian's voice faltered and her throat contracted.

"In that house," she whispered, seeing a shabby one room dwelling with herbs hanging from simple wooden rafters and jars and pouches on every surface available, "there was a wounded fox who I had been tending. Her name...her name was Paddy...and they killed her too. For sweet Paddy was not yet up to walking, splinted up and resting by my hearth she was. And Celandine and Armandine! Oh!..."

Lian gave a heart-wrenching sob.

"They killed them! Defenceless, Paddy was, but strong she would have been had they kept their mindless anger in check. They took her life! And my babies, the two that loved me as a mother! Accch! It is too much to bear! And me, me having only just gone away for one of the few days in my life, gone to that damnable market to be further humiliated by them and their kind! Oh, no wonder they laughed, they knew what was afoot while I was away! Stupid, stupid people! Poor Paddy. I am so sorry, sweetling..."

Alicia cut in, calm and authoritative although inside she felt the hurt acutely. People, the human-kind, could be so cruel!

"Marguerite, how old are you?"

"'Tis my forty sixth year, I think, maybe less, maybe more, I have no need to keep a tally."

"And the year?"

Lian's face scrunched up in consternation "Thirteen...thirteen...the year of our Lord Thirteen Twenty Six!"

"And how do you know?"

"Because they read it out to me when I got taken there."

"There?"

Lian let out a long hissing breath "Avignon, or so they said," she whispered. "Aye, they took me to that hell."

Lian was seeing a jumble of images, of clergymen waving their hands and of corridors lined with ostentatious colourful pennants, the like of which she had never seen before. Then she saw Julien. *The man!*

"He came! He came, after the fire! I was curled up in my torn, muddy old summer cloak, my winter one had been inside and burned like everything else...*oh!*...and I was sleeping on the wet grass outside the ruins of my home, chilled to the very bone so I was, and I felt him near me. I looked up and it was just beginning to get light. I was cold and he bent down, kneeled at my feet, and put his hand upon me. His healing hand filled me with warmth and hope and my heart opened and melted. By the Lady, I loved him, so!

Even in my relief and in my overwhelming flush of love I was aware of how I looked to him. I knew his kindness would be extended to any hurt person and I felt the pain of that for even in his generous gesture I knew I was not unique to him, that I was never enough for him! Oh yes, I knew I was not comely, for t'was given to my younger sister to be the pretty one. Had I have been beautiful perhaps my face or body's allure would have been enough to keep him with me? Could my guile, had I been lovely, have ensnared sweet Julien de St. Pierre perhaps? But I was plain and homely and, worse, I had been bruised very badly by the Lords assault and still wore a little of the Lady's blood about me as a badge of shame. The marks upon me must have stood out as livid wields against my dirty grey-hued flesh and my gown and mantle, such as they were, were disarrayed and covered in their stinking shit. My hair was matted and I need for a sluice in good water but I sat up and faced him, hoping my love for him would blind him to my pitiful body and what had become of me.

"Oh Good Mistress, *Maman!*" He cried out in my pain as if it were his own and he cupped my dirty face in his smooth, cool hands and kissed it chastely. How I longed to draw him down to me, there on the cool, wet grass even as my home still smoked behind us. But it was not to be, instead he sat me up and supported me for a while. There were no words between us for no more were needed, the scene before us spoke eloquently enough. Always the silence with him; so easy it was for us to communicate to eachother inside ourselves.

"We must to the wood," he said, at length, after his presence had strengthened me a little. He was like that, see, a man who could make you feel better just by being there; he had a *sustaining* presence about him, the sign of a true healer. And yes, they had said that of me also, the ladies at the Manor, but I knew that my presence was never as healing as his own loving aura. He was sweet, my gentle peddler Prince. Not mine though, never really mine.

"We must to the woods," he repeated and his urgency got through to me in my torpor and he raised me to my feet although my legs shook.

"Why?" I asked as he half carried me to the shelter of the trees which bordered the land on which my one-roomed dwelling house had stood. Why bother doing anything now all was lost?

"They will not stop at burning your home, my lady, 'tis your very body they seek to destroy. Believe me, I have heard it in the Baronies and seen it on the roads. Too many charred black crosses, still smouldering, and too many questions hanging like a foul miasma in the air! Those who are not as they are, the healers and *seers,* have been taken and used as human fuel.They even take those barely out of childhood's thrall and the old ones who stand in their way; any who defy or obstruct them, any who believe that which is contrary to their bull-headed Christ-following! This burning of your homestead is only the start of it, dear one, for they will stop at nothing. Already I know that a man has been dispatched to Avignon, to report on your folly to that impostor who sits there in pious judgement. Oh yes, I have travelled all night to tell you, for you have been marked as evil, Mistress, aye, even you! Ah! For when has this land known a kinder soul than you, good Maman? Yet we must get you to safety for you are branded now. You see the injustice, the unnecessary evil of it?"

What was there to do but nod an affirmation, defeated and shaken?

"You have a sister, yes?"

"Lucetta, yes, she dwells near the coast, near Marseilles, I believe. I have rarely had word from her since she took with her sixth child, Mathieu, but she fares well there with Frederic, her husband. Frederic is a merchant trader, a wealthy man, and, *may the saints be praised*, a good man too; he will not resent me for seeking refuge there with them. I would like to see my dear kinswoman, indeed I would, but my home...is...is *here*! I only know the Lord's estate, and even Lyon seems a lifetime away to one such as myself. I am not like you, sir, I am not used to travel and the lonely road! Marseilles is *so far away!* Too far!"

"Your home was here, beloved, yes, but now you must flee from the ashes of that life lest you become little more than dust yourself. For they mean to have your blood and *I will not allow it!* See the cloak I have brought for you? It will keep you warm on your journey. And to sustain you I will give you my provisions. Fear not, dear one, for I know that you have no skill with the blade or arrow. Look here, see? Dried salt-meat and fruits,some black bread and a little honey. I bring you all I have, Mistress, for I know the seriousness of your situation," and he tilted up my chin and our eyes met, moss on granite. Me, Marguerite, a middle-aged lady considered well past her prime, a poor specimen who had recently been beaten to a pulp and Julien, a tall, slender, hard-bodied man with a shining countenance and an earnest, open face.

(*Lian and Treeface, Marguerite and Julien...interchangeable! Yes, all time is one moment but oh the pain in those blinks of lives!*)

"And I should make my way on foot to Marseilles to avoid this...this unruly rabble, this *mob*? For why? I am innocent! Of what crime am I found guilty? I did not kill the Lady and her child! We did everything we could...*everything!*..but God took her, may Mary protect their souls, it happens that way sometimes. 'Tis fate is all. And how may we argue with fate? *I am innocent!*"

"Innocence is no longer valued in this world," Julien De St. Pierre spoke into the eyes of his Maman, into *my* eyes, the midwife and lace maker who's fleeting life was in its last days.

(*As was his, if only we had known it.*)

"You must go now!"

"Come with me!" Tears slid down my dirty cheeks leaving runnels like alluvial deposits on my dirty skin. I clutched at him for the first time ever, hanging on to the threadbare sleeve of his loose robe. "I beg you, as a friend, as my only friend, be my guide and protector. Come with me!"

Julien looked away, eyes filled with torment, his hands fluttering, pale, milk-white moths that were useless against the savage lusts of a world gone mad. He had been through this before with his poor sister and he would not risk it again with Maman. Oh, the pain of getting close to people!

"I cannot, my love, for I do not wish to draw attention to you but rather away from you. Please, there is no time to waste , not a moment, and I must go back to the villages before I am missed...or worse, followed...and put them off your scent."

"You will do this, you will distract them, for me?"

"Yes! I will be there for you, even if I am not at your side. Whatever happens I will not let you down! Know this, beloved, that I will be laying false trails and putting the spoor elsewhere. I promise!"

(S*omewhere, far distant, Marguerite heard the strangled sob of another man, a man from another time, perhaps.*)

Alicia broke in. The agony of this moment was palpable, almost unbearable, and she needed to keep Lian's focus to stop her slipping into pure emotion. To attain healing they must *see* the whole memory, experience it in its entirety.

"Tell me what you see as you leave Julien?"

"Oh...don't make me...not yet! I love him, by all the stars in heaven, I love him so! Ahhhh!"

"You want to live, do you not?" Alicia's voice was far more steady than she felt inside, knowing that she was speaking now to a woman marked for certain death. Yet the Marguerite she was speaking to still had hope and she could not take that away.

"Yes...so that I may see him again I will leave. Oh sweet St. Julien! He *is* a saint, *my* saint, may he be blessed! I wear his sister's cloak and carry a pouch of his foodstuffs. So generous has he been to me! Oh, how I wish that we could....that we could *love*...but it seems to me that I shall never knew his sacred bones, will never experience the bliss of our union. Ah, tell me, how do I find the strength to walk away and not look back? He speaks not of futility, my sweet and gentle Prince, he tries to comfort me, to raise my spirits and he said to me..."

"What did he say, beloved?" Lian's memories, as the ill-fated Marguerite, were barely audible, as if she were focused inward, viewing images of separation and filled with a grief so deeply personal that it seemed a rudeness to pry upon them. Yet Alicia had to ask, for she was the guide on this journey. She kept her voice at a respectful volume, loud enough for the woman to respond but soft enough as to be unobtrusive to any harmful degree.

"He says to me '*are we not sure that we have conquered such loss before?*' And I know that he may be right...*he may be right!*...and so I find within me a grain of hope in the dry and arid desert plain I am to become without him. Hope as a speck of sand in the wilderness of my soul, for how I am parched and left as a husk at the thought of losing him! Losing my own life seems but a trifle in comparison for I have never lain with him and now there is no time! Oh the stark terror of that realisation...no time...*time has run out!* So it is for me to go forth alone, childless and forsaken, into a barren world.

Oh God! Oh good Lady...help me!

And he turns and steps away from me, shining as an angel may shine in this lonely land, in this cruel age. And I hear myself praying, even as I stumble on, bereft, '*may safe passage be granted me, Lady, that I may see St. Julien again!*'

But I walk alone and the trees drip for they too are sad beyond sorrowing, yet still able to weep for an age when we may be who we be without fear. Spider webs brush my face as I hurry away and to my eyes they are fashioned into dew clad diadems for the brow of my holy man who came it save me at his own risk. Ah, his simple grace, his true faith! And yes, I must have faith, also!

I weep and time and time again my vision blurs, yet I walk on. And on. And...yes,I must hurry!"

On the couch Lian's head turned from left to right, a haunted, hunted look on her face.

"What are you doing now, Marguerite?" Alicia asked her.

"I am trying to walk but it gets harder for I am tired already and hungry also. The ground is...slippery...shallow soil over hard rock, and I find myself tumbling often, sliding down into piles of dead leaves as the trees stand in silent witness. How many more tears are left in me to shed? All I see are weeping trees and me a single woman hurrying between them as the sun rises and sets.

I am not afraid of the woods, of the shifting mists or the unexpected cries of birds. No, I am afraid of *them,* the nameless ones that maybe pursuing me. They may be behind me even now! How can I not trust Julien? Or maybe he was wrong, after all, I am not to be sought out, not to be pursued, for what am I anyway? I am nothing and nobody, I own no lands, am no threat, have nothing to offer, I have no worth! Surely Julien must be over cautious sending me away like this, surely it will be all an unnecessary prudence? Or perhaps he has, as he promised, succeeded I diverting them from me, after all? I know not! So I walk on, I hurry, and try to keep from falling or flinching.

'*Keep going,*' he told me, '*and cover as much ground as you can. Head south. Do not stop at villages, by pass all settlements. Walk, beloved, for the Lady's sake!*'

So I walk.

And when night falls I make myself a chant to keep me going, a little prayer-song to walk to as my legs ache and my back pains me where I have slipped upon it once to many times. I say:

'A thousand winters shall I walk, all moments then shall be as one,
Until I find the place where love can give without a fear of wrong,
And freedom be rejoiced in there, in thought, kind word and song...'"

Alicia blinked back fresh tears. Again the thought that perhaps this regression had been a bad idea, when the subject was so close to her own heart? But she must press on again.

"That was very beautiful, mistress!" she said to Lian. "But now I want you to move on...go forward in time and tell me what is happening to you?"

"Oh! I've fallen again and this time I've really done something to myself. Ohhh!" Lian twisted a little on the couch. "Damn it, I am not as young as I was and now I can't move. And I was doing so well, too! I've been left weaker than ever by the beating Roger gave me and ''tis a crying shame, for there was never any need for this, for any of it!

Oh NO! *No, no, no!* They're coming! No, it can't be for me! No, surely not, this is too bad....Lady, tell me they are not for me? I will lie still and...no! No, you can't do that!"

"Tell me what is happening lady, try to remain calm and just observe what happens next?"

"A man on a horse, I can't see his face, he just reached down and sort of swept me up in his arms. Quite kind, it seemed, but then...*ooeeff!* Slung on the back of his mount without a word, like a sack of grain, slung across the rump. He knots something about my middle, loosely, to keep me in place. And the pain in my back as I am moved! By all the saints it is unbearable, intolerable! *C'est abominable!* I cry it to him but he appears not to hear. I ask who he is, who sent him? Is he a rescuer or a demon? He just rides. Pointless to scream, he can't hear me, or he won't hear me. None can, or will. We've turned back away from the direction I was headed in. He's taking me somewhere else. How dare he? The pain in my back! Tell him to stop!"

"Let's move on from there, lady, if we may. Go forward again, perhaps a day. Where are you now?"

A silence. There was a perplexed look on Lian's face.

Then,

"Madam, what is this place? Am I in hell, then? By all the saints it surely seems that way, hearing their infernal racket! These people...*who are they?* They climb the walls, moaning and screaming and here am I," Lian winced visibly, "with this pain in my back on a damp stone floor. It is an outrage! Have they no respect at all for an old woman? '*Help me, can't you?*' I call out to the nearest one. He shies away! No, more than this, he does the sign to banish evil! They won't come near me, eye me as if it is me, the Maman, that is the devil here! Yet it is they who yell and act like possessed men, wailing. Babbling and pleading.

Is this a jail? So tired, I am! I shrink back into a corner as another man falls down across the room. The windows are so small, arrow slits, after all, and they can never get through them, they must know that! And so high, they can never climb the walls, yet they do. They fall...often...bodies falling hard onto this cold stone floor. It is so cold in here. I can see my breath, at least I still have breath in my poor body, and I can't sit up. I call out to a woman but she shuffles back from me making the sign...damn it, I am NOT EVIL!

Why do they feel they need to ward off my devilry? What have I done to warrant this? I am a good woman, I am the Maman! The Lord would tell them of my service to him but then where has he gone?" For a moment Lian seemed completely disorientated and understandably distressed. "Oh Lady, where am I?"

"Let us go on to the point when you get out of this place and see what happens next?" Alicia suggested, knowing it was not going to get any better from there on in. Onwards...they had to finish!

"Oh, the light hurts my eyes! Where is this place? It looks like a big barn from the outside and I am being dragged out by men, soldiers, is it? I do not know! Dragged into a kind of cobbled roadway, there's walls all around this place, hemming me in, even out doors it feels like a prison. A city? Dirty! I do not know, I have never seen its like. Fancy buildings all crowding in on me, my head reels from hunger and fatigue and the constant searing pain in my back! I try to tell them I am broken but they pull me harder, almost wrenching my arm from its socket. Terrible cruel devils, they are! *They are the devils, all of them!*

'*Stop it!* Leave me be!' I say but it is as if I don't exist. And now we are inside somewhere and its so fine, rich! Ahh, it is beautiful, yes! Polished, ornately carved, heavy dark wood and sumptuously coloured banners, it's like a church but someone lives here, I think. Dark red velvet and stained glass and a rug...no, a carpet! A *carpet!*

And I'm almost on the floor now, dragged like an old sack because I am too weak and they drop me down. I see pennants of red and gold. Wonderful things! It's like a castle and it's like a holy place...I don't know! Where am I?

Wherever I am, I'm on the floor, dropped so carelessly! Don't they care, these men? Are they soldiers? I thought I saw helmets, no faces!"

"Where have they dropped you, Marguerite?"

"One of them grabs my hair, yanks my head up, my cap comes off and they grab my chin and hold my head so I can see who is before me and the light comes in from the windows behind three men so I can't really see at all. Silhouettes are all they are against the brightness! Almost holy they seem but I know that they mean me harm! They wait for me to speak, I think, so I tell them I hurt and they yank my head further up and then...oh! They push my head down so my head touches the floor and hold it there! They tell me that I should not meet their eyes! That I am a devil and I am to confess!

What? Confess what? I don't understand Oh, who will help me?" Lian seemed to be straining to hear something in her vision.

"What are they saying to you, do you know who they are?" Alicia asked.

"Now they want me to look up so I try to sit and they shout that I must look at what they show me, not at their faces! But all I can see are hands moving and holding up things that do not belong to me but which I recognise...of course I do! Simple iron nails and chains, a hank of horsehair, a holey stone! These are everyday, ordinary things! If that is all they want of me it is very simple! I say yes! Yes, I have seen them before and I don't know, maybe I had even held them. Who was to say? Ordinary things, see? Everyday things, and harmless ones too. They ask me if I recognise these things and I say yes, because anyone would know them!

Then there's babbling and big words, foreign words, and I lose track altogether. Lots of hands, waving, pointing, I think, and voices raised in angry declamations."

Alicia groaned inwardly. This was Marguerite's 'trial'; her hearing to ascertain if she were a witch or devil-worshipping heretic. Yet it mattered not if she were accused of heresy or sorcery for she was found guilty from the start; the specifics were irrelevant for she had simply been condemned for being different...and, of course, for being a poor, old and undefended woman in an age with no respect for such attributes.

"What else do they say and do?"

" I can't really say. I am so tired and my vision isn't so good, the light is almost blinding me and they stand against it, on some sort of elevated thing, like a...a podium, yes. One sits, I think, on a big chair, all fancy. I reach for his foot to beg for mercy because I feel...I *feel* that he isn't a bad man, not like the ones at his side that speak to me rapidly and angrily in a another language, waving their funny little objects, but when I reach for the man he draws back and there is an uproar and they are dragging me backwards and away. But I haven't even spoken yet, no chance to ask why I am here or to find out what happens to me next . And why? WHY AM I HERE?

I try to scream at them but my voice is hoarse. I am a simple woman, an ordinary woman and I mean no harm, only to heal. *A simple woman, I tell you!*

They do not stop. I am being pulled backwards and my skirts catch over my head and I am twisting as they pull and OH MY BACK!" Lian threw herself up and back onto the couch, beads of sweet standing out on her forehead "Help me! What is...oh no! They can't, they shouldn't! Please, I am begging you!"

Silence save Alicia's clock ticking in the kitchen, barely audible. Lian lay inert, panting. "I must get her through this!" Alicia thought. There was no point in reliving this part. The rape, the torture, the humiliation were all best left un-remembered. It was not necessary to remember details, only to understand their effects, to know where the terrible raging anger came from.

And the love.

And the understanding of *how not to be.*

"Go forward no beloved, go past this to the evening. Where are you now. It is dark, almost night. Where are you?"

The voice which replied was dull and flat, painful to hear.

" I am in the cell," replied Lian as Marguerite.

"The cell? A prison?"

"I know not! A cell, a small dark room and I am chained to a seat here. A seat is all there is, a slab of stone. And I...."

"Yes, go on?"

"I have ...lost an eye."

"What has happened to you, lady?"

"No lady now, no mistress, either. They...those men, foul men...did things to me. The two men who dragged me about, they...oh!...I think my arm is broken, dislocated. I am no longer...virgin. I am...hurting now.

I do not know....why."

"Shall we go forward in time?"

Lian only nodded, gulping rapidly. Alicia knew there was no way around the last leg of their psychic journey. Be brave little Lian, child of the Greening.

"It is the morning. Where are you Marguerite?"

"I am still sat against the wall. I cannot feel...bits of myself. I am disintegrating. And...oh, they are coming in. Can I go home now? They reach around me with a key and undo the lock on my chain, like they are afraid to touch me. I can't move. They throw me a rag to put on. I was naked, it seems. I can't move but they do not wish to have contact with my flesh...as if it is corrupt. My poor torn flesh...oh, and the shame of it all! One finally throws the filthy rag over my head and hoists me to my feet. I crumple back onto the stone slab. My soul has shrivelled up, my body is collapsing inwards. Why? WHERE AM I AND WHAT HAVE I DONE?

More pulling, more pain. Outside again and thrown like baggage into a cart. Strange, wooden cart like a cage on wheels. Full of straw? Have I become a beast going to market? Will no one tell me?"

Lian was weeping silently.

"Can you see what happens next?"

"I do not want to!"

"Just a little more and we can leave this place forever. It will not hurt you. You will see pictures but it cannot hurt you. Imagine you are watching a film now, this is not your pain but an imaginary pain, one that cannot be felt in the body. Just watch a little longer and then we can leave this vision for good and all and you will be well."

"Do you promise?" Lian sounded like a child.

"I do."

"Is Julien with you? He promised!"

"Julien is safe, lady, he wants you to be well. Let us look at what happens next and then we can leave the scene. Just a little further. You will feel no more pain...just like a film now...*no more pain...*What can you see?" Alicia prompted Lian, knowing that this would be hard but not impossible.

(*No more pain, please!*)

"I see a market square, we are pulling up there and people, lots and lots, crowds...all peering in at me...jeering...I am caged!"

Suddenly Lian felt as if she were herself again, back as Lian in the Twentieth Century, and was indeed watching a film of someone else with a more detached sense of horror and shock.

" The woman, the Maman, Marguerite, she is looking through the bars of her wooden cage-on-wheels and she sees the market square, thronged with people, waiting and they open the hatch and lift her down and she falls but once again they have her on her feet. And there is an empty stone square, surrounded by buildings and unfamiliar faces and...oh God....NO!" the breath hissed out like steam from between Lian's teeth. "I understand now. Marguerite sees what they have prepared for her even though her vision is going and she knows Julien did not lie to her.

Three crosses, blackened wooden crosses stand stark against the October morning light. Grey and black, shades of death all around, the calling of carrion crows who wait alongside people with doughy, wan faces leering. Jagged, pale stones piled on top of each other to form tall looming buildings, walls everywhere, no escape, hemmed in by bullies and bigots! And...

NOT THAT WALK! NOT YET!! *Please...please...please...*"

Tears ran freely down Lian's face and Alicia felt her own grief, hot and salty.

"Three stakes, yes. One is prepared for her, for the Maman. Marguerite divides herself up now, spirit retreating, body walking onwards towards what is hers, but is really not hers at all. I can hardly comprehend the pain, the travesty. Oh, poor Marguerite! There are two others. WHO? Who are those other two stakes for? But no one will tell Marguerite, the good Maman, and so she is tied with a thick, greasy rope and bound to her fate. I look across and see one stake is already alight. Marguerite cannot see enough though for they have taken her eye and the smoke is blinding and the stench! Dear Lady! The terrible smell...The crowd roars and the waves of sound and cries...I hear Marguerite crying and I know her thoughts. Marguerite thinks, she thinks '*I know her...*'

(I know you!)

She strains against her bonds and sees, or thinks she sees...

Yes, she sees the woman on the first stake die and perceives those violet eyes and her black hair hanging loose and

(*Allette! Marguerite!*)

Allette! they took Allette and killed her too! Oh...she is gone, devoured by someone else's hatred and their choking, stinking fumes.

The second stake...Marguerite wishes that she could see but how can she? How can *I*?"

Sobs wracked Lian's body again.

'*She has to feel this, to get through it!'* Alicia thought as she hung on, wanting with all her heart to spare her friend from this anguish, knowing that it was nearly over and then there would be deeper understanding and healing. Oh sweet healing!

"Carry on, beloved?" Alicia asked Lian, oh so gently.

"They are bringing him out, from another wagon, dragging him and he is screaming and beating at them and I am torn between feeling my grief for my dear, kind, gentle Allette, she who helped in the kitchens, she who assisted me and talked to me and saw me as a mother while I made the lace she so admired and for....oh Christ and Mother Mary let it not be him...

(AM NOT A WITCH! AM NOT A WITCH! AM NOT...)

It is him and his screams...*oh, my darling love!*..his screams are killing me! Tell me, does he see Marguerite? Does he see *me?* Marguerite calls and calls to him but her throat is raw and he just keeps screaming. She tries to lift her hand to make him see her but he just goes on and her voice is so rusty. And she is bound..."

Suddenly Lian went limp and the voice lifeless and hollow.

"He sees her not, he knows her not. Marguerite means nought to him as he dies. They kill him, slowly. And the pain she feels as her blood sings in their flames is nothing. NOTHING!

For he knew her not.

And he is gone. And Marguerite is done too. Dead, all of them. The Maman has gone yet she rises up...I rise up...

...yes, and see three pyres, those of Marguerite and her best friends Julien and Allette, and....and oh God, Julien is gone and I float over Avignon, alone. My soul is deserted, bereft. This is real pain, this is punishment beyond fire and torture. This is my soul, alone, and I drift over their walls, like the smoke and I am...*gone.*"

"It is time to come back now, dear one"

"I know," Lian's voice was small.

"And when you return you will know that you are going to see Julien again and that all the hurt you felt will be wiped away in renewed joy. You will know that we *return* and that all pain passes away and we find, in many ways, another way to be and express ourselves. You will float now, in peace, receiving the light for a few moments, finding healing for your soul, and then you will return the way you came. When you are ready you will find the big wooden door you came though and you will step through it. You will leave this life of Marguerite's behind, for good and all, and you will come back up the stairs into your dwelling. The only thing that you will bring back with you is the knowledge of her gifts, the Maman's gifts, of healing with herbs. You will bring back the wildcraft of the medieval village wisewoman with you, beloved. These are your gifts. All you have done is *re-membered* them.

In your now time now, Lian, accept the healing light and return through your door, bringing that spark of divine healing light with you into this reality."

Alicia sat back, feeling exhausted and sad, for in that telling she had relived, once again, her own demise as Allette, the maid-servant to the Lady Veronique, Marguerite's friend and confidante. It had been hard but successful. She looked over at Lian, she could feel the pure light filling her soul as she floated in the space between worlds, where time was no time. A beautiful glow suffused the woman's aura. Alicia knew that she was, through her own guidance and by Lian's own natural ability, receiving the healing she so needed, in spirit.

"Time to go through the door now...." Lian murmured.

Alicia followed Lian's progress up the stairs, into the hallway and out through the front door of her Tudor house. She gave her guided instructions of how to get back over the grassy bank, across the stream and through the hollow tree. Alicia brought her through the wood and into the open meadow.

"Now, when I count to three you will return to the present, to the moment we experience as the *Now* and you will be fully in your body, your current body of the healer and *seer* Lian Smythe. When you return just open your eyes slowly and remain lying down.

One...two...*three!*"

Lian shook her head vigorously. She found herself back in the room with Treeface, her story completed.

He was crying. Really crying. There was no holding back, now.

"I let you down, beloved!"

Lian took a deep gulp of water.

"I knew it'd be hard for you to hear all that!"

"I didn't get to say I loved you! I didn't let you know how much I cared!"

"But I know now, my darling! We are lucky to be able to *re-member* so that we can put it all behind us, put it to rest."

"But I let you die without even a goodbye, without even an acknowledgement, because of my own blind panic and pain!"

"I know! And it hurt me, it truly did, but I understand *returns* now and the seasons that must pass and fade and the lessons we have in *how not to be* and my pain...well, my pain is no less but it has meaning now, at least. Without it I would not know the pure wonder of our love at its most beautiful and profound. In its depths I find the intense joy of our connection, its strength, its eternal nature. Our eternal nature..."

"We were innocent, though! And we were not..."

"We were simple and ignorant and no, we were not witches, we were just us; Fey souls trapped in human shells, just as we are now. We were different, is all. Nothing's changed, we are just as different now my love only in this *Now* no one can burn us. But witch is just a word, lover, just a harmless word used to describe our essence that can be used as a justification to cause harm. It made no sense to us then and it need not worry us now. Just as I feel no desire to meet my attackers or murderers so do I feel no need to hate the words they used on me. All that matters to me, all that ever mattered in this life of mine, was to meet with those I loved again, not to meet with those who hated me or who harmed me. If they wish to meet with me to make amends then so be it but my links are forged from love, not revenge! They were not of my kind, not Fey-souled, and like called to like for love is stronger than hate in me, to be sure."

"You don't blame me, or even hate me a little, for letting you down? For never letting you know of my love? I was wounded inside, Lian, they took and killed my sister, I accept that now! Before I knew the pain of losing you I had to face the terror of them taking Lilette, she who is now my dear Lydia. They took her because she did dabble in witchery, unlike us, and it was a dangerous game for one so young and beautiful as she, just as it is today! But Lydia won't listen to me now any more than Lilette would back in that lifetime in France."

If Lian felt her usual grief at Treeface calling Lydia beautiful she was determined not to let it show. "But they cannot burn her now, beloved. Lydia is quite safe to practice her natural magic in this age, in this *Now*. You have to let her go!"

Treeface shook his head sadly, a tear dripping off onto the carpet in front of them. "I know, I know, but it's so hard! Loving is hard! And, you know, at the time I was afraid of love for the pain of losing her was unbearable, my impotent frustration excruciating! Oh, God how I suffered, how *Julien* suffered, when they took Lilette to the stake! I had promised my poor parents to protect Lily with my life and I failed them and I failed her her! How could I ever trust myself to get close to anyone again when I was such a useless man, a fool, a loathesome coward? Much safer for everyone if I kept on the move, like a pariah, never settling or getting too close. I lived like I did to avoid commitment, and, in truth, I gave much to others, to strangers who didn't mean much to me, but I gave so very little to you! And why? For fear of attatchment...and the inevitable loss that would follow! There was no bravery in me, Lian, none at all. I drifted and I touched lives lightly but I would never open myself fully lest the awful crippling panic come out and when it finally did, it blinded me. I was struck dumb by the fear! The agony of it made me deaf to your cries as my own were so loud! My terror made me a cripple.

Tell me truly, Lian, do you not feel any anger about my abandoning you? Or...my lack of...oh God! *I let you die*! How can you not hate me?" Treeface's impassioned speech was almost a howl.

"Yes but everything's alright now, don't you see? We have made it alright again and we both understand it and there's nothing to forgive! The love survived....we survived! Our Fey souls are indestructible...isn't that magical? Isn't it worth living for?"

"But I am *so sorry*! You called out to me and all I felt was my own pain, my own overwhelming fear! You needed me and...I am so sorry!"

And for the first time he reached out to Lian, rather than vice versa, and clung to her, sobbing. And they rocked each other as they both whispered their love and their apologies and their vows never to leave each other again.

(*Always, my beloved...whatever happens...I love you all there is...beyond all else.*)

And some bonds were severed and other ones made as they stayed locked together until they both fell back amongst the remnants of their meagre celebratory meal and Lian removed his tattered old collarless shirt, his bright neckerchief, his faded trousers. And her took off her omnipresent black jumper and jeans and reverently, with infinite care and attention, they touched each other, fully, with complete knowledge of who they were.

(*Sweetheart...beloved...mai kae ati!*)

Ah yes, in that perfect *Now* there were eyes, eyes that were green on grey; eyes that eternally reflected souls that were entwined together like ivy on an old sun-warmed stone wall. Tracks of tears that had waited centuries to be shed in eachother's presence escaped those beautiful eyes and washed away delicately drawn copper beech leaves, inscribed on a dear face by a lovers hand. The sound of sighing, like the Equinox winds through the thin branches of crack willow, lifted them and let them fly together as, skin-on-skin, they rocked like a little boat on a calm, clear sea. Long, lean fingers wrapped themselves in fine hair and kisses rained down forever as they floated and flew, rose and dipped, elemental and wild and free.

And, looking deep into each others essence, they held each other's bodies long into the night and cried again as they saw tiny lights sparking across the blackness in the skies over their city. Through their uncurtained windows and behind their own closed eyes there were stars, *there would always be stars.*

And they both knew then that out of their immeasurable pain came a boundless capacity to love, the two Fey souls uniting, igniting the night, creating a third thing born on the Faerytide.

When Lian felt the soul enter her she was not surprised.

Part Three

The Returning

Chapter One

Tall Tales

"I love you."

It was a simple statement, spoken with feeling, and as such it was neither overtly passionate or wheedling. I looked up and saw the now familiar and dearly beloved tree-face, the one permanently reflecting the man's connection with the land, with his own green roots. It was the first time Treeface had ever said those words to me spontaneously and my heart leapt for joy in my chest and the once damaged wings of my spirit unfurled a little more, bright with incandescent tongues of flame.

It was the springtime of our romance; we rode the upswell of our passion and felt the resurgence of a way of being that we had dared not to dream of experiencing again. Despite all of our misgivings and ingrained fears it was a time of wonders, a time to give thanks for blessings bestowed.

It was a time of *returns.*

Outside, the weather was so foul that although it was only two o'clock on an April afternoon we had the light on. A light, I noted with no little sense of satisfaction, that I had managed to find a cheap shade for in a cheerful orange colour.

I had found myself being able to get us all manner of little essentials for our home after realising that if I focused on what we needed then invariably it would turn up, for a small fee, in one of the cities many second-hand shops. I had even learned to take pleasure in bargain hunting and the acquisition of *things*; things which were actually needed though as I still had little time for mindless consumption of goods and the mores of modern society. It was just as well that I was not tempted by Bath's more obvious commercial side with the puny amount I usually had in my purse.

Within the safety and relative security of our relationship, skills and interests were surfacing from deep within me, things that may have been lost or never nurtured previously. My innate Fey knowledge of herbal lore had risen to my surface after my regression to the life of Marguerite and my abilities as a *seer* were burgeoning under Treeface's loving care. I was discovering more about myself in the handful of marvellous months we had spent together than I had ever known in the past twenty nine years. I had, for example, discovered I had a certain flair for design and aesthetics and took pride in furnishing our three small rooms gradually on our limited budget. There was, to my mind, far more satisfaction in kitting out a kitchen in second-hand cast-offs that had taken time and energy to find than buying everything brand new. Not only this but by their purchase through ethical charities I had also helped good causes. My Fey spirit, given a glorious free reign, could not countenance supporting a throw-away society by getting everything I wanted brand new. Alicia's tale of 'the Makers' had touched me deeply and I did not wish to hoard that which was *man*-unfactured for the sake of ownership. I hated being thought of as a 'consumer', it seemed so against my inherent soul-nature, a nature that, from now on, I wanted to be true to. My new make-do-and-mend ethos supported my desire for a Greening of the land and all her children and in so doing it satisfied me.

Our basic way of green-spirited living, and desire our to recycle all we could ,was augmented by spending as much time out in the woods as possible, working simple magics and, with the plants permission, gathering herbs for my teas and syrups, tinctures and creams. Homespun from the golden thread of our philosophy, shot through with the silver of genuine treasures found under stone and in green shade, these were good days...days in which my soul, like an injured bird, took comfort and solace, taking time to grow strong again.

Treeface, I realised, had been watching me for a considerable length of time. I had been so absorbed in my task as not to notice his intense gaze. For once he had caught me behaving un-self consciously and it hid prompted him to speak the only words I ever really wanted to hear. He loved me for who I was. My hand went instinctively to my belly as I settled down next to him.

"Thank you," I put the fullness of my heart and soul into my eyes, or so I hoped, wanting him to know how much a gesture like an unprompted declaration of love meant to me.

"How's it going?" he asked, referring to the sheet of paper I was transforming into a flyer to promote his new business. The little I had learned on my Foundation Art and Design course, years ago when I had first known Robert, still stood me in good stead, although I knew that my simple, hand-drawn lettering and illustrations were out-moded by the standards of the day. We had not had computers when I was studying and even if we had the sophisticated Apple Mac's of the late Twentieth Century I doubted that I would have used them; my resolutely Luddite ways would have prevailed and my resistance to anything that didn't seem traditional would have stopped me from enjoying the real creative advances of living in the *Now.* Perhaps, when things were more settled, I could bring myself up to date with a computer course at college...not that we could afford one. Would we ever be able to?

It was fortunate that the basic, child-like script and pictures that I was reasonable at executing suited the project that Treeface was to undertake. I sought to put together as alluring and evocative a presentation for his work as I could muster with my somewhat elementary skills. I was aiming to put a little extra into it too, centring on the task in hand with a fierce intensity of will so that it should look as irresistible as I wanted it to...hence my total ignorance of his staring at me. Alicia would have said that my creative focusing was an act of magic and I would be tempted to believe her. It did indeed feel as if I was crafting a spell, lost in a dream-like state in which only the task and its message, its *energies,* existed.

That was the beauty of art, making something come to life on the empty page. It was true sorcery, a manifestation of form from the energy of pure thought which was translated into being by my will and skill. It was almost intoxicating.

I couldn't have been that amateur as a designer, even though I was a bit rusty, as I was always being asked to draw up display posters for the Centre to advertise forthcoming outings and events. They had caught me doodling in a distracted moment and had recognised a skill in me that could be utilised. I was no longer 'anti' the mental health care organisation's Centre. In fact, since meeting Treeface I was widely considered to be one of their 'successes' and my doctor, a compassionate if overworked man, had suggested to the staff there that they let me try a little work with them. So I now frequented the Centre twice a week as a supporter to the other clients when previously I had been a client myself. Theorganisation had a hard enough job recruiting paid staff on the meagre wage it was able to pay and so they were glad to accept me in that role, if justifiably wary at first. I had, after all, been a strange and distant client of theirs only a matter of months ago. Yet having learned to 'turn off', or at least protect myself from, the psychic flow I received from those at the Centre who were genuinely and distressingly mentally ill, I was far more able to cope with being of real help to them. All that they wanted, all anyone ever wanted perhaps, was someone to listen to them with full attention. To listen without judgement or salacious curiosity and to really see them...just as Treeface had just really seen me as I had busily gone about my drawing task in complete absorption, free of any artifice or pretension.

It was no end of pleasure to me to realise that, joy of joys, Treeface liked what he had seen so much that he had to tell me he loved me!

I reached over and pulled the piece of paper towards us.

"It's going great because I've realised I can enjoy something when it means something to me, not like when I was studying art and being given projects like 'design a label for a new aftershave'! I was so belligerent then that I would protest that I wasn't going to draw anything that supported animal testing just for the sake of a frivolous product that probably smelled appaling anyway! Even though I was not consciously aware of my innate green spirituality I still acted on it! I spent half my time at college trying to shut off the noise of *the voices* and the free-flying thoughts of a couple of dozen intense young would-be artists and the rest railing against anything they asked me to do which was structured or business orientated! The Greening has always been strong in me, even when I had no name for it, and I was never going to make a commercial artist!"

Treeface stretched over and took hold of the paper I had been working on. He himself had been busy typing out a couple of stories he had thought up years ago but had never gotten around to putting down on paper. He needed to write them out as an aid to helping him with their flow, soon he would have them learned by heart and could reel them off with feeling and emphasis. We also needed samples from each story as a taster of his 'act' to send off with our flyer, as original stories told by the author would be an added attraction. The laboured clack-clack of his old manual Smith-Corona typewriter, retrieved from Jane, had become a soothing counterpoint to the rain drumming on the window pane, lulling me so much so that I had not noticed it stop.

We seldom bothered to listen to music on a cassette recorder even more ancient and temperamental than then one Alicia had in her house and so our days were filled with silence or the natural, repetitive sounds of our existence. There is a rhythm to daily life that is far from mundane. And, of course, Treeface would play his fiddle, also salvaged from Jane's cottage, but usually only out of doors as our dear neighbour, who had now acquired a name beyond 'Mrs Upstairs', was apt to complain about the slightest creak or bang.

Appeasing Mrs ('Upstairs') Evans was one of Treeface's priorities, his aggravating her may contribute to making us homeless in a city already filled with the dispossessed and so it seemed unwise in the extreme. Finding a landlord to rent to us had not been the easiest task, not even with a good helping of Fey will-and-wishing, and we intended to keep our residence now we had been blessed enough to be granted it. I had seen too many of the young homeless people at close quarters after they had blagged their way in to the Centre just to huddle up against the big old Victorian radiator for an hour and scrounge a cup of something hot. I knew that most of these drifters, the unfortunate people who had nowhere to go and no one to go to, were definitely not 'crazy' and therefore shouldn't have been allowed in to use the facilities there which were designated for those sick enough in mind and body to be recommended by doctors and social workers. Yet a few ragged individuals somehow managed to gain entrance, if only for a fraction of their miserable endless days, and I felt their presences come and go with an inexpressible sadness.To them, life had no rhythm and certainly no tune and that made me weep sometimes. The Fey-souled human has a deep sensitivity to injustice and unhappiness that is easily made unbearable by the suffering and pain of others, yet rather than dwelling on such negatives I concentrated on praying for a Greening for them. My own attitude of gratitude for the things I did have was huge and omnipresent.

I tried to put names to their prematurely lined faces. Even wraiths, the lost and the lonely, deserved a name to go by. Even I had needed a name to go by, once, beyond 'Freaky Smythe'. The lost, disenfranchised ones I saw around Bath were simply walking roads I myself had not taken but could have done, easily. They saw me as different to them, more privileged, perhaps, while I saw myself as the same as them, walking a parallel and equally hazardous path that could easily veer off into obscurity or mortal danger at any time. I was only luckier than them, for now.

(If it hadn't been for Alicia, for Treeface...even for my father...)

Treeface was always donating some of his own meagre earnings to fellow urchins who we were only one step away from in terms of social standing. We had a roof over our heads and were always grateful, always fully aware of it, but besides that fact we were as much outcasts as they were, outlawed from a world of mortgages and cars and bank balances by our very nature.

"There but for the grace of the Gods..." Treeface would mutter and touch his forehead in some gesture of protection as we acknowledged the worn out old-young man who was almost indistinguishable from the piles of rough blankets he mounded himself in to keep warm or to cocoon himself from the hostile world. He would draw his primal chalk pictures on the paving slabs around his 'pitch' and collect his pittance from the odd pedestrian whose conscience was pricked by his child-like images.

There but for the grace of someone, for sure.

So, we had good fortune enough to be spending the day in a relatively warm, dry flat working on launching Treeface into business as a storyteller and musician for schools and libraries in the local area. Any establishment catering or caring for children within a bus ride of Bath was considered as a target venue and we had gone through all the phone directories in the library to cover all the ground we could. We would need a phone, for appointment bookings, and had managed to borrow the money off Lydia for that. She had sent us a money order from Norwich where she was temporarily teaching writing for a week and so we were all set to receive calls for prospective clients, thanks to her. I had yet to meet her again, face to face, but for now I tried my hardest to swallow my jealousy and be grateful, not only for the cash loan but also for the fact that Treeface, my beloved Julien, had his sister restored to him again. And despite his protestations and sulks she was doing exceptionally well with her new 'witchy' book. Wasn't modern wild witchcraft just working towards the Greening too, in its own way?

It may seem like an extravagance to borrow money from Lydia when we ourselves were both doing so badly in terms of cash-flow but we were in dire need of a top-up to Treeface's earnings and so her investment in the venture was essential. He had started to busk with his fiddle for money, which he had to do despite the curiosity of the public, but competition was high on the streets of our lovely city and the local council were not supportive to the raggle-taggle element which filled each square or alley with a random assortment of performances...anything from sub-standard Bob Dylan to baroque flute. Regulars to be found busking on the street were a beautiful duo with a dulcimer, a disabled man who had rigged up all manner of clanking, horn-blowing things to become an anarchic one-man band from his wheelchair and even a rough looking lanky skinhead playing the bagpipes with amazing skill. Unless Treeface got a prime spot in the centre of town extremely early in the day, or was out of range of any louder, more persistent rival, and if the council chose to turn a blind eye to him, he stood little chance of making a killing from his unobtrusive, folksy fiddle playing. Although he would have been loathe to admit it, it may only have been his interesting scars, covered in my drawn-on leaves, that drew people over to listen to him in the first place.

The days of people being enchanted by a funny little man who looked like a traveller and played as wickedly wonderfully as the devil himself were, it seemed, drawing to a close and so any saleable gimmick, even his scars, had to be played upon. The life of the impecunious mendicant, be they minstrel or tinker, peddler or poacher, was never and easy on but now...well, people wanted sleek not shabby, they wanted it bigger and better, they wanted it *smart*. And if it couldn't be smart then it had to be so weird or outlandish as to hold their fleeting, computer-conditioned, attention.

Still, the trump card that Treeface would always have to play was that of a genuinely odd figure, seemingly from another age ,which would contrast so strongly with the air-brushed, pixelated 'real world' so markedly as to make it startling, desirably so perhaps. *'A breath of fresh air!'* I had thought to head my promotional flyer for him as that was what he was. *'Like the wind through the wildwood making the leaves dance...Treeface will bring you hours of listening pleasure!'* I wrote in my passable calligraphy, hoping that it wasn't too overblown or unsophisticated for today's children. I wanted to sell the magic of my peasant Prince, with his dancing eyes and clever hands, but not to exploit him, only so that we could eat and keep our roof. I was simply using all the tools in the boxes we had been given and imbuing them with as much Fey starlight as I could to attract attention and enchant people.

I had thought long and hard about the most appealing way I could present Treeface to a primarily 'straight' audience; to the teachers and librarians who would decide if he, was worth paying for or safe enough to employ for an afternoon yet I had also striven to find the most *palatable* way. Treeface was, I was determined to show, no hippy-dippy chap who may be unreliable or drugged up, rather he was genuinely a reminder of a gentler age, a troubadour, a balladeer, a minstrel and a bard. He was, I endeavoured to portray, a *respectable* ragamuffin! And, if that wasn't enough to convince them, to all of this I added the potent enchantment of my wish-and-willing, my Fey enchantment. I wasn't above utilising that for positive ends, not now I had discovered it and fully embraced it as my own, as my birth-rite and my gift to the All.

I had wanted something innocuous as well as charming, eye-catching and memorable without being threatening or weird. This had proved to be quite a tricky blend for me to achieve, especially as I considered the idea of Treeface being thought of as outrageous or dangerous quite offensive. So, I had drawn a man sat on a tree-stump yet subtly blending into it, dressed in flamboyant patchwork and doffing his cap to the viewer while tipping them a cheeky wink. The friendly figure, with leaf-embellished facial scars, was holding out one arm as if he were about to proclaim something interesting while holding his fiddle in the other. It looked fun and colourful, deliciously cheeky as well as traditional, with a real Faery-tale feel that I sensed would enhance Treeface's chances of getting taken on. I felt that this traditional aspect would appeal especially to teachers of a younger age range; children who would still find an innocent delight in the actuality of a man who looked like a cartoon, rather than vice versa. What good teacher wouldn't want to encourage that? They were probably shown the latter on the television at home most of the time but had they ever seen the real thing? The resurgence of interest in the wizardry and Faery magic of 'Lord of the Rings', albeit through a more modern media that utilised technologically superior ways, was on our side at least. We were yet to hear how well the modern myths of Harry Potter would do but it seemed a positive move towards a renewed interest in the ways of enchantment, folk-lore and mystery.

Treeface's rates for a session were to be reasonable and, as far as we knew, no one else had thought of such an enterprise as travelling around schools in our area. *Our* area! Oh, to think of myself as local, as belonging! We had decided that Treeface would introduce himself with fiddle music and tell his wonderful original stories as well as folk-tales and myths. It would be another string to his bow, as it were. He intended to enhance the sessions with a little more fiddle playing, getting the children to clap along if possible, or even compose words for his tunes. He was going to try and write, or find, stories with references to minstrels or just use the fiddle as a way of magically emphasising a particular piece of the narrative. There were all sorts of links in to the session that we would suggest teachers could use as follow ups, in terms of history, music, language and poetry as well as personal and social education focusing on celebrating people's individual differences.

Treeface looked a little unsure of my poster and my heart sank a little. "It's colourful, for sure," he said, " but d'you think that we should have done them in black and white, to save on photo-copying costs?"

"Are you saying it's too bright or something?"

"Ah, now, you know me, I'm nothing but a big worry-wort. If a things worth doing it's worth doing properly and all that but of course I worry about the cost of all this...and..."

"And?"

"And it's not your work that bothers me, sweetheart, I mean, it says everything it's meant to and gets it across beautifully but I am worried that they'll see this man in the picture and think I'll be looking like him when really a man with an old coat and a horrible scar will turn up and might just frighten them all half to death rather than entertain them!"

He twiddled with his moustache, a sure sign he was getting nervous. We had been through everything that had caused him sleepless nights, over and over, the potential police checks on his (hopefully clean) record, the references people may want...

"Well, I may not be a good judge of what the human-people enjoy but you've got the cap to doff and the wink to charm them with!" I said, trying to be bright about it. He may be right about his scars and shabby attire but the thought of him being rejected just because of his face, when he would be so good at storytelling and holding children's attention, was too deeply depressing a prospect for words.

"We could get you some new clothes, I mean, just a few bits...nothing extravagant. Just enough to tart your existing wardrobe up a bit...can you sew?"

Treeface laughed at the use of my word 'wardrobe'. His clothes took up one drawer in the chest he had made for a few pounds out of pine off-cuts.

"I sew as badly as I can ballet dance. Lydia used to do all of that, the mending and all. She had the hands for it, little and nimble. She was a dab hand."

My face fell. "I can't sew either," I sniffed.

"You're right enough though," Treeface knew he had touched a raw nerve by singing Lydia's praises like that and rushed to cover his mistake by sounding more enthusiastic than he felt, "we could pick up a few second hand bits for my act, it would be an investment after all, in the long run. We may have to go without a loaf of bread or two this week but it'll pay off in the end if I look a bit more...the part, you know?"

I covered up my hurt at his previous remark. What would be the point of us falling out just because I was still so stupidly vulnerable and jealous? I had to accept, sooner or later, that Treeface had a life, and other loves, before me and as well as me. There was room for us both in his heart, surely? As long as I had the biggest piece of it...

I swallowed hard.

"We could get a new pair of trousers for a couple of pounds and sew a few bright squares of fabric on them as if they were patches...you've already got a waistcoat even if it is a bit faded...and get you a brighter neckerchief, that'll only be a few pence in a second-hand shop...we could dye some of your old shirts a more vibrant colour...."

"We could get some face paints and get the kids to add leaves to my tree-face, just like you do too! That'd be a nice touch, for the ending of a session. Yes, it'll get them involved!"

"Yes!" I hated to quash the fire of his enthusiasm now it had caught but I wondered if teachers nowadays would be happy with their pupils clambering over a strange man to paint on him? Perhaps now I was being too negative.

"That's a fine idea. And we can collect feathers, acorns, shells, and hang them from ribbons from your walking stick! You'll be a wonderful representative of the Greening, my love!" Treeface had a wonderful staff he used, it was hazel and was naturally formed into corkscrews and curves by some miracle of nature. A beautiful thing which he had made glossy with linseed oil, it would look even more magical if adorned with nature's treasure for his 'act'. We went on enough walks in the local woods to collect an assortment of natural ornaments in a short time period, Treeface came into his own in the countryside and I had no doubts that he could find what he would need among the hedgerows. Our wild Fey spirits *would* shine through and *would* touch people, I had to have faith in that. The Greening was so desperately needed, so terribly overdue...

"Let's do it, let's go out foraging for nature-charms on the next dry day we get!" Treeface beamed at me, "no point in going out in this weather, getting a chill isn't going to help me get on with the work! I hope this bloody rain stops soon though, I need to get down into town and play as soon as I am able. We so need the..." He paused, knowing that he was going to get into another huge fret about money and food and bills and worry me badly. I could see him visibly pull himself out of the gloom that so readily waited for us both when we discussed cash-flow. "Yes, I will really look forward to that, sweetheart, it'll be a lovely thing to do, to go collecting."

I smiled back at him, aware of the games we had to play with eachother in order to 'keep it together' as he put it. The downside of our innate Fey sensitivity was we easily fell into the pits of despair when forced to dwell on how society marginalised us and made us grovel on its outskirts for a means to survive. It was either that or get angry with eachother just so that we could get our panicked feelings out and either of us wanted to do that, obviously. So time and again in the short and precious time we had been together we donned our cheery masks and glossed over our strains and stresses.The funny thing was though, we were so close to eachother, so tuned in, as to know exactly what the other was doing anyway. We were, after all, as one! With that thought I laughed and saw Treeface relax a little again. What a funny pair we were.

It wouldn't be difficult for him to do, earning our living by enrapturing a young audience, would it? If he could only put a glamour on himself, as he was apt to do when we really needed the money from his busking skills, then he'd hold them spellbound. He was charismatic enough as a person, scar or no scar, but with a little extra pizzazz he could be magical to a child used to seeing figures like him only in their picture books. I know I'd have loved him as a child, he would have been like a Hans Christian Anderson character or someone from Grimm's stepping into the classroom with his twinkling eyes and expressive gestures. Had times really changed so much that it would no longer be enough for him to beguile them in a quaint, olde-worlde way?

"Can't you ask the spirit guides for help on this one? For them to give you some astral 'glitter' to make you seem more...er, snazzy?" I asked him, tentatively. Treeface was still very sensitive about words like magic because of the connotations with witchcraft but he may be more open to considering it if it came from his companion spirit guide, an earthy elemental man called Kefli.

I had never 'seen' Kefli but I had a good description of who and what he was from Treeface. He was one of our kindred; a Faery-soul who had lived in the Otherworld since the extermination and persecution of the Children of the Greening but whose presence could be felt strongly in this realm. Even though he no longer walked the Earth in a strictly physical form he could guide us from the *beyond*. He had long ago assumed the appearance of dark twisted bark, a raggedy man made of sticks and twigs with wicked yellow eyes and a hooked nose and four immensely long fingers on each dextrous hand. An impish figure with a fiery personality, Kefli had a penchant for doing tricks and 'tripping up humans' as he liked to call it but he was a thoroughly accurate, incisive spiritual guide for Treeface and highly appropriate in terms of energies.

I had my own companion spirits of course, maybe I should ask them too? And Alicia...why weren't we including Alicia in this? Goodness we hadn't even been to see her yet. We MUST!

"I think that's probably the best idea. Kefli will be able to throw a cloak of 'cosmic stardust' over me and make me seem like a more interesting proposition all together," Treeface mused, drawing his long legs up to his chin and plucking more insistently at his overly long moustache. "I need their help, don't I? I need a little extra something behind me. I really can't afford for this to fail, you know, especially with me having two of you to support..." he looked at me meaningfully and again my hand went to my flat stomach in a reflex action.

There had been no signs as yet that I was pregnant but we were so sure that I would be. Because of what had happened before with Robert's child, and because this one was so important, I had not yet dared go to see my doctor, no matter how lovely and supportive he would no doubt have been. A simple pregnancy test would have proved the prospective child's existence, or not, but they were expensive and I felt, after Robert's child, understandably superstitious. Wasn't it enough of a diagnosis of pregnancy that both of us had felt the rush as the spirit had come into my body even as we cried out in our love-making? Wasn't it enough that we had welcomed the spirit in and felt it accept our offer, that third soul that would share our blood and bones?

(*But, oh God, if it were real could we afford this child?*)

"It doesn't have to be so desperate, I can always get work of some sort..." I trailed off. We had been over it what seemed like a thousand times from all the angles we could think of. Not only would I find it impossible *psychically* to work with the public too much, as the strain of keeping up protection would be totally exhausting, my current record of 'mental health problems' (thanks to my father) and my virtually non-existent work record made my chances of gainfully holding down any work very slight...and that was if anyone would even give me an interview, which so far they had not. Old peoples homes, bakeries, clothes shops...I had tried all the ones I could for part time work and hadn't even been given a reply in most cases. As much as I needed the woods and the land to sustain my spirit and heal me I also needed to be practical and spend the rest of the time making us money. But how? I didn't want to become unbalanced and ill again by doing too much or the wrong thing. Goodness but it was so hard living in the human world!

It was all very well me doing the odd day at the Centre, where I was known, but to hold myself in check *psychically* in a strange environment with less understanding people would be extremely hard on a regular basis. It would exhaust me, in fact, which would not be recommended in my current condition. I had to face facts; soon enough I would be thrity and, as inexperienced and bizarre looking as I was, virtually on the scrap heap as far as conventional employment went. Yes, we certainly needed help on this matter. I had to go and take Treeface to meet Alicia, she would know what we should do. Knowing her she would ask us to move into her cottage. And would that be such a bad idea? I would willingly give up our lovely little flat to be under her tutilege and care! Perhaps then she could make Treeface feel less fear about being himself 'in the world', just as she had managed to do with me, and if she could do it with me, I knew she could do it with anyone! Yes, I'd gladly live under her roof. But would he?

"No," Treeface wasn't reading my mind this time. He was just referring to my finding more 'straight' work in mainstream society. He shook his head and I knew he was adamant, "I know my role in our relationship. I am the provider, little *seer*. And let's not forget that you'll have work of your own to do, soon enough. I don't just mean...Michael Gabriel..."

These last words was almost whispered. We were incredibly reluctant to mention the word 'baby' so we had given a name to what we believed had happened to us. Michael Gabriel was our child, a boy that would bring us even closer together, fated and beautiful, another Fey Star Child who would incarnate to bring the Greening back to the

Earth. He was a huge-eyed being with startling curly white-blonde hair, so unlike us as to be another changeling child; one who I saw in my trance-vision, heaven sent and reaching out irresistibly with his chubby child's arms towards life and hope.

(*Did all prospective parents feel their child was to be special, one of the cherubim? I had no idea but I guessed that it may be so. I only knew what I saw and felt, as regards my own little miracle. I trusted in my* sight *for it had brought me thus far, relatively unscathed, and it showed me a curious boy crowned in the sun that wanted to be born to us. To us!*)

No matter how Treeface told me that he was happy to be our provider deep down, beyond the jovial and encouraging face I would wear, I was scared. He had spent so long being shielded for reality by the stalwart Janey that he hadn't really a clue how to behave or be in society. He was bound to get curiosity, even rudeness, from people and how would he cope? He was being very brave but my heart hurt to think of him wounded by attitudes. And what of our baby? Treeface and I lived in poverty, we were on the fringes of society and he wasn't even quite divorced yet...it seemed madness to bring a child into such a scenario but at the same time it felt *right.* It wasn't selfish desire on my part, I had never felt at all maternal and had long since resigned myself to a single, celibate, childless life. The child was not planned but wanted in the deepest part of me. I hoped, I *believed*, that Treeface felt the same way.

"I don't mean to reject your offers of help, I just mean," Treeface went on, "that you should be working on your psychic skills, little *seer,* so that then perhaps you can start to actually do it as a job, from home here, and be paid for helping people clairvoyantly, as a visionary. You could charge a fair rate per hour that would be far in excess of what I can earn on the street, you can only take selected clients to let you recharge yourself and you can be safe here with Michael Gabriel as opposed to being out of your natural environment without him. People want accurate psychics, proper old fashioned spiritual Mediums, they always will. I know since Hazel Pegg left town for the road there's not been a reliable *seer* in the vicinity but plenty of incoming aromatherapists, reflexologists and counsellors, all the same. I know you can't afford to do a proper training but you could make some herbal simples too, sell a few basic herbal cures, wildcrafted and filled with our starlight vision. Can't you see it, beloved? You'll be a wise woman!

You won't have to chase your beautiful arse round the streets looking for work when you can do these things, *alternative* things, to help folk. You'll be the real McCoy not just some pretender, some black-clad new-ager spouting waffle and platitudes..."

"Can I remind you I wear black!"

"Aye but out of poverty! It's far easier to gather a set of clothes together if they all match!"

"And, ages ago when I bought these rags of mine, I did actually have the logic that if they were going to treat me as an outsider I may as well look like one and slink around gloomily like a stray patch of midnight!"

"Ah, you're no wannabe...w...*witch,*" Treeface let the word come out in a rush as if dwelling on it would be unsavoury. "You would be a natural psychic even if you covered yourself from head to foot in a sack. You can't *man*-ufacture what you are from black velvet and silver trinkets! What you are isn't man-made at all! And you can't shirk from why you are here and your responsibility to your gift in the world...you know that! Ignoring it doesn't do anyone any good at all!"

I thought that this was rich coming from him although I didn't say so. Treeface himself did a mighty fine job of ignoring who he was, a natural and extremely gifted healer as trained by the McAllisters, for the sake of not being persecuted or even hassled, by society. My own lover was afraid of his innate Fey self, of its magic, incase it dragged him into the arena with the proverbial lions again. Yet now was not the time to challenge him and his almost phobic response to his own Fey skills, was it? I knew that reliving our French life together had made him feel more loving and apologetic towards me but it had done precious little to align him back with his own true nature as a magical being. He was just about ok with being the wandering minstrel, the colourful bard, but as for being a healer, forget it! Maybe I would challenge him one day. Soon, perhaps.

"Well, whatever I am, or whatever I can be in this society to earn us cash...it's a way off yet," I continued, the very thought making me flush with nerves. Oh yes, I could empathise with Treeface's fear only I wasn't going to let mine conquer me! I *would* be myself to help others. I *would* stand for the Greening! "I don't even know who my guides are right now, not really. I know I've worked with my spirit guides, asked for their help and felt them, but...who are they? Can we both do a journey to find out? You can ask Kefli for his help in making you seem ultra-appealing to those schools we approach and I can try and see who walks with me, in spirit."

('*Listen to me!*' Lian thought in amazement, catching herself for a minute, '*speaking like this as if this spiritual work was normal for me! All that time not having a clue who I was or what I did and now chatting to my lover about it as if it were quite usual!*')

"Good idea, my love," Treeface nodded, "and the day isn't much good for anything but being indoors, is it?" The rain was coming in almost horizontally again now, making the city of Bath outside our big window seem nothing but a wash of pale greys and sandy browns.

"Do you want to finish the poster first?"

"I can do that after tea this evening, before we lose the daylight altogether, can't I?" I said, popping the lid back on the turquoise felt-tip pen I had been using. We were going to get the poster photo-copied the next day and sent off in the afternoon, we had our list of schools all ready and the envelopes labelled in Treeface's sloping but impeccably neat handwriting. Perhaps we could even go around the second-hand shops looking for bits and bobs to cheer up his wardrobe, scraps of fabric we could somehow utilise to make him look like a brightly patched up tinker. And we could go to the woods, 'go collecting' as Treeface put it. Oh the joy there would be in that!

"Right, so, I'll get set up to do a path-working with you." Treeface picked up the pile of things I had left in a heap where I had been industriously beavering away on the floor like a child and placed it on our only table alongside our empty tea cups. He collected the candle and incense from the mantelpiece, careful to wipe the spilled dust and ash which fell from the from the wooden holder. He also brought me my journalling book from the shelf we had constructed from a plank of wood and a few breeze-blocks, scraps poached from a building site.

We sat opposite to each other, breathing in a united rhythm, quite used now to working one-to-one without any embarrassment. He had his long and in-depth training from the McAllisters and I had Alicia's shorter but no less credible advice and teachings to go by. I would let Treeface guide me through the journey, just as Alicia had done when we did the regression, but at the appointed time he would do his work and I would do mine before we both returned to the present together.

We both began to breathe more slowly, centring ourselves on the breaths we were taking and rooting ourselves like trees into the physical world. It was quite hard to do the rooting when we were in a flat above another flat with the real soil of the Earth somewhere far below us. Such difficult visualisations had made me more adept so that my imagination had strengthened a great deal over the time we had been in Flat Three Carlett Court, and that had to be a blessing in my proposed line of work.

('*And breathe...that's it beloved. And in...hold...and out....gentle does it. Deep and slow.*' I heard Alicia's voice directing me, encouraging me. Dear, dear Alicia, I really must take Treeface to see her, and soon!)

We both went through the ritual of imagining our protection, donning the blue and gold edged spirit-garments we wore habitually before entering the trance state proper. We would find our answers today by means of following a prescribed route into a sacred place within the Otherworlds. It was all in the minds-eye but as real to me as our rickety makeshift shelf was in the world we saw around us on a daily basis. In had no reason to doubt the firm reality of both realms. Not anymore.

Treeface let out a long sighing breath.

"Okay, let's imagine now, as we stand in our protective glow of light, that we are beside a slow moving river. A boat, our own personal boat, waits by the bank for us to step into it to undertake the journey this day." His voice was low, musical, sonorous. I loved it's dark brown, velvety quality. Treeface's voice, like Alicia's before him, made me feel confident and relaxed. It was a great skill they both had and I vowed that when I was ready to lead people into trance I would also moderate my tone to be both as mellow and as strong as an old oak.

I did wonder if I would ever have the confidence to use my own abilities as they could, to guide others; it would be so good to really help people.Then with a start I realised that my mind was wandering from the work in hand and so I focused back on the little wooden boat that waited for me on the silvery waters. The conscious mind did so want to distract! Instead of hearing my own doubts and putting energy into my internal witterings I channelled my intent creatively and saw the reeds move gently as I stepped into my boat and felt it sway a little. Rather than hearing my incessant inner chatter. I heard the plop of a fish as it surfaced and went under again in front of me.

The more I fed my vision the more I experienced it as reality and all else fell away from my awareness. The sun-warmed boards felt familiar and comforting under my hands as I caressed my small boat; the long, white, four fingered hands of my spirit-self shimmered in front of me as I admired their movements. In trance, on a spirit-journey, my astral body was as it had been once in the physical, a Fey, elongated and genderless form made of shifting light and shade. I moved like a being unlimited by any of the things that hampered the progress of Lian Smythe in the Twentieth Century. In spirit-form I was free to run without aching, to bend without breaking, to *be* without any sense of limiting anxiety, pride or phobia.

I felt restored by this. I felt immensely free. Trance work was very therapeutic, a two way exchange of energies, for as I was nurtured so was the Otherworld brought back into harmonious, vibrant being by my input. Once I got past the initial reluctance to immerse myself in the experience, that very human fear of losing identity, it was marvellous.

"Now, take the boat along the river, noting the sounds and smells around you, the quality of the light on the water, the feel of the moving air and continue on in this manner until you reach the stopping place where the mound is." Treeface's instructions filtered into my journey and I enhanced my senses accordingly and headed for the mound.

I pushed the boat away from the side of the bank with my wooden pole and moved off downstream, seeing the reflections fragment and reform as I passed, watching the ripples spread out around me. I heard a moorhen give its funny little call somewhere ahead of me and noted a water vole emerging from the river, scuttling up the grassy bank to my right. There was no driving rain in this landscape as there was in the 'real' world of Bath, the sun was watered gold and the sky was clear and tinted with a wash of palest violet. The trees ahead of me were clad in newly verdant mantles, their tender leaves of softest green still unfurling, speaking to me of resurgence as two swans rose in perfect unison from the reeds and took flight.

Across the field I saw the gentle slope of the mound. Instinctively, as pair-bonded in spirit as the two swans and filled with the grace and fluidity of their nature, Treeface knew that we were at the same point on our journey and continued to guide us.

"Now, we will pull up the boat and tether it so that it will be there for us when we are ready to journey safely homewards after our work is done. In our own time we will get out and walk to the mound which is ringed with silver birch trees. Beyond it lies the great forest and further still, the sea, but today we will not need to journey that far. We will wait there on the green mound and observe our surroundings. After a time we can set up the protective, sacred circle on the ground and ask for the beloved spirit guides to be present, if it is their will."

I did as I was bid, taking special care to make sure the boat did not drift away. In left my pole in the bottom of it. As I bent, I caught sight of my own spirit's reflection in the shimmering waters. Big, black eyes looked back though me, the head tilted quizzically, the enigmatic smile, such a tiny mouth...

('*Like an owl*,' I thought)

Or was it a beak? Feathers, white feathers.

('*Bird tribe*!' someone whispered and I almost knew what it meant.)

There was a barn owl sitting on the prow of my boat.

Instinctively In did what I had been taught (thank you Alicia!) and pointed at the newcomer who had spontaneously entered into my sacred space.

'*Show yourself truly, spirit!'* I said, speaking the words inside my own mind, focusing hard on the little bird which bobbed and weaved, its eyes never leaving mine. '*Who are you?'*

'*Ai raki taki mai*!'I heard myself answer my own question in the old tongue as the owl remained clearly before me. *I am as I am!* It was a true spirit, certainly no cunning, roguish impostor. But why was it there at all?

"You come expecting people as your spirit-mentors, you expect humans though you profess not to be overly fond of them as a species! Ah, you expect to see something you can understand as *normal,* just as you all do! Don't you know that spirit guides can be pebbles as much as priestesses? It's the *energies*...always the energies...ONLY the energies that count!"

I knew the voice as one I had heard in my journey's before, when I had felt presences attributed to my spirit guides but had not seen them. Alicia had never spoken to me of the possibility of guides being less than human, or Faery, spirit forms. A bird? How could we speak together?

"Tsk! I should have pretended to be some Shaman in a wild headdress, or a blessed monk in a cowl, so you'd pay attention to me and give me credence!" The owl let out a loud, unexpected screech. "Have you learned nothing, Elf Child? Know you not of wisdom and the sources of knowledge? Can it really be so, Green One, of starlight born and forged from the same energies as am I, that you attribute the *knowing* only to two-leggeds with clumsy bodies...not the winged ones so akin to your true nature....free flying, night-dwelling...hidden from human eyes?" The owl appeared to shake its head. It's voice, the one I heard so distinctly, emitted from all around it, not seeming to come from its beak...which would have been rather comical, I thought guiltily.

(*An owl with a little beak opening, speaking in the voice of middle-England, an owl with received pronunciation...I wanted to laugh out loud.*)

"Hmmm," the bird eyed me coldly, "perhaps I am not the one to teach you, to protect you, after all? Maybe you should look to those who would seek to trick you, calling themselves Gods, walking in mantles of gold and laying claim to lives as builders of worlds! Remember Henry the Eighth, child! Do you seek such rogue spirits to impress you now or will you take council with me after all? Ho, you human-centric flibberty gibbert; as if the universe is limited to an expression of the sacred only through the image of humanity! Ho, mistress, do I leave you now or are you ready to accept that spirit-walkers may speak truth clad in mantles of fur, feather or fin, clad in nought but ashes or snowflakes, communicating through sound, symbol or sausages if they so choose? Hmmm?" Again an ear-splitting screech. I got the feeling that was done on purpose to make me feel uncomfortable.

I could have sworn, then, that the owl was smiling, albeit a little grimly.

"You have much to absorb, *seer*, surprisingly stupid *seer*, much to know and little time to do the work in. Urgency, there is, about our task. No time for insults, mine or yours, nor for tomfoolery; no more time for fear and belligerence! What say you?"

"No! I mean, I am sorry to have offended you!" My spirit form bowed low to the bird. "I apologise. It is, indeed, short-sighted and foolish of me to expect certain beings to appear for me. Stereotyping, I believe it is called."

"Archetyping! Human-centricity!And so, starlit being, what say you to me now?"

I couldn't believe what I was now seeing, and shook my head as if to clear it. In the place of the owl an owl-woman now sat on the prow of my little boat, seeming to weigh no more than one of the beautiful soft feathers that made up her cloak. I gazed at her silent form in awe and wonder. Should I speak? Was she also the outspoken barn owl? What was expected of me now. I was about to point at her figure, impertinent as it may seem, to 'check out' her validity as a true spirit when I felt a stirring in the air. Something else was happening, I could *feel* it even if I couldn't yet *see* it. Feeling a little fear in case I couldn't handle this new development I perceived another very definite presence nearby. Not wishing to appear rude to the mute owl-woman I none-the-less felt compelled to see who this second presence belonged to and I turned towards it.

There was a Native American Indian man standing on the bank, bold as brass and clear as day.

"Oh no!"

The thought was out before I could stop it. There I was, Faery-soul and child of the Greening, on a green slope leading to a very English looking mound in my Otherworld which was created as a mythical Albion, all wildwoods and clear streams, standing stones and holy wells, and there was...as incongruous as it was possible to be...an Indian in the midst of it! Worse yet, what a cliché to have an Indian turn up as a companion guide!

"Yes, I know what you wanted!" The Indian visitor folded his arms and changed rapidly into a dark haired Elven man in green and grey with tall brown boots and a bow and arrow. I gasped, for the man he had transformed into was exactly the sort that I had desired to meet, one in whom I could trust; a sprite-like Robin Hood, a greenwood warrior for freedom and justice, one I thought that my spirit could resonate with. I had even expected to meet someone a little like Kefli, a Fey soul wearing the form the land itself, clad in a swirl of leaves, shrouded in shining mists.

Before I knew what to do the mysterious and indomitable Indian had returned, bare chested, with his greying hair in braids and his bare legs and feet planted apart, very much the classic Native American. Not only did he stand before me as clear and as bold as any Indian man I have seen in a picture but he then drew a circle of fire around his own feet.

I had forgotten, in my incredulity, to even test him out as genuine or make him stand in the protective ring of fire while I made my checks on his authenticity. It was clearly a day of lessons and no small amount of embarrassment for me.

He shook his head and sighed. "No need to berate yourself," he said, opening his arms to make a gesture which said '*well*?'

I hastily held up my long index finger and pointed at him.

"Spirit, show yourself truly!"

I asked once, twice, three times and there was a flash of light. Had he gone? No, if anything he was taller, sterner, but still undoubtedly Native and yet not native to my scenery. Should I do this 'checking out' procedure with the owl woman too? Was she even there anymore? All I could do was stare at the incongruous Indian man so I didn't know if she was there or not. I felt *compelled* to look at this Indian newcomer; it was as if everything else had telescoped in around him, making him stand out in vivid, startling relief against my green backdrop.

What now? He was undoubtedly present but disconcertingly silent. His obsidian eyes bored into me so much that I was remind of a similar pair of black eyes belonging to the owl.

"Lessons, lessons, all!"

The owl on the boat spoke again, throwing me totally off beam as I spun round to face it again. Yes, it was an owl now and not a woman! It walked a little along the gunnel and dipped its head. "You get what you *need* here, not what you *want*! Ha and ho! At this time you need to grow beyond your present understanding which is getting all bound up in attachments to bodies and countries and identities! These are only forms that suit us, no more or less, for their is nothing amiss with either owls or Indians, thank you very much! And certainly nothing to make them less spiritual than some Wood-Elf! *Ha!*

My lesson to you this day is this; FEEL the energy. *Feel it!* Listen always to the words, heed the gestures, take the symbolism and do not dwell on mantles we wear...EVER.

Heed me and feel me so that you may know me when I speak truly to you again, be that from beak or mouth or the spout of a kettle! Heed me well for one day you will be sorely tested if you think that all that wears green and grey is a good Elf and all that wears a human's armour is a foe. Shells and bells and cones and stones...FEEL IT IN YOUR BLOOD AND BONES!

If it feels right, if it checks out right when you test it then have faith in it...and in yourself! Do not have false expectations or beliefs in only one thing! I shall wear any form I choose, if it is appropriate to my energies and compatible with your learning. This is the first lesson. Good day to you, madam!"

And the owl was gone, just *gone*.

"Now I've offended you both!"

I threw my hands up in despair and turned again to witness the Indian.

"It's just so confusing! I'm in Albion, in my Otherworld place, *here*, and I get an owl native to Britain but which talks like English gentry rather than as an owl, then turns into a mysterious black-eyed woman and then back to an owl! And then I get a man native to America who looks completely out of context! It's *so* confusing! It's true, I expected a Green Man or a Faery Queen...because they are supposed to be of my kind, in spirit, aren't they? I am meant to be a child of the Greening, whatever that really means...oh damn, I'm sorry! In sound really ungrateful, I know you've helped me before now...it's just, oh...how can I work with you if it looks all wrong?"

The Indian man looked at me. Hard.

"Well, it doesn't *feel* wrong, it just looks wrong!" I tried to justify myself.

"What is spirit?" I heard the question as much as I felt it resonate through me, its vibration striking the right chord so I knew the answer.

"An expression of Source energy; a fragment of the All-That-Is"

"What is...*this*?" The Indian gestured at himself.

" A form to wear, no more, no less, and one you feel comfortable in as a spirit."

"Why?"

"You feel comfortable because your energies are well suited to the form, the spirit you are may well once have worn it...on Earth... and found it pleasing?"

"So why the problem with it?" He was man of few words, this Indian. I heard the things he did not articulate as feelings inside me. Feelings about my over-emphasis on appearance.

(*It appeared that I was somewhat hung-up on looks even though I had always been taunted for my own physical mien and had longed to escape the restrictions that it placed on me!*)

"It just makes me feel odd that you look like an Indian because it doesn't fit in with all *this!*" I gestured this time at my landscape, carefully crafted in meditations with Alicia and Treeface.

"Change it, then! It's yours."

('*Or else, change your spirit guide, if you can!*' I heard the challenge inside me.)

The Indian stood still in his circle of fire and stared harder at me, if that were possible. Glittering obsidian eyes speared my soul which flopped like a fish out of water in its discomfort. He was not threatening as such but certainly imposing enough.

" I can't change you against your will!"

He kept on staring.

"Then change...*this*," and he swept out an arm. The world rippled around us and then returned, subtly different to the way it had been before, not unpleasantly so but certainly not my mythical ancient England. The boat was a canoe, the river more reedy, the trees looked more like pines, ('*spruce*' my soul-memory whispered.) The grass was shorter and the land was now flatter. I jumped as I heard a splash behind me and turned sharply to see a beaver disappear into the water.

"Oh!"

Behind the Indian man there stood a small skin tent, a tepee I supposed. Or were they called wigwams? Above us a large bird circled. I sensed snow-capped mountains in the distance and much further on, red rocks and dry plains. ('*We migrated, like birds,*' I remembered, '*to the good lands, with the seasons, nomadic...Oh yes, he truly is of my kind, this Indian, free-flying as any Elf-arrow, of the Earth but not of the world...*')

This new version of my safe Otherworldly space felt like home just as much as my version of Albion had.

"This is very nice..." I really didn't want to sound ungrateful again and besides, it was true! Surely he could feel an honesty from me? A small snake slid past my foot and I looked down, distracted. There were snakes in England, weren't there? But no Tepees! At least, no genuine Native Indian ones. For a moment, what I had established as the truth of my Otherworldly space wobbled and threatened to fall flat.

"Where has...England...er, Albion...gone?"

"Albion was never here!"

"Okay, where is my created space?"

"You are in it," he stated. And I was. Old Albion, land of Avalon, of marsh and fen, hillfort and barrow, had re-appeared. I gasped audibly at the miraculous speed in which things could shift in this realm, according to the speed of ones thoughts or the strength of ones will. Or the clarity of one's vision.

Or the depth of one's knowledge.

Truth wore many shades and shapes of itself, nothing was fixed, everything was energies, spiralling onwards and ever unfolding. Had that not been part of my first lesson from Alicia at the telling of *before*?

('*Change is the natural state of the universe, on all levels, the Great Mystery uses form in so many ways...for expressions of ideas, lending something tangible to a concept for us to experience it fully, using appearance and structure all the better to get the message across! The* knowing *is all there is*!' I could hear Alicia echoing in one of her rambling discourses.)

"Look, er, I think if we are going to work together I need a sacred space here in the Otherworlds which suits your chosen form. Can we go back to your version of things, please? The, er, American version?"

"It is already so."

It was not America, just as it was never England, it was my Otherworld home which echoed the essential energies of those lands for the purpose of feeling comfortable and at ease.

(*This place was like my version of 'the office', I marvelled, it was just the place where I came to work, designed for my working most effectively and efficiently, a pleasing environment! It was no more my true 'home' than any place of work was for a human!*)

As I looked again at the tall, dark forest in the distance and heard the eagle cry over head I wondered what I would look like in this place. It probably didn't matter a jot to this Indian if I looked like an Elf somewhere on the plains of America but, as a incarnate being, it mattered a great deal to me what form I was clad in for the duration of our communion together. In turned and inspected my reflection in the silvery water that flowed under my canoe. I was young, perhaps in my mid-teens, with shiny black hair in two loose bunches and was clad only in a loose shift which reached my bare knees. I had on no shoes nor any other obvious adornment but I was effortlessly, naturally lovely in a way that only a Native woman can be.

In this guise I felt strong and proud, swift and sharp as the eagle above me.

"Running Deer," the Indian man pointed at me. "For the course of our work together you will be she."

"I was once...?" I knew then that Running Deer was me in as much as Marguerite or Lian ever had been. I had been a wild Native girl, fleet of foot and sure, with a fierce love of the land. Just another expression of the Greening's energy, another way for a Star Child to be conceived in a human disguise.

"Indeed."

"And you?"

Our words seemed to be getting more concise and the images the fewer words conveyed and the feelings were more effective than any long-winded discourse in waking up my inner experiences and emotions.

"Red Fox."

"Father?" I stated it as a question I was already sure of the answer to. Neither of us moved. He may have nodded but I needed no affirmations. I was feeling the energies and I felt it as truth as a flood of memory engulfed me. In that life, before my soul had known a needless burning at the stake in another land, I had been happy as an incarnate being, drawing shapes in the sand with a stick by the river as Father fished. This life had been a full one, my senses reeled as I recalled the scent of smoking meat, the feel of sewing the hides, of watching the dance as the sun set, bleeding vermilion and spilling gold into a deep violet sky.

(*...not so very different, then, from a life as a Wood-Elf...honouring the spirit of the land, one and all the same...*)

"I am...very pleased to meet you, Red Fox," I acknowledged him with a sort of curtsy and he gave a shallow bow and put his hand to his chest.

"It is well, for now."

For the first time in what seemed like hours I became aware of Treeface in the room waiting for me to finish so that he could guide me back.

"May I come again...here...to talk with you?"

"You may talk with me anywhere but I shall be here. We have talked already, many times, remember? You have just met with the owl-woman, also, seeing her clearly as if for the first time although all three of us have spoken together often and worked together too. Ask and it is done. Many curious things may happen before you come to see your Albion again. Go now."

And as I thanked him he walked away in the direction of the tepee which had, I noticed, smoke rising from the centre.

(*Just like an Elf-dwelling, a scene from a Faery's simple life!*)

Treeface was speaking to me, asking me to get back into my boat and I turned from a scene that was not so very unfamiliar after all and began to make to row away. Above me I heard the large bird call again and a feather, a huge black, white and dun brown affair, drifted downwards into my boat. As I began to move off, towards the end of my trance, pushing the canoe through the water with a pole that had become a paddle, I thanked the owl who was now perhaps an eagle, a shapeshifting member of the *bird tribe*,and who may, indeed, be anything she so chose next time we met. It was all in the energies, in the feeling of the presence.What a valuable lesson, that appearances are NOT all they seem! *Feel the energies then decide!*

Goodness, hadn't my own life, and Treeface's, taught us that appearances were secondary to the spirit within, to the essence and to the *feel* of that essence? Still it seemed I had needed yet another wake up call to remind me! I knew that in my new life as a Fey *seer* I would never be able to rest on my laurels or become smug and judgmental. Oh no, that was not our way at all and it did me good to remember that as often as was necessary!

Next time I would be open to anything, so long as it felt right and checked out okay as a true spirit. I had met my spirit guides face-to-face!

I smiled as I opened my eyes and instinctively reached out to my journal as Treeface stretched. He looked contented enough, not the usual slightly puzzled frown he wore after a path-working. I hoped he had obtained the help of Kefli with his project in the world.

"Tea, is it?" he asked, a rhetorical question if ever I heard one. It was our way to have tea and biscuits as a means of further grounding ourselves before we even discussed the events of our spirit-travels. Even so, I couldn't resist calling out to him as he headed to the kitchen.

"You'll never believe who I've just been talking to!"

"Not so very long ago, there was a very ordinary family living in an average kind of street on the outskirts of a very dull town indeed.

Every Saturday the family went shopping to the same shops to buy the same things to eat. While they were out shopping they always bought their cat the very same food as they had always bought for him. And they would bring it back every week, without fail, and they would put it in his dish.

The cat would eat it because he was a very polite cat.

He was also a very bored cat with the very ordinary family who never thought to ask him if he ever fancied anything different for his tea for a change. The cat had hoped for a long time that one Saturday they would bring him back a bit of fish or a tasty scrap of chicken but they always brought back the same dried Kitty Crunchies and he always ate them. But how he hated those dull oblong Kitty Crunchies! Always the same! He thought that they were the most dull type of food he could imagine.

And, let me assure you, he was a cat with an *excellent* imagination.

He was also a very extraordinary cat and thought that he had suffered long enough eating his dull, dried food without complaint. It was time for him to speak up about how he felt about his food.

On one particular Saturday, when the little girl of the house had poured out his Kitty Crunchies, the cat looked at her and cleared his throat. He had not spoken to anybody for such a long time that he had almost forgotten how to do it.

'*Excuse me,*' he said, (being a polite cat) '*excuse me, but do you think there is any chance you could get me a little fish next week?*'"

I looked around the room to see the children either staring, mouths open in that endearingly un-self conscious way that children of that age have or openly giggling. Without thinking I placed my hand on my belly. I was so proud of Treeface! I took my eyes from his eager audience and watched him as he leaned forward on his brightly adorned stick to engage them, and me, even more in his home-spun, self-penned story. It was going so well!

"Well, the girl looked at the cat and screamed...and believe me it was not the sort of scream you'd want me to repeat here for you. What a terrible screech! '*Aaeeeiii!*' She dropped the box of dried food and she ran off and when she returned she had brought the rest of the family with her. She pointed accusingly at the cat.

'*He spoke!*' she cried.

'*Indeed I did,*' said the cat in reply, '*and now you are all gathered here together I can ask again....may I have a little fish for my tea next week?'*

The little girl screamed again.

So did her brother.

So did her mother."

Treeface stopped and put his hands to his ears as if hearing a dreadful racket. The children all giggled, more confident about showing their enjoyment now. It was such a privilege to watch him with these responsive, eager children. What a father he would make! It was so sad that he had never had the chance before, with Jane or anyone else. Still, I was glad it was me! Once again my hand slid unconsciously to the invisible bump in my stomach as I fell under the spell of my lover's voice.

Treeface went on, "'*you are not normal!*' yelled the father, hopping up and down in alarm and stepping in the Kitty Crunchies.

'*All this time you have lived in our normal house with us and pretended to be ordinary but you are not!*'

'*You can jolly well get out !*' shouted the mother, throwing her slippers at the cat, '*horrible, horrible creature! Terrible all wrong thing! Don't you know that cats don't talk?*'

Then the little boy and his sister both chased the cat, who was by now a confused and cross cat, right down the hall and out of the front door.

'*And good riddance too!*' they shouted after him as he ran into the street.

Their door slammed."

Treeface paused again as some of his audience, mainly a trio of girls sat cross legged in the row nearest to him, went "arrrr!" in sympathy for the fictional cat and Treeface shook his head and looked sad.

"Our poor friend the confused cat waited for a moment to see if they would open the door again and throw his food out too. He hadn't eaten anything and he was hungry...he would even have eaten Kitty Crunchies. He was *desperate!*

He looked up to see the angry mother and father peering at him from behind the curtains watching for him to leave. He could hear their voices still.

'*Terribly ungrateful sort, that cat!*'

'*So rude too!*'

'*Not at all the sort of cat that we want, dear.*'

'*No, not at all normal.*'

'Quite peculiar in fact, I'd say!'

'Quite!'

With a shrug the cat began to walk off down the street, away from the ordinary house and his insulting ex-owners. He was now homeless as well as being hungry, and he was out in a strange world that he knew nothing about."

Again the "arrrr!" came from the front row while the rest of Treeface's audience hung on his every word. I hugged myself with happiness as the story continued.

"The only things the cat had seen in his whole life were things around his owners neat and tidy garden. As he walked and walked, down other streets and into the town, he began to see many more people and buildings, plants and animals than he had ever known existed. In the big town he saw some people who also had no food and nowhere to go. They were all doing different things to entertain the passers-by so that they would each earn a little money to buy food. There were fire-eaters and dancers, people playing guitars and singing, it was all very interesting indeed. The cat watched them a while and wished that he too could find a way to perform for the people but he walked on knowing he was only a cat. He had no nice tricks to perform to earn himself his food and shelter.

The poor cat carried on going out of town until his paws were sore and his legs ached. When he reached the countryside he came across a barn to spend the night in. He was able to catch a few mice for his tea, which was a great change from dried food. He slept under a heap of straw and was woken in the morning by the first rays of sunshine. As he yawned and stretched and went outside he thought that his new life might not be so bad after all. It may be a hard life but at least it would not be a dull one. The cat then set off to try and find a river so that he could try to catch a fish or two.

As he went across a field he was approached by an old man with a thin, brown, kind face.

The man bent down to stroke him.

'Well, hello there young fellow!' he said to the cat, *'what brings you out here?'*

The cat was just about to speak in reply when he remembered that it was not normal for cats to talk to people. He didn't want this nice smiley man to think he was peculiar too.

'Well, are you hungry then, little fellow?' the man asked.

But all the cat could do was miaow hopefully.

The nice old man laughed and lead the cat to his brightly painted caravan which stood in the very corner of the field, almost hidden away. Nearby, a big handsome horse with hairy hooves was eating from the hedge. The dappled grey horse gave the cat a slow wink as he passed by.

The kindly man set down a dish of milk and...to the cats great delight...a nice plate of fresh fish!

'*I caught those myself this morning*,' said the man proudly. '*Enjoy, enjoy, little fellow!*'

The cat would have just loved to have thanked the man, being a very polite cat and all. But he liked it there and didn't want to risk being chased away. So the cat just purred loudly and looked up at the wrinkled face above him.

'*I must be getting old!*' laughed the nice old man, 'I half imagined you were going to say thank you!'

'*Well, I was!*' thought the happy, polite cat.

The cat gladly stayed with the man for many weeks. The man would tell him stories sometimes and the cat was able to go fishing with him. At night there would sometimes be guests, extraordinary people from passing travelling circuses who wore fantastic clothes and showed off their skills. The cat watched as acrobats and jugglers came to see the old man and he learned from their antics. He would then sneak away by himself into the dark behind the caravan and there he would practice his new skills. He became very clever at back flips and walking on his paws and, if he could find the odd round, smooth stone, he would juggle too.

He certainly was a most extraordinary cat and not at all normal.

But his performing was his secret, for his own enjoyment. Sometimes he let old Ned the horse see a new trick but he kept it secret from the people. He wouldn't want anyone to drive him out of his beloved old man's camp for being strange. He knew now that cats were supposed to be normal and sit by the fire and purr sometimes. That was all ordinary people expected of them. The old man still spoke to the cat, of course, but the cat would never answer him.

It was sometime later that the old man had some bad luck. The chimney in the old caravan had cracked, and every time the man tried to cook on his fire the smoke leaked out everywhere.

'*Oh bless my old boots!*' the man said, scratching his chin and staring hard at the broken chimney, '*we simply haven't the money to get our chimney fixed, my friend. Whatever can I do?*'

The old man thought and thought, and because he could not think of a thing he became sadder and sadder. It was cold in his little van and he was no longer young enough to not mind the chill at night. He was too old to find work in the town. How could he make any money? But the clever cat knew a way how he could repay his dear friend who had always shared his fish and milk freely with him. It may be dangerous for the cat but he had no choice, it seemed, for he would do anything to help the old man.

The very next day he went off early, before the old man had woken up. He set off carrying his tin dish in his mouth and he walked and he walked. He walked past the barn that had sheltered him for a night and back into the busy town. When he found a street he liked he stopped and put the dish down in front of him. He hoped that passers-by might take pity on him and give him a few pennies. Instead they walked by him saying

'*Ahhh! Isn't he so sweet!*'

'*Hey, just look at that cute little orange stripy cat sitting there!*'

But they did not give him a single penny.

The cat looked around himself and saw the other people singing and playing instruments in the street or tumbling head over heels and doing tricks. Those people were getting passers-by to stop and listen to them, to watch them and give them money.

It seemed as if there was nothing else for it. If he wanted money for his old man's chimney then he would have to perform for the people. So he jumped up onto his back legs.

'*Look! Look!*' cried a small boy as the cat began his display.

'*Goodness me!*' exclaimed his mother, as she watched the cat do three back flips in a row.

'*Well, my my!*' admired a passing Policeman, watching the cat perform six perfect cartwheels, one after the other.

The cat was marvellous. He was extraordinary.

A large crowd had gathered around him and cheered when he did something particularly clever, like walking on his front paws with his dish balanced on his back paws. To close the fabulous show, the cat danced a little jig that he had watched the old man dance with his friends. Then, standing on his hind legs, the cat bowed.

'*Bravo! Bravo!*' the people cried.

'*More! MORE!*' clapped the children and their mothers in excitement.

The cat put down his empty tin dish and waited for them to put their money in it.

But even then, when he had made it quite clear what they should do next, nobody gave him any money. People were beginning to walk away as he had finished his show. Now the cat was cross! Polite or not, peculiar or not, he had to speak out. He needed the money for the old man, and he would not go away with nothing. After all, he had performed very well.

He cleared his throat.

'*Ahem! I say!*' he said, as loudly as he could, '*I may be mistaken but do I not see the other performers in this street receiving tokens of your appreciation for their hard work?*'

There was a silence. Nobody moved; everyone that had just turned back towards him just stood with their mouths open. The cat shut his eyes and waited for somebody to start chasing him away. A talking cat? It wasn't *normal!*

Then, a little girl pushed to the front of the crowd and put something in his dish. He opened one eye cautiously.

'*There you are Mr. Cat, that's my most of my pocket money. I thought you were wonderful!*'

'*Well, thank you so much, most kind!*' said the cat, bowing again.

One by one the people came forward with money for the dish until it was quite full of coins.

'*Do you sing too?*' asked one old lady as she popped a pound in.

'*Indeed I can, but not very well I am afraid,*' replied the cat, honestly. He thought for a moment. '*However, good madam, I have a very dear friend who may come with me tomorrow and sing for you, if it would please you?*'

'*Ooh, is he a cat too?*' somebody asked, hopefully.

The cat shook his head. He had remembered that the old man often sang as he played his fiddle in the evenings, and that he sang beautifully too.

'*Well, I shall come back tomorrow then!*' said the lady who had given him a whole pound.

'*Ladies and Gentlemen, if I may just have your attention for a moment longer,*' the cat held up his paw. Everybody stopped again. This really was a most extraordinary cat! '*Please do not think that there is anything wrong with me because I can talk,'* he explained, '*I may be a little different from other cats, but that does not make me strange. All of you good people who have watched me today, are you all not different from one another?'*

The crowd all looked around and nodded, smiling at the cat who was greatly relieved. He bowed once more and picked up the very full dish carefully in his teeth. Then he trotted off in the direction of home.

As the cat went on his way, he passed a lady who looked familiar. She was the mother of the family who owned the old house in which he had lived. She always went to town on Tuesdays to meet a friend. As she went by he heard he whisper

'*Good gracious Doris, that looked like that very peculiar cat we had!*'

'*And a very good riddance to it!*' Doris said.

'*But it couldn't have been him, could it? He must be dead now, without his Kitty Crunchies to keep him going,*' the mother of his old home said and sniffed in disgust.

If he hadn't have had a mouth full of his money the cat would have laughed.

Once back at the caravan, the cat had to explain where he had come by the money, which was enough to fix the chimney and to buy them both a little treat. The cat knew he had to speak, a miaow wouldn't be enough and he didn't want the old man to think he was a thief. He looked shyly at his friend and told him how he had come by his days earnings. Far from chasing him away, the old man laughed in delight.

'*I always knew you understood me!*' he chuckled, '*now I don't have to believe I'm just going mad!*' The man clapped his hands in happiness. '*And I have somebody to talk to every night!*' he exclaimed.

And he emptied the money into a spotted handkerchief and filled the cat's dish with fresh fish, caught that very morning and saved for the cat's return. The next day the man and the cat returned to town together. The cat's promise had been kept and again a huge crowd gathered as the man played and sang and the cat danced and performed his tricks. The old man had painted a sign for his friend on an old piece of wood. It was red, gold and green and looked very smart indeed for something he had produced so quickly..

'*Presenting Dinglebert, the* extraordinary *dancing cat and Jack-the-Fiddle!*' it said in big curly letters.

Dinglebert was proud of his new name which they had chosen

together.

He had never much liked being a normal cat called Tiddles anyway!"

There was a pause while Treeface let his tale sink into the children's minds and hearts. Then he stood up, resting his gaily decorated staff next to a bookshelf and taking up his own fiddle.

"And this," said Treeface to the rapt class of children, "Is what old Jack-the-Fiddle played for Dinglebert! If you close your eyes you may just see him dance! A one, a two, a three, a four!"

And Treeface thrust his old fiddle under his chin, and played a lively little reel, tapping his booted foot. The teacher, a young woman, maybe straight out of University and full of enthusiasm for this welcome diversion to her infants routine day encouraged the children to clap along. Some even had their eyes closed, just as they had during the tale's telling, and were swaying with beatific smiles on their faces. What marvellous pictures could they see behind their closed lids I wondered?

Treeface had his eyes shut too, the bow flying back and forth and the fingers moving swiftly, intuitively. He would clearly never be a virtuoso but he had passion and fire, wit and creativity and his improvised, impromptu tune soared and dipped like a swallow. The character of Jack-the-Fiddle was Jack Tatterkin, I knew, and Treeface would be seeing the wonderful man in his minds-eye, conjuring up his magical presence in the room. Was he alive or was he dead, his gentle woodland wanderer, his saviour? Had he even ever existed at all? Treeface did not know, but he thanked him silently every day of his life. This tune was for him as well as the admiring children.

Flushed and exhilarated, Treeface finished his reel, bowed and returned to his seat. One boy who looked very young indeed began to clap louder and the stopped, looking around sheepishly.

"It's okay, Thomas, we can say thank you to Mr. Treeface now!"

"*Mr.* Treeface!" one of the girls in the front row giggled to her neighbour but they all clapped hard, some getting over excited and stamping a little on the mat. The teacher held up her hand and put her finger to her lips and they were quiet again after a few minutes.

"We don't want to disturb Class Three next door do we?"

"No!" chorused most of the class.

"Yes!" said a single boy with sticky out ears and as many freckles as my own dear Robert had had. Then seeing the lack of support offered by his classmates he fell silent. I smiled. It had been wonderful. Just perfect! Surely Treeface could grow in confidence now, finally, and feel safe to be who he was in public. Surely it would help his self-esteem and quell his fears a little at least? He *was as he was*...and it was well!

I watched my lover, who would hopefully one day be my husband, as he gladly (and wittily) answered the questions of the children. The stories he told were designed to provoke discussion about respect for differences and individuality and with his own dear lined face he also had a way of engaging the children about judgements and prejudices. These children gave me hope for they truly *were* engaging with him and showed a genuine and warm interest in his tree-face as well as his tales. It was a beautiful moment in a successful afternoon and I could feel tears welling with my gratitude. Thank you, spirits, thank you for making everything right for us!

As we stood up to leave we hoped that this young teacher would take up the challenge offered by us, to pursue the issues of respect and tolerance as well as nurturing a love, not a fear, of the unusual and surprising. We ourselves had finished our first 'gig' and it was, I believed, a roaring triumph for my beloved. Just the thing to give a man his confidence back in bucket-loads...if he'd let it.

And so it went on, Treeface's new 'career', with forty well deserved pounds in his hand as he successfully completed one date after another. The word had soon spread about the new entertainer, one that told stories that didn't come from a book but out of his head! The word was, I believe, that he was a magical man who still had the ability to hold the attention of children who had been brought up in the age of computers and videos. What a coup! It was beyond even our wildest dreams! And so the word spread beyond our county and into other shires beyond. We often found ourselves boarding buses and trains to new places. A car would have been nice but out of the question for all sorts of reasons including it not being a 'green' option. I knew sooner or later I would have to stop accompanying him and save money by letting him go alone. Oh, but I loved supporting him!

The story of Dinglebert was interspersed in his repertoire with pared down versions of old stories like 'Thomas the Rhymer' and 'The Swine Herd'. The fiddle usually came out and was as popular as the tale-telling itself. Treeface did it all effortlessly, adopting the cheeky persona to a tee, losing all of his hang-ups about being a poor, disfigured man as he simply acted the part required of him to a receptive young audience. He was marvellous indeed! I sat in thrall at libraries, watching him have his photograph taken with two eight year olds for the local paper. I perched on a stool behind him in the unexpectedly hot spring sunshine at an early school fete. All the time he did this his confidence grew and his sense of optimism returned, every time the phone rang he puffed out his bony chest in pride, knowing our savings were growing enough to see us through the bills for the year.

And all the time Treeface was entertaining other peoples children my stomach remained flat.

We did not discuss that. I had still not had a period and I was, after all, very slender anyway. Best not to tempt fate by having the tests, it seemed. Best to go on as if Michael Gabriel was still within me, nestling deep in my womb, being fed by the good vibrations of Treeface's stories, being loved by the woman who went on her inner trance-journeys and could now do basis psychometry on objects for people who wanted a question answered. One day soon I knew that I just might have my own 'act'. It would have been nice to consult Alicia about it but we never seemed to have the time. If only she had a phone it would have been easier. As it was I knew I HAD to see her soon!

On one of my trance-journeys, Red Fox advised me of a course of action that would facilitate Treeface's healing process, a healing that we had begun so successfully with his very public work as a teller of old tales. Treeface was now comfortable with being a veritable paragon of magical virtue who added to the resurgence of interest in natural enchantment every time he told a story. Would he be comfortable with Red Fox's suggestion that he worked on a story based on the worth of the individual, which was his prime focus anyway, but one steeped in the ways of the Greening... a story which openly mentioned the word witch?

Treeface had become very used to receiving my guidance from the Otherworlds about his 'act'. He was in put in a very difficult position by the latest piece of advice as the other information I gleaned for him on almost a daily basis was consistently correct. Treeface did not dispute my growing aptitude at obtaining clear and accurate psychic information in a safe and disciplined manner with respect for the ancestral ways...the soul-ways of our kind. How could he deny what Red Fox suggested just because he was afraid of the idea?

There was a bit of tension between us on the morning I came back from my trance-journey with the framework for the story. Red Fox gave me most of my information in symbolic form and on that occasion had lead me to the grove we frequented to illustrate his point using the trees we found there. The message was clear, although Treeface would need to pad it out in his own inimitable way.

The idea was to express the need for people to relate to each other as individuals even within the same type of being...i.e. trees...valuing the sacred properties of each divinely bestowed attribute, of each species, and acknowledging their necessary part of the whole. The story was to illustrate not only the inter-connectedness of beings but of their links to the Sustainer...representing Mother Nature as a living part of creation, even if initially it was as a 'humanised' being.

After many nights of agonising and many sheets torn from the Smith-Corona in a frustrated temper, after I retreated to the bathroom to leave him alone with his thoughts and meditations on the matter, Treeface 'birthed' a tale. A hard labour, a reluctant one, but it came to fruition in time for May Day, which seemed auspicious. I had been doing a little reading to boost my own esoteric knowledge, picking up anything in the large local library which 'called to me', be it fiction or no, be it of the native traditions of England or of another country. I knew that the Celtic festival of Beltaine was considered to be a wonderful time for union and to celebrate that union. It seemed appropriate, then, that Treeface, as a direct result of our being together, had created something worth-while and moving that would touch many in a positive, transforming way. That alone was something that would have been inconceivable for him...and, indeed, for me...a mere six months previously.

We decided to preview the tale at the next school we were invited to. With two days notice we had an unexpected and not entirely welcome phone call from a headmistress in a private girls school who sounded 'cool but desperate' as Treeface put it. She didn't seem at all convinced by him as a performer but her usual entertainer had to go away at short notice and Treeface had been recommended to her. Could she hire him? Would he give a show to around twenty girls who had to stay behind while the rest of their year went off to study elsewhere?

Perhaps we shouldn't have taken the private school 'gig', it was against our principles anyway and after all, we were no longer desperate for the money, although as Treeface so rightly pointed out, we could never be sure who the whole thing would dry up. There were the summer holidays in July to consider which meant no work for nearly two months unless he could get summer camps, play-schemes or local fetes and fairs. So, we took the slot for the performance at short notice against our better instincts. Treeface wanted to say no, I know he did, but something in the woman's manner had made him bristle and it had been a matter of his own pride to take on the challenge in her voice. He could and *would* impress her and her girls!

The spirit guides had remained non-committal on whether we should go for the slot or not and even though our intuition said 'no' we turned up at the school together, as ever, clutching the decorated hazel staff, Treeface's fiddle and a bag of assorted other natural aids to his tale. We had, between us, manufactured Dinglebert's sign but we had not brought it to the private school as the girls we were seeing would be too old for tales of dancing cats. That day it would be more appropriate to tell romantic tales of love and heroism...

(*Oh beloved spirits, give us strength, courage and honour!*)

...and the new story. The one of wildwood witchery.

I could tell he was nervous as he began and I sent him all my love and support, reaching out to him soul-to-soul so that he knew he was not alone. *Never alone!* Did he feel me? He could be so unreadable, even now! I just hoped that the tale would fill him and take him along with it, absorbing him to the point where fear was forgotten. His voice betrayed no sign of cracking or quivering but I could tell he was strung as tight as a bow with tension.

"There was once a wood known as Wychwood, where the most wonderful trees grew. The trees were all different in size and shape but they all had one thing in common...they were healthy and they were happy. They all loved their lives and they all enjoyed growing and being the tree that they were.

All except one.

Right in the middle of that wood there stood a huge old oak tree. He was more than five hundred years old, and on certain nights of the year, if you were able to draw close to his trunk, you could hear him tell the stories of the many things that he had seen. He would tell of how, for many, many years, he had heard the first cries of the new born birds each springtime, for many loyal birds chose to build their nests amongst his vast branches. He would tell of how, for as long as he could remember, and even before that, he had provided the acorns for one family of squirrels after another. He would often speak of his conversations with the great-great-great-great grandchildren of the deer that had sheltered in his summer shade.

Oh yes, he was simply a fine tree whose life had been untroubled by death, destruction or pain. His friends, the other trees of Wychwood, some of whom were almost as old as he, had never suffered illness, nor had they been chopped down by greedy, inconsiderate men. It seemed as if the wood itself was protected, and indeed there was an old, old tale of how the wood was bound by an ancient magic, by a spell cast once by a powerful but kindly lady. It was said that she was the same lady that had planted the oak tree himself.

The oak tree, had been very proud of this story, once. But the lady was long dead, and the oak was, for the first time since being planted, very unhappy.

All of his leaves had turned a sickly yellow, although it was not yet autumn. His branches had become so weak and brittle that even the smallest birds were afraid to build their nests amongst his branches. For the first time in many, many years the sound of bird song was missing from his once mighty boughs. The birds had to look for other shelter and the squirrels saw the first signs of his acorns, shrivelled and stunted, and they too decided to move on elsewhere, sad as it was. Indeed his lonely old form seemed to sag and stoop under the burden of his empty branches.

The oak trees old friends, the trees around him, the ash, the chestnut and the beech, could not seem to get him to tell his fantastic tales any more. The oak had known more than any of them and now he would not bring happiness to them as he told his stories. In fact, the oak would not speak to them at all.

The oak did not speak because he was looking at the apple tree.

The apple tree was a fine young fellow who was in his first year of real growth. In the spring he had produced beautiful blossoms and the people who had been out walking in the woods had said how marvellous his pink petals were, twirling through the air all around them. That was when the old oak had noticed the apple tree and had begun to envy it. The fine apple tree did not notice, it simply went about its business of being a happy, healthy apple tree in springtime. It laughed and chattered with the bigger, wiser trees at night although it did not have much to say, being so young. But the little tree was a good listener and loved to hear the older trees talk.

The apple tree wished that the oak tree would talk to him too, as he was nearest to him in the wood but it seemed as if the oak did not like him and so the apple tree did not bother him. The oak just stood in silence, towering over the, smaller tree and making him feel a little afraid. He secretly wished that the old oak would like him and tell him the old tales as he had heard that the great oak once had done.

But the great oak did not dislike the apple tree. No, he was just insanely jealous of him. *He* wanted to have pretty blossoms too! The more the oak stared at the other trees petals, the less his own leaves grew. Usually, the oak had his own glossy new green leaves in spring, but that year he had but a few buds upon his branches.

'*How I wish that I had beautiful blossoms that everybody would admire, lovely pink petals for people to praise,*' sighed the oak sadly. He was looking so hard at the other tree that he did not notice another bird take flight from his own leafless boughs.

Then the fine apple tree began to grow small, hard green fruits and as the envious oak tree watched they grew bigger and better by the day. The oak gazed up into his own branches and saw no fruits there, only the odd leaf that now looked pale and old even though it was summer time.

As the time went by, the other trees became worried about the oak. Perhaps he was sick with some terrible disease that would spread through the wood? Yet there were no real signs of disease upon him, no cankers or moulds. Maybe he was just too old to live and would die a hollow and miserable fellow, allowing all of the old tales of their lives to be forgotten? Surely not? It was unthinkable that the oak should leave them this way! The trees, try as they might to understand the silent and wilting oak, did not know what was wrong with their friend because he would not share his grief or ills with them. He simply focussed his energies, or what remained of them, straight ahead of him with a great sense of wistfulness and hopelessness. The other trees put their branches together and they stretched out as far as the could to one another until they formed a huge circle around the poor oak. Their whispers went from branch to branch.

'*We need to get help*,' began the chestnut.

'*Yes but what shall we do? Nobody listens to the trees anymore*,' said the ash, with a resigned shrug of his branches.

'*Oh, I wish I knew what we could do for our poor old friend oak*,' sniffed the hazel, becoming quite upset.

From down beneath them the hawthorn spoke, her voice a low rumble from the very heart of the Earth, or so it seemed.

'*Do not fear, for I have heard tell from the stars above me and from the creatures that move in the soil around my roots that there is someone who can help us,*' she said.

'*Who is it, lady hawthorn? Tell us!*' begged the wiry hazel.

'*There is still a woman of the woods who has the power to heal us, if only we call on her,*' the hawthorn explained.

The other trees looked down on her in surprise because she rarely spoke.

'*I am not wishing to be rude, my dear hawthorn, but I am afraid that the tale of the wise lady is really only a nice story,*' the larch corrected her.

'*Yes, it's just a folk-story like the oak used to tell us,*' the chestnut agreed.

'*Just a Faery-tale.... that is all. It isn't really true,*' added the elm.

'*Nobody even believes in magic anymore,*' the beech continued.

'*Nor in witches,*' the lime tree finished.

'*Well then, tell me friends, why are we so protected here in Wychwood?*' the hawthorn asked, quietly. Then she said no more.

'*It must be worth a try for us to speak to the witch-woman of these woods...after all it may be the only chance we have to save the oak,*' the walnut tree suggested.

'*But she is surely dead?*'piped up the rowan.

The trees all shook their branches in agreement.

'*You are probably right,*' sighed the larch.

'*Nonsense! What have we to lose by trying?*' the hawthorn berated them. '*Are we trees afraid of looking foolish? Surely not! Let us put any silly embarrasments aside and do this for the good of our friend for there is always hope!*'

And she was right.

The trees stood in silence for a long while, each of them trying to remember the call to the lady of the woods. They had all known it when they were younger but had all almost forgotten. But when one tree *re-membered,* or almost did, then because they were all joined by their branches, their roots and their slow, steady breaths, they passed the memory between them, from one to the next. *Re-membering,* it seemed, involved a call, a wild green soul-song to the lady of the land on which they stood so firmly rooted. Some of them felt a little foolish at first, calling out to this mythical witch-lady in their minds, thinking that it could not possibly work even as they sang out their need to her. Yet as time passed and they kept up their silent chanting, growing less self-conscious and sceptical as they did so, even those trees which had the most doubts about the Faery-stories soon began to feel...*something.*

A musical humming sound began beneath them, above them, inside them and all around them like the sound of many bees singing to the summer time. It joined in their inner singing, accompanying them, encouraging them, strengthening their mighty green connection to eachother and to everything else; to All-That-Is. A passing person may have taken cover from the sound, believing himself to be being chased by a swarm but their were no bees, only trees concentrating hard to make their ancient soul-sound, which they accompanied with the soft '*shhhh*' of their many leaves as they stirred in the evening breeze.

The fine apple tree was too young to join in with the other trees so it stood and watched and listened. The old oak, of course, didn't notice anything at all, except for the fine fat apples that were appearing upon the little tree in front of him.

'*Oh, I am such a failure that I cannot grow such lovely, juicy fruits,*' lamented the poor oak, '*the apple tree is so much better than me. Now everybody will come to him to gather his apples and he will make the people happy again. What can I give? What have I got? Who will come to me to admire my work?*'

And so it was that the great, sad oak tree closed his eyes, not noticing as he did so that another acorn, black and shrivelled, fell from his bare boughs to land in the pile of dead leaves at the base of his trunk. He was indeed dying but he was responsible for killing himself, for his will to live was departing and all because he felt he was not worthy to share the wood with the marvellous apple tree.

Yet far away in a tiny house, a house so small as to have been hidden from the eyes of passers-by within the side of a bank of earth, a woman sat thinking. She had been awoken in her tiny house from a long, long sleep. She had heard the sound of the trees calling to her, their sweet humming coming into her dusty dreams. She had heard their wishes, their needs, and had sat up from her bed of springy moss and leaves, yawning. It had been an age since she had heard the call of someone who *re-membered* her. Once, many moons ago, there had been a time when she walked in the woods, known to all...now she sat in her tiny sylvan home, all but forgotten.

But they had called to her, desperately, passionately, and so she must answer them.

She found that she had been sharing her slumbering place with a little old squirrel who had far more white in his fur than he had grey. He had been snoring away in contentment in his nice, secret nesting place. The squirrel had jumped back in alarm as the pile of leaves he had been nestled down upon took on the shape of a woman. This woman-shape sat up and stretched out her sun-burned, work hardened hand to him and her smile was warm, not threatening. Who was she? Feeling her power and her compassion the squirrel went to her. Whoever she was, *whatever* she was, he fell in love with her there and then and vowed in his heart to serve her. He helped her as she went outside to gather dead wood to make up a fire and he assisted her in building and lighting the fire in her house. He sat and watched as the woman then placed a huge black pot of water onto her fire and when the water boiled he saw the woman move closer to look into the waters seething, steaming surface.

The squirrel did not know what the Lady saw there but her saw her mouth a few words and smile a sad sort of smile. He looked at her and he loved her the more, this Lady with her wild greenish hair full of leaves and the smell of nuts and spices upon her dark skin, skin which seemed to shine like burnished copper. Her heart was so big that it almost made him weep to witness it and he decided he would help her to the ends of the Earth if she asked him to.

The wild woman had looked into her cauldron and had seen many things...clouds passing over a cold moon full of shadows, a tree with bark so frail as to be peeling away from the still green wood...and she saw a man with the head of a deer, his gnarled hands wreathed in ivy, like the tree himself. He was the Lord of the Greenwood, as she was the Lady, and he too had lay sleeping, mostly forgotten but always listening for the call.

It was with this Man of the Trees that she spoke in her vision and decided what was to be done. When they had reached an agreement she thanked him and turned away from his fading picture in her bubbling pot. She turned back to the waiting squirrel and with a voice which became stronger with each word spoken she said

'*Come with me, dear one, nut gatherer! We have not much time.*'

It was the late autumn by now and during the short days the wood was ablaze with colour. The oak did not see, for he had his eyes tightly shut against the sight of the popular apple tree. The apples were long gone, having been picked by people to make delicious pies, or the rest having fallen to the floor for insects and birds to feed on but the oak, unseeing, did not know this. He did not know that his friends, the other trees, were all clad in gold, crimson and honey coloured leaves. He did not see the children collecting the horse chestnuts, the others picking hazel and beech nuts, or admiring the beautifully coloured leaves of the ash and twirling its brown papery seed pods between their fingers.

Night fell. The oak did not feel the woman approaching him. Nor did he see the shape of her willowy form as she drew closer to him. But then nor did any of the other trees witness her arrival as they themselves had become so used to there being no visitors at night in their safe wood-land that their senses were no longer trained to pick up any threat of intruders into their peaceful realm. Yet she came, a woman clad in a cloak of darkness which was embroidered with silver; silver that could have been the dew on moonlit grass or the reflection of the night sky in a shimmering pool. Only the hawthorn opened her eyes and smiled secretly to herself as she heard the lady's footsteps moving by her through the deep leaves.

The Lady approached the oak tree.

'Old oak,' she said.

The tree did not stir, but clenched his eyelids of rotten bark tighter together. He did not want to see anyone or for anyone to see him he thought if he kept his eyes shut against the world that somehow he would not exist. He was so ashamed of who and what he was.

'*I am here old oak, venerable man of these woods, and I ask that you hear me,*' she said, this time resting her hand flat against the tree's huge trunk. Some of the dying bark came away in her fingers but still she kept her hand firmly against him.

All at once, a flood of brightly coloured pictures entered into the mind of the tree. He saw how long ago men had come to gently remove his cast-off wood to make beautiful objects and that the things that they had made from his flesh were still loved and valued by people today. He saw the little girl who, fifty years ago, had chosen him specially to build her rope swing from; she had thought him particularly safe and strong and she had gotten her older brother to make a loop across his broad, solid bough. He remembered too the boy who had collected the oak's unusually shaped leaves to make a print with at school, a picture that his mother still kept for its simple beauty even though her son was now a man with a lad of his own to take for long walks in his beloved woods.

He heard the call of the birds in his branches, especially the songs of his favourite blackbird and his beloved robin. He realised with a start that he had not heard their lovely songs for some while now and he knew that he missed them badly. One big, fat tear slid down his lonely trunk.

'*Leave me! Leave me be, lady, I beg you! For I am not as good and fine as the apple tree!*' he cried, '*and, no, I never will be.So what is my point and purpose? None!*'

'Now then stout fellow, open your eyes and truly *see*, great tree," said the lady quietly and murmured some words into the wood of his trunk.

The old oak opened up his eyes, and what he saw amazed him. It was dark but he could clearly see a woman before him. Very few people ever ventured into the woods at night, as some still thought it to be haunted by a strange old witch from long ago and they were frightened to travel alone there. The oak had never seen a woman out alone at night. She was all but hidden in the folds of her cloak but he could see her eyes, the colour of cool water running over rocks, and he felt comforted.

But he would not raise his gaze to see the apple tree.

The woman removed her strong hand from the trunk of the oak and she reached inside her cloak. From it she pulled the body of a grey squirrel that lay still in her opened palm.

'*Oh no! Please, let it not be so!*' gasped the oak, '*what has killed the poor creature? I know this squirrel of old. Why has he passed away?*'

'*This is the squirrel which used to come to you each year for his supply of winter acorns,it is true,' the lady told the tree, 'and as ever he came to you this year for his winter store only to find you barren and half-dead. He begged you to make fresh acorns for him, for he is old and has not the strength to travel far to the next oak tree, but you did not hear him, nor did you open your eyes to him, so he died here amongst your dead leaves and you, great oak, did not notice.*'

Then the oak tree really cried.

'*Oh , sweet Lady, what has become of me? I did not mean to kill the squirrel, I meant no harm! I just felt so useless as if I had no place in a wood which has such marvellous trees in it such as the wonderful apple tree. I felt so dull in comparison, so unloved and unneeded! I have let my jealousy eat me up and consume me until I am a hulk, a wreck! I did not think I was of any use to anyone, nor any loss...oh, forgive me, small one!'* The oak looked down at the squirrel, ashamed.

'*But see, great one, it is not so,*' said the Lady in her soft, musical voice, '*if you have the eyes to see, if you can let the shroud of your bitter jealousy slip away, then look now!'*

The old oak tree was brave and looked to where the woman looked herself. With a gasp of surprise he saw the apple tree, it's leaves gone, it's fruit gone, it's blossoms gone. It was bare and resting, its work for the year done and with no more to do until the spring it was happy and contented to just be standing there. Although it no longer looked splendid it looked peaceful, serene in the moonlight.

It certainly did not look either beautiful or threatening.

The oak dared to look further around him and saw the other trees were producing their fruits, although for most of the year they had not grown anything but leaves. He saw the nuts, the berries, the seed-cases and pods, the brilliantly coloured leaves all about the wood. Each tree contributed something fresh and lovely to the whole wood...even if it was only the peace of a well earned rest.

'*I see that I have been a fool, a self-obsessed and petty idiot,*' the oak sniffed, looking back to the Lady.

'*Perhaps it is so, beloved, but is a worthwhile thing for you have learned a lesson,*' the Lady corrected him. '*It is worthwhile as it is a valuable lesson for us to share with all who we touch in our lives and it is simply this; that very single one of the trees in my wood has a purpose, every one is a wonderful tree if it does the best it can to produce the gifts I have given to it. Your gifts are many, old oak, but they are not the same gifts as that of the apple tree. Your gifts are yours, and they are special for being different to the gifts of other trees. Do you see? Do you see how all of creation has its own beautiful role, its perfect symmetry, its gifts and its wisdoms to share? Even if we cannot fully appreciate what our gifts may be at any one time, even if sometimes our own pain or insecurity temporarily blind us to truth, we can have faith that it is so! Just by being you are enough, my dear one, just by simply being who you be you fulfil a vital role in the merry dance of life!'*

'*Oh dear, kind Lady,*" sighed the big tree '*what would have hap-*

pened if you hadn't come to me this night?"

'*Be brave and close your eyes once more,*' she replied.

Again she placed her hand on his trunk and again he saw pictures but this time terrible pictures of a wood without his presence in it. It made his whole tree-self shudder.

'*You see, you are not alone in the wood, no being stands alone, especially a Wise One of the Bark,*' the Green Woman told him. '*Your death would have affected all of your friends here, all of those who share in your gifts...*' *She looked down meaningfully at the squirrel, 'your death would bring unhappiness that would have spread, from one tree to the next, for here in the wood we are all part of one another. We can hurt each other by our actions, even without meaning to. If you would have died, old oak, then who would pass on the great stories about the past? The wood would lose its stories and would forget what it was and what it was doing, both collectively and individually. You are part of the wood and the wood is part of you. No being acts in isolation, no, not ever!*'

The old oak tree opened his eyes.

'*It is so, my Lady. I had not forgotten, not really, and I never shall now. How may I now make my wrong right?*' he asked solemnly.

'*Your acceptance of truth is enough to restore balance, old friend,*' she said.

'*But what of dear master squirrel, how may I put right his premature loss of life?*'

The woman did not reply but instead cupped her cool hands around the tiny body of the squirrel and to the oak trees great joy the squirrel began to move. The tree was amazed and delighted.

'*You see, balance is restored, and I can heal you too, old tree,*' she smiled, '*if you vow to keep my friends the squirrels alive and fed until the end of your days...which will not be for many, many more years to come...then I can make you whole and well again also, for the good of the All.*'

'*Oh, good Lady, I swear I will do my best!*' cried the oak, happily.

With that, she placed her hands upon the tree and the squirrel hopped to the floor and sat watching.

The old oak must have fallen asleep, for when he opened his eyes again the wood was bathed in pale winter sunlight.

'*Where is the Lady?*" he asked immediately.

The other trees were surprised to hear the old oak speak, and they exchanged nervous glances with one another. As their attempt to call the witch of the woods had failed and they had believed that the oak was going to die but here he was, almost his old self again.

'*Our dear friend, the oak, is referring to the Lady who came here some nights past,*' the hawthorn spoke in her low, calm voice.

'*Who?*' exclaimed the chestnut, confused.

'*There is no Lady except for it folklore and myth, I know that now; the oak is still half-asleep!*' The larch laughed, just glad to see his old friend the grand oak happy again.

'*Good to have you back,*' called the happy ash to the stretching, yawning oak.

'*Oh thank you, friend,*' replied the tree, who felt a good hundred years younger than when he had gone to sleep, '*if there is no Lady in truth then I must have had a most marvellous dream!*'

'*I would love to hear of your marvellous dream, old oak, please!*' came a small, unfamiliar voice.

It was the apple tree, now looking like a collection of dull old sticks and bare spiky branches. The little tree smiled nervously at the big tree who had been such a silent, brooding presence in his short life.

'*With the greatest pleasure, little brother!*' beamed the oak in return, remembering the terrible pictures of the destroyed woods the pictures that would have happened if he had not lived.

He remembered the Lady of his dream and treasured her wise words. In his dream she had told him how she had planted him long ago to be protector of her woods, keeper of her magic, teller of her tales. He was special too and he was loved. Without his mighty presence the wood may have long ago been destroyed by men, as so many others had been. He was indeed needed.

The trees in Wychwood sighed with relief as the big tree smiled down at the smaller one. The other trees, except for the twisted hawthorn, did not understand but they were grateful all the same. The hawthorn just smiled a small secret smile, feeling warm inside despite the chill air and frosty ground.

The Lady herself walked slowly back to her home in the earth bank, her cloak flashing starlight as she slipped between the trees.

'*Come, dear squirrel, there is much rest to be gained by you and I until next spring; 'tis the time of slumbering and dreaming for us beings of earth,*' she said as she held out her hand to the small creature, in thanks for all of his help.

The squirrel grinned a sleepy grin at his beloved Mistress.

'*Lady, tell me, why do the trees of the wood not believe in you?*' the squirrel asked curiously, before yawning again.

'*They do not have to believe for beliefs only divide us, one against the other, in the end,*' she answered, closing the door behind them, leaving nothing but a grassy bank covered in leaves for the passers-by to see. '*Faith is what we need, dear one; faith in nature and wild enchantment, faith in love and the magical connectedness of all beings. As long as they feel me near, and respect the idea of me, then I will always have a home in the world. For I will always answer when I am called, be it by one who still believes, or by many who have a simple faith, and there will always be that need. Oh yes, our time is not yet over, sweet one, indeed, it may only just have begun.*'

And with that, Mother Nature took off her cloak of stars and settled down to sleep."

Treeface then lifted his fiddle and played a sweet and lilting refrain, evocative of leaves falling gently to earth in a woodland far away. It was truly beautiful and deeply moving and again my slim, white hand wandered over my belly in protective tenderness. Yet as he completed his tune, and indeed his session, he sat down again to silence. The usual applause, when it came, was scanty and the girls looked at each other, confused and, in some cases, disdainful.

"*...babyish*!" I heard one mutter.

This was a sophisticated crowd, perhaps too old, or too world-weary already, for the simple wholesome fare we had offered to them. As I surveyed their discontented faces they seemed very aloof and old-headed in comparison to the boisterous enthusiasm of the junior age range and the innocent glee of the infants. These girls were only in their early teens but already had the scornful manner of those used to getting their own way, I thought; they were hard-nosed, abrasive, privileged girls who were always going to be difficult to please. Sophistication, a *man*-ufactured air of being above that which was earthy, honest and magical, was a trait of the age we lived in and it angered me more than a little. What was it but pretence? A way of blocking out the Greening, of glossing over it with temporary human things, shiny things that would never tarnish or rust, only ever remain as a monument to supposed 'civilisation'. As I sat impotently next to my lover, feeling his unease and sadness building deep within him, I felt my old familiar rage rising in me. Although I had no longer my 'spirit hangers on' that I had once had goading me into depression or temper I still had my own fiery spirit inside me and a need to protect all I held dear...that being the ways of the Earth, of our soul-kind, or of Treeface himself. Yet as I looked around that room I must admit I felt a little nervous of those showy, superior and wholly *refined* young women for they reminded me not a little of my class-mates back in the terrible dark days of my own schooling.

('*Bullies and bigots!*' I shuddered inwardly.)

The girl's teacher had long since left us to get on with her own paperwork in an office down the corridor, I could see her from where I sat and poured out my psychic will to get her to notice we had finished and come back. I felt, suddenly, with a disproportionate amount of fear for a group of adolescent girls, that I had been thrown to the lions. Did Treeface feel this all the time? Oh God, how would I be able to encourage him again if this all went badly wrong for him? His story had been glorious, meaningful, *wonderful*, and now it was as if it had never been told! I prayed for the figure of authority to come back and rescue us, a sense of panic rising at the sensations and impressions I received from Treeface. I knew he was feeling fear...irrational fear and a rush of nervous adrenaline. *Fight or flight!*

It was usually unheard of for any teacher to walk out during a session, they we usually completely spellbound and thoroughly enjoyed the whole performance. It seemed rude, somehow, to just walk away in preference of doing something so mundane when Treeface was a one-off experience.

I knew, as surely as I knew that I loved Treeface, that the gentle magic, resonant teachings and sweet sadness of the story had been lost to the majority of the girls who sat before us. Before I knew what was happening the attention had shifted away from my lover onto me. No one usually noticed me at all! Oh *God!* Could I handle it? By all the spirits that loved me I prayed so.

(*Oh Alicia how I need to see you! Soon, I promise!*)

"Are you a witch, miss?" I was suddenly asked with open hostility.

I threw Treeface a glance and his eyebrows shot up in alarm.

"No, I am not, at least not in the popular understanding of the word, " I said as calmly as I could manage. My hand went to my belly, covering it protectively. If Treeface hadn't been there, or been so damn sensitive about that word, i would have told them that I was a bloody witch, yes. and proud of it too. hell, I would have even used its power to intimidate them a little if they provoked me. But instead I denied my birthrite, shut myself down, lost my power in their eyes.

The girl looked bored, picking at her overly long fingernails idly, "Well if you're not then why do you look like *that*?"

Another group of girls giggled nastily and whispered to eachother.

"*Bloody weird lookin' head!*" I heard one hiss.

"*Like someone's stretched it out of shape!*"

"*Shhh, she'll hear you and put a curse on you!*"

"*She can do what she likes, the freaky bitch! What's she doin' here anyhow? And what does she dye her hair with? Bat's blood?*"

"*Probably uses her own period, if she has one!*"

"*HAAAAA!*"

Their whispers rose so that I couldn't fail to hear every word. Had they so little respect? And should I have protected myself before coming in here? Goodness it had never, ever occurred to me that I would need psychic protection at a children's story telling session! But these were not children, these were...

(*What, Lian? Demons? Inquisitors?Get a grip! They're just rude, cruel, ignorant products of the Makers and not worthy of your anger...or his fear...*)

Treeface intervened hurriedly. I could tell he was close to panic already, the sort that makes you want to bolt for the door. The session hadn't gone at all well, not compared to what we were used to, and now this undisciplined situation was becoming intolerable. Had these horrible girls not absorbed a word of Treeface's story; had they not understood its message of tolerance, reverence and unity?

"My wife is as she is!" he said and I cringed at the defensive tone in his voice...but he called me his wife!

(*Janey was, at least on a pesky piece of legal paper, still his wife. But maybe one day...oh, thank you my love!*)

"You're married then?" There was some giggling.

I actually heard one say to another, with genuine disbelief, "who'd marry her?"

"Or him!"

"Haaaaaa!"

I shuddered again. Had Treeface heard that? I hoped not for I would not want anyone to cast aspersions on our partnership. Even these unbearably cocky teenagers had the power to harm us, it seemed.

(*I felt a flash of my old anger, hot and destructive. Were we really so fragile?Protect yourself, healer man, protect yourself, wise wild woman seer!Do it now!*)

"Why've you got that *thing*?" a dark-skinned, plump girl asked Treeface, pointing, inevitably, at the scars. So far he had managed to get away with genuine interest, a natural curiosity, in his unusual face and this had been used as an aid to the performance as we had planned. Children had actually been allowed to put painted leaves on his bare branches many times. there had been love shown for his difference and even admiration. This was different. I didn't like this crowd, how could I? There would be no face painting for them, then, no rowdy, good natured tussle to get to be first to decorate the branches of the scar as there had been with so many classes so far.

"Mother Nature liked me so much she made me a tree-face!" Treeface had often told curious well-meaning children. Now instead of this he said, defensively,

"It's a scar, is all."

Treeface gestured to his cheek and brow and I noted with horror that his hand shook a little.

Any sign of weakness would be exploited, I knew this pack mentality well! Oh, he had never had a shred of horrible nerves before, but the vibration in the room was far different than any we had encountered previously! '*Welcome to the real world,*' I thought, grimly.

"Why's it there?"

I got the feeling the girl didn't want to know at all, was just being damn impertinent, in fact!

I thought I may get up and fetch the errant teacher back from her study. I sent out a bolt of pure dislike at the girl, much to my own dismay, for putting out raw negative energy was not good practice and she was, after all, little more than a child. However, she was so dense as not to feel it, it seemed for she just stretched lazily, not really caring if there was an answer.

"I have a birthmark!" another girl said cheerfully. She was much nicer looking, bespectacled and gawky but with an honest face. "You just can't see it because its on my thigh. It looks like a potato!"

"Yes, my scarring is a birthmark, you are quite right! " Treeface gestured at his cheek and brow visibly holding onto his jolly persona.

"Right!" the teacher strode in and the girls bolted upright from their insolent, don't-care poses. I could have hugged the woman for all her rudeness. Thank you for saving us, you old bat; for rescuing Treeface from the questioning he so hates.

We both stood up hastily, Treeface dropping his stick in his hurry to depart. It clattered noisily to the tiled floor and there was stifled snigger. The girl in the glasses leapt to her feet and picked it up.

('*If it only touches one heart, ever, if it only sows one green seed...then it was worth it*!' I heard Alicia's voice, wise as ever, reassure me.)

"Thank you!" Treeface was genuinely grateful. "It's been a pleasure to meet you..." he left a pause for the girl to give her name.

"Candia!" the girl said and one of the bigger pupils whispered a snide comment and snorted.

The mistress clapped her hands sharply. "Right, two o'clock, down to the auditorium. Lena, Natasha, hold the doors please," and the girls also stood, suddenly obedient and docile, and filed out. Candia turned and threw one shy glance back at my 'husband'...

(*Was it possible to feel jealous of some poor, picked upon slip of a girl? Oh, how very little experience I had of relationships and of human interactions!*)

"Well!" the teacher said, briskly "See Valerie Marchant at reception on your way out would you, she deals with payment."

And she too was gone leaving us standing in a cool room filled with chalk dust and bad feeling. Not a word of thanks between them!

"Let's just get out of here," Treeface said and I needed no further encouragement. My guts were turning over and bile had risen in my throat. I could feel the anxiety coming off Treeface in sickening waves.

('*Let him not blame the new story!*' I prayed to myself as we went down the dismal corridor to the receptionists office.)

What I really meant was, *let him not blame me.*

Or wild green witchery.

"So, what's all this about storytelling?"

"Storytelling now, is it?" Treeface's mother looked down her nose as if it was the first she had heard of such a strange and disgusting concept, rather as if we had just announced that vintage wine could be made through distilling rat droppings. She dragged on her menthol cigarette aggressively and eyed her errant son with disdain. No wonder he had delayed taking me to meet his parents! We were sitting around their kitchen table, next to the Aga, the first proper one I had ever seen. The Reynolds's seemed to live the idyll of middle-class England, a three storey house in a village equi-distant from Bath and Bristol and in the commuter belt for both, surrounded by countryside but close to the cities. There were two Range Rovers parked up on the gravel drive, a duo of clean green Barbour jackets and matching wellingtons in the porch and a fat Labrador flopped on the mat. There was money here, real money, yet Treeface was so poor! Didn't they care about their son? Hadn't they ever wanted to help him out, to make a life already blighted by scarring a little easier? Apparently not. For these were two of the most smug, self-righteous and resolutely *cold* people I had ever met. In fact the more I looked at them the more I struggled to think of them producing the wonderful, odd looking, magical Treeface between them. And how had they ever created the passionate, ethereal, willowy Lydia (for much as I hated to admit it that was what Treeface's sister was)? I decided that the two Reynolds offspring, like me, were changelings. Fey born through human parentage into human bodies that couldn't help but reveal their true soul-nature.

Yes, only Treeface, their strange son, seemed to detract from their overall image of rural domesticity...oh, and me, of course. There was no way you could say I looked like a typical landowner's wife, or even a stockbroker's. I was in my early summer variation of my all-black theme, the cotton jeans with baseball boots and a too tight, wash-faded T-shirt which was only slightly ripped under one arm.

Treeface's father, a man who was an intimidating cross between Santa Claus and Brian Blessed, had been addressing his son whilst blatantly assessing my chest. No doubt he would find it failed to impress with its stature. I was a skinny, if reasonably proportioned, woman and no match for his own wife's curvy solidity which no amount of Laura Ashley cardigans could conceal adequately. The woman was like the typical matriarch of a well ordered rural estate and I found it very hard indeed to picture her having the nervous episodes that Treeface had related to me when discussing his childhood. Apparently his father's many ill-disguised affairs had sent her close to the edge of sanity and health on many occasions in his youth and I had expected to meet a frail and brittle woman. Instead I was greeted coolly by this bustling, efficient and dismissive woman who looked as if she didn't care about much at all. Maybe that was all an act, I wondered, trying to be charitable about another woman. But I doubted it.

And clearly Vic had not put aside his philandering ways as he was obviously prospecting for something younger, but certainly a little plumper breasted, than me. What if I had met his physical criteria, would he have had no qualms in trying to poach me from his only son? I had not a shred of doubt that he would. Damn my *sight*, it always revealed to me what I would rather not know! I should have done more psychic protection before agreeing to visit the Reynolds's at home. I knew I wouldn't fit the bill for this bluff, boarish man; I rarely did for men used to the standard images of modern women offered as sexual objects. I almost smiled though, Treeface's father was so obvious, I could read his thoughts as if they were written on his forehead!

(*How had Treeface grown up here, I wondered, as the conversation drifted around me as insubstantial yet irritating as Mrs Reynolds's smoke? How had the boy that had lived in this respectable, restrictive place become the man I knew and loved? It was as baffling to me as how I myself had emerged from my own father's semi-detached house on a fairly tidy but bland and regimented estate...a house devoid of colour or excitement, which betrayed no signs of individuality or flair.*

What was missing from both backgrounds, I mused to myself, was any sign of an interest in things mystical or even remotely alternative, the things that made Treeface and I uniquely ourselves. Our respective homes were almost ludicrously stereotypical in format ...my own culturally and aesthetically bereft, stultifying for a child needing freedom and stimulation, whilst his played up exclusively to a rustic dream that was as cold and dead as a fox ripped apart by the huntsmen's hounds. We were sat in a farmhouse kitchen in a house that definitely wasn't on a farm while the Reynolds's certainly bore no resemblance to happy or capable landowners. It was almost surreal, a charade of a life-style that I found unsettling. Were we all just characatures of ourselves, the fuddy-duddy parents, the rebellious outcasts?)

"When are you going to get yourself together, boy?" Treeface's father prized his eyes from below my neckline and poured himself another shot of whiskey even though the rest of us had tea. I knew Treeface himself would have liked to have been offered a shot to calm his not inconsiderable nerves but it had not been forthcoming. Something in Vic Reynolds kept his son resolutely in the role of silly, mildly annoying little child.

"Thought once that dreadful little woman left you you'd get a new lease of life! Jane was pretty enough, there's no doubt about that, but when she opened her mouth, ye Gods!" his father shook his head dramatically and continued, "I suppose with that bloody thing you've got on your face there's precious little hope for you, really. But I've offered you desk jobs and old Bob down in the office in Bristol, he's offered you positions where no bugger would have to see you much. trouble is you don't know which side your damned breads buttered on, lad, and you never have!" Vic shook his head again as if his son was completely incomprehensible to his older, wiser, infinitely more capable father. "That bloody thing on your face, I'd have it lasered off if I were you, there's a reputable clinic in Berkshire and I've offered to pay, although why I should fork out for you I don't know."

I was open-mouthed; to have so much open contempt for your son! how could his own father despise him when he hadn't even done anything wrong but be born 'disfigured' and be himself! Really, if Treeface would have given me any sign it was okay to do so I would have answered this gross man back in this own terms! But instead Treeface sat, head bowed, defeated and almost cowering from his father.

Vic cleared his throat noisily. "You think it's too late now, eh, boy? Think there's no point in changing your face now you've let yourself get old and unemployable? Humph! You'll never get a decent woman or a decent job and God only knows where you are living these days! You're a disgrace boy, always have been, always will be. I don't know why your mother and I wasted a single penny on your education. Pfftt!"

Treeface said nothing; he gave no sharp retort and uttered a resounding nothing in support of his choices. I knew him well enough by now to realise that there would be no placating statement, nor any spirited defence of himself, or of me, to the virulent Vic. Treeface looked down at his hands and an atmosphere you could cut with a knife conjealed around us. Even Vic fell into an uncharacteristically brooding silence.

"And what do *you d*o?" Isabel Reynolds looked vaguely in my direction but didn't meet my eye. I was glad as I had no desire to I felt myself getting very angry indeed. My pale face was going red, I could feel it.

"Lian's helping me, for now!" Treeface butted in defensively, his voice going up a register from his usual bass note. His father seemed to have usurped him in the deep booming voice department. God help us, Treeface was intimidated by the old bully!

"Yes, yes but what *are* you, eh?" Vic Reynolds half leered at me, clearly oblivious to my discomfiture...or perhaps glad of it.

"Lian's a *seer*," Treeface said and I could feel the waves of terror coming off him as he spoke the truth in the face of his over-bearing patriarch.

"Hells teeth and God's balls!" Vic spluttered. "Well, I suppose its better than a prostitute. Or a bloody writer of feminist drivel that seeks to make women restless and discontented with their lot...humph! Why can't your sister stop cavorting around and find herself a proper man to start a family with, eh? God knows we've got to get our grandchildren from somewhere!" Vic took a slug of his drink. "Suppose anything's better than stirring things up like Lydia tries to...hmmm? But then I'm not so sure...What's *seeing* all about, anyway, eh? Getting the unsuspecting punters to tell you their secrets and then tarting them up so they think you've found it out *spiritually...*" he said the last word with contempt, waving his large hand in an exaggerated way at the ceiling, "and then charging them for the privilege! Filling people's heads with stuff that'll never come true, I reckon that's what *seeing* is! Waste of bloody time, either way!"

We had been there for over an hour, not long when visiting a partner's parental home, I supposed, but I didn't know if I could stand any more. And I thought that *my* father was bad with his dismissive, throw-away attitude to his only daughter and his complete lack of understanding as to who or what I was! This man was worse than I had ever imagined, a blatantly rude, intolerably ignorant monster! How could Treeface bear to be in the same room with him on a regular basis? My lover owed this vulgar man nothing...*nothing*! He did not need to take his insults and slurs.

(*What was worse, I knew he would take slurs on me, too, and not defend me at all. Why, he already had!*)

My own Papa had seemed to drift even further away from me since Treeface had come on the scene, thinking as he would that someone else could take care of me now, all his responsibility absolved. Apart from the odd bit of cash to assuage the last of his conscience I heard little from him. I think he must have adopted my cousin, Maureen's lad, as his own. I guess he had always wanted a boy anyway or, at the very least, a *normal* girl that he could parade around. Just as well, there was nothing I had to say to him anyway. If more parents and children agreed to part company quietly and without fuss when it was obvious there was nothing in common between them as adults then the world would have been more harmonious all round, I reckoned. I didn't tell my own father that we had a phone, which was listed under Reynolds anyway, and the odd note was acceptable if I switched off the horrible impressions that came with it...

(*The ones of his shame and thinly veiled dislike for the flame-haired progeny he considered a changeling at best, a curse at worst. The ones in which he regretted chasing after my wonderful, wild mother or ever impregnating her at all.*)

...and pretend, just as he did with me, that we were passing acquaintances that had fallen out of contact, not blood kin who had, as each one thought, spurned the other willfully, spurning all the values that the other held dear. Why did parents have such unlikely children and then feel disappointed? Could they not accept that we are all souls on our own journeys, not dolls for them to play with and show off? And could we children not accept our own parents as individual souls also and not expect them to be Faery-tale folk free of faults? It seemed to me ever so sad. But yes it made me angry too. Why did we waste time on it? Why wasn't I now with Alicia rather than spending a valuable second more with these two horrors? Yes, I MUST see Alicia! I felt so damn guilty about that. And I missed her, I truly did. although we had only met a few times each time was a lifetime to me, filled with magic and meaning, in which we connected at a level far deeper than any other.

I snapped out of my reverie to hear Vic's baritone booming again.

"What's to be done with you both, then, eh?" Vic drank a slug of whiskey that would have made a lesser man cough, even though it was a respectable single malt and probably very palatable. He positively relished being an intimidating figure, I thought.

"We don't want anything *done* with us!" Treeface began, his voice rising yet again, his defences up. Then he added "thank you, anyway," in the deferential manner he had apparently always adopted in Vic's presence. I cringed inwardly. Where was my hero, my wild and strong Green Man? This man, despite his desire to be who he was in the world, at long last, was now falling back into his long-held, fearful, whining and submissive mode!

"Tea, more tea?" Isabel stood up bombastically and knocked over the ashtray that she had balanced precariously on the edge of the scrubbed pine table. She tutted loudly as if it had been our fault for distracting her as Vic grumbled, oblivious to the fact we were there as guests.

"It doesn't matter, Ma!" Treeface leaned over and put his hand lightly on the woman's wrist. I felt brief pang of jealousy at the tender action but I could clearly see she would immediately shake him off. The woman was highly unmaternal, it seemed. No wonder with such a rampant boar for a husband! She would have been better off dedicating her life to growing roses or breeding horses than having children.

Isabel sat down again and scowled darkly to herself, Treeface and I both caught the look. I knew it hurt him.

"Have you met Lydia then Lynn? Blonde sort, small, smaller even than Rory, I'd say. Lovely looking piece, could have been a model but for her height, I suppose. Simon, that's her agent, bloody sensible sort of chap too, plays golf over at the club, took some photo's of her I think. Do you know where they are Isa?" Vic gave a chesty cough and I could barely stand the angry discomfort I had welling in me, never mind the pain Treeface was feeling. Oh, how Treeface KNEW I was desperately insecure and how awful the mentioning of the loveliness of his sister made me feel! Well, to have my nose rubbed in that and to be called Lynn, as if his father couldn't be remotely bothered to get his girlfriend's name right, was intolerable! Oh *God!* Couldn't we just go home?I despised Vic and didn't want to tolerate another second of him, let alone see glamourous press photo's of the 'lovely Lydia'. And how on Earth could this man call his only daughter a 'piece'? I had tried to find Vic sad or inept but I couldn't, not when I saw how his bumbling brashness cut his poor willow-wand of a son to the quick and not when he paid me so little regard, not even as a guest in his home. How could he pour scorn on Treeface's honest attempt to make a living when he obviously was proud, albeit in a dubious sort of way, of his younger daughter's attractiveness? It was abhorrent to me. How much longer had we to sit there?

(*And how could we face each other after this debacle?Why hadn't he said 'her name's not Lynn, it's Lian, L-I-A-N , as in lion!'*)

I sat and retreated into my own head, absorbed by my own thoughts as Isabel droned on and on in a flat, emotionless voice, about comings and goings in the village these days and Vic boasted and bragged about business and golf scores and took the occasional side-swipe at his scarred else son for not joining the family firm or being a chip off his old block. No one seemed to notice my withdrawal, much less be bothered by it, and beside a quick squeeze to my hand under the table by Treeface I was pretty much left alone, which suited everyone.

How could he let them treat him like that? Had he no sense of worth, no pride to make him defend his own actions in the world? How could he let his father eye me like a...a thing to be weighed up for its physical merits like a cow in the ring on market day?

And how had he ended up born to such people?

('*Now, now, pet. That's no way to look at your fellow incarnate beings, now is it? Where's your Fey compassion?That's an us-and-them attitude developing, that is! You take care you don't pass too many judgements, mind. You don't know their backgrounds in this life, let alone their other lives...you don't know their pain or their patterns. Just sit, cariad, just sit and be still. This is something you are doing for your lover, not for yourself. Let him fight his own battles, deal with his own problems, wait 'til he asks before you go offerin' an opinion on any of it. Like as not he's feeling embarrassed enough as it is, look! Just bide your time and sit it out. Now's a good time to ponder that question though...do we choose the parents or do they choose us or do we all agree on it, for many, many reasons long before we all incarnate? What do you think, beloved?' Alicia's voice, clear and clam, cut through my grumbling thoughts. Oh, what would I do without her? And, moreover, when would I get to see her? It had been months now and I hadn't managed to take Treeface over to see her. Next week, I hoped. It was only as bus ride away, after all. Maybe we could visit some schools while we were over in her area? I felt suddenly ashamed. Who was I to criticise these people, as trying as they were, when I couldn't even be bothered to go and see the only other person who had ever showed me any kindness? Especially as she only lived a matter of miles away from me!*)

I forced out a smile as Treeface sought my eyes across the table. Yes, it was hard maintaining one's honesty and integrity in front of family, I knew that, especially when you were having a very different life-experience and had changed so very much since you had last met, in ways they may never know or understand. But did they need to? Blood ties may not be as strong as spirit links but they still counted for something in the world, even if I couldn't quite grasp their meaning as yet.

As we made our way wearily back to the far side of Bath on the bus there was an awkwardness between us that had not been there before. If it hadn't been for Alicia's words reaching me in my black mood then I would have been horribly damning about Vic and Isabel Reynolds to Treeface. As it was, I held my tongue and kept my own council, for once. He was being very chatty and trying to over compensate for the fact he had let me, and himself, down. I told him it didn't matter but I knew that it did. It mattered that he had not learned to speak his truth to the people he knew as his parents and it mattered that he was more worried about upsetting them than he was about defending me.

Treeface was also nervous because we were going home by public transport and that meant stares, whispers and maybe worse. The public were tolerably polite when they winessed him as an entertainer, a quirky figure froma folk-tale come to life, but on a bus, seeing him as just a man with a strange face and an even stranger energy...

And despite Alicia's wise words about not passing judgement I knew that I had made one on him that day, one that was, perhaps, irreversible. For in some small way the seemingly trivial events in the Reynolds family home had echoed the lack of commitment Julien De St. Pierre had shown to protecting me in France. It was just symbolic perhaps and probably, in the scheme of things, nothing to cause me alarm as Treeface was still by my side, still going home with me to lie with me. He was not going to leave me.

Yet, if everything was energies then our energies, as the united whole we made together, were wrong. It hurt me terribly this knowledge, a cruel cold stabbing in my chest that felt like death come for me, too soon. For I knew with dread certainty that his energies were not as mine, his were still those of the appeaser when it came to anyone who he feared could hurt him whereas I was willing to leave the victim I had been behind...only he was holding me back.

It sickened me and it pained me to know that anyone in authority...the teachers in schools, his father, the landlord at Carlett Court, even the driver on the bus...they all held power over him and to keep some sort of safe stability in his life he was willing to let himself be trampled verbally by any one of them. Rather that than unsettle the status quo, upsetting the apple cart and, heaven forbid, drawing their attention on him he would let them trash him, making little of him, making light of all he was.

Alicia was wrong, the re-telling and *re-membering* of the burning of Thirteen Twenty Six had not healed Treeface. He had come into this life with a choice...with visible scars that spoke eloquently of who and what he was...with the challenge to be proud of himself, no matter what, because they could only kill the body, never the soul. But he was still afraid. He was still choosing to hide himself, in fear.

And his fear would allow him to be insulted and me with him, as ever.

And with that knowledge, something beautiful died in me as we sat on the grubby bus seat in our very first uneasy silence, going back to the city I had began to think of as home. Such a small thing to let it get me down, I reminded myself.

Just a small thing.

And I knew as surely as I loved him that I was not carrying his child.

Nor, perhaps, would I ever be.

Chapter Two

Time of No Reply

I tried my best for her, I really did, but, like Janey, and indeed Lydia, before her, it was never enough. For what she needed was a man with the confidence to push beyond his self-imposed limits and fulfil the promise of his wild soul. I wondered, truly, if I could ever provide enough for any loved one, be that woman...or child.

(*What child would incarnate to be fathered by me? To live below the poverty line with a man incapable of feeding and clothing himself adequately, with no real place in society? How could a child be expected to choose to be born into that circumstance? And how could a child desire a father that was impotent, confused, a-feared? Could I, as a man, allow it to happen*?)

It was a simple, raw fact that all of the women who had ever been close to me had found me lacking and had been brought low by living in the shadow of my pain. Even my own mother despaired of me, maybe even despised me, and seemed to veer away more and more from the reality of her only son on every occasion we met, referring to me by turns as a teacher or a scholarly writer, depending on her mood.

She would hardly meet my eyes these days. Indeed had she ever? She just evaded the truth of her son as she had always done, letting Vic take the lead in expressing their sentiments. I always felt that trying to connect with my mother was like scratching on glass.

My own father, meanwhile, was never backwards in coming forwards about how he felt. He was a man given to blunt proclamations and bald statements of (often hurtful) facts, as he saw them. My father never felt any need to hold back the truth for fear of upsetting me and so often claimed he was deeply ashamed of me, a shame that was non-negotiable. Mind you, what chance did I have when Vic even showed disdain and perhaps, on occasion, disgust for my successful sister? What had he hoped we would be that we had turned out so badly for him...or would it not have mattered how we had turned out when he would always have considered us lesser than him somehow?

I could hope for no sibling camaraderie to form a barrier against him and his inevitable litany against me (and anyone who was close to me) as Lydia wasn't going to hang around the matter of our family too long when there were deals to be done with that creep of an agent Simon Matthieson. So, as with so many things in life, I was alone with my the pain that my family caused me by their dismissive and coldly callous attitude. My only option was to exorcise them totally from my life and perhaps one day I would manage that, somehow. For now, though, it seemed as if I were stuck with them as even if I ceased to see them, which I had done many times to elude the hurting, their voices haunted me with words of dismissal and embarrassment. Even in their absence they taunted me. Yes, my parents were ever the ghosts in my machine.

So, what with one thing and another, I was made to wonder it whether anyone knew, or truly valued, who I was, at all? Everyone I cared for seem to want me to be something other than I was, or, more to the point, saw me as something that suited them, be that a wild and thrilling outlaw or a romantic visionary. Even Kefli, my dear companion spirit and wild woodling man, seemed more willingto blindly accept me as his kin than to witness the cowardly truth of me. Yet even those who had seen me as dashingly different or romantic, a wolfshead from another age, would inevitably end up viewing me as something sad and tatty. Or, worse still, contemptible and weak.

With this in mind can you imagine how I felt when the two of them, Lian with her jaw set in that hard-faced way she adopted when she was afraid and Lydia wringing her hands and looking moon-eyed and mystical, both sat down at a table with me to discuss 'the future'? It had been bad enough dealing with Jane and the divorce but somehow talking of the future with my sister and lover was more stressful and draining than all my dealings with Jane's almost-sneering solicitors. You know, it all seemed so ludicrous, divorcing Jane, or her divorcing me as it turned out, when our marriage had been built on so very little to begin with. Marriage had only been the order of the day as Jane had badly wanted children from me back then and she couldn't countenance a child out of wedlock. Jane had been brought up by staunch church-going parents and, although she herself did not practice any religious devotions, her childhood conditioning loomed large in her life. And yes, we had thought they would indeed be children along within a few months of our union, such as it was. Instead Jane and I discovered within mere weeks of being wed that we were physically as incompatible as we were spiritually and emotionally. We didn't talk about it, it was too painful, but Jane soon morphed from my would-be wife and lover to my reluctant protector and benefactor...and little else. No children came. And I was glad, to be honest. How could I be a father, coward as I was, when all children meant to me was cruelty and torment, bullying and brutality? My own conditioning on the matter of children was strong too. How could it not be? No, I was not sorry that we remained childless.

What a farce a solicitor's debate over our shared worldly goods, a motley collection of second-hand furniture and worn-out household implements, had been. How sad that the last vestiges of the friendship that Jane and I had maintained through thick and thin should be disposed of so easily, along with a set of knives or a sagging sofa. Divorce was hard, yes, even when there was no love lost, not really. And yet, in direct contrast to that lingering sadness over Jane and our lost life, what a colossal pain I felt, somewhere deep and unnameable, as my flame-haired *seer* and my pale haired enchantress met properly for the first time. They were women who must have had something in common, surely, for me to have found them both so wonderful, so compelling? Yet they seemed locked in some private battle of their own, oblivious to the man that had brought them both together, and were acting as if each were the polar opposite of the other, diametrically opposed to all the other was. In this way my past and my present were united for one mercifully brief, yet wholly unbearable, time at a pub table in early June...and I would have gone through ten divorces to avoid the anxiety and discomfort of it.

.I didn't understand the energies that flowed between my beloved sister and my current red haired lover but they disturbed me. It seemed to me that their feelings, and especially Lian's, went far beyond the jealousy and rivalry I would have perhaps expected. I couldn't explain, either, the wordless panic that filled me as I watched them interact, no love lost between them either yet sparks flying, an incredible intensity uniting them, attracting and repelling them simultaneously. I did not fancy for one moment that it was their love of me that brought them to such a clashing of wills, such a swelling cacophony of feeling! Indeed, I may as well have not been there for all it seemed to matter to them!

Strangely, the suave, sophisticated Simon, Lydia's agent and now, apparently, her lover, was the only one who seemed to acknowledge me at all beyond a cursory glance or question. Lydia's *boyfriend,* as I now had to accept him as being, was a tall spare man with the hungry, aesthetic look of a priest combined with an elegant, urbane edge. Typical of Lydia's 'fans' he wore crumpled linen and sported a foppish strawberry blonde fringe which fell into his eyes at annoyingly regular intervals, lending him the air of an actor from a period drama trying to look alluringly rakish. But the seemingly casual yet carefully arranged reddish-gold hair was thinning! I know because, believe me, I looked...looked for any fault or flaw I could find in him. I knew that such thinning hair would bother Lydia, sooner or later, aesthetics were so important to her. Just as I knew as soon as she had arranged the meeting for the four of us (how civilised!) that she would have already cast aside her shabby mis-matched wardrobe and taken full advantage of her literary agent lover's backing fund.

I was right, and, by the Gods, she looked good!

I felt a pang of guilt as I assessed the small, slim form of the woman I knew so well, inside and out, as she sat on the slatted wooden seat in the pub's beer garden opposite to me. She had reverted to her youthful penchant for rich velvets, even in the heat of the day, and wore a flowing sleeveless shift which glanced temptingly across her small, neat breasts and over the firm belly and lean thighs. Lydia was a prize to be sure, the burgundy eyes like old port, the blonde hair silvered in the sun and spilling across the shoulders. She wore a sun hat in black straw with dusty pink cloth roses pinned to the rim and a wide swath of maroon silk satin round the crown to set them off. Lian, on the other hand, wore a holey black vest top and a wash-faded black cotton fringed skirt for we had not the money for clothes. Just as Lydia had worn faded corduroy and washed out wool mere months before, before *Simon*, when I was her best friend and confidante...

By Christ! I gathered a hold of myself and tore my eyes from Lydia's obviously seductive attire. Is that what I did to a woman, render them shapeless and threadbare like the old cardigan Lydia had to wear on the day I met Lian? How could I compete with the elegant, casually witty Simon, he who sat smoking his thin cheroot, buying our drinks when I could only have bought us all a glass of squash, perhaps, so short was our money that week. How could I judge poor Lian against Lydia's finery when it was my fault that by comparison she looked so drab and drawn? That was what worry about money and genuine fretting over psychic work did for you. Lydia too had once looked pinched and anxious hadn't she?

But the delightful little Lydia, brilliant writer and evocative poet as she was, was not a psychic like my lover. A *sensitive* perhaps, and certainly a soul-poet, but not a *seer*. It wasn't only money, or lack of it, that made Lian anxious. It was what she *felt*. Lydia would have killed to have Lian's gift of *sight*, to have been a 'proper' witch with real natural powers, but as it was she had the gifts of word-craft, and of charm and beauty, instead. Lian had the burden of all her *seeing* and *knowing* on her each and every day and with that reality rarely experienced it as a gift at all. How amazed she would be to discover that Lydia actually envied her something too! But I would never tell her and Lydia certainly wouldn't!

All Lian would ever see, in comparison, was her own strangeness compared to Lydia's charming, childlike poise and sweetness. Yes, Lydia did indeed seem to become more lovely, more ethereal and attractive, as the years went on. I stared at her, mesmerised for a few moments, as most men who ever came across her were. The only man I had ever known to truly resist her was my father, thankfully; I dreaded to think what might have happened if his own revolting rampancy may have gone to far in her direction. Even Shay Donnelly had known her worth and adored her even as he raged against her. Looking at Lydia was like moon-gazing, I thought; she was lithe Lady Luna in her first quarter, a slender dancer, a ripe crescent. Then, as if to shake me awake from my stupid infatuation with my her splendid appearance, Lydia opened her subtly rouged mouth. And when my sister spoke it grated on me like no other voice ever had before.

For the voice was not hers.

Oh yes, I knew Lydia was highly skilled at whatever she set her mind to and I knew why she had adopted that horrible voice instead of her own. She had set her sights on wooing an American audience and for making an impact in the States. For this she had clearly decided, or been told, that she needed to have a cut-glass English accent. More doors would open for her, be that for work or for finding her son, if she could appear like a proper cultured, and obviously beautiful, English lady, like a piece of picture book history come to life. Gone was her warm West Country burr that overlaid our more distant origins in the shire to the north of London. In its place was a clear ringing tone like a piece of good silver hitting a Waterford crystal decanter.

"Simon and I are moving to L.A., of course, as there's no use in us being here now when the future lies in the States, is there darling? Of course we will pop back over from time to time for tours and so forth; Simon has a perfectly good little place in Chesham which he only uses at weekends at present and that can be our home in England. In today's market he can sell his London place at the drop of a hat!"

I wondered when Lydia had ever learned anything of the property market? She was usually highly impractical and unconcerned with matters pertaining to bricks and mortar, such as bills, I thought ruefully. The only thing she had ever put her mind to in a focussed way was finding her boy Donal...oh, and getting published. I should have known she'd only do something if it suited her to. Half the time she had spent with me she'd feigned complete bewilderment, even if I had even asked her to get a money order at the post office she had acted like I had been speaking in another language, as if ordinary run-of-the-mill things were from another planet to hers.

I stared hard at my sister, the very same woolly, silky sister that had asked me, mere months before, to stand behind her as she spoke to a London audience, whilst knowing how stressed it would make me. Oh yes, I had stood behind her then and countless times before, and I would do it again a thousand times too...and she knew it! This was my apparently will-o'-the-wispy, Fey sister who had rubbed my nose in her foolish witchery even though she knew how sore it would make me. Damn her! Had she always been so manipulative? But she was beautiful and gentle and creative wasn't she? I couldn't hate her, not ever! And *I couldn't lose her*! Even with that man...*that lanky lounge lizard!*..sat next to her I could not give up on her. Not on my Lyddie! I WOULD NOT LOSE HER AGAIN! Not to witchery, not to anyone or anything!

"I'll be putting my share of royalties for this quarter in with his money and we can probably get a wonderful place there that'll be handy for us flying to London, New York, Europe...which I'll have to do far more, obviously..." Lydia licked her rose-madder lips and smiled winningly at Simon.

"Why can't you stay here? Er, both of you?" I asked before I had time to think any more.

Lydia smiled at me as if I were truly soft. Had she always done that?

"Oh, Bath's fine, in its way, but I really wouldn't want to cramp your style, Rory, with you starting out in the city afresh. I'd hate for us to be constantly bumping into each other, it wouldn't be right...You need your freedom and our closeness may hamper your new relationship...and I need my freedom to express myself in a wider way..." Lydia paused and flashed her dark eyes appealingly in my direction. I could feel Lian at my side stiffening with barely suppressed rage.

Something in me withdrew even further than I had found myself doing of late.

"I think I need a change of scene, anyway," Lydia went on, stretching languidly as if to emphasise how contented and refined she had become, "there are a fascinating set of people in L.A., just like Bloomsbury all over again really, and just *exactly* the types I've been looking for to bounce new ideas off, apparently. Witchcraft, *modern* witchcraft, is huge in the States and its definitely where I need to be. I've already been invited to host a monthly group that meets to discuss women's mysteries at the University, and there are ongoing opportunities for seminars, thanks to Simon, so there'll be plenty of work. It's going to be very exciting!" Lydia stopped, her eyes shining in a way I had seldom seen before, and then seeing me blanch she visibly got a hold of herself. Her excitement at leaving was obviously too great to be expressed decently in my presence, she had to pretend to have other more honourable motivations for her choices. "Yes and er, and *of course* I'll need as much of my money, and our time, as I can manage to locate Donal. I have to be in America both my work and for him, I hope you understand that, sweetheart?" Lydia smiled winningly, her horrible new voice ringing in my head " Yes, it's for my work, and naturally for Simon's, but it's for Donal too. For his life and mine. And when Simon and I get married..."

(*Married? To that...that dilettante? To that slimy extra for 'Brideshead Revisited'? Oh Lydia!)*

"What do you mean, married? And how can you go to America and leave me like this when I'll never be able to afford to come and see you? You can do all your work and research from here, Lydia, don't let him convince you otherwise! *How can you go when I'll never see you?* After all we've shared...after all I've done...*I'll never see you!* You can't go!"

I trailed off, horrified at myself. I sounded like a parent guilt-tripping a child who wants to break away from the nest. Again my words had flown out before I could think about what I was going to say. My feelings spilled from me like sour wine and Lian, stung by their clinging, cringing sentiment, jumped in, cheeks flaming, eyes flashing. I knew she was dying to tell Lydia what she thought of her and this seemed to be the opening she had sought. Old jealousy and righteous indignation mixed to create a potent, unpredictable and highly volatile brew.

"Yeah, you've used Treeface all your life and now you are going to swan off with *him...*" Lian jerked her thumb dismissively at Simon; he was just the sort of man she detested on sight and I loved her for it "...without a thought for your own brother! He's been like a bloody husband to you! God, he even had to sit and baby mind you the day I met him. And you knew how much he hated that whole publicity thing, especially about witchery, yet you forced him with your wheedling and guilt!"

"Is that what you told her, Rory? Is it?"

Lydia looked genuinely shocked. and hurt. Oh God I couldn't bear it! I shrank away, my head shaking of its own accord, and I put my hands up as if to ward off their words. By Christ you are such a coward, Reynolds! What would Tatty and Ana and Meggy think of you now, eh? Why does Kefli stick around with such a fool as you?

"I say, steady on there! Woah! I hardly think, *with all due respect of course,* that you can call what Rory, or Treeface, here did for Lyddie er, *support* in any true sense of the word!" Simon puffed on his thin cigar and looked horribly smug. "Surely support is more than standing behind someone a few times like a spare prick at a wedding?" He laughed at me, braying like an ass, and I wanted to throttle him. "And if its a matter of money, and it usually is, then we, Lydia and I, can arrange a little something for you both. Yes we can certainly pay you in arrears for your time, Rory, if that is what this is all about, this silly bickering! Lyddie's going to be huge out in the States and I am sure we can manage to give you a back payment."

It would have been comical if it weren't so offensive but, as ever, when someone insulted me I found my lips glued fast and my hands clenched into ineffectual fists. I said nothing. I would let them all denigrate me and I would not speak. A pattern learned long ago, hard to let go of. Argh! My terrible impotence!

"How *dare* you speak of Treeface's honour and intentions when you don't know him! He has integrity and credibility and authenticity...not like you, Mr Flash Harry, and certainly not like *her*, his using sister! Treeface just wants to see her...he hasn't got much in his life, only me and...her...and he needs to have access to his sister. You can't take her away, and you can't go Lydia, not when he's too poor to fly round the world after you! Accch!"

They both stared at Lian as if she were an interesting specimen that they were viewing under a microscope. God, let them not insult her! But then I wish Lian hadn't made me sound so needy and pathetic even if it were true. My head was spinning with it!

There was a moments uneasy silence and then Lydia's horrible, artificial Joanna Lumley/Henley Regatta voice sounded again; cool, calculated. and *all wrong!*

"May I remind *you,* Lian, that you yourself have only known my brother for a mere handful of months! Let me be the judge, as his closest member of family, of what is best for him!"

Lian eyed my sister with contempt and puffed her skinny chest up as her words sprayed out indiscriminately. She had suffered all her life and had only just found something, and *someone,* to care about. She would not have it threatened in any shape or form! Her anger, if misplaced, was formidable.

"Yeah, well that's as may be but I do know this, that he looked after you, Lydia, even if it meant himself going without food or sleep! And even if it meant that he dropped his own principles and wrestled with his fears to do so! And you *knew* that! You knew it even as you used his kindness and loyalty! Well, go on, bugger off on him then! *I* will love him, *I* will take care of him now! Better than you ever did, or anyone else for that matter! Accch!"

Lian glared daggers at my rapidly blinking sister and even though she was defending my honour, as it were, I wished she would just let Lydia and the snaky Simon get on with it.. But instead of backing down and shutting up now, as was wise, my lover had found her stride and was yelling now, this time back at Simon who looked like a study in nonchalance in comparison.

"He did what any man could for Lydia, just like he does for me, and she damn well knows that! If she's such bloody feminist, always going on about woman-power..."

"I take it by '*she*' you are referring to Lyddie?" Simon enquired, suddenly haughty, putting a protective arm on his girlfriend's (*my sister's!*) shoulder. Lian bristled and I wished I could move my hands to hold her protectively too, but I was frozen in space and time. I remained inert and Lian continued on alone. And Simon had called my sister Lyddie! Oh how could she let him? That was my name for her...mine alone!

"Yeah, *her*! Bloody Lyddie! So why the hell couldn't she look after herself? Now she's got you to run round after her lily white arse she just drops her stupid doting brother like a stone!"

In direct contrast to Lydia's ingratiating cut-glass voice Lian's accent got thicker and more northern the more she lost control. Where was this anger coming from? Was she really so indignant on my behalf or was it instead an irrational jealousy that spanned centuries finally spilling over into this life? It was as if someone had uncorked her again and all of her old pain was spewing out like a volcano, erupting with the intent to kill or, at very least, maim. Her anger may have been justified somewhere else, with someone else, but did my sister's foolishness and desire to do well really warrant this outburst? I felt ashamed and so uncomfortable in my own skin as to feel queasy.

Seemingly unperturbed by Lian Lyddie went on demurely, "I had my creativity to think of but as you don't seem to have any creativity Lian I don't suppose you'd understand. And I had been through so much with the loss of my child and my partner that Rory was always willing to help me out and back me up....but again you've never had a child, or even a brother, so..." Lydia trailed off meaningfully, cruelly. I had never told her those things. Where had Lydia got such information? I could feel the pain emanating from my lover and I wished that the ground would swallow us both up, right there and then, for good and all. But instead Lydia began again.

"I only ever asked for Rory's willing support, I certainly never demanded it...I was just so grateful when he supported me and I am terribly sorry if I have to move away from him but...oh!" Lydia suddenly stopped and looked appealingly and tearfully at Simon. Was it genuine? I watched in terrible mute fascination as he squeezed her shoulder in affirmation of her rightness. And I also knew Lian had seen this gesture and that it would make her rage the harder.

"Oh don't go all pathetic on us! You're as hard-nosed as anyone else, Lydia Fentley, or whatever your name is. You just use men, you make them be your servant just to allow you to get where you want to be. Admit it! You use your beauty and your charm like a crowbar to break into men's lives and steal what you want. And your claiming to be an empowered witch and a feminist icon...well, let me tell you, that makes it you even worse! You are a hypocrite, Lydia! What kind of magical woman needs to lean on a man, to *use* a man, that way? And what sort of an equal liberated male-female relationship is it if one has to suffer because of the others gain? You *know*, because you're not stupid, damn it, that because of you leaning on Treeface, making him go out and stand behind you like an unpaid bodyguard, you've been able to write and get published and earn shitloads! You'll be earning even more now and be a kept woman too and Treeface's got no chance of ever doing better for himself 'cos of society's bias and injustice, because of who he is...Accch!" Vicious spittle flew from Lian's wide scarlet lips and I cringed. "Call yourself a Fey, mistress? Claim hearth-rite with witches, do you? *How dare you claim our lineage!* I bet you aren't even very good at writing! It's only your shallow, fickle beauty that gets you by in the end. Its like prostitution dressed up in fancy language!"

I listened to Lian's disjointed and miscalculated rant as if the subject was someone else, not me at all, and certainly not my sister. I heard her spit the word *Fey* out as if it pained her when used in association with Lydia. I couldn't take any more of this! I took to examining my broad square nails under the table, hands trembling badly, my Guinness going untouched.

"Well at least I have my beauty! I'd rather be a bitch than a dog..." Lydia hissed, meaningfully and Simon laughed, his hoarse braying grating on me, taking off yet another layer of my protective skin.

Did Lian hear? How it would cut her to have yet another slight on her looks, no matter how indirect! Now I felt ashamed of Lydia in her crown of dusty roses and plummy velvets. How low would they all stoop to assuage their personal grievances on one another? I knew only I could stop it. After all, I could have taken Lian's hand and simply left. Or could have stood up and asserted my balanced viewpoint on the situation. I could have demanded apologies, sought explanations, poured oil on troubled waters or simply stilled them with a raised hand. But I didn't and I wouldn't would I? Oh no, not Treeface.And certainly not Rory.

"Anyway, I don't give a toss about your looks Lydia." Lian continued as if Lydia's jibe had gone over her head if she had heard it at all. How could my lover say that? Nothing seemed to matter more to her than her own perceived ugliness and others beauty! Her feelings of inferiority had ruled her life and almost ruined it, there was no way that Lydia's looks were irrelevant to my lover! But she went on none-the-less. "All I care about is your brother, *my* soul-love, *my* one-ness! *I* am the only one to know him, and the only one to care about him, too. So yeah, sod off to L.A., swan round in your fifteen minutes of fame, we'll be fine, just bloody fine!"

"*How can you say that?* You've only known Rory for a few months! And he is called Rory, not Treeface, you know! You don't know me or him at all! I've known him all my life you silly little...oh, this really is intolerable!"

Lydia got a hold of herself. Her accent and manners had slipped and that couldn't be allowed.

"*D'you think I don't know that!*" Lian interrupted through clenched teeth. "Do you think it doesn't goad me every single day that you had all that time with him, a life time, and you squandered it while I have been searching..."

Now Lian trailed off, panting, while Lydia rolled her soulful eyes. Simon patted her indulgently, I noticed my sister was also trembling a little. But that was nothing compared to Lian who was breathing hard and who had gone paler than ever. Her flaming hair burned too brightly against her clammy milksop skin and again I felt confusion and shame. If only Lian were less abrasive, more willing to play at being the fluttery eyed, sensitive woman as Lydia was she probably would have gotten further in her own life. Instead she seemed not to care how she appeared to others, be that mad fire-brand or Elvish mystic. Lian was woman used to being disliked, insulted, feared even, so why change now? Even when she knew she was loved, for I did love her even as she raged, she felt insecure and defensive. And did I help her feel anything but?

Why did I not back her up? Or even try to calm her? I don't know! I just sat and shook and poked at my fingernails while they railed on and on about me and what was best for me. I went off into a dream, an unseeing, unfeeling dream. It was only when I became aware of Kefli poking me in the leg with his bony finger that I came back, just a little, to the matter in hand. I saw my elemental friend's familiar astral form and heard his hissed words '*rightly or wrongly, up-sy down-sy, Lian is suffering! Twigling brother, if you can't speak to her then at least try and send her some healing!*'

I looked at my scarlet-haired lover, seeing the sun-bleached scene before me as if I were behind glass...muffled voices, mouths opening then snapping shut and looks of seemingly venomous hatred being exchanged. I observed the energies of anger, fear and confusion thick between us all, connecting us whether we liked it or not, hostility even emitting from the apparently laid-back Simon. I picked up random words and thoughts....

(*Greedy*!

Bitch!

Stupid!)

and 'tuned into' Lian, who sat stock still to my right. She was, I knew, experiencing a terrible pain in her right temple. Lian was an inveterate migraine sufferer, I was used to helping her deal with these attacks but this one appeared to be on the 'wrong' side of her head and unusually strong in its relentless pounding. I saw her hand reach up and rub ineffectually at the spot before without another word she abruptly got up and made her way into the pubs darkened interior, leaving the three of us sitting in a sudden silence.

In my shock I instantly saw clearly again...bright colours almost dazzling me, the noise of a wasp buzzing around Lian's abandoned glass of juice sounding inordinately loud....and became aware of Lydia frowning in consternation at me. I could read her thoughts, the same frustrated railing against my woolly headedness as she had always felt. How could I have been entertaining such doting, protective thoughts of her when I was thinking so little of my true love? What sort of a spell had I always been under with my sister, anyway? I silently thanked my trusted spirit mentor Kefli for his assistance in breaking my inertia and alerting me to Lian's pain.

"What's going on?" Simon leaned back with a mildly quizzical look on his pinkish freckled face, as if he were watching a performance with a difficult twist to the plot-line.

"She's not feeling too well," I explained, my voice sounding rusty to my ears. I heard Lydia sigh, she hated my cracked, defeated voice, the one that came out when I was particularly distracted or fearful, or had been absent from the previous proceedings in a trance-like way. "Er, no, she's not feeling good."

"How the hell do you know, she didn't even say anything!" Simon blew out the smoke of his cheroot and I longed for the pipe I had long since abandoned or for something of my own to calm me and occupy my hands.

"I just...*know*. As is possible when you are close to someone."

And I knew, as surely as I had known Lian was under a migraine attack, that Simon found me and my funny little girlfriend infinitely contemptible.

"Bit of a clairvoyant are we?" The indulgent smile on Simon's face was revolting to me. How could Lydia love him? *How?* Or was she, as Lian had accused her, simply using this callow man as she had previously used me, her brother? I blanched at the possibility. Oh, surely not?

"Darling, Rory simply knows things like that. He's a bit of a witch. Aren't you, *Treeface*? A bit of a sorcerer on the side."

Lydia gave me such a bland look but behind it was a cruelty that I had had no idea existed. Was she really a shallow and manipulative woman who used her beauty and guile to claim accolades and acolytes? If it were true then would my sister find the seemingly suave but imminently calculating Simon as easy as I to manipulate as she had me? Would he be her biggest, least questioning, fan in order to keep her happy enough to produce new work for him to sell? Oh, what did our human relationships cost us all and what were we prepared to compromise?

Lydia knew that I would not respond to her jibing but that I would be shocked by it. I felt myself crumple a little more. She knew, had possibly always known, that I was weaker than her.

Then as if the previous exchange had not happened at all my sister sat up a little straighter and began to speak in that false, pretentiously proper voice again.

"While Lian's not here then, maybe I can get a clear word in," she said crisply. The demure fluttery woman that had previously languished before me was snapping rapidly into a more business like, entirely more focused, mode that I had known of late. "I may as well tell you that I went to see Alicia. Yes, *Lian's* Alicia. She's a very well respected Medium in local circles and I was given her name, hoping she could give me some psychic insights into Donal's whereabouts or my future." Lydia stared at me, almost triumphant, allowing this information to filter through, knowing it had surprised me but that it would shock Lian much more. "And was I passed on Alicia's name by chance, as a coincidence? I don't think so! For Alicia's my Fey-kin too, and yes she's *my* Alicia now; she doesn't just belong to that red-haired harridan of yours! Alicia told me all about my past lives and I am clearer than ever on what I have to do in the world. I am sorry, Rory, but I have a *mission*, a meaningful life-dream to fulfil, and family ties can't be allowed to interfere with it."

"Terrific!" interupted Simon, clapping his hands together like an over-enthusiastic child. He was clearly loving every moment of this. By the Gods I could see now that he *wanted* a rift between she and I, had probably even engineered it! Oh, it wasn't Lyddie's fault then; he had somehow brain-washed her...

But Lydia was continuing, a slight frown only marring her flawless face for a second.

"I am part of the Greening too, and I have to bring Fey witchery, wild green witchcraft, back into the hearts and minds of many. It is *needed!* And if that makes me single-minded and, well, *different* than you have known me to be before, then so be it because the Greening is bigger than all of us, beloved. Oh yes, of that we can be sure! We three, four if you count Alicia, are Fey souls returning with our jobs to do...Lian and the old woman to *see*, you to heal and play the bard, me to introduce wild witchcraft into the mainstream. *That is how it is!* Only I am lucky enough to have Simon to help me make it a reality, a *magical* reality, and no one, not you, or *her*, or any other dissenter like our sad, twisted father, can make me stop now!

Your old fears can't hold me back beloved, not now or ever again. I wouldn't be stopped in our life in France and I will not be stopped now, whatever happens! I am brave, my love, brave and strong! I *remember* my own burning and it will never hold me back, never crush my spirit as it did yours, oh no! The flames have *forged* me, Rory! I am a phoenix and am going to rise! Yes, for my own sake, and my son's too, but for the sake of magic and mystery, for a poetic resurgence of all my soul holds dear, for the Earth and all her children. And who can stop me? Not Shay Donnelly and his swinging fists, not Vic Reynolds, and hell, not even *Rory* Reynolds no matter how much I love him! Because I love the Greening more, beloved. And if that makes me a bitch then so be it!"

Lydia stopped for a second to get her breath. I could see she was exhilarated, drunk on the rising bliss of her own power.

"So I am going to America because Alicia says it is where my future lies as a soul-poet and teller of green truths...as a *wild enchantress!* Not to spite you, or abandon you, Rory, but because my own soul sings that I have to! And yes, I need to go to America to find Donal too; not only because he is my son and I need him with me but because he is *one of us*; because, believe it or not, he also has a Fey-soul! Irish blood and a Faery soul...a fine combination for him! And I hear him calling me...*I hear him*! He and I and you and Lian, if she can get over her ...her *madness*...have so much work to do in the world. the world *needs* what we do! Oh, Rory, Rory beloved, you know it to be true..."

"Do I?" My voice was a rusty croak just as it had been all those ashes of years ago when I hid in old Talius the oak.

"Yes! Doesn't he Simon? If he used his intuition like I do and didn't hide from it he would know! There's a place in the wider world for us, a place where we can have a real influence, make big changes...help bring the Greening to bear!"

Simon was smiling indulgently as if all of this was just a big pile of fantasy concocted to see her books and ideas. He obviously had no idea about the Greening at all but was willing to help her sell it, whatever it was. Money was his motivation and success his passion and if Lydia thought any differently she was fooling herself. Simon knew he had an excellent product in my sister, one which came ready-wrapped in a beautiful package, and he would humour her for as long as it took to sell her and make a big, fat profit. Oh that she had come to this pretentious lizard, this foppish cad, for advice and counsel...aye, and love...instead of me! Yet how could I hate her, even for a moment? Even if she was cruel and cold and manipulative how could I hate Lyddie? And if she was a Fey-soul, as I had long suspected myself....yes, if she were truly our Fey-souled kin...

Lydia looked at me, reached for me across the table, and I looked away. Try as I might to meet her spirit-to-spirit, and to rationalise and seek a balanced view of what she did, I was afraid of her. Afraid of her self-assured conviction, her future success, and yes, afraid of her Fey witchery and what it may bring this time. All of it, all that she was brave enough to be, reflected badly on me. I felt so....

(*lost, useless, worthless, beaten!*)

...then I remembered Lian.

"Excuse me, I'll be back in a minute," I said stiffly and got up, my wiry heron's legs tangling under the bench table. I could hear Lydia huffing to Simon, probably incredulous that I could not embrace her and accept her new identity there and then. Instead of saying '*oh how marvellous, I fully understand!*' as I usually would make myself do I had actually got up and walked off instead! Even I knew that Lydia didn't like anyone ambling off when she was disseminating about her work or ideas. But we lived in different worlds, she and I, and perhaps we always had, be Fey-souled kin or not; her world was bright and golden, mine was full of lengthening shadows.

I went in to the gloom of the bar area, the coolness of the interior was welcome. I took a deep breath, the familiar, comforting smell of tobacco smoke and beer filling my nostrils. I could see that Lian was not inside the pub. Was she outside at the front, on the high street, had she simply got up and gone home? I doubted it. I went to the rear corridor and I rested my head against the tiled entrance to the public toilets for a moment. Everything spun around in my vision and settled. I was deeply disturbed by the meeting but needed to think of my Lian, not of myself.

I must be stronger! God, yes!

It was then that I picked up a sense of Lian close by. I knocked on the main entrance to the ladies lavatories and heard a toilet flush inside and a shuffling as someone came to the door.

"Lian?"

The door opened and a waxy, wan face peered at me, all big eyes and trembling lips. "Been sick," she sniffed, wiping her mouth on the back of her hand, abstractedly. "Pain in my head! Pain because I know she met Alicia! I felt it, I *saw* it when I looked into her lying eyes! *Alicia is mine!*" She winced at her own sharp tone, feebly lifting a hand to indicate the side of her head. "Oh, it hurts! And it hurts in my heart because I have so few things to call my own and she has so many! Lydia has possibilities that are open to her, have always been open to her, because she is so...lovely....and it will ever be so for her and never be so for me! And now she takes my only other friend from me! Accch!"

Lian's face was pinched and pallid, the naked hurting so terrible to look at. Despite her obvious agonies she continued, breathing raggedly and with her voice pitched low, barely audible over the rushing of the refilling toilet cistern and the bar noises from behind us.

"And you seem to worship her even though she is casting you aside now for bigger and....well, bigger...things. And you do nothing! You let her hurt you, and me and *you do nothing!* You should let her go! We don't need her, *you* don't need her! You have me now and *I won't leave you...*"

Lian coughed, retching,and her eyes opened wide in alarm. I knew how she hated to be sick. I reached out and held her arm, pouring all the energy I could into her as a temporary boost. When I pulled away she looked as if she may have a tiny bit more colour in those milk-white cheeks of hers although her eyes were still burning too brightly in her unnaturally pale face. She slowly, unsteadily made to come out of the toilet and I hugged her to me, a little self-consciously. I wanted so much to protect her but here she was, psychic as a fish and exposed to all that animosity, that intense energy. Some of it, hell, *most of it,* was her own though. I didn't know why she seemed to find Lydia that goading, it couldn't have been simple jealousy alone could it? Another incarnation of rivalry and resentment, maybe? I neither knew, nor really cared, where the apparently bitter feud had originally come from, I just wanted it over and done with.

"Do you want to go home, sweetheart?" I asked her.

"Yes...no...no, I just want you to help me! To forget *her* and focus on *me*! I won't leave you, not ever, I won't let anyone harm you!"

I looked at her, her ashen complexion and her huge brimming eyes and something in me snapped.

"Oh GOD! God, sweetheart I don't know which way is up!" I stumbled further into her embrace, desperate to help her and ,in so doing, to help myself somehow. We were one, she and I. Yes, we were! "Oh Lian...God, Lian...I am afraid...AFRAID! I have so little that is mine too and I don't want to lose it and yet I don't know how to keep it either! I can't bear if it she goes away, because of witchery, just like last time in France, and she doesn't come back! What if they get her for it all over again? How will I feel if I didn't save her, protect her,

ALL OVER AGAIN! If she goes I am so terribly afraid that she will never come back, not alive! I feel for her and I feel for you and I am drowning all the time, especially now...oh God, yes...and I am always *resisting*...resisting suffering, resisting my *self*...and always and every minute of every day I am a-feared! *Re-membering* has not healed me, it has made me worse; it's given me more reasons than ever to be worried about each passing second and what it may bring to us all, to us Fey ones, over and over!"

Lian's eyes were closed now and my mouth was in her hair. I was glad I could no longer see those fathomless green-grey eyes, burning with such a passion that I myself could never dare to reveal lest it turned on me and hung me, drowned me, burned me up...

"Are we not sure...that we have conquered fear before? Such loss...and death...and suffering...are we not then sure? Are we not?" she whispered, turning again into a Fey *seer* in my arms, and my heart was breaking for all that I had ever put her through too. Suddenly she was my eternal priestess, my holy soul-love, my bright and canny *seer*-mistress, not just a jealous tortured woman.

"Oh fair one, help me!" I reached for her face blindly, instinctively and she reached for me.

"Help *me*, beloved!" she responded, her voice no more than a sigh now.

And wordlessly we clung together in a city centre pub, oblivious for a moment to all else. I could feel us both silently reaching for eachother, soul searching for soul, hoping that in so doing we may find our true selves again; selves that were not a-feared or angry or jealous or twisted with pent-up grief. Ahhh....

Then, to my surprise, Lian pulled slowly away.

"Yes, well...we have to sort this...can't let her..." she rubbed at her temple, "it really hurts though. Jesus, it does."

"What can I do for you? How can I...?"

"Sugary tea...please!"

"Coffee, they only do bad coffee in here. Is that any good to you, beloved?A cup of over-brewed sweet coffee?"

Lian nodded and sat down heavily on the steps leading back into the bar area. What was I to do now? I had to make a choice, a quick choice, whether to stay with Lian and abandon the pointless yet compelling meeting with Lydia or to go back and leave my poor sick girl alone. My head was reeling! So I did what I thought was best.

I ran to the bar, ordered the coffee and told the barman where to take it and what it was for. I don't know if he fully understood me but I put as much psychic will behind it as I could so that he would at least understand why Lian looked so poorly. It wasn't through drink, that was for sure. People were so funny about illness, it made them awkward and squeamish, especially men. I had grown up with a mother who had, in those days, preferred to languish in bed, relinquishing her responsibilities, than to be at the kitchen sink as my father had wished. Oh yes, I knew how to be a carer. I had gotten used to looking after Lyddie if she ever caught a bug as she, dear old Ma, was rarely willing to rustle up much beyond a cursory bowl of soup. Plus I had been ...damn it, no, I *was*...a healer and had an empathy with those suffering pain or discomfort.

Yet even though I knew that most men were not as good at being a carer as myself I allowed Lian to be at their mercy that day. Neither the young man behind the bar, nor his colleagues, would treat Lian with the gentle care she deserved but I let them get on with it. I just hoped they'd try. I visualised them seeing Lian as a poor little thing in distress, a pretty if pallid damsel who needed help, rather than a strange, haunted looking waif who may make them feel uneasy. I threw the last remaining ounces of my will behind that thought.

Then I ran outside. I saw the backs of my long adored sister and her lover, his expensive linen jacket on the seat beside him, his arm snaked round Lydia's narrow hips.

(*A jolt of pain, a pang of regret, no more than that.*)

"Lian and I have to go, as soon as possible" I said to the couple, facing them breathlessly. My heart lurched in my chest and I felt as if I too would be sick. "I'll have to accept that you'll be emigrating Lydia and that's how it is. I will accept it so we can all move forward without ties or regrets or recriminations. I want what's best for you, you know I always have. But I...

(*I love you and will miss you terribly! I am always so afraid, Lydia, so afraid for us all!*)

...wish you...well. And you'll...keep in touch?"

(I picked up a thought... *'if that girl had been here we probably wouldn't have been able to get him to say that...'*)

"Amen to that!" Simon said, smacking his open palm on the wooden table, making the reminder of our drinks, now renedered warm by the sun, jump in their respective glasses. "Of course Lydia will be in touch. Obviously! And we will let you know when all of her tour dates in the UK and Europe are, so that you can pop along. You will always be welcome to stay with us, eh darling?"

"Yes! And thank the Goddess for your wisdom and kindness!" Lydia echoed, almost demure but failing to hide the flush of pleasure that stained her creamy complexion.

"Excellent! Well, we'll send you a ticket for the wedding as well., next May. We thought Hawaii actually, what do you think? Wherever it is we can't expect you to get there under your own steam, eh old boy? You may have to get a hotel for a few nights because our wedding may be a very *large* affair and we can't have help everyone stay with us. I'm sure you understand!"

"But I'm her only real relative...her only true bit of family..."

"Absolutely! Blood's thicker than water and all that, eh? But you simply have to accept that Lydia's life has *expanded* and there are all sorts of other people close to her now...or that want to be. Ha ha!"

Simon was mercifully interrupted from this offensive little speech by his shrill mobile phone; if he hadn't then I felt as if I may have punched that duplicitous bastard. The man was a liar, a hypcrite, a manipulative fraud! Yet Lydia smiled adoringly at him as he said "Two ticks!" and answered his no doubt state-of-the-art phone.

"Yeah, Jeremy? Alright, my man, how are things? Good, splendid! Yes, I've done all the paperwork for you, its in the post. Listen, remember the matter we were discussing last Tuesday? Yeah...Mmm..."

For every one of Simon's 'ticks' I was aware Lian was alone and in pain. Sod him and his meaningless schmoozing, I had to get back to her!

Lydia and I were left looking at each other as Simon arranged an appointment with his solicitor. I thought of Lian sitting by herself at the rear of an unfamiliar pub and felt a wave of sorrow.

"So how's the new book doing?" I found the words spilled out of my mouth even though I was thinking of anything but her blessed career, the very thing that had divided us and was sending her to...

(*to her death?*)

...to America.

"Better than I could ever have hoped, actually, thanks. I have a teaching slot at the Winchester literary festival and a batch of weekend workshops booked in Edinburgh and then its off to Seattle and then

Washington in September. I don't know how far we will be into our move then but its all rather exciting! I really want to back it up with...*connecting*...with my readers, you know? Oh Rory, the Greening is so important! Its so vital we get out there and be who we be. It really is! I wish you'd..."

I shook my head in a vague up and down, left and right way, trying to stop her saying whatever came next.

"Oh *Rory*! What I do is needed and what you *are* is needed. We must gather all our resources and bring the magic back to life! Wild enchantment is ours by right; it is up to us to bring it through into the world in words and deeds and by being who we are, naturally!"

She must know, despite her urgings, that I did not know, nor would I ever know, what it was to be needed, wanted, respected in the world. What I was, *who I be*, would never have the warm reception that she and her precious, dangerous work did. I was like a stormy night on the wild moors compared to her sunlit afternoon in a nature reserve; I would be avoided, shunned, spurned whilst she would be embraced. That was just how it was. I just hoped to all the Gods in heaven that they, whoever *they* turned out to be, kept on embracing my darling sister and didn't turn against her. Not again!

"So, it's doing well then?" I said, feeling dumb, feeling redundant.

"Yes Rory, it's doing very well," she said quietly and as her eyes met mine I could see they were swimming with tears.

Real tears? Somewhere in there, I thought, there's a gentle, supremely lyrical woman who cares about more than fame and the praise that goes with it. Somewhere inside Lydia there was a girl who had once charmed me with her jingle-jangle hippy looks, like a young Stevie Nicks with her skirts billowing in a field of poppies. It was at that person I smiled with as much warmth as I could muster.

"Good luck, then!" I wished her, like a stranger, knowing my own aspirations were so meagre in comparison to Lydia Fentley's; they rarely went beyond hoping some one would fill my cap with coppers enough to keep Lian and I in bread and milk. The summer season for storytelling wasn't exactly going to be brimming with gigs due to the children being off school. Maybe next year once I became more organised, established in my field...

Yes, maybe.

Simon had tuned off his cell phone. I did so dislike the intrusive electronic ringing and beeps that those modern gadgets made! Yet it suited him, this supercilious creep that was now my sister's lover and mentor. To me his energy was also shrill and loud and blatantly state-of-the-art and it did not mingle with my own energy so much as to seem to want to absorb it, to swallow it gladly. I recoiled from him and his brittle, shallow concerns with all my will. *May his vibe never encroach on my life and may my dear beautiful sister be protected from it too!* God, could I trust her well-being to this plastic phoney with his crocodile smile?

I had no choice.

"All settled!" he said, with the air of a man used to settling things briskly and efficiently said and he shook my hand. He wasn't even sweating in the heat while I felt damp and grimy. The man had no qualms about appraising me frankly as our hands connected.

My throat suddenly filled again with ashes. Let me go, for God's sake, will you!

Lydia gave a tinkling laugh that was not hers. Had she not the heart, or the respect, to be herself for me? Another drop of my unquestioning, almost romantic love for her evaporated in the burning urgency I suddenly felt to get back to Lian. Lian was real, no matter how badly she could behave. She was as she was! Oh, leave me be, the pair of you! *Go home wherever that may be!*

"Right then, Lyddie darling, shall we go on to Bryony's?"

"Yes, okay."

Lydia adjusted the brim of her hat and I wondered if she too would shake my hand.

"We'll know about the move in a few weeks," she said.

"That'll be grand, perhaps you can let me know then, you know, so I can say goodbye and....er, stuff," I replied, flatly.

"Yes indeed."

And then they were gone in a swish of velvet and a whiff of after-shave which reminded me of sea breezes.

Sea breezes in another country I would never visit.

Things had started to go wrong for Treeface and me.

Our days together days were still golden but a certain chill had entered them, an as yet unseasonable crispness. There had been no time to really dwell on this unsettling feeling in the air between us though for we had been busy even if our industry had not been rewarded in monetary terms. We had done a great deal of promotional work for Treeface's bardic business, primarily for charities at local events where no one could afford to pay us more than expenses. We had plenty of good will and promises of recommendations from these well-meaning people, who sadly were running things on a shoe-string in their own lives, but good will didn't put butter on our toast, let alone jam. If it wasn't for the fact that our city had many tourist visitors in the summer who were all happy to pay buskers if they were entertaining or unusual enough then we wouldn't have even had the bread to put butter on.

It was just a slack time, perhaps, and over the summer holidays it might indeed get worse, but who knew? Maybe other avenues would open up for us if we focussed on a positive financial outcome with our will-and-wishing? We really had to rely more on our magic, and have faith in our inherent power, rather than wasting time on panicky schemes and pointless, draining worry! Regardless of the fiasco of that last private school venue we had mistakenly taken, Treeface was still a master of his art and had been acclaimed by almost everyone else we had encountered. To get kudos from the people of the sophisticated city of Bath was no mean feat but, as ever, Treeface wanted to dwell on the '*what ifs?*" that may never happen, like him not getting another paid job and having to rely on scratching a living from his fiddle alone.

After much deliberation Treeface had come up with another scheme to supplement us. I could certainly see his point about taking his storytelling to the people, as the streets of our city would be heaving with tourists in late summer to early autumn, but it did not sit easily with me. Treeface's idea was that while they sat sunbathing, or relaxing in the city's squares on benches and at cafe tables, he could regale them with his traditional tales, this time spiced up for adult palates, and embellished as ever by his fiddle playing. He had even considered taking up residence at the Saturday flea-market or the Sunday outdoor art exhibition that happened in a local square.

The idea made some practical sense yet it somehow alarmed me on a deep instinctual level; my lover was now used to a captive attentive audience in schools and his tale-telling to a dismissive, indifferent or even openly disparaging audience may distress him. Not everyone would sit still and quietly and listen; a lot of passing people would disturb his flow and there were bound to be those pressed for time who would just get up and walk off in the middle of a story. It was different when he was playing his fiddle in the streets, people would always be walking past and not stopping, but a story required attention and the presence of an attentive audience. People in the street did have places to go and things to do, after all, and although they would appreciate having a lovely lilting refrain on a fiddle follow them down the street it may be a bit less appealing to walk past as the man was in the middle of a tale. All they would hear would be a random selection with no meaning behind it.

I imagined Treeface being incredibly disheartened at being talked over, roundly ignored and walked past. He would have to suffer heckling too, no doubt, and some of it was bound to be addressed at his scarred face. As much as some folk would warm to the opportunity of being entertained, others would find it intrusive and all sorts of jeering was likely. How would he handle cat-calls after years of lying low and avoiding attracting any attention to himself at all? And how would his gentle, whimsical tales stand up to city streets? It seemed a risk for such a vulnerable soul as he and I wished perhaps he would have just put more effort into a fiddle session as the streets were more suited to rousing and catchy tunes than to reams of meaningful verbiage. I was, however, touched by the bravery he had shown in suggesting such a risky venture, for the sake of our ongoing survival. I fully appreciated how hard it must have been for him to offer his neck up in this way for a chopping block that may or may not exist.

Oh why was it so hard for our kind to fit in in society; a society which appeared to have no real use for the Greening or its children? And why was it that even though I had found my soul's own love and discovered my life's purpose that things were still hard...perhaps even harder than ever before? On a human level life was extremely difficult even as on a soul-level it was much clearer and brighter. Perhaps eventually, if I didn't back down or lose heart, the two worlds of Faery and humanity, Otherworld and 'real' world, would merge more harmoniously for me. Maybe with perseverance I could help to bring a Greening, a resurgence of living in harmony with the land and with each other, just by this integration in my own life. It was part of my work to weave these strands of seen and unseen, the mundane and the magical, together using wish-and-will and practical everyday action. As ever I needed to talk more to Alicia about this!

So, I would not add to Treeface's fears about his ability to provide! I didn't want to hurt him and I couldn't bear the thought of him giving up. There was always 'social security', the government handout of a benefit to keep us above the poverty line...just. But how, as green-spirited individuals, could he and I accept a handout from a government that we so despised, taken from the taxes of a society which was so against our ideals and principles? No, it was survive or die for us; we wanted none of their benefits. Stubborn as that may have been, and foolish too, it was how we both felt now and we had to hold fast to things that we held dear or our sense of self and purpose would have just faded away into obscurity again. Faced with the shiny onslaught of the modern world and is values we had to say no and carve our own niche and so no, *we would not let the Makers fund us!* Instead we would bring them our magic and compassion and change things from within.

We *would!*

Yet even though Treeface held fast to his heart-principles and made plans and kept on with the idea that he would succeed as a wandering bard, he was still often maudlin, sometimes deeply morose. It was as if some great nameless melancholy was always waiting to absorb him and if he let his guard down for a second he would be overcome. I hated to see him lost in thoughts that I knew would be spiralling down out of control into even more desperate territory, creating bleak scenarios, playing them out behind those green-grey eyes.

As much as I was disturbed and often angered by his constant dwelling on the darkest possibilities I hated the idea that I would take my frustrations out on him more than I hated his behaviours. So, rather than yelling at him to snap out of it or making a scene about how I felt abandoned while he spent his days off in another, more gloomy, reality, I let fly about all manner of other things which annoyed me. I was too sensitive, and my thoughts and feelings were too keen for them to dissipate, unexpressed. Instead of my being able to let go of how I felt by talking it through gently, I opted to just get mad at any old thing as it was, in the short-term, more of a satisfying release of my emotions.

Yes, I was getting angry again.

My anger was the sort that needed to come out as because of my soul-nature I needed to let things flow through me. I was a channel, not just for psychic emanations but for all energies, all emotional currents, be they my own or another soul's. If I pent them up they took on the form of a blockage in my system and if I became 'stoppered' by such a blockage then I would be ineffective at what I did. Basically, if I held on to things and did not let them pass naturally through me and out into the world then I became 'corked'. And, just like a fine wine with the same problem, I would go 'off'. And, like a sour old wine, I would no longer be of use in the world.

And to be of use was my purpose for incarnating, wasn't it?

No, I was well aware now of how to act in accordance with my nature, thanks to Alicia, and so I began to get angry at anything...*anything but Treeface!*...just to get some of it out.

Although my way of dealing with things was just as wrong, I preferred it to what I saw Treeface's fear doing to him. His fear turned rank and gnawed at his guts, eating away at him day by day. He squashed down all of his anxiety and distress at the injustices he saw and had experienced and allowed his raw emotions to simmer inside him instead. He put a lid on how he felt and, again as the invaluable Alicia had taught me, when you block one thing, everything is affected; you cannot do anything in isolation and expect it not to affect the whole of you and, by direct reflection, the All. So, we became locked in a cycle, Treeface moping and repressing his fearful feelings and effectively closing me out as well as he shut his own panic down...and me responding to that by venting my spleen willy-nilly, which in turn made him feel even more attacked and so he shut himself down further...

('*Everything is energies, our energies are everything*!' *Oh yes, I hear you beloved and I will see you soon Alicia, I promise*!)

My anger had really started to rise again on the day we had met Lydia. I knew it was going to be bad meeting with the woman that I felt so threatened by, how could it have been otherwise? But I had thought that at least I would have my own creation with me...something which she did not have, nor had she ever had. I was positively looking forward to showing up at the meeting with the physical proof of my love, the product of my union, my child with Treeface. I was beginning the family she and he had never had, the family that *I* had never had, a flesh and blood unit forged from spiritual ties far beyond those she and Treeface had ever experienced as a sibling partnership.

I wanted to show her my swelling belly.

My being pregnant was my only means, it seemed to show that he loved me more than her, to in some way prove my worth beyond her talents and looks. Yes, I know how it sounds! Is it any wonder the child was not willing to be born to a woman who ha*s* thoughts such as these? For shame! But, oh God, why did I envy Lydia so? Why did she matter so much to me? Was this animosity connected to soem other life she and I had yet to recall, linked to soul-dramas we had yet to *re-member*?

The truth, which was plain for anyone to see no matter how I tried to disguise it with other issues, was that I was plain jealous. Not only was I jealous of the love Treeface so blatantly and unquestioningly had for her, and all their closeness and time together, but I felt that as long as she existed then by comparison I would be as much a failure as she was successful and as ugly as she was graceful and lovely. It was bizarre and it was irrational as only soul-links can be...if only I had acknowledged it as such a link and looked into it in order to put it to rest! How could it not be a soul-bond that Lydia and I had when we were both Fey souls in bodies such as these? If only I had addressed all of my feelings from a spiritual perspective, just as Alicia had taught me in our short time together, and seen them for what they were! But I would not, even though I was quite capable of it, psychically. I preferred to have her in my life as the object of all my bitterness than for it to be a situation which became healed by my innate wisdom. And I continued to deflect my growing dissatisfaction away from Treeface and onto the bonfire I was making. I was behaving, to all intents and purposes, like a spoilt, blinkered and patently stupid human instead of the enlightened, spiritually literate and shining being I was inside my temporal body. But how tempting it was, I discovered, to ignore the soul and go with the ego, how much more *satisfying!*

I discovered that it could be very addictive to hate someone.

But, like all human wants and gratifications, the satisfaction it gave was only fleeting. I knew that, really, but was prepared to absolve my responsibility to my Fey soul just for a short while, even though I knew that I'd have to face up to my true self sooner or later.

Meanwhile, I continued to cry out in outrage that Lydia had more than me, and that Treeface somehow loved me less than her, and in doing so I dis-empowered myself more effectively than any enemy, any supposed rival, ever could have done. Oh yes, I had let my anger out which was healthy but I had still gone against my true nature, over-riding what I knew to be right, and so my *sight* became dull at best, blurred and warped at worst.

I was lost without it! Lost without the very thing I had spurned and cursed for so long! *For my sight was me!* Without it what was I but a confused and strange little woman again, purposeless and disturbed?

And surprise, surprise, feeling that way made me angrier still! It became a self-perpetuating cycle and one that was no doubt encouraged by less than scrupulous (unseen) outside influences. For people such as ourselves, such influences were never far away, just waiting to feed off our plentiful energy and breed yet more of those bad feelings in us for them to gorge on.

So, in the glorious fleeting days of summer, my first summer with my true love, I filled up my time with negativity. At least my wailing over having killed Robert had been real, born of a genuine belief that I had been responsible and fuelled by my howling pain at his loss, but this...this terrible ranting was unnecessary! This time my demeanour was self-inflicted and avoidable but like my misguided railing over Robert's 'murder' it stopped me from reaching my own potential and working with it to bring about inner, and therefore outer, peace....a peace I had managed to achieve, briefly it seemed, so short a time a go.

Obviously the more I ranted the more withdrawn my lover became, and the more he closed down his energies, battened down his psychic hatches, and brooded, the more angry it made me that he didn't really love me...not like he loved darling Lyddie. And then he thought each bit of anger was directed at him, even when I purposely deflected it at Lydia, such was his own deep-seated victim status. Well, it wasn't just that, was it? The man was a sensitive, a child of the Greening, as much as I was and he *knew* that I was really mad at him even though I shouted on about his sister...and his dreadful parents too.

(*Oh the pain and the beauty of a true soul-mate link, no secrets could be kept, no feelings truly hidden!*)

Instead of such wasteful squandering of our energies we should have been building up my psychic skills, continuing our training as psychics and healers, yet instead I we were wilfully letting our power drain way into the ether through fear and anger.And do you know what I thought, even as I knew the truth of our ridiculous situation? I thought that Simon was willing to back Lydia, to be her champion, yet what did I get? A man who pulled away from me! A soul-love who retracted his affections so easily! A wild howling rose from within me at the genuine pain this caused, a desolate sound rising and falling, shattering the peace of my inner realms. Why did Treeface not love me as much as he could? WHY? Lydia and Simon, they weren't soulmates and we were and yet we had not a fraction of what they had, of their luck, of their working partnership in the world...

Yes, they would marry, Lydia and Simon, and she would have a second husband where I would have none for Treeface had decided...no, *decreed*...that we didn't need marriage and that legal marriage was a curse on a perfectly good relationship. To seek the sanction of the very establishment who rejected 'our kind' would be folly, surely, he stated, categorically. How could anyone of 'our kind' ask for the Church or State's blessing after all they had done to our human selves, and our Fey spirits, over the centuries? He had determined that our love should remain blessed with the passion of freedom, that all that would bond us were ties of love and spirit, that we needed no public proclamations to confirm what we already knew. In this he was as stubborn and pig-headed as the father he claimed to be so unlike. Just as Vic Reynolds couldn't see what his own bully-boy tactics had done to his wife over the years so Treeface could not, or would not, countenance how this made me feel as a woman.

Part of me, the delicate, romantic part of my being, the bit of me only recently thawed by his love, melted by trust and hope, began to freeze over again slowly. My old cynicism gradually returned, hard-edged and spiky, as I went looking for any reason to vent my anger. In my irrational need to project the blame onto someone other than Treeface I sought a way to express my pain. I could not, would never be, angry with him. He was doing his best, I knew that...

Yet he even rejected the idea of a greenwood marriage, a 'handfasting', a renewable match made for a year and a day, between lovers, without the sanction of Church or State. It was 'too openly pagan' he explained, it may make us subtly, energetically connected to the 'witch' tag. And, he went on, it was still just a ceremony that we truly did not need, did we? Oh, how could I think otherwise than he didn't really want to be joined to me, in any shape or form? Not in France, not in England, not ever!

Who could I make the focus of the searing pain I felt inside me when his kiss was brief and dry? How could I not feel the rage boiling over when he sat, entirely separate to me, pondering the possibility some distant disaster?

Oh, Lydia! Lydia was my perfect scapegoat for all my hurting. Compared to me she seemed so cool, so together, a woman that was going somewhere in life. How I had desperately needed to feel I had produced something of my own to counteract the terrible insecurity and sense of failure that she made me feel about myself in her presence. I had a choice, the bigger part of me knew that, but it was easier, and perversely, more fun, to rip her to shreds than to learn from her, even to reach out to her in friendship as I could have done, I supposed. I felt sad, on some level, that I had not taken the option offered to me which offered wisdom and serenity, maybe even sisterhood, and had taken the cowardly route instead, the one of reacting to the fear I felt rather than responding to it.

As it was, before that day of the meeting in the pub when I had suffered the most appaling head pains, the mere mention of Lydia's name by Treeface set me into spin. But when I knew we had to meet her...

"I can go alone," Treeface had said, and indeed he could have for it was his business as I wasn't even married to him...

(*Oh, oh, oh! Nor would I ever be! Why did it matter to me? Since when had I become so conventional as to need society's approval? Or a formal rite to show we were pair-bonded? But it hurt me so much!*)

No, I wasn't married to him or anything, I was just his girl, his live-in lover. But I had wanted to go, not only for the chance to observe Lydia and to try and pick up some tips on how she managed to be so successful, so attractive and engaging, but also to show *It* off.

It. The lump, the bump. Michael Gabriel! It...*he*...should have been visible by then!

But it wasn't, of course. *Because the baby never was.* The soul that had entered into me on the night of my passionate love-making with the man that had once been Julien, had turned tail and fled when it had truly witnessed, from deep within my womb, the reality it was to be born into with us. And so I had bled and become nothing but an empty vessel. Just like on the fateful night of the Ouija in Manchester, I had lost that which should be most precious to a spirit incarnated in a female form. As I perceived myself to have so little of anything anyway that I took this as a personal slight. I couldn't even provide a suitable host body to bring a spirit into the world and even the most stupid, the poorest, the most congenitally ugly...they could all have children!

(*Terrible thoughts, absolutely terrible! But why not me? Why did spirits reject my woman-form? How could I make myself different, better, more acceptable? Oh Alicia I need your help again, so soon, and I will come to you...I WILL...when I feel stronger again, less in pain, for I do not want to take my anger out on you again my beloved soul-sis-*

ter. By no means! So I wait but I yearn to speak with you my lady.)

So, I was no published author, no mother-to-be, just a *seer* with no prospects, a twenty nine year old with no husband, a woman with no child inside her. And worse, a Fey spirit who was not living as she should be, with compassion and wisdom!

No child, it seemed, would come to us to join us more fully, to be our creation, our symbol of togetherness and passionate being, while we struggled with ourselves, with our deep-rooted terrors. Already in our love-making there was a little touch of frost, I noticed, with a heart that hurt so much. Oh, but there was still love, so much love, but there was no spark, the ardour dampened by some flat, unyielding hand of fate. A little light had gone out in the world, one we called hope perhaps, and so what was making love, in theory, became going through some desperate motion, in practice. Our bodies joined, they heaved and we moaned, while the sense of a bereavement never honoured clung around our naked bodies like a clammy fog and made us shiver even as we sang out in pleasure. A sigh became an echo of something...

(*NO! No, please...no!*)

...something that had perhaps already gone.

We could have gotten psychic guidance on the matter of our child. Hell, of course we could have! We could have both gone straight to Alicia and begged her forgiveness for our absence and sat at her feet, listening to her as she re-introduced our spirits to truth and beauty, drinking in her lilting arcane words as she restored us to harmony and peace. We could have done so much but as it was we two, the little *seer* and the bardic healer, we didn't even seem capable of talking about it. No, Treeface and I were not able to talk about the huge, life changing fact I was no longer pregnant, if indeed I ever had been. And if I hadn't been then how could we trust our intuitions and spiritual guidance anyway? It was an all-encompassing vicious circle we were locked in, one fed by each new misunderstanding, each gesture of withdrawal or pain.

My angst and Treeface's depression certainly got worse when we stayed in the flat, especially in the evenings. A shift in the atmosphere, subtle at first but becoming more tangible as the weeks went on, usually occurred after sunset. One of my greatest pleasures so far in that lovely, light room had been to watch the sun go down. I had charted its progress across the sky up until midsummer and had watched it start to move steadily back across the sky, setting further round on the skyline, disappearing in as stunning display of crimson and gold, the likes of which I had never witnessed before. Sadly this particular phenomenon was created by the vantage point we had, being above the city and looking as we did at the horizon through a haze of pollution. Bath may have been beautiful but it was congested with too much traffic belching out fumes and it sat, geographically, in a natural 'dish' surrounded by hills, thus collecting the effluvium effectively. The bluish mist that seemed to be omni-present made the sunsets even more magnificent, the glowing orb descending, it seemed, through layer upon layer of lavender, plum and midnight blue, spilling honeyed lemon light onto mellow stone and turning the canal to a flat rill of molten gold. It was after this display that I knew things may start to get uncomfortable in our little room.

Because of this strange atmosphere indoors in the evenings we strove to stay outside as long as possible, going walking in the woods most days after Treeface had done his ubiquitous stint in town. It was summer still and so the environment supported a healthy, outdoor existence even though there was often a nip in the air come sundown. We often tramped along the canal path to the pub just to eke out a half pint of juice, or we crossed the new, and much contested, by-pass to climb Solsbury Hill, just to avoid being in our own home rather than for the pleasure of it. In fact we often walked in a glum silence, Treeface striding out on his long legs without holding my hand as he had before, lost in dark thoughts, oblivious to scenery and wildlife.

I had even spent my twenty ninth birthday tramping without purpose up hills and between verdant oaks with a silent man who would often leave me behind and not notice. I often wept as I saw him disappear into the shadows between the trees, not realising I had fallen behind. His gift to me on my birthday had been a new mug that would hold what seemed to be a pint of tea...that and a new fissure in my heart as he neglected to hold me and give me the real treasure I knew he had within him. He failed to yield of himself and so no amount of gifts, had they been heaped on me, would have mattered one jot.

So it was that I became older but no richer, realising that the ever-rolling wheel of the year had turned and something had not been realised. Or, worse, that we had moved on in space and time into a new cycle yet I had failed to take up the challenge offered to me in the last one, thus missing the opportunity to be me and to effectively grow as me. The prospect of being stuck in that groove of self-reproach and denial for another year, let alone the next seven as astrology and physiology apparently dictated, was totally appalling, no matter how much temporary relief I got from flouting my true calling and letting my anger spew forth instead. Oh, we needed no external enemies for we functioned well, he and I, as our own.

Treeface and I became I study in avoidance tactics. The more the money dried up to a feeble trickle, the more he walked alone, head bent, as I stumbled on behind him lost in my own savage day-dreams of revenge. The more I tormented myself over him not showing me the affection he once had...the affection Lydia had, moreover...the more I wanted to escape what I saw was the breeding ground for all of my ills, the flat that had been our sanctuary. How quickly things can change and invert for a *sensitive*, if bad energies are allowed to go on unchecked!

What a shame our very human behaviour was; what an insult to the Creator who fashioned us as bright, shining beings with the potential for such wild enchantment!

We had bright beacon souls, Treeface and I; all of our kind did. We shone between the worlds like stars. This was our kind-light, our Fey spirit-energy that was there to inspire and guide, to illuminate those who had lost their way and to bring them home to the truth of themselves. Yet our beacon could also act as a candle to any passing moth who was lost in the darkness between the human world and the Unseen ...or worse, one who was greedy for what we had to offer. Oh yes, they came again, the thought-forms, the *nasties.*And others came too, the lost and the confused, human souls wandering in the ether seeking a sign, something that could en-lighten them. Oh yes, we attracted many intruders to our home for it was no longer just my beacon that attracted them but *our* beacon, a doubly powerful lamp in the darkness. With a positive outlook and a harmonious way of life that centred on soul-full practices and psychic work we could have used our joint force for great magics and much good. Instead we let it slide, squandering energy in negative thoughts and pointless arguments, dwelling on pain and anguish and fear. With our guard down and our psychic muscles weak, but with our soul-energy flaring brightly as ever, we let the invaders in. For ones such as us it needed to be a continual thing ,our psychic discipline and our living an green-spirited life, and every time we abandoned it, and so our true selves, we allowed our inherent power to be wasted. There were always those who would come to take it if we let it fly unchecked and who can blame them? It is a law of nature and it was solely our fault.

Due to our lack of money, and the endless walking we did, our physical energies were low enough by the time it got dark. We were tired and added to this our psychic reserves were depleted because we were not doing any real trance-journeying or meditation as we should have been. Being as we were, two Fey souls in human shells, we craved the outdoors anyway but in summer we often got disturbed when we tried to work our spirit-journeyings out-of-doors. It sometimes seemed as if there was no inch of the glorious land of South West England that wasn't owned, or managed, or 'policed' in some way! Yet we still spent as much time as we could outside in nature, away from the city, even if that time wasn't as dedicated to *seeing* and psychic working as it no doubt should have been. If it wasn't for the fact that being in all that green countryside, or next to the river, had boosted our etheric energy a little then we would have been weak on all counts and very easy prey indeed. As it was, our natural need for earth-energy and a closeness to the elemental forces gave us the opportunity to have a stronger spiritual essence even if our ability to *see* was impaired by lack of frequent use. If we had not been absorbing nature's raw supplies of power so often then our whole make-up would have been dangerously weak. The fact we kept topping up on the verdant life-force energy freely given by trees and the land itself as we walked was probably what saved us from really disintegrating when we were attacked psychically.

Because when they assaulted us they really did have a huge amount of back up. And the great army of entities chose the sleeping area of our tiny studio flat as an obvious way in, heading for the place where the sexual energy was, where we were most likely to show any feelings for good or ill, as a target to feed on. The built-in cupboard next to the makeshift bed was, I felt, was becoming a dark place, like a portal, where they came through from the astral realms and sucked in our etheric energy, our life-force (what there was of it) as an aperitif before they really got started on working on us.

For any other human it may not have been so bad but because of our nature we could *see* these lost souls as well as they themselves perceived us in what they considered to be their own space.

This included the wandering spirit of Eleanor Finch.

That morning, as Treeface brought me my customary large cup of tea and hunkered down by me I could see he had made his mind up about something. We had taken to sleeping elsewhere on the floor as we now had an inflatable mattress, bought at the height of Treeface's school earnings, and so we simply dragged to the other end of the room, sadly away from the window. As I lay there looking and feeling dishevelled and disgruntled (it had been a particularly trying night and I had managed to sleep sometime around three a.m) Treeface took a swig of hot, sweet tea. I ran my hands through my shock of flame-red hair which somehow managed to make itself into an impenetrable thicket overnight. I looked through my matted fringe at the man I loved more than anything, despite my stupid griping, and was pleased to see him looking so motivated. Most mornings he had taken to sitting in silence, hugging his knees, deep in thought. This was different, there was a new light in his eyes and a definite sense that he was more 'present' rather than off in some potential disaster elsewhere. I sat up and the covers fell away from me.

Treeface appeared not to notice. He was intent on telling me how he felt, for once.

"Lian, I am so sorry that you've had another disturbed nights sleep, too. I was troubled by the presences as much as you, I shouldn't wonder. I don't know what the big black figure means that we both witnessed last night but we're both aware of this psychic attack, this invasion, and I'm not having it anymore, it's tearing us apart! I provided this home for you and I will see to it that it's habitable!"

The night before, after we had returned from a jaunt to the woods, a particularly canny, extremely disturbed, spirit had managed to rap me smartly on the head. Never before had I experienced a 'ghost' that could actually make such a profound physical contact. It was not pleasant and, if it was able to do something as relatively harmless and hit me on the head with the equivalent of an astral fist, what else could it do, in time, when it had gathered up even more of our bright Fey life-force to feed it?

I took my tea and pulled the covers back around me even though it promised to be another sultry day at the tail end of what had been a glorious summer. As usual I was still 'white with a hint of Lian' despite the sunny days we had spent out of doors, having managed to stay in the shade for most of the time. I felt quite embarrassed at the idea of displaying my naked body while Treeface, oblivious to any of its charms, wanted to discuss poltergeists; *nasties* as Alicia would have called them...

(*That settled it; we were going to have to go and see Alicia! Today? Tomorrow!*)

"What do you propose to do about the entities...or whatever we have attracted?" I asked, warily. I was on very shaky ground when it came to dealing with restless spirits who could make physical contact like that. It still frightened me and made my head buzz with confusion. I *had* to see Alicia, only she could help me!

"Well, I won't be afraid of 'it', or *them*, anymore. We're being edged out of a flat I pay for by my own toil, yes and yours too beloved, and we're living on the corner of our one room rather than upset it...whatever *it* is! It's a spiritual bully among many such energetic tyrants and I can deal with those! I'll sit and meditate on it, go to the place where its strongest, by the built-in cupboard in the corner, and call up the spirits responsible so I can banish them. It should be easy, I don't know why we've let it go on this long!"

Come to think of it, neither did I. What was wrong with me to have become so lethargic and lax, what had Alicia taught me as regards to doing daily psychic cleansing? I knew the procedure yet I was letting the attack go on around me, becoming as intimidated by the unseen presences as I ever had been. And I had abandoned my companion guides in favour of fretting over what the spirits could do to me. It seemed that while we were in that flat we lived in some horribly gloopy dream-time, brains all fogged up and as weighed down and heavy as if we were trying to walk through a thick broth.

"I'm up for it, I can do a meditation in this corner while you do one in the other?"

"Lian, it's not your place to have to clear up this mess. It's mine! I got us this place, I am responsible!"

"Oh, sod responsible!"

Was there no end to this man's pride?

"I am your partner, this is a working relationship, and I am 'a formidable psychic'...aren't they your own words, used over and over? Were you lying?"

Treeface shook his head, looking sheepish.

" I can do it! I am a *seer* even if all I have been truly seeing lately is the end of my nose. I can help you by getting information and seeing if it ties up with yours...then we'll know for sure that what we did independently was valid and true if we both see the same things and get the same guidance on it! You go by the cupboard if you want to and I will stay here."

"Sorry my love. I shouldn't forget that you are who you are and you do this work better than me! It's just that lately, well...you've...you know..."

"Been difficult? Angry? Prickly? Oh, you name it, I've been it. I know that! I'm just...grieving a bit, I guess..."

That wasn't the half of it! Besides all of our other silly human gripes and insecurities, Michael Gabriel's non-existence was still an issue we could not discuss. It sat between us, the sheer weight of it forcing us apart. I hoped I could broach the subject with him now but I felt him pull away from me even before he made as to stand up.

"Yes, well, I am sorry, I do know.." he busied himself with plucking lint from his sleeve.

"WHY CAN WE NOT JUST TALK ABOUT IT?" It came out as a wail of pain. I wanted to repress it but it was out in the world.

I wish I hadn't responded but part of me had hoped it would be okay, that he would reach for me and we could cry together...or something, *anything*! Treeface looked as if he had been slapped hard or had had my hot tea slung in his face.

"I am doing my best, I am just doing my best!" His voice took on that familiar defeated tone and the light in his eyes dimmed again.

And I knew as I heard him speak that he was in torment for not being able to provide. No money, no proper home anymore...no child.

"I'm sorry too," I whispered. When ,when would we truly be close again, he and I?

('*And why are you so far apart now?*' Another voice, the still small voice I liked to ignore of late, piped up. '*Is it because he doesn't want a child? He blocked the spirit! Treeface doesn't want to be a father, he thinks he will only let a child down too. So he sent Michael Gabriel away with his thoughts and his feelings...he willed-and-wished him gone with his Fey magic! Treeface wants to run away, to be free, not to be tied to yet more responsibilities that he cannot meet. And you, how would you have coped with another Fey soul in your life when you can't even stay connected to your own bright essence? Not to mention your jealousy if Treeface gives time and energy, and yes, love to another! Would you be jealous of your own child,* seer?*For shame! You both rejected the spirit that was coming to be your child. In your own ways you both made it unwelcome...*')

Now that I really couldn't bear, not now or ever! I would block it!

"I'm sorry!" I reached out to Treeface but I had broken the spell again, the all too brief closeness we had achieved replaced by a business-like efficiency

"I'll prepare the space for a serious psychic session," he said, his face an un-readable mask. "We will get this sorted out, you'll see. And then.."

"And then?"

"And then...and then I really don't know."

I was left alone, in a second hand sheet, clutching the tea as if it were a talisman.

(*Come back, my love, come back to me! Don't leave me again!*)

It could only get better after we got rid of the omni-present astral and cosmic detritus, couldn't it? We were not over, he and I. It was just a blip, a temporary hiccup before we truly bonded in mind, body and spirit. Just a misunderstanding, really. Even soul-mates must have those. Oh yes, if soul-mates could burn and not cry out for love of one another even as the flames rose, then soul-mates could surely have a little glitch...

Suddenly I was on my feet, running naked after Treeface down what we considered to be the 'haunted corridor' between our one room and its separate bathroom and kitchen. Who cared if we hadn't got proper curtains, who cared if my body wasn't perfect! I loved him! He had to know that!

"Ooeeff!" I rushed at him and leapt, jumping up and wrapped my arms and legs round him as he struggled to find his feet and stay balanced. He stood with me enfolded around him, clinging as if for dear life. I rained kisses down on his beautiful lined face.

"I won't let you slip away from me!" I cried.

And I looked at him, I truly looked, and I saw a tall thin man with a strange meandering scar, lines running like the tributaries of foreign rivers in a child's atlas, and eyes I could drown in. His eyes, always the green-on-grey, their deep waters clouding even as I looked into the murky depths, seeing fronds of green weed clinging as I clung, draped over slippery, silvery mottled rocks. *Into the green*, beyond time...

Always.

"Don't hurt me!" he gasped and for a moment I took it that he was speaking to my heart.

"I will never hurt you! Not ever!" I looked into his face, his beloved face with all its furrows and whorls, and realised what he meant.

Slowly, filled with my own unfathomable pain, I slipped down to the floor and stood away from him.

"Sorry," I said dully.

"You were gripping me so hard! Pulling me..."

But I was sobbing now, there was no holding back, and I saw him reflected and refracted back at me as my tears broke free and brimmed over. My whole world turned to glittering sparkles, like the first rays of sun hitting a subterranean lake, and I was blinded by my own shimmering waves of grief, held in check too long. I would not mention his name, I would not, but I held out my hands to Treeface for him to hold me.

"Beloved!"

"I am..so..."

"So am I!"

Yes we were always sorry, so sorry.

We were sorry and we rocked each other, me small and naked, he whip-thin and bent, and although he was not mentioned I felt him pass through us as he had the first time, the moment when we had cried out in the bliss of our union. And the laughter of a golden haired boy that may yet be, one day, bubbled up and poured through me like real sunlight when all I had gotten used to was artificial light and we rocked, we just rocked.

No words, none at all.

And when we stopped rocking we just held each other until the tears stopped.

Then Treeface reached down and picked up a piece of his notepaper he had dropped, the sort of cheap loose-leafed lined stuff he used when I had my nice bound book for psychic note making...

(*Alicia!*)

And he wrote in his almost elegant, archaic looking, slanted hand

'Whatever happens...I love you.'

And taking it from him I kissed his hand and moved away. The moment was too fragile, too precious, to use words. Too many words, of late; harsh and hateful, vague and vapid. Just words Now it was time for silence for we had work to do in the world, my lover and I. We had work to do together that expressed who we were and what we truly did. And so, clutching the most valuable thing anyone had ever given to me, I went away from him to set myself up for some psychic work in the living room.

I slipped on my T-shirt and cotton jeans and settled myself down in front of the window with my psychic note-book at my side. The view over the city was uplifting, the mist thinning over the hills a little revealing an azure sky. It was going to be another scorching afternoon, we were having an incredible year, weather-wise. The summer was stretching out langorously into early autumn with little sign of relinquishing its grip. Perhaps once the schools went back in the first week of September then the phone would begin to ring again and Treeface and I would be happier with him getting work. If we were more contented then maybe the flat would calm down and be more friendly too?

But I knew, somehow, that the flat was now 'too far gone' to simply revert to a peaceful abode of its own accord. Things had been attracted there that wouldn't simply wisp away if we smiled more. No, we needed to clear them and then, with any luck, our increased optimism and security in ourselves and each other, would infiltrate and stop any more psychic imbalance. I wanted only to attract spirits by being a pure light; I didn't mind being an astral beacon, like a psychic lighthouse, to the genuine lost souls who needed me to help them. What I didn't need, nor did I want to encourage, was my being a crazily flashing light that shone far too brightly, burning out of control due to my indiscipline and ignorance. I could well do without the hangers-on that just wanted to feed for their own sake.

There would always be genuine cases who had become trapped, poor human souls that for one reason or another had become Earth-bound, but the ones that deliberately stayed 'in situ' after death for means of revenge, or the ones that were never human but had only ever been the product of someone's particularly sordid thoughts, would always be prevalent too. I sighed. It really was a work in progress, this life of mine. I could not afford to switch off my senses, or rest on my laurels as I had been doing, for one more minute.

I closed my eyes and realised that for the first time ever I was alone in the work. I had no guiding voice, no stern Alicia or gently authoritative Treeface. I was just left with my own knowledge and instincts to be my own leader through the labyrinth of the Unseen. I had to take myself through the process of protection, relaxation and make my own journey to meet the companion guides. I took my first of three deep breaths. I *knew* what to do and I would not let fear make me hesitate.

I was a *seer* and so I would *see*.

I followed all the prescribed steps of the route I had been taught by Alicia, that which had been developed both by Treeface and by my own subsequent, if patchy, work with the two main spirit guides. I knew we probably all had many 'spirit mentors' but that only a few were able to draw close enough to our 'level' to be tangibly experienced. On this occasion I asked for my companion guides to draw close to me to help me with the work in hand, that of identifying any intruders in our home and banishing it, or, more likely, *them,* to the place in the universe best suited for their purposes at that time. I had grown a little rusty in my ways to say the least but I still went through the rigorous procedure of asking both of my guides, Red Fox and the bird spirit-woman, testing both out for authenticity. With the sort of task I was about to undertake I had little time or space for pranksters or impostors.

My 'testing' of them convinced my spirit guides further of my true intent and they drew closer to me, reassured that I considered both myself and my work as worthwhile. I asked for their protection, and for the powerful energy inherent in both them...and my own Fey spirit...to be leant to the proceedings. They then helped me to strengthen my protective blue-gold aura that I used to keep myself astrally safe.

(*Oh, if only I had done this each day, instead of wasting time griping and raging, then none of this would have happened! With the guide's help I would have been able to stay balanced and in touch with my own powerful Feyness! I wouldn't have needed to feel so insecure as to hate Lydia and so I wouldn't have been randomly firing off such disturbed energy for* nasties *to feed on! And I would have spent time keeping myself astrally cloaked from any spirit or energy that did not come for my highest good, with great love for me. What a fool I have been! With all the tools at my disposal, and all the advice I have on hand to use them well, I instead chose to remain impotent and disempowered!*)

Not wishing to waste another precious moment I drew the first protective circle on the ground around me and then a second, asking that any spirit who bothered my home should show themselves inside its boundaries. Yet despite this safe practice I was ill-prepared for who appeared. A little thrown, I was reminded sharply of Alicia's warning, '*do not get too involved in how they appear!*' Although this had initially been a search to retrieve, and send on, squalid grimy interlopers and psychic detritus, I was aware I was initially to be dealing with a very human spirit, a genuinely trapped soul. She was no *nasty.*

I knew that there was more than one reason why I shouldn't get to hung-up on the look of this particular spirit. She was human, she was female and she was distraught...three things I could relate to in varying degrees! I was in danger of getting too caught up in her story and I would therefore be at risk of manufacturing information as I was too emotionally involved with the subject matter. Not only that but I would also be open to letting all manner of other external *nasties* creep in, attracted by our bright astral light, if I didn't get on with the task in hand. I was there to send her away! So despite her feeble and distressed air I went ahead and 'tested her' and when I had identified the very pathetic, vulnerable vision in my circle of flame as ' a true invader in my home' I was in the position to get her moved on.

"Show yourself truly!" I intoned this three times, as was proper for a Fey, for were not three wishes, or three kisses, often mentioned in our Faery-tales? Three is our magic number, our key to the eternal mysteries, and so on the third occasion she shuddered, grew a little clearer in my vision, but remained a young woman, slender as a willow-wand and fair as a mythical Guinevere. However, the dark rings under her eyes revealed her condition.'*Laudanum poisoning*!' I heard from somewhere.

The voices! Did they speak truly, also?

"Let only the truth be spoken here!" I commanded. "Who are you, child, and why are you in this place?"

"Please!" She peered at me with watery pale blue eyes. Her skin had an unhealthy dull pallor that made mine look almost radiant and blooming. I held myself in check, not wanting to feel to much for this intrusive spirit although that in itself was hard. She was so *sad.*

"What brings you here?"

"Do not attempt to extract answers from her," Red Fox stepped forward and held up a hand. "She is at her wits end and would be deemed quite mad by today's standards. She has been systematically poisoned by her family. She wanders here as this land beneath us was once the orchard where she last saw her lover. She has been kept here in death by her insanity in life and by her over-riding desire to see him again. Tell her she must move on if she wishes to meet with Oliver...tell her he is in the light."

"Eleanor Finch!" I intoned with as much authority as I could muster. The woman did not look at me but groped blindly around her instead. How did I know her name? The bird-spirit, sometimes owl, sometimes eagle, my *familiar*, had whispered it on the wind to me, perhaps.

"It is time for you to move on, to be at peace. Your beloved waits for you elsewhere, it is time that you went to him."

"*Noooo*!" she wavered in and out of my vision, flickering like a pale candle in my circle of protective blue flames.

"Oliver!" She gave a pitiful cry and reached out into the air around her hopelessly.

"Do not attempt to cajole her!" Red Fox spoke sharply. "Send her! Tell her to go! Call on her companion guides and the spirits who love her to help her move on to the place which has long since been prepared for her."

"Miss Finch, Eleanor Finch, I send you to the light. May your guides and loving guardians be at your side to show you reality, to bring you peace and safe passage. May you step on into the light, may you be taken to the place in the universe which is right for you at this time. Move on, spirit, with love, for you have no place here any more!"

I felt cruel saying these last words but they came out anyway, with renewed conviction, and I sensed a whole host of forms surrounding the poor waif in my circle. I saw a beautiful white light in the distance, appearing out of nowhere, a tunnel of pure love formed of incandescence. Is that what happens at the moment of death? I seemed to remember otherwise. Maybe that was what happened to lost or trapped souls? Or maybe everyone experienced the passing over differently?

"Go now and be at peace!" I said and with a rush the woman blurred and began to shrink, moving towards the tunnel in an odd gliding motion, surrounded by glowing pinpricks of golden energy, her loved ones and spirit guides. My eyes filled with tears. When she had nearly vanished I heard my familiar, the shape-shifting bird who was sometimes called Rides-the-Wind.

"Do not hold on to her! Wish her well now, let her go! For that is how you may show you truly care. This is not where she should be, beloved, let her go now!"

And with the words I felt myself give a psychic burst of energy, pushing her away from my realm with all the love I had in me for her, and she vanished. I released my breath in a rush.

"That was hard," I said to my spirit friends who remained by me.

The circle of flame still stood on the ground but it was empty.
"Is she truly gone?"

"Is it your will that she is truly gone?"

"Of course!"

"Then there is no reason for her to return, unless you will it so,and even then there are stronger forces than yours..." Red Fox smiled wryly and bowed slightly.

"Are there more?" I asked

"What do you think?"

"Many? I know there are some, certainly, but I sense a line, a queue...how many? I can't deal with loads of them? And why so many?"

"Too many questions. One answer. Yes, there are many. And you should deal with them, all of them, but not now."

"When?"

"You ask, I tell you. If I tell you, you will be obliged. Hard work, never easy! Work with your beloved, join forces. Send them away and seal the portal. Then tend to your own energies, *seer*, keep yourself in check and the work will be less! The portal needs to be closed, things put to rest, and then you need to be who you are, completely, and accept what this entails. No more hate and fear, no more anger and despair. Do not waste power but conserve it, save it for wish-and-will of a healing kind, for all beings! Focus...and do it for the Greening, kindred of mine! Yes, always for that! Return when you have topped up your energies. Go now; go *into the green*!"

"Thank you!" I said, and nodded my gratitude to both of my supportive spirit mentors.

"It is well."

I felt exhausted as I followed my procedure to return from the sacred place, back to the present, making sure at the end of the session I was grounded. As I began to write some key words down in my book for reference I sensed Treeface standing behind me having left his corner of the room. I held up a hand to gesture he should wait a minute. I wanted to write down what I had, in brief, as to corroborate his findings. If I had 'evidence' before he told me what he knew than there would be no danger of me simply copying what he said.

Such was the beauty of two psychics working in unison, yet separately, as there was greater scope to both substantiate each others findings and bounce ideas around as to solutions.

After a few moments of scribbling I turned and beckoned him to me. I stood and reached out to hug him before he joined me on the floor. He looked as perplexed as I felt. There had been no simple answer. One woman had appeared who bothered us, yes, but who were all the nameless others waiting in the wings. Eleanor Finch (I must be careful not to dwell on her!) hardly seemed *compos mentis* enough to have caused all of our 'haunting' problems.

"A woman?" Treeface asked.

"Young, fair haired, pale and wan, waxy complexion, dark circles under her eyes."

"Poisoned by Laudanum?"

"Yes, but I haven't a clue what it is!"

"I'll explain later. Her family kept her under control with it after finding she had become with child by a local man called Oliver Prentis, a man who she met in the meadow here."

"Yes, where the flats now stand. I got the impression that this land used ton be an orchard, not a meadow, but no matter. It was clearly a green space, either way. Yes, she would meet him illicitly on this common land. We're talking about the Victorian era, right? And they...buried her...*here*? I don't know for sure and I don't want to go into it! Their house was over the road, the big one opposite the flats with the long driveway. Very flash! Very austere and forbidding too!"

"Yup, she was kept prisoner, to all intents and purposes, in the front bedroom, overlooking the land where the flats now stand. She dwelled on this land a lot, visualising it in her captivity, mooning over her lost love. Making psychic links to it where she already had physical ties to it at the time of her previous thwarted passion! And the child she conceived by Oliver? Did her child die? Was it bricked up in their house or buried here? I don't know!" We both shuddered, knowing that it was unwise to focus on these details when she had gone on, knowing that to endlessly mull over things we need not know, or could do nothing about, was to make unnecessary links with her soul.

"Oh, we get the general gist, don't we? Same woman, all in white, looked sick, seemed mentally ill? Yes?"

"Yes but she isn't all there is, or was, here, is she?"

"Not by a long chalk, I'm afraid."

Treeface made us more tea and I drank mine while fighting the tangles in my hair. As I was lacing up my old baseball boots I asked him if he had any idea where we should start clearing the real *nasties*? I suddenly felt so close to him again, in a different sort of way, as if we were equals and friends instead of jealous, insecure lovers. I was quite excited...this was my first psychic mission and it was to be with my true soul-mate! Ha, Lydia would never be able to...

But I stopped myself. Lydia was just my beloved's sister and that was all. She wasn't here; she would never be here! He wasn't comparing me to her; we were just us in the moment, he and I. If only I could hold this happiness, these positive, balanced thoughts...

Alicia would help me maintain this sense of centred peace, yes, I knew she would! I wouldn't hold it against her that she had consorted with Lydia and she wouldn't hold it against me for being absent from her for so very long. We were old, old friends she and I, such trivial things, transient *human* things, did not matter to our souls. Hell, she had forgiven me for being the rudest woman she had ever invited in to her home so my absence would be nothing to her, not in the scheme of things. Alicia Owens was a strong, beautiful, compassionate woman and a wild Fey spirit and she had room in her heart for me and many more besides! Oh, I would just be so glad to see her, and she me; so glad to see the fine hair like spun moonlight and smell the cinnamon-and-roses scent of her skin, to hear her call me *child* again. Yes! She would be so pleased to hear I was doing my psychic work, just as she had taught me. She may even help me! And she could meet Treeface, in the flesh at last, and we could thank her, truly thank her, for her guidance that brought us together.

It had been too long but tomorrow...

Alicia!

Chapter Three

Blind Vision

I touched the worn metal of the gate. It sang out to me strongly...

(touch me!)

...and as I touched it with both hands, as if I were giving it a blessing, it showed me a picture. This was nothing new, objects had been revealing their secrets to me for years. Yet why did this picture seem to me to be more important than any other, more keen to be witnessed in detail? Who was in it? A younger woman, older than me but fit and strong. Yes, a hard, tanned athletic sort who reminded me of a physical education teacher of some type. Or a tennis player? Taller than me too. Dark hair, almost black really, cropped short. Was this Alicia, perhaps, many years previously? Surely this rather fierce looking woman was too tall to have been Alicia, even in her straight-backed youth? And why would I see her this way now? No it wasn't Alicia, definitely not; the woman in my mind-picture had her hands full of shopping and it was in plastic carrier bags. 'Safeway' bags were modern things, not green-spirited things and certainly not of Alicia's youth! I knew for certain that my friend would never have entertained plastic carrier bags even if they had existed when she were younger, in fact she probably used the same old cloth bag or woven basket, over and over, all her life.

So, if the image I received from the gate was a true one, and I had no reason to doubt it, was this black-browed, grim looking vision Rhiannon, returned to see her mother at last?

Was she indoors with Alicia right now, having a reconciliation over a mug of soothing linden flower infusion, fresh picked from the lime trees that grew on the edge of the back garden? I didn't know if I wanted to meet her, not after all she had done to her mother. But then I was glad she had returned to see her, for whatever reason. That was good surely? And yes, who was I to talk about how my friend should be treated when I myself had abused our friendship so very recently by temporarily abandoning it? But she must be in there, my psychic sight, even when it was not being used as often as it should be, would never just throw up such a clear image if there was no reason for it. I gave my own wise Fey spirit more credit than that!

Swallowing any urge to turn on my heel and leave them alone together I pushed the gate shut behind me and stepped onto Alicia's path. Then I was still again, waiting, watching, *feeling*. Something wasn't quite right...what was it? Where there any clues? Yes! I looked down and saw there were no weeds growing up through the cracks in the paving of the path. Alicia had never called them weeds, they were her *allies,* her green companions in wild magic, and she allowed them to grow as long as they agreed not to get any bigger or more unruly. Alicia had an *arrangement* with the intrusive, invasive plants in her garden. Now it seemed as if someone, not Alicia surely, had poured a lot of noxious chemicals all over the path to render it smooth, uniform and unblemished by the cheeky heads of dandelion or clover. Had this damnable daughter of hers bullied her mother into behaving 'normally'? Rhiannon had certainly left her mother because she was ashamed of her 'difference'; of her wonderful uniqueness and ability to help and heal and enchant. Good grief, had this loathsome Rhiannon, keen to have everything tidy and ordered, sent Alicia away...to a rest home? To an old people's ghetto? *'Oh my Lady!'* as Alicia herself would have said at the very thought! Why, Alicia was more sprightly and spry and better equipped than most middle-aged folk to be caring for herself...and for others too!

I stood and scented the air. A few remaining blossoms, the suggestion of the fruit to follow, mingled with hot tarmac and recently cut grass....but there was no delicious scent that spoke of Alicia. No tang of magic in the air, nor of baking or brewing, activities that were as usual to Alicia as breathing. Alicia's cooking and creating her brews were her *spells*, each creation imbued with her Fey will-and-wishes for healing or inspiration or creativity. She could never go a day without giving her everyday acts a healthy dose of Fey enchantment! Perplexed I looked up and saw the curtain in the living room twitch (pale pink draylon? Since when had Alicia had a penchant for such things? It seemed to me then that maybe I had never known the old woman at all!)

And then my eyes went to the empty space where the besom, Alicia's old faithful broom, had stood against the wall...

(*No!*)

...and I knew before I pressed the doorbell that it would play a tune, no longer just the cheery 'ding-dong' of old. And the brass fox door knocker had gone too.

Oh God! Alicia! Had I left it too long? Please, please...Oh God! Wouldn't someone have told me? But who?

My heart lurched painfully. I hadn't bothered to see her for so long, *seven months* it had been! What could have happened in that time? Lots, that's what. Treeface and I had met and fallen in love again, he was almost divorced and we shared a flat, a *home*, together! I had gone from mental health client to care worker and he had started facing the world as storyteller and musician. Lots could happen, for sure. Whole lives could change!

Or they could end.

Death. Death could happen in the twinkling of an eye...of a violet eye, now faded chambray...now blind?

I pressed the bell again, frantic. I knew that there was someone home, why didn't they answer?! Oh God, oh Goddess, oh my drea spirit guides, let it be her, let Alicia come to the door! Someone help me!

(*Spirits who love me, spirits who come for my highest good, be with me now, I beg you!*)

If only Treeface had come with me! But no, he had said that this time I should go alone, just to make sure that I could really give Alicia one hundred percent of my attention after being away so long. Treeface would come with me next time, he promised, but this day he was going to use the time alone to get rid of more of our astral *nasties* from the flat. He had said that, in the long run, we needed her help to cleanse the flat as our effort would never be so effective as our joint effort, the effort of us three, reunited...

(*The reunion of witches, of Fey* seers *and healers, we three!*)

Oh, how I needed my lover's arms around me now!

"Please answer! I don't care if Rhiannon's with you! I don't care if you are mad at me for leaving it so long! PLEASE!" I urged Alicia, talking in my head to her. I knew that she could hear me, she had always been able to read my thoughts.

And the door opened.

The woman of my vision, that determined, sober and very straight looking woman, eyed me with barely concealed dislike and mistrust. She opened the door just wide enough so that I could see the new floral wallpaper and hear the child yelling within the house somewhere. She said, with impatient iciness,

"Yes? I'm very busy!"

"Mummeeee!" the child shrilled.

I saw myself through her eyes, all wild wilful hair and mad green eyes.

Did she think I was a Gypsy come to flog her a hand-made clothes peg and curse her or something?

"Rhiannon?" I tried to look around her, past her, into the familiar house which now looked deeply unfamiliar in its bright bland decor. Everything about the place exuded the air of modern banality, a formulaic sameness that I had observed in every family home from my dear Papa's onwards. There was no character here, none of Alicia's quirky charm. Oh Alicia! In seven months have you been eradicated? Wiped clean away by this monstrous woman? How on earth had you ever birthed such a person?

(In my head *the voices* asked me '*and how did your dear old Papa ever father you?*')

"I'm a friend of Alicia's. I'm sorry to..."

"Who? What? Oh be quiet, Gillian! I'm coming!" The baby yelled the louder and I stepped forward.

"Stop right there!" The woman barred my way, "I'm not Rhiannon. You've got the wrong place, I'm afraid. Now excuse me I really am very busy!" She said this as if my kind, a scruffy little woman with a strange haunted look, could ever be as busy as she, an upright citizen, a good housewife and mother, was.

"But you *are* Rhiannon! Where's..."

"I assure you, I am *not*!"

"I'M LOOKING FOR ALICIA OWENS, YOUR BLOODY MOTHER!" I asserted loudly, close to a yell, knowing she was going to shut the door on me. Then my resolve broke and a tear rolled down my cheek.

(*Echoes of another time...was it really ten months ago when she had seen me, had called to me? Oh Mother!Oh dear, dear Lady!Alicia! Where are you, beloved?*)

"Look, I don't know who you are or what you want,and I don't particularly care! Please leave!"

Fresh tears sprang unbidden from my eyes and streamed down my face. I held my hands up in front of me, reaching ineffectually.

"Please tell me where she is?" I begged.

"Look," the woman looked both remorseful and disturbed by my tears, "but I live here with my husband and son! There is no Alish..."

"She was called Mary Alicia Owens but she preferred Alicia," I said, looking at my scuffed boots as they blurred through my endless tears, "She invited me in last...oh God!"

Snot and tears mingled on my face, just as they had done after Robert's death. I could see this woman flinching from me. Was I so horrifying? So visceral as to cause real repulsion? I couldn't afford to make her turn from me, I needed to know!

"Please, *please*, tell me where she is?"

"Ok. Alright. Stop! I'll tell you and then you'll go away, yes?"

She didn't wait for my response. I doubted I was capable of one.

"My mother is dead," the woman said, tonelessly, as if reading from an autocue, "she has been dead since late January. But to me, she died a long time ago. There *was* no Alicia Owens, I have no mother! And there is no Rhiannon Owens either! What a ridiculous name, I ask you! I'm Stephanie Klein now and I'd ask you to remember that, thank you very much! Now, if you'll excuse me...yes, I'm coming Gillian! *Be quiet!*"

The baby, left alone, was howling in protest. I wished I could howl too, but I knew where that would get me. Medication...social workers...no Treeface, no job...but...

(*Oh, oh, oh, she was gone. No! NO!*)

Please, no!

"There's nothing to be done. She's been cremated long enough. Now I really must ask you to leave."

"Cremated!"

No, no, no, this was all wrong! Alicia would never have wanted that. To be in the earth, giving life, helping trees to grow from her wise old bones, not thrown in the flames again.

(*NO!*)

"Now I really would be grateful if you'd let me get back on with my work!"

And the woman, this stiff brutal stranger who was Rhiannon, yet not Rhiannon, made to shut me out.

"Did she...did she...oh God!" I couldn't see for tears and my nose ran uncontrollably. I didn't care how I looked, how much more repulsive I was than other people! I wanted to die too! Oh, *I didn't say goodbye!* I didn't tell her...

(*I love you! I love you Allette! I love you Alicia! All the time I have been promising to come and see you and you've been dead!Oh mother!*)

...no, no, no, bring her back. Please!

"It can't be true!"

(She must be lying! She hates me and my kind, she won't tell me the truth! She's put Alicia in a home for old folk and stolen her home from her! Oh, the bitch! Alicia is alive somewhere...she must be! But where? But then...Oh God!...but then there was that empty feeling I had been avoiding all year! I had been diverting myself from it's terrible truth with anger and jealousy but now it came flooding back. A knowing, *the realisation Alicia had died shortly after our last meeting*

together. Slipped away she had, her work done for this life. That was why I had put this day off, lied to myself, conspired with myself to stop myself from coming here, from facing...this! I had diverted my own attention away. Oh God!)

"It is true," Rhiannon/Stephanie said. She was regal, cold, totally unlike her beautiful mother.

"Did she leave any...how...?"

"What? *What*!? Oh, I see! Stop right there! Have you come here wanting a hand out? Is that what you're up to? Money for drugs is it? Who *are* you?"

"I'm..her...friend!"

"Friend!" the woman snorted in derision. "What sort of friend are you that doesn't come round for six months and then appears asking if she's been left anything in the will? Jesus! Well, that was typical of my mother, associating with the likes of you! Taking in every waif and stray and fobbing her own children off with platitudes! Pah! Well, we live here now and you'll get nothing from us, you cheeky madam! So go back to the coven you came from, or the gutter, and spare me any more of your pathetic, phoney tears!"

And the door slammed. A door without a brass knocker in the shape of a fox. A door painted in white gloss, not the grass green paint that had been peeling and flaking, having been applied many, many years ago by a woman who still had strands of black in her hair.

A future slammed shut and the heart that I had thought to be pink and whole again thudded dully in the cavern of my chest, returning to the pitted pewter of the days before...

(*Before Alicia!*)

...now the days after Alicia.

And I walked. Of course I did.

I got as far as the end of the road before my knees buckled and down I went, collapsing like a house of cards, nearly pitching straight into the road. And there I stayed in the dark and silence.

Until the sirens brought me back briefly.

(*I don't want to come back! I don't want to face it! Don't make me! Don't...*)

"Don't touch me!"

"Come on now love, that's it, lets have a look at you now, *that's* it. That's better, eh? Good girl. Do you know who you are? What's your name, love?"

They sat me up, the two of them, and me a sad, empty rag doll thing. Rhiannon/Stephanie had cut all my strings and I was a broken puppet, neither use nor ornament.

I told them my name. They could have it for all I cared.

(*Alicia, Robert...take me with you! Treeface doesn't need me, he doesn't even want me and perhaps he never really did! Take me out of this world for good and all, I'm so tired of the pain...the hurting...the yearning...please! Take me to the children I never had, let me stay with them, and you...*)

I heard someone else repeat my stupid, redundant name into a radio, a radio crackling with more exciting things than a stupid *seer* who hadn't seen what mattered most.

"How are you spelling that love?"

I shrugged bonelessly, a dirty broken marionette on a cracked paving slab. Bleeding. I stared at the drops of blood on the grey concrete. Perfectly round they were, crimson pennies scattered at my feet. From where? I didn't care. They were very pretty.

"Did you faint? Hello? Lian, stay with us, love. Hey, hello! That's it lass, stay with us! Did something happen? Any pain? Did you hit your head? Where's it hurting, Lian?"

"Can you remember anything? No, don't worry, that's it, were going to take you in the ambulance. Are you on medication, is there any condition we should know about?"

"Plenty of time for remembering later, eh? This is Bill and I'm John, love. Can you stand? Let us help you..."

Too many words.

"*Words can charm and create harm and a rope will make me dance...*" I said, not knowing why.

They were checking for signs now, of drugs, alcohol.

(*I'm clean! I'm just a* seer, *a terrible broken* seer *who cannot, will not, see!*)

Oh God! She had been there for me...*been there for me!*...that was all I knew, that was all I needed to know.

Their radio crackled with life, someone else's life. I moaned.

Why hadn't she come for me? Why hadn't I seen her spirit as he passed over? WHY?

(*She did come, you didn't want to see! You didn't want to lose a second mother, not now, not ever! She did come! But now she's moved on, passed over, gone!*)

"Come on now love, one, two, three, that's it! Up we come! Lovely, well done Lian. And just let us help you, over here, good. One step and then you're in...okay?"

And they assisted my rag-body into their ambulance and took me back into the city where somewhere my love waited for me. My love who hadn't seen Alicia's death either! Or had he?

I didn't know anything but the fact that Treeface waited for me. But would I ever truly return?

Who would have thought less than three months later I'd be in another ambulance on the other side of that very same city, heading for the hospital again?

After Alicia...

(*God, how it hurt me to say that!*)

...I had thrown myself into anything, *anything,* that would take my mind off my guilt and pain, take me out of myself. I shopped frantically for bargains for the flat, coming home dazed and foot-sore, with little to show for my travels but a head full of nothing and maybe a cheap item for the kitchen or bathroom. I worked hard at finding new things for us to eat that would cost little but fill our bellies well, scouring bookshops for fat, expensive tomes on meat-free cooking which contained recipes I could jot down when no one was looking. I walked all over the woods, seeing nothing, feeling nothing, and I tramped the canal path for miles, passing many, seeing no one, an exercise which gave me blisters and no memories at all. I pursued clients for Treeface, sometimes I even I made love to him mechanically, but I rarely spoke. The matter of the haunted flat and our financial future had been lost in the aftermath of my loss...and his. For although he coped with it better than I, I knew that it tore him apart in a different way. How could he trust his own intuition if he hadn't known of our soul-friend's death? How had he not heard Kefli, his companion spirit, warning him of this? And how had he not encouraged us to make the effort sooner so that he could have met the woman who had shared his soul-nature, and his fate, in Thirteen Twenty Six?

More than this I started spending extra, unpaid time at the mental health charity's Social Centre with the clients, trying to focus on their needs and worries, not mine. I myself hadn't lost my own mind, sadly, so the only way that I could deal with it's contents, and the continual aching in my heart, was to think of others and their ills. I became a 'befriender' as well as a support worker of the lowest order and sat with the schizophrenics and the ones with paranoid delusions and convinced myself that those were *real* problems. So distressed was I that I was lax with my psychic protection and got too involved, on all levels, with their fear and torment. The slide into their madness was something I would have entered into almost willingly, longing for some of their medicated oblivion or their total abstinence from personal responsibilities. The irony was that the more I did this, ignoring my ability to *see*, the more Alicia would have been upset at me for forgetting her training and who I was, inside. Even my way of mourning for her would have hurt her!

Yet although I knew all that she had taught me was true and real I still I craved their derangement like I had never craved nicotine. I watched the clients dragging hard on umpteen cigarettes and imagined I could do the same with their latent insanity; if I could I would become another woman entirely, one who lost her *knowing and* her impotent *seeing* and only experienced life as a constant spinning in darkness like a whirlygig beetle trapped under a bucket, in permanent night, in constant confusion. I disregarded the spirit-entities, the *nasties*, that buzzed around the confused, sick and disenfranchised like fat flies and I let them land on me, drain me, turn my mind. Oh so easily it seemed I could regress back to the Lian I had been before Alicia!

('*I am here because I do not wish to be there. Is that the only reason?...And for me I ask, which people do I have to see and where shall I go?...Because wherever there is, whoever there is, I have to take me with me!'*)

And every day that passed I thought '*where are you now, Alicia? I know you think I am strong enough to cope with this, with these decisions, on my own now but I'm so frightened I'll make the wrong choice! And yes, I am supposed to know that there are no wrong choices but...help me!*')

And as I listened to the clients problems, their petty gripes, their rambling and almost incoherent mutterings, I noticed one man. A man who was in seemingly perpetual motion and who had the bluest eyes I had ever seen; a man who had been brought up exceptionally well, educated and feted...and then somehow discard by both society and his family when he had made the cardinal error of getting mentally ill.

Yes, I, Lian Smythe, the little *seer,* fell straight into the biggest delusion, the oldest trap of all...that I could *help* him, that I could *change* him. He distracted me, you see, he gave me something else to dwell on. I could not dwell on my own lover because whenever I thought of Treeface and our life I thought of the empty space in it left by one of our kind, one that should have been with us, and so I could not...*would not*...think of him!

I thought of blue-eyed Stevie instead. He was a strangely blank canvas for me to paint on.

Stevie was very handsome. I had never really thought this of any man before. Robert had been beautiful inside and Treeface, well, he was my soul-love and my soul saw beyond appearances. Even if he had been an old, old man, or disabled in a terrible way, or grossly overweight I would have seen his eyes and melted into him. But Stevie, my sad little distraction, he was physically very appealing His surface appearance was pleasing to me, like a pretty enough picture that I could stare at and not think. I heard tell that several of the other clients of the Centre's facilities had dated him, even had relationships with him. One, Sandra, a rotund but milkmaid-pretty blonde, had claimed that he hit her and that he was 'a real nutter'. As this woman herself was in no fit state to cast aspersions I held my better judgement over his merits back. Oh yes, I did what a thousand other people have done when unhappy, or trapped or desperate to have some light relief from their own trying situation. I became *obsessed* with him.

Well not with him, never that. With the *possibility* of him and the possibilities he offered to me as a means of escape.

Seemingly overnight I was fantasising about a man called Stevie about who I knew almost nothing. Not in a sexual way, oh no, more in the way of a painter who wants to find the meaning of life in the contours and shadows of another human being....just so they don't have to look too far in the harsh outside world, or worse, *inside themselves*. I wanted to find everything there in his presence so the cruel killing world beyond him may dissolve and, along with it, my pains and worries. And those of Treeface.

Where did Stevie go? Where did he live? What was his story? My mind filled itself with fresh tangents and logarithms just as it had so long ago in the presence of a strange, sick girl called Jocelyn. How did other people live? How did this Stevie live? Perhaps as a Fey spirit the human world would always fascinate me, as well as repel me. I could never find out much about Stevie from his own lips though as he would leave the room when I joined in his group discussion or opt out of a card game if I came to watch. Once he simply walked out of the Centre and did not return at all, leaving his coat behind in his haste to depart. I was not able to go in to the Centre every day and so I would have to wait a whole week to find out what had happened to him....and even then I may never know for it was frowned upon and could even be a matter of severed disciplinary action, (even for me as a once-client, barely paid carer and volunteer) to get to personally involved with the 'users'.

I hated that, the 'us' and 'them' attitude. It was only, well, *afterwards*, that I saw the point in it at all.

So, while Treeface strived to put a crust on the table with fiddle playing for which he could find little heart, or stories in which he could find little meaning at present, I mooned aimlessly after a man with a mental illness who reputedly beat up his girlfriends but who, I tried to reason, had a beautiful sonorous voice and the most startlingly blue eyes I had ever had the misfortune of falling into at such a vulnerable time.

Yes, I focused with whole-hearted intent on meeting Steven Henry Clements of Flat Two B, Number Sixteen, Berryhill (oh, I had looked through his Centre registration documents, I had to admit it). I so wanted to meet Stevie, the man who I thought of to the exclusion of all else, outside of the Centre and then maybe we could go for a coffee and he would tell me all about himself....a self that I was dwelling on, habitually, night and day to blank out my own reality. You see, the slide into my stupid, blind actions had been swift and all consuming, and no doubt encouraged as ever by those vindictive, greedy spirit entities who rejoiced at my foolishness. I had put aside my gifts, for they had dried up and gone silent and blank anyway it seemed to me, in favour of being haunted, even possessed, by the *nasties* that dwelled everywhere for me...but nowhere quite as much as within the walls of a Centre dedicated to helping those with mental health problems. My human self, it seemed, couldn't help itself while my Fey soul retracted itself like a tortoise into its shell come winter.

I know, I was deliberately going against my spirit-self in all ways possible and against my loyalty to Treeface, but it seemed I couldn't help myself and, with Alicia dead and gone, who would come to my aid?

So, I would see Stevie twice, maybe even three times a week at the

Centre and then the rest of the time I would do some more focusing on him, just to block out anything else. My imagination, strengthened by trance-vision and through spirit-journeying, was excellent and my day-dreams were extremely vivid. Oh, I could have used the will I was using for my meeting with Stevie outside the Centre for more *useful* ends, couldn't I? I could have used it to get Treeface work, to strengthen his self-confidence and public appeal, or to find us more regular money! I could have used it for the Greening, to heal and offer comfort and hope! But I squandered it. I used my potent psychic potential, the one I had thought corked up and ineffectual, the one I reasoned had abandoned me like everyone else, on a strange man. I was truly harking back to my same old victim's patterning, believing everything and everyone had abandoned me, even my trusted spirit-mentors! *As if they would!* No, it was I who had abandoned them in my despair but old habits surely do die hard, that is if we ever manage to kill them at all. I had given up Robert, and lost him for ever, on the strength of my soul-link to Treeface and here I was, reunited with Treeface, my oneness, and yet I was wasting my valuable, vital enrgy on someone I didn't know at all!

No, I did not know Stevie Clements but I pretended that I did. I saw us meeting, as if by chance, in the street of shops that ran down past his flat. I knew which shops were there, I had looked down that road often since finding his address, so far in vain. Then he would invite me for a meal, the sort of meal Treeface and I could never afford, not in a million years, and in a lovely restaurant he would talk and I would listen. He would tell me about his life, his childhood as the son of a judge, his boarding school years, maybe at Marlborough college, and his unfortunate slip into gambling which ruined his promising career in medicine...and how his wealthy father had had him put on medication to try and shut him up. Oh yes, in my head Stevie was so many things, urbane and witty, motivated and full of fun, keen to share with me his privileged life...

(*What a fool my human self, that willful being encouraged by those omnipresent* nasties, *could be! Oh for shame, Lian! Why couldn't you just face your pain, get angry, let it out as Alicia taught you? Why couldn't you honour her memory instead of hiding* from *her death?)*

..and all the while I thought these ludicrous thoughts, none of what I was concocting matched with the truth of a man who rented a scruffy flat on a busy high street in Bath. All I truly knew of Stevie was that his eyes were sky-blue and mesmerising. Indeed, they may have been bluer than the most beautiful summer sky but they were wild, wilder than was safe or sane, or sometimes heavily hooded and clouded, albeit briefly, shielded by soft drugs and psychosis, from all reason. Stevie, despite the truth of him and for the want of another, was a perfect foil for all my attentions, attentions fuelled by my own grief, confusion and rage.

(*Why did Alicia have to leave me, just like my mother? Why? And why hadn't I known she was dead? Why? And why was my relationship with my soul-love not bringing us happiness and security and a child born with a Fey soul? WHY?*)

Yes, there was a lot of energy behind my misplaced focusing, for sure.

I should have known much better than to direct that blast of fiery energy at anyone, let alone a stranger with psychosis! For he *was* ill. Hadn't I read his registration documentation at the Centre, albeit in secret? The records were for staff only and were confidential, so as to stop any prejudicial treatment of clients who had backgrounds of violent behaviour or abuse. I betrayed that trust placed in me as a volunteer and supporter. How would I have liked someone else peering at my own dubious 'case history' for their own ends? And I accused Treeface of only seeing what he wanted to see in Lydia! Had I forgotten the words '*psychotic episodes*', '*violent rages*', '*delusions and hallucinations, apparently demonic in nature...*' in Stevie's records? When I had read my own notes (again in secret) they had said I heard '*voices*' and '*saw things*' too. So I thought...

(*Or I didn't think at all*)

...that I'd ignore those comments. I was harmless and they said I had delusions, or, at least, had once experienced them. Surely then Stevie was not really mad or sick either? Like all foolish people who enter into a situation where they think they can 'save' a person, change them by their own loving care, I was destined for a fall. I thought I knew Stevie better than they when all I knew was my own pain made manifest into a distracting fantasy. But witches...*seers*...aren't safe to play such games that others may get away with. I know that now.

I *know* it.

I don't resent what happened or what he did to me. I wouldn't say I deserved it, well who ever deserves violence? But I would say that I was at least responsible in part and how significant a part depends on how much store one puts on my psychic ability. For that was what truly drew the man to me and made him behave as he did. That was what made him come to me, in all confusion; pulled by my unseen will and the influenced by his own entities, and drawn to the flame of my absolute and overwhelming grief and pain, the dumb voodoo of my anger. I thought that I needed Stevie, with all of the distracting possibilities he gave me, and I thought that he may need me to help him. Yet I did not need Stevie H. Clements as he truly was, at that time, I just needed to save *someone*, to turn my head and heart away from saving myself. And all he needed was professional care.

Who knows, he may be well now. They may have given him a lot more psychiatric help after what he did to me.

And what did he do? Well, he came to me, of course, as I wanted him to...just not in the sort of way anyone would really want.

I had been at the Centre three times that last week. The regular clients didn't seem to care if I was there more than usual, or to care if I was there at all; it was only the staff who were surprised to see me again. Ostensibly I was covering for someone who wanted a day off, only, of course, I wasn't going to be paid for my services...services which had latterly included doing the food shopping for the communal lunch and even cooking with the help of a very mumsy woman called Tanya. Cooking for twenty or so adults was all new to me and I felt quite accomplished afterwards, even though the meal itself had been basic fare.

"Why you want to be here when you don't have to be beats me!" Tanya said jokily. Didn't she really not know why I was there? I had wondered if my lingering looks at the lovely Stevie had alerted her attention? Or, indeed, anyone's? I wouldn't be the only psychic with a background of mental health issues, after all. Maybe in ordinary circumstances the clients would have wondered at my behaviours but with them being the way they were no one really saw a great deal of what anyone else did, really. Their psychic faculties were open but they were too open in some cases and they had just gone flying off on many surreal tangents from tedious reality or else they were so firmly 'shut down' and fuzzed up by prescribed drugs (as I myself had once temporarily been) to be almost spiritually inert, one step from coma or death. It was only the staff, it seemed, that I had to worry about.

But I would say that Tanya was the most sharp eyed and curious about me than all of them and yet she had not put together why I wanted to come to 'work' so often when I got precious little but a free lunch for the privilege. Maybe that was because Stevie seemed, especially that last week, entirely reluctant to stay in the same space as me, to occupy any situation I joined in. He would stride off to another corner or retreat behind a magazine if he saw me approaching. Anyone would think he hated me! And if he did? Maybe he did!

Did the possibility that he hated me change how I was? Did I get a grip when I realised he may not either need, or want, my help or interest? By no means! Instead I watched him take a reluctant turn on the Karaoke machine that last, ill-fated afternoon with Celia, a very lonely, usually withdrawn lady who, we all discovered, had a marvellous high, fluting voice. Stevie's own singing was resonant enough and hit all the right notes and a number of the watching women got all flustered watching him perform another Beatles duet with the blushing Celia. He was, after all, conventionally very handsome and the horizons of those who attended the Centre, ostensibly for company, were very limited. I myself tried not to stare at him too much; I did not want him to notice my intent gaze and sit down again. And as I stared at him a funny little mantra popped into my head:

'Stevie steps upon the wind,
Stevie is Nothing and Nothing is King!'

On and on I repeated it to myself, round and round it went in my head, blocking out my own distressing thoughts. I knew that night Treeface would come back to the flat having spent a day in a school that probably would have been difficult for him. He may have been able to buy us some food for tea but the rest of his earnings would go towards the rent, just as my meagre money did. Either that or council tax, or water rates. Then we would have to sit in a flat in virtual darkness, using our stubs of candles to save cash, witnessing all its ghosts and atmospheres. Not only this but there was no seasoned wisewoman to consult about the ongoing, and still rapidly increasing, problems in our home. We may even have to leave it soon! Could we afford it now winter was just around the corner and could we tolerate the spirits in it even if we could afford it? I resented the thought of having to move out again and it upset me deeply. It was my first real home and it should have been one that made me deliriously happy, living with my soul-love at last in a beautiful city, high on a hill, and yet...

Oh God, it hurt me to say it but why hadn't my finding Treeface made everything better? If one's soul-love didn't make it all alright then there was no hope...no hope in life at all! And what sense was there in anything when I had gained a soul-love but lost a beloved soul-friend? What point or purpose in that? And then there were the constant spirit-entities, and the lost souls that flocked to us both in our home,and the discipline of psychic maintainance al the time, just because of what we were, inside...Oh, it was unbearable, all of it!)

Yes, I was in despair, for sure, and so the song went on and on, round and round,

'...*Stevie is Nothing and Nothing is King*!'

Indeed, I was still singing it when I left the Centre that night. Stevie had left just after three, slinking off into the misty afternoon to the sound of applause for his contribution to the afternoon's singing session. He put on his grey jacket and had wound his burgundy scary around his neck and I had noticed the slight wave to his short brown hair and the darkness of the brows and lashes which made the eyes seem bluer. I imagined, not for the first time, but probably for the last, resting my head in my hands and watching him from across a candlelit table as he entertained me with his endless banter.

(*How did I ever imagine this reticent, sullen man for all his nice accent could become a witty raconteur when outside the Centre? Was it me who was mad, after all?*)

Stevie may have looked beautiful and, to all intents and purposes, seemed composed, but I had seen the doctors recommendation on the confidential Centre entry forms. He was a fully paid-up member of the Centre and you didn't get to be that for being completely well and happy! Even if the reasons were only that no one understood you and your latent psychic gifts they still had to have some 'evidence' against you...

(*like the fact I believed I had killed Robert*)

...they didn't just write you off as a 'nut-job' for looking surly.

Part of me, the dumb, smashed-up human part, insisted on seeing himas self-possessed, fabulously amusing, sparklingly intelligent...and willing to let me help him somehow. The fact that if he were so perfectly together that he wouldn't have needed my help seemed to have entirely escaped me but then even if I had seen this fact I would have convinced myself that only I could understand him! Maybe I thought he needed help to get people to recognise he wasn't ill, rather instead he was really healthy and mentally on top form? Yes, I must have reckoned that he was just seriously misunderstood, as I had been, and now

I alone could help change things for him.

But another part of me, the Fey part, my eternal wise self, always knew the truth of that situation and that was the bit of me that should take responsibility for what he did to me. It wasn't all his fault, it really wasn't. I had inadvertently *bewitched* him.

I had made him crazy about me.

Very crazy, indeed.

'*Be careful what you wish for, Faery child!*' Alicia would have said, but she had been stripped away from me, like everything seemed to be that I loved or valued in my life, laying me bare.

The Centre shut at five and by five thirty Tanya and I had cleaned up the mess of cigarette butts and burned plastic cups, discarded newspapers and sweet wrappers and had locked the doors of the part of the larger office building which served as the charity's daily meeting place. Tanya was waiting round the corner for her husband to pick her up and I knew it was time for me to go back home while I still had one that I could recognise as such. Time for me to go home and face music of a very different kind.

So, I was still singing when I turned to walk along the back route to the flat from the centre of town. I sang other songs too, about the rain-washed rosehips I saw glistening darkly in the hedgerows as I left the town behind and headed out towards the canal path

'Buckleberry, hedge-pedge, fruit of wilder roses,
Brimble-bloom, bramble-boon, hedge speaks of pixie's noses,
Cat-whin on the hip-tree, you haws with bright red lips,
Heddy-grinnel, nippernail, sweet pixie pips!'

I would have tried anything, sung anything, to block out all thoughts of Treeface's expression when I got in. Would I feign happiness or weep all over again? Oh God!

So I stepped onto the path that ran down by the canal still singing. And I reached the empty bridge, walking slowly in the semi-darkness.

It may have been before six, or at least that's what I said in the police report.

And there was Stevie, as if by magic and indeed, it *was* by magic, for whether I acknowledged it (or worked with it) or not I was a *seer* and I had unwittingly enchanted this man, this very sick man, by my relentless focusing. The repetitive use of my little song, the supposedly harmless 'Stevie mantra' had been the end of it, a magical chant par excellence to focus my will on him even more. And for what purpose?

For us to meet, for me to help him! All else had been unclear after that.

And so it was as he leapt out of the shadows under the bridge. We met.

"Who are you?" he asked. His blue eyes were dull and his fingers clenched into claws. "Why do I want to do...this?"

Was he talking to me? He had been crouching, hunched over in the shadows before he sprang into my path. How had he known that I would walk back that way that night? I never usually did; I had just wanted to waste a bit more time before going home and facing the reality of my life...my life without Alicia and with a man who would never love me enough to champion me, or so it seemed. Had my psychic pull been so strong on him, so magnetic, that he had just gotten drawn there?

Yes it had.

Later, in the shadows, they found a small bouquet of flowers. He had not written on the accompanying florist's card but I assumed they were bought for me in his complete bewildered state. A bunch of flowers bought when the man had been clueless, to all intents and purposes, as to why he needed to buy them at all. He just had to.

Looking at him as he stood there in front of me, devoid of all reason, beyond reasoning perhaps, I suddenly understood that mental illness, like being a real witch or *seer*, isn't 'glamorous' at all. No, it isn't artistic or dramatic or exciting. It isn't something to play at. You were either ill or you weren't. You were a witch, born so, or not. He was a sick man and I was a witch, of sorts; a very foolish *seer* indeed. So we did have something in common after all; we were both authentic outcasts, both misunderstood by society and by ourselves. And neither of us were ever going to sit at a restaurant table and recite poetry or share a coffee in a well appointed flat in Bath. Yet even our being outlawed from the 'normal' world of humanity, from 'straight' society, was not enough to unite us...no, not even a little.

He didn't really hurt me although I thought he might do, at the time. What was in his clenched hand? That was what bothered me. I didn't want to run because I, like all the do-gooding people who I had once so despised at the Centre, thought I could still help him, still talk him out of it. But these circumstances were different to any other 'psychotic episode', for how could I effectively disarm what I had only just primed so completely? I almost had to let the attack take its course in slow motion, playing out before my eyes in stuttering, crackling black and white. A silent movie.

I didn't even know what he had put on me until later, down at the police station.

He only had a pen in his hands ...

(*A pen! Thank God, or rather thank my guides, thank Alicia and everyone in spirit that I had temporarily abandoned!*)

...but he pressed hard. He wrote badly and with exaggerated precision for all his supposed education. He pressed hard enough to break the skin. And I lay dead still, my face shining like a moon-flame to the mindless moth of his own charmed will, while he finally, deliberately made his mark.

Red pen, a bit of blood, it looked worse than it was.

"Hexy hex," he muttered over me as he held me with his left hand by the throat, the right hand carving each letter slowly. "Sixty, sexty hex's. Six. Mmm. Umm."

'*He's mad!*' My own mind had screamed it at me, at last. Had I really only just realised? Wake up and smell the roses Lian...or at least smell the dogshit under the bridge and hear the dirty canal water lapping the bank greedily and taste the horrible mettalic tang of blood and fear. Yes!

A bit of me watched, detached and oddly curious, as the grotesque drama unfolded, and the floating Fey bit of my self chided me for being such a stupid, stupid human little girl.

And then...

How had I gotten onto the floor? Did we fall? He had strong hands and a vice like grip and his burgundy scarf flapped in my face and smelled of musty rooms. A drip of his spittle fell onto my cheek as he concentrated somewhere above me.

All my clothes remained intact. There was no other damage done. He did what he needed to do to express what had built up in him.

You see, everything is energies, I simply passed mine on. How blatantly irresponsible! So I won't blame him even though I had to name him.

('*Yes, it was him, Officer, it was Stevie Clements of Flat Two B, Sixteen Berryhill...*'

'*Another stay in hospital for you then, young Stevie!*')

And I won't blame myself too much because I was distressed at the time I enchanted him. I won't hate him, or myself, I'll just take some responsibility for both of our actions, albeit belatedly. Maybe the only things to blame are those damn entities, the *nasties,* flapping round us all, made of human hurting, human ill-wishes and whims, waiting to act as vampires on our energy, to turn us to bad choices, to drink our doubt and magnify it a thousand fold for us. Damn them! And damn my refusal to deal with them promptly, every day of my life.

For that is what *seers* have to do.

How long had it taken for the man walking his Golden Retriever to spot me lying there on the edge of a dream, in the muddiest, most hidden part of that canal path route out from town? Ten minutes? How long did it take for a man to smoke a cigarette? Stevie had done that first, you see, before he kind of stumbled off, mumbling.

'*Why do I always attract men who are unstable, unhappy?*' I wondered as I lay there staring up at the white painted bridge. I lay and thought thoughts which I can no longer remember with a generous abandon as my forehead pulsed and throbbed sickeningly. And then the man with the dog asked me,

"'Ere love, are you alright?"

I saw a gentleman of about seventy, muffled up against the cold and damp, peering down at me as I lay prone and in pain. I smiled up at him crookedly.

"Probably not!" is all I can remember of our exchange.

Then, after a while there was a very bright light and horrible strong tea with lots of sugar but no love in it, in a white plastic cup, just like ones I had so recently been clearing up from the Centre's tables. There was an ambulance and, later, a police station, the first one I had ever been in. And there was me, feeling sick and somehow ashamed all at once, while mediacl staff, then police, milled about and phones rang. I was asked, between them having to deal with a hundred other more pressing things, who had etched the word 'WITCH' into my forehead? They took all of my scanty details, nodding all the while, and I wanted to tell them all about it...about the fact that the address I gave them would soon no longer be mine and the man I told them was my 'next of kin' was not my husband and that the circumstances of the attack were all mixed up in my own projections and fantasies and that I missed alicia and felt so very bad about it...but would any of it help?

What was real? Was I qualified to tell them? So I pared things down to the basics; to dry, unemotional facts, easily digestible chunks...to things humans, especially human men, can understand.

And I can remember Treeface's expression of shock and horror and fear as he confronted what had become of his partner. And, more importantly for him, as he confronted authority figures in the shape of police men. Inquisitors in a white room with wooden chairs! I can still see his white, haggard face clearly as he first saw me and feel my renewed shame and guilt that he had to go through something which was the reverse of what had happened to him as a child...him seeing someone attempt to put something on my face rather than him having something wiped off his. More than this, I can remember the police officer's barely disguised look of amazement to see a man with a facial scar of such a blatant variety come to collect a woman who had just had her own face forcibly marked by someone else.

The thoughts I could read from those well meaning but completely baffled, and, in some cases, quite disgruntled police officers were so unwelcome to me. Too familiar, too upsetting...

('*What the hells going on here, she says she was attacked yet in comes this...freak...who's walking round with that on his face! Ironic!*'

'*What's he meant to be, anyway? What a bloody odd pair!*'

'*Whatever she's been up to it's caught up with her then!*')

...and I wished once more that my *seeing* and *knowing* would die back, saving me from this very human pain of being ostracised, disbeleived, mocked and rejected. For one moment I wondered myself if those officers of the law who judged me silently...

(*I could hear them, damn it!*)

...while smiling politely, had been there in Thirteen Twenty Six when a woman was dragged into a barn and raped and beaten and broken...

Returns!

Yes, Alicia, dear one, I know that there are always *returns*!

And, if I have returned, as I truly believe, then I am stronger now and *we* are stronger too, as a society. We do not, on the whole, stand by and watch people tortured and burned anymore, or even condone their being verbally, let alone sexually, abused. We have broadened our minds and our horizons a little by foreign travel and television and films. We no longer subscribe to Roman Catholicicm, *en masse,* nor do we live by its limiations out of unbridled fear. Yet we do still have our own personal xenophobia, deep within us, that makes us all recoil from one that is *other,* and we do this even if we find the notion of ourselves doing it repellent. And there I was, an *other,* in a room full of police who had sworn to protect those who were not *other*, the tax-paying, pension-owning populace of our fair city. I think that the only thing that let me off the hook for not having somehow caused my own crime, as it were, was the fact that the man I had blamed...and I had to blame someone...was already noted as being involved in several confirmed incidents of domestic violence and several unprovoked attacks. He was also an *other,* maybe more so than me.

Stevie Clements was arrested for my assault but ended that night not in a cell but in the local secure unit. Was there much difference? Stevie hadn't gone far, they found him just walking in meaningless loops across the nearby park, out of his head or so it seemed. Poor man! Had my power, my potent, and very real, soul-magic, pushed him over an edge that he had managed, through his own efforts and via medication, to stap back from a little of late? If that is so I will forever carry the guilt, not only for the death of my Robert, and for the lonely demise of my dear friend Alicia, and possibly for the loss of my Mama too, but also for Stevie, who may take years to recover from my influence over his already broken mind.

Stevie had been splintered before I came along but he had been repaired, how ever temporary that repair may have been, and I succeeded in shattering those pieces of him that had been painstakingly fixed togther by nurses and carers. Like tiny fragments of an ancient urn found buried at a round barrow, his mind now lay in meaningless fragments for someone to try and fit together again. And all so I could escape myself!

Well, no more!

Chapter Four

A Hard Road

The morning after the attack my obsession had gone...and so had Treeface's hair. I got up late from my nest of old blankets on the living room floor and padded off to find my absent lover. I could hear him even if I couldn't immediately see him but he was easy enough to find. He had left a trail; a trail of hacked off clumps of smooth nut-brown hair shot through with silver. I picked up one handful, then another, blearily moving towards the small, cold bathroom from where the noise emitted. The flat was filled with a sound that had gone beyond crying into a terrible, almost unbearable, keening wail.

The man who turned to face me was bald; he was an old man, his face contorted in a paroxysm of grief, the tree-lines more clearly defined than ever against a new landscape so suddenly and drastically revealed. He was a man who had let the fear of persecution conquer a love that could have been true, perhaps, in a very different time and place. Whereas I...

I *knew.*

It was late autumn, the season of mists and sighs, and my love stood, shorn of his hair, like a tree who had let go of its last leaves for the sake of the new cold, dark season that was upon us. Swathes and swags of his once collar-length hair had been left where they had fallen, around the sink, all across the bathroom floor...and I walked through them like leaf litter, feeling the soft skeins shift under my bare feet.

He looked naked and afraid, his head only adorned with a few random tufts. To all intents and purposes this was new man, a strange and alien man whose eyes I met.

"I mourn," he all but shrieked.

I knew that.

"You cut me off along with your hair because I now bear a witch-mark? Is it that bad?" I asked him, as calmly as I could, even though I felt like screaming too..

"No! I cut off all ties to the past, to the hurt it caused us both. I honour what happened to you and I shed my hair, as the tree sheds its leaves, for the coming of a new season. We will never suffer the things we have suffered for *who we be* again!"

"You are right, we will not."

"For we will be where no one will ever find us, we shall be free to move from those who would torment us, free to escape any impending capture..." his voice rose still further, a shrill sound. Did he no longer care about disturbing Mrs Evans et al? Apparently not, for we were moving out soon anyway; I knew it to be so. Even in my pain and trauma I had known and when I had returned from the police station last night I had seen the letter, opened and deliberatly placed on the kitchen worksurface, to confirm my *knowing*. I knew what that letter spelled out for us.

Treeface was going.

But was I going too?

"So, you sever all responsibilities to your own eternal self? To your Fey soul and all that it may bring you?" I gestured at the precious hair. I even stopped to pick up a strand.

Oh, even in the aftermath of my own pain he had to make his own gesture of suffering! In my own sadness it was he who'd tried to reclaim the stage and make a declaration! Could he not just be there for me, *just this once*? No, he clearly could not! I looped the soft brown hair around my ring finger, feeling its silky embrace around the bare flesh. Let him sweep his own leaves up! To me he was only Jack Frost now, peering myopically through a starry-leafed veil, spangled with hoarfrost and the sparkling filigree of empty spider webs. He was not Jack-by-the-Hedge for me, no man of the bright Greening, instead he was cold and I was just another lonely sun that could never warm him enough.

I had done with running, with sweeping things under the carpet. I wanted new life, yes, but not at the expense of my own self-esteem, for our kind did not revoke our promises, nor should we no matter what it cost us...or cost 'the me that is Lian Smythe'...personally.

He went on crying, his arms and legs seeming thinner than I remembered them, his face more full of hollows. He looked embittered and battered, already an empty husk of himself who was moving on blindly towards the release of death. Did I know this man? Did I want to? I noted his apparent anguish with an almost clinical detachment and thought only that it was shame he was so overwrought rather than genuinely impassioned. It was a shame. While his real passion lay sleeping, hibernating under the security blanket of his deep seated pain, his mind ruled, steering the leaky, rudderless boat that was his mortal body, tricking it into blind alleys. He was up shit-creek without a paddle and I wanted out of the choked gulley in which we spun, rudderless, directionless, before we both sank without a trace.

I was still frightened, oh yes that had not changed, but for once I was glad that I was always a little bit angry too. At least the fire still burned in me...

(*even if I was still a bit unbalanced, even if I wasn't quite right yet!*)

...and I didn't want any self-indulgent despair, not mine nor his, to put it out.

I was as I was, damn it! And I would become better at being just that. I wasn't about to quit the classroom and spend the rest of my life 'bunking off' the school of life. I may have a belly full of fight, and the urge for flight was still strong within me, but I was alive!

And, from now on, I intended to behave as if I was.

What if Stevie had had a knife instead of a pen? What if his demons, those omnipresent *nasties*, had encouraged him to go a bit further than just carving me up a little? What if my own companion guides weren't so wonderful and the spirits who loved me were not so vigilant in their care of me? Then I may be dead and gone and this day may never have existed for Lian Smythe.

Would I have really wanted that, even in my pain, not to have had this day?

Thank the spirits, I was *alive*!

But my head hurt badly. The skin was broken in many places and it needed tea tree cream rubbing into it again. I put my hand to it and could still feel the indentations where the pen had made its own grooves, turning me into an arcane alabaster sculpture carved with hieroglyphs. But these glyphs on my forehead could be deciphered couldn't they? People would be able to read their message! So, just how bad was it I wondered? Turning from Treeface for a moment I picked up the small wooden backed mirror that I kept on the shelf in lieu of a proper bathroom mirror. That lovely mirror had belonged to a set my mother once had owned; a brush, comb and mirror all with carved and painted wooden handles and backs. It had always reminded me of something a gypsy would have had, with its wild roses climbing across the wood in glorious relief. Now it was mine and as I picked it up I felt, just as I always did, a *frisson* of my lost Mama, a tingling of her which spoke of love and support and infinite patience and care.

(*Are you looking out for me too Mama?*)

I brought the small mirror up to my face and met eyes with the Lian Smythe I saw reflected there. She was crying, just a little. Stevie, in his own delusion, had been right. I was a witch! Now I had a label, a visible marking, to prove it, just as Treeface had his lines to prove he was...

(*or should have been!*)

...a Green Man. The witch-word was there on my brow in scratchy red letters, tattooed into my white flesh. So now, as with everything in life, I had a choice. I could wear these new lines, freshly cut into my human skin, as a curse, something I needed to push my feathery red fringe over, a new burden that would make me shrink from the gazes of passers by...or I could wear my marks with pride. Not an easy choice, granted, but a neccessary one! I was a *seer,* a reincarnated Faery, a *witch*! Whatever you called it it amounted to the same thing, in essence, and I *would* keep the faith of my wild spirit. I would chose life; chose integrity and faith and the Greening! I would be proud of my new birth-lines, etched there by a man who had doen me a favour rather than a disservice. I was born again; once more pain and suffering had pushed me back into the world. Only this time I *knew*! There would be no more kicking and screaming from me, no more protesting that I wanted to go home and not stay here amingst these cruel, stupid humans, for now I had no choice but to own who I was. Yes, it seemed a good day to honour that, taking it on rather than casting it off.

And Treeface, he was right too, it was a good day for him to be rid of anything that would hold him back for his own dream. It was a good day to make or break with past pledges. A good day for things to die, for leaves to fall, for...

I knew not what else to say. I knew was there was work to be done, in the world but I did not know, right then, how I would do it.

I just knew what I would not do.

"I shall not run away from myself, beloved!" I said to the spirit inside the man called Treeface.

A spirit I had loved for so very long.

And I knew that for a time there may be terrible pain, a pain that seemed beyond bearing, but that love...

(*my love*)

...conquered all things, as all things must pass save love and love alone.

I let go of the ring of his nut-brown hair I held and watched it fall to the floor.

When I saw her afterwards I thought my heart would break. She had been branded as effectively as if she were a Jew in Hitler's Germany except this was a kind of branding that would never, ever come off; more akin to the tattooed numbers brutally scribed into forearms than to yellow stars sewn roughly onto coats. Now people would always know her for what she was, or what they thought she was, just as they did with me and just as they had with all those poor innocent Jews. Didn't she know, or accept, how hard it was to be marked permanently? Lian, my lovely, impetuous little *seer*, now had a mark that identified her; a mark that could get her hung, tortured, dismembered, stoned, raped, boiled, burned...

Couldn't it?

They say that such things could not happen any more, not in this day and age, but people are cruel and that does not, *will not*, change.

Oh Lian, my precious Fey-child, what did you do to him to provoke this? How did you enchant him to make him behave so? Beloved, have you been disloyal to me as I have been disloyal to you with thoughts of my own sister? Not sexual thoughts, no, never those, but thoughts of an otherworldly love, a pristine and perfect devotion, that no human can ever match in reality? Did you hold this man, this poor insane man, in as high regard as I did Lydia? For shame on us both! Yet we cannot help it, can we, beloved? For it is the Fey nature in us that calls to that which is beautiful and unsullied an makes us crave the Summerlands with its promise of transcendant bliss. Our soul-nature makes us romantic beyond bearing and often renders us so bitterly disappointed with our intimate human relationships. Yes, we find it easy to fantasise about perfection, you and I, and so very hard to deal with eachothers human mistakes...

Yesterday could have been a good day for us, for me and my fair one, but fate thought otherwise. That morning, when Lian had gone off to the Centre again, no doubt unsuccessfully trying to bury the truth of Alicia's untimely passing in the grief of others, the letter came. It had been a recorded delivery and even as I accepted it from the postman I felt the power it contained. This one letter had the ability to change our lives.

Things, ordinary human things, can act as a pivot on which futures hang. For a moment, between accepting the letter and rejecting it, I too was suspended on the quitet wave of destinies, turned upside down like Odin on Yggdrasil as those futures held in the balance...

'*Handle with care!*' that envelope should have read.

And so inevitably I took the letter, feeling the weight of the probablities it contained even when the postman gave it over so lightly. To him it was another letter in a brown business envelope. To me it was everything, or maybe nothing, who knew. Because of this I sat with it unopened in my lap for an hour, gazing out over the city which I had come to love so well over the years. I would be saddened to leave; each alleyway held a memory, each tree knew my face and I theirs, but now, with Lydia gone and us with a flat that we could barely manage to keep running, a place full of irrate spectres and clinging spirit parasites, it was time to move on. We needed a new start, a chance to live cleanly, in harmony, without ghosts and endless pressing financial worries. It was time to go into the *wild green beyond*, for good and all.

I slit the brown envelope and watched the single sheet fall into my lap. Solicitor's paper, good quality. I picked up my pipe, the one I smoked now only when Lian had gone out (for how could I justify my needless expenditure on tobacco otherwise?) and lighting it I watched the smoke wreathe in its inevitable blue spirals around me. I drew some of its rich, dark cherry-scented essence down deep into me, tasting the coltsfoot I always burned along side my hand-blened 'baccy. I felt my hand on the wooden pipe stem and felt the tree spirit that once dwelled within its grainy folds, acknowledging it's part in my dance of life. And then I stared at the cream sheet again , not wanting to unfold its secrets...at least not yet.

I had known that Jane would do right by me, in the end. She was ever the practical one and with no small measure of kindness in her; how could she have worked at the hospital if this were not the case? One of the things that had originally attracted me to her, besides her ability to appear so damn capable of looking after people, was her compassion for those in need, for the weak like me. No doubt the absence of her feeble, damaged ex-husband and all his woes, fears and foibles had softened her opinion of me and leant a fonder air to her memories. But it wouldn't just have been her feeling remorseful after the harsh send off she gave me. It would also be that she would want to live with Pete, for the sake of their unborn child, and the need would be strong in her, strong as her need for his divorce and their marriage. So she would have to sell our once-home, her house, not least because what man would want to live in the house in which a couple had lived together, ostensibly as man and wife, for so many years? Not macho, salt-of-the-earth Peter I shouldn't think. And probably my maudlin, defeatist air had tainted the house too much for Jane too; who could blame her wanting a new start either? So she would sell the place for sure. And he would be selling his old family home too, obviously, and dividing the proceeds with his beleagured (ex)wife?

I had no rights to Janey's money, I knew that. But lately, I have to admit, I had been using my Fey will-and-wish on her, just a little. With Kefli's help, and on his advice, I had been astrally asking Janey to give me a fair amount of the clear profit she made. Nothing ostentatious or unbalanced, just a gesture that said that our marriage hadn't been the collosal waste of time she had thought it to be, after all. Something to say that what we had shared was probably not all bad, even if it were not that good, and so she wanted to offer me a gesture to say goodbye, good luck and have a nice life, Rory. Because Jane herself considered that she had had very good luck meeting Pete (although I was not so sure, a man who would leave one young family for a woman would no doubt do it again) she would, I knew, feel guilty if she didn't give me *something*. It would be guilt mixed with a sort of superstitious feeling about the success of her new marriage that would make her give me a token gesture, a bit of cash to make me happier in my own future. God, the Devil and all the spirits between knew that she thought I had precious enough chance for either success or happiness as it was. So I had been talking to her, astrally, *psychically* you may say, soul-to-soul, and she had agreed that something would be forthcoming to myself and Lian.

And here it was. How much?

How much was my future happiness worth to you Janey, Janey that was once Reynolds, perhaps soon to be Jancy Lattimer?

How much? Enough to buy Lian and me the tiniest of tiny cottages? A two up, two down affair if we were lucky, which I thought we would be if we went *into the green.* Enough to get us that new start, away from manistream society, away from landlords with their unreasonable regulations and neighbours with unrealisitic expectations?

Enough to take us away from prying eyes?

Into the green, to the wild green beyond!

Yes, enough for sure.

We could leave Bath and follow the wild path to the Greening, thanks to my ex-wife...and to a little bit of will-and-wish which was, after all, the only bonus I had out of being *other*.

I could go down to the solicitor's tomorrow and arrange the payment, Jane's guilty, kindly payoff. Yes! And then I would take Lian for a meal, a really lovely one in a cafe she had always expressed a wish to visit one day, never really thinking we would ever be able to, and then I would tell her!

How happy I thought she would be, how incredibly grateful! I knew how much the spirits here in this tiny, lovely flat were getting her down, and our psychic indiscipline in our home had been a worry for her along with the rent and bills. Well, I could change all that for her in a way that she thought I never could. I did have the power, after all. Oh yes!

We could have a brand new start!

So wrapped up in the dreaming of a new future was I that I never picked up those warning signs from the ether. I smoked and stared out of our windows, gazing beyond the rooftops and steeples into a new beginning, and I missed Kefli's wise, warm voice in my ear, asking me to wake up from the fantasy and go down to the bridge to meet Lian from the Centre. No, I didn't hear him, I didn't hear *anything* in the present as I was gone, flying into a future, fashioning it lovingly from the very air around me. Imagining a world where we could live freely, in peace, with security; using my green-spirited will-and-wish, *envisioning* it to be so! And instead of going to her, as my own soul and my spirit-mentor said I should, I stared through the moment, disregarding the warnings present in the *Now.* It grew dark around me and still I stared, oblivious, drifting on a tide of blissful imaginings. Yes, I stared while all the time, in a reality that was inescapable, my beloved, my foolish Faery lover, my darling one-ness who I so longed to protect and make happy, happier than she or I had ever been before, was being branded.

It was only when the police came knocking that I woke up.

'*Wake up and smell the coffee!*' they always say, those contemporary humans who make 'life-style choices' and shop at Ikea; those who are resolutely 'normal' by design and not in the slightest bit *other.*

Well I woke up and smelled the blood.

And felt the terror all over again.

I wanted the 'old days and the old ways', if they had ever existed, as much as he did, believe me! I wanted the return of the Greening, I was *committed* to it, but the way of the Greening was not a way which required opting out; instead it required hard work from the inside of society, bringing our wisdom, healing and *sight* to those who needed it most...

And who were 'they'? Why, the very people who made up society of course, those trapped in lives they saw as pointless, those with diseases and those who felt unbalanced, those who were the real victims for they lacked the insights that we had to make the changes needed for themselves. It was not our role to go gallivanting off into a perfect sunset, it was ours to get involved by assisting those who were living out of harmony, bringing clarity of vision and healing to them. Our work was to be with those who were slumbering, not with those who had already awoken!

Taking our own selfish route into the distance, leaving some supposed 'them' behind, was not an viable option for he and I, not any longer. We had to help the very folk that were most unhappy and unfulfilled; the 'sleeping ones' who suffered in silence within society's very fabric. The Greening was a process of *becoming* and we, as Star Children who wore human forms, had key roles in that unfolding. We had to encourage people to see them selves as part of a whole again, to understand and work with their own inner spirit, so that they may once again be active contributors with a purpose...be that through organic gardening, weaving with hand-spun fleeces, creative child-care or *seeing*...oh yes, we had to face up to our responsibilities in the *Now* and live by example!

How would running away into relative obscurity serve any purpose but our own? How would our separating the two-leggeds out into 'us' and 'them' bring about the Greening?

If we could not even be at peace with ourselves then how could there ever be peace on Earth? Everything had to start somewhere...*as within, so without!* If we gave into our own fear how could we play our valuable part in the returning of a balanced, peaceful harmonious Earth? If we truly wanted the Greening then we needed to be a representative of what we wished to see reflected in the whole world. If we tried to live outside the community, rejecting it, at war with it almost, then how could we ever hope to walk peacefully between all worlds without judgement or apprehension?

Alicia was gone, and oh how I mourned her, but I was still here, determined to carry on the tradition of the Fey ones, whatever that personally cost me. How else may I honour her memory? Why, hadn't I had my own wake up call to stand strong and proud of my soul-nature? I couldn't run from a message etched into my own forehead, now could I?

All this was running through my mind as Treeface eyed me with incredulity. He looked so strange, so *revealed*, with his badly shorn head and cleanly shaved face. It was so odd that someone who wanted to hide so very badly had done the very thing to himself that would make him stand out even more! His symbolic gesture had potentially difficult repercussions in the world, even if he wore his hat! He looked to me right then like a mad monk of an obscure order who had renounced the world and chosen to meditate on fear all his days, in solitude...solitude excepting me, I supposed. And here he was, staring at me as if *I* was losing *my* grip on reality!

"You'll love it! Outdoors, away from consumerist Britain, out in the sacred landscape..."

"Running away into the countryside rather than working *with* the land, it's not what I want! It's not who I be! Goodness, we can get an allotment here in Bath if we need to live more self-sufficiently! I'm amazed, you who have encouraged me so long and hard to be myself, you who have supported my unique way of being so whole-heatedly, can now ask me to forget my psychic work and concentrate on surviving in a way that is alien to me! It would be laughable me trying to live like my ancestors, or worse, like some former self hundreds of years ago! I've been there and done that! I can't get on and be a *seer* for people if I'm living in the middle of a lonely moor trying to eek a living out of the soil, twenty four/seven! It'll be a job of work for me to just survive day to day, fetching wood, digging, mending, scraping things together...how would I manage that, eh? And if I had to work so hard at just being alive, harder even than here, how on earth would I ever find time to develop my skills as a *seer*?"

"Yes, it is a hard life but it's a good one, it's the best, most wholesome one I have to offer you! We'd soon get into a way of being, we'd get quicker at doing everything..."

"How do you expect me to suddenly learn how to be a totally self-sufficient peasant at the age of twenty nine when all I know is a roof over my head and taps that make water come out and even lights that come on when I flick a switch? I only know how to cope in the Twentieth Century, I only understand, in practical terms, how to get by with the blessings we have in this age! I may remember other lives but I don't remember exactly how to make lace or deliver babies or even make a decent fire!"

Treeface looked at me in disbelief which just goaded me to carry on my spiel.

"And yes, I do think there are blessings in the modern age, the good things that run along side the corruption and the pollution in our society. There was nothing noble about bubonic plague, outrageous tithes or sewage in the streets...or about superstitions or inquisitions either! We have moved on, in some ways, and if we could find ways of living as we do sustainably then all the better!"

"I thought you were against modern society and so-called civilisation because of what it is doing to the Mother Earth?" Treeface looked at me beseechingly. "What about the Greening beloved? We can't re-green the land when we live in a flat, our feet not even touching the land when we walk!"

"The Greening is *symbolic* as well as literal, you know that! It's about changing attitudes, finding balance, coming home to our true spiritual natures and encouraging others to do the same! It's as much about a resurgence of compassion and experiencing a deep connection to all beings as it is about growing good root vegetables! I am *terribly opposed* to the destruction of a planet I pledged to defend and honour, you know I am, and I am completely committed to finding solutions to the mess we are making with our mass-production and use of fossil fuels..."

"So why won't you leave it all behind?"

I sighed in exasperation. We just weren't getting each other! I suddenly felt like we were two trains on parallel tracks, passing in the dead of night, in no danger of colliding but still aware of the other rumbling along in the opposite direction.

"I won't leave it all behind, my love, because I am *a part of it,* born it into it! I have to be responsible and use my gifts where it matters, within the structure, no matter how I dislike it! For all of my life I've used 'their' transport, as you would put it, and drank 'their' water and eaten 'their' pre-packaged food. What's 'theirs' is mine, too, in essence! I've been a part of the system I so dislike and I can't shirk that completely now! I have to work *with* it, no matter how hard I find it, because I still want to bathe in water heated by their electricity and I still want to cook on my gas cooker so that I have more time to do the stuff that matters...communing in the woods with the Tree-Beings, learning how to be a better *seer* through talking with my spirit guides, making my own medicines, reading about what other people are doing and going to meetings so the isolation doesn't bring me down!

I want to have these things so I can do the really important work which needs to come first. And that, as you well know, is changing peoples attitudes and perceptions, as well as my own. That's where the *sight* comes in and I can't give anyone clear spiritual guidance from a ditch knee deep in mud! I need this way of life for now so that I can do what I came here to do, playing my small part in the world so that with my help people wake up, *re-member* and look beyond all this..."

"I can't believe what you are saying! You want to play along with their ways? You've said so many times how you hate living isolated in units, in these little boxes away from the Earth, you know it isn't natural or beneficial! Why can't you do the work from a cottage in Penwith? Why can't you join an alternative community down in Cornwall and help them?"

"Because," I thought for a moment, "well, because I *know*. You'll have to trust me on that just as I trust the *knowing* of it myself. I am needed where there are phones, trains, buses, post offices and so forth so I can be contacted. I know the people that really need my insights are working in shops, in banks, all over the city...don't look at me like that, yes they are! Even if they reject me now, I just know that in the long run I am needed here, in the midst of it. And the sacrifice I make to be of service in the world is living in this way, not in some obscure place out in nature...as much as I may have liked that, once.

If I'd have been meant to be a small holder, or a farmer, or even a dedicated vegetable grower I'd have been born one, in the country! I'm a child of cities, Treeface, and that's a fact! And so, to a lesser degree, are you! How can I possibly learn to be me, a *seer,* and learn to be something I am not at the same time? I'll not be effective at either and then...and then what's the point of being me at all? If you give up on yourself, and hide yourself away, then you may as well be dead!"

Treeface flinched away as if I had slapped him. I knew I had inadvertently hit on a raw nerve. So, he did know, deep down, that he was efectively talking about disappearing from modern society, becoming, to all intents and purposes, null-and-void? If he had been meant to be a land-worker he would have been born one just as if he were meant to be scar-free he would have been! Was he just kidding himself that another life, over six hundred years ago, gave him some sort of right by default to be a country dweller, regardless of his birth circumstances this time around?

I spoke more gently.

"My love, you can't be Julien and the world can't be like *before*, not totally. Can't you see that its dishonouring Treeface and what he was born to do?"

"And what exactly was he born to do, my one-ness, live in fear? Live hand-to-mouth in a hostile city?"

"No! Be the healer you are, Treeface, in the community, proud and strong, healing with words and music as well as with your hands! Be someone that doesn't let the foolish, ignorant words of those who are lost wound you, rather letting any harsh words strengthen your resolve to bring peace and understanding instead! Bringing magic back to people's lives as the beautiful, original Fey bard you truly are! A tree-faced enchanted man with the Fey power of the Greening! Can't you see how wonderful it is, what you are? Oh my love!"

"We could go to Ireland, to Eire, then! There's more space there! The populations smaller, there may still be cheaper cottages and good land and less restrictions..."

"Once again you miss my point!"

"No, I just want us to go somewhere magical, to get...*to get it back!*"

"But you never lost it, there's nothing to look for! It's already here, in potentiality. The real way to bring the magic back to life is to understand *returns*, by *re-membering*. What can be more incredible and beautiful than the fact that nothing dies, everything lives again? We need to share that, in the world, hands-on!"

Suddenly I was aware I was part-channelling the information, a stream of consciousness pouring forth. I let it flow, hoping he wouldn't interrupt me, or it, too much.

"That magic is to be found in a prison cell as well as on the wild and windy moor! There's magic here, magic in modernity, there's enchantment in making that which is dirty and polluting cleaner and more sustainable! And how? Well, it's only by changing peoples attitudes and outlooks that circumstances change! It's people that need a fresh perspective and so *this* is where the magic is needed, *this* is where we have to bring it back to life! It's not the country so much that's in need, despite what the greedy farmers are doing, it's the people in towns and cities that need transformation! Modern life needs us Fey-spirited humans, beloved! There's a balance to be struck between advance and retreat, modern and ancient, traditional and technological and we are the ones to help strike it! It's self-defeating to draw such rigid, straight lines to make judgements like '*new is bad*' and '*traditional is good and pure*.' Just as there is good and bad, in potentiality, in all situations and in all people, so there is in all ways of being, in all possibilities. We simply need to re-balance ourselves and our way of being; there's a pleasing blend to be achieved from every opposite force in creation!

To pretend this human race never became so technologically advanced...whether you agree that it is an advance or not...is to block the truth, to hide from it, and that is against the Way!

Think about it, beloved! Think what a privileged position we have in terms of a linear history! How fortunate we are to live in an age with perspectives on so many eras of human existence! We can digitally reconstruct the faces, dwellings and lives of the ancestors! We can put dates on our oldest artifacts, we can even know what the weather was like in ancient times by looking at ice, soil or rock cores and tree data! We now have the option, given the knowledge available to us, to choose how to adapt all ways that have been in order for them to be made more harmonious! There's much to be said for the past and the present, a fusion of both would be preferable as opposed to the complete denouncing or obliteration of either!

We were born to be a part of this process of *re-membering* ourselves and were meant to bring a regeneration to the Earth by helping to re-integrate all that is holy and good. We can't do that if we stand apart and shun that which is healthy and beneficial in today's technologically advanced world along with that which is damaging!"

I ceased abruptly, my own logic cutting across my spiritual connection. Was I being harsh, trashing his dream? It wasn't mine, that was all I knew. It may have been, once, but now...

"I hate it when you lecture me! You never used to be this dictatorial, or so ..."

"So what, exactly?"

"So...*straight*! I thought you wanted to live outside the rules, that was all! I thought we were alike, you and I? I honestly misunderstood you because I thought you wanted what I did, a return to how it was before the separation...*a return to the old ways.* You're always going on about *returns* but you deny the opportunity to actually return to a way of being that would suit us perfectly! We know what our spirit's need, what they have always needed, in fact! Why can't you just go with that when I offer it to you?"

I felt my anger rise as he rode roughshod over the *Now*, and over the wise words that had been channelled through me, in favour of some romanticised *then* which had long since vanished over some mystical, mythical horizon. Vanished into the Otherworlds, maybe. *But we are alive in this world!* Treeface, this is *Now*! I suddenly felt as if I would defend this certainty to the last, for somewhere...somewhen...I had vowed to do so.

I looked at my man, ready to attack him again. His face, his dear lined face, now so blatantly exposed to me like the sacred puzzle inside an ancient oak as it was cruelly felled with a chainsaw, was a study in genuine anguish. As he sat there, still clutching my blanket to him as if he were naked and protecting his modesty, I felt nothing but sorrow for him. Poor Treeface, I was running down his dream...the one that revolved around a derelict cottage and a bit of land in remote Cornwall.

The one that was all about running away.

The one he had been a hundred percent sure I'd leap at, in delight.

God, being a *seer* could be a terrible thing! Sometimes it would have been nice to remain in blissful ignorance about what my man was planning, what he wanted so badly. It would have been nice to have remained oblivious about what he felt about his sister, those feelings that had sparked my insane jealous rage, or about how horrified he was at my own drastic facial scarring. But when I laid my hands on his soft skin, when we were both open and vulnerable to each others energies in moments of love-making or rare closeness, I felt what he felt, I saw the pictures in his mind that he saw.

And I did not like them, not one bit.

I had known about Janey's money for some time; I had known his witching secret, his desire to will-and-wish her, and felt very guilty about it. But what could I do? I *saw* and I *knew*. I was as I was, damn it, and so was he!

"Okay..." I said, trying to deep-breath myself into a state of calm clarity, "Treeface, buying a derelict cottage with Jane's money would be akin to me wanting to find the reincarnation of my torturers or executioners in this life, just in order to have my revenge on them! It'd be as futile...because its *gone*! That time has passed, beloved. The only reason I recalled the incident at Avignon was so that I would understand where the fear came from and know why I yearned for you so."

"You don't understand! I want to make things..."

"Right?" I interrupted.

"No, you're wrong! I want to make things *good* again, to re-weave *what was* into *what is* and to carry it on because I think that what were doing was curtailed by bullies, thieves who stole our lives...and Alicia's...and that now fate, and Jane, have given us the chance to do what we would have done. To live together in isolation as healer and *seer*! To be a part of the land's cycles and have a deep relationship with its wild spirits! I can't make right what was but I can make good what is..."

"So you've already said," I commented dryly. "I just can't agree or see it that way."

To me it seemed like a very hollow game indeed. Pick up where we left off a good few hundred years ago? Why? For what reason? Should we start wearing dirty cloaks and not wash too often while we were about it? Oh sure, I hadn't liked being Lian much before I had understood her unique gifts but surely now I understood who I was, and what I could do in the world, then I would be dishonouring Lian's chance at a full and rounded incarnation, whatever that may entail, if I were to carry on by walking Marguerite's old road?

Treeface's frustration and disappointment was palpable. It hung between us like a curtain of chilly fog, reducing our visibility to the ends of our noses. Oh, what was wrong with our relationship and our way of relating? It was a roller-coaster ride of extremes, one minute expressing profound love and the next experiencing raging tempers and cold withdrawals. It was a tempestuous thing, our connection, one that see-sawed dramatically. Even in the course of one conversation, one interaction, it swung between grief and strife, deep love and seeming indifference. Were we so out of balance? Did we need to find harmony, as he suggested, but removing ourselves from everything and everyone we deemed as a threat or harmful?

If we did then it was hardly a strong, enduring love, rather one that could not cope with real life as opposed to a beautiful, altogether convincingly rendered oil painting of a by-gone age.

A question came to me, one of the hardest I have ever posed to myself.

'*Are soul mates meant to be together, in the world? Can it last or is it but a brief 'touching base' with that which is most dear, a glimpse of 'home and hope' to keep us going for the rest of that incarnation? Do soul-mate relationships falter because we expect the bliss that we experience in spirit, between incarnations, to translate into the Earthly existence and it never can?*'

I had never thought of it that way before. I had struggled with understanding why our connection in the world, our physical being together, hadn't made everything right and perfect. I had never considered, not for one moment, that soul-partnerships weren't meant to last, nor were they able to make things glorious and glowing in an incarnation. They were, like everything in these lives of ours, tools for growth. They were part of what affected us most deeply and so gave us the most profound opportunities to change and to move on in our understanding, in our *becoming*.

And if that were so, this stark supposition, what were its implications for he and I in the long run?

"Can't you just agree to try it with me? What have you got to lose? I have this money coming, we have it coming ..." Treeface was totally perplexed.

"It's nothing to do with me, I'm not your wife!" I could never resist the opportunity to remind him, I just couldn't let that one lie.

('*Serves him right,*' some petty bit of my shrieked, '*for being so presumptuous of what I want or need when he doesn't even want me, not properly...*')

"That's not fair! You're my *partner*! A partner is equal and respected and, yes, loved all there is! How many times must I reassure you of my love and commitment?" Treeface looked aghast that I could mention that old chestnut again.

"And, Treeface, what I have to lose is Lian Smythe's life! If I agree to follow you then I am opting for Marguerite's over hers!"

" It's our money to use as we please, a one-off gift. Why can't you accept that? And I want you, as Lian, to come with me, not Marguerite! I want to do what's best for you, for your soul-nature! And with what little money I will get from Jane, for it surely isn't a lot in today's world, I want to get the most suitable thing. It'll not buy us a fine house, her paltry fifteen thousand pounds, but it'll get us a shell, something we can build on! It'll give us the perfect kind of home for two wild spirits but it'll not give us a chance to own fabulous bricks and mortar in a city because it's not enough! Think of the wonderful challenge it will be to put a home togther from the basics. Imagine how rewarding it will be to interact with a place like that! Who said that doing that, working with the land and the local area, isn't a huge part of the Greening, beloved? Who?"

I did not answer. I could not! I didn't know. Suddenly all the events of the last two days had caught up with me and I felt so defeated; exhausted! But Treeface didn't seem to notice my sudden sagging.

"Besides, why should we buy into *their* society, into *their* property market, getting involved in high rents and draining mortgages and ridiculous notions about 'property ladders', when we can get out of the rat-race altogether and own our own space outright, for good and all?"

How could he still see people as 'us' and 'them'? Hadn't a belief and experience of re-incarnation shown him that we can be, or could be, anyone if that guise taught us what we needed to know? The were different soul-types in many different kinds of body but only one Source for all. To make divisions like 'us' and 'them', as if 'they' were evil and altogether wrong, seemed petty and reactionary. Wasn't that what started wars...a belief that we were pure and noble while some 'other', some 'they', was nasty and rotten...

Wasn't that how we, the Fey-souled, got branded *other*, and persecuted, in the first place?

Wasn't that sort of 'black-and-white' thinking responsible for the Nazis killing six million Jews? And many, many true gypsies, *seers* and radicals?

I got even more cross. Us and them? Why perpetuate such needless divisions? And this from a pacifist! Yet I knew him as a good man, an honourable and kind man. I took a deep breath.

"Perhaps you should look at this?" I crawled across the room to the free newspaper we got delivered every Thursday. I had left it by the door so we could recycle it when we went out into town and I grabbed it in my haste to put my own thoughts across. I rifled urgently though it to the back and pointed at the property section.

"Look! I can see one, two...three...places that we could at least look at within a twenty mile radius of this city! Yes, they're asking twenty thousand but you never have to pay the asking price! We could haggle, or whatever it's called. You'd be good at that! We can compromise and live in a run down place but nearer to big towns and major cities and *people* than Penwith! Maybe we could even borrow a bit to top up Jane's contribution..."

"Oh Lian! We can't afford proper houses!" Treeface squinted at the pages I held in front of his face. "Those are...horrible...anyway!"

I looked at the properties under twenty five thousand pounds. Yes, they weren't exactly 'roses around the door' type dwellings, there was a 're-possession' on an housing estate way outside Bath and a derelict shell of a cottage in a disreputable town up for auction. I also saw a mobile home for sale on a secure residential site which we could have easily afforded with Jane's 'donation'. If he wanted to move then we could do it that way, having the benefit of town and the 'good life' with a garden we could cultivate. And, more to the point, why did we have to move at all? Couldn't we just live more comfortably with our savings behind us and stay in our lovely flat, spending time on psychically cleansing it, and ourselves, properly?

"We could focus on getting more money to add to Jane's?" I suggested. "If visualisation and meditation works when I focus on a us finding a cheap new rug or a flowerpot then I imagine it'll work if we really needed the money for a home! We could share a dream rather than me running off after yours!" I said, with a brightness I did not feel. I was adamant that I would make some sort of point about the benefits of staying in a regular house or flat. I continued, sounding as optimistic as I could."We have work to do in the world, you know that as well as me, and for that we need a stable place to eat, sleep and to work from. Psychic work needs a established backdrop, not some where neither of us really know. I mean, you only know Penwith from your childhood visits..."

"And a holiday when I was seventeen, that was the one that made a difference!"

"Yes, but you have no idea of the dynamics of really living there! You don't know the attidues of the locals, or what its like in winter, or how it is surviving the weather conditions! We could move and be ostracised as 'incomers', having lives that are still filled with insecurity! I can't do my best work under the threat of always being unwelcome!

Oh, can't we just find a nice place with running water and sound walls...things I'm used to...so I can do my spiritual work, like you want me to? I can be a good *seer*, you know that! Think of all the good I can do, all the people I can help! And if I help them then it passes on and I will contribute to the All in an active, positive way! I can't do that if we run away, Treeface! I need a known home to work from! Can't we find a bit of land locally if you want to get into self-sufficiency, can't we live cheaply near here and grow our own stuff too? It's the first time in my life that I have felt at all settled and I am not ready to abandon that yet...not because of my scarring, not because of the spirit presences, not because of anything! *I like it here!* I love being with you and

I love Bath, too! And what about your storytelling in schools? Surely you don't want to let all we have built up to slip away? It'd be such a waste to give up on that now, it brings so much joy and understanding to the children."

"Ah, but what better home for *seeing* than the old cottage? There's been village wisewomen for generations! Look at Alicia!"

"Yes, but I would never have found her if she had been stuck out on a moor somewhere like a hermit!"

I blanched but he continued, desperate as he was to convince me.

" That's as maybe but people *will* come in droves no matter where you are if you put out your will-and-wish; it'll be very appealing to them, the little house on the bleak wild moor! And what more appropriate an existence for a fiddler and bard than a rickety castle made of local stone! And our clients, our visitors, can come and go and leave us in peace, away from harmful 'people-ish' energies, out *in the green*!"

Oh God! He obviously saw the whole thing in such a rosy glow that he imagined that people would be drawn to us rather than it being a two way exchange of us making ourselves available to the widest possible clientele.

"I am as I am, a city-dwelling, Twentieth Century woman! I can't just suddenly start living like someone who grew up in a wood or on the road when I've lived all my life in houses, in cities. I'm nearly thirty! I wouldn't know where to begin, making fires, drawing water from a well, living by candlelight alone and bathing like my gran probably did, in a tin bath! Can't you see I'm not the wisewoman you want me to be? I am a *seer* woman from near Manchester who doesn't understand the country, not really. I love it but I don't *know* it, in my blood and bones!"

"You could learn!"

It was true, of course I could learn! Yet for every thing he could say to me I could have a sharp retort. I just *knew* that this course of action was not the right one!

"I haven't been given your freedoms in this life, Treeface, I just don't have that back-up knowledge about trees and horses and...well, you *know* my life story! It's been limited and isolating, frustrating and solitary; it's been set on an urban stage, it's been the very opposite of what you now want me to be...some wild hedgerow angel like the mythical Meggy! I can't be that wild woodling woman, not ever, at least not in this life. Can I? Look, maybe we'll 'book in' for that next time around, eh? As much as it might appeal to me I can't just become a toiling peasant any more than I can become a brilliant mathematician, virtually over night! And, oh yes..."

I saw him flinch back, waiting for my next barb, and I wondered if I was approaching this all wrong? My anger could just sweep me away sometimes, I knew that.

(*Oh Alicia, I feel so on my own even though I knew you are with me, somewhere, somehow. If only you were still around to advise me, face to face, as you were before. What is there for me to do but take a breath and carry on as I think best. Oh, guide me! May I not to be too harsh or too acquiesscent! Give me both wisdom and strength!*)

"And do you really think they'd accept us?" I asked, my voice noticeably less shrill than it had become moments earlier.

"Who?" Treeface looked genuinely puzzled.

"The real Cornish people, the true Kernow folk! That's if there are any left on the moors at all that don't live in ex-council houses in towns; houses with net curtains and satellite dishes like everyone else!"

"Why shouldn't they accept us, they'd know we were like them in spirit! And I could do all the hard graft, the chopping wood the carrying water, until you felt able to help. You love the outdoor life, Lian, you're learning, I mean *re-membering*, all the names of the herbs and flowers round here. You'd take to it in no time and we'd be accepted because we are genuine!"

"Treeface," I said, sweetly, "How would you know where to go?"

"I'll make connections, I'll find out! There are ways! "

I shrugged dismissively then scowled. I could see I was genuinely hurting him but what could I do? I wasn't Marguerite; nor was I Meggy or the marvellous Ana of his childhood visions. No, I was a spikey red-haired woman with a involuntarily 'tattooed' head and a strange face wearing ancient drainpipe jeans and baseball boots, not a folksy woman in a shawl with a wicker basket full of herbs! Couldn't he see that? Was that what he had wanted all along, a middle-class hippy-girl? Someone like Lydia perhaps? If it was I felt insulted and rejected and even angrier. Oh, my stupid temper!

I couldn't go back and live a previous life! I *wouldn't*!

"We don't need to hide now! There is no burning! We don't need to run! We are blessed because we *know* that we have work to do and we have the space to get on and do it. Oh yeah, people insult us occasionally because of who and what we are but so what? We have each other, we have our purpose! *They can't hurt us anymore! It's time to stop running and break the pattern!*"

My final words rang out in the room, surprising us both. It was as if someone else, someone far more authoritative and impressive than I, had spoken. The voice that I spoke in after that outburst was not nearly so awe-inspiring but I still meant every word.

"And you, have you broken your cycle, your pattern?" Treeface asked me, quietly.

"I hope so! I want to! I may not be up to the job yet but at least I recognise the pattern and want to change it even if I haven't quite got the ability to achieve it yet! Believe me, I have no desire to lock myself in to a never-ending set of soul-dramas! We have been part of the *forgetting* for so long, isn't it time we fully *re-membered* and woke up to ourselves, for good and all, *no going back*?"

"And why would we be continuing a pattern if we seize the opportunity to have happiness as Julien and Marguerite never did? Surely that is breaking the cycle of misery and tragedy by us actively talking the role we want rather than our being forced to do things against our will?" Treeface looked me in the eye and I held his gaze.

"Yes, but it's still feels like running away, only society at large is now the enemy rather than the Pope or his minions! Julien and Marguerite may not have had things to do in the world but we...*our spirits*...have moved on since then. There's work to do, here, *Now*...as us! Life, incarnation, isn't an escape...it's our *work*! We don't need to be 'the victim' or 'the one who opts out' anymore! We can confine our escapism to our stories and songs, to our entertainments. We can choose to get on with the job of *becoming* in this reality 'cos, to all intents and purposes, its the only one we've got and it's a damn shame to waste it!"

Treeface rubbed his exposed face where his lovely moustache had been and could have screamed. Here we were arguing pointlessly about a tiny sum of money when we should have been thinking about, and processing the pain of, the last forty eight hours...most notably my incident with Stevie and my new 'tattoo' and Treeface's self-inflicted baldness. Instead he distractedly picked up his empty tea cup and put it down again and I glowered at him. It was getting dark outside, a bad sign. The flat still became strange and hostile after dark, thanks in the main to our continued psychic indiscipline.

"You'll not even give it a go then?" he asked finally.

I knew that for all my hopefully eloquent speeches, for all my impassioned protestations, he was still genuinely surprised. I realised that in his enthusiasm for re-discovering our basic, earthy past that he had not picked up my own feelings at all. I couldn't help but melt a little, at his pathetic downcast dejected look. I loved him, didn't I?

"What you do with the money isn't my business, I know... but...well, couldn't we at least look at some houses here?"

The tugging of the ghost of his facial hair went on and there was a silence.

"We could look, I suppose...but only after we go down to Penwith and look there first. Please Lian? I can ask Matt to take us, I know he's back in town. You'd like him, he's...fun. And you'll love Penwith, I promise you that. For a wild soul its a fine place, a fine home..."

Treeface trailed off and I sighed heavily. I felt so tired again! I would conceed this one thing to him, yes.

"Ok, I'll come but only to look, out of curiosity. It'll be nice to get away. I'll treat it as a break and no more than that."

"But there'll be no joy in it for you?"

"None," I looked up at him in the half-light, our gazes as ever locking, making something shift in the pit of my stomach, touching me deeply.

"This is a partnership beloved," he sighed, "so then, yes, in truth we should both look at each others suggestions. It's just...well, I thought..."

"You thought I'd want to live in a derelict pile on the moor with you? No questions asked...hurrah and off we go?"

"Yes, I did," he said simply, his eyes shining with unshed tears.

"But I'm not Marguerite!" I cried.

"And I'm not Julien," he said quietly.

We could have held hands then, placed one hand over the other as the light faded and the evening was upon us, but neither of us moved.

"Why is it so hard?" I asked, at length.

"Our being together?"

"Yes, why do we seem to find it hard, as soul-mates, in the world.? I thought it'd be so different this time, didn't you? I thought everything would become clear, become *easy*, once we found each other..."

"You thought it'd be okay? Perfect, even?"

"I did, I really did!"

"Maybe we should meditate on that question?"

"Maybe, but no now, eh? It's dark enough for...*them*...to be active."

"Is that an excuse or a real reason?"

"It's real! I can't afford to open up to them when *they're* at their most virulent; we'll have more of *them* on us before we know it. I can't turn down my astral light, can I? I'll be ineffective and then we'll get no answers anyway."

"Tomorrow I can phone round estate agents down there?" he asked.

"Tomorrow, for sure," I replied, feeling washed out and hung up to dry. Surely I should be having a restful time after my ordeal with stevie? Surely I should be being looked after and indulged? Yet I believed, I *knew*, that my attack was partly my fault and so even if Treeface had wanted to lavish care and love on me all day I would have felt deeply uncomfortable. I sighed again.

What we would do, or say, now after such a heated debate, one that revealed the wideness of the cavern that had somehow opened up between us?

I said nothing, for I was wilting by the second. Yet, as ever in times of greatest stress,Treeface relied heavily on the simplest tasks.

"More tea, then?"

"More tea, yes...thank you," I said, courteously, as if to a stranger.

I nearly added '*with lots of love in it*' but it seemed inappropriate now.

We didn't sleep much that night, what with our own absorbing thoughts milling about in our minds and the psychic atmosphere of our flat which fluctuated somewhere between mildly uncomfortable and downright hostile. Our flat had simply gone from bad to worse while we two did little to stem the flow of disturbed, disturbing energies. Even using the bathroom between the hours of eight p.m. and eight a.m. had become an exercise that required extensive psychic protection as it was situated down the corridor which seemed to act as a passageway between the realms. That particular night the level of psychic intrusion was predictably high; we were quite stressed personally, to say the least, and so the flat was bound to mirror that in terms of 'paranormal' activity. Typically, the more anxious and upset we got the less we did to combat its intrusions and then we ran the whole gamut of 'haunting' tactics...the slamming doors, the knocking noises, the horrible smells and sudden icy chills, the curtains that blew in a wind that should never have been there and the alarming crashes with no discernible source. I had long since been trained to deal with such eventualities and yet I still failed, as ever, to protect Lian...or myself. I was locked in a cycle; the more distressed I became at my own impotence the more the energies turned wayward and nasty, and the more nasty they became the more distressed I got.

What could be done but move out and start again? Didn't Lian realise that we needed to be away from human interferences and energies? Couldn't she accept that our very soul-nature's demanded we were out in the wilds with as little opportunty for human interaction and, therefore, energetic disturbance as possible? We needed Faery energy, undiluted, pristine green power; the elixir of the uincivilised, untamed South West! Not for us the cities and towns, crammed with dangerous people and raw human-energies! And yet how irresponsible it seemed to run away to the beautiful countryside, leaving the problem for the next tennant to deal with! How disgraceful! I was meant to be a healer and help folk, how could I just run off and hope the next person to live in the flat would be completely insensitive to the dank, repressive energies we had somehow attracted to ourselves? For shame! After all, it was *our* soul-natures, mine and Lian's, that had 'awoken' the rogue spirits and nasty energies in the first place! You know, perhaps I should for once face up to my crippling fear, own who and what I *be,* and sort this problem out; I could make it my priority, maybe even my life's work! But...well,were there were just too many of these rogue spirits here for two people to sort out effectively? Was the work simply a case of 'too much to soon' especially for Lian as a relatively 'new' psychic? It must be prudent to know one's own limitations, surely, and dangerous to be full of false pride about one's skills?

And yet the spirits would never let us experience something we couldn't deal with, would they? They only ever give us what we can handle, don't they?

Gods, I didn't know! How could I know? I needed help!

(*Spirits who love me, spirits who come for my highest good be with me now and guide me, I pray you! What shall we do about this flat, about our lives as spiritwalkers, about moving away? Oh, help me, I beseech you! And in return I vow that wherever we are I will commit myself afresh to acting as a caretaker of the land, working with it, aiding the Greening...by all the trees that ever touched the sky and by all the leaves that ever drank the light so I will! But oh, please help me!*)

And spirits, will I ever be free of my crippling fear? Now I even wear the shaved head of some sort of bizarre penitent to show how low I feel! It was Lian that had been branded and a man, (a handsome, unscarred man?), named Steven who had been the aggressor but it was me, Treeface, who took the blame as ever. I bore the guilt of all Lian's hurting just as I had with my mother, and Lydia. And even Jane. And where did it get me? It made me old before my time, bent and gnarled, turning me ito a parody of a medieval hermit or a particularly worn-down, wind-beaten Tibetan Lama.

Yet I should count my blessings shouldn't I? We all should! I should look at the recumbent form of my flame haired soul-love and smile. And give thanks. Yes!

But even as I did so I felt the cold, insiduous energies of another spiritual intruder slide round me like rancid oil. My smile became a rit-cus and my heart sank, stone-like, in the seemingly endless cavity of my chest. I lay down and stared at the ceiling.

Both of us curled up on the inflatable mattress in our second-hand blankets in relative silence. Although the atmosphere between us was not bad it was distinctly uneasy. Once in our makeshift bed we would usually always visualise a protective 'circle of fire' around ourselves, or our sleeping area, or even the whole room, but even that no longer seemed to have much of a lasting effect. It seemed that some things in the universe were not 'fluffy' and that some certainly had quite the opposite of our best intentions at heart. If it weren't for our trusted and trusty guides coming to our aid time after time then I doubt if we could have kept our nasty, invasive spiritual adversaries beyond our own physical selves. I would pray, or *invoke* as Alicia may have put it, for protection from my companion guides, asking that only those spirits who loved me or who came with my highest good in mind may come near me. It worked, for sure, but there was only ever a stand-off, never a full retreat of that oppressive and somehow coldly *gelatinous* energy that the flat conducted so well.

For all I knew that very flat could have been built on a cemetary, the site of a mass execution or a battleground, anywhere that would explain its seeming unique ability to manifest a flow of 'apparitions'. More likely it had been the latter as such things were prevalent on the outskirts of our city, apparantly. Only a few days previously I had opened the walk-in cupboard in the hallway, thinking I would be safe to do so in broad day light, and found a dis-figured, horrifically wounded soldier apparently standing in it, in full battle dress, replete with a smell of cordite which had been so pungent as to make me gag. That vision had been by far the most graphic although I had become well used to the angry, bitter, confused souls who shared our space and to the strange, scavenger-like entities who preyed on their energies, and, as a consequence, ours.

It couldn't have been just our Feyness and our personal upsets that made such things happn in such abundance, could it? It had to be partly the land's fault and if that were so then if we left it couldn't follow us!

(*And if it was mostly the land's fault then we couldn't be blamed for leaving the next tenant with it...could we?*)

It was way past midnight and as I lay there my mind wandered, picking over facts and fictions, looking for those illusive answers that I knew would be shining brightly under some unturned stone of my memory. I recalled the last time that we had sensed a full-on psychic invasion. Then we had both been on better terms with each other and so more tuned-in to both our own energies and that of 'it', the *nasty* as Lian so endearingly called it. We had decided that the best course of action, on that occasion, had been to get up and had walk all night through the streets of our slumbering city. In other words, we had both agreed to run away from the threat.

It had seemed like a silly adventure at the time because we were in much better spirits ourselves but in reality it had been just another excuse to avoid confronting 'it'. We had walked in pointless circles, part of us loving the unique experience of having Bath 'all to ourselves', *sans t*ourists and shoppers, watching the seagulls periodically rise like more friendly ghosts from the roof tops into the night sky, and part of us resenting our loss of sleep and the inconvenience of having to do something we had not wished to do. But the weather had been warmer then and it had seemed like a novelty, if we looked at it positively, that we were doing something that no none else seemed to be at such an hour of the night. The spirit intrusions had, after all, enabled us to have a one-off experience of a deserted city. That night, with Lian and I feeling so far removed from each other, there was nothing novel about the psychic intrusion, it was simply the last thing that we needed. What we had needed, in fact, was a good nights sleep to make us more amenable to further discussions in the morning. So we both ignored 'it'. And each other.

And who could blame us? It was hard work, our 'gift' of psychic awareness, for just as we thought we had sent one bunch on 'to the rightful place in the universe' then along came another poor wandering spirit in a state of denial or high distress. It was like a never ending queue. It seemed so sad to me, when I was feeling open and compassionate, that so many souls ended their lives in confusion, pain, fear and torment so that they never moved on naturally themselves but remained locked 'in situ' until someone like me, or us, came along. This had to be especially pertinent on the site of a battle and it did indeed seem that our little purpose-built block of flats had been built on an ancient battleground of some kind. Perhaps this would explain why Lian and I were so often locked in battles with eachother without quite knowing why; as if the old wars fought there had infected the very energetic fabric of that area with conflict and suffering? How sad! Yet as ever my other more cynical, less patient, human aspect would then rail against the inconvenience of having all this psychic disruption and my compassion would evaporate. It was humanity's own stupid fault things ended up like this, after all, especially if it were the result of another bloody war! And so I would throw up my hands in a gesture that meant it was just too much and why pick on me to deal with something grim and negative, yet again?

Sometimes the *knowing* was a huge responsibility which meant my fearful, narrow human parts could no longer dominate me and I had to give in to the less gratifying, infinitely less selfish spiritual essence which spoke to me of empathy and patience. Lian could have had a point there, for how could I expect to experience a world in which there was no disruption or warring elements when I too still harboured clashing factions of my self? Wouldn't I just be taking that inner turmoil and disharmony with us wherever we ran to? Maybe my own body was a battlefield of sorts; a portable one that I carried with me?

That night, with all of those questions whizzing round inside my head, I clamped my eyes shut and tried to do the same with my senses, sealing what I could of my energies up in a protective bubble of bright blue impenetrable glass. It was best, as Alicia had taught Lian , to make ones protective bubble or cloak from an organic, free-flowing material that moved and breathed as you did the Earth's own atmosphere and so therefore glass seemed inappropriate. But I could think of nothing else that would be clear and bright yet solid enough to contain my essence as I hopefully, eventually, slept.

I lay there with my brain zipping along at a rate of knots, aware of the woman I loved lying stiff as a board next to me, saying nothing, doing nothing. I was aware only of her shallow breathing. She too was awake but we remained locked in our own isolation, prisoners of confused thoughts and treacherous feelings, sensitive victims of a psychic war that waged all around us. How those invasive spirit-presences resented our life-force! They hated us for our living energies which invaded the dull, turgid world they had made for themselves between realms, in the place where they had died in their last body.

Were they too scared to move on into the Otherworld? I could relate to that! Too angry? Well, Lian could relate to that! Were they too far gone to know who or what they were any more? You know, I think we could both identify with them there.

But I didn't like to ask the spirits what their problem was.

I did not want to *dwell.*

So I turned my mind relentlessly to the issue of soul-mates while the room seemed blacker than it should have been and the sense of being watched grew stronger and the temperature dropped a few degrees below what was reasonable or seasonable. And the woman by my side may as well have been a million miles away than a hair's breadth. Could Lian really be my soul-mate, my spirit's closest kin, if she seemed so distant to me even when I lay by her side? With a horrible irony I realised there and then that I had felt closer to her when she had been unknown to me, when she had been, perhaps, only a fantasy...the red-haired *she* of my imaginings.

(*Oh the Fey addiction to Otherworldly love! And our urge to flee when things got difficult, to flit away on gossamer wings to a place of perfection!*)

....surely I would not wish her to be unkown to me again so that I could exist in that state of perfect yearning?

Within the framework of my pristine protective bubble I did the sensible thing once more and handed the question over to my guiding spirits. I would let their wisdom flow into me. Why not? I'd only be lying there awake, nervous and cold, if I didn't do something to occupy myself. When I spoke to them, my unseen friends, I felt less lonely anyway and I could do with them around me when I felt so vulnerable and at the mercy of Lian's rejection on one hand and intrusive, invasive and thoroughly aggressive forces on the other.

"What are soul-mates?" I asked my spiritual guides inside of myself, breathing as steadily and as deeply as I could manage.

I waited. I breathed more deeply.

"What is the nature of incarnation?" came the reply.

"Is this a riddle?"

"What is the nature of incarnation?" the question remained.

"To *know*, to know *who you be* through experience which leads to growth. To learn in order to...er..."

"You are tired, wired woodling! No questy-quest, now you should rest!" came the familiar voice of Kefli from somewhere deep within me.

"No! I mean, I need to know! And I can't sleep..."

"But this isn't the best time, or space, to get clear answers, now is it?"

My second guide's voice cut in, clear and true.

"No...but..."

"Sleep now! Snoozy woozelings! Too many questings...vexings!"

"In dream-time we give the necessary information. Be at peace."

And I was falling. There was a soft, woolly darkness now that I welcomed and, after a seemingly boundless time, I began to dream.

And in the dream we were in a little covered wagon, she and I, on the winding, endless roads of Ireland, with a big bay pulling our little home to our next camp. Oh the joy of it !

(*Had it been so long since I felt truly warm inside?)*

And then there was the inevitable pain as the scene faded and I lost that vital sense of joyous freedom...

(*Free of fear!*)

...but then almost immediately the feeling was replaced with fresh delight as the scene changed. Such bright colours! Scents and sounds! I was playing the fiddle at a camp with Tatty and Meggy and Ana and I was relaxed, more relaxed than I can ever remember being, and I was laughing and joking with the people around me...

(*could I ever be so at ease with myself and with other people? How marvellous if I could be!*)

...and I turned to share the joke, expecting to see a small, skinny red haired girl sitting behind me but instead I saw a man with a face covered in tattooed branches...

(*I see myself!*)

...and I had no idea...none at all...that I was dreaming,...

(*falling!*)

...and in this reality I was aware of myself being in a kind of floating library, one with no walls, one with many levels. I appeared to be on a high level but there were people below and above me, all reading voraciously and quite unconcerned that I was suspend on a floor above them, seemingly on a level with no stairs up or down. How did I get so high? There were no stairs! And how would I even get down again? I began to feel afraid of the height I had reached. I looked down and saw the top of a man's bald head as he studied a reference book far below me. Perhaps he could help me if I attracted his attention?

But I was distracted by a whimpering sound. I was surprised and amazed to see others crouched down next to me, holding onto the small square of flooring, our section of the floating library. I asked one man why he was there and he replied,

"I am studying the laws of physics, as we understand them, but I am afraid I won't be good enough for the tests! *There's so much to know!*"

Did I know him? He seemed so familiar! I felt simultaneously sorry for him and relieved to have company at this disconcerting level. But it seemed such a shame that he was so unhappy at the situation we had found ourselves in and the overwhelming urge to help and support came upon me. As I becamse aware of this need to give him comfort and aid, the others also turned to me, looking up from their desperate attempts to cling onto the strange floating floor. And...my heart will burst, it will surely not be able to contain all the love!

(*Meggy! Ana! Oh, Tatty! And Kefli! It's you! All wearing different bodies; strange, wonderful human selves, wearing suits and ties and formal skirts! Oh and Alicia, Allette! And Lydia and...little, little Lian, just a child now, holding hands with a freckle faced boy and...oh God...!Our boy, Michael Gabriel, reaching to me across the square of carpet on which we balance...a man with curling hair and wide slanting eyes...*)

Can we help eachother down of should we go higher?

(*Higher!*)

And I am flying over mountains and out to sea, keeping pace with the eagle as it soars and swoops, riding the wind gladly. Tiny droplets of water bead my face as we pass through a low cloud. I feel kissed by moisture like a petal in the first cool dew of morning and then a voice says;

'*We are one and within the One there are many. We are ocean and we are droplets and we are the patterns made by droplets as they flow towards being an ocean again.. We are all expressions of water and we are the water itself. Sometimes we know only ocean, sometimes only the singular isolation of the droplet. Sometimes we collect as puddles, rock pools, clouds and other times we are all waterfalls and all rivers and all seas, unmindful of our singular aspect, merely being, in unison. And sometimes our single droplet splits, so that it may reflect its self back, mirroring the other part of itself. And at other times the droplet remains whole, always seeking to merge with its greater self, yearning for the wholeness, craving to connect with all droplets. You are water, as we are all water, and we all flow like streams into the greater ocean and yet we are that ocean. It is how we flow, and where, and with whom that makes up the dance of droplet to ocean. The sea...see?*'

'*Seeing is believing!*' I answer, seeing a rainbow reaching out from sky to sea to land, embracing each but remaining whole in itself, showing each its potential to be *other*, to be glorious, connecting all in a shower of bright knowing.

And I was awake again, lying next to a starnge, fabulous woman; the droplet who had split apart from me in order to offer me a mirror. She lay on her side, a miracle of precious cells and atoms, facing away from me, snoring very gently. I was so glad she could sleep, my beloved. I hoped she dreamed of oceans teeming with wonderful life. The dawn was coming and Lian slept on.

"Life is for expanding, for pushing boundaries, for climbing higher and stretching yourself...for becoming things you thought you never could be!" I said to my self in jubilation. "Just as a pool of water spilled on a table top will seek its edges, exploring the space that defines it, and then overreaching it, so should I be!"

I *knew*!

"Security stifles growth, wilfully remaining in old, known patterns stop necessary changes! The true soul-mates, our spiritual friends, are those who enable us to undertake life's challenges, hard as they may seem. They are those who spark with us to achieve deeper understanding, new heights of personal achievement, for the good of the All! They are not those who encourage us to opt out or run away, for they are also striving to be the best they can be, not looking for get out clauses! This is true team work. As a Child of the Greening, as a soul incarnate, I have obligations and so I must break the patterns which are too strong and too damaging...my long-term and oh-so comforting bad habits... and step out of the cycle of the past!"

I knew that my companion guides were close by and I let Autumnus, a trusted mentor, speak to me.

"We were discussing choices this night, and choices are never right or wrong, as such. Suffering and separation, the glamour of love thwarted by cruel outsiders, these have become your themes and life-patterns. You have long since been tempted by the chance of having a 'perfect love', a divine bodily experience on Earth, one which is never allowed to become 'ordinary'. That is, you have been looking for that which is purely 'of the spirit' and not tainted by the long-term familiarity, sullied by the world's touch, ruined by cruel folk...and so you opt for it being thwarted by some seemingly loathsome enemy rather than let it turn sour or drab! Oh, how tempting is the romance of the love denied! But how easy! To continue in this pattern is to reject the option of growth by interaction with those who are not like you, in essence, who will not agree with you, who may even oppose you!

How easy it is, dear friend, to run away even though you may make it seem like a terrible chore or a necessary evil! It is but a *choice*! Change the pattern now and you shall be free. Remain so tethered and you shall repeat the model; life will conspire against you if you make the choice to continue with this delusion, just as it has always done. You may deliberately step out from this circle or wilfully keep it so, for it is familiar and safe. Such are the choices given to you at this time. Be aware!

Strain to hear your soul's song above the babble of those who would seek to keep you a-feared...including your human self! And look in your beautiful mirror often and know her as what she is...for *she is you*, dear one. And you, turn and turn about, are her source of reflection. Give her a true, clear vision when she gazes into the scrying bowl of your eyes! And by doing so you will be granted the vision of where you may be, of where you might go, in time, with love. We will never fail you, kin to those of bark and bud and branch, Treeface, so give us your fear! *Let go*! Let us carry you a little way. Leave the baggage with us and get on the train!"

Ah, choices!

"Thank you, my dear, dear mentors," I said.

And I knew, in as much as I ever was alone, that they had gone.

I got up and, for the first time since we had been in that flat together, I made but one mug of tea, I even put some love in it for myself, and then stood quietly watching the sunrise over the city. It was well past the Autumn Equinox now and I noted with sadness how far back around the sun was in the sky from when we had first glimpsed its appearance over the slumbering City of Bath. I was still standing at the window, lost in possibilities and probabilities...watching the tiny figures of strangers start to appear on the roads below, seeing curtains open in houses I would never enter, hearing distant cars staring up to travel who knew where...when Lian woke up.

"Looks like another fine day!" she yawned and stretched. A pale, watery sunlight touched her face, creased from the pillow, made fuzzy with sleep. Oh, the dear, dear girl!

I bent down to kiss her, not expecting her to respond. She didn't much like touching in the morning. I knew how she felt, touching often reminded me of being held down, or somthing similar, and so I had to make a real effort to reach out, even at the best of times.

(*Oh Treeface, can't you let go of it all, all that stuff that weighs so heavily on you, and come to your lover as a free man? She loves you;* she is you! *She loves you all that can be! She just doesn't love all you've brought with you...not any more. And, no, you can't walk with a pocket full of broken stones as your soul shrinks and fades like a forgotten balloon left tethered to a tree after a party. No, not now, not ever again.*)

I didn't want her to see how I felt. And if she noticed she did not say. Only a little surprise showed in those marvellous slanted green-on-grey eyes, so like the eyes of that young man in my dream.

I would not lose her!

"Yes, it's a beautiful day, beloved," I affirmed, walking way from her slender prone form to make her a drink. "We could even go outside to meditate if it stays so clear and bright; it may warm up later by the look of it, and if we wrapped up well..."

I was aware that I should not to push her. Maybe she no longer wanted to meditate on our situation? Maybe she had had her own thoughts and dreams in the night and decided to give me up as a bad lot?

Ah, choices indeed.

I feigned a gaiety I did not feel.

"Anyway, it should be an interesting day! Did you sleep well?"

"Not too bad, after a fashion," she replied. I couldn't tell if she were simply tired and hungover from unrefreshing sleep or if she were sullen. Or worse, indifferent.

So I just nodded and went off into the kitchen clutching my own empty mug.

I knew she was surprised to see me up and about and almost cheerful. I was he who had shaved his head and face in howling grief at seeing her so defiled with....*that word;* he who had advocated running away like a rabbit from a fox. Yes, I was he that was weak and cowardly and damaged, ravaged by the experience of life to the point of being useless. Was she wondering what had happened to my doom and gloom, to my dread and my dread-full anxiety?

But, as was her way sometimes it seemed, she said nothing.

If I were a tiny rivulet at that moment, bubbling up, keen to become a fast flowing tributary, or maybe a stream, she was deep, dark water.

She was still, unfathomable and holding no reflections that I could see. But I would not give up looking, I would simply look harder.

"Humph! Well, I could have told you, another shit-hole! May as well have spent that hour in the pub. Waste of time, wild goose chase after nothing but a stringy, tough old bird....*ha!*"

Matt was talking loudly.

It seemed that he always had something to say which had to override both me and his older, wiser friend. He punctuated most of his sentences with curt little '*ha!*'s. He reminded me, standing in the driving rain and wind in that strange little Cornish village, of some bluff old pirate who had tried to turn himself into a debonair man about town but could never quite stop his blunt edges from showing through. If I was being even more fanciful about him I would say that Matthew Jordan-Mailer was a man who had lead a wild, hard life, a rum sort who now needed to drink to forget all the amazing, yet terrifying, things that he had seen. Maybe he had been lost at sea, maybe seen dreadful things in some mythical war...

God, I was always so full of escapist, romantic drivel when I was upset! I would rather think of some fictitious plot for Matt's life than focus on the reality of that dreary day, a day that may already had an inevitable conclusion even though it was only early afternoon.

Matt was easy to fantasise about, easier than Stevie had ever been. He purposely cultivated a witty, charming air and presented himself as a devil-may-care man with a hint of mystery and danger lurking somewhere in his past...or perhaps even his present. He was both an open and closed book; some subjects you couldn't shut him up about while others, like the topics of his family or his feelings, were strictly taboo. I could see through his cultivated persona (both psychically and as a cynical woman) to his more insecure and blustering core yet I could also quite easily go along with his loveable renegade act just as his more gullible, less affable, friend did. When Matt spoke, Treeface listened to him as if he was about to impart some gem of wisdom he himself could have never quite fathomed. He clearly idolised his infinitely more casual, and seemingly care-free friend, which had probably been a part of Treeface's problem all along.

I looked at my lover, standing slightly bent and cowed, and the tree-trunk sturdiness of Matt.Talk about chalk and cheese! How could Treeface have ever matched up to his parents high expectations, especially as he had been born at a disadvantage anyway, when this ebullient, golden boy had been around as a childhood companion? I bet Vic Reynolds had loved Matt and coverted him, not so secretly, as his own progeny, even as Matt's own father found him lacking. How large their respective fathers, both misogynistic bullies, must have loomed in their lives! I guessed that Matt was Treeface's only long standing pal because Matt didn't mention, let alone notice, it seemed, Treeface's scars and *differences.* In fact, Matt hadn't even commented on Treeface's new and drastic scalping, unless you could count a cursory up-and-down glance and a resounding 'humph!'.And, in turn, Treeface did not remind Matt of the horrors of his own youth under the domination of Colonel Anthony Jordan-Mailer. Nor did he comment on his friend's apparant alcoholism.

To say I found Matt attractive would have been an incredible overstatement. He was tall and lightly tanned and his damp, wind-tossed golden curls framed his large, open face. He did indeed look as if he could have spent his life so far out at sea, only perhaps on yachts rather than fishing boats or galleons. He was broad shouldered and strong armed with only the first hints of a beer belly and a slight suggestion of a double chin to mar his otherwise impressive physique. He wasn't my type at all, was he? '*Too cut and dried altogether, not enough magic in him at all,*' I reasoned with myself as I found my gaze wandering over his resolutely stout body. Yet I found the notion of being protected by this strapping man oddly appealling. How could it not be when all along I had been faced with my lover's fearful avoidance of an active guardian's role? Maybe such a need for a protector was inescapable as a woman, especially in one as prone to persecution and bullying as myself. But I could protect myself couldn't I? Damn it, I could! And I could stop my pointless day-dreaming about this broad-beam of a man right now, too! Why, he didn't even believe in enchantment!

'If I can't hit it with a hammer, I'm not interested. *Ha!*' was one of Matt's favourite retorts to any attempt by Treeface or myself to discussing the spiritual aspects of life. He could be curt and dismissive but when he had a few drinks inside him (which was, to be fair, all of the time) he could also be more engaging and genuinely funny than any man I had thus far come across. And he was just a bit nearer my age than Treeface...oh God, was I actually comparing the two long-term pals for my own purposes? It was so hard to resist doing so though, Matt dominated the space around him and although Treeface was undoubtedly the more articulate and sensitive of the two men, next to his vivacious, gregarious friend he appeared weak and indolent. Both in terms of what he did and what he had to say for himself in Matt's company, Treeface came over as the lesser man of the two.

(*But he isn't! Treeface isn't weaker or lesser than anyone! He is of Faery, his energies are more subtle than the blunted human-kind! How can I think otherwise, looking at the human-kind more favourably, blinding myself to true enchantment by looking at the surface only? Accch!*)

I caught a hold of myself once and for all, in complete disgust for my thinking such disloyal, unfair thoughts. How could I make such a judgement concerning who was the more attractive, the man I loved or his own long-standing pal? I had to admit that I had definetely viewing Treeface unfavourably against this tousle-haired man, asking myself why the Reynolds ability to be forceful and forthright (as well as the less desirable attributes of being cutting and crude) had somehow by-passed my own lover and landed squarely on the shoulders of a boy who was quite often present in their home? And now it had to stop! I would not make a scenario happen again like the one that occured with Stevie; I *would* acknowledge the power of my own thoughts and desist immediately! I was a magical being and as such I could affect change with the slightest direction of my intent; I had to take responsibility for myself and my actions *right now*!

Good grief, how could I be even wasting valuable headspace on such deliberations? Treeface was *unique*! I felt such shame at making needless comparisons. A few months ago I wouldn't even have given Matt house room, after all, and I certainly wouldn't have been doubting my own soul-mate's attractiveness in the face of his own bluff friend! I immediately transferred my attention to all the things I found objectionable about Matt; the impending layer of puffy fat that would soon cover his body as a result of the high living he so enjoyed in and around town, his dismissiveness, his lack of depth or understanding of spiritual matters...

(*his human soul!*)

...but, I had to admit, even in my shame, he reminded me of real life, of ordinary people who had enthusiasms and drive, something beyond insupportable visions and nameless fears...beyond our strange life on the fringes.

Oh, how I wished Matt wasn't around! Without Matt we would never have made it to Cornwall, and that would have been a blessing, surely? But then, would I have wanted to have missed Penwith and the moors of Bodmin? The landscape of the deep south west of England only had a cursory veneer of 'the world'; its true essence was far more ethereal and mysterious than that. Cornwall, or Kernow as it was known to the local folk, with infinite pride, *pretended* to be of the Twentieth Century whilst secretly remaining elsewhere altogether. I had no doubt that here was a true wild land of Faery, that in walking this land one could have one foot in the modern age and one foot in the Otherworlds. Had Treeface known this when he had suggested that we live here? Or had he just wanted to run to the furthest point from established 'civilisation' in England?

I caught tantalising glimpses of ruins and tumbled stone quoits as Matt's big, fast car rushed past open field and moor alike, spraying dirty water in its wake. Blurred figures leapt in the rain-washed half-light and the spikey hedge-trees reached to us with brittle fingers from between tumbledown walls. Ah, the terrible, wonderful soul-poetry of such a bleak, broken but infinitely beautiful land! Even the vague hint of what this area had to offer made my heart leap and pound inside me, filling me with some as yet unnamed longing of its own. I had no idea, at that moment, that it truly was a land with more than it's fair share of standing stones, Faery rings and cool, dark underground passage-chambers that no one really remembered the purpose or meaning of.

I felt as if I could indeed fall in love with the essence of Penwith. Just driving through it thrilled me and woke the wild spirit in me as if for the first time. Why had no one ever told me of this marvellous place before? I felt the need to roll around in it's mud, grasping great handfuls of the darkly wet earth to me, smothering myself in the sodden essence of this craggy, mysterious place. I wanted to steep myself in its secrets and taste the rolling mists on my tongue, burying my face in the low clouds that shrouded it's rocky outcrops...

(Come, come and join us, dance into the dreaming! Cry out like a gull flying into the Greening! On high tor and low moor, we're drifting, revealing! Come join us, my lover, and drink down this feeling!)

...and maybe I could have, had it have been a very different day altogether. But did I want to live there, away from people, away from the challenges of bringing the Greening to those who needed it most? No, I didn't. At least, not in the way we would have had to have lived there.

So, Matty's presence was a boon but also a curse. There wasn't a hope that Treeface and I could have seen half the properties we had seen in Cornwall if it hadn't been for Matt...yet I wouldn't have seen this much of the glorious wild land either. There simply weren't the trains and buses to take us to these far-flung, isolated, badly situated destinations. Matt had been the real enabler of Treeface's short-lived, and rapidly dying, dream yet I had Matt to thank for the fact that it *was* dying, as his belief that our house-hunting was a flagrant waste of time influenced Treeface greatly. Matty's dismissive thoughts were almost audible, '*why are we squandering precious drinking time when we all know that there's too little cash to find a decent house*?' and Treeface was sensitive enough, of course, to have picked up Matt's unvoiced opinions.

I shook my wet hair from my eyes as I heard Matt say, predictably,

"We'll go to the pub for a while and dry off. The next appointment isn't until..."

"Two thirty! And it's a good forty miles back up the coast!" I butted in, my voice sounding shrill and unfamiliar to my ears.

We were going to see a bungalow back up on the north eastern side of Cornwall next; it was not exactly on the wild moor as Treeface had hoped but it was within our meagre price range. I didn't much care one way of or the other if we missed it, and better for me if we did, but nor did I wish Matt to get so drunk in the time we had to spare that he couldn't drive us anywhere at all, let alone home. I suspected he was over the limit already; he had been supping from a bottle of juice on the drive down but I wasn't altogether convinced that it was the innocent beverage it appeared, it was more likely a concoction involving some sort of alcoholic spirit. Matt seemed a little too convivial so early in the day for it to have been just pure fruit juice.

"Come on Lian, let's go for a beer!" Matt clapped me on the back, oblivious as usual to the fact that I couldn't take alcohol, which was quite inconceivable in his world view. Despite his encouragement I stood back and watched as he and his puppy-dog pal bounded off into a dark little pub. Besides the post office which served as a general store it was the only utility building in the village. What would it have been like to live there? I would never know now as the property we had looked at had been awful, thankfully.

I was rapidly getting used to looking at tired little shells of houses that were permeated with the smell of damp, overlaid with poverty, misery and despair. I felt a deep sense of regret for all the folk who had once lived and often died in all of the shoddy, run-down, poky properties we could afford. And so few of them even had a garden, let alone the acres of wild land Treeface had envisioned for a self-sufficient life for us! Treeface's own back-to-the-land dream had been drowned in the deluge of Cornish weather, and a tide of Matt's caustic comments, and didn't look set to make another appearance. We were outpriced by a long way and had no hope of owning anything, not even rough land, for the figure we could offer. Gone were the days when a few thousand could secure you a plot with a derelict shell. Welcome to the real world Treeface!

No, our house-hunting had been nothing more than a series of pointless, depressing expeditions to ruined or frankly uninhabitable dwellings which Matt would drive us to, he having come to stay for the duration of our search. Some of the places we had seen had been an eye-opener in the extreme and once again I thanked my lucky stars that I was who I was and hadn't been born into complete and utter penury. In Somerset on our way down to Penwith we had seen a two roomed cottage with no running water or electricity which had been on the market for a seemingly ludicrous for twenty thousand pounds. The miasma of desperation that had hung in the air there had been almost overwhelming. Matt had not entered in to the rickety building but Treeface and I had braved the squalid little dump and, as we were shown around the site by the pompous Estate Agent, it's dismal atmosphere had seemed to seep into our very souls.

"How on earth can a place with no water or sanitation be priced at twenty thousand pounds?" I had asked the man whose face was fixed in a kind of permanent sneer as he lead us round the tiny space. '*And,*' I had wanted to ask, 'h*ow did some poor old lady live like this, with no toilet and no way to wash, until so very recently? What sort of a society allowed that*?'

"We're selling this property for its land, clearly!" the Estate Agent attempted a smile at me but it looked like a twisted grimace. "I thought it should be obvious this is not a house, as such, but rather an opportunity for *re-development.*"

The man had an air of a busy chap deigning to waste his precious time on such a half-wit as myself and I longed to slap his supercilious face. What a condescending person! The Estate Agent was obviously was as sensitive and compassionate as one of that crumbling house's large red bricks...in fact the bricks were probably the better receiver of psychic impressions of the two judging by the amount of melancholy feelings they had stored and emitted.

'*Ironic, isn't it,*' I considered to myself as we stepped over the piles of mildewed newspaper and human detritus that littered the cottage's uneven stone floor, '*that this place is in worse repair than my home in medieval France ever was and it's only marginally bigger*!'

Treeface had said nothing, just stared around him with his face set in a grim rictus of disgust. It was left to me to deal with the contemptuous, haughty Estate Agent, and to Treeface's understanding of the situation, why shouldn't it be? Treeface had never suggested we stay in Somerset! It was true that the further we got from the City of Bath the cheaper cottages became but the habitable ones were still nowhere near cheap enough!

Even right at Lands End, in Penwith, as far from civilisation as we could go in the west of England, we could not have afforded to live, not really. It wasn't just that the places we saw were in dingy towns ,with precious little scope for living self-sufficiently, but we couldn't have afforded the level of renovation that the ones out in the middle of nowhere needed.

Some of the Cornish houses we saw had no windows or doors;

clearly the last impoverished owner, in a fit of pique for being so rudely evicted, had gone on a rampage of destruction before leaving, as if to say '*if I can't have it, then nobody will!*' Or maybe bored teenagers bent on acts of vandalsim, or the wrath of the elements, angry at having humans encroach on their wild territory, had seen to the place being a windswept open shell, who could tell? And what wind it was on the moors! Certainly the place was awesomely elemental, and compared to the city we had come from it was raw and untamed in the extreme, but that wasn't enough to make me want to eek out an existence there. It was '*too weather-ish and un-peopled*' as Matt put it as we were buffeted, rained on and then shown glimpes of startling blue sky through the rapidly scudding clouds.

Yes, I liked the wildness of the region very much, it had to be acknowledged, in fact I felt quite passionate about it, but that wasn't enough to persuade me that it would be worth ditching the active, commited side of the Greening and braving a harsh life there. And it would have been harsh, terribly so, as with our meagre funds all we were shown were houses that smelled more like public toilets, houses with gaping holes in their roof and walls, places which were really huts with only one primary room and cramped, dank places with mildewed walls situated on main roads, with their windows rattling as the lorries thundered by. As we drove round I saw suggestions of homes that others had tried to build up from nothing, badly constructed frameworks resting on original stone foundations, and felt great sadness for their dreams broken on the unyielding granite back of this proud and feisty land. Combining such dereliction with the harsh reality of the weather , not to mention the terible car-less isolation, it woud have been madness to attempt such a move.

Wouldn't it?

But what must Treeface, his mouth set in an unfamiliar grim line have thought of this, his own lovely rural dream, being quashed so rudely and obviously? What did he make of the snide, condescending , unhelpful people who showed us round? What did he make of the evidence of other would-be small-holders, their attempts at existing reduced to little more than smashed glass and brutally snapped timbers? If Matt hadn't been present I could have got him to talk about his feelings but with Matt there, bumbling and making jokes, it was impossible to know what my lover's real emotions were. It must have been soul-destroying for him, surely, and as embarrasing for him as it was reassuring for me. *We wouldn't have to leave our city! We could work there and bring hope and healing!* And even if Jane's money would never buy us a home, and nor had it ever been meant to, at least it could cushion us, act as a barrier between us and destitution while we did what we were born to do in the world!

Yet all along I had a feeling, a *knowing*, that there may be something else out there in store for us. Something besides housing.

Something, yes. But not what I had expected.

As Matt and Treeface went into the pub, Matt trotting eagerly with his tail up whilst Treeface looked like a whipped dog, I took a stroll round the village. It seemed all but deserted and I wondered, not for the first time, if such places were actually inhabited by any locals at all? Had they all left and was this a place full of holiday home-lets and weekend dwellings for the rich city folk up-country, a place with no real residents at all? Or perhaps it was like a ghost village without even holiday makers or weekend trippers? Even if I hadn't wanted to walk and get some air I wouldn't have fancied that brown-looking pub at all; I hadn't wanted to witness folk eyeing me and Treeface up and down as if we were aliens, no matter who they were. Even if we were aliens, *earth aliens,* I didn't want to see it on these stranger's faces! That's if there had been anyone in there at all. Either way I would rather get wet than watch the two men sink pints! With Matt paying, Treeface would only get merry and then, very quickly, maudlin. Oh please let Matt not become to pissed to drive home!What a day! Still, I had agreed to come and look and I had done just that. And now the pointless experience was nearly over...well, almost pointless. My introduction to the wild land of Penwith was something that I would carry that with me wherever I went from now on; such energies weren't for keeps but for holding lightly, with constant awareness that they were not ours to own. I thought that I could make a loving pilgrimage to the 'un-peopled' and fierce peninsula of West Penwith...but nothing more. Some lands were never meant to be settled and tamed, just as some feral beings could never be domesticated by human 'civilsation'.

I stomped through a large puddle, soaking my only remaining pair of black jeans with reddish water and headed toward a gate. Water seeped into my baseball boots and my socks made unpleasant squishing sounds inside them as I moved. Ugh! Maybe I would find a nice tree to shelter under, to sit and think about things. I had both Alicia's death and Stevie's attack, not to mention my own stupidity, to mull over and the last thing I had really needed was to complicate how I felt with such a strange and pointless exercise as house-hunting! I also had a whole new 'look' to contend with. I was lucky that my fringe covered my scars, more or less, but it was still a bizarre and disconcerting experience, having a word, or part of it at least, etched into my head. Somehow, despite my long-held, and often upheld, views of my own ugliness, the fresh red lines on my brow didn't bother me as much as I thought they should. I didn't exactly like them but then I didn't hate or resent them either. If I really delved inside me for how they made me feel I would say that they felt okay. Not terribly wrong and not right either, they just *were*. Like some half-finished statement of intent they sat on my skin, my scarlet hair framing and mingling with them.

It was Treeface that disturbed me more with his wide open face and exposed skull. So far, with his newly ploughed and furrowed face, he had attracted some adverse interest in our generally open-minded city but I wondered what sort of reception he would get in such a parochial place as the Tinner's Arms, the squat little pub that he and Matty had juts entered? Oh, how could he have ever thought that us too oddballs could ever sit nicely in a rural community, especially an isolated one like this? And how was he feeling when he had made himself so *visible* when it was all for nothing? Treeface had exposed himself in a statement of mourning for something that didn't bother me that much and I thought that he must have had huge regrets about the dramatic nature of his gesture. He *hated* to draw attention to himself! So how did my lover feel about himself now he was so revealed? And how did he feel about us, about Cornwall and his dream...about anything? Surely I should know?

I stomped through another puddle but hardly noticed, for what worried me more than wet legs or feet, or indeed my own scars, was this-that Treeface was set on one thing, and one thing only, and I knew his will, like mine, could change worlds. And with that realisation I had another, more profound one. Relationships only really worked if the couple, or group, had a shared dream. Only then was it a *partnership*. Only then was it something more than playing out some soul-drama, a psychic tug-of-war between complex physical needs and psychic wants. Was this supposed rural idyll still what Treeface wanted? He hadn't really said. But here we were looking at cottages, or what remained of them, and so I guessed it was what he wanted? I mean, he had called up Matt and got him to come over almost immediately after our 'talk' so what was I to think? And if it was what he wanted then where would he stop in order to see it through...how would he strive against the odds to make it happen? Once again, as it often did in personal matters, my *knowing* remained resolutely dim, as if one of those big fat Cornish clouds had scudded across my inner vision an dampened down any ability of mine to *see*.

Would Jack Tatterkin have thought it so right for us to live out here in obscurity, I wondered? Pity he wasn't there to ask. All we had was Matt as a sounding board and he was a man who seemed to have a '*live for today and hang tomorrow*' attitude par excellence. He was so opposite to Treeface in that respect, and many others, that I really hadn't a clue how their friendship had survived this long. There was no way he would contradict anything that he knew would make his beleaguered pal happy. Matt's attitude was '*do what thou will shall be the whole of the law and sod the consequences*'; a devil-may-care stance he had adopted as a boy to escape his own father's overbearing control, so Treeface seemed to think, and which had been augmented ever since by his one-sided love-affair with the bottom of a beer glass. I guess that dominant fathers may once have been their middle meeting ground, as friends, but now? Habit? A weird mutual safety and support? Who knew? Trying to discuss Matt with Treeface had always proved impossible; his loyalty to him, as his sister before him, was absolute.

Was he like that about me I wondered? I doubted it. But maybe that was my insecurity and conviction in my unloveable status.

I reached the gate and stopped in surprise, for instead of a nice neat field, *ala* north Somerset, there was infact an expanse of open moor; a wilderness playing hide and seek with the omnipresent mist. The gorse and browned bracken became visible as I stared, then was veiled again. Lumps of granite sprang up along with hummocks of dry grass, sparkling with rain and quartz, then disappeaerd into billowing white. A sudden urge, as strong as any I have ever felt, pulled me closer. *I had to go in there!*

Suddenly all other thoughts became null and void and my *knowing* was back on full alert; I was picking up signals from everywhere. Protect yourself Lian...something's happening. There are *presences*!

(*Earth presences! Earth aliens! Faery-kin! Oh!*)

I clumsily mounted the gate, my boots, with their sole's worn slippery, giving me little purchase on wet metal. Oh, oh, oh, I had to get in there!

"*Psssst! Oi there, humany sort! Half-Fey! Psssst!*"

With one almighty effort I climed up and dropped heavily over into the springy moorland grass.

"*We's can see you and you's can hear us but we not meet yet! All wet!*"

I looked about me, senses snapping into new life even as I cursed my dull human form. I could scent them on the wind and they smelled *sweet*!

"Where are you?" I asked into the billowing mist.

"*Round and about, insidey out!*"

There was laughter, a surprisingly gutteral sound, and then the musical voice continued, poking fun of me as I spun on my heels, boots squeaking and squelching comically, searching for them.

"You's is making a piggy's ear from a silky's purse! You's can't see! Hee hee! Poor piggy! Spins more for us, we likes dancin'!"

I sniffed the wind and moved, trying to tune in to my Fey soul-self, accessing bits of me that had slumbered long in the *forgetting*. The mist made everything harder and it came down heavily all at once, a fat white curtain obscuring what little I had previously been able to see with my human eyes. Sighing I closed my useless eyes, moving in my own world, my inner Faery-realm, seeking my kin. The body of Lian stumbled with her arms outstretched over rocks and into hawthorn trees, fingers brushing painfully off gnarled bushes both sturdy and spikey, even as my old Fey soul got wind of them.

"*You's is gettin' warmer, bumbly boo! We's is still over here, waiting for you...over here!Whys has you's let yer self get so slow and human-sloppy, hey girlie? Whys you not up and dancin' with us properly-like?*"

There was a pause, a silence that seemed enormous, and I took the opportunity to tune into them further. *I had them now, I was sure of it!* My heart raced madly. Feys! Real live Fey-kin in their Faery forms! Ah, what would Alicia do to see me now, me the sceptic, the angry ranting girl, making her way towards her lost race, her own people?

Oh Alicia, I do this for you! You were right! All things have purpose and poetry, all meetings are well-met. And they exist, our Faery-kin...THEY EXIST!

"Coming, ready or not!" I said, under my breath, knowing they could catch my slightest whispering nuance.

And with that the mist lifted, as if heralding a new act on the stage of life, and there they were.

Two of them, maybe three. A red-capped, child-sized Fey, running and laughing. Then two. A squat Faery, leaping, frog-like, clad in gorse. So fast! So fast they were, my precious lost siblings! And so very, very bright!

Then one. Like a pale sun, blinding me.

"V'ridian," she said, simply.

"Lian," I replied, moving to take her hand in mine.

"I know," she said and when she smiled I heard the ice cracking on deep water at midnight and the sky lit up to the sound of swan's wings, beating.

Oh my racing heart!

Her hand was thin, impossibly long, almost boneless with four fine fingers that tapered into smoke.

She shook her head as I reached for this hand and pulled away from me.

"Oh!" was I not clean to them, untouchable?

"Too powerful," she said, eyes of shadow-fire meeting mine, growing wider. "We do harm if we touch the humany-kind without fair protectioning; it burns, see?

"Like...acid?" I felt foolish, and clumsy, and oh so humanly gauche.

"No, *soul*-burn. If I touch you, Fey kindred, without you and I first protectin', shielding our energies, you will never be able to go back to human-forming. Two live wires meet and you would need to abandon your body and...."

"Die?"

"And come with us."

"*Come with us! Come with us!*" I heard them ,the Faery throng behind her, all around us, hissing, wishing.

"No!"

"No? But for so long, kindred, you have wanted to die, to go home, have you not?"

"*Not, not!I forgot*!" came the hissing.

"I no longer wish to leave my life," I said, and swallowed hard. It was true! "And I no longer wish to leave Lian's body for she and I have work to do, in the world, I think. I no longer hate Lian, or her life, I simply want to *know*. To *help*, To *love*!"

"*Ever never no more...pooh!*" came the hissing, like a dozen naughty children, hidden. Watching...

"This is good!" V'ridian said to me, directly. Holding my gaze, filling me with ancient starlight, waking my latent, lambent self from the dark sleep of *forgetting.* "She would be proud of you, now, child. *Cariad.*"

I started and the mist came down again, obscuring the thin, pallid form for a moment. Tears came in to my eyes.

"You know of Alicia?" I asked into the mist, my voice an awed whisper now.

V'ridian stepped forward from the rolling clouds. Her hair, if it was hair, flew back from her own pointed alabaster face. It was many colours of green, too many to ever count, and it shot upwards and outwards, crackling madly, only to dissolve into the whiteness of the mist. It was so hard to tell where she began and the untamed land around her ended.

"Please?" I begged her. "Tell me! Tell me Alicia is okay, that she doesn't hate me? Tell me that...oh! *Please*!"

"There is a message here for you, child," said the wraith-like image of the Fey, flickering like a guttering tallow candle in the strange afternoon half-light.

"*Message! Pessage! She's not deservin' one! She won't dance for us no more! Pooh pah!*"

"Please tell me! Please! I have to get back, I am a long way from home and..."

"You *are* home!"

V'ridian looked at me, her almost featureless face was still and unreadable save for those eyes, wide and full of mysteries.

"No, you see I can't stay here, it's not..."

"YOU ARE HOME."

"Oh!" I jumped back, surprised. Her voice was so absolute; I heard it echo in each chunk of granite, each browned leaf and broken stem, in each glistening haw on the stunted,wind-thrashed tree. Beyond this, beyond each individual part of the moor, I heard it *in* the moor, down deep in the earth; those words found roots and grew strongly all around me.

"Here is the message, child. Here is Alicia's message to you...and our message this day, too. For we all need you. Yes, we do. We are the violin, seasoned and well tuned, and you are the bow that can free the hidden melody from the perfect instrument. Fey music comes from our connection, from a well-rosened bow on taut strings, and how may we best connect?"

"By me working in the world, not hiding myself away in some obscure..."

V'ridian contuinued as if I had not spoken and I shivered, half the damp and chill and half from her disconcerting unstudied authority. Her strength was the strength of snow capped mountains and of icy rivers gushing gladly, unstoppably, into the sea. She was as affecting as a single strike of lightening on a dry corn field; her true power condenced into a solitary flickering form but not truly contained by it. Energy flew out from her hair, fingertips and even the points of her ears in cold blue showers. I blinked and her intense after-image dazzled me.

"We may best connect by your being *everywhere*, as are we, in essence. You may best work for the Fey by working for the land herself. How to do this? Not for you the big garden or small-holding, cariad, not for you the static home in the same old place, but by keeping in motion, as the old wise ones ever did. Travellin', see! Your home is wherever you choose to stop! Your home is *everywhere!* Travellin' is the best way of gettin' your message to the widest audience, across the miles! By travellin' you do not deplete the land on which you live and in this way you meet many of us, awakening us in the land as we awaken you, feeding off eachother's force, drinking deep of eachother's inspiriational presence in the world. This is the way of the Greening for you, child! Not for you the confines of one house, one garden, one set of aquaintances, one locale. No! By travellin', movin' on, bringing healing and seeing to towns, villages, cities, and then leavin' again you give much, learn much, *take little!* See? It is so easy! So beautiful! So right for us Fey. For we are of the Earth, not of the world, and we may only pass through it gently, leaving only tracks in our wake, touching lightly, gently, powerfully...then moving on like a restless breeze at twilight. Such is our true nature, such is the Way."

I had no idea if I were talking to Alicia now, or to this strnage willowy wraith, or to any number of my Fey-kin. And it didn't matter for the message was clear to me.

"But how? How do I travel? I have no means! I can't survive! I don't know how, I am a city girl! Oh, why does everyone want me to be something I am not!"

My stupid human protestations were cut short again by her calm, clear voice which cut through me like an east wind.

"You speak of 'I'? Oh no, not *I*, not anymore. There are two of you now, maybe one day three if you can keep on the path and welcome the soul in fully! You and your lover must travel. There is a wagon for you, already waiting. She had bought it for you, the wildwitch Alicia, knowing that she was soon to leave the Earth and travel spirit-wards. She has bequeathed you a wagon, child and you must take it, *take it and go*! In the taking of this four-wheeled you will free yourself from all past patternings and start again; faith can do this, faith wipes slates clean. Love conquers all things! You will become free, become whatever you want to be, moment by moment! City girl, no more! Angry girl, no more! Instead now, Star Child, you be a Fey wildwitch, on the road, moving lightly across the land, learning to be, in harmony, giving...*Take the wagon and go!*"

"A wagon?" I stood, flabbergasted, shivering a little as the mist clung to me in a way I found overly familiar. Even the mist here had a mischevious spirit.

"*Wagon? Pesky wesky piskie child, knows not what a wagon be, so she don't! Pah and poohsey! She soft, she not good Faery-warey-type, no, no! Won't dance, knowses of no wagons!*"

"Look, who are you? Show yourselves!" I exclaimed, suddenly bothered by these Fey invisible antics. "Show yourselves as it is my will!" I thought that if I may command the spirits in my Otherworldly travels maybe I could do the same here.

Not so!

"*We's not comes out 'tils we are good and ready and that be never-not-ever so...poooh! Pah! We no speak to you now anyways not! So!*"

"You cannot *ever* command a Fey!" said V'ridian, cooly. "You should know that, dark-bright mistress."

"I am sorry," I hung my head, feeling foolish and frustrated. Ah it was ever so! Why was I so stupid?

"You are not a fool, madam!" I looked up, startled. V'ridian was using Alicia's voice again now.

"You! You shouldn't play games with me like that, tricking me! Oh I miss her so!" Tears sprang from my eyes and spilled down my cheeks before I even knew how sad I was.

"No more trickery and no more commands," said the pale flickering Fey before me,"truth though, yes plenty of truth. For in a moment you will be bidden back to the earthly-world although for you now things will never be the same. For one, I will be walking with you, in spirit, and for two, you have been touched by the wild soul of Faery, the real live essence of *who you be*, and so all is transformed. Do you hear me, Fey-kin? My words are en-*chant*-ment and my presence in your life is pure magic...the magic of *before* and *beyond*! All is changed now; all is new! You may always ask for transformation, child, for you are never alone. Know this: you can ask for help! So here, I help you, even unbidden as I was. When you walk out of the mists this day you walk out of the fog of the *forgetting* for good and all. And you will be as you are, a shining star-ling, a Fey *seer* of great skill, a witch-mistress of great charming, a healer girl of formidable powers. And you will know how to survive...*and to really live*...on the roads, in the hedgerows, by the streams, yes, even as they freeze in winter. Now, to find the wagon..."

"Yes?"

"She, the spell-wife Alicia, left a note inside the hollow tree at the back of her garden, the one at the edge of the footpath."

"The ash?"

"Indeed, it is so. And it is still there, strong singing magic holds it hidden, and in it are the directions and instructions. She loved you so she gave you the best gift you could have. Better than her house, which she knew would be claimed anyway, and better than money. It is part of her dream and if you use it, own it, love it and take it on the road then her dream may live on and grow in the world. It waits for you, your wagon, at Penny Farm, her directions will guide you. There is a man there, a fellow Fey, Ed is his name, a Sturwick he is, and he will tell you all there is to know. She prepared the ground well for you, beloved. Ground her dream for her now, Lian, and keep the Faery-faith, always, for it is *who you be...*"

V'ridian was fading, the flickering becoming more rapid, her form disintegrating into lines and flashes and then reforming faintly.

"Why did I find you here? Why not before? Why not when I so needed you!"

I implored the empty air where she had been, a static charge which crackled with ghost-fire was all that remained of her.

'Its the wild land, cariad, the untamed soul of England, of Albion. and you may ever seek us in these forgotten, human-less places... know we live there still, waiting! We have never gone away, you just didn't know how to find us! Amongst dry bracken and flowering gorse, bare stone and pure water, will we rise to greet the day with you. It is ever so, beloved! We are of the untamed, 'un-peopled' land, walking *within*, hidden in the *wild green beyond.* By the soul-full eloquence found in every glossy leaf and ferny glade we walk within you too! Fey-kind, little Lian, be our voice in the world, we implore you! Be the voice of all that is magical, all that is lyrical, all that is ethical...For you are changed beloved; *changed*!"

"*Yes, yessss! Do our bidding witchy-mistress, yessss! We loves you really! Yessss!*"

"...and go, go now! Go! Do not bring that man to us! Go!"

"Oi! Ginger whinger! Misery-me! D'you want to go home or what?" Matts' voice drifted to my ears, sounding as if he were from another age, another land.

"*Keep the faith!*"

"*Be's who you be!*"

"Thank you!" I said, pouring heart and soul into the two simple words as I turned on my heel.

No time to linger or feel regret. No time to walk deeper into Faery, into the *wild green beyond.* I had to go to my lover and his friend. I had to! I didn't want to bring that man there to them; Matt was far too 'peopley'.

"Coming Matt!" I yelled, my voice sounding loud and strong to my own ears.

I walked steadily, surely, through the white fog which lifted and fell like the heavy white petticoats of a Victorian can-can line. This time I did not trip or stumble for I *heard* the rocks and the trees call to me before I walked into them; I *heard* the land singing its warnings and its greetings! Ah, for the first time in this life of mine I was *awake!*

(Oh Alicia! They exist, they truly do! Thank you so much for telling me the truth about my soul, about the Fey-ness within me and the Feyness without that is still here in the world. I am just so happy! OH, THEY EXIST! And how I wish you were here with me to share this glorious moment! Mae a ka ta kei ie, my dear, dear Alicia!)

And then I was out of the billowing whiteness and I could see clearly. The whole day seeming washed clean and fresh. Things sparkled! Even Matt, standing outside the pub rolling a cigarette looked bold and bright and beautiful. And Treeface...

Treeface, his bare face wreathed in smiles and those dear, dear lines, shone the most brightly of all things. He was alive and luminous with spirit and I loved him and he loved me! And, do you know, his shaved head and his bare face both looked right! How could they not be? They were as they were. Perfect.

Climbing the gate easily this time I dropped down into the lane and ran lightly through the puddles towards them. Matt kicked me up the backside and laughed which came out as a sort of burp. He wiped his mouth on the back of his hand and smiled endearingly. I smiled back. How could I not? He was like some amiable but quite dangerous character I may watch in a film of someone else's more exciting life. Maybe he could have played a Saxon lord with all that blonde hair? Or maybe he would make a good Viking, broad and forthright? He suddenly seemed so full of possibilities and choices; I could almost see the life-lines stretching out from him into the ether, making connections in potentiality. And I knew, for good and all, why treeface liked him so for he had a kind soul, human or no.

Oh, I was transformed and so was my experience of the world. I had seen the Fey and everything was different, richer, more vibrant!

"Everything's different!" I said.

"Did you find some magic mushrooms in that field?" Matt peered at me, unable to tell why I had gone off so surly and returned so sprightly. "Did you pick us some too?"

"No, she's been with the Faery-folk, haven't you darling?" Treeface was mellow, blurred by booze and glad to see me. And he *knew*, of course he did.

"I have indeed been with the Fey!" I said, no longer having a single human care if Matt, or anyone else, thought me to be mad.

"And what did they say to you beloved?" Treeface met my eyes and despite the drink he locked into me, soul-to-soul, waiting. Did he fear what I would tell him? If so he stood bravely, my precious oneness.

"That its all going to be alright!"

"Oh purple-please, ladies and gentlemen, how do you work that one out? You've not got enough money to buy a shack and you're both on the poverty line! You're both as mad as..."

"Shh, let's hear her, Matty, c'mon now!"

Was this the first time Treeface had ever contradicted or stopped his larger, bluffer friend? If so I felt proud for him. In its own way it was a valiant thing to do.

"They said it's okay, beloved, that there's a home for us just waiting back in Somerset, just outside of Bath.!"

"Back there?" His dear face fell. "But we can't afford something there, in the city, you know that as well as I do! Oh, damn the Fey and their unrealistic meddling. They don't understand, they never..."

"Its *in* the city at the moment but its certainly not *of* the city!" I smiled into his eyes, "We can find it there but it doesn't have to *stay* there. It can be everywhere! On the road..."

I could see Treeface drinking in the thoughts and images I was sending him. In my mind I focussed on a wagon, a little moving home pulled by a hairy, hardy horse. Treeface knew about horses, he was good with them, and so he could tend it whilst I rode beside him towards whichever place needed us next. I saw the gaily painted wagon rolling down a winding lane across the Levels, moving past baleful-eyed heron who gave their mournful, almost comical, cry in acknowledgement. I saw us tending and mending, giving and never really taking, moving on. It was better than a house in the country, or a flat in the city; far better! Now we could be *everywhere*, anywhere we needed to be! The Earth was our home and I would learn, yes, I would, to live as a traveller, a Fey witch, a *seer* walking lightly on the land. It was the perfect compromise, the middle way for Treeface and I, for we could go to the people, to help them, but not be of them. Our place would always be with the trees, for sure and now we could travel to the people without having to stay with them, returning home to ourselves, to the *wild green beyond*, every night.

"On the road? Really? But how?" Treeface stared at me, his moss-on-granite yes wide, and I could have hugged him for the sheer joy of seeing him there with me.

"Look what are you two on about? I don't get it? What are you saying? Sounds bloody barking to me..."

Treeface held up his hand to silence Matty. Amazing!

"Really!" I replied to Treeface, also ignoring Matt. "It's the perfect solution! The one that means we will be running *to* something, not just running *away* from something!It'll be good and healthy because it's not a life to be lead amongst people-energies yet it doesn't avoid people; it travels to them and then leaves again, moves on! It's a life lead in the wild, green energies of the *beyond*, beloved, and yet it means we can reach many more people, and creatures, than if we just lived in one place. It's *perfect*! She was so kind, so thoughtful..."

Treeface swallowed hard.

"Alicia?"he whispered.

"Yes!! YES!" It was all I could do to stop myself leaping around in joy.

"By all the Gods!" Treeface shook his head in amazement. "I never even thought of that! By heaven! Of course she would have considered you before she died, of course she would have catered for our needs. Oh, bless the dear soul. It solves everything. But...is it...?"

"Is it true? YES! Yes, beloved, of that I have no doubt. Our kind do not lie! All we have to do is to go back to the old ash behind Alicia's house and find her instructions. She hid them in the ash's hollow, bound by strong protective magics! All we have to do is get back and find those instructions!" And I couldn't help myself. I was so overcome with love and thnaks that I flung my arms around my darling man, little caring what Matt throught or felt...if anything.

"I would never have dared to hope that they Fey would find you here," Treeface, equally moved, whispered words into my hair. "Oh my love after all we have been through, all the hurting, we are to be saved by one dead woman's love and a race that is also considered to be dead and gone, if it ever existed at all! *Our* race...even I thought them to be lost. It was my last hope that they'd still be present here in the wild west!"

"They're not lost and nor are we!They *do* exist, its all true! I saw them, beloved! I SAW THEM! And I *felt* them and, oh, they've woken me up, truly!" I stood back from him as if to show him I were different. I noticed, from the corner of my eye, that Matt had wandered away and was sitting on a low wall, smoking. He didn't look too bothered, bless him. If he loved his friend as much as Treeface loved him then he'd be glad that Treeface had at last had a true soul-partner, a special lover of his own, and a happy, fulfilling future ahead of him.

"Oh sweetheart!" We needed no more words. Locked into eachother in a way we seldom had been before we held hands and breathed togther, drinking in the essence of our union, breathing out all the old fears and angers of our division. If I were transformed then so were we...and so was the land, for we were one, in truth. Then, slowly, savouring each second, we walked to where Matt sat.

"Right mate," Treeface announced. I had never seen him so up-front, so *animated.* "The gig's off down here. Much as we love it in Penwith you are quite right, we are wasting our time here; bricks and mortar are not for us, not here, not anywhere. Take us back to Somerset and we'll buy you the best meal you've ever had in Bath!"

"Yes, and all the drink you can take!" I added, cheekily.

Matt raised an eyebrow. "I doubt if anyone's pocket could stretch to that," he said, archly. "Okay, I'll take you back. But don't expect me to have a clue about what's going on!"

And we all smiled, made new by the wild westerly wind and the relentless rain of a land that was still alive, still vibrant with the sparkling energy of Faery. We could all be different from that moment on if we so chose, for in all moments were renewals and chances for the Greening to begin. And there could be magic in each seemingly mundane situtaion if we chose to see it...

(*Keep the faith!*)

...and feel it in each thought, kind word and loving deed. Yes!

"To Bath then," Treeface cried.

And we linked arms, the three of us, like Dorothy, the Tin Man and the once Cowardly Lion, and strode splashing through the puddles to Matt's kingfisher blue Rover.

After

Is there really such a thing, such a place or time as *after*? Are there really endings? Can a beginning ever truly exist as such? All I knew was that I *was*. I was awake, fully present again, and everything else was simply the duration when I had not fully *re-membered.*

Oh, but I am here now and, do you know, it is harder to be in this conscious condition than to be living in the semi-cognisant, half-hearted way I was before! Harder but infinitely better! I had taken the deadened, dimmed version of living I had endured in the first half of my incarnation as the sum-total of existence and now, well now it seemed like nothing but a tunnel vision, a half-life viewed from the wrong end of a telescope. For my first twenty eight years of dwelling in the body of Lian Smythe I had seen the world through a filter of her inherent and acquired fears and her self-imposed limitations. How sad! But how neccesary too, for this was the unique journey that had brought me to this moment, and, for all the pain it had caused me, I was glad.

The world she had seen, this Lian, this befuddled wild spirit clad in mortal form, had been almost desolate and in it her body had wandered in confusion and isolation even as her soul had tried so hard to shine. Yet every time the spirit-light got too bright her human-self panicked and threw a mantle of dusty black incomprehension over it. It was self-sabotage, for sure. The human-self is good at that.

But believe me, living like a somnambulist, however grim it sounds, is easier than being a willing participant in your own process of *becoming*. Yes, *re-membering* is the tougher option by far! Life without *re-membering* is like a dull trudge with snow-blindness, walking in a whiteout from one point to another, head down and focused only on a narrow goal, a pre-ordained idea of a destination. It may be unpleasant but it requires little thought or effort, not in comparison to how it is when a decision is made to actively *be*. Even though it had seemed hard at the time, my half-living had been miserable but not challenging, not emotionally stretching, as I had never really been fully present enough to fully feel.

Without the *re-membering*, life is indeed a struggle but with *re-membering* life is REAL! No more 'just getting through it', no more staggering from 'a' to 'b', no more excuses! *Re-membering* requires commitment and dedication with no opt-out clause whatsoever! Although there are always choices, and some of them are easier than others, there is also *response-ability*. An ability to respond, not react; to act with compassion, not fear. A responsibility to the true essence of our spirits; a responsibity to each creature-teacher who walks or grows, swims or flies beside us on the journey; a responsibility to the Earth Mother who allows for that journey to be possible at all. A hard road indeed but, as with fragments of glittering quartz crystal within the grey granite, there is much beauty to be found in such an tough thing.

These were my thoughts as I sat in the tattoo studio, watching my lover be *re-greened*. At last his tree-lines were sprouting real leaves,; he was to be permanently verdant, beautifully bold and bright.With each buzz of that clever needle my man was becoming green, greener, *greenest*! No more hiding for him, or for me. No more apologies for being! No, my lover, my precious one-ness, was becoming a real foliate man now; a wild bard crowned in the glory of nature, the majesty of his *own* nature, and I was so, so proud of him!

I knew that the process did not hurt, not really. Especially if you focussed on the intent of the permanent skin-marking, the magical will-and-wish of it. I myself had put every ounce of my sylvan soul into the tattooist's lines and whorls as she had worked on me. And what a tattooist Sally was! We had tried very hard to find her but it had been well worth the questing! Sally was one of the few artists in the south claiming to be a sacred skin artist, not just a run-of-the-mill, designs-from-off-the-wall kind of tattooist, and as such we wanted her to be the one to bring our full transformation to fruition. We had searched through magazines and phone directories, travelling to many small towns, and several cities, across the area, meeting with tattooists who gazed at us with blank incomprehension, much amusement or even open hostility. But when we came across Sally, in a small but neat studio in a Wiltshite market town, we had known immediately she was right for the job. A lot of tattooists we had come across simply wouldn't even consider working on faces but Sally, over tea in her back room, had given every consideration to our own considered propsal. She could understand what we wanted to do, and why, and that was enough in itself.

I had known immediately that she would be right for our *re-greening* as Sally too was Fey spirited. Of course, she did not know it yet but after laying her hands on us she would do, soon enough! Her companions spirits and ours would see to that, for sure. With her tight bobbing curls, dancing black eyes and delicate pointed chin she was already bearing the marks of our kind clearly through her fair human skin. Oh what a joy it was to see that in another! And what a joy, a deep and moving joy, it was to work with her. The process was fascinating and its arcane nature, fused with modern mechanics and technology, blended seamlessly with the energies of what we were doing. We were bringing the magic of the Otherworlds through into the modern hectic world of humanity; we were combining the etehreal with the corporeal, the magical with the mundane, as was the way of the Greening.

I had known instinctively that Sally would be fully supportive of the act of commitment and courage we were making together and that she would add her own desire for a *re-greening* into her work. And what work it was! Just a brief glance into the mirror to my right showed my own face as a verdant hedgerow on a May morning. I was a green woman, for good and all! Where Treeface had oak leaves and tiny acorns sprouting from each natural branch-mark on his brow and cheek, my own lines revealed a gnarled hawthorn, her leaves glossy in spring sunlight, her boughs laden with delicate yet deeply vibrant blossom. We were really doing it! Here was enchantment in action, here was a statement of personal power and unrepentant glory! Oh, the Faerytide was rising fast now...and it was wonderful!

(*You cannot hurt us now! Strip away the skin and you'll find the same beneath, eternally...returning! Burn us, would you? Bury us? Scrub our faces raw? Well, we'll rise again! For we are the seeds that cannot stop reaching for the light and no matter how dark you make it for us we will always find it as rich loam for our germination! We cannot be contained, not now and not ever again, and we are breaking though into the light, over and over, ever-reaching for the Greening!*)

I watched Treeface as he sat, head tilted back, his posture showing he was deeply relaxed. He was breathing slowly and in a measured way even as Sally worked on parts of his face that must have stung if not hurt. Occaisionally his skin twitched but that was the only sign he was in discomfort at all. Oh, the bravery of him to put himself through-what must be painful! The inner strength of him to overcome a fear of physical hurting! I knew that like a phoenix he would rise from the ashes of his past pain and terror, moving towards new bright dawn, a free-flyer riding the winds of change gladly, and that this was as much an initiation for him into authentic, fear-less being as it was for me. Oh how proud I was of him! And now how proud he could be of himself!

(*Are we not sure that we have not conquered loss before? Aye, in morning I find strength...*)

I would have held his hand, or called out to reassure him, but his stillness detered me; had he gone a-journeying? I knew that if he had then he would more than likely be conjuring up the enduring spirits of Tatty and Meggy, Ana and Kefli in his minds-eye and deep in his soul. He could finally stand and meet their eyes as *one of them*; he could now meet them as an equal fit to walk the wild road along side them. Only his own desperate fear had kept him tethered for so long. But even as he was bound his constant straining on the cords that held him had frayed them thin and as soon as he put enough presure on those bonds one last time they snapped! My lover was free, thanks to a meeting on a moor in the mist, and we were rising fast on the Faerytide, held only by love and an indominatble strength of conviction. We had faith in our own Greening, and that of the All, and now, thanks to our spirit-kin and our own resurgent souls, we were unstoppable!

I examined my face in the mirror again, fingering the raised surface of the freshly inlaid ink. How strange and beautiful this miracle of human ingenuity; the manipulation of a simple electrical machine which allowed for magic to be fused into skin and beyond. How intense the experience of making that which lies *within* be seen *without!* Surely meaningful tattooing was unique in this process? With gentle, eager fingers I could feel a little dried blood around my blossoms and leaves and I was glad to have shed some of my body's life-source for the honouring of my soul. Giving my blood in this rite of passage was my temporal way of gifting that which was the eternal and enduring beyond flesh. It made the whole experience seem much more like an initiation, a long and painful a journey deep inside ourselves to be expressed by blood and beautiful scarring in the outer world. It was indeed a rebirth and it was usual at any birth for their to be blood.

Sally said we would have to wait until the tattoos had settled down and stopped bleeding, or oozing watery blood and lymph, before she could let us leave. Would that be a hardship, being forced to spend more time with our Fey sister? Indeed not, I for one would be glad of it. Where before I would have felt jealousy when I looked at her, or even hate for her success and beauty, now I felt nothing but admiration and respect...as well as kin-ship beyond skin. I loved her! Sally had said that usually she would put a dressing on the tattoo-wound and then we could leave immediately but on our faces this seemed impractical. Apart from practicality it also seemed to us so very important to walk out of those doors changed, revealing to the world who and what we be without any last trance of fear or, in my case, any shred of defiant anger. We were as we were, only now more so! My fingers traced the buds and the blossoms that so well disguised the clumsy attempts of Stevie to brand me and I was glad, glad for each and every moment, every single thing, that had lead me here, now.

What would Lydia think of this brave act on behalf of her brother, I wondered? Although she had now been gone for several months she still came into my head as regularly as ever and I knew she must certainly have haunted Treeface's waking hours, although he never said as much. When Lydia walked out of his immediate life it had almost been like he had lost his own child rather than a sister but he had, to his great credit, not let it affect him too adversly. Where I had expected him to become even more dismal and defeated he had persevered with amazing fortitude, and now...well, now there were other things, and greater dreams, to occupy him.

I myself had come, especially since Penwith and finding our beautiful wagon, to see Lydia Fentley, soon to be Matthieson, as more of a role-model than an adversary. Lydia had always had the courage of her convictions and, despite her being so lovely to look at, she had still needed to battle against many odds, such as her own cold-hearrted parents, to get to her elevated position. She too had once been through *the burning*, long ago, as had we, but she had never let that stop her expressing her beliefs, her *faith,* publically. No, Lydia was no longer a figure of jealous hate for me and instead had shifted position in my conciousness to someone to admire. After all, her work on natural enchantment, women's emancipation and personal witch-power was, in its own way, as much a part of the Greening as what we two would do. This shift within me had lead me to know, deep down, that Lydia would be overjoyed by her brother's metamorphosis into his true self. For Treeface to have found his power, and be prepared to stand by it, publically, as did she, was something that would please her greatly. I knew that when we met again there would be much rejoicing. And yes, I would forgive her for the cruel words I had indeed heard her utter on that distant day in the pub garden. And why? For I knew that she too, in her own way, had been jealous and that the insiduous spirit of jealousy can make us all behave badly, out of soul-character, from time to time. I was no saint; I just had faith now, for good and all.

However, I doubted Jane would have felt so charitable about her ex's bold statement. It was her money that was enabling us to transform ourselves with these tattoos and I very much doubt he would have had a penny from her if she'd have known what we would do with a small sum of it. But then, did she have to approve of what we did? At the end of the day did anyone?

Sally looked up from her intense working and met my eyes in the mirror. She smiled, a mischevious grin in a pointed Pixie's face, and I smiled back from beneath my own laden boughs that spoke of renewal. 'Okay?' she mouthed at me as she swilled her needle around in a plastic cup full of water. I nodded my affirmative, watching as the water in the beaker turned from vivid lime to jewel-bright emerald. As I kept watching the water kept on swirling, filling my vision, taking me deeper and deeper into the green.

Re-membering.

I have *re-membered* and now I have a purpose.

A purpose...does that make me sound as if I am deluded, as deluded as Stevie? By no means! I don't have any delusions of grandeur nor any sad illusion of being more special or 'chosen' than any other incarnate being, any other unique spirit currently en-bodied on this Earth. I am neither blessed nor especially cursed, I know that now. All I have is a role, a set of steps in the dance of life which only I can perform. In this particular lifetime I may only weave my own individual glittering strands of the web and of that I am proud but not boastful, nor am I shameful. I know my place and am glad of it; I am no longer humble to the point of wishing for obscurity or angry wishing for extinction.

I have only the *knowing*, the inner knowledge of what my soul agreed to do this time around, and in that innate *knowing* is my purpose, just as the purpose of the marigold lies dreaming within her small and resolutely spiny seed. And my gift of *sight*, of *knowing*, is no greater, no less needed, than that of a healer, or a potter, or a dressmaker... or than whatever *your* gift may be! I simply agreed to be who I be as a child of the Greening so that the Way may be experienced on Earth again. That is Lian Smythe's job, regardless of worldly titles or labels. That's what this wild spirit, housed in this wonderful body, booked in to do!

All of that which I have experienced as an incarnate being so far has been part of the process of *re-integration*, to reclaim all the parts of myself that I gave away, thinking others knew better, to assimilate all the parts of my self that I hid out of sheer terror or shunned for lack of understanding. Now I have come to an acceptance of all aspects of my being, of my wild spiritual nature, and even if I cannot love all aspects equally at least I can acknowledge them as parts of an integrated whole. Just as I cannot love every being that walks the Earth, or swims or flies, so can I accept them, with compassion. *As within, so without!* As night follows day, as the lush fruit eventually withers and the seed falls to ground, as the moon shows her dark face and the tide turns, so do we heal ourselves by embracing all the shades and shapes of our selves, externally and internally.

I now know that I am a cell in a larger body and to make all parts of me whole and functioning in a unified way is to enable the greater whole, the bigger picture, the larger cycles, to move with grace and in harmony. I have a purpose!

As do you.

As does my beloved, a Green Man being made the greener in a tattooist's chair. Ours are small steps, lightly taken, and our voices add to the swelling song of the universe. My part of the tune is carried, in eddies and swirls, onwards and upwards, blending with yours and twining and twisting like tenacious ivy around the song of my lover. I am in euphony with myself and so my note is true and pure. And so the dance is more enjoyable, the refrain more melodious, and creation's resonance is sweeter...not because of me, but not in spite of me either.

I do what I can. I take responsibility for me. *I am as I am.*

As are you!

As is my sweet soul-love who even now shifts and opens his moss-on-granite eyes as Sally stares down into his precious face, etching his soul lines the deeper and sprouting leaves on their empty boughs. I reach over and gently lay a hand on his arm so that he knows I am with him, supoporting him through this the most permanent, the most affecting, gesture he can ever make in this world. All his responsibilities to the land, as well as to his soul-kin, to Mother Nature's myriad creatures, and, most of all, to a small blue-green planet herself, are etched into these patterns. That which he long ago pledged his allegiance to is now made flesh; his vow to guard her and cherish her with his heart's blood and his soul's eternal essence are now made as visible. He has, after all that has been, kept faith.

Yes, even when I felt as if he would crumble, hide away, run and run again, he has stood firm. Finally he has shown his faith to be that of the mightiest oak, its plunging roots finding such deep purchase in the world, its branches lifting towards eternity, reaching, seeking the golden light of truth and unity.

A tear of pure gratitude spilled down my cheek, running over my frothing white blossom and pooling in my tender new leaves. Each tear was a spring rain, warm and nourishing, to sustain that which grew in me, and on me, eternally.

(*And each leaf remembers your name Alicia! Each petal is a prayer to your holy spirit and each twigling stem tells me we will meet again. Oh yes, beloved, so may it be!*)

Sally, as if sensing my heart's overflowing, looked up again and met my swiming gaze. Fragmenting in my watery vision she turned into many, all smiling gently, encouraging, open and wild and free. She had returned, beyond their torture, beyond the persecutions and the barren times! Yes, beyond the cruel fires, beyond any torturous experience at a simple wooden stake, beyond the systematic hurting, we had all returned! Though we had been lost for such a very long time we had come home to oursleves at last.

Some words sprang into my head, unbidden...

'Wild wood, wild blood, moon and star,
You'll be loved for what you are.'

...and I sang them softly too myself, knowing that soon I would be singing them as I sat next to my beloved, driving a beautiful yellow and red bow-topped wagon down unfamiliar lanes. I would be singing it as we camped by tangled hedges laden with Autumn's bounty and I would sing it to the rabbit in her hole and to the tree's stark black silloutettes on a December afternoon. I would sing as I learned to go wooding, taking only that which was dead and never green and I would sing it as I learned to lay a fire with respect to the selflessly giving trees and to the spirit of dancing brother flame. I would sing it to the dispossessed who needed healing, to the troubled who needed guidance, to the lost who needed to be sung back home. But most of all I would sing it to my beloved who would be feeding a stout bay mare on a piece of common land, or playing his fiddle at a local fayre, or mesmerising another group of childen round a campfire in a wood. Yes, I would sing and all creation would be singing with me, a small red-haired *seer* with a fierce spirit, just like a lion's.

All I had to do, all we ever had to do, was to have faith.

Our future was waiting for us in a barn at Penny Farm, guarded by Ed Sturwick, he who had lovingly restored the '*Romany Rosa*' to her former glory. She waited there, our jaunty, stately wagon, just waiting for adventures, waiting to carry us to where we were needed. Yes, our destiny had been so lovingly bequeathed to us by our Faery-Godmother and soon we would be living the dream on the highways and by-ways of England.

We would be bringing the Greening!

I looked up form my dreamy reverie to find the tattoo machine had stopped it's angry wasp-like buzzing. Both Sally and Treeface were looking at me, expectantly.

"Its finished!" said Sally, happily, wiping at Treefaces verdant brow with a paper towel.

"It's only just begun," said Treeface and I, with one voice.

And Sally smiled at us with all her soul's Fey magic shining through her dark, dark eyes.

I could see them through the trees.

Through the bars of hazel and elder I witnessed them, the intricate patterns of the branches echoed on their own dear faces.

Had it been foolish of me to come? But how very neccesary!

Autumnus and V'ridian were with me, guiding me, giving me their support. They had lead me here, to this clearing, covering for me as I wandered away from my parents to stare at the couple who sat laughing and joking outside their pretty covered wagon. My own parents favoured a standard touring caravan, which was parked up at the official site on the Levels, but I was much more interested in that lovely red and yellow bow-top. It had been beautifully and painfully restored for this happy tree-faced couple by Ed Sturwick of Penny Farm back in the Nineteen Nineties, that I knew. There weren't many of these stately wagons left now, nor folk who'd be willing to restore them, but Ed had been such a man, gentle-man, a craftsman...a Fey-human, like us. Yes, I had chosen Ed, so long ago it now seemed, to be the man to put together my own heart's-dream for these two tangle-browed lovers. I had so wanted to have the chances in life I never did, see? The '*Romany Rosa*', that jaunty little wagon, had once belonged to my husband, to or rather to *Alicia's* husband, Will Owens, but his lengthy and devastating illness had lead to the wagon's imminent decay...and, ultimately, the loss of Rhiannon and Davey too. Will's lingering, like a wraith between worlds, had almost been Alicia's undoing as I recall, but she endured, grew stronger, kept the faith.

And now here she was, here *I* was, back again! My Faery-faith had the power to pass beyond death, to move through time like a glittering salmon through fresh water, to bring me back to where I needed to be. Yes! But oh how hard it was, but how *right,* to see them there, my beloved kin, and not be able to tell them, to hold them...

(*Treeface! Lian! Feel me near you, I pray! Know me beyond this child's body that I now wear and know that I love you beyond all human boundaries. I am so glad, so very, very glad, to see you there in my beloved wagon! Bless you! May the* 'Romany Rosa' *be a good home for you, my beloved ones, and for your child...when he comes. May it carry you safely along the highways and by-ways, across common land and down winding streets, and may its path always be that of the Greening. Always!*)

The presence of those sweet, keen guiding spirits, they who had always been with us three in one shape or form, made me feel comforted beyond measure. If it had not been for them, for their focus, their firm but tender support, I would have run into that clearing, perhaps screaming, perhaps crying with sheer confusion and frustration. I wore a girl-child's body, that was for sure, yet my soul was also her soul, *Alicia's* soul, and the feelings that my soul experienced, there in the trees, were overwhelming.

I had not thought it to be as hard as this! Should I run, bolt for them and hope that they could feel the woman, their soul-kin, behind my child's eyes? And what would that have achieved, eh? A child of only four, an unknown girl with mousy hair and a plain, open face, hurtling towards them out of a copse? A girl who would have to be returned to er parents, after all, for her presence with them, these two wild-looking strangers, could bring them trouble. A girl who would never know them, never share hearth and heart with them, not in this life. And yet one who would never, ever be parted from them, not really.

Would they have known me for what I *be*, within, beyond my human form, or would they have merely seen me as a minor, a wee lost child? I would never know.

Something so precious in me that it had no name rose up and filled me watching them there. They both looked a little older, of course, but their haunted, drawn looks had left them and their energies sparkled like sunlight on dew. Oh Lady, how I loved them! And how they loved eachother and the life I had given them.

The life that Alicia had made sure that they have.

These two had no wilful, disruptive, unsympathetic children to consider when they took to the road. These two had no invalid among them whose needs grew more and more complex by the week. No, these two could travel freely as Alicia could never have done, bringing the Greening to each new village or town, spreading a little of their love and care far and wide but never spreading it too thinly. No, there was nothing to hold them back! Ah, it felt good, and yet terribly sad, even to a tiny child, to know that someone else was experiencing what should have been her's once, in another life, another age. An age when witchery and the *sight* had not been accepted as they are now. An age when 'psychic phone-lines' and bestselling spiritual books and magazines about the unexplained had no place in the world at all.An age in which children left you, abandoned you, for being *who you be* and for using herbs and spells on a dying man. A man who, they refused to believe, was always going to die anyway.

Ah yes, Davey and Rhiannon always felt I had killed him with my *unnatural abilities*, as they saw them.Just as society told them it was true, reinforcing their prejudices and fears of their own strange mother. Our kind were always a scapegoat for other folk's pain and confusion, always open to the misplaced anger and undealt with fears of others.

I sighed, a high, childish sound to my own ears. V'ridian, whose form was always a clear and very dear reflection of my own emotional state, flashed and faded from my vision only to appear again, shimmering at my side. She was clad in shifting shades of softest green, in deep mauve and cold, cold grey. She moved constantly, spiralling round me and then manifesting for me as a long-limbed, shock-headed shadow. I saw her become a zigzag of crackling light as the pain of my hurting zipped through me again, ripping me open.

"It *hurts*!"

I needn't have spoken for they were both my mirror, V'ridian, she who had once appeared as an owl, an eagle and a butterfly, was now revealed as an almost-female, a wavering reflection of a weeping willow in a deep, secret pool. She knew my sadness inside and out and reflected it back at me so I knew that I was not alone, was never alone. She glimmered with the cool light of a thousand ancient mornings, with the bright darkness of uncountable, unfathomable twilight hours. She reached out to me, flickered, shone, was gone.

Then I felt her impossible fingers infuse me with a golden light and caress me with a touch as sweet and gentle as summer rain. I felt *loved,* even as these two, this precious couple of unearthly, yet deeply earthed, tree-faced beauty, would never love me in this life. Yet still I watched them, mesmerised it seemed, reluctant to let these two familiar figures out of my sight as they sat outside of the '*Romany Rosa*', chatting companionably just as she and I used to not so very long ago.

Linden blossoms fell into my hair like confetti.

I could not go, not just yet, for I had brought them a gift that must be given, and given swiftly lest my emotions get the better of me and I run to them...

Stooping I placed '*The Lovers*' card in the water and set it to sail, pushing it with my small, eager fingers towards them. My dear familiar spirits had brought the card to me and had placed it under my pillow, a gift from the Faeries to a child. They would always help me, my

Fey guides, and of course they had told me what I should do with this card. So here it was, cresting each swell of the water like a proud, colourful little vessel, going to its rightful home.

Even as I watched the card move from me my Otherworld friends sensed the acuteness of my grief, and the depth of my joy, and held my hands, as much a part of me...more so...than either the frustration or the emptiness.

Autumnus wore his mantle of leaves which crackled and rustled and spoke to me of death and re-birth. In that raiment he looked to me to be be-decked in jewels which flashed as the sunlight caught them, ruby red and amber. Underneath his leafy cloak his elemental body was fashioned from dark earth. He wore the guise of the land at winter's turning, built of hard ground with frosty eyes and a mouth like a cracked acorn about to melt back into the soil after a whole cycle of resting under the oak that had given it life. Autumnus, this wild guardian of mine, reminded me of my pledges and pacts with the planet. And my promise to be fully in the life of this little girl now. I had promised to walk away, once my gift had been given, and to not walk back. Yes, and he would help me. He *would*! He was more, much more, than just a child's imaginary friend. I squeezed his ephemeral hand, never doubting in his presence, in his *reality*, for a second.

Then I stood for a moment longer and kept my council.

I would not disturb them, not this day or any other, but *I would not forget*. And I knew my parents would not bring me this way again and that their little girl's will-and-wish would not, *could* not, move them to do her silent bidding again. I would not be on the trail of these beautiful remnants of a dead woman's life again, oh no. It had been a one off. And now I must go!

V'ridian passed close to me and I got a sense that I was doing the right thing, if it was by far the most painful. She was less tethered to human-levels than either myself or Autumnus, hence her previous shape-shifting into bird or winged insect form, and her voice rang with truth, her communications crystalline and quivering through me. She was all enchantment, a bright darkling, and just to know her was to fly with her, lacy winged and fashioned of filaments and fragments of dreaming. She waxed and waned at my side, a creation of pure inspiration and flights of fancy, and I knew that she would guide me well in my own futures, just as she would with them. Like rainbow circles around the moon, like the rising mist over the marshes, she spoke to me of mystery and I responded to her now with a child's glorious enthusiasm. Oh, there was still so much to learn, to do! Yes, I had other things to do now and I would make sure I did them. I began to walk away, my little hands held by the two Fey who were now my best friends.

And,

'*Resurgence!*' called a blackbird to its mate.

'*Resurgence!*' sang the river that flowed between us, myself and my oldest, dearest companions. And, in my mind's eye, I saw that colourful scrap of printed card being moved along by the current of the bubbling waters. It was sodden and a small snail was riding it like a raft but it could still be recognised for what it was...for what it once had been and now would be again. I was a magical gift,flowing from one witch to another, a symbol which stated that they may take control of their own relationship, and of their own lives, without fear. With this act of sympathetic magic they could embrance eachother and their furture, freely, with joy and thanks.

And even though my back was now turned to them, as each step took me further away, I felt her pick it out of the water. And oh, I felt her hold it up to her face, felt the amazement of my dear, flame haired witch-kin.

"*Alicia!*"

I heard Lian even as I kept walking; moving surely into another life and another hope for the Greening. Yet I did not turn, I could not!

(*Dear spirits, give me the strength to carry on!*)

Instead I smiled, knowing that they had their gift, a card that meant so much to them both, this time in tact, whole again.

'*Go well, beloved*' I said, half to myself, in a child's sweet, plaintive voice.

And as I walked back towards my parents I heard a heron call out somewhere across the Somerset Levels, a cry which pulled at the starlit strands of my soul, strands which still shone even though I had thought them lost within that hollow place within me. And I *knew*.

I followed the sound of the bird's forlorn cry and I knew my new life was over there...

Somewhere.

Begun Summer Solstice 2001, completed Imbolc 2005

For Gary, my soul-love

For more information on green spirituality, wild witchcraft, natural enchantment and spiritwalking please see:

'Green Spirituality' *

'Craft of the Wild Witch'

'Spiritwalking'

'Spellcaster'

Details on publication etc. given at the front of this book.

Or e-mail

poppypalin@gypsymoondesign.fsnet.co.uk

or visit the website

www.poppypalin.org

for more details

* *Poppy writing as Rosa Romani*

And go well, for the Greening. *Keep the faith!*

You've read the book, now plant a tree!
In honour of the wise ones of bark, branch and bud
who gave their lives that we may share
ideas and dreams.

Cover illustration:
St. Paul's in the Blitz, 1941
Courtesy of Popperfoto

Geffrye Museum
Kingsland Road
London E2 8EA
Tuesday–Saturday 10-5
Sunday 2-5
Closed Monday

Originally published by the
Inner London Education Authority, 1974.
Publication ISBN 0 7168 **0628** 2

UTILITY

FURNITURE AND FASHION

1941-1951

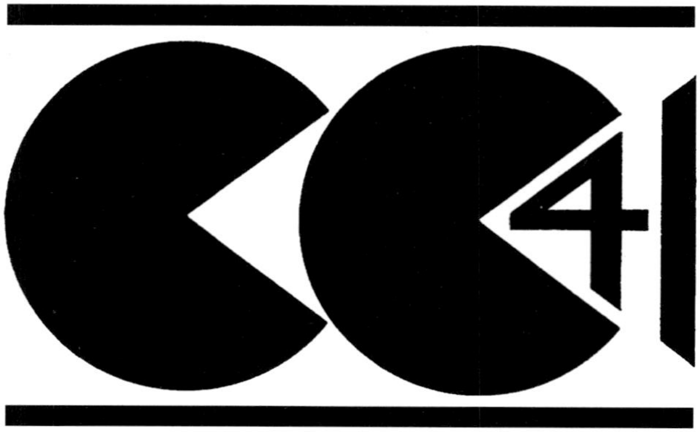

The best-known aspect of the Utility scheme is undoubtedly its symbol, but information as to its precise meaning and origin is tantalisingly scarce. Fortunately, Lady Watkinson, the widow of Sir Laurence Watkinson, who was at the Board of Trade from 1931 to 1946, and launched the Utility scheme, had kept a group of cuttings from the Sunday Dispatch in which the full story is told. The 'CC' stands for 'Civilian Clothing' and '41' for the date 1941, but the designer, Reginald Shipp, who is otherwise unremembered, was apparently instructed 'to design the double C so that the public should not recognise the letters as such'. Sir Laurence's secretary at the time was Alison McInnes, now Lady Peck, who recalls that the symbol was referred to as 'the cheeses'. It was she who christened the clothing 'Utility', a term that was in due course also applied to the furniture made under the scheme, and which is the main subject of this exhibition.

Jeffery Daniels

Contents

Foreword 3
Acknowledgements and list of lenders and donors ... 4
Introduction... 5
Utility Furniture - Chronology 7
Hugh Dalton 24
Sir Gordon Russell 25
The attitude of the Furniture Trade 27
The attitude of the Unions 29
Enid Marx 30
Wedgwood Victory Ware 32
Utility Fashion 33
The image of Utility 37
Posters 39
'Dig for Victory' 42
Post-war Design 44
Miscellanea 45
Bibliography 47

FOREWORD

1995 Foreword to Utility Catalogue

Twenty-one years on from the Geffrye Museum's exhibition on Utility Furniture and Fashion, the catalogue continues to enjoy steady demand. It remains one of the most useful reference works on this extraordinary period in British design history, and for this reason we are publishing a second edition, with no alterations or revisions. As a clear, concise and authoritative description of the Utility schemes, particularly for furniture, it has proved hard to beat.

David Dewing
Director

ACKNOWLEDGEMENTS

Sir Gordon Russell, Professor John Vaizey, Lady Ashton, Christopher Heal, Enid Marx, George Dixon, Gillian Naylor, Mark Brutton, David Mellor, Barry Kitts, Victoria and Albert Museum, Imperial War Museum, Vestry House Museum, Public Record Office, Department of Trade, Design Council, Design and Industries Association, Building Centre, London Borough of Hackney Library Services, London College of Furniture, London School of Economics.

The exhibition has been mounted with financial help from the London Borough of Hackney and the Area Museums Service for South Eastern England.

The catalogue, which incorporates much unpublished material from the Board of Trade Archives, was compiled and written by Richard Sword, deputy curator of the Geffrye Museum, with contributions from John Vaizey, Gillian Naylor, David Mellor, Jane Ashelford and Bob Carter. The exhibition was designed and executed by Bob Carter and Richard Sword.

Lenders

Items

Victoria and Albert Museum B1-10, C1, 17, 18, E1
Imperial War Museum C5, D1-28
Vestry House Museum F11
Enid Marx B11-17
Christopher Heal A24
Mrs L S Nash A25
J Crux A26
Jane Ashelford C12, 14, 16
Jacqmar Ltd C15
Robert Opie D29, F6, 7, 8 (part), 10
Rosemary Hards F8 (part), 9
Richard Sword E2, F4
Ann Roy E5, 7
P Pickard Jenkins E8, 9
Paul Edwards E10
B Kelly Espinosa F5
Katherine Howard E3

Photographs

Imperial War Museum 36-38, 41-49
Design and Industries Association 1-6
Design Council 7-10, 12-14, 18-22, 25-29, 34
The Labour Party 35

Miscellaneous uncatalogued material is lent by Vestry House Museum, Robert Opie, Rosemary Hards, Mrs N Brown, J Crux, Dennis Howard, Ronald Roles and Mrs E M Holland.

INTRODUCTION

When war came in 1939 timber was hard to come by because there was an acute shipping shortage. Other imported goods, notably staple foodstuffs and petrol, were rationed, and the size of the rations grew smaller as the war progressed, becoming, ironically, smallest of all in the acute economic crisis that gripped the world after the war was over. Paradoxically enough, the families in that third of the population of Britain who in 1938 were chronically undernourished had their first adequate diet in 1940 and 1941. The incidence of deficiency diseases, and notably infant mortality, dropped dramatically.

Some foodstuffs were not things people eat daily or weekly, like tea, sugar and fats. They were miscellaneous tinned and other goods. They were put on a points system – so many points were allocated to a family each week, and every rationed commodity was given a 'points' value. The same was true of clothing. It wasn't possible to say that people should have a suit or a pair of shoes every so often; but it was possible to say that they could claim a certain total quantity of garments in the course of a year, by weighting the points value of each item of clothing until it roughly represented the quantity of cloth and amount of labour involved in its production. Here again, war socialism meant that for the first time many people were decently clothed. It wasn't absolute equality of course, because people who had full wardrobes at the beginning of the war had a reserve to use up, while young adults (at least, those not in uniform) were barely able to clothe themselves except on the second-hand market.

Furniture represented a special problem to those who were trying to control civilian consumption, and to regulate industrial production. In principle it had a very low priority as it used timber, and the country had large stocks of furniture when war broke out. But furniture was needed, for the services, and to replace the homes destroyed by bombing, and for people who were setting up homes for the first time. True the marriage rate was very low in the war, but even so half a million or so marriages took place every year. The usual way people furnished their own few rooms was by buying second-hand furniture, and true enough, second-hand prices shot up – there was virtually nothing that couldn't be sold. Even so, some new furniture had to be made.

The question that arose was apparently simple but in practice most complex, and the solution was bold. It was the same for furniture and for clothes. Both terms covered a very wide variety of products – beds, tables, chairs are all 'furniture' – and each kind of product itself had an enormous range of shapes, sizes and styles. It wasn't possible to ration them in such a way that everybody got – say – one table, one bed and one chair a year; some people would need far more (if they had been bombed out, for instance) while others would need hardly anything – for many people over 40 the problem is how to get rid of furniture, not how to get hold of it. The first solution, in the case of clothing, was coupons, of variable value (26 for a suit, 1 for a handkerchief), and allocation in the case of furniture. You were entitled to buy it if you could prove you needed it.

But even if the Board of Trade said who could buy it, the prior question was who could make it. Timber and carpenters were both scarce in wartime Britain. The use of scarce timber to make enormous baroque objects for the rich was obviously to be forbidden. At the same time, however, the opposite danger was greater. It was that furniture manufacturers would produce shoddy stuff that wouldn't last and sell it at exorbitant prices to customers who just had to have some furniture whatever its cost or quality.

Prices could be controlled as all prices, except second-hand prices, were controlled. Quality offered a more complex problem. A chair could have its maximum price fixed at, say, £2 10s. But how could you ensure that people got £2 10s. worth of chair? The answer was, of course, a standard design, which could be relatively easily checked, and which would by its simplicity avoid unnecessary use of raw materials and labour, and by its high quality give it a long and useful life. This was the origin of utility furniture, utility clothes, utility household goods like blankets and sheets. The utility sign CC41 soon became recognised as a guarantee of high quality material and workmanship and sensible design, at a moderate price.

It is at this point that the response to wartime and postwar shortages meets the century old movement to overcome the catastrophic consequences of industrialisation on design and taste. From William Morris on, craftsmen had protested against the debauching of taste which mass production had brought about. Part of the remedy was a return to honest craftsmanship for one-off objects. But that could only be a remedy available to the relatively affluent for more than a small proportion of the things they used. For the rest of the people, better design had to be built into the industrial system.

The co-operative movement, and firms like Boots and Marks and Spencers, specialised in selling mass-produced standard formula high quality products at a reasonable price. The poor, it seemed, had a thirst for frills and furbelows which gimcrack producers satisfied with shoddy, cheap and nasty things. The system was as ugly as it was tasteful.

Progressive local authorities, like the London County Council, brought good design to the people through their housing. London's pre-war cottage estates, and its blocks of council flats, pioneered good housing at low rents. London Transport under Frank Pick specialised in good quality transport, from the tube trains and stations, to the posters and litter bins. The war provided an opportunity for the philosophy of the economical, practical, utilitarian standards to be applied to the taste of the nation as a whole – and this opportunity lasted right through the war, until the early 1950s, with the end of the Atlee government in the autumn of 1951.

It was a philosophy that flourished in that austere age when shortages were widespread, and the ethic was strong that what was available should be fairly shared. Its living memorial is the National Health Service. Its celebration was a conscious reincarnation of the Great Exhibition of 1851 – the Festival of Britain of 1951, held on the South Bank, then (as now) a barren treeless spot. In that Festival, opened by a dying king, sponsored by a dying government, and attacked by an opposition hungry for an end to austerity and rationing, the best architects and designers and artists produced a Celebration of Utility, a chaste festival that Bentham himself would have been proud of. The people who created those transient tests, devoted to science and discovery, built the London we now see around us. Its sheer ugliness prompts the question – what was it in the Age of Utility that led to the appalling monstrosities that Casson, Shepherd, and other famous men, have inflicted upon us? But that is for another occasion – this furniture is from the Innocence of Utility, before the buildings of its frightful maturity were more than aspirations.

John Vaizey

UTILITY FURNITURE-CHRONOLOGY

Of all the war-time Utility schemes that for furniture was an unparalleled example of the total state control not only of the supply but more importantly, the design of an essential commodity.

In our society it is perhaps only possible to impose such controls in war-time, and in the case of the furniture industry it was the sheer magnitude of the problem of rationing the at times almost non-existent supplies of timber that led to the adoption of so drastic a measure. No other items were controlled in the same way with the exception of such relatively unimportant things as pencils, radio receivers and cigarette lighters, all things to do in some degree with wood (matches were in short supply so a Utility cigarette lighter was devised). Other Utility goods were merely limited in the amount of material and/or labour which might be used in their manufacture, as with clothing and pottery.

The significant events leading up to the introduction of Utility furniture at the beginning of 1943 are dealt with in the chronology which follows, as is its subsequent development after the war and its eventual demise at the end of 1952.

Two of the key figures in the scheme, Hugh Dalton, President of the Board of Trade 1942-45 and Gordon Russell, who headed the Utility furniture design team, are considered in greater detail at the end of the chronology.

Abbreviations used in the text:

BoT	Board of Trade
MoS	Ministry of Supply
MoH	Ministry of Health
CPRC	Central Price Regulation Committee

1937 April 11th

Publication of the Council for Art and Industry's report on 'The Working Class Home, its Furnishings and Equipment'.

The Council for Art and Industry had been set up in 1934 under the chairmanship of Frank Pick who as chief administrator of the London Passenger Transport Board had done more to bring designers into industry than almost anyone else.

Its report is of crucial importance in the development of the Utility furniture scheme six years later since, although the latter would not have happened without the war, many of the ideas behind it are contained in the Report: it may justly be said that the design morality of Utility derived from the Council for Art and Industry's attitudes.

In its definitions of 'good design' for instance, in the statement that the committee was most favourably impressed by 'items in which the design was simple, of good proportions and without dust-collecting features', in the use of phrases like 'simple construction' and in its reluctant recognition that popular taste might well demand more ornament, it foreshadows Utility. The report's conclusions as to the amount and type of furniture deemed suitable for the working classes were of great use to the BoT officials and members of the Utility Furniture Advisory Committee in 1942, as were its cost yardsticks. In fact the Report's figures were later used by the BoT to show how well Utility compared to similar pre-war furniture. It is also significant that one member of the committee that produced the Report, Elizabeth Denby, an expert of Dalton's Utility Furniture Advisory Committee, and that their secretary H A R Binney, a BoT official, was also to be closely involved in the scheme.

1939 September 3rd

Britain declares war on Germany.

September 5th

Control of Timber (No 1) Order made by the MoS under the Defence of the Realm Regulations. Timber Control was set up as a department of the MoS, quickly followed by other controls, all of them affecting the furniture industry in some way. These were Silk and Rayon, Leather, Wool, Cotton, Iron and Steel, Aluminium, Non-ferrous metals, Flax, Hemp, and Jute. Under this legislation a system of licensing for industrial consumers, such as the furniture industry, was imposed: what was left after defence, export and other essential needs had been satisfied was in effect rationed. The supply position rapidly worsened although it was not apparent immediately since many manufacturers had stocks of timber.

December 1st
First meeting of the Central Price Regulation Committee under its Chairman, Raymond Evershed. The CPRC was set up to administer the Prices of Goods Act and became the chief means of controlling the prices of civilian goods. There were seventeen regional committees, each responsible to the central committee.

1940 June 10th
Price Control extended to furniture and furnishings. However, prices at this time were not, and could not be, controlled rigidly. Rises in the costs of raw materials had to be passed on and increasing shortages gave rise to a certain amount of profiteering, instances of which could at least be reported to the local Price Regulation Committees by the public for investigation and possible prosecution.

July
Timber supplies to the industry withdrawn completely. Furniture production continued to some extent however, from stocks of timber held by the manufacturers.

September
Early in the month the Blitz ended the 'Phoney War' and the Government announced that it intended to introduce an insurance scheme whereby 'payments for damage to the furniture of persons of limited means' (up to £400 p.a. income) would be made, up to 100% of the damage. The scheme was to be administered through the local Assistance Boards and District Valuers.

Towards the end of the month Timber Control very slightly relaxed its restrictions on supply and a small amount of timber was released to the industry. This was prompted by the damage caused by the first serious German air-raids of the war.

October
Early in the month the Government introduced its insurance scheme for property, including furniture. Its provisions were to be expanded under the War Damage Act of March 1941.

October 21st
Purchase Tax introduced on many items for civilian consumption, including furniture. Its purpose was to reduce consumption as well as raising revenue and the rates varied between 16⅔% and 33⅓%. In considering this it must be remembered that many people had what was termed 'surplus' income because there was so little to spend it on.

December 1st
Quotas for the manufacture of many domestic items were introduced and were applied to some sorts of furniture, notably wicker and metal, and bedding. The supply of some items was cut drastically, aluminium holloware being reduced to nil. This was especially unfortunate in that Lord Beaverbrook's misguided 'Saucepans into Spitfires' campaign had induced many people to part with their cooking utensils for salvage. The shortage was mitigated two years later with the introduction of the Utility kettle-cum-saucepan.

The Quota system was a much-used economic weapon and it operated by the Government's deciding that production should be restricted to a percentage (almost invariably lower) of that for a corresponding period in a previous year. For example the production of some metal furniture was reduced to 25% of that for the corresponding half of 1939. Production was of course cut by the fairly simple expedient of cutting the quota of raw materials.

During the second half of 1940 the domestic furniture industry had been very badly hit by the supply situation. However many manufacturers were beginning to move into essential war work making things as diverse as Bailey Bridges and parachutes as well as furniture for local authorities and the forces. One Government contract was the supply of hundreds of thousands of air-raid shelter bunks – nothing could have been more utilitarian than that.

1941 January 24th
Major A I Harris, Timber Controller at the MoS, gave a Press Conference at which, to quote *The Cabinet Maker* 'he gave

advance information on the subject of Utility furniture' together with promises of a release of timber to make this 'domestic furniture of a simple type' for evacuated families and those who had lost their homes in the continued bombing. Although this may be one of the first references to Utility in connection with war-time furniture, the word was in fairly common usage, meaning standard or basic. Indeed a furniture manufacturer's advertisement the previous year had described its dual purpose bed-settee as 'double utility'.

February
The first week of this month really marks the beginning of some sort of Utility furniture scheme, for it was then that the Government announced its 'Standard Emergency Furniture'. This was born out of the extreme shortage of timber which had all but been withdrawn since July 1940, coupled with the serious damage caused by German bombing. The idea was for the MoS, as an agency service of the MoH, to provide replacement furniture to bombed citizens (or bombees as they were called) who would be helped to buy it through the Government insurance scheme.

The emergency furniture was extremely basic and totally undistinguished, unlike the later Utility furniture. It was to be made by firms on a Government list, mostly those already engaged on contracts for canteen, office and hospital furniture. Indeed the emergency furniture bore a remarkable resemblance to that already being made for the Ministry of Works and Buildings.

Specifications were issued for basic items such as wardrobes, cupboards, dressing chests, cots and tables. Unlike Utility furniture two years later, 80% plywood was used in its construction, as the shortage had not yet become acute. Plywood's advantages in economy of material and in lightness were obvious and in any case the furniture was envisaged strictly for emergencies, meeting a relatively limited demand. Contracts were issued quickly and it was in production by the end of the month. It must be remembered that the rest of the domestic industry, provided it could get the timber, was still free to make whatever it liked.

March
Later in the month BoT plans for the concentration of industrial production were well advanced and it was expected that the furniture industry would be involved. Concentration meant that industry was directed to where it was most needed and in the case of domestic furniture this was away from areas where the labour demands of, say, the armaments industry might compete. Firms were encouraged to co-operate, even to the extent of joining forces, while large firms with many branches were expected to concentrate their production in fewer plants. In this way nucleus firms, as they came to be known, were established. Concentration had not gone very far at this stage of the war, especially as there was no direct compulsion, but it assumed overwhelming importance later in the following year when it became part of the whole strategy of Utility production.

April
Income Tax raised to ten shillings in the pound.
From now until towards the end of the war only men over forty and women were eligible for employment in the furniture industry. Younger men were liable to be conscripted or moved to reserved occupations.

June 1st
Clothing and footwear rationing was introduced and extended almost immediately to furnishing fabrics and carpets. The exception was blackout material, which was also one of the few things free of purchase tax. Rationing was extended to furnishing fabrics to prevent people making coupon-free clothes out of them, but after protests from the trade some of the heavier fabrics (over 7oz per square yard) were taken off coupons, as there was little danger of their being used for clothing. The furniture trade feared that rationing would come to them as well before very long.

September 2nd
Limitation of Supplies (Cloth and Apparel) Order, 1941. This extended and altered the rationing regulations of June but is mainly significant as introducing one of the most famous 'trade-marks' of all time, CC41, although the name Utility was not used in connection with the mark until the following month with the Utility Cloth (Maximum Prices) Order. An explanation of its meaning and origins is given elsewhere in the catalogue.

November 1st
Main Quota Scheme for domestic furniture manufacturers introduced. This was very important in the development of Utility furniture for a number of reasons: Timber Control, announcing the quota for the ensuing six months, was already talking of 'domestic furniture of a Utility type'. From this date too, the Raw Materials Department of the MoS stipulated that henceforth only twenty specified articles of essential furniture could be made, and also laid down the maximum amount of timber that could be used in any one article. It was rather a crude way to control the consumption of timber, and no attempt at all was made to specify actual designs for the twenty items, nor were prices to be controlled any more rigidly than was then possible under the Prices of Goods Act.
Only those firms registered with the Timber Supplies Committee of the Furniture Trade (a branch of the MoS's Timber Control) would receive further supplies of wood. It is perhaps significant that the members of that Committee included W Johnstone, A G Tomkins, Lucian Ercolani and Frank Austin, all of whom later had a direct concern with the Utility scheme.

December
BoT goes ahead at last with its plans, announced in May, for the concentration of the industry and the establishment of nucleus firms. Once again there was no absolute compulsion but the mechanism by which the industry was now supplied under the Main Quota Scheme introduced in November made it virtually impossible to avoid: the way to Utility production was opening up.

1942 January 1st
Timber quota cut by one third.
Plywood, increasingly used in aircraft production, was withdrawn early in the year.

February
Early in the month, the Vice-Chairman of the CPRC, Professor Ford of the MoS and Mr Hooper of the Ministry of Works and Buildings discussed the possibility of devising a Utility furniture scheme around the MoS's 'Standard Emergency Furniture', with strict price control.

February 21st
Hugh Dalton becomes President of the Board of Trade.

February 24th
At a meeting of the CPRC it is stated that 'details of the (Utility) scheme are being prepared'. The CPRC was engaged in trying to price the twenty pieces of furniture whose manufacture had been allowed since November 1941, and finding it virtually impossible. It concluded that the only way to control prices would be to specify the actual design of the furniture as well as its timber content. The CPRC also recommended that factories also be designated to make it and that it be exempted from Purchase Tax.

This pressure from the CPRC, prompted by its shock at the prices then being asked, was clearly one of the most important factors in the development of Utility furniture. The other factor, one which had become endemic, was of course the timber supply situation.

April 14th
Professor Ford of the MoS tells the BoT that the supply position is grave. He said his Ministry could no longer guarantee any timber for furniture that year and that they would in any case have to make 'some substantial reduction'. The MoS wanted to see the twenty permitted items of furniture cut down still further, and it was only the representations of the MoH who had to deal with the bombees that made the MoS take a wider view instead of cutting off timber supplies altogether.

The situation with regard to furniture had now become really desperate, with rising prices and profiteering on the one hand and the threat of a drastic reduction in supply on the other. Hugh Dalton had to act, and behind the scenes he and his officials were working hard on the possibilities of a Utility furniture scheme.

May 5th
In the House of Commons Mr Leslie, MP asks Hugh Dalton 'whether, in view of the excessively high prices now being charged for household furniture, he will consider fixing prices for same, so as to protect persons compelled to re-furnish their homes after losses caused by enemy action?'

Hugh Dalton:
'Yes sir. I signed yesterday an interim order prohibiting increases in prices above the current level. This order will be published on Thursday. I have asked the Central Price Regulation Committee to submit further recommendations on the subject'.
Mr Watkins:
'Are any arrangements afoot by which good substantial furniture at reasonable prices will be provided for the public, under Government control?'
Hugh Dalton:
'We are advancing in the direction of the production of more Utility articles of various kinds, but I cannot say that we have yet got as far as furniture.'

May 7th
Furniture (Maximum Prices) Order 1942.

This was the order mentioned by Hugh Dalton in his answer to the Parliamentary Question above. It froze prices at their May 1st level, and included secondhand furniture, although antiques, defined as being made before January 1st 1900 were exempted.

By this time Hugh Dalton and the BoT wanted to press ahead with plans for Utility furniture. It was stressed that the Furniture (Maximum Prices) Order was an interim measure, and that care should be taken not to call any of the goods controlled under that Order Utility. The CPRC agreed to try to fix maximum prices for the twenty specified pieces of furniture, and also to fix the margins on secondhand pieces.

Already the BoT was envisaging Utility Furniture being available to bombees and newly-weds only, under a 'certificate of need system', and it produced a minute to that effect on May 8th. Dalton, after he had seen the minute on May 9th, noted 'Prices should be reduced as soon as possible and Utility production speeded up. The public is rightly impatient.'

June
Early in the month the BoT was able to formulate its ideas for Utility Furniture in great detail, making the following proposals in a minute dated June 10th:

1. Prohibition from July 1st of the manufacture of any furniture except the twenty pieces in the MoS list (it was still possible for manufacturers to make pieces outside this list if they had legitimate supplies of timber).

2. The prices worked out by the CPRC were to be applied from July 15th.

3. To appoint 'one or two of the best available designers of furniture' to help the BoT, with the Ministry of Works and Buildings, to compile a booklet of specifications and prices of Utility Furniture. The BoT was thinking also of temporary furniture of paper and basket work and hoped that the booklet could be published by September 1st, together with an invitation to the trade to apply for licences to manufacture the furniture.

4. Utility furniture only to be produced under licence from October 1st.

5. 'Certificate of Need' to be introduced, without which it would be impossible to buy the furniture.

6. Utility furniture to be free of Purchase Tax if possible.

While the time scale of some of the proposals was a little premature, these did correspond to the final form of the scheme, and met with Hugh Dalton's approval. He commented 'Now sound out the trade on the policy proposed and let me hear how these react. Let us have a good panel of advisers on utility furniture and let me see a list of names proposed.'

June 30th
CPRC produced a report on the situation following the price freeze announced by Hugh Dalton on May 7th. Their findings were disturbing and revealed many abuses and evidence of profiteering, reinforcing their view that only a full-blown Utility scheme would be effective.

July 3rd
Lord Forres, who was in charge of the concentration of industry at the BoT, met the trade and told them of the decision which had been taken. The trade was very opposed, not to the idea of Utility specifications, but to the revolutionary proposal to specify actual designs. They felt that

they knew better than the BoT what the public liked and should therefore be allowed to supply it. They felt that purchasers would dislike having to have the same furniture as their neighbours, and made a strong plea that retailers should be represented on the proposed Advisory Committee as only they knew what the public would accept. But the mind of the BoT was made up and the reasons it put forward, mostly of a practical nature, were unanswerable. It is worth noting one of the reasons mentioned by Lord Forres, that the BoT valued the possibility of 'influencing popular taste towards good construction in simple, agreeable designs to the benefit of our after-the-war homes.' Those sentiments were undoubtedly Hugh Dalton's.

July 8th
It was announced to the Press that 'The President of the Board of Trade has appointed the following Advisory Committee on Utility Furniture.'
'The function of the committee will be to produce specifications for furniture of good, sound construction in simple but agreeable designs for sale at reasonable prices, and ensuring the maximum economy of raw materials and labour.'

Chairman: Mr Charles Tennyson CMG, Vice-Chairman of the Council for Art and Industry, Chairman of the Board of Governors of the National Register of Industrial Art Designers, Secretary of the Dunlop Rubber Company and Late Deputy Director of the Federation of British Industries.

Members: Miss Elizabeth Denby ARIBA Specialist in the planning and equipment of low-cost housing.

Mr John Gloag ARIBA Consultant on Industrial Design.

Revd. Charles Jenkinson Vicar of St John and St Barnabas, Leeds. A former Chairman of the Leeds Corporation Housing Committee.

Mr W Johnstone Furniture Manufacturer. Member of the Executive of the Furniture Committee of the Scottish Committee of the Council for Art and Industry.

Mr Herman Lebus CBE Senior partner in the firm of Harris Lebus, furniture manufacturers.

Mr Gordon Russell Furniture Designer, Director of Gordon Russell Ltd, of Broadway, Worcestershire.

Mr V Welsford Manager of the Furniture Factories of the CWS.

Mrs E Winborn Member of the Tenants' Committee of the Kensal House Estate.

It is interesting to note that three of the members (Tennyson, Johnstone, Denby) had, or had had, some connection with the Council for Art and Industry which produced the 1937 Report on furnishing the working class home. Russell of course was one of the 'top designers' mentioned by Hugh Dalton, John Gloag was already well known for his books on Industrial Design, Lebus and Welsford represented the trade, while the Revd. Jenkinson and Mrs Winborn in effect represented the consumer.

July 11th
The concern of the CPRC over prices, mentioned in their report of June 30th, was backed up by a Press statement by Sir Douglas McCraith, Chairman of the North Midland Region Price Regulation Committee. He was perhaps the best known of the local Price Regulation Committee Chairmen and was not given to mincing his words. He was talking about furniture and recorded that 'in many cases the prices being charged were out of all proportion to the value of the goods', that 'undue profits were being made in many quarters', prices being sometimes '300% in excess of pre-war' and that quality was often inferior: 'In many cases they consist of plywood with cardboard sides and bottoms.' McCraith welcomed Dalton's announcement of the Utility scheme and sent him a copy of his Press statement on July 13th.

July 14th
The first meeting of the Utility Furniture Advisory Committee took place, attended by Hugh Dalton, who commented 'They look quite a good bunch . . . they should do well,' and after a later meeting H A R Binney reported to him that 'some

members were pleased as punch to be on the job'. In drafting a reply to Sir Douglas McCraith's letter, Dalton wrote appreciatively and added 'My aim is to secure the production of furniture of good, sound construction in simple but agreeable designs and at reasonable prices.' According to a BoT official who had attended this meeting Dalton had left things rather open in his remarks to the Committee and it was now clearly up to them to interpret his intentions, which are best summed up in his remark above.

The Committee met weekly and by the end of the month it had been agreed that they would ask for drawings from nine designers by August 24th. The first Utility Furniture catalogue, published January 1st 1943, gives the names of eleven designers who had 'assisted the Committee in their work' and this presumably included all nine who had been asked to submit drawings. The eleven were L J Barnes, Edwin L Clinch, Walter J Cornell, H T Cutler, John Grey, Kenneth Holmes, J C Macneill, Brian O'Rorke, Victor Ruben, Grey Wornum and C V Worth.

Of the drawings submitted on August 24th those by Clinch and Cutler were amongst those selected. Edwin Clinch has said that about 65% of the first Utility furniture was designed by himself, about 25% by H T Cutler and the remainder by someone 'who worked for Lebus.' But according to *The Cabinet Maker* the third designer was L J Barnes, like the other two a High Wycombe man (Lebus's factory was in Tottenham). Walter Cornell later designed some of the Utility woven-fibre chairs. Clinch and Cutler knew each other, Clinch being a designer with Goodearls and Cutler also a lecturer at the High Wycombe Technical Institute. After their briefing at the BoT in late July they decided to collaborate on the project, working extraordinarily long hours at the Imperial Institute to the amazement of officials there.

Clinch and Cutler had a very clear grasp of their brief and were well aware that any inadequacies in the design or construction of the furniture would reflect badly on the BoT and reduce public confidence in the scheme. They were also aware of the need to prepare very concise specifications, leaving as little room for error as possible on the part of the sometimes relatively inexperienced workers who would have to use them.

Although to Edwin Clinch it was an exercise in 'plain common sense' their application to the problem without any preconceived ideas resulted in some of the best furniture designed this century, well conceived and well made. To quote Clinch again 'All that you see with Utility furniture is pure, it's good', 'the more simple the furniture the more precise must be the workmanship' and, perhaps summing up the place of Utility in the design history of this country, 'Furniture never went back to what it was like before the war – thank God.' Interestingly, much of their original range continued in production until the end, whereas many of the immediate post war pieces from the Design Panel, of which Clinch and Cutler became members incidentally, had a comparatively short production run, being phased out in 1948.

The design parameters were that the furniture should be strong and serviceable, not in any way temporary, and that it should use the minimum raw material. Only hardwoods – oak or mahogany – were to be used and all joints were strongly mortised or pegged. Because plywood was unobtainable veneered hardboard had to be used for panels. Characteristically most of the cabinet furniture stood on plinths rather than legs; wood sections were relatively thin and panels were often subdivided. Plastics were needed for the war effort, so that knobs and handles were of wood, but in spite of the shortage of steel, screws were specified in the construction, contributing greatly to the strength of the finished piece. Wardrobes were deep enough for clothes to be hung side-ways; this was certainly not always a feature of pre-war wardrobes and is an example of the thought that went into the way in which the furniture would be used. Springing in the easy chairs was minimal, 1 lb of steel wire having to do the work of 7 lb. Partly because of this particular shortage no settee or three-piece suite was designed, although a bed-settee was made for those who had to combine their living and sleeping accommodation.

August 24th

Charles Tennyson showed Hugh Dalton the drawings and models which had just been submitted to his Committee. Dalton impressed on him the need to stick to standard designs and not to give the manufacturers any leeway in this.

September 22nd

Hugh Dalton inspected the prototypes at the Imperial Institute, commenting 'not bad, but a little too uniform'. But he was satisfied enough to want to press ahead with production straight away. On the face of it there was now no real need to keep his Committee in being, but with an eye to the future he saw that he would eventually need to expand the scheme, and he wanted then to be able to 'strike a balance between undue "regimentation" and undue variety'.

October 14th

Hugh Dalton attended the preview of the Utility Furniture exhibition at the Building Centre, Maddox Street, W1, with G L Watkinson (later Sir Laurence Watkinson) of the BoT, who felt that the furniture would establish standards that would outlast the war and influence taste in all sections of the community.

October 19th

The Utility Furniture exhibition opened to the public. It ran for three weeks, attracting over 30,000 visitors. The furniture was displayed in a number of room settings but was not priced as the BoT was still working on the costing. At the same time Hugh Dalton was trying to get the Chancellor of the Exchequer, Sir Kingsley Wood, to exempt it from Purchase Tax. Wedgewood's 'Victory Ware' (described elsewhere in this catalogue) was also shown, with examples of Utility cooking utensils, including a combined kettle and saucepan. On the whole the furniture was well received, especially by the popular press, which praised its 'serviceability' and the prospect of low prices. They also sang the praises of the down-to-earth Mrs Winborn, representing the 'ordinary housewife' on the Advisory Committee. Some of the 'quality' periodicals were less enthusiastic, however, and the Architects' Journal commented: 'Very ugly to look at'. The public's main interest on the other hand seems to have been in when it would be available.

Throughout October the BoT had been working on the monumental task of pricing the furniture. It had to be done within six weeks from the time of the exhibition so that the catalogue could go to press in time for publication on January 1st 1943. The CWS cabinet factory in Enfield and Joseph Johnstone Ltd of Lochwinnoch had made some of the exhibition furniture, and their figures, together with data amassed by the CPRC, formed a basis for costing. In addition tenders from 850 firms had been received, 45 of them being investigated in great detail by BoT accountants. A comparison was made with the Council for Art and Industry's 1937 report on furnishing the working class home, showing that whereas up to the introduction of Utility, prices had risen about 150%, with its introduction it would be possible to furnish a home for only about one third more than in 1937 – £54 9s. 9d. as against £39 14s. 5d. for a double bed, wardrobe, tallboy, dressing chest, dining table, sideboard, easy chair, three dining chairs, kitchen table and one kitchen chair. This comparison was for Utility furniture in oak; in mahogany the cost would have been £72 19s. 6d. The trade was unhappy with some of the costing proposals: it wanted a 50% profit margin rather than the 33⅓% which the BoT had decided was generous, and fearing that larger traders would undercut the smaller it wanted the maximum selling price to be also the minimum. The BoT felt that if some traders were able to sell below the maximum, and in the event some were, it would indicate that the 33⅓% margin was sufficient, and in any case could only benefit the consumer, for whom the scheme had been devised.

The BoT was at the same time hard at work on the equally difficult problem of designating manufacturers to make the furniture. The 1,200 firms which had been drawing their quota of timber before October were reduced to 32 by December 1942, although the number designated had risen to 72 by January 1st 1943 and to 150 by March 1943. It was to continue throughout the war, with a big jump afterwards as firms returned to furniture making from war-work. No one firm was ever designated to make the whole range: for greater efficiency different items were made by different firms, spread as evenly as possible throughout the country (before the war London and High Wycombe were the major manufacturing areas) to save on transport costs and to avoid any duplication of effort.

November 1st

Domestic Furniture (Control of Manufacture and Supply (No. 2)) Order 1942.

This Order instituted Utility and prohibited its manufacture except under licence from the BoT. Non-Utility furniture already under construction had to be finished by January 31st 1943 and could not be sold after February 28th 1943.

November 11th
The Utility Furniture catalogue went to press.

November 16th
The Chancellor of the Exchequer agreed to exempt Utility furniture from Purchase Tax, provided Hugh Dalton did not ask for remissions on anything else. This exemption, and price control made it necessary to apply the CC41 Utility mark to the furniture and very specific instructions were given to manufacturers as to where and how it should be applied.

With the ending of the exhibition at the Building Centre arrangements were made to hold similar exhibitions in major towns and cities throughout the country, starting with Glasgow. By the end of March 1943 there had been showings in Birmingham, Bristol and Cardiff, with further exhibitions planned for Liverpool, Leeds and Newcastle.

1943 January 1st
The Utility Furniture catalogue was published.

It was divided into five sections – living room, bedroom, kitchen, nursery furniture and miscellaneous items like book-shelves and a bed-settee. Each piece, often with a choice of oak or mahogany, was illustrated and priced.

Following the BoT recommendations of the previous year it was only available by permit to bombees and newly-weds, although no permit was needed for nursery furniture and exceptions were allowed where couples had to live with their parents. The prospective buyer had to get an application form for the permit from the local Fuel Office, and after scrutiny this was issued by the district Assistance Board. Sixty units were attached to the permit, which was valid for three months, and each piece of furniture had a unit value varying from eight, for a wardrobe, to one, for a kitchen or dining chair. A special fifteen unit bed-settee permit was issued only to those who lived in bed-sitters. People with houses or flats were not allowed to buy the bed-settee. Unit values were not given in the catalogue as it was felt that they might be varied from time to time. In the event they changed remarkably little for the duration of the permit system. Since retailers could only get the furniture from the manufacturers against the units they had got from the customer they could not hold any stocks, and the choice had to be made from the catalogue. Sometimes however a retailer was able to display the furniture in transit to the customer, and there were cases where retailers persuaded or even bribed a customer to let them hold an item for a time in order to display it; in a situation where demand far outstripped supply competition for custom could be fierce. 18,500 permits were issued in the first two months of the scheme, and furniture to a total value of 25,000 units had been supplied by the end of February.

The Utility programme was now well under way, with the Advisory Committee still in being to keep an eye on any difficulties that might arise in production and to suggest improvements where necessary. As has been mentioned it was also Hugh Dalton's intention that the Committee should eventually evolve other designs itself as well as from suggestions put forward by the trade. This period immediately following the introduction of Utility was not without incident, for in February Lord Beaverbrook tried in the House of Lords to get the maximum prices order annulled, a move which, had it succeeded, would have made the scheme very much less effective.

During the Spring of 1943 Russell was thinking hard about the role of the Advisory Committee and in particular about whether, from the designers' point of view, they had done all they could. They had worked hard to try to discover what people really wanted and how they used their furniture. Russell was very active, helping to organise a meeting at Toynbee Hall in the East End to find out public reaction at first hand and during the year attended other meetings with a similar concern. To quote Russell, writing in 1946, 'I felt that to raise the whole standard of furniture for the mass of the people was not a bad war job. And it has always seemed sound to me, when in doubt as to people's requirements, to aim at giving them something better than they might be expected to demand.' He continues '. . . surely it might be possible to use the Utility specification as the basis of a quality mark in the post-control period. To this end I felt it was essential to carry on intensively with research into design. To leave everything until new designs were called for, and then take in a few designers and work at the frantic speed of the last few months (of 1942), could not give the best results.'

May

With these ideas in mind Russell then wrote a short report for the Chairman, suggesting that a panel of not more than six designers be set up under the chairmanship of a 'knowledgeable man', preferably an architect, familiar with metals, plastics and other materials besides wood. He also suggested that the Chairman of the panel should have a seat on the Advisory Committee so that he would be able to state the designers' views. Tennyson and Dalton studied the report and early in the month the President asked to see Russell and told him that he wanted him to head the proposed panel. This came as a great surprise to Russell, although it is hard to imagine anyone more qualified for the job at that time, and this was clearly Dalton's opinion. Russell's request to be able to select his own panel and to have prototypes made when necessary was agreed, and he began his search for suitable designers. He already had Clinch and Cutler ear-marked, but with so many others in the forces he had a hard job and some of those chosen were only able to attend meetings sporadically.

June

The Design Panel's first meeting appears to have been on June 3rd at Neville House, although it was not until the full Advisory Committee meeting on June 23rd that the Panel was formally reconstituted under Russell's chairmanship. The list of members given in the Advisory Committee minutes includes Brian O'Rorke, Grey Wornum, Edwin Clinch, H T Cutler, Eden Minns and R D Russell. O'Rorke and Wornum, both architects and heavily committed in other areas, were only able to attend a few of the early meetings, Eden Minns was conscripted into the Navy and Gordon Russell's brother, R D Russell was sent to India after attending a few meetings. Although when the war situation eased O'Rorke and Wornum were able to help the Panel again, it was rather a desperate time for Russell. He still had his mainstays, Clinch and Cutler, who were able to help in the design of the first post-war Utility furniture, but perhaps his most important subsequent additions to the Panel were Jacques Groag, a Czech architect and pupil of Adolf Loos, and Enid Marx, the textile designer. Groag in particular had a great influence on the design of the post-war ranges while Enid Marx designed the furnishing fabrics between 1944 and 1947.

The first stage in the Utility furniture programme was now complete. The Clinch/Cutler designs were in production and although few actual changes in their range were to occur until after the war, the Design Panel was far from idle at its weekly meetings. On the one hand there was the need to keep an eye on the production of the existing designs, devising modifications where necessary, and on the other it was vital to plan and make prototypes for the future, all the time bearing in mind what the supply situation might be, and what new or substitute materials might have to be used. Early on the possibilities of purely temporary furniture made of paper were explored and just before D-Day the Panel was told that it might be necessary to go over to softwood. Fortunately, as Russell commented, this did not happen, although they did some preliminary work.

September 1st

To dampen demand the number of units issued for each furniture permit was reduced to thirty. Although production was rising it still could not keep pace with demand, which rose even faster. To soften the blow, purchasers of Utility furniture were allowed to buy 15 sq. yds of coupon-free curtain material.

1944 June 6th

D-Day. The invasion of Europe by the Allies.

June 13th

V1 (buzz bombs or doodle-bugs as they were popularly called) attacks on Britain began. These, and the later V2 rocket attacks continued almost until the end of the war and caused damage on a scale unknown since the Blitz of 1940, destroying or damaging nearly one-and-a-half million houses and creating an even greater demand for Utility furniture.

August 1st

The sixty unit allowance was restored by Hugh Dalton, although only to those who had had thirty units since the allowance had been reduced. Those becoming eligible for permits after this date had sixty units, but thirty of them were 'deferred units', usable only after some months' waiting.

August 28th

Utility furniture was introduced in Ulster, 32 manufacturers being designated. The trade disputed the necessity for its introduction after nearly five years of war.

December

The Council of Industrial Design was launched by Hugh Dalton to 'promote by all practicable means the improvement of design in the products of British Industry.' The first director was S C Leslie, who was succeeded by Gordon Russell in 1947. Russell meanwhile was one of the 24 original members.

1945 April

All-steel bedsteads were introduced into the scheme, in two qualities, black only for a single size, and a single and double bed in a choice of brown, grey, pale blue, and green. Like the existing Utility furniture they were not subject to Purchase Tax and the unit requirement was the same as for wooden beds.

The end of the war was in sight. Russell and his design team had been working hard experimenting with designs using blockboard and plywood, which were expected to be available before long. Hugh Dalton's and Gordon Russell's foresight in keeping the Advisory Committee in being and in creating the Design Panel meant that on the design side at least, the scheme was ready for the changed conditions of peacetime. At the BoT, on the organisational side, things were moving. Internal reports were produced on the post-war future of the scheme, and one such report, dated May 3rd 1945 and entitled 'Miss (later Dame Alix) Kilroy's Survey of Problems arising on Utility Furniture' set out most clearly the original reasons for establishing the scheme and the possible lines of its future development. Her report, which obviously summed up the whole thinking of the BoT, was prompted by the fact that production was lagging badly and would need to be greatly increased with the ending of the war, and by the fact that materials in short supply, like metals and plastics, would once again be available. She made a number of proposals, all of which were ultimately taken up: the Advisory Committee should be asked to provide for greater variety in the future (as we have seen, Gordon Russell was already in a position to do this); 'approved' designs should be introduced; metal furniture firms and the plastics industry should be allowed to make furniture, provided their designs could be approved as being within the Utility scheme; 'wicker' furniture should be introduced; the zoning of factories should be abandoned, for with the end of the war furniture making capacity would be vastly increased as hundreds of firms returned to the industry from war-work, and lastly, furniture should be imported, provided the exporting countries did not reduce their supplies of timber to this country in proportion to the wood content of the furniture.

May 8th

VE (Victory in Europe) Day.

The war was over and the BoT announced that it would allow people to buy red, white and blue bunting free of coupons until the end of the month.

At the same time an exhibition 'Design for the Home', designed by Milner Gray and organised by CEMA (Council for the Encouragement of Music and the Arts) was held at the National Gallery. Some of the prototype furniture which Russell's Design Panel had been working on was shown, and attracted favourable comment from the Architectural Review, which said that some of the pieces were 'very attractive indeed'.

May 23rd

The war-time Coalition ended, and was succeeded by Churchill's Caretaker Government. Oliver Lyttelton returned to the BoT until the Government resigned in June pending the General Election.

July 26th

The result of the election of July 5th was finally declared and a Labour Government with a massive overall majority of 146 had been elected. Clement Atlee, Churchill's Deputy during the war-time coalition, became Prime Minister, Hugh Dalton, Chancellor of the Exchequer, and Sir Stafford Cripps went to the BoT to take up where Dalton had left off in May.

October

Sir Stafford Cripps appointed a Working Party to report on furniture. Its brief was 'To examine and enquire into the various schemes and suggestions put forward for the improvement of organisation, production and distribution methods and processes in the furniture industry, and to report as to the steps which should be taken in the national interest to strengthen the industry and render it more stable and more capable of meeting competition in the home and foreign markets.'

Its first meeting took place on the 29th with Eileen Strudwick as secretary. She was well versed in the problems which would be discussed since she had also been secretary to the Utility Furniture Advisory Committee. In addition, the Design Sub-Group of the Working Party included Russell and Cutler. Its report was published almost a year later, on August 31st 1946. Among other, very detailed recommendations on the running of the industry, it proposed that so long as the supply of furniture lagged behind demand price control should be continued, and that to be effective it should still be linked with fixed specifications and designs. It recommended that the range of furniture should be greatly increased and that Utility should eventually be made available to people outside the priority classes. It was felt very strongly that the scheme should not end until these proposals had been carried out and until production was sufficiently high to make price control unnecessary. As with Alix Kilroy's report, many of the recommendations were carried out; indeed, that for widening the range of Utility furniture had already been carried out earlier in the year.

1946 March 1st-23rd
As part of Gordon Russell's work for the Design Sub-Group of the Working Party, Cripps sent him to America, not only to study and report back on its furniture industry but specifically to find out about their use of aluminium, which was increasingly being thought of in this country as a substitute for wood because of the large amount of scrap left from the war. Russell did not find his visit very helpful – the Americans were using aluminium for 'porch' furniture, and as their wood supply during the war had not been too bad they had had less need to explore the possibilities of aluminium. Even so, for a year or two quite a large amount of the metal was used in this country for such things as kitchen cabinets and beds, some of them specifically within the Utility scheme.

March 13th-23rd
While Russell was away the BoT held an exhibition at its Millbank headquarters of over fifty pieces of prototype Utility furniture which it was intended to produce in the near future. With important exceptions these marked the first real changes in the scheme in the three years since it had started. Introducing the furniture Sir Charles Tennyson said that with the return of more labour, a better supply position and the experience of three years work, the Design Panel under Gordon Russell had been invited to produce these further designs. Three different ranges were shown, all designed by the Panel:

'Chiltern', which continued the existing range with a fair number of additions and refinements. It was named after High Wycombe, Edwin Clinch and H T Cutler being its main designers.

'Cotswold', a completely new range using rather more materials and labour than Chiltern and therefore more expensive. It made much greater use of the now available blockboard and plywood than Chiltern, which had originally been designed with their absence in mind. The Cotswold range was characterised by a lightness which was opposed to the solidity of Chiltern, and by an extensive use of flush panels and veneers. It was named after Gordon Russell, whose own furniture workshops were (and are) at Broadway in Worcestershire.

'Cockaigne', which was intended to be mass produced with a much greater use of machinery than either Cotswold or Chiltern. For this reason it would also have been cheaper. There was obviously a great deal of uncertainty at the BoT about this range; it was renamed 'Cheviot' and then it either never went into production or was quickly discontinued.

Enid Marx had produced further designs for furnishing fabrics in wool as well as cotton and examples of these were also shown at the exhibition. The three prototype ranges of furniture were shown at the Daily Herald Modern Homes exhibition, held from March to May 1946, and with the exception of Cockaigne went into production soon after.

May
Aluminium divans were added to the Utility range, designed by

C Rostgart, a member of the Design Panel in 1947, according to H T Cutler.

To ease the poor supply situation six pieces of furniture were now being imported from Finland, and the possibilities of obtaining furniture from other countries, such as Poland, were also being explored. This furniture was stamped CC41 and marked with the country of origin.

September 24th
Britain Can Make It exhibition opened at the Victoria and Albert Museum, and remained until the Festival of Britain in 1951 the most important post-war exhibition held in this country.

This survey of British industrial design was an enormous popular success, in spite of it being called by some 'Britain can't have it' because of the number of exhibits that were either for export only or not yet in full production. Its closing date had been extended by two months until the end of the year and in that time it had 1,432,369 visitors.

It was Sir Stafford Cripps's idea and he diverted London's entire supply of glass for two months to repair the war-damaged windows of the museum. The exhibition was organised by the Council of Industrial Design and designed by a team headed by James Gardner. It showed just everything that was being, or could be, made in this country and one popular exhibit was 'Things in their Home Setting', a series of rooms, many furnished in Utility and designed to be inhabited by a whole range of imaginary people, from the kitchen for a Yorkshire miner and his family to the bachelor flat of a BBC commentator.

December
Units were no longer needed for kitchen cabinets and woven fibre furniture. The unit values of other items were reduced.

1947 March
The first Ideal Home Exhibition since 1939 was held. Dutch furniture was now being imported to supplement the Utility range.

May
By this time the BoT had examined ways of widening the Utility scheme still further, possibly by expanding the range and also by inviting the trade to submit designs which could then be approved and accepted as Utility. In its invitation to manufacturers in May the BoT suggested that 'simplicity and refinement of design are qualities which will be looked for by the assessors'. It was also proposed that if such designs were accepted then only 'dimension stock' should be used in their manufacture, i.e. the dimensions of the component parts would be laid down by the BoT. These proposals, which appear to have come to nothing, foreshadowed the freedom of design which was to come at the end of the following year.

June
The second Utility catalogue was belatedly published, illustrating the Chiltern and Cotswold ranges, together with metal and woven fibre furniture. Some of the items illustrated in this catalogue but not in the 1943 catalogue had already been in production for two years. The catalogue was not of such great importance to the purchaser as was the earlier catalogue since traders were able to display items from the two ranges in their showrooms by this time.

September
Gordon Russell left the BoT's Directorate of Utility Furniture Production to succeed S C Leslie as Director of the Council of Industrial Design, his work on the scheme over. Frank Austin now headed the Design Panel which included C Rostgart, Clive Latimer, N Ward, Jacques Groag, Miss W Cloos and H T Cutler, who also became 'Trades Relations Adviser, Utility Furniture'.

December
The BoT announced that production of Cotswold would cease the following April and that manufacture would be concentrated on one range only – the 'Diversified' range.

1948 January 1st
Prototypes of the Diversified range were shown at the BoT, designed by the Panel under Frank Austin.

April
The Cotswold range was withdrawn, except for the upholstered furniture, dining chairs, beds and occasional furniture. The Chiltern range continued, with some deletions but also with a fair number of alterations which manufacturers were allowed to make at their discretion.

May 1st
The deferred unit system which had operated for permit holders since August 1944 was abandoned, and the full sixty unit allowance was restored.

June
The President of the BoT, now Harold Wilson, announced that units were no longer required for Utility: furniture rationing was at an end.

Further relaxations in the observance of the Utility specifications were announced: walnut veneers were to be allowed provided they cost no more than mahogany, and any type of handle could now be used.

November 29th
Freedom of design within the Utility scheme was introduced.

1948 had been a year of increasing dissatisfaction on the part of the trade, which wanted more freedom. The BoT was obviously uncertain of what to do and in the end decided not to put the Diversified range into production but to allow manufacturers to design their own Utility furniture. They had to keep within the limits imposed by the rather strictly defined dimensions not only of the finished furniture but also of many of the component parts. The manufacturers' ingenuity was such that from the end of 1948 until the end of the scheme nearly three years later, the CC41 mark was applied to an extraordinary variety of furniture, although if manufacturers preferred it, and many did, they could continue to make Chiltern to BoT specifications. At the same time the BoT realised that many manufacturers would not have design staffs able to cope with the new-found freedom, and accordingly they made working drawings of a range of designs available on request. The designs were illustrated in a small BoT booklet produced at the end of 1948, and many of them very strongly resemble the never-to-be-produced Diversified range of a year before. Whatever they chose to do, their work was subject to inspection by the BoT, the Utility mark being very much a guarantee of a certain minimum quality, as well as an exemption from Purchase Tax. Its price was still controlled too. Non-Utility furniture, which had been manufactured in gradually increasing amounts as the supply situation eased especially by firms too small for the economic production of Utility, including the so called working masters, was subject to tax–at first at $66^{2}/_{3}\%$, although this was reduced to $33^{1}/_{3}\%$ at the same time as the introduction of the legislation giving manufacturers freedom to design their own Utility furniture.

1949 January
The Furniture Development Council was established, with Sir David Waley as its first chairman. This was one of the results of Sir Stafford Cripps's report on furniture of 1946, and in many ways was a natural successor to the Utility Furniture Design Panel.

1951
Festival of Britain.

Planned in the years of austerity it marked a turning point in the attitude of designers; its romantic and consciously light-hearted approach contrasted sharply with the austere functionalism that had informed the Utility furniture scheme in its early years.

1952
The Conservative Government appointed a Committee to enquire into the Utility schemes, with particular reference to the increasingly vexed question of its exemption from Purchase Tax. The Committee reported in February 1952, and its recommendation that 'the present exemption from Purchase Tax of Utility goods be replaced by a system . . . applying to Utility and non-Utility goods alike' marked the beginning of the end of Utility. The Government acted on the recommendations and on December 15th 1952 the Utility Furniture (Marking and Supply) (Revocation) Order 1952 and related Orders came into operation. However the Labour opposition forced a debate on the ending of the scheme, particularly on the abolition of any effective quality control, and this took place in the House of Commons on Wednesday January 21st 1953. In spite of a reasoned and at times passionate defence of Utility from the Labour benches, notably from Douglas Jay, Austen Albu and David Weitzman, the cause was lost by 37 votes when the House divided at 9.13 pm. The Utility furniture scheme was at an end.

Postscript
Sir Gordon Russell recalls that the only furniture being made in Sierra Leone about fifteen years ago was Utility: the BoT sent designs to help them start a furniture industry, and it is thought that this was done in other countries as well.

Furniture

Dimensions (height, width and depth) are in feet and inches. The items marked * were called *Chiltern* after 1946.

A1 Wardrobe

Purchased from Binns of Newcastle in about 1942 it closely resembles the Government Emergency Furniture which was introduced in 1941 to cope with the demand caused by bomb damage. Its extensive use of plywood and its poor construction make an instructive contrast with the Utility furniture of the following year.
Plywood 5′ 7″x 2′ 9½ x 1′ 2″

Utility Furniture

A2 Dining table*

Model 2, illustrated in 1943 catalogue.
It has a panelled top with extending leaves. The legs are laminated from three lengths of wood owing to the impossibility of obtaining timber of sufficient thickness at that time. CC41 mark and CWS label.
Light Oak 2′ 6″ x 3′ x 3′ (extending to 3′ x 5′)

A3 Dining table (plate 19)

Cotswold range Model 651 illustrated in 1947 catalogue.
It has extending leaves and the top has a grooved border, adding to the impression of lightness which is a characteristic of the Cotswold range introduced in 1946. CC41 mark.
Mahogany 2′ 6″ x 3′ x 2′ 9″ (extending to 5′ x 2′ 9″)

A4 Sideboard* (plate 12)

Model 1, illustrated in 1943 and 1947 (with metal handles) catalogues.
It makes extensive use of veneered hardboard in its panelled construction and like most of the early Utility cabinet furniture stands on a plinth rather than legs. CC41 mark.
Dark Oak 2′ 9″ x 4′ x 1′ 6″

A5 Pair of dining chairs* (plate 10)

Model 3a, illustrated in 1943 and 1947 catalogues.
Three vertical slats in back, with shaped back rail. Loose padded seats covered in original green leathercloth. CC41 mark.
Light Oak 1′ 5″ x 1′ 5″ x 1′ 3″

A6 Dining chair* (plate 10)

Model 3c, illustrated in 1943 and 1947 catalogues.
Three vertical slats in back. Loose padded seat covered in brown leathercloth (restored). CC41 mark.
Dark Oak 1′ 6″ x 1′ 5″ x 1′ 3″

A7 Dining chair* (plate 9)

Model 3, illustrated in 1943 and 1947 catalogues.
Two horizontal slats in back, loose padded seat covered in original brown leathercloth. CC41 mark.
Dark Oak 1′ 5″ x 1′ 5″ x 1′ 3½″

A8 Occasional table

Model 7, illustrated in 1943 and 1947 catalogues.
Veneered hardboard was used originally for the top and shelf, and plywood after the war. CC41 mark.
Dark Oak 2′ 2″ x 1′ 8″ x 1′ 8″

A9 Fireside chair (plate 21)

Cotswold range Model 1450, illustrated 1947 catalogue.
It has show-wood arms and is upholstered in the original woven cotton fabric. CC41 mark.
Oak 3′ 3″ x 1′ 11″ x 2′ 1″

A10 Kitchen cabinet

Model 907, illustrated 1947 catalogue.
Unlike the 1943 cabinet, it makes full use of plywood in its construction. It is in two halves, which could be purchased separately, has an enamel work top replacing the linoleum of the war-time version and aluminium handles. CC41 mark.
5′ 9″ x 2′ 9″ x 1′ 8″

A11 Pair of kitchen chairs

Model 4a, illustrated in 1943 and 1947 catalogues.
This design assimilated the traditional Windsor chair into the Utility scheme, and (with dining chairs) was the only furniture made in High Wycombe during the war, when most of its factories had gone over to essential work. CC41 mark.
Stained Beech 1′ 5½″ x 1′ 2″ x 1′ 2″

A12 Child′s bedstead

Not illustrated in 1947 catalogue, but similar to Model B1.
Tubular steel bedsteads were introduced into the scheme

towards the end of the war as the supply situation eased. This example has a wire mesh mattress support and the tubular head and foot are painted in the original pale blue. CC41 mark.
Length 4′ 3½″ x Width 2′ 6″

A13 Tallboy* (plate 14)
Model 5, illustrated in 1943 and 1947 (with metal handles) catalogues.
It has a hanging cupboard below and two drawers above. The cupboard door panels are subdivided vertically partly for decorative effect but also to compensate for the relative weakness of the veneered hardboard that had to be used originally. CC41 mark.
Light Oak 4′ x 2′ 9″ x 1′ 6″

A14 Dressing table
Chiltern range Model 3003, illustrated 1947 catalogue.
The top is stepped down in the centre and has a wooden shelf. Like much of the post-war furniture it has metal handles, in this case turned brass and probably designed by R Y Gooden. CC41 mark.
Oak 2′ 4″ (4′ 9″ to top of mirror) x 3′ 3″ x 1′ 6″

A15 Woven fibre chair
Model 3, illustrated in 1947 catalogue.
The 'fibre' is in fact paper, twisted and woven into a cloth, the warp threads being re-inforced with 18 g. steel wire. The resulting cloth is then attached to the bentwood frame. This example, painted in its original Naples Green, was made by W Lusty and Sons Ltd (Lloyd Loom). CC41 mark.
1′ 4″ x 2′ 2″ x 1′ 10″

The following are photocopies of working drawings prepared by the Board of Trade for the Utility scheme. They were sent to designated manufacturers who had to follow the designs meticulously.

A16 Dining chair (plate 11)
Model 3a, October 1942.
12¾″ x 15¾″

A17 Kitchen chair
Model 4a, October 1942.
12¾″ x 15¾″

A18 Tallboy
Model 5 June 1944.
This drawing, by Edwin Clinch and H J Cutler, slightly revises their original design of Autumn 1942.
28¾″ x 38″

A19 Dressing tables
Models 3, 3001-4, 5 December 1947.
The drawing shows the alternative methods of veneering the drawer fronts permitted at that time. Bracket feet have also replaced the earlier plinths in these drawings.
31″ x 20¾″

A20 Occasional tables
Models 2052/3 and 2056/7, August 1st 1945.
Model 2052/3 is chiefly interesting for its splayed bobbin shaped legs, foreshadowing the 'contemporary' coffee tables of the 1950's. Model 2056/7 is a simple drop-leaf design.
20″ x 40″

A21 Typical joints for table work
Dated October 1942 it shows two methods of jointing a table frame, one mortised, the other dowelled.
13″ x 8″

A22 Aluminium structured divan
Models C1 and C2 (3′ 0″ and 4′ 6″ wide).
This divan, probably designed by C Rostgart, is the only piece of aluminium furniture to be listed in the 1947 catalogue.
12½″ x 8″

A23 Aluminium structured dining chair
Model 4303.
This chair does not appear in the 1947 catalogue. The sketch includes a note that the upholstered seat and back were detachable and that the structure was coloured either cream, light or dark beige, pastel green, saxe blue or light chocolate.
12½″ x 8″

A24 Catalogue (plates 23, 24)
The second Utility furniture catalogue, published June 1947. It illustrates every item of furniture then available within the scheme.

A25 Utility furniture buying permit (plate 15)
Dated November 1945, it has some unused units attached.

A26 Priority dockets
These allowed the holder to purchase 20 square yards of linoleum and 15 square yards of curtain material free of coupons. Holders of Utility Furniture Buying Permits could be issued with these dockets from September 1943 when the number of furniture units had been halved to thirty. The Utility Furniture Office of the Board of Trade was also able to issue dockets for the coupon-free purchase of mattresses, blankets and sheets.

'My Utility Furniture was now coming forward well, with great economy of material and clean lines without fussy ornamentation' (Hugh Dalton, *The Fateful Years* 1931-45).

Just as one of Herbert Morrison's war-time catch phrases had been 'go to it' so Hugh Dalton´s must have been 'see to it': Dr Dynamo, as he was dubbed by a colleague in S.O.E. accepted Churchill´s invitation and became President of the Board of Trade on February 21st 1942. From that moment Utility as a whole never looked back and there is no doubt that the rapidity with which the furniture scheme was initiated and the energy with which it was subsequently pursued owed most to Dalton's dynamism. After all, unlike his predecessor at the Board of Trade, Oliver Lyttelton, he was a socialist, and the underlying idea of state management came more naturally to him. The mood of the country too was on his side, a mood of which much of the readership of the influential 'Picture Post' was aware and which would lead directly to the Attlee administrations of 1945-51. This increasingly 'socialist' aspect of the country was well expressed by one Conservative businessman to John Wilmot, Dalton's Parliamentary Private Secretary, when he said 'You socialists are getting in everywhere. I must say I do admire you. One of you is Deputy Prime Minister (Atlee), and you have got control of the Navy (Alexander) and the Police (Morrison) and Scotland (Johnston) and all our Trade (Dalton) and now you have worked in one of your members as Archbishop of Canterbury (Temple).'

Dalton was very proud of his Utility schemes, especially that for furniture, and several times expressed a wish that he was in one of the priority classes so that he could get some for himself. He remained at the Board of Trade until June 1945, and when he became Chancellor of the Exchequer in Atlee's administration, it was left to his successor, Sir Stafford Cripps, to begin the adjustment of the scheme to peace-time conditions.

Plate 1 Utility living/dining room, photograph taken at the first exhibition of Utility furniture at the Building Centre, October 1942

Plate 2 Utility living/dining room, photograph taken at the first exhibition of Utility furniture at the Building Centre, October 1942

Plate 3 Utility kitchen, photograph taken at the first exhibition of Utility furniture at the Building Centre, October 1942

Plate 4 Utility bedroom, photograph taken at one of the BoT exhibitions of the furniture organised early in 1943

Plate 5 Utility living/dining room, photograph taken at one of the BoT exhibitions of the furniture organised early in 1943

Plate 6 Utility kitchen, photograph taken at one of the BoT exhibitions of the furniture organised early in 1943. The Utility combined kettle and saucepan can be seen on the stove

Plate 7 Utility dining room, photograph taken in 1945 showing the original range of furniture

Plate 8 Utility kitchen, photograph taken in 1945 showing the original range of furniture

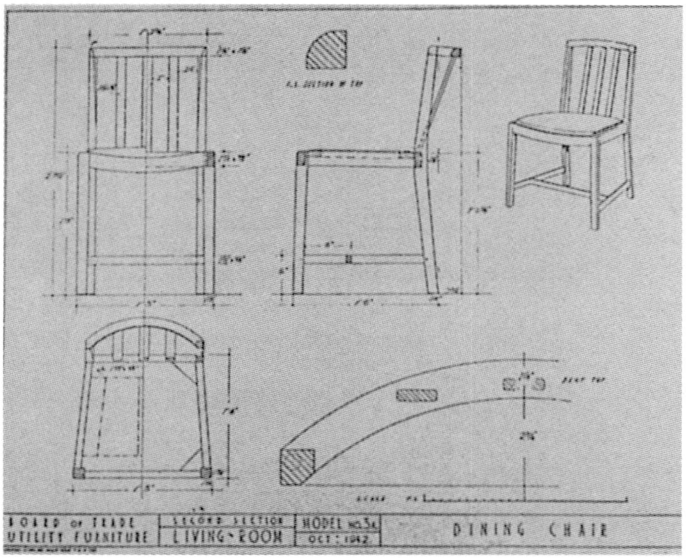

Plate 9 Dining chairs, 1943
left: Model No 3b (this was discontinued later in favour of the other three designs)
right: Model No 3 (See A7)

Plate 11 Working drawing for dining chair, Model No 3a (see A16)

Plate 10 Dining chairs, 1943
left: Model No 3a (see A5)
right: Model No 3c (see A6)

Plate 12 Sideboard, Model No 1, designed in 1942.
This example is post war as it has metal handles (see A4)

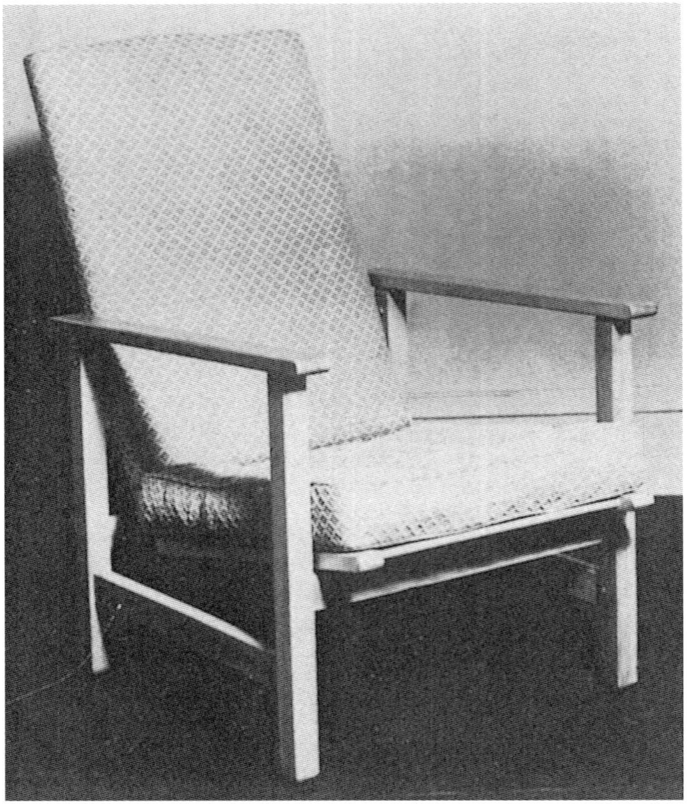

Plate 13 Fireside chair, Model No 1, 1943. The back can be adjusted to two different angles

Plate 14 Tallboy, Model No 5, 1943 (see A13)

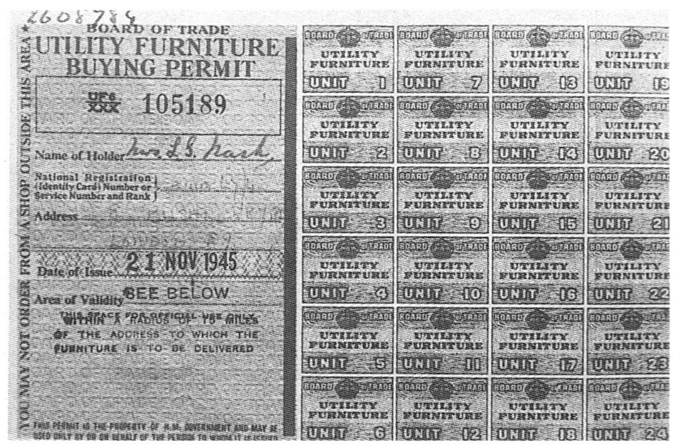
BOARD OF TRADE
UTILITY FURNITURE
BUYING PERMIT
105189
Name of Holder
National Registration (Identity Card) Number or Service Number and Rank
Address
Date of Issue 21 NOV 1945
Area of Validity SEE BELOW
WITHIN A RADIUS OF 10 MILES OF THE ADDRESS TO WHICH THE FURNITURE IS TO BE DELIVERED
YOU MAY NOT ORDER FROM A SHOP OUTSIDE THIS AREA
UTILITY FURNITURE UNIT 1 … UNIT 24

Plate 15 Utility Furniture Buying Permit

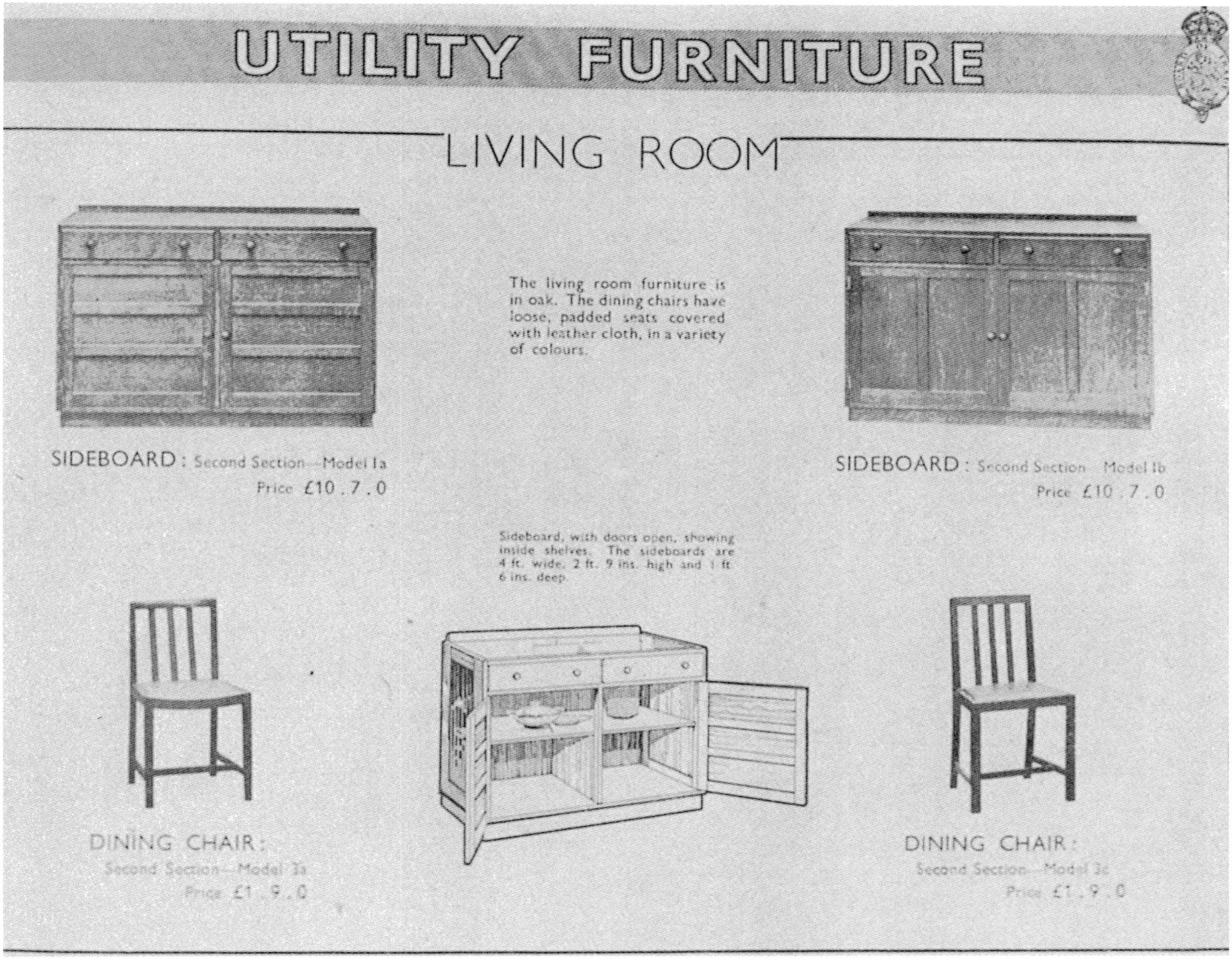

Plate 16 A page from the 1943 Utility Furniture catalogue

Plate 17 A page from the 1943 Utility Furniture catalogue

Plate 18 Metal bedstead, Model B2 introduced May 1945

Plate 19 Cotswold dining table, Model No 650 (oak), 651 (mahogany) 946 (see A3)

Plate 20 Cotswold occasional table, Model No 2054 (oak), 2055 (mahogany) 1946

Plate 21 Cotswold fireside chair, Model No 1450 (see A9). 1956

Plate 22 Chiltern dining table, Model No 605 (oak). 1946

Plate 23 A page from the 1947 Utility Furniture catalogue, illustrating two Cotswold sideboards

HANDLES

(Wood and Plastic)

H 1000 (Wood). Finish : Polished Oak or Mahogany.
H 1001 (Wood). Finish : Polished Oak or Mahogany.
H 1002 (Wood). Finish : Polished Oak or Mahogany.
H 1003 (Wood). Finish : Polished Oak or Mahogany.
H 1004 (Wood). Finish : Polished Oak or Mahogany
H 1061 (Plastic). Ivory, Black, Brown.
H 1064 with H 1062 plate (Plastic). Ivory, Black, Brown.
H 1064 with H 1063 plate (Plastic). Ivory, Black, Brown
H 1065 (Plastic). Ivory, Black, Brown.
H 1059 (Plastic). Ivory, Black, Brown.

16

Plate 24 A page from the 1947 Utility Furniture catalogue, illustrating some of the wide range of handles allowed by that time

Plate 25 Cockaigne wardrobe, 1946

Plate 26 Cockaigne chest and tallboy, exhibited at *Daily Herald* 'Modern Homes' exhibition, 1946. The chest (R) is a Cotswold model

Plate 27 Diversified range, sideboard and occasional table 1948

Plate 28 Diversified range, sideboard 1948

Plate 29 Diversified range, sideboard 1948

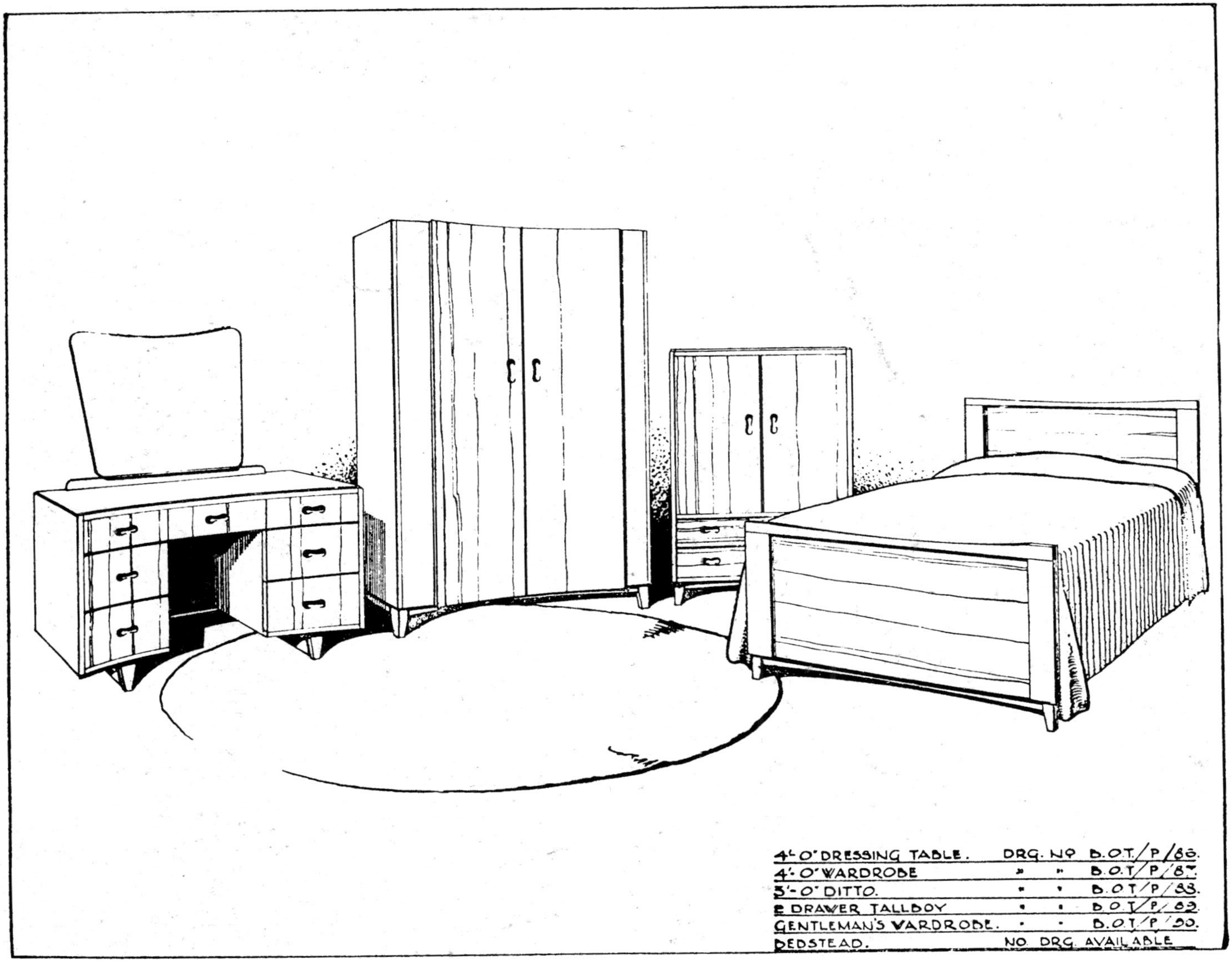

Plate 30 Bedroom suite, BoT drawings, December 1948. The designs were made available to manufacturers if required after freedom of design had been restored at the end of 1948. They resemble the Diversified range of early 1948, which was never produced

Plate 31 'Spot and Stripe' (see B7)

Plate 32 'Chevron' (see B8)

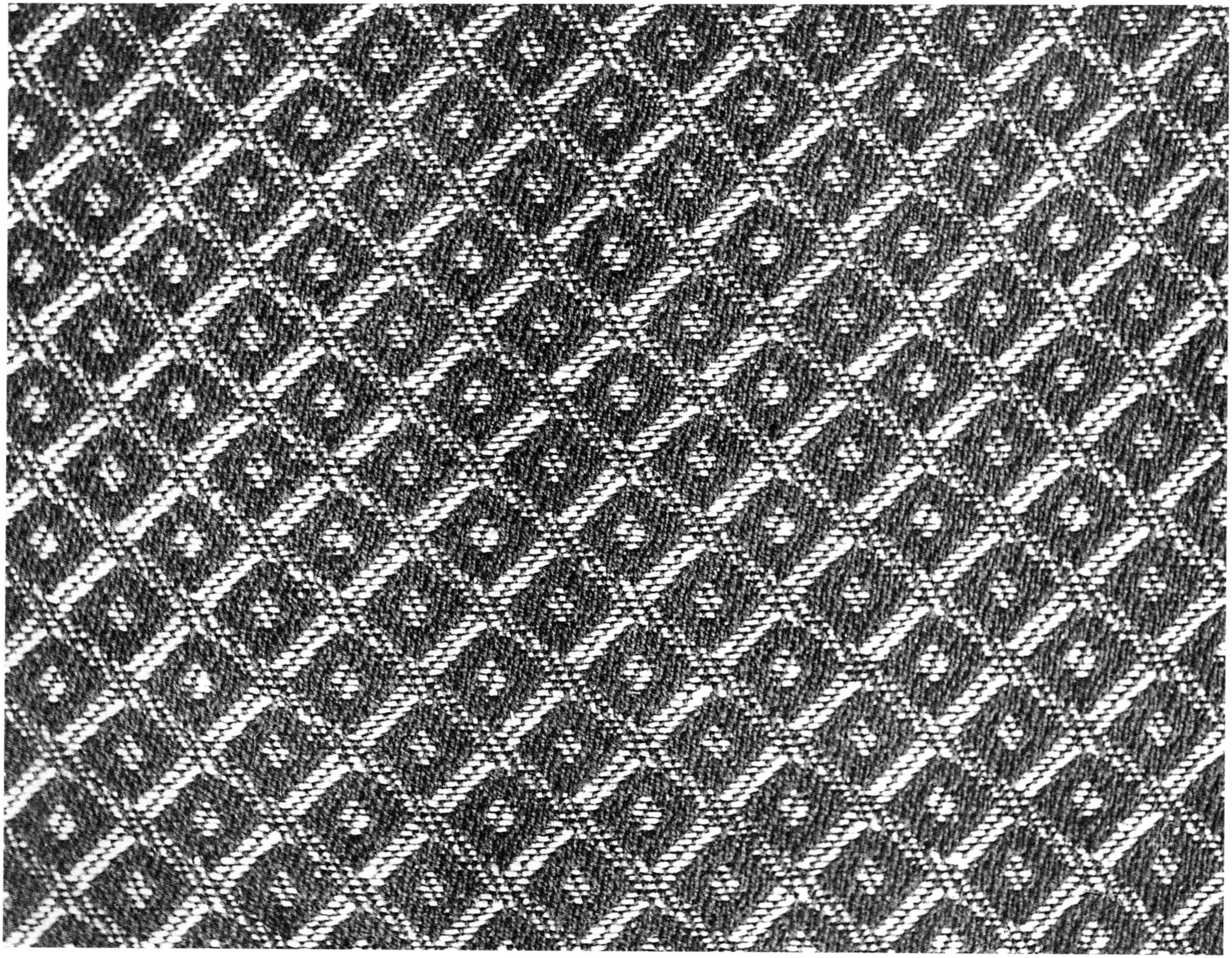

Plate 33 'Dot' (see B9)

Plate 34 Sir Gordon Russell CBE MC RDI FSIA

Plate 35 Hugh Dalton

Plates 36 & 37 (left) Utility clothing designed by members of the Incorporated Society of London Fashion Designers, 1942

Plate 38 (right) Suit designed by Victor Stiebel, 1942 (see C1)

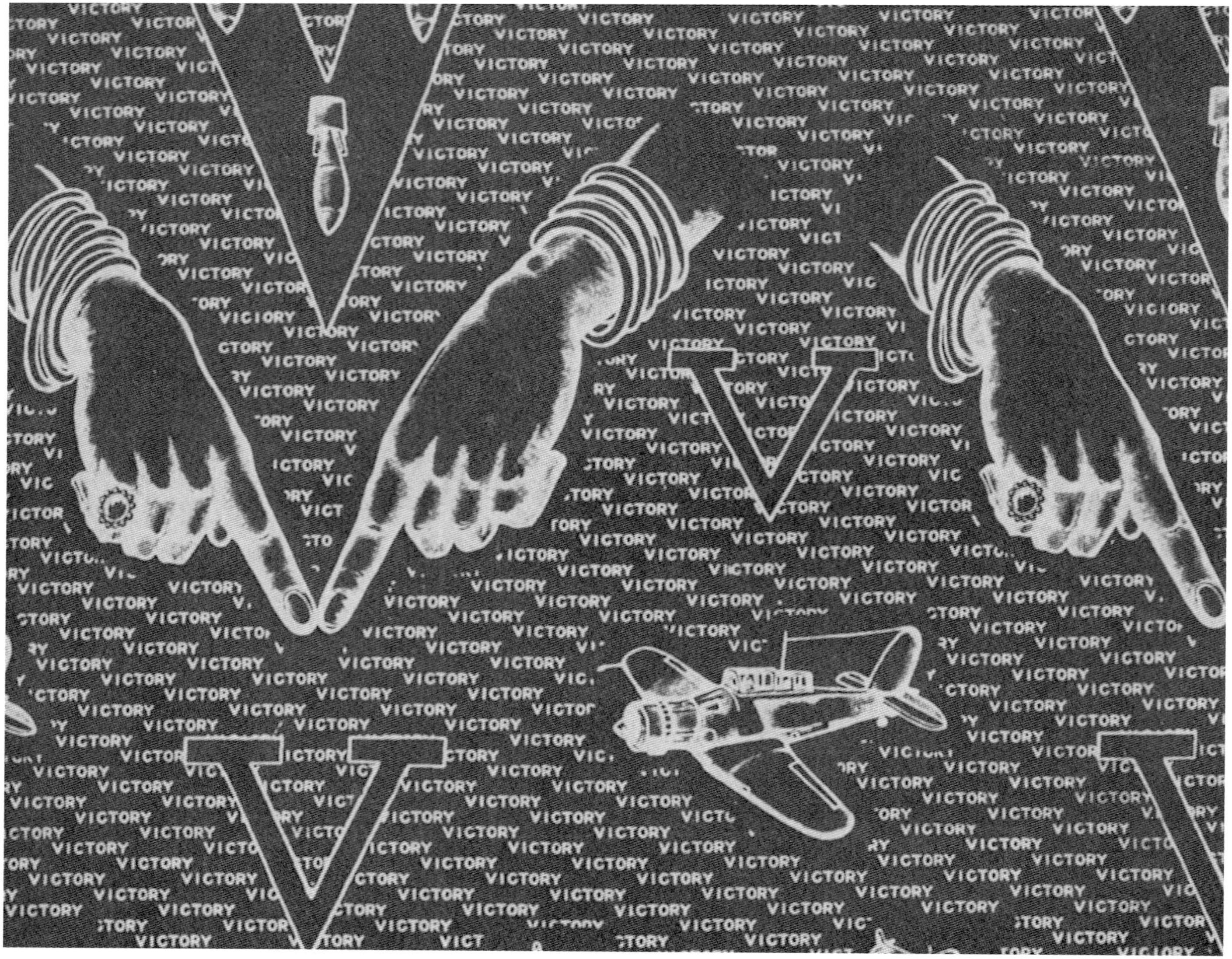

Plate 39 (see C18)

Plate 40 (see C17)

Plate 41 A ´lumberjill´ member of the Women´s Land Army

Plate 42 (see D1)

Plate 43 (see D13)

Plate 44 (see D16)

Plate 45 (see D17)

Plate 46 (see D18)

Plate 47 (see D20)

Plate 48 (see D21)

Plate 49 (see D23)

Plate 50 War-time civilian radio receiver (see F3)

Plate 51 Bush radio (see E2)

Plate 52 'War-finish' electric fire (see F4)

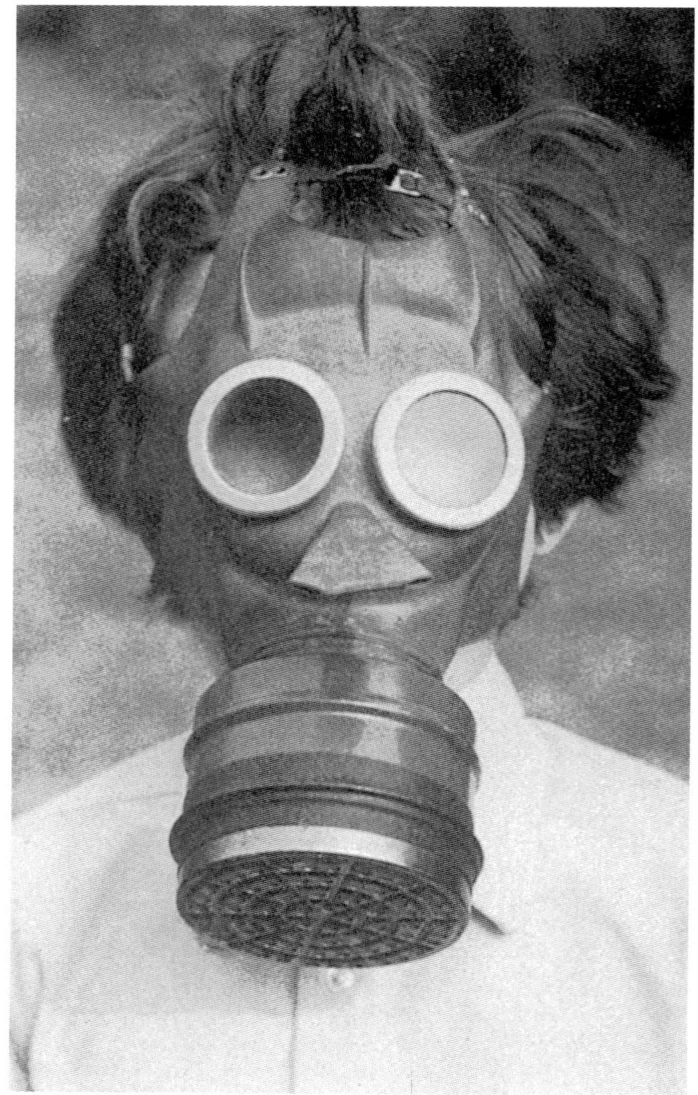

Plate 53 'Donald Duck' gas mask (see F11)

As a designer and a campaigner in the cause of good design Gordon Russell continues a tradition of commitment that has been inherent in British design theory and practice since the mid-nineteenth century, when William Morris and his successors first demonstrated the necessity of survival through design. But in spite of his associations with the Cotswolds (several of the Morris-inspired craftsman were still working there when he was a boy) Sir Gordon´s convictions were based on personal discoveries and experiences rather than on any conscious decision to emulate or extend the achievements of Gimson or Ashbee. He taught himself the designer's trade by trial and error, his apprenticeship being the practical experience of helping to restore and furnish the Lygon Arms, the magnificent but dilapidated coaching in that his father had bought in Broadway when Gordon was 12.

In these early years at the Lygon he made as well as restored furniture, since this was, as he explains in his autobiography* 'all in the day's work'. ('As far as I remember', he writes 'I didn't attempt to make it look either old or new: I was just trying to solve a problem, finding out the snags for myself and endeavouring to resolve them'). These experiences, however, were interrupted by the war, which resolved any doubts Sir Gordon might have had about his future career. His four years' experience of destruction convinced him that the survivors had 'a constructive duty to perform'. 'Somehow or other' he wrote 'we had to hand on to those coming after us good things of our own creation'.

The impetus, therefore for his becoming a designer was similar to that which inspired the Arts and Crafts generation; like his predecessors in the 19th century Gordon Russell was determined to promote and maintain a living tradition of humanism in design; like them he was convinced that the survival of this tradition was a measure, as well as an instrument of civilisation, and that it was demonstrated, as far as the designer was concerned, by a respect for natural materials and honest construction. There was, however, one important and fundamental element of Arts and Crafts philosophy that Sir Gordon could not accept, for he was convinced that humanistic standards in design could be achieved by means of quantity as well as craft production, and that the machine, that *bête noire* of the 19th-century idealists, could and should be used as a civilising rather than destructive tool.

During the Twenties Sir Gordon was fighting on various fronts to establish and explain these ideologies. In the first place he had to build up his firm, which entailed training designers and craftsmen, defining design standards and evolving techniques for producing work in economic quantities. And then, of course, he had to sell the work, and this involved him in a national campaign to promote theories which, as far as he was concerned, were based on sound common sense. He began to explain his ideas in talks and pamphlets as early as 1923; he also became a leading member of the Design and Industries Association, and the success of the firm's practical achievements during this period was reflected in growing sales as well as prestige. Then the pioneering work of the Twenties was consolidated in the Thirties following the return to the firm, after architectural training, of Sir Gordon's youngest brother Dick (R. D. Russell). Production during this period tended to be concentrated on the domestic market, and more machinery was introduced to increase the output, a factor that was reflected in the rationalisation of the ranges, and in the design of the furniture itself, which with its understatement, careful detailing and precision of form and finish established a vocabulary that was to be used by British furniture designers throughout the 1950's.

It took a war, however, and a national shortage of materials to confirm the validity of this vocabulary, which prior to 1939 seemed totally alien to the majority of the British public, and to the 'trade'. The introduction of the Utility scheme, was, as far as Sir Gordon was concerned, a total vindication of the theories he shared with the handful of pioneers of design

* *Designer´s Trade,* Allen & Unwin, 1968.

reform in Britain. The brief, to ensure 'a supply of furniture of the best quality available, at controlled prices, to meet a real need' might have been written for his own firm; and the fact that it could only be met by designs that were simple, straightforward and soundly constructed proved, as he pointed out, 'the basic rightness of contemporary design'.

The fate of these certainties in post-war Britain is another story, for the past thirty years have produced as many concepts of 'basic rightness'. During the whole of this period, however, Sir Gordon's convictions about the nature and purpose of design have never wavered. The Council of Industrial Design which he directed from 1947 until his retirement in 1960 was formed to promote these ideas on a national level, and now, after 14 years' retirement Sir Gordon still holds his own where values and practicalities are concerned. And as he himself pointed out 'As one who has spent his life trying to do something like the equivalent of pushing a tank uphill I have discovered that there are occasions when holding one's own can count as progress'.

Gillian Naylor

The trade was fundamentally opposed to any form of control over its activities whatsoever, and in the early months of the war, after Timber and other Controls had been set up to license the supply of raw materials, its attitude as expressed in a trade journal such as *The Cabinet Maker*, was that it was engaged in a 'struggle against officialdom' and that 'officials were taking the profit out of business'. At the same time the trade was aware that it had good opportunities to improve its position relative to other consumer industries, such as the motor trade, which were much more hard-hit by Government restrictions. That was before materials shortages began to bite. When they did, price rises were inevitable and as ever the retailer, totally at the mercy of suppliers in this instance, bore the brunt of public discontent. The wholesale trade meanwhile hoped that the Price Regulation Committees set up under the recent Prices of Goods Act would not turn their attention to household furnishings. It noted with alarm the growing opposition on the part of the public not only to increased profits in industry but even to any profits at all being made and *The Cabinet Maker* expressed the trade's feelings about the redistribution of wealth which was beginning to be brought about by the war by saying 'The great middle-class, on which the brunt of the seven and sixpenny income tax will fall, staggers silently as well under official controls and restrictions of every kind.' Charges were made that the Government was in danger of becoming totalitarian: 'Nothing could be more fatal in the present struggle than to put British industry in the same fetters as those in which German industry is gripped' and this was during the first few months of the war, over two years before the Utility scheme was planned. It is difficult to imagine what the reaction might have been had the trade foreseen not only total price control and concentration of the industry but also total design control as well.

Its *bête noire* was the Prices of Goods Act. Under this legislation it was intended that the public should be protected against profiteering but it was felt that this Act and the Price Regulation Committees which administered it had as their target legitimate profits, and that the trade as a whole was being tarred with the brush of the profiteers. Certainly the Act gave the public the sort of redress against unfair and dishonest trading that it had never enjoyed before and many cases of profiteering were brought before the Committees. The trade felt that the legislation was 'foolish' and in the case of its own industry, totally unnecessary. The Government disagreed, and the Committees assumed increasing importance throughout the war especially in connection with the pricing of Utility goods. The stated aim of the trade to 'curb the controllers' was of no avail and they had to come to terms with increasingly effective legislation especially, in the case of the furniture industry, after Hugh Dalton became President of the Board of Trade in February 1942. Its real fear, of backdoor socialism, is made clear in *The Cabinet Maker's* editorial of February 17th 1940, which suspected that policies were dictated by 'people who are the open advocates of a system of society different from that under which we are accustomed to live.'

The growing seriousness of the economic situation, leading to an almost total withdrawal of timber between July 1940 and February 1941 brought home the need for controls of some kind and the end of the 'phoney war', with the Blitz of autumn 1940 marking a turning point: from then on the trade was acutely conscious of its contribution to the war effort, and whatever private reservations its members held, they were seldom voiced and when they were, they had a gloss of constructive criticism, with none of their previous stridency. Relations with the Board of Trade improved throughout 1941 as each side got to know the other more thoroughly than ever before. The Board tried hard too, and the trade press carried Board of Trade advertisements such as 'Hats off to a nation of shopkeepers' which retailers were invited to cut out for display in their shop windows.

When the Utility Furniture Advisory Committee was appointed in July 1942 *The Cabinet Maker* commented favourably (and prophetically) 'Our guess is, and our hope is, that the Committee will plump for sound, plain and functionally satisfactory furniture. If it does so, it will have left, after the war, a solid and nationally characteristic mark upon style' and admitted that 'Austerity and Utility have useful astringent qualities'. Three months later, with no news from the Advisory Committee, the trade began to doubt that the Utility scheme would get under way before at least April 1943, but the Board of Trade exhibition of the prototype furniture in October 1942 took it by surprise and the extent of the preparations became apparent. Its reaction to the furniture was on the whole favourable, especially with regard to its construction and finish but 'Good, solid and sensible . . . that's just what the public doesn't like' was one comment on its appearance. The trade could not hide its alarm at the concentration of the industry which would come about when the furniture went into production. The number of manufacturers designated was a mere 150 at first, employing about 5,000 workers as opposed to over 100,000 before the war, although it must not be forgotten that the great majority of the better equipped firms were fully occupied on war-work, the manufacture of aeroplanes such as the 'Mosquito', built mainly of wood, being a prime example. There was then, no option but to fall in with Government plans; gradually the number of designated firms was increased until with the end of the war much of the capacity which had been engaged on essential work returned to furniture making, in many cases having gained greatly in technical expertise from the war-time experience. But with peace and the election of a Labour Government calls for the abandonment of Utility grew in stridency; what had been tolerated in time of war was no longer acceptable, especially as the trade feared that the restructuring of its industry which had already come about would be extended irreversibly, with the bogey of nationalisation just around the corner.

With the ending of Utility in 1952 'freedom' won the day, but some sections of the trade were reluctant to see it go. For one thing the variety of styles that could be made had expanded enormously and for another the public estimation of the trade had been raised from the nadir of 1941 by what in effect had been a guarantee of quality: it had been virtually impossible, because of the stringency of the specifications, to make a structurally poor piece of furniture during the Utility era, and its qualities had become widely appreciated, leaving an indelible mark on the design consciousness of a generation.

THE ATTITUDE OF THE UNIONS

The Second World War was a period of full employment and as far as members of the furniture trades unions were concerned there was little objection to the massive alterations imposed on the industry since jobs of some kind were always available. The work-force actually engaged in furniture making was less than 10% of the pre-war figure, but those displaced found themselves either in the forces or working on Government contracts, sometimes in the very factories where they had previously made furniture: with the sole exception of the manufacture of Utility kitchen chairs this was the case in High Wycombe, the very centre of the industry, while Wrighton of Walthamstow was making 'Mosquito' aeroplanes which of course used a great deal of wood in their construction. These examples are typical of what happened to the industry all over the country. With conscription the number of men under 40 working in the severely curtailed and relatively non-essential domestic furniture industry dwindled and the remaining workers for the duration were largely older men, and women of all ages.

The major union, the National Union of Furniture Trades Operatives (NUFTO) was directly involved with the Utility scheme in the person of its Secretary, A G Tomkins. Hugh Dalton invited him to become a member of the Utility Furniture Advisory Committee on January 29th 1943, and in Dalton's opinion he became one of its most valuable members. The unions were not represented in the original composition of the Committee and Tomkins's experience in labour relations and his necessarily extensive knowledge of the trade were clearly useful in promoting cohesion between the Board of Trade, the manufacturers and the workers. Hugh Dalton paid several visits to furniture factories with him, notably in the East End. He was one of the Government's bitterest critics when the scheme was dismantled at the end of 1952 and wrote in the NUFTO Record for January 1953 '. . . we have found pleasant satisfaction in the knowledge that our work in the factories has supplied inexpensive, soundly-constructed, well-finished articles of furniture, with a guarantee backed by Government licence.'

After Gordon Russell had been given the go-ahead to set up his Design Panel of the Utility Furniture Advisory Committee he quickly began a search for suitable designers to serve on it. There was a particular need to have a textiles expert, since the Committee had been forced to use up existing fabrics for its upholstered furniture, some of which were felt to be unsatisfactory. By mid-1943, at about the time the Panel came into existence, these original stocks had been used up and on September 24th Russell went to see the Yarn Controller in Lancashire about further patterns. Time was short and he was forced to select three or four designs for which cards had already been cut. This must have been particularly irksome to him, concerned as he was with seizing the opportunity afforded by the Utility scheme to do something about every-day design standards. But by this time he had got what he saw as absolutely necessary for the continuance of the scheme – a design panel, able to give it a dynamic impetus which it would otherwise certainly have lacked.

Russell next sought the advice of Anthony Hunt, who before the war had been manager of Edinburgh Weavers, on the feasibility of producing suitable fabrics: eventually Enid Marx, already well known for her pre-war textiles, was appointed to the Panel. At first she was asked if she could select from existing designs. Not surprisingly, in view of Russell's recent experience, she found this impossible, and with the backing of the Panel, began to design her own. Her earliest designs for the Board of Trade, including 'Skelda' and 'Flora', date from 1944 and she was subsequently designed a large proportion of the Utility furnishing fabrics until the scheme was relaxed at the end of 1948. This applied to the cotton fabrics, but the woollen ones, except where her designs were used after the war, had to be selected from manufacturers' patterns, and Gordon Russell has commented that while there were many excellent ones, others which had to be used to keep production going could hardly have contributed to the reputation of the Board or of the furniture trade.

There were a number of important limitations which affected Enid Marx's designs for cotton furnishing fabrics, all of them related in some way to raw materials shortages. Repeats for example had to be small to avoid wastage in matching up the pattern when covering a fireside chair or settee. They were usually not more than three of four inches and sometimes smaller. 'Pyramus', with a repeat of around twelve inches was never used in the end for that reason, according to the designer, although the Victoria and Albert Museum has a pre-production sample. There were limitations on the types of yarn and naturally on the amounts that might be used. This affected both the weight and wearing properties of the finished fabric. Two types of yarn were used, Egyptian cotton for the warp and condenser yarn for the weft. The latter had a slub which helped to give body to the cloth, a very important consideration when its weight was lower than the ideal. This was a problem of which the designer was well-aware, and she made full use of the differing properties of the two types of yarn to obtain a richness and body with limited means.

Until the *Britain Can Make It* exhibition at the end of 1946 when a yellow was introduced, only four colours were allowed her, rust, blue, green and natural (cream). This was not only due to a shortage of dyestuffs, which affected the density of colour attainable, but also to accounting difficulties; any further choice and the Board of Trade would have been involved in even more paperwork, a fascinating example of the sort of indirect design control caused by the war.

Enid Marx's preference at that time was clearly for rather formal, geometrical, patterns which in any case lent themselves easily to small repeats. However, she did produce some more naturalistic patterns after asking her charlady, who had been bombed out, what she would like, and her preference had clearly been for something floral. Incidentally, a new Utility mark had been proposed in 1946, and Enid Marx prepared seven designs for S C Leslie, the first Director of the Council of Industrial Design, although none was adopted, the famous 'CC41' mark being retained.

Textiles

The fabrics catalogued, all by Enid Marx, are what are known in the trade as 'feelers', or samples produced to give an idea of the finished cloth, while others, in different colourways, had been submitted to the artist for approval or comment. They were machine woven in all cases by Morton Sundour Fabrics.

B1 Skelda
Designed 1944
Rust and blue 24″ x 24″

B2 Ring
Designed 1945
Rust and natural 15″ x 24″

B3 Pansy
Designed 1945
Green and natural 24″ x 8″

B4 Star and Stripe
Designed 1945
Rust and natural 15″ x 12″

B5 Thisbe
Designed 1945
Rust, blue and natural 15″ x 24″

B6 Squib
Designed 1945
Blue and natural 22″ x 12″

B7 Spot and Stripe (plate 31)
Designed 1945
Swatch of eleven different colourways, some with notes by Enid Marx attached approving or requesting minor colour alterations. Each approx. 12″ x 12″

B8 Chevron (plate 32)
Designed 1946
Blue, rust and natural 12″ x 12″

B9 Dot (plate 33)
Designed 1947 15″ x 12″

B10 Catseye
Designed 1947
Blue and natural 15″ x 18″

Textile Designs

All the designs in this section are by Enid Marx, in water and body colour on paper.

B11 Flora
One of her first designs for the Utility Furniture Scheme
9″ x 7$^1/_2$″

B12 Ring
15$^1/_2$″ x 11″

B13 Squib
6″ x 8″

B14 Spot and Stripe
8$^1/_2$″ x 7$^3/_4$″

B15 Pyramus
This design has an unusually large repeat
9$^1/_2$″ x 16″

B16 Dot
6″ x 6″

B17 Catseye
With notes and weaving instructions
13$^1/_2$″ x 12″

From June 1st 1942 the prices of domestic pottery were controlled. There was no rationing but the manufacture of all decorated and 'inessential' ware for the home market was prohibited.

In April 1942, with growing shortages of pottery, Hugh Dalton had directed that designs were to be chosen for 'simplicity of manufacture and minimum breakage' and that only the glazed but undecorated natural clay colours, white, cream or brown, were to be used. Additionally, and contrary to general practice at that time, the customer was to be allowed to buy single pieces, such as a saucer without a cup, or a teapot lid, if required.

Wedgwood, which had moved from Etruria to its new factory at Barlaston early in 1940, became one of the nucleus firms for the manufacture of 'Utility' pottery and in fact turned over the whole of its output to it from Autumn 1942. War-time pottery was not strictly Utility since apart from prohibiting decoration and inessential pieces the Board of Trade did not lay down any specifications, and Wedgwood's production was specially designed by their Art Director, Victor Skellern ARCA. It was named 'Victory Ware' rather than Utility because the firm felt that the latter was inappropriate for pottery designed and made to its usual standards. This was of course at a time when Utility still had connotations of being second best and before the example of furniture had made it a guarantee of quality.

Victor Skellern's designs were beautifully simple and some ingenious devices were adopted which made for ease of manufacture, storage, durability and cleaning, and increased its adaptability: the teapot, and similar jugs, had a low centre of gravity and a wide mouth for cleaning; its lid, with recessed handle to minimise the risk of breakage, would fit the jug, teacup and beaker; the serving dish with tab handles could be inverted to cover another, thus making a casserole for the oven or a storage bowl for the larder; the rims of the plates were designed to stop condiments running down; the cups and beakers were designed to stack, and both fitted the saucer. In July 1942 the Design and Industries Association commented 'Good design – or the lack of it – has never been so apparent as it is under the new restrictions, and Wedgwood have come unscathed through the Utility acid test'.

The following items, all in white earthenware, were available:

plate, in three sizes; meat-dish, in two sizes; soup dish; dual-purpose bowl; cup and saucer; beaker; bowl for sugar or jam; jug, in three sizes; teapot, in two sizes; egg-cup; sauce boat.

'UTILITY' FASHION

Clothing during the war years was almost entirely utilitarian and completely conditioned by the demands of war work. Uniformity was imposed by Government regulation so that there were no real fashion changes in the period. An article in the June 1942 edition of *Housewife* commented on the non-existence of fashion: 'Slowly the essence of our attitude towards clothes has changed. Now at the end of our third year of war a bandbox reputation is not only unimportant but undesirable'.

Sex appeal was almost entirely focused on make-up and hairstyles, red lips and permed or waved hair were accepted as necessary concessions to female vanity. The advice in *Housewife* was to 'Put on your best face', for keeping up appearances meant keeping up morale. The Ministry of Supply realised the importance of cosmetics to its female munitions workers and in August 1942 gave them a special allowance of high-grade foundation and face-powder together with a special booklet entitled 'R.O.F. Beauty Hints. Look to your Looks.' Great ingenuity was needed to eke out the meagre supplies of cosmetics. A teenage girl working in an aircraft factory used the 'dope' from the paint shop as clear nail varnish whilst another trick was to add a 'few drops of warm almond oil to melted down lipstick ends to use as a cream rouge' (*How we lived then* N Longmate, 1971). Stockings were extremely scarce during the war for in 1941 the use of silk was banned and in 1942 socks had to be worn due to shortages. Undaunted, some women coloured their legs and painted the seam down the back of the leg with eyeliner.

On Whit Sunday 1941 (June 1st) the Government introduced clothes rationing. The aims behind this were threefold; to control consumer spending, to release workers in the clothing industry for more important work and to yield more factory space. Twenty coupons were allowed in that year, each garment being allotted a certain number of coupons. The more material and labour needed to make a garment meant that it carried a higher number of coupons. A woman's coat, for example, needed 14, a woollen dress 11 and a blouse 5. Up until 1942 style had not been subject to regulation but in that year the Civilian Clothing Order introduced Utility clothes. The Board of Trade asked each member of the Incorporated Society of London Fashion Designers (Hardy Amies, Creed, Bianca Mosca, Digby Morton, Peter Russell, Victor Stiebel, Hartnell and Worth) to submit four specified basic outfits–a top-coat, suit, afternoon dress and cotton overall dress. The thirty-two models were pooled and the most suitable selected by the Board of Trade and then mass-produced, appearing in the shops by the spring of the following year. The garments had to conform to their regulations, be made from Utility fabrics, and be labelled with the Utility mark, two 'cheeses' and the number 41. Jackets had to have three buttons and as there was no superfluous trimming or decoration allowed this severity of style meant that the cut was all-important. The designs were shown at the Board of Trade in September 1942, and in the October issue of *Vogue* the scheme was praised because now 'all women have the equal chance to buy beautifully designed clothes suitable to their lives and incomes. It is a revolutionary scheme and a heartening thought. It is, in fact, an outstanding example of applied democracy'. The suits were in fact extremely smart as the Stiebel suit in the exhibition shows. Vogue was very optimistic about the state of British couture describing it a 'fighting trim' and that the dress restrictions instead of shackling fashion 'simply pare away superfluities'.

By the end of the war most women felt differently. Clothes rationing became more severe as the war went on; in 1942 sixty coupons were issued but in 1943 there were only forty and in 1944 forty-eight. Extreme care was needed in choosing clothes, since once the coupons were cut from the ration book the owner had to wait until the following year for a new issue. As certain clothing items and materials became scarce ways were found to 'make do': hinged wooden-soled shoes were introduced in 1943 to supplement dwindling leather supplies, hats, which in pre-war days, were a vital part of an outfit were considered frivolous and unnecessary in war-time, and turbans, snoods and head-scarves proved a practical alternative; magazines gave advice on how to knit and crochet caps. Slacks became an indispensable item in a woman's wardrobe: usually made of corduroy velveteen they were worn with double-breasted jackets. Another practical innovation was the siren suit (which Sir Winston Churchill made so popular) with a zipped or buttoned jacket, large pockets and hood and matching trousers.

'Make do and mend' was the Board of Trade's slogan for the war; it issued booklets which gave advice on the mending and care of clothes, how to combat moths, how to unpick jumpers and re-knit them and how to make decorative patches. Some materials were coupon-free and women used their ingenuity to devise garments out of black-out material, parachute silk, curtain-net and butter-muslin.

The British textile industry received much encouragement at the beginning of the war in the hope of encouraging exports. In 1941 a number of artists, designers and illustrators were commissioned by the Cotton Board's Design and Style Centre to design a series of exclusive fabrics. The scheme received a Government subsidy and the designs were shown in 'Vogue'. Among those who contributed were Graham Sutherland, Duncan Grant and Ben Nicholson. Sutherland's design *Green Roses* anticipates the floral designs so popular in the 1950's but a print which reflected the spirit of the time was Fougasse's series of *Careless Talk* campaign posters which were printed on Jacqmar silk.

In March 1942 a series of propaganda prints appeared. They were designed by Arnold Lever of Jacqmar using the slogans and stories of wartime England. Some of the titles were *Happy Landing, The Navy's Here, Fall in the Firebomb Fighters, Home Guard* and *Dig for Victory.* They were made into aprons, blouses and dresses by Bianca Mosca. Jacqmar also produced scarves with similar motifs for two coupons each. Other patriotic gestures were V for Victory brooches and the Victory-roll hairstyle in which the hair was rolled up tightly round the head with a swept-up curl on the top.

By the end of the war women were beginning to tire of the severe, square-shouldered suit worn with heavy, wedge shoes and shoulder bags and were longing for a softer, more feminine look. Hips became slightly more rounded and there was a hint of more fullness in the skirt.

'The New Look' and after

In 1946 the Council of Industrial Design put on an exhibition at the Victoria and Albert Museum, London entitled *Britain Can Make It.* The fashion section featured the latest designs of the Incorporated Society of London Fashion Designers. These clothes being intended for export, the London collections were put on a week before the Paris collections in the hope of catching overseas buyers in transit to Paris. The emphasis on export is also apparent in the textile industry, the magazine *The Ambassador* being the British export journal for fashion and fabrics. As in 1941 artists were asked to design fabrics and the results were shown in the exhibition. It was hoped that the combination of top artistic talent and the high-quality English wools would make an effective export product.

Henry Moore and Graham Sutherland were among the exhibitors. Audrey Withers in her introduction to the *Dress Fabrics* section of the exhibition comments on the important point that the manufacturers have realised that 'through mass-production and a raising of the level of wages–ways of dressing and living enjoyed formerly by the few have become available to the many and alongside this there has emerged a strong and universal desire for more change, variety, more comfort and convenience.' It took a few more years before any real benefits were felt for although the fashions displayed in the exhibition were *chic* they were all intended for export. Export figures of British fashions rose from £98,000 in 1938 to £507,000 in 1946 (figures from the 1946 edition of *The Ambassador*). Clothes for the home market remained strictly rationed with the Utility models the only ones available. The enormous expansion of the ready-to-wear industry in the 1950s and 1960s owed not a little to the war-time and post-war activities of the Incorporated Society who gave British fashions a 'stability and elegance which hitherto was possessed by Paris alone' (*Silver and Gold* by N Hartnell, 1955).

In 1947 the fashion world was stunned by Dior's Spring collection. He showed dresses with nipped-in waists, heavy padded pleats and a very full skirt which was only twelve inches from the ground. The soft, rounded lines were a complete contrast to the skimpy, austere look of the preceding years. In the October issue of *Vogue* the revolution that was the 'New Look' was observed in an almost reverential tone: 'There are moments when fashion changes fundamentally.

When it is more than a matter of differences in detail the whole attitude seems to change – the whole structure of the body. This is one of those moments'. In England, as in France, there was an enormous outcry over the extravagance of a garment which needed 25 yards of material and new foundation garments which were then classed as 'luxury garments'. The look was exactly what women wanted and their demand for it triumphed over Sir Stafford Cripps's disapproval (he wanted it outlawed) for within a year the 'New Look' was worn all over England. It was a considerable fillip to the reputation of British couture that Norman Hartnell was chosen by Princess Elizabeth to design her wedding dress.

In the Autumn of 1948 a more slender 'Directoire' line was introduced, flourishing side by side with the full-skirt look. There were a variety of coat styles to wear with the slender look including swagger coats and the 'long-waisted' coat. British manufacturers brought out some very exaggerated versions of the 'New Look' which were worn with high-heeled ankle-strap shoes and rather fussy accessories including handbags with loop handles and rolled-up umbrellas decorated with bows.

In February 1949 a large range of garments became 'coupon free', which generated the opportunity and demand for more variety in fashion. Day costume again offered the choice between a slim and a full-skirted line. The slim skirt had pleating on one side and was worn with either a bolero or a short cape. The full-skirted dress flared out from the hip-line and evening dresses were extremely decolleté and dramatic. In the spring Dior showed slim-line dresses with floating panels which fell from the hip accompanied by a short 'gamine' haircut. Very small or very large hats were worn with the new hairstyle.

1950 brought the 'pencil-slim' skirt and low-cut necklines. The full-skirted dress made a feature of wide collars and a tiny waist. *Vogue* commented: 'The New Silhouette needs a New Figure. It demands above all, a figure to emphasise the smallest, neatest whisper of a waist that can be clasped between two handspans'. Taffeta became a very fashionable material and was used for dresses and matching coats.

1951, the year of the Festival of Britain saw little change from the lines of the preceding year. The halter-neck re-appeared, the long-line skirt continued with the introduction of the 'sheath skirt' and 'trumpet skirt', together with a diagonal emphasis which was achieved by seaming, buttoning and tucking. Jackets were either fitted or a contrasting 'fly-away' or 'swing-back' shape. The popular colours were grey, black, navy and neutral.

Fashion during the post-war years had become increasingly feminine. Soft, curved lines accentuated the bust and hips thus ensuring an enormous boom in the foundation garment business. With the rapid growth of the media, fashion began to change faster than ever before and the rise of the ready-to-wear market meant that everyone had a chance of wearing it. The last coupon issue was in September 1948, and although the Utility specifications continued until 1952 they were increasingly unspecific, becoming little more than a means of exempting goods from Purchase Tax.

Jane Ashelford

C1 Suit (plate 38)
Designed by Victor Stiebel 1942.
Blouson jacket of blue woollen frieze with darker blue flared skirt. One of the sample Utility garments designed by members of the Incorporated Society of London Fashion Designers for the Board of Trade. Shown to the Press in September 1942, and featured in *Vogue* in October 1942. The maximum selling price was £4 2s 2d.
Hip size 36″

C2 Hat
Black felt with veiling.

C3 Court shoes
Blue suede.

C4 Handbag
The clutch bag which was so popular in the 1930's continued to be worn during the first years of the war. Shoulder bags appeared in 1942 and were far more practical.
Black leather.

C5 Women's Land Army uniform
Greatcoat, size 9, with armband or brassard, denoting four years' service; corduroy breeches, lacing below the knee, hip size 40″; thick woollen knee socks; brown leather lace-up

shoes; cream 'Aertex' shirt; green tie; green woollen jumper; khaki felt hat with WLA badge.

The Land Army was run solely by women and its headquarters were at Balcombe Place, Sussex, the country house of its honorary Director Lady Denman. It was started in June 1939 with the compilation of a register of women who would be willing to give up their ordinary jobs for farm work in the event of war. By 1943 its numbers had risen to a peak of nearly 90,000 land girls, aged eighteen to forty. The work was badly paid and hard, but in spite of these drawbacks many girls joined especially from the industrial areas, avid for the freedom of out-door life. Some went into the timber corps, where they were known as 'Lumberjills'.

Miscellaneous accessories

C6 Child's pyjama case.
C7 Maroon suede hat with grey/maroon bow.
C8 Six wood and steel hair combs, two each in blue, red and black.
C9 Metal compact with embroidered design.
C10 'Vinylastic' braces, in original wrappers.
C11 Woman's plastic rain-hood.
C12 Green plastic V for victory brooch.
C13 Canvas Utility beach sandals.
C14 Brown suede Utility court shoes.

C15 'Shoulder to Shoulder' Jacqmar artificial silk head-scarf. Patriotic head-scarves were popular during the war, usually carrying some sort of slogan, as in this example. See also C18.

C16 Three hats:
Straw, with spray of leather flowers and black net bow.
Straw, with Petersham ribbon brim.
Home-made, felt with black velvet bow.

C17 Rayon crepe fabric, illustrating various articles of clothing with the number of coupons required for each. The background is formed from repeated 66's, the total number of coupons per year allocated to everyone under the Utility clothing scheme (plate 40).

C18 'Victory' printed cotton, probably for manufacture into head-scarves. The selvedges are decorated with the morse-code signal for victory (plate 39).

THE IMAGE OF 'UTILITY'

From 1941 onwards, official Home Intelligence reports, supplemented by the surveys of Mass Observation reveal a radical shift in the popular perception of the war: Dunkirk, the Battle of Britain and the Blitz formed a break with the 'phoney' war. Total war conditions created an ideological cleavage with the past, which was perceived as fantastic, frivolous and delusory, compared with the bleak, heroic realism of the present.

This was expressed in a preference for the tangible and actual, rather than the abstract or symbolic, an example of which is the Mass Observation discovery, (November 1944) that public opinion no longer favoured orthodox stone war memorials, preferring practical memorials such as schools and houses, objects useful to the community.

This shift of opinion towards use-value – a utilitarian mentality – had several elements in its composition. Despite the threat of invasion, people's preoccupations were still primarily domestic, and the populist deification of the 'ordinary person' engendered a corporate spirit of 'millions like us', which in conditions of austerity produced a vogue for patriotic shabbiness as the antithesis of conspicuous consumption. In 1942 an ex-teacher told a Mass Observation investigator, 'War time restrictions and changes of habit have been rather a blessing for me. Now it is patriotic to be darned and patched." This socially sanctioned dowdiness was enjoined by the propaganda slogan, 'make do and mend', which however became very unpopular by the end of the war and the expectations of better things that this brought with it.

It was war that was educating people in the assumption of a planned future and in fact, the words 'Reconstruction' and 'Planning', which became early 'peacetime hopes' were the ideological imperatives of the wartime total society. Perhaps this was first crystallised in *Picture Post's* January 4th 1941 issue, *A Plan for Britain,* which mapped by photo-features, a Utopian peacetime organisation of 'the new Britain'. In 1942, Abram Games designed a series of posters for the Army Bureau of Current Affairs, called *Your Britain, Fight for it Now.* They embodied the war aims of a hygienic, well educated, well housed future, based on the limited range of pre-war exemplars of architectural modernism such as the Finsbury Health Centre and the Tecton Block.

The conscription of the population and wartime co-ordination of labour generated an image of the nation as an efficiently organised team, and Britain was projected as 'the finest example of teamwork in the world today'. Housewives, as much as any other group in the population realised their interdependence and function in society as the necessities of total war impinged upon the individual and the home. A large Knightsbridge store headlined its sale announcement: 'A sewing machine can be almost as much a weapon as a spade'. This tendency is best illustrated in the Ministry of Information's 1940 poster of a human chain of boiler-suited workers, servicemen and civil servants, grouped round a central anonymous silhouette with whom the spectator was intended to identify, by means of the slogan: 'It all depends on me'. This kind of propaganda for war production concentrated on the individual who 'went to it', represented as a component in the war effort–as a link in the national chain, and a certain social equality was visually signified by this, just as in the widely used synonym for utility–'standard'–a social levelling was also implied. It was Gordon Russell, one of the chief designers, who contended (1947) that 'Utility' furniture was a sign of a general 'social experiment' in wartime.

From 1942, this has to be set against a strong simultaneous current of cultural pessimism and inertia, a low state of morale in sections of the intelligentsia who projected a depressing bogey figure, 'the utility man',–uniform, functional, standard and essentially dull, who was destined to be the prototype for the overalled party members in George Orwell's *1984*, portrayed against a decor of banners proclaiming the virtues of increased production and the tatty sub-functional drabness of Victory Mansions.

But there were more optimistic images counteracting fears of a social 'levelling down'. In May 1943 Tom Harrisson of Mass Observation lectured at the Building Centre on 'Public Taste and Public Design', pointing out that the masses in Britain had had little opportunity to see modern paintings and well designed furniture until the intervention of government agencies like CEMA. His conclusion was emancipatory and typical of the 'Utility' era in linking the imperatives of efficiency, information, health, hygiene and planning. These imperatives of austerity were paradoxically levelling up assumptions and goals: 'the whole tone of M.O. results convinces all of us who have worked on it, that the potential private taste of the public is far more advanced than is supposed or at present appears.'

David Mellor

Note: the author is engaged in research and teaching at the University of Sussex and the Mass Observation Archive. All quotations are from material lodged at the Mass Observation Archive, University of Sussex.

During the Second World War a great variety of posters was produced in very large numbers for the civilian population and for the armed services. They were displayed in factories, canteens, post offices, service installations, and less frequently and perhaps, less successfully, in larger versions on hoardings.

The posters in this exhibition were aimed at the civilian population or Home Front, although of course the message in many cases was just as applicable to service men and women, especially those stationed in this country or on leave here.

The themes of the *Home Front* posters generally referred to or illustrated the well known campaigns of the war years, such as *Dig for Victory, Make do and Mend, Lend a Hand on the Land, Coughs and Sneezes spread Diseases, Lend to Defend, Careless Talk costs Lives, Salvage* and *Is your Journey really necessary?*

Many of their designers were employed by the Ministry of Information, whose campaigns branch was an important source of posters, although other ministries such as Health, Agriculture and Supply together with quasi-official bodies such as the WVS were also involved. The Ministry of Information was formed in 1940 but never managed to attain a great popularity, possibly because, with the example before them of Goebbels' Ministry of Propaganda subjected to constant ridicule in the Press, people were suspicious of anything that smacked of propaganda. At any rate it was variously nick-named 'The Mystery of Information', 'The Ministry of Mal-formation' and 'The Ministry of Muddle'. In spite of this apparent mistrust however, the work the Ministry of Information was fostering in the design field was crucial: apart from its posters it had formed an Exhibitions Unit, one of whose functions was to design touring exhibitions (usually relating to the various campaigns already mentioned). The talent concentrated at the Ministry included among others Milner Gray, James Fitton, J K Henrion and Misha Black and it is hard to imagine that the two great post-war exhibitions, *Britain Can Make It* 1946 and the Festival of Britain 1951 would have been possible without the war-time opportunities and experience of many of the artists and designers involved in those two ventures. Technically many of the posters are brilliant, making full use of typography as an integral part of the design, and exploiting to the full the various media–letterpress, lithography and photo-lithography. The last facilitated the use of photo-montage, a technique pioneered in Germany before the war by such artists as Moholy Nagy and the anti-Nazi John Heartfield. The technique was much used by J K Henrion and Zéró (Hans Schleger).

The subtlety and at times humour of many of the posters, compared with the xenophobic crudities common in the First World War, was due not only to the ability of the artists involved but also reflected the solidarity that had developed in the population as a whole, starting with the Blitz and reinforced by the entry of America into the war and the realisation that with the German reverses at the hands of the Russians the tide had at last begun to turn: the enemy, Nazism, came into sharper focus and the necessity for its total defeat became paramount; posters played their part not only in spurring the population on but also in giving it a vision of the 'New Britain' which would come into being after their defeat.

D1 Wait! Count 15 slowly (plate 42)
G R Morris
Blackout warning poster issued by the National 'Safety First' Association. Probably 1940 (The NSFA became the Royal Society for the Prevention Of Accidents (ROSPA) in 1941). From 1939-44 ROSPA produced four to five poster designs a month, often printed on both sides of the paper for economy.
Offset-lithograph $14^3/4''$ x $9^1/2''$

D2 Wear or carry something white
Zéró (Hans Schleger)
Blackout warning poster issued by the London Passenger Transport Board (LPTB).
Lithograph 25″ x 20″

D3 ARP calling you
Pat Keely
Issued by the Air Raid Precautions (ARP) Department, Home Office 1938.
Photo-lithograph 14³/4″ x 9¹/2″

D4 Air raid danger
Police notice asking for lights to be concealed. Probably 1939.
Letterpress 22¹/2″ x 17¹/2″

D5 Enemy invasion
Instructions in the event of an invasion issued by the Birmingham Invasion Committee. Probably 1939.
Letterpress 15″ x 10″

D6 Hitler will send no warning
Poster exhorting people to carry their gas masks at all times. Issued by the Ministry of Home Security. Probably 1939.

It was widely believed in the first two years of the war that gas attacks were imminent. That this did not happen was possibly due to the fact that the civilian population, trained to expect it, was better prepared than the German, which would consequently have suffered more in any reprisal attacks.
Letterpress 30″ x 20″

D7 How to put on your mask
Instructions issued by the Ministry of Home Security. Probably 1939.
Photo-lithograph 30″ x 20″

D8 Post before lunch
Zéró
Issued by the GPO, these horizontal posters were displayed on the sides of Post Office vans.
Lithograph
10¹/2″ x 42″

D9 Salvage still wanted
Probably designed by Reginald Mount
This, and numbers 10, 11, 12, are some examples from a series issued by the Ministry of Supply asking people to save rags (for furnishings), paper (for containers) and bones (for fertilisers).
Photo-lithograph 14³/4″ x 9³/4″

D10 Rags
Lithograph 14¹/4″ x 9¹/4″

D11 Waste paper
Photo-lithograph 14³/4″ x 9³/4″

D12 Bones
Photo-lithograph 14³/4″ x 9¹/2″

D13 Dig for Victory (plate 43)
This was one of the most successful campaigns of the war, and its story is told by Bob Carter at the end of this section of the catalogue. This poster is one of the best known of a large number produced for the campaign.
Photo-lithograph 30″ x 20″

D14 Food from your garden
Pictorial instructions for making a compost heap. Issued by the Ministry of Agriculture.
Lithograph 30″ x 20″

D15 Rabbits can be fed on
J K Henrion
This shows graphically how rabbits could be fed on a wide variety of vegetable material, from kitchen scraps to hedgerow weeds. Many rabbits were kept for their meat, but apparently it was hard for people to kill what had often become a much-loved pet.
Photo-lithograph 30″ x 20″

D16 Eat greens (plate 44)
Zéró
Photo-lithograph 30″ x 20″

D17 Grow your own food (plate 45)
Abram Games
Subtitled 'every available piece of land must be cultivated'.

Games produced some of the finest war posters and was later responsible for the Festival of Britain symbol.
Lithograph 30″ x 20″

D18 A clear plate means a clear conscience (plate 46)
James Fitton
Subtitled 'don't take more than you can eat'.
Lithograph 30″ x 20″

D19 Lend a hand on the land
Eileen Evans
Issued by the Ministry of Agriculture, it asks for volunteers for farming holiday camps.
Photo-lithograph 30″ x 20″

D20 Women wanted (plate 47)
Jack Mathew
Issued by the ARP Department of the Home Office for the WVS, it asks for women to volunteer for evacuation service by applying to their local council or WVS branch.
Lithograph 30″ x 20″

D21 Women of Britain (plate 48)
Zec
Poster exhorting women to come and work in the factories. With more and more men conscripted into the services factories were increasingly staffed by women and older men.
Lithograph 30″ x 20″

D22 Coughs and sneezes spread diseases
H M Bateman
One of a series by this artist, well known for his 'the man who . . .' cartoons, which depicted social blunders. His coughs and sneezes series for the Ministry of Health (Central Council for Health Education), is in a similar vein.
Photo-lithograph 30″ x 20″

D23 Wanted for sabotage (plate 49)
The Squanderbug ('Hitler's pal') was invented by Philip Boydell for the National Savings Committee and the swastika-covered bug quickly became a potent symbol in the campaign to increase savings and reduce consumption.
Photo-lithograph 19 3/4″ x 14 1/2″

D24 Fire danger
Cusden
This warns purely graphically, with no text, of the danger of fire from cigarette ends. Produced by ROSPA and issued by the Ministry of Labour and National Service.
Lithograph 30″ x 20″

D25 Shelter at home
Depicting a Morrison or table shelter. These shelters were introduced early in 1941 and were named after the then Home Secretary, Herbert Morrison, just as the Anderson shelter had been named after his predecessor in 1938. They were more successful than the Anderson shelter for the simple reason that being indoors people were more inclined to use them.
Photo-lithograph 30″ x 20″

D26 Hello boyfriend, coming my way?
Reginald Mount
Issued by the Ministry of Health in its campaign against VD.
Photo-lithograph 14 3/4″ x 9 3/4″

D27a-h Careless talk costs lives
Fougasse (C K Bird)
This series of posters became one of the best known, and was certainly amongst the funniest, of the war, its popularity paralleling that of 'ITMA'. In each case the talkers are being overheard in some way by Hitler, who is sometimes accompanied by Mussolini.

The economy of means employed by Bird was an important factor in the success of these posters, designed in 1940.
Photo-lithographs each 12 1/2″ x 8″

D28 Think before you speak
Sticker designed to be placed in public telephones as part of the *careless talk costs lives* campaign. Issued 1941.
Letterpress 6 1/2″ x 5 3/4″

D29 Join your savings group now
Pat Keely
Issued by the National Savings Committee, 1940.
Lithograph 30″ x 20″

The experience of the First World War made it immediately apparent that another war would mean renewed food shortages, and it was therefore only a day or two after September 3rd 1939 that plans were put into operation to encourage the public to grow their own vegetables. Under powers given by Defence Regulations the Minister of Agriculture made the Cultivation of Lands (Allotments) Order, 1939 which permitted councils to enter upon unoccupied land to provide allotments. (Later under Defence Regulation 62A councils were authorised to convert to allotments any other land including bomb sites, parks and playing fields.) 1939 also saw the publication by the Ministry of Agriculture of *Growmore Leaflet no. 1* which incorporated the first vegetable cultivation plan for a ten-rod garden or allotment. This prototype, which provided for all year round cropping, gave gardeners throughout the war a basis for endless discussion, criticism and suggested improvement, and by the end of the war literally thousands of computations of it had been devised to suit personal gardening convictions and changing circumstances like the seed or fertilizer position. After Dunkirk the home food production effort was intensified and on September 10th 1940 the Minister of Agriculture appealed in a broadcast for half a million more allotments while launching the *Dig for Victory* campaign proper. The campaign's slogan was chosen with no little difficulty; *Grow More Food* was thought too stodgy and the Ministry of Information Slogans Department worked overtime to find three word phrases that would stir enthusiasm without frightening anybody. *Dig for Victory,* however, was actually coined in an Evening Standard leader of the autumn of 1939 and subsequently taken up by the Ministry.

The campaign's role was twofold – to exhort and to advise. A major feature was the *Dig for Victory Week,* a series of which were arranged successively in most major centres. These employed posters, lectures, films, *Food Production Brains Trusts,* vegetable cooking demonstrations, competitions and prizes, and they were surprisingly successful in increasing allotment lettings and the number of private gardens turned over to food production.

Demonstration plots were also set up, the most famous of which was the Ministry of Agriculture and Fisheries' own plot in Hyde Park. These created considerable interest and it was felt that, in company with so many aspects of the campaign, a post-war continuation would be at once certain and beneficial. The 1969 Report on Allotments, however, reveals that less than 5% of towns still provided model plots by 1969.

As in the First World War a welter of garden literature, both official and commercial, appeared; the *Growmore* series of Ministerial pamphlets, some of which had been aimed at farmers, was later supplemented by the *Dig for Victory* series, while bodies like the Royal Horticulticultural Society and magazines like *Good Housekeeping* also published basic manuals intended both for the beginner and the experienced gardener. A number of books were published which dealt specifically or in passing with the design and organisation problems involved in turning over the pleasure garden to vegetable production. These works are united in suggesting that at least some aspects of purely ornamental gardening should be retained, and the idea of reserving the front garden of the average suburban plot as a flower garden is often mentioned, it being stressed that wartime austerity made the appearance of at least a few flowers especially welcome. *Practical Gardening and Food Production in Pictures,* by Richard Sudell, which supplies designs for the wartime garden, is typical of the encyclopaedic kind of work, while C. H. Middleton's *Your Garden in War-time* deals with the problems of re-organisation in greater detail.

C. H. Middleton, prolific garden writer though he was, was primarily a broadcaster and his *In Your Garden* programmes, which began before the war and continued through it, became popular and did much to stimulate general interest in horticulture. In 1942 *Radio Allotment* began – a series that catered for totally inexperienced gardeners, it broadcast the weekly state of an allotment near Broadcasting House cultivated entirely by BBC staff. It was encouraging in its implication that innate skill and years of experience were not essential to successful vegetable growing.

The necessities of wartime food production introduced large numbers of school children to horticulture – an activity which had previously been mainly confined to rural schools, but which through evacuation and utilisation of all spare urban land had become more generally feasible. The possibilities of both general and specialised horticultural education began to be realised and a number of experiments were carried out. A Birmingham school evacuated to Cannock Chase allocated small individual plots to each pupil who was allowed to cultivate the land unsupervised and with a completely free hand (although tuition was given on a separate larger plot and advice was available if required). The children's response to the experiments was both enthusiastic and creative and seemed to point to the inclusion of such activities in post-war curricula – a situation which never really materialised despite the post-war opportunities for replanning urban space.

The concept of the stock allotment emerged during the 1930's as a means of helping the unemployed supplement their meagre resources by keeping small livestock. Vegetable and stock allotments, with careful planning, could be successfully combined – the waste products of each being mutually beneficial. After 1940 under Defence Regulation 62B all allotment holders were permitted to keep pigs, hens and rabbits on their plots – a concession that was eagerly taken advantage of in view of strict meat and egg rationing. In villages Produce Associations were formed which were usually representative of all the food producing groups of the community: again efficiency was increased by the amalgamation of interests. In towns pig clubs were popular, the expense and maintenance of the animals being shared by the members. Even in the West End of London space was found by police and firemen's clubs to house animals.

Changes in the statistics for tenanted allotments in England and Wales will give some idea of the effect of the *Dig for Victory* campaign. During the First War the number of allotments increased from 600,000 in 1913 to 1,500,000 in 1918. At this time the major growth was in cities and the rural emphasis which the allotment movement originally had gradually changed to the urban one which it has today. After the First War the demand continued unabated (contributing factors were the economic condition, the return of servicemen and wartime publicity). By 1929, however, there were again fewer than 1,000,000 plots – the effect of the return of war requisitioned land and the pressure of building on allotment sites. On the eve of the Second World War there were 740,000 allotments, a figure which by 1942 had doubled and by 1944 had reached 2,000,000. The output of millions of private gardens and cultivated army and air force land included, non-professionally produced food in 1944 reached a total of 3 million tons or 10% of all food produced in the country.

The tide of interest in gardening and allotments which the war had fostered continued for some time, spurred on by post-war economic difficulties. Broadcasting in 1947 the Chancellor of the Exchequer stressed the importance of allotments, and the Minister of Agriculture, speaking at the 1948 Conference of the National Allotment and Garden Society declared, 'Today we are digging for our very lives, for food, for dollars and for our self-respect'. Numbers of allotments, however, did considerably fall off during the 50's and 60's, not only because of the economic boom but also because of increasing development of allotment sites. In 1967 the NAGS prompted by the *We're Backing Britain Movement* began a *Dig for Britain* campaign and distributed 250,000 leaflets. The current allotment renaissance, however, is not so much a product of this patriotic campaign (increasing vegetable prices have themselves made home production desirable), but is a result of increasing dissatisfaction with the quality of commercial produce and rationalised farming methods. Organic Gardening and the Alternative Culture have at least temporarily saved the allotment from the superimposition of the debasing and pointless leisure garden image offered by the 1969 Departmental Committee of Inquiry as the only salvation for the movement.

Bob Carter

The *Britain Can Make It* exhibition of 1946, inspired by Sir Stafford Cripps and organised by the two-year old Council of Industrial Design, marked a turning point in design consciousness in this country: virtually the whole current production of consumer industry was on show and, significantly, the role of the industrial designer himself was thoroughly explored, notably in displays by Misha Black. There was even a section called *The Designer looks ahead,* with prototypes of such things as a streamlined electrically-assisted bicycle and an air-conditioned bed, photographs of which are shown in the exhibition.

A characteristic of design in the early post-war years was the incorporation of surplus materials such as aluminium: Ernest Race, Robin Day and Clive Latimer (a member of the Utility Furniture Design Panel) used it effectively in cast and sheet form for non-Utility furniture, and many people who were of primary school age at the time will remember the cast aluminium and plywood school furniture designed by James Leonard, much of which is still in use. Christopher Heal experimented with the possibilities of laminating wood and sheet aluminium and even improvised rugs from war-surplus cordage and parachute silk. The constraints imposed by the anomalies of shortage and surplus were fully exploited and the solutions that resulted, helped in many cases by the technical advances of the war-years, gave a valuable impetus to post-war design.

The objects shown here, while not intended to be comprehensive in their scope, are nevertheless representative of design in the early post-war years.

E1 Poster for 'Britain Can Make It' exhibition 1946
Designed by Ashley Havinden
Photo-lithograph
30″ x 20″

E2 Radio receiver (plate 51)
Case in bakelite designed by Frank Middleditch for De La Rue Plastics Ltd and Bush Radio Ltd.
Exhibited *Britain Can Make It* 1946

E3 Ensign 'Ful-vue' camera
Made by Barnet Ensign Ltd
Exhibited *Britain Can Make It* 1946

E4 Hand-drill
Made by Leytool Ltd
Exhibited *Britain Can Make It* 1946

E5 Opal glass ashtray
Probably designed by R Y Gooden (an identical one in clear glass is illustrated in *Designers in Britain* (SIA/Allen Wingate 1947).

E6 Utility dining chair
Model D732. Designed by J Christopher Heal 1950 and made for Heal and Son Ltd. This chair, in beech, is an example of what could be done within the specification limits of the Utility scheme after design control had been abandoned. The loose seat has its original cover

E7 Electric fire
Made by 'B and T' in tubular and sheet aluminium.

E8 'Pin-Up' home perm packaging (photograph)
Designed by P Pickard Jenkins for J Walter Thompson Ltd.

E9 'Pickard Tuscan' photo-typesetting alphabet
Designed by P Pickard Jenkins in 1950 for W S Cowell Ltd it anticipates the decorated alphabets popular at the time of the Festival of Britain.

E10 'Ubilda' toy car
In a field dominated now by plastics this 1947 toy by Chad Valley in painted tin plate (with its original box) is a continuation of pre-war manufacturing methods.

Examples of war time ephemera too numerous to mention individually are shown and include such things as Ration Books, Identity Cards, food packaging, ARP equipment, gas masks, incendiary bomb casings, Government booklets and parts of both Anderson and Morrison air-raid shelters. However, a selection of items, especially where they have been lent by individuals in response to appeals for material, are listed below:

F1 Music in the National Gallery 1942
H Scott Harrison 1942
The painting shows part of the audience at one of the well-known war-time concerts at the National Gallery. It is painted on the back of a piece of American cloth - canvas created with linseed oil to make it waterproof, and much used at that time for kitchen table-cloths. The stretcher is home-made.
Signed and dated 'H Scott Harrison '42'.
Oil on American cloth 13¾" x 17½"

F2 Girls drilling 1943
Rupert Shephard (b. 1909)
It shows women engaged on war-work at EMI's factory in Hayes, Middlesex.
Signed and dated 'Rupert Shephard 1943'
Oil on canvas 16" x 22"

F3 War-time civilian radio receiver (plate 50)
The only receivers produced during the war were made to a standard pattern under Government licence by a group of manufacturers including EMI, GEC, Marconi, Murphy and Philips. This example is a medium-wave instrument and the dial is marked solely with 'Home' and 'Forces' stations, although it was no doubt still possible for listeners to tune into the Bremen broadcasts of 'Lord Haw-Haw'–after Tommy Handley one of the great entertainers of the war years.

F4 'War-finish' electric fire (plate 52)
Simply but solidly made in pressed and strip steel it has two individually switched elements and its designed for wall-mounting.
Made by Berry's Electric Ltd

F5 Child's Diary 1939-1941
Written by B Kelly Espinosa and started when she was ten years old. A typical entry (for Sunday 27th October 1939) reads 'Cold morning so I am staying in bed for a time. Hitler is ill and has a bad throat. Spent the afternoon cleaning the drains . . .'

F6 Toy acrobat
Made from scraps of wood and linoleum, it is typical of the improvised and home-made toys of the war years.

F7 Weigh your Mummy's Meat Ration
Toy metal scales in original box. In spite of their small size it would have been possible to weigh the miniscule meat ration on them.

F8 War time postcards
Seventeen examples, many of them in the British sea-side postcard tradition, including 'I've just been showing Miss Jones our air-raid shelter'; 'How was I to know you were a conscientious objector' (husband to his bride in a bedroom at the 'Hotel Bliss') and 'We had an escaped German prisoner hiding in our house last night. . . . I heard Mum tell Dad there was a Jerry under the bed'.

F9 Envelopes
Three examples, civilian, RAF and Active Service, of letters examined by the censor.

F10 Struwwelhitler. A Nazi Story Book
A brilliant (and similiarly macabre) adaptation of the well-known cautionary tale Struwwelpieter.
One episode shows Hermann Goering ('Guns before Butter') daily shrinking away as he insists on trying to spread guns on his bread rather than butter.

F11 Gas Masks
More correctly called respirators, they include an all enveloping type for babies, with a hand pump operated by the person holding the child, a 'Donald Duck' mask for young children (plate 53) and civilian and ARP examples.

BIBLIOGRAPHY

Author	Title and Publisher
Jean René Bernard	*Le Système Utility* (Paris 1953)
Misha Black (Ed)	*Exhibition Design* (Architectural Press 1950)
Denise Bonnett (Ed)	*Contemporary Cabinet Design and Construction* (Batsford 1956)
Angus Calder	*The People's War* (Cape 1969)
Hugh Dalton	*The Fateful Years, Memoirs 1931-1945* (Muller 1957)
Joseph Darracott and Belinda Loftus	*Second World War Posters* (HMSO 1972)
Monica Felton	*Civilian Supplies in Wartime Britain* (HMSO 1945)
Norman Hartnell	*Silver and Gold* (Evan Bros 1955)
Roy Hay	*Gardener's Chance* (The Garden Book Club 1946)
J. Hurstfield	*History of the Second World War, The Control of Raw Materials* (HMSO and Longmans 1953)
David Joel	*The Adventure of British Furniture* (Ernest Benn 1953)
Gordon Logie	*Furniture form Machines* (Allen and Unwin 1947)
Norman Longmate	*How We Lived Then* (Hutchinson 1971)
Fiona McCarthy	*All Things Bright and Beautiful* (Allen and Unwin 1972)
Russell Meiggs	*Home Timber Production 1939-1945* (Crosby Lockwood and Son 1949)
C H Middleton	*Your Garden in War-Time* (Allen and Unwin 1941)
Michael Moynihan (Ed)	*People at War* (David and Charles 1974)
M Pleydell-Bouverie (Ed)	*Post War Homes* (Daily Mail 1944)
Gordon Russell	*Designer's Trade* (Allen and Unwin 1968)
	The Things We See: Furniture (Penguin 1947)
Michael Sissons and Philip French (Eds)	*Age of Austerity* (Hodder and Stoughton 1963)
Richard Sudell	*Practical Gardening & Food Production in Pictures* (Odhams, n.d.)
Richard Titmuss	*Problems of Social Policy* (HMSO and Longmans 1950)
William Webb	*Garden First in Land Development* (Longmans Green 1920)
F R Yerbury(Ed)	*Modern Homes Illustrated* (Odhams, n.d. but c.1947)

Miscellaneous:

Allotments. Bulletin No. 9 of the Ministry of Agriculture (HMSO 1936)

'Britain Can Make It' Exhibition Catalogue (HMSO 1946)

Departmental Committee of Inquiry into Allotments (HMSO 1969)

Design 46 (HMSO 1946)

Designers in Britain Vols 1 and 2 (Allan Wingate 1947 and 1949)

Dig for Victory, series of war time pamphlets issued by the Ministry of Agriculture and Fisheries (HMSO)

Domestic Furniture, Designs and Specifications for Licensed Manufacturers (HMSO 1947)

Furnishing Show Book and Directory (National Trade Press 1948)

Furniture Board of Trade Working Party Report (HMSO 1946)

Furniture Design Typescript report of conference organised by CoID and held at RIBA July 1949

Furniture and Furnishing 1880-1955 (The Cabinet Maker 1955)

General Specifications for Utility Furniture (BoT 1948)

Growmore series of war time leaflets and bulletins issued by the Ministry of agriculture and Fisheries (HMSO)
Hansard's Parliamentary Debates (HMSO)
New Home No. 1 (HMSO 1946)
Report of the Purchase Tax/Utility Committee (HMSO 1952)
Statutory Instuments and Statutory Rules and Orders relating to the Utility schemes (HMSO 1941-1952)
The Cabinet Maker Year Book (The Cabinet Maker 1948)
The Furnishing Trade Encyclopaedia (The Furnishing World 1949)
The Vegetable Garden Displayed (Royal Horticultural Society 1942)
The Working Class Home Report by the Council for Art and Industry (HMSO 1937)
Traders Leaflets relating to the Utility furniture scheme (HMSO, various dates)
Utility Furniture Catalogue (HMSO 1943)
Utility Furniture Catalogue (HMSO 1947)

Periodicals:

Architectural Review
Art and Industry
ColD Annual Report
DIA News
Housewife
Ideal Home
NUFTO Record
Picture Post
The Ambassador
The Cabinet Maker
Vogue
F A Talbot World's *Work Those Amazing Allotments* (January 1919)
News cuttings relating to Utility Furniture

Unpublished Sources:

Board of Trade files, series BT 64 and Bt 94 relating to the Utility schemes, Price Control and Rationing.
Hugh Dalton Diaries
Subject files

Designed by GLC Supplies Department, Printing & Graphic Design Division
and Printed by A. McLay & Co., Ltd. 27077/62446 8/74